ZENITHISM

Studies of the Harriman Institute

HARRIMAN INSTITUTE

The Institute sponsors the Studies of the Harriman Institute in the belief that their publication contributes to scholarly research and public understanding. In this way the Institute, while not necessarily endorsing their conclusions, is pleased to make available the results of some of the research conducted under its auspices.

ZENITHISM
(1921–1927)

A YUGOSLAV AVANT-GARDE ANTHOLOGY

Edited by
Aleksandar Bošković
and
Steven Teref

Library of Congress Cataloging-in-Publication Data

Names: Bošković, Aleksandar, 1977- editor. | Teref, Steven, editor.
Title: Zenithism (1921–1927): a Yugoslav avant-garde anthology / edited by Aleksandar Bošković and Steven Teref.
Description: Boston: Academic Studies Press, 2022. | Includes bibliographical references and index.
Identifiers: LCCN 2022025306 (print) | LCCN 2022025307 (ebook) | ISBN 9781644697214 (hardback) | ISBN 9781644697221 (paperback) | ISBN 9781644697238 (adobe pdf) | ISBN 9781644697245 (epub)
Subjects: LCSH: Yugoslav literature--20th century--Translations into English. | Experimental poetry, Yugoslav--20th century--Translations into English. | Experimental fiction, Yugoslav--20th century--Translations into English. | Creative nonfiction, Yugoslav--20th century--Translations into English. | LCGFT: Experimental poetry. | Experimental fiction. | Creative nonfiction.
Classification: LCC PG584.E1 Z46 2022 (print) | LCC PG584.E1 (ebook) | DDC 891.8/2090052--dc23/eng/20221018
LC record available at https://lccn.loc.gov/2022025306
LC ebook record available at https://lccn.loc.gov/2022025307

ISBN 9781644697214 (hardback)
ISBN 9781644697221 (paperback)
ISBN 9781644697238 (adobe pdf)
ISBN 9781644697245 (epub)

Cover design by Milan Dragojlović with Ivan Grave
Book design by Konstantin Kuzminsky, Mykhailo Fedyshak, with PHi Business Solutions

Published by Academic Studies Press
1577 Beacon Street
Brookline, MA 02446, USA

press@academicstudiespress.com
www.academicstudiespress.com

Contents

Acknowledgments

Even the most assured falter in their convictions. When one thinks of the major avant-garde movements of European modernism one tends not to think of zenithism. We have aimed to change the conversation on European modernism in the English language with this book and there were days when the task overwhelmed us. You would not be holding this book in your hands were it not for the long list of people who unflaggingly supported us in this endeavor.

The initial vision behind this anthology was simple. It would comprise translations of key texts from *Zenit* magazine and all the books published by Biblioteka Zenit press. *Zenit* and Biblioteka Zenit, after all, were the main publishing vehicles of the zenithist movement. Although these two publishing arms of the zenithists serve as the central nervous system of this book, they only tell a small part of the story. The zenithists not only published outside these two venues, they also documented their ideas and history through their correspondence. And, of course, there are decades of scholarship on zenithism and its influence both within the former Yugoslavia and beyond its borders.

Carrying out the mission of transporting zenithism into English, however, ballooned into a project that extended much deeper and wider than we anticipated.

Again, we tried to simplify the goals of the anthology. This book had to answer two questions: One: What is zenithism? Two: Why is it important? To this end, we would pepper the anthology with short introductions for each section. What those sections would be and how long they would be ended up being the windiest serpent for us. The introductions were not short, but sharp, striving, and piercing.

We have at times felt like the one-eyed among the blind. Other times, we have felt like the blind among the one-eyed. We have been the whorl of scythes in a land of decapitated dolls. We have not lived by half measures. That, in the end, is the spirit of zenithism.

Joining us have been a growing cast of characters who have kept their heads and lent sanity and order to the proceedings. Without these people the anthology could not have happened. We are in their debt.

Ellen Elias-Bursać is the godmother of this anthology. Without her, this book may never have been seen by the bright eyes of the reader.

The nascent stage of what would eventually become this anthology began as two parallel anthologies on a survey of all the avant-garde movements of the former Yugoslavia: Croatian futurism, expressionism, Sumatraism, zenithism, Yugo-Dada, the Travelers, hypnism, Slovenian constructivism, and Belgrade surrealism. We each wrestled separately with assembling our own anthology, completely unaware of each other and our respective efforts. When Ellen learned of both projects, she introduced us and, with that, we combined our efforts and were able to make significant headway on lifting the project off the ground like a lumbering albatross.

Our team of translators, who have been an absolute pleasure to work with, have made an otherwise unmanageable task attainable. We owe an extraordinary debt to our core team of Bosnian, Croatian, and Serbian (BSC) translators: Samantha Farmer, Vesna Jevtić, Dragana Obradović, Maja Starčević, Maja Teref, and Suzana Vuljević. We are honored to have worked with these women who stand in stark contrast to the masculine energy of zenithist authorship. Their unfailing hard work, open minds, and graciousness in receiving and providing feedback have been a godsend.

Another key member of our team includes Ronald Meyer who volunteered his time and editorial expertise on the introductory essays. He tightened the essays when they needed it most.

We want to thank the peer reviewers at the National Endowment for the Humanities for their invaluable feedback on an early iteration of what would consequently become this book. They were the ones who recommended that we steer away from attempting a survey of all the avant-garde movements of Yugoslavia and instead focus on one movement. We also want to thank the peer reviewers for Academic Studies Press who provided us with insights on how we could further improve this anthology.

We want to thank Danijela Lugarić for helping with the scans of Vida Golubović's articles on zenithist correspondence. We are ever grateful to Saša Ilić for graciously sharing the manuscript of Anuška Micić's and Ljubomir Micić's correspondence he edited and for being of crucial help, together with his colleague Velibor Prelić, with allowing us access to the Legacy of Ljubomir Micić, special collections at the National Library of Serbia.

This anthology is a marriage of translations of a wide range of primary zenithist texts and a wealth of scholarship on zenithism. The scholars whose access and guidance we have utilized in assembling the texts and composing the essays have enormously enriched the depth of what we have been able to bring into English. The venerable Gojko Tešić has been indispensable for his generous sharing of the secondary literature on zenithism and the avant-garde, and for assistance with locating an original copy of *Damn Your Hundred Gods.* The irreplaceable Irina Subotić, a lifelong scholar on zenithism, has been critical for her generous help with materials and resources, and for her enlightening conversations about zenithism. The incomparable Aleksandar Petrov has been vital for sharing his research and for his kind recommendations. We want to acknowledge Stanislava Vujnović for her assistance with and recommendations of current scholarship on zenithism.

Bringing the complex work of the enigmatic MID into English has been one of the biggest challenges of this anthology and we are indebted to all those who assisted us in this leg of the book's journey. Andrea Bogojević and Jennifer H. Zoble played a vital role for their help with the translation of MID's *The Metaphysics of Nothing.* Igor Perišić's assistance with scans of the republished editions of MID's books, edited by Gojko Tešić, acted as a valuable check against the original editions. The members of the Third Coast Translators Collective (TCTC) provided crucial support and feedback with Steven and Maja Teref's translation of MID's *The Sexual Equilibrium of Money.* TCTC helped them break out of their translationese funk when it was most needed. Naoko Fujimoto has been an indominable champion of the Terefs by publishing "Dust in the Sunlight: Translating Light," their essay on the experience of translating MID into English. Miodrag Milovanović deserves the greatest praise for sharing a scan of the 1925 article on MID from *Vreme.* This article provides the most extensive sense of MID as a person and thinker.

Although most of the texts in this anthology were translated from BCS, other languages were represented, and we are grateful for the language experts who helped us with non-BCS language support: Jed Rasula for his translation of Yvan Goll's *Paris Burns* and Boško Tokin's "Cinema Poems." Meghan Forbes for her help with translating survey questions from the Czech journal *Bytova kultura,* Neil Blackadder for his German, and Caroline Chapman Giberson and Luna Giberson for their French. And perhaps the most daunting language for us was that of economics. The economist Veroljub Dugalić helped us with economic terminology, namely, the term *LORA.*

We are grateful for the support of the owners, curators, and staff of galleries and museums who supplied us with high resolution images of zenithist texts and images. Namely, we are indebted to Adam J. Boxer and Ubu Gallery in New York and the Galerie Berinson in Berlin, Nevena Martinović and Aleksandar Milojević at the Gallery RIMA in Kragujevac and Belgrade, and Milica Cicmil, Biljana Djordjević, and Bojana Borić Brešković at the National Museum in Belgrade. Likewise, we are grateful to Sonja Martinović at the National and University Library in Zagreb and Vladimir Pištalo, Acting Director of the National Library of Serbia, for their assistance with zenithist sources. The visual story of zenithism could not be told without them.

Special thanks go to Milan Dragojlović for his help with the the front cover design.

We are likewise grateful to collectors who have shared their collections with us. Darko Šimčić was generous for sharing his private collection of zenithist texts and providing information on an original copy of *Archipenko: New Plastics*.

Thanks to the journals and publishers who have published and otherwise supported this work. Action Books were kind to give us permission to reprint Boško Tokin's "Cinema Poems" from *Burning City: Poems of Metropolitan Modernity*. MIT Press and the Los Angeles County Museum of Art were gracious in giving us permission to preprint numerous indispensable zenithist texts from *Between Worlds: A Sourcebook of Central European Avant-Gardes, 1910–1930*.

Numerous translations in this anthology first appeared in the following journals: *Asymptote, Brooklyn Rail, Columbia Journal, Conjunctions, Harriman Magazine, LIT, Spoon River Poetry Review,* and *Vestiges*. We are indebted to the editors for supporting this work.

A special thanks goes to the following institutions without which the publication of this volume would not be possible: The Collegium de Lyon, an Institute for Advanced Studies within the University of Lyon, and the Harriman Institute at Columbia University. We are truly indebted to their steadfast support.

Despite our convictions that this book would be a seminal text for zenithism in English, we could not have persevered without the support of our stalwarts who believed in us when we doubted ourselves. Tony Trigilio has been the wind under our wings for his counsel and encouragement. Likewise, the editors of *RHINO* have been unflagging in their encouragement and enthusiasm when we have been at our most tentative. We especially want to thank Virginia Bell, Angela Narciso Torres, Naoko Fujimoto, Jacob Saenz, Jan Bottiglieri, and Darren Angle. The edge is frightening but less so when someone dear holds your hand.

Last, but not least, we give our heartfelt thanks to our colleagues and friends who helped us persevere and build this unshakeable web of indominable support.

Aleksandar Bošković

Steven Teref

List of Translators

Andrea Bogojević
Aleksandar Bošković
Samantha Farmer
Meghan Forbes
Vesna Jevtić
Dragana Obradović
Jed Rasula
Maja Starčević
Maja Teref
Steven Teref
Suzana Vuljević
Jennifer H. Zoble

List of Illustrations

The Barbarians are Coming, or a Savage Rhythm

The Barbarogenius, the Balkanization of Europe, and Cultural Nihilism

The First Road of the Barbarogenius: Cinépoetry and the Radio-Film

The Second Road of the Barbarogenius: The Hybrid Novel, Prose Poetry, and the Serpentinella

The Third Road of the Barbarogenius: Conceptual Writing

The Barbarogenius at the Gates: Zenithist Theater, Soirees, and Public Interventions

The Nadir of Zenithism

Sources

Archives Michael Ilk, Germany
Collection of the National Museum in Belgrade
Collection of the National and University Library in Zagreb
Gallery RIMA, Kragujevac & Belgrade
Legacy of Ljubomir Micić, Special collections, National Library of Serbia, Belgrade
Ubu Gallery, New York & Galerie Berinson, Berlin

Pronunciation Guide

Here is a helpful American English pronunciation guide for some of the letters in Bosnian, Croatian, Serbian (BCS) to assist readers when encountering the names in this book.

C, c	as in the **ts** in **tsetse** fly
Č, č	as in the **ch** in **church** and **ch**urn
Ć, ć	as in the **ch** in **ch**ess and **ch**eese
Dž, dž	as in the hard **g** in **g**eneral or the **j** in **j**oke
Đ, đ	as in the **j** in **j**iu-**j**itsu or **j**uniper
I, i	as in the **ee** in n**ee**d
J, j	as in the **j** in f**j**ord or the **y** in **y**ellow
Lj, lj	as in the **li** in bil**li**on
Nj, nj	as in the **ni** in o**ni**on or the **ny** in ca**ny**on
R, r	as in the trilled **r**
Š, š	as in the **sh** in **sh**eet
Ž, ž	as in the **s** in plea**s**ure

Introduction: You Have to Be a Zenithist

Aleksandar Bošković and Steven Teref

Among the assorted avant-garde movements and modernist tendencies which emerged in the newly established Kingdom of Serbs, Croats, and Slovenes after World War I, zenithism occupies a special place. Zenithism was an avant-garde movement in its complete form with a founding ideologue, a group of followers, manifestos, a periodical, a press, multidisciplinary activities, and a clear sense of its place in society and Western culture at large. Zenithism stood apart from other early twentieth-century movements by seeking to unite the separate strains of experimental literature and art into a pan-avant-garde. Established by the artist couple Anuška (née Kon) (1901–1961) and Ljubomir Micić (1895–1971) and his younger brother Branko Ve Poljanski (1898–1947) in 1921, zenithism revolved primarily around the magazine *Zenit* and the publishing house Biblioteka Zenit. Although *Zenit* published work from most of the concurrent avant-garde movements sprouting up across Europe—a feat remarkable in itself—it was the press that best highlighted what made zenithism unique—namely, hybrid writing. Though the zenithists did not invent hybrid writing (and they were certainly not the only ones producing it), they were the first to make it a central feature of their poetics.

The foundation of the zenithist movement, that is, the magazine *Zenit* and its publishing house Biblioteka Zenit, form the backbone of this anthology. But the movement was much more than a literary endeavor. The zenithists held several fine arts exhibitions—in Zagreb (1922), Belgrade (1924), and Moscow as a part of Western revolutionary art (1926). Zenithists promoted their work with a series of readings and performances (in 1923 and 1925), which included multimedia poetry readings and polemics. The performance group Travelers staged zenithist works. Zenithists even staged numerous political actions and demonstrations, such as protests against Alfred Kerr in Paris (1925) and Rabindranath Tagore in Belgrade (1926). Zenithism was represented in the visual arts through linocuts by Mihailo S. Petrov (1902–1983) and abstract paintings and constructivist-influenced art by Josip Seissel (1904–1987), who went by the nom de guerre Josif Jo Klek.

Beginnings: It's Healthy to Drink Electric Milk

The emergence of zenithism was contingent on historical, cultural, and material factors. Coming forth after World War I as one of the early avant-garde movements in the newly established Kingdom of Serbs, Croats, and Slovenes, zenithists, like avant-garde artists across the continent, experienced the same disappointment in bourgeois society for being unable to prevent the war. Established by the artist couple Anuška (Kon) and Ljubomir Micić, the movement was formed during the period of vibrant aesthetic activities of European avant-gardes. Initially following his poetic worldview informed by a strong expressionist orientation, Micić merely intensified zenithism in a collision with real life at the crossroads of two epochs and the changed historical, political, and social circumstances. He was primarily interested in the problem of complex poetic inner constellations and the revolutionary principle of internationalism, in solving the issue of aesthetic revaluation of old spiritual values with the help of ideological constructions about Europe and the Balkans. Reflecting on the postwar origins of the movement from the perspective of its five-year anniversary, he writes:

> An adequate expression had to be found for this new state of mind and soul: it was necessary to unconditionally give this new somersault of the Balkan spirit a new name, it was necessary to unconditionally emphasize the external difference from similar European movements of modern times. It was necessary

> to decisively cut through all traditions, European and domestic, in order to ruthlessly and under a new flag declare war on the investigation of everything that stinks of a disgusting past. The most important thing was to find the way to this first struggle for the cultural independence of the Balkans and the new creation of humanity. [1]

Through zenithist publications and activities Micić wanted to shape and promote the formula of the Balkan avant-garde movement, which, with its original program and accompanying creative practice, would be on the same level with other progressive tendencies in Europe at the time. To achieve this, he advocated for the artistic and cultural emancipation of the Balkans from the West in general and Europe in particular, the dethronement of its traditional values, and the reversal of the process of Europeanization of the Balkans in the direction of the Balkanization of Europe.

Ljubomir Micić's correspondence allows us to trace the origins of *Zenit* to the fall of 1920 when Micić contacted Boško Tokin (1894–1953) and Yvan Goll (1891–1950) with a call for cooperation. [2] Boško Tokin, who lived in Paris from 1916 to 1920, played an important role in sharing his knowledge about the cultural and literary phenomena of French and Italian modernism and avant-garde to a Yugoslav audience and vice versa. [3] He wrote reviews of foreign books and magazines, and published them in Yugoslav periodicals challenging domestic reactionary criticism from the standpoint of French *l'esprit nouveau* (the new spirit) and true futurist revolutionism, directed against opposition to the establishment of a new order. He was interested in diverse phenomena such as the Renaissance, the internal monologue (as an attempt to resolve the role of artists in the modern world), the futurist theme of aviation, and even miracles. But first and foremost, he was interested in cinema and its significance for new, avant-garde approaches in literature. Tokin contributed both to

---

1 Ljubormi Micić, "Film jednog književnog pokreta i jedne duhovne revolucije," *Zenit*, no. 38 (February 1926): n.p.

2 See Vidosava Golubović, "Časopis *Zenit* (1921–1926)," in *Zenit: Internacionalna revija za umetnost i kulturu 1921–1926*, ed. Vidosava Golubović and Irina Subotić (Belgrade: Narodna biblioteka Srbije, Institut za književnost i umetnost, 2008), 17.

3 Tokin selected and translated modern Yugoslav poets for an anthology on contemporary Yugoslav poetry in French, which he edited and published in 1919; see *Anthologie de Poèmes yougo-slaves contemporains*, trans. Philéas Lebesgue and B. Tokine (Paris: Édition de la Revue Littéraire des Primaires "Les Humbles," 1919).

establishing cinematography as "an integral part of a new poetic technique" and introducing film as a narrative theme in Serbian literature.[4]

In Paris, Tokin met Yvan Goll, a French-German poet who frequented the same artistic circles, and introduced his recent poetry inspired by cinema to a Yugoslav audience in the inaugural issue of *Zenit.*[5] As with Tokin, Yvan Goll started contributing to *Zenit* from the first issue, where he published his poem "Der Mensch vor dem Meer" (Men in Front of the Sea) in German. Soon after, he formally joined zenithism, accepted its program, and contributed to its formation and promotion. Goll became actively involved in the development of the term *zenithism*, publishing his contribution in a manifesto of the movement in German on the front page of the fifth issue of *Zenit.*[6] He joined *Zenit* as a co-editor for West Europe and ran it with Micić from October 1921 to May 1922, embracing the East-West editorial concept.[7] As a declared zenithist and co-editor of *Zenit* for issues 8–14, Goll helped finetune the poetic practice of zenithism. In addition to contributing poetry and theoretical articles, he published the long poem *Paris brennt* (*Paris Burns,* 1921) in German, as the second publication by Biblioteka Zenit.[8]

As partners in the zenithist enterprise, Ljubomir and Anuška each played a distinct and vital role in making the movement successful. While Ljubomir was the poet, critic, writer of manifestos, and editor of *Zenit* and Biblioteka Zenit, Anuška's managerial and organizational role was paramount: without her the printing of any zenithist publication was unthinkable.

Due to Anuška's connections with her uncle and the main shareholder of the paper factory Lipa Mill in Zagreb (Croatia), Matija Frojnd, and her work in this enterprise, it was possible to produce *Zenit,* publish Biblioteka Zenit books, as well as later to finance Micić's

---

4 See Radovan Vučković, *Poetika srpske avangarde* (Belgrade: Službeni glasnik, 2011), 212; Gojko Tešić, "Kontekst za čitanje pripovetke srpskog modernizma i avangarde," in *Antologija srpske avangardne književnosti,* ed. G. Tešić (Novi Sad: Bratstvo-jedinstvo, 1989), xv.

5 See Boško Tokin, "Evropski pesnik Ivan Goll," *Zenit,* no. 1 (February 1921): 5–9, and Jovan Kršić, "Zenitizam," in Vojislav Maksimović, ed. *Sabrana djela,* (*Književnosti naroda Jugoslavije*), vol. 2, (Sarajevo: Svijetlost, 1979), 21–25.

6 Yvan Goll, "Zenitistisches Manifest," *Zenit,* no. 5 (June 1921): 1–2.

7 See Zoran Markuš, *Zenitizam* (Belgrade: ID Signature, 2003), 48–49; Golubović and Subotić, *Zenit,* 17; 31; 84–87.

8 Goll published the second, French version of the poem *Paris brule* (1923) in 1923; see Yvan Goll, *Le nouvel Orphée* (Paris: La Sirène, 1923), 139–155. For more on the differences between the two versions, see Johannes Ullmaier, *Yvan Golls Gedicht "Paris brennt"* (Tübingen: Max Niemeyer Verlag, 1995).

long exile in France.[9] Anuška ran the Belgrade branch of Lipa Mill, which was the main source of income for her and Ljubomir, and also provided the funds that the Micićs needed for zenithist publications, promotions, business trips, and art purchases. The Lipa Mill factory was primarily involved in the "production and sale of paper, cigarette paper, packaging, and cardboard, as well as confectionery products. *Zenit* was published from leftover paper that Anuška managed to set aside from the large quantity that passed through the branch office, which resulted in the issues being of a different format, weight, and color" over the course of its history.[10] The Biblioteka Zenit press most likely used the same resources.

Anuška's input was crucial; nothing would have been possible without her mediation, approval, consultation, editing, and translating zenithist texts into German. As Saša Ilić writes, "With her advice and talent, she combined two important spheres: finance and culture, or, in modern jargon—advertising, which was present in almost every zenithist publication, mainly on the last pages or on the inside of the covers."[11] Various companies that advertised in the pages of *Zenit* were an important economic resource that appeared and developed in Zagreb and Belgrade between the two wars. As Ilić convincingly argues,

> It is in this broader economic context that a real picture of zenithist production is obtained, which, due to Anuška's cultural horizon and commitment to the avant-garde, arose from the *surplus value* that she redirected to a common cultural product—*Zenit*. This means that one of the most important anarchist and anti-capitalist literary journals of that time in the Kingdom of the Serbs, Croats, and Slovenes appeared in the heart of capitalist production. This kind of work required an outstanding person who would be able to redirect the 'material base' into a revolutionary production. Anuška Micić was just such a person. Self-contained and versatile.[12]

---

9 Anuška's uncle Matija Frojnd (1969–1935) "came to Croatia in 1903, while in 1907 he took over the recently founded Golub cigarette paper factory which served as the foundation for the Lipa Mill factory established in 1910." See the recent collection of correspondence between Anuška and Ljubomir from the post-zenithist period: Saša Ilić, "Ljubav i smrt posle avangarde" [Love and death after the avant-garde], in *Strašna komedija: Prepiska Anuške Kon Micić i Ljubomira Micića 1920–1960*, ed. Saša Ilić and Dragana Peruničić (Belgrade: Narodna Biblioteka Srbije, 2021).

10 Saša Ilić, "Ljubav i smrt posle avangarde," in Ilić and Peruničić, *Strašna komedija*, 37.

11 Ibid.

12 Ibid.

Besides Anuška, Micić's younger brother Branko Ve Poljanski played a significant role and provided valuable support both in the work of the magazine and in the promotion of zenithism. Poljanski's early work was linked to Ljubljana and marked by theater acting and the launch of the futurist-expressionist magazine *Svetokret* (Worldwhirl, 1921). In addition to publishing his works in *Zenit* and through Biblioteka Zenit, Poljanski was often involved in the agitation and backing of magazines and movements in Yugoslavia and European capitals: besides Ljubljana, Zagreb, and Belgrade, he promoted zenithism in Vienna, Prague, Berlin, and Paris. It could be argued that the groundwork for *Zenit* was laid by the appearance of *Svetokret*,[13] by endorsing futurist-expressionist novelty, paradox, and revolutionary ideas, while denunciating the sluggishness of the human spirit.

While in Prague, Poljanski worked closely with Dadaist Dragan Aleksić, who was formed in the artistic environment of Prague where the two met, and whose manifestos, poetry, and Dadaistic essays were published in *Zenit*. In Zagreb, Poljanski and Aleksić co-edited the magazine for film culture, *Kinofon* (twelve issues between 1921 and 1922), in which they published essays about international cinema.[14] Aleksić's intense cooperation with *Zenit* lasted from March 1921 to May 1922, and ceased when the Micić brothers combatively disassociated zenithism from the former's Yugoslav branch of Dadaism.[15]

From the very onset of the movement, Ljubomir Micić enlisted many domestic and foreign associates—representatives of Western and Eastern cultures—who contributed to zenithism's ideological platform of humanism, pacifism, and the international brotherhood of artists. Many well-known Serbian modernist writers, such as Rastko Petrović, Stanislav Vinaver, Stanislav Krakov, and Miloš Crnjanski, published their work in early issues of *Zenit*; however, it was a short affair since they soon broke with Micić and stopped contributing to his review, announcing their decision publicly and collectively as the Belgrade literary

---

13 *Svetokret: List za ekspediciju na severni pol čovekovog duha* (January 1921). Republished (Zagreb: Ranko Horetzky, 2008).

14 Aleksić himself was an avid film lover. He collaborated with Boško Tokin in founding the Belgrade Club of Film Lovers (1924), as well as on the shooting of the unfinished Serbian avant-garde film *Kačaci u Topčideru*, directed by Dragan Aleksić and Boško Tokin (Belgrade: Klub Filmofila, 1923).

15 See the two issues of the anti-Dada magazine *Dada-Jok* (May 1922), edited by Poljanski. Republished (Ranko Horetzky, 2008). Due to growing misunderstandings with Micić, Aleksić's Dadaist novel-grotesque *Provala gospodina Hristosa* (The Burglary of Mr. Christ) was not published as the third volume of Biblioteka Zenit as was advertised in the April 1922 issues of both *Kinofon*, no. 8 and *Zenit*, no. 13.

group *Alpha,* in the journal *Kritika.*[16] *Zenit* has played an important role in introducing new art forms by artists such as Vilko Gecan (contributing to the pre-zenithist phase), Mihailo S. Petrov (the early phase), Josip Seissel or Josif Jo Klek (the mature phase), and Jovan Bijelić—all early abstract painters in Yugoslavia, along with a Jewish Croatian artist, Vjera Biller, as well as the Slovenian constructivists, August and Thea Černigoj with Eduard Stepančič, whose works have been preserved in Micić's private collection, now owned by the National Museum in Belgrade.

Besides poet Yvan Goll, who served as one of the initial pillars of zenithism, many renowned European avant-garde artists appeared in the pages of *Zenit*: Alexander Archipenko, Henri Barbusse, Franz Richard Behrens, Marc Chagall, Fortunato Depero, Theo van Doesburg, Ilya Ehrenburg, Albert Gleizes, Wassily Kandinsky, Lajos Kassak, El Lissitzky, Louis Lozowick, Vladimir Mayakovsky, Filippo Tommaso Marinetti, Hannes Meyer, Geo Milev, Laszlo Moholy-Nagy, Jaroslav Seifert, and Karel Taige. They all more-or-less shared the poetics that largely departed from the accomplishments of the early European avant-garde, which also contributed to the affirmation of a new potentially global movement—zenithism. As Micić wrote, "New art from before the war (meaning fauvism, cubism, expressionism or futurism—author's note) can never continue where it was interrupted. [. . .] That is why a new mobilization of the post-war atmosphere of spirits is needed, because new art is not timeless."[17] This "postwar atmosphere of spirits" was in fact the same disappointment in the European bourgeoisie, as found in Miloš Crnjanski's bitter poems in *Lyrics of Ithaca* (1919).

In addition, progressive artists of the time were caught up in the technical progress of mankind, and were drawn to new, modern phenomena such as the airplane, radio and film, or the general development of electrical engineering. It is likely that this modernity of ideas—manifested in the pages of *Zenit*—was one of the crucial reasons for the fervent affirmation of zenithism by West European artists (and avant-garde movements, namely De Stijl in Holland, the futurists in Italy, Devětsil in Czecholovakia, the Hungarian avant-gardists around the magazine *Ma,* and other members of international constructivism.[18] This allowed *Zenit* to transcend its Yugoslav borders.

---

16 See *Kritika: književno umjetnička revija,* nos. 11–12 (November and December, 1921).

17 Ljubomir Micić, "Savremeno novo i slućeno slikarstvo," *Zenit,* no. 10 (December 1921): 11.

18 Emile Malespine, for example, started the journal *Manométre: Revue polyglotte et supernationale* in Lyon in July 1922, which was modeled after *Zenit.* See *Manométre. Collection complete: 1922–1928* (Paris: Editions Jean-Michel Place, 1977).

Zenithist Publications: *Zenit* and Biblioteka Zenit

The Micićs started publishing *Zenit* magazine and books through the Biblioteka Zenit press in Zagreb in 1921, but then had to move the editorial office to Belgrade in 1923. In Zagreb, *Zenit* had a steady monthly publishing rhythm until the definitive break in May 1923, which was caused by a politically provocative article about Stjepan Radić and Croatian culture.[19] After the May 1923 issue of *Zenit* no. 24, the editorial office relocated to Belgrade.[20] During the Belgrade period, the publishing schedule was inconsistent due to the financial and administrative hardships Micić had to face, including endless attacks on *Zenit* in the Serbian press; thus, to overcome gaps in publishing, the editor sometimes combined several issues. Nonetheless, Micić tried to preserve an uninterrupted rhythm of *Zenit* with publication-related activities, such as public appearances, zenithist lectures, soirees, and exhibitions. Under Micić's editorship, *Zenit* magazine was published with occasional interruptions until December 1926 (a total of 43 issues were issued), when, due to an attempt at a Marxist interpretation of zenithism, the magazine was banned and Micić was forced to leave the country.

Zenit was a major forum for avant-garde authors who fought for new forms in literature, architecture, film, theater, music, and fine and applied arts. Initially, the periodical was influenced by expressionism, but soon after post-cubist, futurist, and Dadaist elements entered zenithist aesthetics and changed Micić's approach to new media and the magazine's design. Russian avant-garde artists—particularly Ilya Ehrenburg and El Lissitzky, editors of the magazine *Veshch' = Objet = Gegenstand* in Berlin—became important collaborators and guest editors of the *Zenit* double issue, nos. 17–18 (September–October 1922). *Zenit* increasingly leaned toward the aesthetics of constructivism and Bauhaus, while some proto-surrealist texts were later featured. During the Belgrade years, *Zenit* was heavily indebted to socially engaged art.

---

19 Issue 24 of *Zenit* was the last to be published in Zagreb: the reason was the publication of Micić's pamphlet "Parrot and the 'Croatian Culture' Monopoly," written as a response to the following statement of Croatian politician Stjepan Radić: "We [the Croats] used to be the vanguard of European culture, but now we are trying to be the rearguard of Balkan non-culture." Micić later "translated" his pamphlet from Croatian into Serbian and published it in *Zenit*, no. 39 (March 1926). Due to the sharp reaction of the Zagreb community, "Micić fled to Belgrade unprotected and lonely," as he himself wrote.

20 Golubović and Subotić, *Zenit*, 151, 347.

As the main platform of the zenithist movement, *Zenit* adhered to anarchism, internationalism, and the revolution of the spirit. In the opening text of the inaugural issue of *Zenit* (February 1921), Micić put forward that "the SPIRIT or the demiurge, Anarch—wishes to rule chaos—to be all powerful (*vsevolod*), to be a god. He lusts to create *action* from chaos."[21] The first Biblioteka Zenit publication, *The Manifesto of Zenithism*, by Ljubomir Micić, Yvan Goll, and Boško Tokin, published in June 1921, repeated the slogan: "We are led by the mystical demi-god ANARCH."[22] Micić later explained: "Zenithism is a free spirit, a spirit independent in its search: for its form—its style—its "I"—its *individuality*. [...] Zenithism, in its striving for the liberation of man, in its striving for individualism, is also *anarchy* and its *religion* is to create new forms and relationships as a spiritual basis for the future Balkan-human art and to destroy the inhuman and non-spiritual past we all share with its positive aspect."[23] In another instance, Micić asserted: "New poets are fanatics of new creation. Spiritual rebels and anarchists. Their anarchy is a vow of the spirit for the liberation of man from pathos, the matter of egoism and dark crime. [...] The poet's anarchy and flame is THE WORD."[24] Micić's short prose piece "De Gidi bekjar budala" (Come on, you stupid fool), published in 1926, describes a character named Anarch Hunger—the author's alter ego—whose last name probably reflected the economic hardships Micić went through in 1924.[25]

The header of *Zenit* stated that it was an "international" magazine, and true to its claim, zenithism was recognized and accepted in Russia, Belgium, Holland, France, Germany, Czechoslovakia, Hungary, Italy, and elsewhere. To that end, the magazine printed work from across Europe in the original language sans translation in an effort to draw the international readership it sought. In his manifesto published in *Zenit*, Yvan Goll proclaims: "MAN! We are neither French, nor Serbs, nor Germans, nor Blacks, nor Luxembourgers! We are

---

21 Ljubomir Micić, "Čovek i umetnost," *Zenit*, no. 1 (February 1921): 1; emphasis in the original. See "Man and Art" in this anthology.

22 Ljubomir Micić, Yvan Goll, and Boško Tokin, *Manifest zenitizma* (Zagreb: Biblioteka Zenit, 1921). See *The Manifesto of Zenithism* in this anthology.

23 Ljubomir Micić, "Duh zenitizma," *Zenit*, no. 7 (September 1921): 4; emphasis in the original. See "The Spirit of Zenithism" in this anthology.

24 Ljubomir Micić, "Delo zenitizma," *Zenit*, no. 8 (October 1921): 2–3.

25 Ljubomir Micić, "De Gidi bekjar budala," *Zenit*, no. 40 (April 1926): 4–10; "Hvala ti Srbijo lepa," *Zenit*, no. 36 (October 1925): 4; "Za slobodu misli, za slobodu stvaranja," *Zenit*, no. 41 (May 1926): 10.

Europeans, Americans, Africans, Asians, Australians!"[26] This proclamation not only referred to the various origins and languages of those who published in the magazine, but also to the ideological orientation of zenithism. In the first issue of *Zenit,* Micić declared: "Our fight will be against crime—for Man. Workers of the world, unite—against killing."[27] In the pages of *Zenit,* Micić gathered a vast number of associates not only from Belgrade, Zagreb, and Ljubljana, but also "from almost all other European countries in which there were avant-garde movements, from North and South America, and even Japan."[28] Micić's journal connected the Balkans with the world.

Zenit positioned itself as a revolutionary magazine from the beginning. Its first issue featured the article "Proletkult" by Anatoly Lunacharsky, the Soviet Commissar for the Ministry of Education, and Micić's definition of art as "eternal revolution."[29] The zenithist revolution began as a poetic expression of indignation at World War I as the origin of European history that demanded change:

> The path of the poetic revolution, which the zenithists started at the beginning of this decade, is partially expressed here. It is progressively imposed more and more as a postulate and a categorical imperative, directly as the second link of social revolutions, which shook and partially endangered the foundations of capitalist society.[30]

As such, *Zenit* made room for topics related to the Russian revolution.[31] *Zenit* was critical of the political and cultural practices of capitalism, the heritage of European colonialism, the authority of political power and the church, social injustice and ossified institutions,

---

26 Yvan Goll, "Zenitistisches Manifest," *Zenit,* no. 5 (June 1921): 1–2.

27 Ljubomir Micić, "Čovek i umetnost," *Zenit,* no. 1 (February 1921): 1–2. See "Man and Art" in this anthology.

28 Irina Subotić, "The *Zenit* Magazine and Ljubomir Micić: Ideas, Programs, Achievements," in *Balkanization,* ed. Žarko Aleksić and Jelena Micić (Vienna: Friday Exit, 2016), 16.

29 A. Lunačarski, "Proletkult," *Zenit,* no. 1 (February 1921): 11–12; Ljubomir Micić, "Čovek i umetnost": 1–2. See "Man and Art" in this anthology.

30 Ljubomir Micić, "Radio-film i zenitistička okomica duha," *Zenit,* no. 23 (April 1923): 2–5. See "Radio-Film and the Zenithist Vertical of the Spirit" in this anthology.

31 Maxim Gorky, "Povodom revolucije" [On the occasion of the revolution], *Zenit,* no. 34 (November 1924): 13–14; no. 35 (December 1924): 11–12. On the occasion of Lenin's death, the review published Leon Trotsky's text "Lenin," *Zenit,* no. 26–33 (October 1924): 25–27. Also, Micić and his wife, Anuška,

and the unchanged traditions in the Kingdom of Serbs, Croats, and Slovenes. Although he insisted that zenithism was fighting for the "revolution of spirit" rather than a class revolution, Micić viewed poets as rebels and "spiritual anarchists," not as social revolutionaries. He attacked the decision by the Kingdom to break all diplomatic ties with Soviet Russia following the October Revolution.[32] Moreover, "in commenting upon the October Revolution, Micić praised Russia's ability to overcome 'sentimental politics' and to break with the past in order to set the foundation for a radically new social reality."[33] As the Bolsheviks regained power and emancipated Russia from Western influence, Micić saw the Soviet Union as an example of a successful social experiment by a Slavic people; Micić believed that Soviet avant-garde art had, for the first time, put Russia ahead of Europe as the model of Slavic "authenticity and originality" in the sea of Latins, which he suggested the Balkans should aspire to. This quest particularly resonated with Marijan Mikac (1903–1972), a young poet and Micić's follower, who in his essay "The New Zenithist Art" proclaimed,"Zenithism is a new movement in art. As such, Zenithism is revolutionary."[34] According to Mikac, the "revolutionary" aspect of zenithism should be understood by its open-ended, ever-changing, and anti-finalizing character: "zenithism is proto-dynamic in its development: the basic elements are evident everywhere, but the movement is in constant creation, progression, and evolution."[35]

The core contributors to *Zenit* also published their work through Biblioteka Zenit.[36] In addition to Micić, Goll, and Tokin, three other authors—Branko Ve Poljanski, Marijan

translated Lunacharsky's *Proletkult* in 1924 and published it with Micić's foreword (which was translated into Bulgarian and published in the journal *Plam'k*).

32 The state's decision had been driven by Western European governments. Micić wrote extensively on this matter, arguing that by falling in behind its Western European allies, Yugoslavia had, "to its great Slavic disgrace," turned its back on Russia, whose political support was critical to the success of the Yugoslav project. Micić, "Protiv jugoslovenskog antirusizma" [Against Yugoslav anti-Russian sentiment], *Zenit*, no. 15 (June 1922): 36; and "Protiv sentimentalne politike" [Against sentimental politics], special issue, *Zenit* (September 1922): 1–2.

33 Iva Glišić and Tijana Vujošević, "I am Barbarogenius: Yugoslav Zenitism of the 1920s and the Limits of Performativity," *Slavic and Eastern European Journal* 60, no. 4 (2016): 736–737.

34 Marijan Mikac, *Fenomen majmun* (Belgrade: Biblioteka Zenit, 1925), 59.

35 Ibid., 64. The Belgrade surrealists in a similar manner a few years later conceived their own experimental literary and art practices connecting them to dialectical materialism. See Vane Bor and Marko Ristić, *Anti-zid* (Belgrade: Nadrealistička Izdanja, 1932), 8.

36 The press existed under different names such as Biblioteka Zenit [Zenit Series], Izdanje "Zenit" [Zenit Edition], Administracija "Zenit" [Zenit Administration], Izdanje međunarodnog

Mikac, and MID [Mita Dimitrijević]—published multiple works with the press. Biblioteka Zenit's programs, ideas and aesthetics, as well as the typographic and graphic design, offer more than a cross-section of *Zenit* and its development from 1921 to 1927. One of the key features of the press was its collaborative nature, which included writing introductions, contributing illustrations, and designing each other's books. But there were also examples when all those jobs were done by one person. A prominent feature of the fourteen books Biblioteka Zenit published in its seven-year run was hybrid, or cross-genre writing, which became the signature zenithist contribution to the European interwar avant-garde movement. Another striking feature of Biblioteka Zenit publications and promotional materials, as with *Zenit*, was the press's commitment to innovative typography and graphic design, which made reading a new and transformative experience. However, before we address the innovative printing practices and cross-genre writing as hallmarks of the movement, let us briefly describe zenithism as an idea and the key features of its aesthetic-ideological program.

Key Zenithist Tenets

At the outset, zenithism was marked by an expressionist mood: Micić defined it as "abstract metacosmic expressionism," founded on a hymnic faith in man, as a mystical hope that he will reach the zenith—"the highest incarnation of Allexistence." [37] But this quickly changed into a programmatic (and pragmatic) eclecticism, the key tenet of utmost importance for the entire zenithist literary production. As Goll stated in his essay "The Word as a Beginning, an Attempt at New Poetry," published in *Zenit* in November 1921: "Take off on the airplane and see a narrowing globe from the Zenith. ZENITHISM is the taming and accumulating of all 'isms,' and one should take the best from all of them: futurism, cubism, creationism, ultraism, Dadaism; and I would also suggest: Africanism, Mongolism, Dervishism, Internationalism." [38] The fundamental

časopisa "Zenit" [Zenit International Review Edition], and Collection des Zénitistes Internationaux [Zenithists International Edition], but Biblioteka Zenit was the first and most frequent name used for the press. Scholars have settled on Biblioteka Zenit as the standard name.

37 See Micić's contribution in *The Manifesto of Zenithism* in this anthology.

38 Yvan Goll, "Reč kao počelo, pokušaj nove poezije," *Zenit*, no. 9 (November 1921): 3. Goll's essay was reprinted in the German magazine *Die neue Rundschau* under the changed title "Das Wort an sich. Versuch einer neuen Poetik," where, as the title suggests, the emphasis was placed on the independent poetic

eclecticism of zenithist poetics and its program of "synthesis of new art"[39] or "synthesis of all rebellious -isms"[40] led to the proliferation of zenithist eclectic-synthetic constructs and cross-genre writing.

The aesthetics of a modern, urban, mechanist, and spiritual verticality was the most suitable for zenithism's aspirations, as outlined by Goll in the same essay: "Today's form is vertical. Our time is steep. We're moving up. We are airplanes. Elevators always live vertically in skyscrapers. Telegraph poles and antennas and chimneys. We are approaching the ZENITH."[41] To this end, the Eiffel Tower ("the platinum needle"), as much as Tatlin's *Monument to the Third International* (1920) or any other radio antenna rising high to reach the zenith, along with the wireless telegraphy (*télégraphe sans fil* or TSF), achieved mythical proportions in zenithism.[42]

Zenithism was also driven by primitivism and the idea of the new zenithist man—the artist-barbarian. Drawing on Goll's and Tokin's poetic convictions, Micić conceived the *Barbarogenius* (*barbarogenije*), as a great Balkan primitive, something like Nietzsche's Superman and D'Annunzio's Superhuman, who finds his superhuman strength in the self-owned (re)source of southeastern Slavic folklore. Zenithism made "a paradoxical-eclectic leftist/rightist cut in Western traditional universalism" and envisioned the Barbarogenius as "the potential of the modern local"—a superior force that introduced new, fresh, unadulterated, unknown and pure culture, philanthropy, and mutual understanding, with emotions and compassion—"which should motivate or anticipate the new universal."[43] Zenithism

---

word, as in *Zenit*, putting the entire idea in close proximity to "The Word as Such" (1913) by Russian futurists Aleksei Kruchenykh and Velimir Khlebnikov.

39 See the slogan "Zenitisme est le movement pour la synthese de l'art nouveau" on the last page of *Zenit*, no. 25 (February 1924).

40 Risto Ratković, "U Sandžaku san na crvenoj travi," *Zenit*, no. 38 (February 1926): n.p.

41 Yvan Goll, "Reč kao počelo, pokušaj nove poezije," *Zenit*, no. 9 (November 1921): 2.

42 "In the nineteenth century the first transmitters could broadcast only Morse code, and radio was first known as a "wireless telegraph," or *télégraphe sans fil* in French. [...] Until the 1950s, the French used the acronym TSF—which could refer to either wireless telegraphs or telephones—as shorthand for radio. [...] Apollinaire was one of the first avant-garde figures to write enthusiastically about the TSF [...] and 'Lettre-Océan,' one of his most famous calligrammes, is a literary homage to the effects of radio broadcasting on modern poetry." Rubén Gallo, "Jean Cocteau's Radio Poetry," in *The Sound of Poetry, the Poetry of Sound*, ed. Craig Douglas Dworkin and Marjorie Perloff (Chicago: Chicago University Press, 2009), 215–216.

43 Miško Šuvaković, "Eklektični avangardizam: Zenit," in *Istorija umetnosti u Srbiji XX vek: prvo tom, radiikalne umetničke prakse*, ed. M. Šuvaković (Belgrade: Orion art, Katedra za muzikologiju Fakukteta muzičke umetnosti, 2010), 87.

aimed toward a synthesis of earlier avant-garde movements, combining futurist-Dadaist-expressionist, and constructivist elements, but unlike them, the zenithist movement openly opposed everything Western European and with it, everything imperialist and capitalist by promoting barbarism and the Balkan civilization. In other words, the avant-garde culture of total "revaluation of all values" in zenithism was reinforced by local heritage.[44]

Micić launched the provocative idea to undertake a "Balkanization of Europe" by means of the metaphorical figure of a Barbarogenius, considered to be a "decivilizer" and the "holder of non-sentimental, raw vitality, of pure faith—a non-affected soul, an open and good heart."[45] Unlike the contemporary understanding of "Balkanization" as fragmentation along ethnic lines that arose from the breakup of socialist Yugoslavia, Micić sought in "Balkanization" to return the repressed "unconscious of Europe" (the Balkans) to a fresh, primitive, and positive creative force of the awakened Barbarogenius who would conquer and rejuvenate tired European culture. Micić sharply criticized national and class divisions, especially limitations in terms of borders, appealing for openness, subverting the meaning and inverting the position assigned to the Balkans by hegemonic Western European discourse, and asserting that the emancipation of "the stale [. . .] culture of Madame Europe" was contingent on the raw energy of the Balkans.[46] Micić's struggle against the old and degenerate Europe manifested throughout his work, most prominently in his book of poetry *Anti-Europe* (*Antievropa*, 1926), which was published by Biblioteka Zenit and immediately banned by the police. Micić set himself the task of using the principles of avant-garde primitivism to "wipe out the web of dreams" and to tear off the "cultural mask of the God-bearers of the lacquered West."[47]

The zenithist position was set apart by its cultural nihilism: the negation of European (in Micić's opinion: obsolete) culture, sharp criticism of European political and cultural practices and outdated tradition, embodied in old, tired, and incompetent institutions that refuse to face the new demands of society and contemporaneity. Zenithism's destructive cultural nihilism was marked by a joyful, childish, and fantastic vitalism, as if following Russian philosopher and activist Mikhail Bakunin's credo that "the passion for destruction

---

44 The revaluation of all values or the transvaluation of all values is a concept from Friedrich Nietzsche's philosophy, introduced in his *The Anti-Christ* (1895).

45 Ljubomir Micić, *Barbarogénie le Décivilisateur* (Paris: Aux Arènes de Lutèce, 1938).

46 See also Glišić and Vujošević, "I am Barbarogenius".

47 Risto Ratković, "Zenitizam," in *Ćutanje o književnosti* (Belgrade, 1928).

is a creative passion, too."[48] Zenithist cultural nihilists embraced contradiction, ambivalence, and paradox as their central principles. As art historian and theoretician Miško Šuvaković wrote, Micić's zenithism "has paradoxical, eclectic and excessive ideological characteristics, and, in the most general sense, it can be defined as an anarchist approach that uses different strategies of provocation within great ideologies of Slavism, nationalism, Nietzschean superman, Bolshevik revolutionary rhetoric, Trotskyism and anarchist nomadic strategies of a permanent change of views, forms of expression, values and ideologies."[49] The embedding of zenithism in the "leftist" ideological matrix, as well as the radical departure from any Western European paradigm, are two essential determinants in its developmental stage.

Micić saw a model for a zenithist cultural nihilist in the figure of the *haiduk-komitadji*, a proverbial outlaw from both Balkan folklore and geo-political reality.[50] Originating from small bands waging guerrilla warfare against the Ottomans, *haiduks* were troops of the Austro-Hungarian military border (*Militäegrenze*) used in war against the Ottomans and in wars of the seventeenth and eighteenth centuries, which Habsburgs waged against other European powers, or the so-called border troops (*graničari* in Serbo-Croatian); while *komitadjis* were formed by the Bulgarian IMARO (Internal Macedonian and Adrianople Revolutionary Organization) in 1893 with the ultimate goal of acquiring full political autonomy for Ottoman-held regions of (Northern) Macedonia and Adrianople, these paramilitary groups inspired Micić's construction of avant-gardist zenithists.[51]

---

48 Mikhail Bakunin, "The Reaction in Germany" (1842); see https://www.marxists.org/reference/archive/bakunin/works/1842/reaction-germany.htm.

49 Miško Šuvaković, *Istorija umetnosti u Srbiji XX vek* (Belgrade: Orion Art, 2010), 73.

50 See translations of the following Micić's works in the anthology Exercise III of the "The Categorical Imperative of Zenithist School of Poetry" (*Damn Your Hundred Gods/Rescue Car*, 1922), and his poem "bim bam boom" (*Anti-Europe*, 1926).

51 In 1918, *komitadji* were "troops of the Internal Macedonian Revolutionary Organization (IMRO). In response to the rise of Bulgarian influence in Ottoman Macedonia, Greeks and Serbs formed *chetniks*, small guerrilla warfare units that were sent across the border with the task of organizing inhabitants of pro-Serbian areas and villages in Ottoman Macedonia to oppose *komitadji* bands from the rival IMARO as the main agents of the same activity on the Bulgarian side (8). *Kachaks* were traditional Albanian outlaws, who emerged in Kosovo and Metohija as agents of the Kosovo Committee in 1919 (84). *Komitadjis* and *kachaks* represented the paramilitary structures of the two organizations (IMRO and the Kosovo Committee) and were the most pressing security concern in the Yugoslav south (84, 89)." See Dmitar Tasić, *Paramilitarism in the Balkans: The Cases of Yugoslavia, Bulgaria, and Albania, 1917–1924* (Oxford: Oxford University Press, 2020).

If *haiduks* and *komitadjis* were characterized by their intense political engagement, zenithists were known for their intense cultural commitment; if the former showed a strong inclination toward guerrilla warfare, the later did as well, but in the field of culture; if the former actively participated in armed conflicts, political crisis, and coups, the later actively waged cultural wars, public actions, and scandals; if the former were the bearers of paramilitary violence, the later exercised violence *in* and *with* language in their poetic and programmatic works.

Finally, both *haiduks-komitadjis* and zenithists had specific practices in common that were related to their status as outlaws. For example, both groups made personal allegiances rather than organizational or institutional ones. Furthermore, they both transgressed borders and boundaries, whether between countries and territories or between literary genres and the arts. More importantly, both were committing banditry, whether by attacking and robbing oppressors (*hajdučija*) or through texts, that is, by practicing literary banditry. Only by revolutionizing each and every form of writing and by 'dissolving' or 'disorganizing' every literary genre were zenithists able to transcend their reality. Only by employing literary banditry was the zenithist artist able to address the modern distinction between spirit and matter, subject and form, positivism and nihilism, politics and spirituality, art and 'anti-art', with an ironic reformulation of this dualist thinking. Due to the free exercising of these two 'outlaw' practices—hybridization, bastardization, cross-pollination between the arts and the literary banditry—zenithists were able to question the very premises upon which Western (European) cultural values had been established and promulgated, enabling the colonial dominance of Western economy and culture appear justified and lawful.

Radical internationalism and supranationalism, which ran simultaneously with the functionalism of a new national art as the Barbarogenius concept suggested, represented zenithism's key tenets. This eclecticism involved, on the one hand, a pluralism of ideas and movements and, on the other hand, epigonism and kitsch. Nonetheless, it is the eclecticism—which promoted bastardization, transgression, and the crossover between different arts and between art and life—that positioned hybridization in the center of the zenithist program. The push for hybridity as the main feature of zenithist literature marked a shift in the system of representation (from *mimesis* to montage) and representational practices which dynamized the artwork's spatial dimension (the page), and thus called for a more active reader-viewer.

Cross-Genre Writing

The zenithists experimented with genres, often creating hybrid texts that upended traditional literary forms. The cross-genre nature of their texts—in books, pamphlets, brochures, posters, and flyers—reflected a radical vitality, but frequently exhibited ambivalent tendencies, both affirmative and critical, which zenithists developed in response to the surrounding avant-garde movements. Zenithist experiments extended to manifestos, multi-authored texts, and typographic exercises that were often constructed using montage techniques.

As an avant-garde movement, zenithism announced the shift from mimetic to the montage principle of art and strived to reevaluate and de-hierarchize the notions of both literary genre and literary system to establish an *open genre* (the open work of art) paradigm.[52] In other words, avant-garde and zenithist authors experimented with different forms of writing, aspiring to alter the literary work in its classic meaning with the so-called "avant-gardist manifestation."[53] This open genre system paradigm did not manifest itself only as negation and fusion of previously existing literary structures and conventions, but also as the ceaseless desire for limitless expansion, unrestricted experimentation, and the perpetual invention of forms regarding its explicit *poetics of the new*.

Zenithist innovative cross-genre writing experimented with artistic texts as much as with non-artistic texts and non-literary forms. As for artistic texts, *Zenit* published inventive crossover "genres" such as the grotesque novel, the synthetic novella, electro-film projection, constructivist zenithist poetry, the paradox-story, neo-zenithist acrobatics, comic-tragedy, the ultra-novella, a machine-like march, dramatic synthesis, and the serpentinella.[54] Some specifics of these innovative forms were the erasure of borders between literary genres (poetization of prose and prosification of poetry) and different arts (through intermediality); the verbal-graphic organization of texts (so-called montage interaction of visual and

---

52 See, for example, Umberto Eco, *The Open Work*, trans. Anna Cancogni (Cambridge, MA: Harvard University Press, 1989).

53 "Instead of speaking of the avant-gardist work, we will speak of avant-gardist manifestation." Peter Bürger, *Theory of the Avant-Garde*, trans. Michael Snow (Minneapolis: University of Minnesota Press, 1984), 50.

54 See: Gordana Slabinac, *Hrvatska književna avangarda* (Zagreb: August Cesarec, 1988), 43.

verbal elements and "polygenres"[55]); and the influence of film, reproductive arts (posters, advertisements) and more low-brow forms of entertainment (music-hall, circus, spectacle, fairgrounds); and the erasure between low and high art (dehierarchization of arts). On the other hand, non-artistic texts consisted of reports, news, literary criticism, newspaper articles, legal texts (bans), pamphlets, letters, as well as greeting cards.[56] Finally, non-literary forms involved materials from the visual arts (reproductions, photographs of cities, film stars, masks, and architecture), caricatures, posters, as well as sheet music, advertisements, forms of process block prints, and other typographic means.

Cinema proved a lasting influence on zenithist experimental cross-genre writing. The zenithists practiced cinépoetry, a hybrid form with roots in the telegraphic writing of Italian futurism and the visual poetry of French cubism and Orphism (Guillaume Apollinaire, Blaise Cendrars, Max Jacobs, Jean Epstein, to name a few). With cinépoetry, the zenithists strived to produce cinematic effects in writing: dynamism, abrupt changes of perspective and point of view, and a rapid montage of different sensory experiences. Tokin wrote several "cinema poems" inspired by Blaise Cendrars' poetry and Jean Epstein's two 1921 books, *Bonjour cinema* and *La Poésie d'aujourd'hui*, which upheld cinépoetics as a set of strikingly different notions of poetry, cinema, and thought in its spectatorship and readership.[57] Tokin also published a short book review in *Zenit* no. 4, "Mierendorff: Haette Ich das Kino" (If I Had the Cinema), in which he emphasized Carlo Mierendorff's belief in the cinematograph as a perfect tool for propaganda, as it was able to revitalize poetry, spiritualize matter, and materialize spirit, to establish a new balance with its inherent dynamism and movement, and thus to birth a new era for the arts. Inspired by Apollinaire's poem "Zone," which describes the experience of the French metropolis from early morning to late night, Goll published his cinépoem illustrated with eight postcards, *Paris Burns* (*Paris brennt*, 1921), in the second publication by Biblioteka Zenit, developing a poetic form akin to the cinematic

55 For the term "polygenres," see Aleksandar Flaker, *Poetika osporavanja* (Zagreb: Školska knjiga, 1982), 35.

56 See for example Micić's *Airplane without an Engine* (1925), which included documentary material: a text from the daily *Politika* from September 23, 1923, declaring the death of zenithism a few months after Micić's arrival in Belgrade, as well as a document on the seizure of Micić's book of poetry *Damn Your Hundred Gods* in Zagreb in 1922.

57 Boško Tokin, "Kinematografske pesme," *Crno na belo* [almanac], edited by Monny de Boully (Belgrade, 1924). This text was translated by Jed Rasula [in the *Burning City* anthology]. See also Tokin's text "Pokušaj jedne kinematografske estetike," in *Progres* 1, no. 120 (October 1920): 120–123.

genre of a "city symphony."[58] Goll's cinépoetry book *Paris Burns* was considered to be one of the most characteristic zenithist editions. According to Micić, it combined anti-European statements, futurist synthesis, film projections, questions of time and contemporary life, including (for that period) a very rare use of documentary photographs (postcards) as illustrations. Micić's hybrid cinépoetry collection, *Damn Your Hundred Gods/Rescue Car*, published in 1922 as the third book issued by Biblioteka Zenit, combined prose and poetry with illustrations and offered a syncopated rhythm of divergent readings of the text, "allowing readers to be at different locations simultaneously, as if they were watching a film, rather than reading a poem."[59]

The zenithist group also produced several examples of radiograms and radio-films. The former was inspired by Marinetti's telegraphic poetry and "wireless imagination" as well as by Goll's writing, where both the Eiffel Tower and Tatlin's draft for the *Monument to the Third International* (1920) play a significant role as icons of technological modernity, its urban culture, and zenithist aesthetics of verticality. While Micić demanded that "a zenithist work must be a radiogram," Goll proclaimed that the sign of modernity was the ascending line: "The sonnet was—a square / Classical drama—a triangle [. . .] / Today's poetry is / VERTICAL / It is climbing toward the ZENITH with airplanes, elevators, automobiles, Eiffel Towers, chimneys / Man climbs vertically / OBELISK."[60] By extension, the zenithists celebrated Nikola Tesla as an experimenter and scientist and embraced him as a true Barbarogenius with Serbian and Balkan origins—an "electrogenius" who patented basic radio applications three years before Marconi.[61] *Radiogram* was the title of an Yvan Goll's poetry collection that was meant to be printed by Biblioteka Zenit, but the concept did not make it into print. Instead, Branko Ve Poljanski launched "Zenith-Express Radiograms" as a combination of news, poetry, and advertising to mark the special occasion of his trip

---

58 Some of the well-known films of this genre in the 1920s are Alberto Cavalcanti's *Nothing but Time* (*Rien que les heures*, 1926), Walter Ruttmann's *Berlin: Symphony of a Metropolis* (*Berlin: Symphonie einer Großstadt* [Berlin: Fox Europa, 1927]), and Dziga Vertov's *A Man with a Movie Camera* (*Chelovek s kino-apparatom* [Kiev: VUFKU, 1929]).

59 Dijana Metlić, "Zenitist Cinema: Influences of Marinetti and Mayakovsky," *International Yearbook of Futurism Studies*, ed. Günter Berghaus et al., vol. 9 (Berlin: de Gruyter, 2020), 263.

60 See translation of "The Zenithist Manifesto" by Ljubomir Micić, Yvan Goll, and Boško Tokin in this anthology.

61 See the unsigned write-up "Nikola Tesla an 'Engineer,'" published in the "Makroskop" section of *Zenit*, no. 40 (April 1926): n.p.

with his brother to Berlin in 1922. In another example, Micić's hybrid text "Shimmy in the Graveyard of the Latin Quarter: A Zenithist Radio-film in 17 Acts" was published in *Zenit* no. 12 (1922) and was structured like a newsreel, or a cinematic collage, which served as a novel example of Eisenstein's "montage of attractions" which relied on Marinetti's principle of "simultaneity and interpenetration of different times and places on film, Rodchenko's early 1920s collages, and the hectic rhythms of Mayakovsky's poetry."[62]

Zenithist cinépoetry and radio-film works showcase eclecticism as the main feature of the movement most responsible for synthesizing aesthetics of verticality (cosmism of zenith and sun), a cultivation of primitivism (the East-West polarization), and a renewal of poetic language into experimental cross-genre writing. Zenithist cinépoetry and radio-film forms unfold following the dictum of the "telegraphic style" of Italian futurism (Marinetti), French paroxysm (Nicolas Beauduin), and literary cubism (Apollinaire, Cendrars),[63] as well as the "naked, unambiguous" poetic word, combined with syntactical ellipsis, overall brevity, simplicity, and an elemental "lone sentence" in place of a solitary verse freed of traditional form and rhyme. Goll articulated the following on futurist poetics: "Our language should be: steep, narrow, rocky like an obelisk. As steep as the rays of the midday sun. Hard. Naked. And above all, unambiguous, because the telegraph office does not have time to issue the phrase: Electricity is too expensive."[64] Following Marinetti's "liberated words" (*parole in libertà*) and a telegraphic style of poetry combined with experiments in typography, Micić developed his "words in space" (*reči u prostoru*) as a new artistic practice.[65]

---

62 Dijana Metlić, "Zenitist Cinema: Influences of Marinetti and Mayakovsky": 263.

63 The zenithist embrace of a telegraphic idiom was a platform for its renewal of poetic language: "The lyrics will be electro-radio. [. . .] Therefore, the deepest experience should be captured in a telegram in shorthand. The greatest possibility of content should be expressed in the most acute and at the same time the simplest form. [. . .] Another direction: the laconic Japanese *tanka*. Again, Asia and proto-poetry. [. . .] Such a Spartan cablegram of the soul is read in the elevator between parting with a woman and a feverish stock market report." Yvan Goll, "Reč kao počelo: Pokušaj nove poezije," *Zenit*, no. 9 (November 1921): 3.

64 Yvan Goll, "Reč kao počelo": 2. Also: "A lone sentence. [. . .] Each verse as a sentence placed in its own atmosphere, sentences all isolated as telegraph wires and each carries its own news, and all together represent the nervous life of a city. Each verse is solitary . . . therefore there is no more rhyme, no stanza, etc. [. . .] Simplicity: to say things simply. The new man, who telegraphs, reads only the titles, the indicated nouns: the development [of a story] is banal." Ibid.: 4.

65 Ljubomir Micić, "Reči u prostoru," *Zenit*, no. 7 (September 1921): 10; "Reči u prostoru 10–16," *Zenit*, no. 9 (November 1921): 1, 5–7, 11–13. Micić's poetic cycle "Words in Space" resembles Goll's essay "The Word as Origin: An Attempt at a New Poetics" in the way it transmits the independent poetic word

The serpentinella was yet another zenithist hybrid form, a Dada-like created category or quasi-genre invented by Poljanski, likely modeled after a serpentine line he found on Tatlin's counter-reliefs and his draft for *The Monument to the Third International* (1920). The short rhythmic story "33 sEcoNdS," published in *Dada-Jok,* has as its subtitle "a spinning wheel in the serpentine" (*kolovrat u serpentine*), while Poljanski called it a serpentinella—a form of a story in curves or shifts. One of the key characteristics of this zenithist quasi-genre is the entropy of expectation since it is impossible for the reader to predict what to expect after the next curve and shift in the story. In other words, nonsense and paradox are at home within this zenithist Dada-like genre par excellence, as it is almost impossible to retell the story or its plot.

Similar to these short rhythmic stories, the longer zenithist prose works—Poljanski's *77 Suicides* (*77 samoubica,* 1923), Marijan Mikac's *The Monkey Phenomenon* (*Fenomen majmun,* 1925), and MID's *The Sexual Equilibrium of Money, or A Trade Correspondence on The Currency Question* (*Seksualni ekilibr novca ili Trgovinska prepiska o valutnom pitanju,* 1925) and *The Metaphysics of Nothing* (*Metafizika ničega,* 1926)—demonstrate that mixing genres, styles, and codes, that is, shifting the established boundaries of literature, is, by all accounts, the basic intention of zenithist prose and writing in general, and that the anti-narrative orientation is an integral part of that intention. Zenithist prose is not exclusively narrative; Poljanski's novel is, for example, a hybrid form that cinematically confronts prose and poetry in a discontinuous narrative, while MID's books are based on mixing narration with essayistic, journalistic, pseudo-scientific, prophetic, poetic, and other forms of expression of linguistic functions. All this resulted in a strong emphasis on the construction of the literary text, whereby the smaller prose segments of diverse character gathered as a whole via the procedures of editing, juxtaposition, genre mixing, and semantic opposition. Thus, the diversity of prose material leaves the impression of constant play with both the presented reality and narrative conventions. According to literary historian Ivan Negrišorac, "zenithist prose is one of the first attempts of the Yugoslav avant-garde to constitute a distinctly non-referential prose-artistic language, a language that will remain at

---

into the plane of space. See Yvan Goll, "Reč kao početo: Pokušaj nove poezije," *Zenit,* no. 9 (November 1921): 2–4. More importantly, Micić included the revised verses from the cycle "Words in Space" in his book *Damn Your Hundred Gods/Rescue Car* (1922).

the level of signifiers as much as possible."[66] He astutely concludes that "zenithist prose exists as an intertextual parasite," and that it "could not exist without 'organisms' whose juices it sucks and whose existence it constantly questions."[67] This is particularly relevant for MID's works, which are seminal examples of early proto-conceptual writing.

In the zenithist attempt to step out of the space of certain types of art, one can find its connection with Dadaism. In zenithist prose, this affinity is also manifested through the desire to expand the semiological space of writing, which implies the introduction of various visual signs (iconic signs, various typefaces, horizontal and vertical bars, and lines that underline and emphasize certain fragments) that enter into a special relationship with the verbal aspects of the text. MID's books, for example, indicate best this transition from the world of symbols in the world of signs themselves.[68]

Furthermore, zenithist prose is ludic in character and the zenithist style relies on its humorous foundation. For example, Poljanski uses Dadaist-like grotesque-humorous exaggerations in *77 Suicides* to address existential issues in the world he denounced, while literary jester MID deliberately misattributes the famous quote from Shakespeare's *Hamlet*—"To be or not to be"—to Arthur Schopenhauer, the German philosopher of philosophical pessimism and quietism. The tendency to play with facts in a fictional world is evident in almost all planes of the literary structure. The composition of longer zenithist prose works is loose, inconsistent, and carried out according to the logic of collecting fragments, where individual chapters are indicated to be extremely independent and diverse wholes. If there is a narrative backbone, it is very fragile and does not seem so crucial that it could not be reshaped, changed, or even abandoned. It is similar with the characters of these prose works. Zenithist playfulness subverts the construction of either characters or action. For example, instead of focusing on the psychological profile of the novel's main protagonist, Nikifor

---

66 Ivan Negrišorac, "Zenitistička proza kao osporavanje romana," *Polja*, nos. 342–343 (1987): 352, 347–374. "At the same time, the intertextuality of zenithist prose will not be realized so much through certain forms of ironic and parodic attitude toward other texts (although there are some: Poljanski's attitude toward the *Book of Genesis*, for example) inasmuch as zenithists care about determining the literary type of novel in whole." Ibid.: 373.

67 Ibid.: 373.

68 "What makes MID's books an important contribution to the 'mystery of the author,'" according to Šuvaković, "is their non-contextualization. Unlike other zenithist books that have a literary status, regardless of radical innovations or transgressions, they are indeed uncertain artefacts of writing. MID's books do not present references to literary genres but are a presentation of 'graphic' writing itself, which moves between the visual and the verbal." Šuvaković, *Istorija umetnosti u Srbiji XX vek*, 98.

Morton, Poljanski uses the number as a carrier of the language's expressive function to grotesquely distort traditional readerly expectations of the novelistic hero, described as a multiplied character: "On every continent, a few of Morton's airplanes crashed at 77 airports. Seventy-seven bodies exited those planes in 77 cities. Seventy-seven unusual visitors were **He Nikifor Morton**. Morton stood in 77 squares. He was in impossibly profound thought. He stood. A minute. An hour. Hours. Till the evening. Motionless. A man of stone"[69]—and the description is followed by the list of 77 cities, among which small Balkan cities are placed on par with major world metropolises. This insistence on constant humorous twists acquires a quite marked ironic-parodic and disputing-negating features. The zenithist style is prepared to humorously play with the seriousness of any image of the world, and even the form of the novel in general.

Zenithist Graphic Design

Our anthology features translations of Biblioteka Zenit publications with their original graphic design, page layout, typeset, and pagination. The graphic design of zenithist works, including the posters, brochures, and leaflets reproduced in this anthology, play a semantically important role in articulating, understanding, and contextualizing the zenithist program and the ideology of its aesthetics. The visual effects of typographic and graphic solutions featured in the books published by Biblioteka Zenit reflected the radical nonconformism, militant activism, and psychological use of assertive words and signs with the desire to encourage the viewer or reader to think and join in a given—zenithist—world of ideas.

Inspired to embrace the word as a visual medium, zenithist authors, together with their artist confederates, sought to empower the visual to be "read" as if it were a text. Zenithist publications and works on paper were to result in new and transformative experiences—*reading-as-seeing* and *seeing-as-reading*—both through and beyond their pages. Zenithist print matter offered its readers not merely aesthetic stimulation, but also guided them to see the materialization of radical socio-aesthetic reorganization of human behavior and political formation, thus enhancing the relationship between the arts and social

69 See, for example, our translation of *77 Suicides*.

dynamics, as well as between art and politics.[70] Through the *Zenit* review and press, zenithism developed its own eclectic visual idiom in an endeavor to cultivate a local audience.

Zenithist graphic design both reflected and propagated a positive attitude toward industrial and mechanical innovation, for example, railways, machines, and photographic cameras, and consequently experimented with photography, radio, film, and industrial design. For example, the design of the cinépoetry book *Damn Your Hundred Gods/ Rescue Car* (1922)—one of the most radical zenithist works within the Yugoslav publishing scene at the time, was created by Micić—as stated in the edition itself, using the procedures of constructivism, suprematism, and futurism. Micić designed the front cover with interpolated letters, numbers, words, and geometric forms of red and black, thus rendering typographically the futurist rhythm of electricity, the theme of railways and railroad switches, and the simultaneous permeation of surfaces. In this edition, the empty, censored text-spaces from the first, banned edition of the book are singled out and graphically designed according to architectural laws: separated by rectangles made by the process block prints, thus reflecting suprematist expressions, "white on white" and "black on black." In principle, by leaving black and blank surfaces in place of the words the police banned in *Damn Your Hundred Gods*, Micić was able to create political resistance through the redacted spaces of the ciné-poem. The typographically innovative use of different letter types, grades, and sizes, dynamically distributed throughout the page, was combined with the illustration of an airplane without an engine (a glider), a motif that will later serve as the title of Micić's eponymous 1925 book of verse published through Biblioteka Zenit.

Photography was celebrated and utilized throughout zenithist publications along with cinema, as both a symbol of modern technology and a precise, immediate means the most suitable for mass communication with an international audience.[71] The typographic

---

70 Micić made a similar argument in his defense, on December 15, 1926, prior to the police arriving to his apartment to arrest him for the dissemination of Marxist ideas in the text "Zenithism through the Prism of Marxism" (the police failed to arrest him due to Anuška's help), in which he stated that he believes that Marxism is not a political idea, but a humanistic approach and social idea.

71 For example, *The Manifesto of Zenithism* (1921) includes a photograph of Ljubomir Micić as well as his *Airplane without an Engine* (1925), dedicated to Anuška Micić and illustrated with a photo portrait of the author from his younger days, prior to zenithism. Goll's *Paris Burns* (1921) incorporates eight post-cards, most of which are photographs of well-known Paris locations and sites. Also, in Micić's *Damn Your Hundred Gods/ Rescue Car* (1922), positive zenithist attitudes toward mechanics and film are illustrated by photographs of film cameras and modern printing, while the album-monograph *Archipenko: New Plastics* (1923) includes fifteen luxurious black-and-white photo reproductions of Archipenko's work.

design of zenithist publications and advertisements promulgated the futurist ideas of dynamic movement, belief in progress, and an orientation toward the future. They championed new achievements in science and technology, such as radio, telegraphs, airplanes, electric energy, Tesla's inventions and Einstein's theory of general relativity. They were imbued with the new spirit of electricity, ascent, and movement: both *Zenit* and Biblioteka Zenit editions featured the Eiffel Tower and Vladimir Tatlin's draft for the *Monument to the Third International* as icons of the new technological modernity, wireless telegraphy, and zenithist aesthetics of verticality.[72]

Functionalism of the constructivist and Bauhaus type became more and more pronounced in typography, in the design of headings, title pages, and in the layout of texts, especially in the last years of publication of the *Zenit* review and Biblioteka Zenit. In some cases, such as the covers of Poljanski's *Topsy-Turvy* (*Tumbe*, 1926), the graphic art is highlighted by letter shapes and evenly distributed horizontal lines.[73] The introduction of new typography

---

72 In zenithism, Vladimir Tatlin appeared in the early twenties as both a model and a leitmotif, a symbol, and paradigm. First, in 1921, Dragan Aleksić in Dada fashion denied traditional aesthetics using the term "Tatlinism" as "machinism," and the following year Tatlin was recognized in the context to which it belongs. Zenithism embraced the ideas of Tatlin's constructivism. His draft for *The Monument to the Third International*, published several times—in *Zenit*, no. 11, even twice, then in the double Russian issue, no. 17–18, in Micić's book *Damn Your Hundred Gods/Rescue Car* (1922), on the poster of the "Great Zenithist Evening" (1923), and so on—is identified with the highest technologic achievements of the twentieth century, with the ideals of internationalism, Bolshevism, communication possibilities, the use of non-artistic materials, great artistic imagination, cosmic movement (year–month–week–day–hour), uninterrupted dynamism (spiral flow), planetary proportions (slope, height) and geometric order, as a possible expression of esoteric premises. Tatlin's *Monument* was given an important role in Micić's programmatic texts, "Shimmy in the Latin Quarter Cemetery" and "The Categorical Imperative of the Zenithist School of Poetry." According to Micić, *The Monument to the Third International* speaks of social engagement and international spirit; it is a macrocosm in action, a look into the future, connecting people and conveying the news with an impressive tribute to the Russian Revolution. It is especially important to master the space and establish the East-West coordinates, necessary for the realization of the idea of Balkanization of Europe. Acceptance of Tatlin's ideological solution, paradigmatic for the entire Russian avant-garde, and to a large extent for the entire modern art of the twentieth century, meant consciously identifying zenithism with the utopian model of the *Monument* itself and the entire Communist International in conditions that did not provide for immediate realization. The photograph of the Eiffel Tower one finds on the front cover of Goll's *Paris Burns* (1921), and at the beginning of Poljanski's ciné-novel *77 Suicides*, in reference to the T. S. F. (*télégraphie sans fil*).

73 "The front covers are stylized in a constructivist-Bauhaus manner, using horizontal and vertical parallel black lines on a red background (in some editions this background is white). The back cover varies

in zenithism was functional for accentuating the most important parts of their numerous programmatic texts and, at the same time, had a new plastic dimension where letters and the whole layout became visual symbols.[74] An illustrative example is the graphic design of the front page of the album-monograph *Archipenko: New Plastics* (*Arhipenko: Nova plastika*, 1923), close to constructivist in terms of type and color (red and black), while the page layout featuring black and white photo-reproductions of Archipenko's sculpture-paintings and drawings, with the thick lines and geometric forms of the process block prints on the opposite side, resembled constructivist-like postcards.[75] Additionally, the design that Micić made for the covers of his collection *Anti-Europe* (*Antievropa*, 1926) featured nonobjective typography, similar to what we find in El Lissitzky's PROUNs.[76]

Both *Zenit* and Biblioteka Zenit editions exhibit a wealth of graphic solutions in an avant-garde language that employed graphic frames of varying size and thickness, arranged

---

the zenithist theme: triangular shapes in the cadence, one of which breaks through the black circle, most closely related to El Lissitzky's Suprematist poster, "Beat the Whites with the Red Wedge" (1919), a procedure already used in earlier zenithist editions. The idea of a world turned upside down is associated with the name of the collection of poems and its twice repeated title—*Tumbe*—once as a word broken in a mirror, and another time as an inverted reflection in a mirror." Golubović and Subotić, *Zenit*, 228–229.

74 This care in the typography and graphic aspects in general of all zenithist editions was evident, even in some of the commercial advertising in *Zenit*. The black triangles and parallel lines, sometimes in rhythmic and dynamic relations combining futurist movement and constructivist forms, are zenithist signature signs. It is a visual rendition of zenitosophy that, according to Micić, "connects three crucial points in space: earth—sun—moon. that metacosmic triangle is the only zenithist symbol." See his text "Zenithosophy or the Energetics of Creative Zenithism" in this anthology.

75 It is likely that Micić's monograph was enabled by the contact Branko Ve Poljanski made with Archipenko in Berlin during the fall 1922. At the time, Archipenko was a collaborator of Berlin's *Der Sturm* and his works were considered a paradigm of modern art in Europe: similar monographs were written by Karel Taige and Yvan Goll; the avant-garde magazine *Ma* of Lajos Kassàk also writes about Archipenko; among Yugoslav authors, Dragan Aleksić addresses him within the process of Dadaist stylization, as well as Rade Drainac in a short note on the occasion of the publication of Micić's album with Archipenko's sculptures and drawings in the fall of 1923. That was the time when Archipenko sent an invitation to *Zenit* to join the International Society of New Artists in New York, which was led by Catherine Dreyer and Wassily Kandinsky, and in which Marcel Duchamp was one of the presidents (this was the Société Anonyme—the core of the future Museum of Modern Art in New York).

76 According to Irina Subotić, the system of PROUNs is an "agonistic and dynamic, not meditative immersion in the multi-layered spatial and temporal representation as a model of the modern world." See Golubović and Subotić, *Zenit*, 72.

in vertical and diagonal directions. In visual terms, these devices underline the flow of textual content and add to the texts' persuasive strength and dynamism. The zenithist typography exercised negation and violation of typographic norms, creating a "modern comedy," in the sense that it placed the beginning and the end of the graphic construction in the center, arranging all other elements separately in a straight line toward the edges.[77] For example, the graphic design of the front covers of Poljanski's and Mikac's books, created by Poljanski and Jo Klek, communicated zenithist negativity as a recuperation of spearheaded dadaist negation and de(con)struction, along with the constructivist celebration of geometric surfaces and "mechano" elements.[78] Finally, the most illustrative example of the typographic solutions employed in the conceptual deconstruction (and destruction) of meaning through the zenithist poetics of negativity have been the mentioned MID's books. Not only is it possible to read *Sexual Equilibrium* from end of the book, as suggested by the reverse pagination, but it is also possible to read *The Metaphysics of Nothing* as its sequel.

Structure of *Zenithism (1921–1927): A Yugoslav Avant-Garde Anthology*

Our anthology showcases the poetry, fiction, and nonfiction of zenithism, pulled primarily from the magazine *Zenit* and the Biblioteka Zenit press, along with introductions connecting the literary works to other avant-garde movements of the time. Unlike other

77 See Ivan Matičič, "V svojo smer!" and Dragotin Kosem, "V svojo smer!," published in *Grafička revija za pouku i promicanje grafičkog rada*, no. 2 and no. 4 (1925), respectively.

78 On the front cover of the ciné-novel *77 Suicides* is Poljanski's abstract visual work—the apocalyptic situation with polemical effects, summarily supplemented by cosmic symbolism with the help of typographic angular lines reminiscent of the dynamics of the multiplied man of futurism. Jo Klek designed the front page of Mikac's *Effect on Defect* with intertwined machinist ("mechano") elements and geometric surfaces. Klek's book design introduced typographic novelties by emphasizing certain signs and letters of poster size with the task of strengthening the semantic power of certain poems (for example, in the poem "the guard on the rhine predicts" the letter *o* is reminiscent of a cannon barrel). Jo Klek also created the front cover illustration for Mikac's *The Monkey Phenomenon*. It is a drawing of a one-eyed monster or mutant, depicted through a destructive instinct: the curves of his body are confronted with geometric urban structures that he destroys with his raw power. A similar motif is found in the "film novel" *The Mad Corpse* (*Bijesna lješina*), published in Branko Ve Poljanski's film magazine *Kinofon* in 1922.

anthologies in English which have featured only a small selection of zenithist texts, this anthology is solely devoted to zenithist source texts and authors, most available to English readers for the first time.

All the key zenithists are represented here: founder Ljubomir Micić, his brother Branko Ve Poljanski, French-German poet Yvan Goll, early contributor Boško Tokin, the sailor poet Marijan Mikac, and the enigmatic MID [Mita Dimitrijević]. Additionally, every Biblioteka Zenit book is presented here in its entirety with the exception of two works: the photographs of Aleksander Archipenko's works from *Archipenko: New Plastics* have not been reproduced nor have we included Mikac's novel *The Monkey Phenomenon.*

This anthology highlights two signature features of zenithism. One element that separated zenithism from other experimental literary and art movements in the early twentieth century was its synthesis of the various current avant-garde strains into a pan-avant-garde aesthetic. A second, more important trait, is zenithism's emphasis on cross-genre writing as its most significant contribution to the European interwar avant-garde, a unique feature in the crowded field of 1920s experimental literature.

The introductory essays for each section and accompanying footnotes and endnotes draw on existing scholarship on zenithism's literary and artistic contributions, references in the work itself, and the movement's history while also adding to the conversation by capturing untapped currents in zenithist work. The selection and division of the translated texts in the seven sections serve to re-contextualize the movement's historical, ideo-political, and conceptual development into their discrete parts, resulting in an accessible roadmap to zenithism's major features.

Zenithism (1921–1927) outlines the movement's developmental arc, which began with its search for an authentic and original contribution of Balkan (Yugoslav) culture to the European avant-garde, and eventually created its own novel form of conceptual writing that questions authenticity and originality as the very premises upon which the notion of cultural value had been created, reproduced, and re-capitalized as a cultural means for colonial oppression and economic domination.

The first section, *The Barbarians are Coming, or a Savage Rhythm,* lays out zenithism's key concepts that made the movement unique from other avant-garde groups circulating in early twentieth-century Europe. "Man and Art" lays out the argument that zenithism is the successor to expressionism. *The Manifesto of Zenithism* is the fully articulated vision of zenithism as a movement and introduces the archetypal artist-barbarian figure of the Barbarogenius, the Balkan version of Nietzsche's Superman.

Section 2, *The Barbarogenius, the Balkanization of Europe, and Cultural Nihilism*—the most wide-ranging section of the anthology—can be succinctly summarized with Risto Ratković's[79] essay "Barbarism as Culture," according to which the barbarian (i.e., non-Western European) is the creator of culture. If the Balkans or Slavs in general are treated like barbarians by Western Europeans because they are the Other, then artists from the Balkans and artistic Slavs in general can reset the conversation on their own terms. The young Croat Marijan Mikac can be an avant-garde poet rivaling the best avant-garde poets. The Ukrainian Archipenko can redefine what constitutes both sculpture and painting. Zenithism as a movement can make Western Europe take notice, as is evidenced in *Nemo propheta in patria*. Zenithists have their own philosophy ("Zenithosophy"). The Balkans are presented as rich in culture and history as Western Europe (*Airplane without an Engine* and *Anti-Europe*).

Sections 3–5 focus on the three aspects of zenithism's experimental cross-genre writing. The idea behind the three roads image unifying these sections is appropriated from a line in Marijan Mikac's poem "effect on defect": "From every Christ three roads of Hercules." Obviously, the Barbarogenius is a more suitable figure.

The First Road of the Barbarogenius: Cinépoetry and the Radio-Film, marks the first phase of the zenithist cross-genre program, fusing concepts of cinema, radio, photography, and newspaper layout with poetry. Goll's *Paris Burns* applies the fast-cut action of film editing to poetry. In *Damn Your Hundred Gods/Rescue Car*, Micić treats the page like an action-packed film frame or a densely structured photograph.

The Second Road of the Barbarogenius: The Hybrid Novel, Prose Poetry, and the Serpentinella features a wide range of work by Branko Ve Poljanski, who experimented with hybrid literary styles and forms in prose and verse. This section showcases the versatility of Poljanski's talent, from the (anti-)Dada gestures of his Dada-mocking journal *Dada-Jok*, to the poetry-prose and expressionist/proto-surrealist fusions in his zenithist novel *77 Suicides*. Perhaps one of the more striking features of this section is witnessing Poljanski's radical transformation from the expressionist-leaning *Panic under the Sun* to the fully realized zenithist cross-genre work *Topsy-Turvy*. The lingering question for the reader will be whether the serpentinella is a real poetic form.

---

79 Risto Ratković (1903–1954) was a Serbian avant-garde writer, associated with both zenithism and surrealism.

The Third Road of the Barbarogenius: Conceptual Writing showcases the entire opus of Mita Dimitrijević, who wrote under the nom de guerre MID. His two books, *The Sexual Equilibrium of Money* and *The Metaphysics of Nothing* act as halves of a whole conceptually, the word *nothing* acting as the thread tying the two works together. The two works are so interlinked that one can be forgiven for referring to the works as *The Sexual Equilibrium of Nothing* and *The Metaphysics of Money*. They are early examples of appropriation as a creative act and what would eventually be called *conceptual writing*.

The sixth section, *The Barbarogenius at the Gates: Zenithist Theater, Soirees, and Public Interventions*, addresses zenithist evenings and performances which included multimedia representations in the form of poetry readings and polemics with local audiences; the performance group Travelers which performed zenithist plays; concrete political-activist actions and zenithist demonstrations, such are their protest of Tagore's 1926 lecture in Belgrade.

The last section, *The Nadir of Zenithism*, features a single work: Poljanski's final book *The Red Rooster*, the last publication by Biblioteka Zenit. Though *Zenit* was shut down the year before by the authorities, Poljanski's last book marked the end of the press and the movement. The eponymous sequence poem is a farewell to a movement, literary endeavors, and a city, all symbolically rendered as a lover lost.

The afterword, *The Zenithist Legacy*, argues for zenithist (dis)continuities and illuminates the paths taken from recognizing zenithist works as the "conceptual unconscious" of later Yugoslav experimental art practices from the second half of the twentieth century.

The Barbarians are Coming, or a Savage Rhythm

Introduction

Aleksandar Bošković and Steven Teref

Manifestos were the foundation of many early twentieth-century avant-garde movements in Europe and zenithism was no different. Although founder Ljubomir Micić wrote numerous manifestos about various aspects of zenithism over the course of its existence, three early manifestos illuminate the core of what zenithism stood for in its nascent phase.

The first zenithist manifesto in this section is Micić's editorial "Man and Art," which was printed in the inaugural issue of *Zenit* (February 1921). This marks the first appearance of the term *zenithism*. Micić's despair and resignation, as a veteran of the Great War, is apparent, as he lays the groundwork for zenithism's aspirations: "We will bring forth a new ember to illuminate Yugoslavia's darkness. [. . .] We are entering a New Decade and need to go beyond Yugoslavia's borders. [. . .] May our entrance into the third decade of the twentieth century be a battle for humanity through art. [. . .] We will use it in our decisive fight against all traditions, all regionalisms and borders: for art and man there are no borders!"[1] Pointing out that contemporary death is "the furthest from classical beauty and from l'art pour l'artism," Micić concludes not that "Art belongs to nations," but that "Art directs its

1 See "Man and Art" in this anthology.

own movements [. . .] That is why we fight for both the freedom of the individual and the affirmation of individualism."[2] As "the incarnation of the sublime," zenithism is defined as "*abstract cosmic expressionism*," that is, "the imperative to create the most powerful expression possible in a work of art" and "a drive toward creating the most sublime forms."[3]

The Manifesto of Zenithism (*Manifest zenitizma*, 1921), the first publication by the Biblioteka Zenit press, is perhaps the most important statement on zenithism. According to the tripartite manifesto, authored by Ljubomir Micić, Yvan Goll, and Boško Tokin, primitivism and the artist-barbarian define the main programmatic orientation. Micić launched the term "Barbarogenius" in *The Manifesto of Zenithism* as an incarnation of barbarism that will "destroy suburbs of big and plague-ridden West European cities, shatter windowpanes of gilded courts [and] the high towers of National Stock-markets and Banks."[4] For Micić, the revelation of the "naked man Barbaro-genius" overlaps with "the catachrestic space" of Šar Mountain and the Urals to form an individual myth about a new apocalypse within the story of the decline of the West and its material and spiritual culture: "Close your doors West—North—Central Europe—The Barbarians are coming! Close them, close them, but we shall still enter."[5] Both imperatives—the destruction of Western culture and salvation from evil—are based on radical activism: "the first is contained in the formula of the barbarian invasion of the Balkan Southeast to the West, and the second in the act of saving man, a phenomenon comparable with the salvation of the Son of God. The metaphor of that salvation is the rescue car; its movement evoked by alliteration: 'Hotblooded horse hoofs hitting.'"[6]

Yvan Goll, a French-German poet and one of the authors of *The Manifesto of Zenithism*, was even more radical in his call for barbarism: "Let us destroy CIVILIZATION with the help of A NEW ART . . . The entire literature of the civilized old age is nothing but an expression of such false feelings and phrases which have estranged us from primeval nature . . . Back to the primeval source of experience . . . back to barbarism! We need to become the BARBARIANS of poetry once more."[7] Goll saw the emergence of avant-garde

---

2 Ibid.

3 Ibid. Somewhat later, in his essay "Traveling Expressionism and the Anticultural Bridge," Micić writes: "Above expressionism rises zenithism—art that is affinitive—mortality that means totality." See Ljubomir Micić, "Putujući ekspresionizam i antikulturni most," *Zenit*, no. 3 (April 1921): 9.

4 See *The Manifesto of Zenithism* in this anthology.

5 Ibid. Vida Golubović, *Biblioteka časopisa* Zenit (Belgrade: Gallery RIMA, 2021), 7.

6 Golubović, *Biblioteka časopisa* Zenit, 7.

7 See *The Manifesto of Zenithism* in this anthology.

neo-primitivism in the Scythians, the subject of the eponymous poem by Alexander Blok, printed in *Zenit* no. 3 (April 1921) in the original Russian. In an undated letter to the Czech writer and *Literární skupina* vice chairman Zdenek Kalista, Goll claimed that "a generation of young barbarians is advancing in Hungary and Yugoslavia, and rotten Europe needs boiling blood. You will bring it to her if you are what you are, if you sing about your destiny and the pain of liberation. We want a wild proto-poetry, fresh languages and feelings."[8]

In his contribution to *The Manifesto of Zenithism*, Boško Tokin suggested that zenithists follow expressionism in its quest for spirituality and the dynamics of mysticism, emphasizing their need for such a practice: "the expression of essential constructions, the emanation of a healthy, pure, barbaric dynamism. *One needs* to be *a barbarian*. This is what it means to be a barbarian: beginning, possibility, creation. (Nietzsche, Whitman, and Dostoevsky are barbarians because they are beginnings.) We, the Yugoslavs, are barbarians."[9] For Tokin, a zenithist is a personified synthesis of "barbarian + aristocrat + metacosmician + surrealist"—concepts with origins in different movements and aesthetic programs: "Barbarian and aristocrat are the terms I implemented in *Zenit*, *surrealist* is an expressionist as much as a zenithist term, only the term *metacosmician* belongs to Micić."[10] According to Tokin, this neo-primitivist barbarian-aristocrat should be founded on the barbarism of Prince Marko, the South Slavic epic hero, and Balkan civilization.[11]

All three authors presented their conception of zenithism in accordance with their beliefs and poetics. Micić's projection is dominated by an emotional cognition of the world as opposed to a rational one ("You cannot 'understand' *zenithism* unless you *feel* it"), by self-citation, intertextuality, the tendency to an apocalyptic and utopian way of thinking, and mysticism.[12] Yvan Goll, on the other hand, especially in the second part of his text, insists on the independence of the poetic word, reevaluating the traditional understanding of

---

8 Literární archív, Prague 1967, no. 2. Quoted in Golubović and Subotić, *Zenit: Internacionalna revija za umetnost i kulturu 1921–1926*, (Belgrade: Narodna biblioteka Srbije; Institut za književnost i umetnost; Zagreb: SKD Prosvjeta, 2008), 97.

9 See *The Manifesto of Zenithism* in this anthology.

10 "I worked on aristocratic aesthetics and philosophy together with Mr. Lacaze-Duthiers (founder of that aesthetic) in 1918 and 1919 in various studies, which appeared in French journals." Boško Tokin, "Moj zenitizam [My zenithism], *Jugoslavenska njiva* 34 (August 1921); 539–541.

11 On September 8, 1921, in the Belgrade *Tribuna*, Boško Tokin writes about the seventh issue of *Zenit*, claiming that "(Micić) did not think about all that before, only after reading some of my things." Boško Tokin, "*Zenit*, no. 7," *Tribuna* 2, no. 205 (September 1921): 3.

12 See Golubović, *Biblioteka časopisa* Zenit (2021), 5.

the poetic form, advocating for primitivism and barbarism in poetry, in order to theoretically devise the postulates on which the new art of zenithism rests.[13] Boško Tokin's thoughts in *The Manifesto of Zenithism* move within the limits of French modernism, expressionism, and futurism. He rejects some of these directions and schools and includes some in the synthetic definitions of Micić's zenithism. To approach the demands of zenithism, Tokin re-evaluates cubism, futurism, and expressionism by drowning them in a single undifferentiated movement, while he is also inclined to affirm Slavism, dynamism, and barbarism. Syncretism in the group around *Zenit* came to the fore in *The Manifesto of Zenithism* through the cooperation of writers and painters.[14]

Micić's manifesto "The Spirit of Zenithism," published in *Zenit* no. 7 (September 1921), promotes avant-garde revolt and a rebellious attitude toward traditional forms of art and life, establishing how zenithism, through its ideology of destruction linked to construction, differed from futurism: "Shattering the old, not as an end in itself, but as an imperative of the positive force, which is a new affirmation [. . .] Each shattering provokes a *new* creation—a *new* form—a *new* construction."[15] The Dadaist "destruction of all traditions" is inscribed in zenithism, since "it, too, must be mercilessly destroyed once it becomes a tradition."[16] Openly against imitators and pseudo-creators, Micić is critical of Western civilization's "false humanism"; he writes: "the West has no religion of feeling, only religion of thought. And this is the cause of the fall of Western culture and its false humanism!" At the same time, he supports a Yugoslav-Balkan newborn culture, represented in the figure of the "Barbarogenius" as a bearer of the Balkan ethics and "heroism of the spirit":

---

13 Ibid., 8.

14 "In addition to the traditional connection between literature and painting, the rise of syncretism can also be observed in the field of photographic art. The first order of syncretic phenomena is a portrait photograph of Ljubomir Micić. [. . .] Similar to the portrait of Micić, the portrait of Yvan Goll on the drawing by Albert Gleizes is given 'in strict frontality.' In doing so, Gleizes' cubist technique made a significant difference in the treatment of Goll's portrait; the novelty is that his compositional parts compete with the styles of early and late cubism. [. . .] In the semi-profile of Boško Tokin (the work of Slavko Vorkapić), a transition was made from the static nature of the portrayed characters of Micić and Goll to the dynamism of the artistic expressiveness of the drawings. [. . .] To conclude: these artistic contributions are especially significant because of the connection of their formative actions with the central programmatic ideas expressed in the manifestos: in Micić, priority was given to mysticism, in Goll to cubism, and in Tokin to dynamism." Golubović, *Biblioteka časopisa* Zenit, 9–10.

15 Ljubomir Micić, "Duh zenitizma," *Zenit*, no. 7 (September 1921): 3–5.

16 See "The Spirit of Zenithism" in this anthology.

> "We are naked and pure" means this: in a clean cradle, in a Yugoslav-Balkan cradle, a new spirit—an integral, independent spirit of *creative individualism* was born, and only such a spirit is capable of bearing and creating new values. A new spirit of a strong race has been born, a race that has been without art and culture until now. [. . .] Our advantage lies in the fact that we have no 'cultural tradition.' Our only tradition: Prince Marko and Kosovo. [. . .] *ZENITHISM : THE ETHICS OF MAN. Heroism of the Spirit: Barbaro-Genius.*[17]

So, who are the barbarians? If culture is a duel between East and West, as Micić writes in "The Spirit of Zenithism," and if zenithism implies the destruction of all traditions and the aspiration to create "new forms and new relations as the foundations of future art," who are the forces that should represent a radical purgatory and carry out an integral transformation of art and society?[18] Whose incarnation is the Barbarogenius? Since Micić's text in *The Manifesto of Zenithism* expresses a sincere faith in man and an almost mystical hope that he will reach the zenith, "the highest incarnation of Allexistence," one should look for the origins of "barbarism in the incarnation of the Barbarogenius" in zenithist cultural nihilism and its incessant and uncompromising questioning of both the conventional values and the very premises upon which these values were established.[19] We explore in more detail both of these genealogical aspects of the zenithist infatuation with the joyfully vital and nihilistically destructive barbarism in the second section of this anthology.

17 Ibid.

18 Ibid.

19 Slobodan Markuš, *Zenitizam* (Belgrade: ID Signature, 2003), 49.

Man and Art

Ljubomir Micić
from *Zenit*, no. 1 (February 1921)

MAN—That is our first word.

From the loneliness of stiff walls and cursed streets, from the dark abysses of the unconscious and from monstrous nights we approach you as apostles, as prophets and we preach ART TO MAN.

Man is the center of the macrocosmos, while art and philosophy are the circumference of his most sublime understanding, his most sublime consciousness. The most sublime manifestation of the spirit and the soul—the SPIRIT or the demiurge, Anarch—wishes to rule chaos, to be all-powerful, to be a god. He lusts to create *action* from chaos. But the only creator is the artist, who always embodies Man in his creation, his work of art. The artist is both the embodiment and a passionate desire for the revelation of *Man*. The artist is the Revelation—the Annunciation—the Last Judgment of: *Man*. The artist is an endless horizon without beginning and without end on Earth's deadly savage hurdle through space. The ZENITH is the center—man's only salvation—his only redemption.

The artist, as the incarnation of the *sublime*, suffers from the combustion of his own or humanity's pain. He is a humiliated soul's cry for salvation, a metacosmic cry, a cry from the depths of our innermost spheres.

Having sunk deep into the abyss of the soul, we want to emerge from ourselves with a New Man and shine a new light into the darkness of the black old days, of our sad non-youth. We will bring out a new ember to illuminate Yugoslavia's darkness.

We wish to bring out our inner face.

We are entering a New Decade and need to go beyond Yugoslavia's borders. We crossed them in the past decade as soldiers of war and murder for the "freedom of nations," but from now on we wish to be soldiers of human Culture, Love, and Brotherhood. We enter haggard, yet transformed. We enter deformed and hurt, but we have the strength of those who have suffered and been humiliated and stoned on the pillory of Europe. May our entrance into the third decade of the twentieth century be a battle for humanity through art.

Our martyred generation is dying out. It has been trampled and destroyed. The red monster of war has dug graves for us all, for millions of people, with its murderous claws. One corpse for every two soldiers. We must never forget that the last decade witnessed the death of thirteen million people, that ten million died of poverty and one hundred and fifty million became diseased. And we, who have been left as the rear guard, we carry our pain in our hearts, our common souls are full of desperation, and our common protest is: *No more war! Never again! Never again!*

The silence of our nerves has been shattered by grenades and fear of death. The joy of our souls has been darkened by the monstrosity of mutilated human bodies. The peace of our hearts, now choking on bloody tears, has been shattered by the inconsolable mothers who died of hunger and grief for their innocent children. Oh, you, you who have seen the eyes of the people you killed while they begged for their lives in agony, you who have seen the widow's weeds of mothers dying of grief—you must never, you shall never go forth to kill another man. You are the only ones who know what man really was in this insane asylum of a cursed century.

Man—was as crucified and as spat upon as Christ, but he *was not* Christ.

Man—was as forsaken and as humiliated as a beggar knocking on closed doors.

Man—was created to be God—and then killed as cattle for slaughter.

Thieves!

Your bloody spurs have pricked him, horses' hooves have trod over him, heavy chains of dark prisons have bound him, deadly torrents of sharp bullets and the thunder of stupid cannonry have pummeled him.

Man! Everyone renounces you at the last moment just as Peter renounced Christ, in the name of murder and in the name of your blood. Do not forget this, do not ever forget it!

Every word we have uttered has been against this crime—the crime against us—and against our times. The poet's words of damnation were too weak. That is why everyone must know that our pain is the fire we carry within. We believe in the birth of a New Man. Our first commandment is: IN THE NAME OF MAN—DO NOT KILL!

Our fight will be against crime—for Man.

Workers of the world, unite—against killing! Raise consciousness of Man in *Man!* Today, the non-human is an evil-doing deity—the great inquisitor, who has built black gallows for us all over the world.

All of us poets bear the night's darkness, which is our great punishment for being poets in these times. We have all been pushed into space and we know not whether we are insane or above time. Like apostles of the crucified Man we preach faith in the New Man and wait for his revelation. We are no longer waiting for the czar; we are waiting for Man!...

Man!... Man!...

The tragic power of our new art lies in a desperate cry: Man! And that is why it is the furthest from classical beauty and from *l'art pour l'artism.* It is a New Spirit which creates, and the artist's eternal urge has always been creation. Art, which to us means expressionism, is a strong desire to create new values, new forms. It is our love's cry. It is a cry for salvation and exaltation.

Art is general—human. That is why there is no specifically national art, much less class art. We, the poets and artists of this country, extend our hands to everyone who thinks like us, *to everyone, for everyone* above shattered human skulls.

Art belongs to nations. That does not mean that a nation has a right to dictate what direction art will take. No! Art must follow the path of its creators, because the collective or the public is in this sense limited—inferior. Art directs its own movements. The public merely takes part passively by reflecting on the works. The public can never experience them. To have an absolutely artistic experience one needs to be an artist. That is why we fight for both the freedom of the *individual* and the affirmation of *individualism.* It must not be destroyed. Only a strong individual is creative. Every artist must be an *individual.* He must create *from within,* not *outside himself.* Otherwise, he is a parasite who feeds on *others* like a pseudo-individual. That parasite has a common name: *dilettante.* The cult of dilettantism is quite well established here, and its players are the experienced mystifiers of an unknowing and uneducated population. Gravediggers that they are they block all progress. Many decades, this one included, have been their playground, but let this Third Decade be our playground. We will use it in our decisive fight against all traditions, all regionalisms and borders: for art and man there are no borders! The pages of *Zenit* are open for this purpose to all the apostles of art and humanity from the North Pole to the Cape of Good Hope. These are the words *Zenit* has chosen to represent it to Young Yugoslavia and to announce its rebirth:

New Man! New Spirit! New Art!

Oh, the sun is so great and brilliant in its ZENITH. When the heavens ring the great zenith noon, our eyes rise up to you, our souls open like a festive Muscovite temple. Our hearts dance the bloody rhythmic dance of man's desperation on earth. The man we are looking for on earth has his ZENITH as well. We long for it—for the most sublime power of the inner cosmos.

Oh, zenith sun, you burn like a fire sacrifice. Our eyes are yellow with its flame, and we long for the highest throne, the throne of the SPIRIT. Our souls yearn for revelation, and art is the great revelation of the Spirit, the great fulfillment of all man's longings. It is our eternal unrest, eternal dynamics, eternal anarchy, eternal revolution. It cannot and must not rest. Our tragedy of unrest and death has reached its Black Peak and directed our art into a new movement. Today we enjoy a *Second Renaissance.*

It has found its strongest affirmation in *expressionism. Expressionism* is the soul's imperative to create the *most powerful* expression possible in a work of art.

Zenithism is a drive toward creating the *most sublime* forms.

Zenithism is abstract cosmic expressionism.

Zenithism and expressionism are mirrors in which we shall see our terrible inner pain—the drama of our souls. For a long time yet these mirrors will remain cursed for the still unborn generations begotten in blood. They will not be able find themselves, but they will find—us. For a long time to come they will look for themselves, but again they will find—us. And we, like monstrous ghosts and phantoms, will roam bloody-handed through their dreams and their nights.

We are a pledge of the future sons who will sacrifice themselves for the salvation of Man, and we leave them our Golgotha and our Mount of Olives in our works—a clear path to resurrection.

Our cry: MAN.
Our faith: ZENITHISM.

Translated by *Maja Starčević*

The Manifesto of Zenithism

Ljubomir Micić, Yvan Goll, Boško Tokin
Biblioteka Zenit, June 1921

Translated by *Maja Starčević*

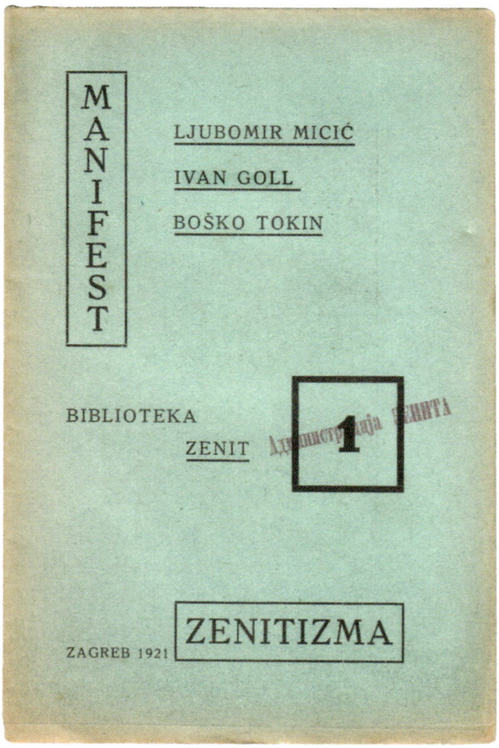

1.1. Lj. Micić, Y. Goll, B. Tokin, *Manifest zenitizma* [The Manifesto of Zenithism], Biblioteka Zenit, no. 1, Zagreb 1921. Front cover, printed on green paper. Courtesy of Gallery RIMA, Kragujevac, Serbia.

LJUBOMIR MICIĆ

Ljubomir Micić

You cannot "understand" Zenithism
unless you feel it.
The electricity we do not "understand"
but feel is perhaps the greatest
manifestation of the spirit—
Zenithism?

We are naked and pure.

Forget hatred—sink into the naked depths of Yourself!
Dive and fly to your own heights!

ZENITH

Fly above this criminal, fratricidal Present!
Show your astral being to the visionary eyes of Superlife!
Listen to the magic of our words, Listen to Yourselves!
There—on Šar Mountain, on the Urals—stands

THE NAKED MAN BARBARO-GENIUS

Fly above the Šar Mountain, above the Urals and the Himalayas—
Mont-Blanc—Popocatepetl—above Kilimanjaro!
We are now floating high, high above the bodily spheres of the Globe.

Break, bound chains! Fall, suburbs of big and plague-ridden
West European cities! Shatter, windowpanes of gilded courts,
High towers of National Stock Markets and Banks!
Return to your fat stomachs, war profiteers!
Hide your bought concubines deep in your dirty pockets!
Have you no shame?
And you, blind mothers, and stupid fathers, selling your innocent daughters for bundles of money!
And you, black underground spiders, spinning your webs around pure souls Freemasons!

Have you no shame, you drunk lodges!?
You—the soul profiteers of art and culture—are the greatest liars of all!
Against you—*for Man*!
Close your doors West—North—Central Europe—
The Barbarians are coming!
Close them, close them but

we shall still enter.

We are the children of arson and fire—we carry Man's soul.
And our soul is *combustion*.
Combustion of the soul in the creation of *sublimity*

ZENITHISM

We are the children of the Sun and the Mountains; we carry Man's spirit.
And our spirit is the life of cosmic *unity* held together by Love.
We are the children of the *Southeast barbaro-genius*.

It is coming. . . It is coming. . .

THE RESCUE CAR

Hotblooded horse hoofs hitting
the ground galloping to a savage rhythm.

Underground channels rumble
Cramped hospitals moan.
City churches—streets and cathedrals
celebrate Easter
1921.

Moscow pours blood.
Far away bells of assumption thunder.

A closed yellow car is rushing
Cutting through space of sinful and colorful streets
where war battalions of fratricides once passed.
— — — — — — — — — —
Oh, mortuary music of those gray battalions!
Oh, bloody burials of attack trumpets!
Oh, dull thuds of men's bodies
remember:
! Man is your brother!
! Man is your brother!

The sun is spurting.

Astral bodies of the universe are dancing.
Floating up there in the endless circular spheres
of the new planet.
* * *Alpha and Pons* * *
And the red-colored crosses
on the milky glass of the yellow cars
have hoisted high their visionary flag of Redemption
and are singing the E a s t e r n S l a v i c song of Resurrection.

Countless crosses of our defeated land are trembling.
The wooden gallows above our skulls are falling.
Bloody ropes are snaking above the fratricidal Black Peak.
And through big cities, cars with red crosses are rushing
EAST
SOUTH
WEST

The Yellow Rescue Car is rushing
Carrying a hidden corpse—Man.

Man is dying everywhere.

The Sun has fallen into my soul
into the limitless spaces of All-love.

Red glass crosses have shattered
Man has died in the yellow car.

Letters are dancing, thrown above the crosses

R S U C R
E C E A

Black flags, brothers, flutter in our souls
because
Man is dying everywhere. . .

* * * * * * * *

It is magic, the word *Zenith!*

Man, a brother and father of gods, was born somewhere in the jungle.
Man created God, for he saw terrible storms and arrows,
heard thunder and desired the *Sun.*
One magical and deep night he discovered Himself—Man.
The first weakness of Man created God—*The First Empire.*
The first Egyptian and Greek cultures (Greece and Macedonia are both in the Balkans!)—*The Second Empire*

ZENITHISM = THE THIRD UNIVERSE

A graphic picture of Zenithism = an incarnation of the metacosmos' bipolarity:

ZENITH

Z
E
ETHER N ETHER
I
T
H

ASTRAL **I** ASTRAL

ASTRAL BODY **S** ASTRAL BODY

M
MAN

EARTH EARTH

Man is the center of the macrocosmos—the Earth's North Pole.
Zenith is the center of the metacosmos—the Universe's North Pole.
Zenithism is a magical and electric interval between the macrocosmos and the metacosmos, between—Man and Zenith.

Man is thunder thrown into space—on Earth:
Man is our starting point.
Man is a victim. The victim is always central.
Man is tragedy. Tragedy is always sublime.

Man—Spirit—Metacosmos—Sun—Phenomenon—Zenith

ZENITHISM = THE ORIENT OF AIRPLANE SPIRITS

Zenithism is an idea of art.
Zenithist art must be an art of ideas—affinitive.
A Zenithist must create.
A Zenithist must create new things.
Zenithism is an artistic affirmation of the Allspirit.

ZENITHISM = ∞ = TOTALITY

Zenithism is absolute supernatural *individuation,* the only creative one:
it must contain the artist + the man.
Superman
it must incarnate the bipolar metacosmos
Phenomenon

Zenithism is more than spirit = the fourth dimension
Zenithism is beyond dimensions = ∞ or the tenth dimension =
Eternity.

Magical zenithist word = radio station A
Man's fluid feeling and jolt = radio station B

Manifestation = Radiogram.

A Zenithist word must be electrification
A Zenithist work must be a radiogram.

This is not a Gospel. This is a Manifesto.
The people of the future, who come after us, they will write the Gospel.
And they will come... they will come...
The future Man!
He will be the son of the Sun and Zenith.
He will speak the Zenithist language.
All... all... will understand.

This is not a philosophy.
The philosophy of Zenithism is still being created.
It is emerging... happening...
Zenithism is mysticism and there is no philosophy of mysticism. There is only the mysticism of philosophy—the mysticism of *New Art.*
Zenithism is a discovery of the hundred and twentieth century.

Expressionism, cubism, futurism are dead.
We are an extension of their lineage—to higher ground.
We are their synthesis, but as an arrow pointing upward, a reincarnation
—the plusexistence of their philosophical ideas:

> The soul of souls of those who have died but lived one hundred and twenty centuries ago and yearned for the Zenith.
> The soul of souls of the nameless ones whose proud children we are.
> Sons of creation—togetherness—unification—traveling
> through chaos—the sons of the **Oriental Sin**.
> The Eastern Sin must have occurred, for that is how people came to know Themselves.
> There would be no Zenithism without the Oriental Sin!

We, who have discovered Ourselves—Man—we are Zenithists
You should be that too!
Our only *thought* is the ZENITH—*the highest incarnation of Allexistence.*
Our path is only—ahead—above—over everything
that has been.
Down with pale traditions, systems, and borders! Borders are for the limited!
We keep going... going...
Travelling from chaos to create an *Oeuvre.*
Led by the mystical demi-god

ANARCH

You come too, though woe unto them who stumble and are left by the wayside.
We will not come back.

Poets! Brothers! Zenithists as yet unknown!
Throw down the coat of lies!
Awaken Man and exalt him!
Sing of flames, fire, the burning, and thirst for the Zenith!
Put a stop to Man's fall. That will be our greatest oeuvre. That is
the vertical line that will pierce the heavens above. And *sunny blood—*
sunny blood shall flow.

The poets of the Zenith! Sing of Man, not of a murderer.
Man is made for Love and for Exaltation.

Above shattered human skulls we extend our hands to all,
over all borders, to all who think like us: *to people!*

And then, when the last Nonhuman dies
then
in all the countries—in all the cities—on all the towers

—ships—planes—palaces—courthouses—hospitals
—academies—insane asylums—seaports—
hang clean white flags and greet the *Future Zenithist Man*
then
in all the pavilions—churches—halls—playhouses
—circuses—streets—roofs—railways—submarines
—army barracks—
in all Zenitheums
sound your trumpets—
organs—timpani—drums—fanfares—
sing your hearts out
sing... sing...

THE ANTHEM OF ZENITHISM

THE ANTHEM OF ZENITHISM

Earth is for Man the Brother, not for Man the Murderer!

Zagreb, in the Balkans, June 12, 1921

IVAN GOLL

Each morning at about five o'clock, on all the continents, the same NEWSPAPERS raise their hungover gray heads and shout the black lies of life:

PEACE CONFERENCE—MURDER IN CHEESE SHOP—JUMPED FROM HIS DARLING'S HEART—BUY GILLETTE RAZORS—BERGSON IN CHICAGO—VOTE FOR NERO—

HOORAY!

Oh, dear Europeans with your narrow foreheads, women with corsets too tight, children playing with the Trojan horse: enemies, enemies of yourselves and of one another, enemies to your brothers and fathers: all of you, the crowns of creation wearing paper crowns and American-style haircuts: Socialists and Royalists, shabby proletarians in gold mines, smiling bankers from London:

Oh!

No, we don't like you! We won't approach you with words of love. No, comrades and brothers with plaster heads, no, addle-pated professors, alcoholic clerks, infected surgeons of the skin and the soul: no!

We hate you! Hate you! Hate you!

But we will tear the masks of the capitalistic carnival off your faces. We are tearing your cynical suits off your bodies. We are tearing off the fig leaves: We will blaspheme and flood your brains which are as dried up as old sponges and your hearts which are as dried up as three-day old bread.

And then

all of you, born animals, born criminals, born militarists, nations grown strong in the midst of hymns of war from Homer on down to Marinetti, your civilization determined by the Bible, grammars and instruction manuals: Nations, high above your army barracks and Halls of Justice decorated with the ridiculous gilt-lettered motto: Liberty Equality Fraternity high above your walls and your morality

we shall show you

THE ZENITH

and hand you

THE SUN

and the cataracts of truth, millions of Volts in heavenly light.
Our first-rate thinking machine
will pour a poisoned generation into your condensed milk cartons—
Liquid Sun

THE TRUTH

No! No! No! We definitely do not like you
We won't embrace you, you charlatans, you politicians, you syphilitics,

you goody-goodies, you, sentimental mini-nationals!
Nationalities! Origins! Older generations! Weeds!

MAN

We are not French, nor Serbian, nor Black, nor German, or Luxembourgian.
We are **Europeans Americans Africans Asians Australians.**
So, in these times of unavoidable trusts—here is a strong cosmopolitan document

ZENITH

We will use ozone, hydro-superoxide and radium to wash out your mouths and hearts, so you can come forth as people, without markings, with your heads bare—with no top-hats, driver's hats, or hard hats—so you can come before the open **Sun of Truth** with no sleepache or sunstroke.

Let us destroy CIVILIZATION with the help of A NEW ART.
You are partly to blame for Europe the has-been:

for the pathos of its everyday life
for the falsity of its sentimentality
for its slavery to tradition.

The entire literature of the civilized old age is nothing but an expression of such false feelings and phrases which have estranged us from primeval nature

Down with all kinds of pathos!
Down with Clichés!

Back to the primeval source of experience—SIMPLICITY
THE WORD
back to barbarism!

We need to become the BARBARIANS of poetry once more.
The Barbarism of Mongolians Balkanites Blacks Indians

Your poems above Europe
A most beautiful lyricism comes from you
The only kind of lyricism
PRE-BLOOD
PRE-SUN
We need modern BLACK SONGS
filled with electricity, telephones, stenograms
MACHINE DANCE
Dynamite—Moon
PRIMEVAL SOUND

ZENITHISM
is
intensive—radial—electromagnetic
SUCKLING ON THE WORLD'S HEART
International
Interdivine

Each century has *its* form:
    The sonnet was—a square
    Classical drama—a triangle
    Shakespeare and Whitman—parallel lines

Today's poetry is
A PERPENDICULAR
It is climbing toward the ZENITH with planes, elevators, automobiles, Eiffel Towers, chimneys.
Man is climbing vertically
OBELISK

The Globe would appear to be shrinking
The poet can hold it in his hand
    like an apple
The New Poet is always INTERNATIONAL
    He sings SIMPLY
    for all Nations
    for PEOPLE

Again and always the *first words of worlds.*

Paris, June 1921

BOŠKO TOKIN

Boško Tokin

The new artistic movements—cubism, futurism, expressionism—are actually three different expressions, three shapes of a single movement. Three shapes of one possibility *(creating a higher reality)*, of one direction that cuts through dogma, logic, façades, and other barriers to the freedom of spirit and action. A higher reality—dynamic, surreal, and cosmic—is being created.

However, the modern epoch and classicism are still in their infancy. Just beginning. Another plus and impulse is needed: the Slav world.
The present: destruction, gestation, climbing and successful attempts at creation, listening to and feeling oneself. Thence: projecting oneself onto the world and into the world of others.
Cubism and futurism have got lost in materiality and repetition.
Expressionism has yearned and still yearns for spirit, spirituality, and the dynamics of mysticism. It yearns for dynamism in its ideas as well, but Expressionism has not been able to realize it all and has thus lost something of its vitality and impetus. New movements which are surreal in principle are not always such in practice, and we need this kind of practice: the expression of essential constructions, the emanation of a healthy, *pure*, **barbaric** dynamism.

One needs **to be** *a barbarian.*

This is what it means to be a barbarian: beginning, possibility, creation. (Nietzsche, Whitman, and Dostoevsky are barbarians because they are beginnings.)
We, the Yugoslavs, are barbarians.
Impetus, dynamism of ideas our own consciousness projects us high, far, straight at our target, into implementation, into the

ZENITH

Barbarian + aristocrat + metacosmician + surrealist = zenithist.
Zenithism = ism par excellence, the only one corresponding to us (humans).
Just as one man differs from another, so one ism differs from another.
Zenithism boils down and unifies all earlier isms by surpassing them. The magical term *zenithism* is quite simple—as Columbus' egg is simple. Yes, it had to be found. We are the ones who've found it.

Do you feel (you do feel, you will feel) the meaning of all nuances, variations:
The Zenith of my feelings, emotions, ideas
The Zenith of my being. My Zenith.
In the Zenith of your (our) aspirations and exaltations.
Your Zenith.

Zenithism—sublimity. Going higher than oneself.

And behold: a new star is rising to the heavens from Yugoslavia, a new country is projecting itself onto the heights: the journal ***Zenit*** and **Zenithism**. An electric current. A current dangerous for diseased people.

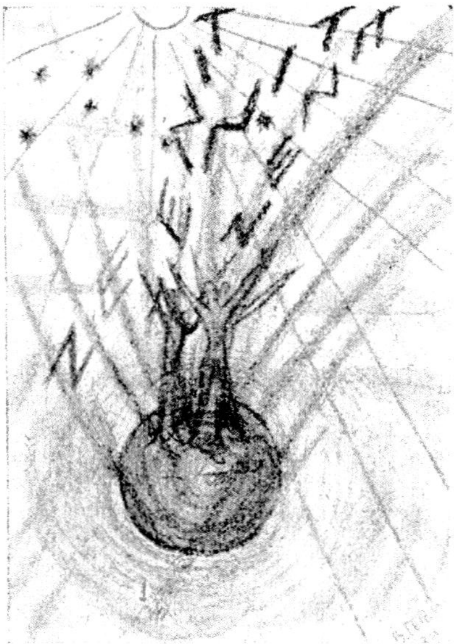

We project ourselves

in all directions.

We project.

Accept it!

Absorb it!

You who can:

Long live the stars.

Stars.

New stars.

It is being made in all parts of the world, at every point on Earth. We are making a style, a heart, and a spirit, a *zenithist* ideology, a *zenithist feeling of the Earth*. The Earth has chosen us to sublimate it and to create its new meaning.

Europeanness + Asianness + Africanness + Australianness + Americanness + new yet undiscovered continents + Mars + the stars (all the stars) + the Pons comet + ∞ =

ZENITHISM

The aestheticization of all dynamisms and mysticisms = Zenithism.

The zenith everywhere and in everything. In you. New people, fly! . . .
Flying.
Going higher. Stepping over. Making real.
Climbing.—**Zenith.**

Early June 1921

The Spirit of Zenithism

Ljubomir Micić
from *Zenit*, no. 7 (September 1921)

The spirit of Zenithism: revolt and creation.

The spirit of every creation: revolt.

The spirit of every revolt: shattering the old, not as an end in itself but as an imperative of the positive force, which is a new affirmation.

Zenithism: a new artistic affirmation!

By dint of its expansion and instinct—its *inner* activity and movement—its superior nature and elan as a *spiritual* element of new relations in art—it shatters the matter of stiffness.

Its *creation* topples everything though this is not its goal.

It is merely the result of new relationships and new values.

Each shattering provokes a *new* creation—a *new* form—a *new* construction.

Each new and great idea causes rebellion and hatred in the weak.

*

Why do you hate Zenithism?

Because it is new and active.

The crowds have always hated anything new and grand.

Why don't you "understand" Zenithism?

1. Because Zenithism is art.

2. Because your spirit is poor.

3. Because you have learned only old ideas, and we are creating a NEW IDEA.

This has always been the case: the poor in spirit hold on to old ideas because they are all they have: *what has been.*

Their souls are a museum of dusty old objects and books.

Finally: Why are we new?

Because we have been scoffed at by you and never recognized. And your recognition—that is, the recognition of those who should be *students* and not teachers—would be the negation of all new values; it would be a negation of Zenithism. Your tragic inferiority lies in the fact that you are always "teachers" of values *unknown* and *new* to you, never students of those values.

We are new because of the richness of our soul and spirit.

The new art (futurism, cubism, expressionism most of all!) is a precursor to the *scientific* theory of relativity. The artistic *theory of relativity* has been in existence for over ten years. The *scientific* aspect has found its strongest affirmation in new art. (This is for you "teachers" who are hearing it for the first time!)

The people who audaciously deny the possibilities of *new art* (and there are plenty of them!) are weak and mediocre. And they are the ones who most vigorously defend the traditions and mummies they so slavishly adore. (Only mediocre men are slaves!)

An epigonic generation that lives dishonorably, they sponge on those who *create.*

Imitators and pseudo-personalities find themselves *in others* who have created *their own* faces. Because it is easier to imitate and create algebraic-artificial variations than to create independently—*anew.*

It is easier to be a "defender" because defenders are always characterized by their *collectivity* and great numbers.

Only the strong go on the offensive! (If most people in the world were not idiots, there would be no logical explanation for its tragic fate!)

People who do not think like us do not think like us only because they *do not think* or *cannot think* at all. We cannot think like you because it would be a failing—a great failing.

That is as it must be. There would be no conflicts otherwise, and conflict is eternal and bears an eternal flame.
There have always been "madmen" who were prophets and "sages" who were idiots.

*

Zenithism is the destruction of all traditions. It too must be mercilessly destroyed once it becomes a tradition.
We must step backward to move forward! That is why we turn a deaf ear to the requests of those who have not stepped backward.
Spiritual manifestations cannot have specific forms and directions!
The form of biological man is not determined in any way, so much less is the form of spiritual man.
No two people are alike!
There are hermaphrodites just as there are dwarves; there are giants just as there are hunchbacks. (But the moral hunchback is the most common variety!) There are people who have hearts on their right side. And there are the barbarians.
If this is superfluous, if no one "understands" this, then I believe in Zenith's prophecy: that most people in Yugoslavia are bulls (*Kulturträgers*![1]) whose heart is on their *right* side and brains in their *feet*!

Each spirit creates its unique forms independently.
That is why there cannot and must not be monotony.
The lines in your forehead (if you have one) cannot be the same as the lines in a poet's forehead. And a poet is by no means what you think a poet to be. A poet is what you, dear "teachers," call a "madman," and "madmen" are poet-apostles you cannot feel.
The person who wants to know them and know the difference between them also must be borderline brilliant and borderline mad.
And you will never reach that border.
Besides, who knows—if the border even exists?
So where do you get the cynical audacity to measure everything with the silly spectacles and microscopes you look through with blind or closed eyes?

---

1 Kulturträger: culture bearer, or one who passes on culture.

Your eyes are closed and filled with dust.
Your eyes are blind even when open.
Why do you laugh out loud?
Because you want to drown out the laughter echoing in your own faces. You laugh out loud because you refuse to feel your poverty and our pity.
And we have enough pity for all the people on this Earth, an Earth which is not good to us. The Earth is your mother—our stepmother and a baby killer.
Go upward into the sublime heights, where there is no laughter or hatred or cynicism, and your eyes will be opened: you will see your days as vain and your words as empty; you will feel the blush of your own shame because you destroy all who do not resemble you and drive them into asylums and prisons.
There have always been "madmen" who were prophets and "sages" who were idiots.

*

Zenithism is right for a man of sublimity and heights—for a man who can go upward and reach up, reach up tirelessly—for a man who does not suffer from vertigo when looking deep down below—into the abyss.
Zenithism is right for a man who will not fall dead from sunstroke—for a man destined to look inward into his soul, who is exalted in his spirit and whose head is touching the clouds and who carries the Sun on his forehead.
He knows and is aware of the fact that he is above the crowds whose laughter is just dogs howling at the full moon.
He hears and feels his stride and his words echo far into space.
He knows that a crowd does not have itself, and that it never had itself.
He is dead to the empty "I" of the crowd.
One has to come to know and discover oneself.
Zenithism is abstract and it discovers the spiritual elements within and outside man: it is the new spirit of the earth, a child of the cosmos and the Sun.
Zenith is an *abstract* term for the most *sublime* heights of man's artistic spirit.
Only those who have come to know and discover themselves can be individuals: *elevators.*
The other kind don't have their own souls and they live a lie thinking they are their own.
They are *pseudo-individuals.*

That is why you who can drown out foreign souls, let your own souls be born, free yourselves of the foreign spirit, let your own free spirit be born.

Zenithism is a free spirit, a spirit independent in its search: for its form—its style—its "I"—its *individuality.*

"We are naked and pure" (*The Manifesto of Zenithism*) means this: in a clean cradle, in a Yugoslav-Balkan cradle, a new spirit—an integral, an independent spirit of *creative individualism* was born, and only such a spirit is capable of bearing and creating new values.

A new spirit of a strong race has been born, a race that has been without art and culture until now.

Therefore:

Zenithism, in its striving for the liberation of man, in its striving for his individualism, is also *anarchy* and its *religion* is: to create new forms and relationships as a spiritual basis for the future Balkan-human art and to destroy the inhuman and non-spiritual past we all share with its positive aspect.

Because:

Art must be spiritual—abstract.

Music alone has always been a true art because it is abstract and does not "represent" anything.

Art should not "represent" anything except itself.

All that we have *is not* art: it is only a point of departure.

It is only rough matter and craftmanship, while generations of people have lived a lie, not knowing what art was.

We still do not know what art is.

But we will find out one day.

*

Yugoslav "art" is the onanism of brains and captured souls.

Despite the protests of virgins, professors, and journalists, let us destroy wagon loads of false artistic fabrications that travel through the Balkan lands.

Yugoslav "culture" is a foreign wild and rotten apple.

Our advantage lies in the fact that we have no "cultural tradition."

Our only tradition: Prince Marko and Kosovo.

That is where our "art" is now. That is our yesterday—our barbaric yesterday, and we do not want to be barbarians any longer.

One should not be a barbarian!

That muscle and heart heroism of ours has ended its epoch under Rudnik and on Kajmačkalan.

That was the time when the Balkan-Serbian man died as a slavish barbarian for *physical* freedom and the freedom of our borders, for the freedom of an oppressed race.

But there is no art in that.

Only a dead and bloody chapter.

Today we need to fight for the freedom and affirmation of an all-human spirit.

The last barbarians are nothing but the forefathers of the first Zenithists.

Let a new day begin: THE HEROISM OF THE SPIRIT.

Let a heroic fight for spiritual freedom of man begin, everywhere where people live, as well as the fight for their brotherhood.

In the spirit of a new beginning: ZENITHISM: A NEW TODAY.

The spirit of Zenithism transforms and is all-human.

I do not say humanistic, because there is no humanity.

Only people.

Humanity has had its difficult birth for centuries now, but the West had no strength to give birth to it, because the West has no religion of feeling, only religion of thought.

(And this is the cause of the fall of Western culture and its false humanism!)

Religion of feeling and thought is being born in the SOUTHEAST which has raised and will carry the flag.

Zenithism is a religion of thought and feeling—a flag of future transformation.

*

Let our strength of transforming spirit and our religion of Zenithism help man discover man within him and help the song of tempests announce the birth of the future New Man!

Let the power of our faith in the New Man help others realize that humiliated souls are still souls, that shattered hearts are still hearts and that the BLOODFLIGHT of the Spirit will dance as a winner on the carcass of matter and lies!

Let our Heroism of the Spirit help the birth of the New World!
Our greatest song will be: HUMANITY

*

: Thus spake the Balkan man—the first Zenithist:

Cosmos is chaos.

*

The spirit rules chaos but is not its master.

*

Chaos is eternal.

*

Chaos has to exist.

*

The spirit is not absolute because it has not yet performed its final deed.

*

The final deed of the Spirit will be the death of Earth.

*

Without chaos there would be no creation.

*

Without creation there would be no chaos.

*

Novelty always causes chaos.

*

The Spirit of Zenithism: The Ethics of Chaos

*

Man is in eternal chaos.

*

Man is chaos.

*

ZENITHISM : THE ETHICS OF MAN

*

Heroism of the Spirit: Barbaro-Genius.

*

Barbaro-Genius: the most sublime strength of the spirit—
a term for Maximal Spirit.
Such is the new world: METACOSMOS.

Our poems must be the clatter and clang of factories where machines and workers sing:
MAN
Our poems must be church bells tolling the song of altars and bell towers: GOD-SPIRIT
Our poems must be stone roofs of high hills and a welcoming explosion of: THE SUN
Our poems must be clouds and storms thundering the song of lightning: THE ZENITH
Our poems must be bloodflight singing its anthem:
COSMOS—CHAOS—WORD

Our greatest poem will be: MANKIND

Our poems are not poems of feminine flirts.
Our poems are the stomp of cities, streets, squares, the thunder of tempests and abysses.

Our poems are not poems of meter and rhyme.
Our poems are rhythms of highly strung cosmic arches in a world of astral visions.

Our poems are not poems of whorish women and profane muses.
Our poems are movements of future spaces and worlds on the other side of Life and Death.

Our poems—dramas—words—symphonies—lines—notes—movements—have no laws.

Law: SPACE
Poem: WORDS IN SPACE
Religion: ZENITHISM

Translated by *Maja Starčević*

The Barbarogenius, the Balkanization of Europe, and Cultural Nihilism

Introduction

Aleksandar Bošković and Steven Teref

Zenithism has frequently been reduced to its concept of the Barbarogenius or, more precisely, to "the barbarism incarnate of the Barbarogenius, both destroyer and creator."[1] This narrow view is understandable since the self-mythologization of Micić and his movement through the construct of the Barbarogenius—along with his veneration of the Balkans and the accompanying critique of both local and European bourgeois culture, expressed through the call for the Balkanization of Europe—was ceaseless throughout more than a decade of zenithist publications (culminating in Micić's novel, *Barbarogénie le Décivilisateur*, published in 1938).[2] As art historian Slobodan Mijušković recently put it:

1 Slobodan Markuš, *Zenitizam* (Belgrade: ID Signature, 2003), 49.

2 See Nikola Dedić, "The Agony Called Europe: *Zenit* Magazine and the Historical Specificities of the Yugoslav Avant-Garde," in *Sto godina časopisa Zenit 1921–1926–2021 / A Hundred Years of Zenit Magazine*, ed. Bojan Jović and Irina Subotić (Belgrade: Gallery RIMA, Institute for Literature and Arts, 2021), 62.

> In the end, what is consistent in zenithism, what it does not give up, and what does not change, concerns, of course, the radical anti-European, anti-Western and anti-capitalist cultural, ideological and political attitude, the idea of the Balkanization of Europe, and the "symbolic figure" or "construct" under the name of the Barbarogenius, whose mission is to translate that idea into reality."[3]

Just as the zenithist ideology, which moves between anarchism, Bolshevism, Marxism, and nationalism, is ambivalent, so is the Barbarogenius, "the most fantastic and the most controversial symbolic figure of new Serbian culture," castigated by Yugoslav writer, critic, and philosopher Radomir Konstantinović, as the epitome of dark and retrograde Serbian nationalism.[4] It is, therefore, important to address the specificities and context within which this "symbolic figure" was constructed and to critically assess the cultural and ideological repercussions of its subsequent deconstructions and vindications, as well as accusations and apologies in an open-ended intellectual debate. Micić's concept of "barbarogenius" is best properly situated in its interwar (not to mention avant-garde) moment, rather than read through the prisms of World War II-era or late-Yugoslav political antagonisms, as often was the case.

The title "Zenith Manifesto 1922" clearly echoes Tristan Tzara's "Dada Manifesto 1918." Micić offers an original vision of the Balkanization of Europe with the Barbarogenius as the central character: "We don't want to be Europeans. We are Balkan—Easterners. [. . .] We want: the BALKANIZATION of EUROPE."[5] With the slogan "EAST vs. WEST," Micić betrays the earlier motto about the dualistic relationship between the Orient and the Occident, permeating all positive and negative assumptions in the terms "Balkans" and "Balkanism."[6] Micić follows the Italian and Russian futurists in their quest to abolish traditional literary values. However, while the Russian futurists—in a call to "throw Pushkin, Dostoevsky, Tolstoy, etc., etc. overboard from the Ship of Modernity"—renounced their own classics, Micić called for a coup against the classical literary and philosophical tradition of Western

---

3 Slobodan Mijušković, "Top Hat, Peasant Shoes and/or Bare Peasant Feet," in Jović and Subotić, *A Hundred Years of Zenit*, 33.

4 Radomir Konstantinović, "Četiri pesnika (Sifon–soda–krv Ljubomira Micića)," *Treći program* 4 (1972): 214, 211–250; "Ko je barbarogenije?," *Treći program* 1 (1966), 9–21.

5 Ljubomir Micić, "Zenit manifest 1922," *Zenit*, no. 11 (February 1922): 1. See translated text in this anthology.

6 See Vida Golubović and Irina Subotić, *Zenit: Internacionalna revija za umetnost i kulturu 1921–1926*, (Belgrade: Narodna biblioteka Srbije; Institut za književnost i umetnost; Zagreb: SKD Prosvjeta, 2008), 28.

Europe embodied in Molière, Dante, Shakespeare, and Kant.[7] Moreover, the performative aggressiveness of Micić's graphically violent, impassioned, and sensationalistic language embalmed in the grotesque seeks to shock and provoke by internalizing the European stereotype of the rebellious, aggressive, and barbaric Balkanites and directing it back against that same European culture and its (mis)representations of the Balkans. In this radical cultural shift from Europe to the Balkans, zenithism was unequivocally proclaimed by Micić as "the new art of the awakened Balkans and the liberated Barbarogenius."[8]

The manifesto's very form and layout coded this radical shift typographically, introducing the orthography as a marker of difference. As art historians Iva Glišić and Tijana Vujošević have argued, "Zenith Manifesto 1922" is

> comprised of an outer layer of Latin-character text surrounding an inner column of Cyrillic, all in varying fonts and character weights. In the central column, Micić outlined an imaginary conversation between himself and members of the newly ordained Soviet leadership—Vladimir Lenin, Lev Trotsky and the Soviet Commissar of Enlightenment, Anatoly Lunacharsky. They discuss whether the young, impoverished student Raskolnikov from Dostoevsky's *Crime and Punishment* really had committed a crime by killing the rapacious pawnbroker and stealing her money which he planned to use to good effect, or whether in fact his actions had been justified. "Zenith Manifesto" ultimately celebrated Raskolnikov's actions as positive and progressive, equating them with the smashing of the skull of Western European capitalism and culture by the Soviet leaders in a supreme act of emancipation.[9]

The central column ironically celebrates "death" as a "national pastime" of Balkanites who became both poets and barbarians ("our men still carry a flute and a knife between their teeth with blood in their eyes") due to their "tragic trauma nurtured by an evil history of empires' selfishness and self-interest."[10]

7 Micić announces that these classics should "rest in the museums, embalmed for eternity." See Ljubomir Micić, "Zenit-Manifesto 1922," Zenit, no. 11 (February 1922): 1.

8 Ibid.

9 Iva Glišić and Tijana Vujošević, "I am Barbarogenius: Yugoslav Zenitism of the 1920s and the Limits of Performativity," *Slavic and Eastern European Journal* 60, no. 4 (2016): 724.

10 Konstantinović, "Ko je barbarogenije?": 21.

It is telling that Micić began forging zenithists' poetic self-awareness and articulating their cultural mission in the outer layer of Latin-character text and in dialogue with the Europeans, that is, with those who call the Balkans "barbarians": "We zenithists are the first to listen to the commandment of our wild blood in art. (You call us barbarians!) We are the first to discover that there is a land of the Barbarogenius—the Balkans! So far, it has *given birth* to us, and as of today, we *create* it in the atmosphere of the Balkan spirit and Balkan culture."[11] The text's layout thus unconsciously confirms Konstantinović's remark about Micić's "great misconception: that the being of this barbarism (its irrationality) can be separated from the language in which it is structured and, consequently, that it is possible to express its authenticity in a foreign language that it finds inauthentic."[12] At the same time, it is in this outer column that Micić extends the limits of poetic language—opening it to bastardizations with Esperanto and cinema, as well as to its interactions with the visual features of the script—and promotes his concept of zenithist poetry as hybrid writing: "Zenithist poetry = WORDS IN SPACE. Words as meaning—the concept." It is in this unpremeditated promotion of hybridization and eclecticism that one should acknowledge the marriage of barbarity and geniality in the poet-Barbarogenius, since the practice of bastardization (barbarism) as an unconscious (irrational) but key tenant of cultural nihilism consequently engendered zenithism to foster a conceptual writing that radically questioned the premises of authenticity, originality, and authorship, upon which the notions of (Western European) cultural values were established.

In his 1923 essay "Zenithism as the Balkan Totalizer of a New Life and a New Art," Micić further developed his program, specifying the relations between Europe and the Balkans, old culture and barbarism: "Europe can only be reborn if it is fertilized with raw powers and new seeds, but never entirely on its own."[13] This historical mission will be carried out by the Barbarogenius, who is "the carrier of an unsentimental, coarse vitality—pure faith—an unadulterated soul—a good, open heart, which with a lot of universal love we, along with the Russians, bring to the new life of a new humanity."[14] The categorical belief that the Balkan Barbarogenius will fertilize Europe by destroying ancient forms and

---

11 Micić, "Zenit-Manifesto 1922": 1.

12 Konstantinović, "Ko je barbarogenije?": 18.

13 Ljubomir Micić, "Zenitizam kao balkanski totalizator novoga života i nove umetnosti," *Zenit*, no. 21 (February 1923): n.p. See translated text in this anthology.

14 Ibid.

introducing barbaric raw materials is the essence of the period starting late 1922–early 1923 of zenithism, which remained intact until Micić's departure for France. But the idea of barbarism and the incarnation of the Barbarogenius should be seen in light of the conflict between East and West, Moscow and Paris—the principles emphasized in Micić's texts—because they reveal the sociological and political-ideological positions of zenithism. In Europe, zenithism saw not only a sclerotic and tired culture ("dusty ancient European academism and its anti-human fungus; [. . .] bleak academism of Western European moths; [. . .] the false, empty vision of 'culture,' [. . .] the tarnished brand 'Europe'"), eager for new juices and the need for rejuvenation, but also its economic and political base: capitalism and imperialism.[15] In the Balkans, on the other hand, Micić saw, or more precisely, projected his belief in the creative and transformative power of pure, original primitiveness and barbarism inherent in, as he saw it, the Balkan man.

Everything that makes up the meaning of the aforementioned zenithist constants (the Barbarogenius, the Balkanization of Europe, anti-capitalism, and anti-imperialism) relates to Micić's persistence of "the *ethical* dimension of barbarism, which he often describes using categories such as naivety, purity of faith and soul, an open and good heart, direct compassion, heroism of spirit, justice, humanity, brotherhood, etc. Whether all these characteristics really belong to the ethical vertical of barbarism/primitiveness, in which the 'religion of thought' (West) is opposed to the "'religion of feeling' (East), is a secondary question," asserts Mijušković in his essay in response to Konstantinović's remark about Micić's "great (European) misconception" that produced distinctions and divisions between the primitive and the civilized, the barbaric and the cultural; according to Mijušković, these divisions "did not remain on the paper of cultural-anthropological studies, but were materialized in practical politics."[16] In other words, the construct of the Barbarogenius and the zenithist program of the Balkanization of Europe was a response to the question of how to position the region and how to define a shared cultural identity of the politically-united South Slavs (Yugoslavs) with respect to major European powers.

Micić's response to "the challenge of developing an authentic voice independent of West European models, and the realization that cultural and intellectual authenticity

15 Markuš, *Zenitizam*, 53.

16 Mijušković, "Top Hat, Peasant Shoes and/or Bare Peasant Feet," 33.

directly translated into political confidence"[17] was not a single case, but represented yet another of his eclectic-synthetic constructs. As Glišić and Vujošević summarized, Micić constructed the "symbolic figure" of the Barbarogenius by appropriating "the political myth of the young, fresh, and original Balkan genius who would defy 'rotten' and 'decadent' Europe,"[18] a concept that literary critic Jovan Skerlić had already examined in his 1912 survey of nineteenth-century Serbian literature, as well as by drawing on the work of anthropogeographer Jovan Cvijić, who allocated a special place to the "Dinaric type" among different Balkan personality types: "An embodiment of the unique Balkan ethos, the Dinaric type was a man easily angered because [he is] ruled by his belief in freedom, honor, justice, and pride. Cvijić saw the Dinaric type as an agent of political and cultural liberation for the Slavic peoples, as his feisty temper was complemented by a rich imagination."[19] The myth of a young virile *Homo balkanicus* enamored with the "ethics of cultural barbarism,"[20] as exemplified by both Cvijić and Micić, was ready to depart on a mission of Balkanizing Europe. The zenithist poet Marijan Mikac was, for Micić, the living, breathing example of the Barbarogenius. In his foreword to *Effect on Defect* (*Efekt na defektu*, 1923)—the first poetry collection by Marijan Mikac—Micić introduces Mikac as an authentic, nineteen-year-old Balkan poet deprived of the influences of foreign literature and cultural traditions, expressing "real Slavic-Balkan strength" in its naivete, roughness, youth, and willpower for the

17 Glišić and Vujošević, "I am Barbarogenius": 727; Zoran Milutinović, *Getting Over Europe: The Construction of Europe in Serbian Culture* (Amsterdam: Rodopi, 2011), 81–118, 261–66.

18 Glišić and Vujošević, "I am Barbarogenius": 727.

19 Ibid.

20 In a very instructive text "Barbarism as Culture," in which he promotes barbarism as a (new) model of healing, rather than the antipode of culture, the zenithist poet Risto Ratković writes about the "ethics of cultural barbarism," the ethics of "those who do not a priori respect anything and are still meek and good." Emphasizing in barbarism the potential of liberating the person against all normativism, he says, among other things: "Our innocence made us mad and we became barbarians. What a paradox! But here it is: we oppose all savagery, indignity, meanness, all repulsive things so neatly masked by culture; we oppose them with pure goodness and joyful freedom." Risto Ratković, "Barbarstvo kao kultura," *Zenit*, no. 37 (November–December 1925). In "The New Zenithist Art" essay accompanying his first novel *The Monkey Phenomenon*, Marijan Mikac listed the following "important elements of Balkanism, which Ljubomir Micić highlighted 1) Purity of primitivism 2) down-to-earth humanity 3) heroism of spirit and heart 4) integrity of soul 5) universal brotherhood 6) justice 7) ethics." Marijan Mikac, *Fenomen majmun* (Belgrade: Biblioteka Zenit, 1925), 67; see the translation of Mikac's essay in this anthology.

creation of new values.[21] The front cover's graphic design by Jo Klek, a zenithist visual artist and creator of the first costumes for zenithist theater, showcased the seriousness of the movement's attempt to bring the innovations of "our young, rebellious, and unarticulated race" into the Yugoslav literary scene.[22]

According to Micić, "the Balkanization of Europe, in short, means: the formation of a new type of culture and man from a Balkan trademark of ethics and genuine humanity—which at its furthest extent means: to create a culture of life and not a culture of lies and paper—to create a new life and a new culture within that life for every man and not just for the privileged, for libraries, galleries, and museums."[23] As already noticed, Micić's program simultaneously expressed pro- and anti-European tendences, while this "tension between rejecting and longing for Europe is resolved defining the mission of Balkanizing Europe as a *performance*, in which the attack on Europe simultaneously entailed the use of barbaric energy to breathe new life into the very continent under attack, thus creating a modern Europe that would elevate the Balkans to a more prominent status."[24] Micić conceived the project of the Balkanization of Europe both to exploit and invert Balkanist stereotypes and thus enter the European cultural domain on its own terms. He demonstrated that the stereotypes are nods to which it is possible to suture separate, contradictory, and often antagonistic fragments into a collaged and, in (t)his case, chiastic form: "By this process, the role of the Balkans as imitator of imposed *European models* would be replaced by a European imitation of the *Balkan ethos* by transforming Europe into a fragmented continent and a cultural war zone in which a host of militant factions would fight for domination."[25]

---

21 Mikac's poems, according to Micić, celebrated the "constructive expression of mechanized life and radial speed of modern work and great labor" which found expression in zenithism's embrace of paradoxes. Published in only thirty copies, this typographically playful edition represented the aesthetics of defect that sprang out of a deeply anti-poetic, anarchic, and revolutionary spirit that Mikac shared with Micić and propagated in his poems on both thematic and formal levels, extensively using paradox, free associations ("žena mlaka ne vole ludaka," or "a lukewarm woman doesn't like a madman"), and simultaneity, including sequences of simultaneous but unrelated events. See: Ljubomir Micić, "Vo imja Zenitizma," [In the name of Zenithism] in Marijan Mikac *Efekt na defektu* (Belgrade: Biblioteka Zenit, 1923), n.p. See *Effect on Defect* in this anthology.

22 See *Effect on Defect* in this anthology.

23 Micić, "Zenitizam kao balkanski totalizator novoga života i nove umetnosti," *Zenit*, no. 21 (February 1923): n.p. See translated text in this anthology.

24 Glišić, Vujošević, "I am Barbarogenius": 728. Authors' emphasis.

25 Ibid. Authors' emphasis.

Such imitative performance within which the representations and their cultural, political, and ideological effects (European models) switch places with a Balkan ethos (naivete, purity of faith and soul, an open and good heart, direct compassion, heroism of spirit, justice, humanity, brotherhood) was employed to encourage one area of thought to consider an opposing area's perspective, as in a chiastic structure. However—and one could argue, exactly because of the chiastic structure—Micić's project of the Balkanization of Europe can be perceived as both "an active and a reactive vector within an avant-garde network and topology of forces," as media scholar Jovan Čekić claims.[26] He writes, "When this barbarian, with his purity and innocence, is reduced to one community, nation or ideology, then a false choice is introduced between 'them' and 'us,' between the civilized and the barbarians, between the 'blinded' and those who 'see.'"[27]

Nemo propheta in patria, a supplement to *Zenit* no. 25, which contains statements on *Zenit* and zenithism from foreign periodicals, is a good example of how zenithism was viewed from within the avant-garde network to which Čekic refers. Zenithism was known and written about in Moscow, Paris, Leiden, London, Brussels, Antwerp, Munich, Berlin, Rome, Warsaw, Budapest, Prague, and Sofia. Zenithist works were translated into a dozen languages, published in top avant-garde European magazines, and included in world anthologies during the 1920s.[28] *Zenit* was at that time one of the few European magazines to publish articles in their original languages; it was in a real sense international. It is difficult to find a person among the 1920s elite of the European avant-garde whose name could not be found in the pages of *Zenit*. For some, it served as a window and a door to the world. Others validated their views through it. It is not without reason that *De Stijl* named it one

---

26 Jovan Čekić, "*Zenit*: The Avant-Garde Network Hub," in Jović and Subotić, *A Hundred Years of Zenit*, 54. "If observed within the avant-garde network, zenithism provokes and seeks new connections, and protests in the spirit of the avant-garde. If observed outside the avant-garde network, however, provocations flow into Micić's individual national-political interventions, which threaten to retroactively suture the entire activity of zenithism. In the first case, we have a 'surplus of meaning' coming from the network, where every provocation calls for openness and new connections, while in the second case, we have closure and negative reterritorialization to the national as the only valid one." Ibid., 54.

27 Ibid., 53.

28 For example, zenithist works appeared in Yvan Goll ed., *Les Cinq Continents–Anthologie Mondiale* (Paris: La Renaissance du livre, 1922), as well as in the magazines such as *Blok* (Warsaw), *Bouwkunde* (Antwerp), *Les 7 Arts* (Brussels), *Der Sturm* (Berlin), *De Morgen*, *Helmond* (Holland), *Lumière*, (Anvers), *Manomètre* (Lyon), *Wohnungskultur* (Brno), *Ma* (Vienna), *25* (Gorizia), *Plam'k* (Sofia), *S 4 N* (Northampton), but also in *Inicial* (Buenos Aires), and *Mavo* (Tokyo).

of the five world magazines crucial for the development of the avant-garde at the time.[29] "The emergence of *Zenit* and zenithism, on which an entire generation across the globe collaborates, has garnered attention in twelve countries, in more than sixty journals and newspapers," writes Micić in his 1923 essay. In the same essay, he spells out that his experience of being unrecognized and unwelcomed in his home country—the Kingdom of Serbs, Croats, and Slovenes—equals being outside the avant-garde network.[30]

Following Deleuze and Guattari's denouncement of transcendence as "a typically European disease,"[31] Čekić perceives "anti-Europeanism, anti-Christianity, anti-art, anti-capitalism, anti-war, anti-humanism, and all other anti-, for the avant-garde to denote only different angles of observation and detection of symptoms of European disease—transcendence."[32] In this anti- is also inscribed the search for the "new man" and, thus, the zenithist fantasy of a new uncorrupted barbarian—the Barbarogenius. For Čekić, the avant-garde demand for erasing the boundary between art and life "implies non-acceptance of such an understanding of art for which transcendence is a constitutive moment. In contrast, for the avant-garde, art is inseparable from the *flux of life*, understood in almost a Deleuzean sense, as 'pure immanence,' as something that cannot be coded in any way."[33] According to Čekić, the search for new images of thinking is connected with artistic provocation within the network. Regardless of "how sometimes offensive, naive, militant or inconsistent," this search is inherent in the avant-garde, it represents "an effort to establish new ways of artistic connection with 'networks of life,' which are hybrid, eclectic, volatile, fluid and elusive,

---

29 See Markuš, *Zenitizam*, 61; Maja Stanković, "*Zenit*: Predecessor of Networked Activity," in Jović and Subotić, *A Hundred Years of Zenit*, 77–91. See also Meghan Forbes, "Advertisement as Collaboration in the Central European Avant-Garde Magazines," https://post.moma.org/advertisement-as-collaboration-in-the-central-european-avant-garde-magazines-2/.

30 "I mention this only to emphasize that it is precisely in our country that this journal, the only one of its kind in the world, publishes works in all the original languages, and for it to be known to all what a shame it is that our country (state, society, press) treats us like an evil stepmother, while we zenithists selflessly carved out quite a bit of space on the international battlefield, where the finest do battle to claim victory for a new art and a new panhuman culture." Ljubomir Micić, "Zenitizam kao balkanski totalizator novoga života i nove umetnosti," *Zenit*, no. 21 (February 1923): n.p. See translated text in this anthology.

31 Gilles Deleuze and Félix Guattari, *A Thousand Plateaus: Capitalism and Schizophrenia*, trans. Brian Massumi (Minneapolis: University of Minnesota Press 1987), 18.

32 Čekić, "*Zenit*: The Avant-Garde Network Hub," 45.

33 Ibid.

sometimes even mystical and incomprehensible, but always turned to life as 'pure immanence.'"[34] As soon as this search is reframed and reterritorialized to the national and ideological, it returns to the transcendent, "the elusive, beyond comprehension, which is embodied in the ideologies of the country, people, spirit, or something that encodes the whole field."[35] This is perhaps most evident in the example of the Barbarogenius: within the avant-garde network, it acquires the meaning of rebellion and disagreement of the procedural minority, while outside the network it grows into a minority reduced to local and national frameworks, which end in a "narcissism of small differences."[36]

What is perceived as problematic with Micić's concepts of the Barbarogenius and the Balkanization of Europe was, actually, his agitation for the prominent anti-European, anti-Western, anti-Latin, pro-Balkan, pro-rebellious ideology of "haiduk-komitadji barbarism" within the new state of united South Slavs in a specific geographical, historical, and cultural space and in a distinctive socio-political context 'outside the avant-garde network.' This space and this context are connected with the unmediated experience, cultural-historical memory, and understanding of the Balkans and the complex internal circumstances of the then-Kingdom of Serbs, Croats, and Slovenes. Paradoxically, it was exactly here—outside the avant-garde network and within the newly established state of South Slavs—that Micić strived to shift from performing and representing the Orient for the West to calling for a Balkan identity among Balkan populations themselves and renegotiating the presence of Orientalist stereotypes among the Balkanites. And it was exactly here that he famously failed.

Micić's 1922 manifesto "The Categorical Imperative of the Zenithist School of Poetry" beautifully illustrates the subtleties of this distinct socio-political context and geographical, historical, and cultural space 'outside the avant-garde network':

---

34 Ibid., 54.

35 "It is no longer an event as an experiment with the real, but a fall into the old picture of opinion dominated by not only the 'spirit of the parochialism,' but also the phantasmatic hegemonic spirit that 'knows' the solution to all the problems of humanity." Ibid., 54. Also, see Radomir Konstantinović, *The Philosophy of Parochialism*, ed. Branislav Jakovljević, trans. Ljiljana Nikolić and Branislav Jakovljević (Ann Arbor: University of Michigan Press, 2021).

36 Sigmund Freud, *Civilization and Its Discontents* (New York: J. Cape & H. Smith, 1930); see also Michael Ignatieff, "The Narcissism of Minor Difference," in *The Warrior's Honor: Ethnic War and the Modern Conscience* (New York: Metropolitan Books, 1998), 34–71.

> Do not forget that I am a BANOVITE-BALKANITE like Nikola Tesla. I am not even afraid of the crack of a haiduk's pistol nor of the stench of poisonous gas, not to mention your billy-goat bell. Quickly remove the corpses so they do not begin to smell of Latins. Your dear Molière is a real twit. Ah, and your imaginary Shakespeare Mister Lloyd George! You've driven me to madness you measly, plagiarizing sycophants![37]

This quote is important for two reasons: first, for Micić's anti-Latin and anti-Western European attitude, directed against the notorious cultural mimicry of the Balkanites (and their attempt to imitate the West through adoption and perpetuation of Western ideology) as the essence of their self-colonization; and second, for Micić's self-characterization of a "Banovite-Balkanite," that is, a member of a Serbian minority from Banovina (Banija)—a geographical region in central Croatia and a part of the Croatian Military Frontier within the former Habsburg monarchy and Austro-Hungarian Empire.[38]

Micić reacted against both the cultural mimicry of Croatian cultural elites he witnessed in Zagreb and the reactionary parochialism of a Serbian servile mentality and culture he found in Belgrade. Micić was frustrated by the tendency of Croatian cultural elites to "parrot" diverse elements of European culture and—since they transferred the sense of *shame* from culturally superior Europe into a feeling of *disgust* toward the Balkan other—for distancing themselves from other Balkanites within the same unified state, especially those that had been under Ottoman rule and who were therefore supposedly hopelessly backward, uncultured, and barbaric, that is, positioned further South-East (Serbs, Macedonians, etc.), as Bakić-Hayden aptly described it in her concept of "nesting orientalisms."[39] Not long after he moved from Zagreb to Belgrade with his wife Anuška, Micić encountered a very similar mentality to "that which he had thought he had left behind in Zagreb."[40] He was attacked

37 See the translated text in this anthology. Micić first published his manifesto in *Zenit*, no. 16 (1922) in German and included it in his *Damn Your Hundred Gods/Rescue Car* in Serbian later in the same year.

38 Nikola Tesla, a famous American scientist of Serbian descent, and Svetozar Pribićević, a Croatian Serb politician, both of whom Micić compares to himself, originate from different regions of the same Military Frontier in Croatia (Lika and Banovina).

39 Bakić-Hayden, "Nesting Orientalisms: The Case of Former Yugoslavia," *Slavic Review* 54, no. 4 (Winter 1995): 917–931.

40 "In fact, in Serbia Micić faced an even more intransigent parochialism. His disappointment with Belgrade resulted in the essay 'Thank You, Beautiful Serbia,' published in *Zenit* in 1925, in which he

in the press, accused of offending public morals, persecuted by the police and government officials in the courts, and suffered from State bans and censorship imposed on zenithist publications.[41] The reaction to these constant persecutions, and especially to the ban on the book *Airplane without an Engine* (*Aeroplan bez motora: antievropska poema*, 1925),[42] can be found in *Zenit* no. 40 (April 1926): first, the ban on *Zenit* is ignored and ironized with the words in the form of an advertisement: "Do not read the 39th volume of *Zenit* because it has been banned by the police"; second, a censored version of the *Airplane without an Engine: An Anti-European Poem* was printed in its entirety; and third, on the back cover in the form of an advertisement, we read in Serbian and French: "Don't forget the banned anti-European poem by Ljubomir Micić, *Airplane without an Engine*."[43] In relation to this poem, court bans, and police persecutions, for the first time a letteristic work in the form of a typogram appeared in the former Yugoslavia. It represented the figure of a man hanged over bureaucratic paragraphs, composed of a text in French: l'auteur de la poème anti-européenne AVION SANS APAREIL LIOUBOMIR MITZITCH, below which is a pedestal of five lines called: ZENITHISM; at the bottom is a text in French and Serbian stating

---

attacked the 'servile' mentality and culture that he found in the Serbian capital." Glišić and Vujović, "I am Barbarogenius": 734.

41 See Irina Subotić, "Micić u svetlu novootkrivenih dokumenata," in *Ljetopis* (Zagreb: Srpsko kulturno društvo *Prosvjeta*, 2016): 349–378.

42 At the end of 1925, Biblioteka Zenit published Micić's anti-European didactic poem written in 1922, *Airplane without an Engine*, dedicated to his partner, Anuška Micić. Its introductory part included documentary material: a text from the daily *Politika* from September 23, 1923, declaring the death of zenithism a few months after Micić's arrival in Belgrade, as well as a document on the seizure of Micić's book of poetry *Damn Your Hundred Gods* in Zagreb in 1922. An aviation motif with futurist effects appeared in *Airplane without an Engine*: to turn the power of a poem into an airplane. The collection was confiscated by the police, by order of the Governor of the City of Belgrade (based on a decision of December 16, 1925). The Court of Appeals filed a lawsuit under the Press Law, which Micić appealed on December 18; but the Court of Appeals upheld the ban, on December 22, 1925, for "grave breach of public morals"—Micić used erotic expressions to speak of his love for his wife (*Zenit* covered in detail the banning process in the text "My Poetry and 'Public Morality'" in 1926). Furthermore, Micić's polemical collection of poetry *Anti-Europe*, published as the ninth edition in the Biblioteka Zenit series in 1926 and dedicated to Dr. Dušan Popović from Zagreb, contained a rich fund of subversive ideas. In the poems he emphasized his love for his wife, Anuška, while in opposition he expressed his hatred for Europe, which is also a female character, personified on the basis of an ancient myth. See both books in the anthology.

43 See *Zenit*, no. 40 (April 1926): https://monoskop.org/images/1/14/Zenit_40.pdf.

that the poet Micić was "put on trial" for his anti-European poem.[44] The State eventually passed a definitive ban on *Zenit* on December 15, 1926 for the text "Zenithism through the Prism of Marxism," which was signed by the pseudonymous author Dr. M. Rasinov (most probably Micić himself). The text draws an explicit parallel between the barbarians (the Barbarogenius) and the world proletariat, echoing Micić's call for the destruction of anti-social art in his response to the questionnaire posed by Czech journal *Bytova kultura* in October 1924, published in *Zenit* no. 35 (December 1924).[45] In the end, Micić had to leave the country and spent the next ten years in exile in France. Keeping in mind that "Micić is not talking about anti-Europe and anti-capitalism from Zürich, Berlin or Paris, but from the Balkans, Zagreb, and Belgrade,"[46] his request for the Balkanization of Europe as "the formation of a new type of culture and man from a Balkan trademark of ethics," and his call for erasing the boundary between art and life to create "a culture of life and not a culture of lies and paper . . . for every man and not just for the privileged," appear to have a sound emancipatory goal and an attainable utopian vision for Balkan identity among Balkan populations themselves. As historian Nikola Dedić has aptly demonstrated, zenithism was the only art movement on the 1920s cultural scene in the Kingdom of Serbs, Croats, and Slovenes that accepted, embraced, and promoted the Balkans as a genuinely authentic civilization through the "zenithist myth of the Barbarogenius;" it was the zenithist way to struggle for hegemony within the artistic field, that is, the sphere of cultural production which was under the control of the "comprador bourgeoisie," the plutocratic and exploitative Yugoslav bourgeoisie that helped the colonizers and lived off sales.[47]

---

44 See Golubović and Subotić, *Zenit*, 225.

45 "Barbarians are the entire world proletariat. Barbarians are the idea of total proletarian strength, which has the power of volcanic lava about to explode. [. . .] Barbarians are 'Moscow vs. Paris'—'East vs. West' [. . .] Barbarians are Micić's barbarogenius [. . .] The barbarogenius is the fighting proletarian, the only one who can make the appearance of the new man possible." Moreover, the slogans of zenithism overlap with the Marxist slogans: "Down with today's tyranny. DOWN WITH EUROPE! Down with the exploitation of man by man. Down with country borders. Greetings to all workers of the world LONG LIVE BARBARIANS! Revolution is our poem. Long live new liberated society. Long live the new man." See "Zenithism through the Prism of Marxism" in this anthology.

46 Mijušković, "Top Hat, Peasant Shoes and/or Bare Peasant Feet": 37.

47 Dedić, "The Agony Called Europe: *Zenit* Magazine and the Historical Specificities of the Yugoslav Avant-Garde": 59–74. According to Dedić, "intimists advocated for the modernization and Europeanization through a narrative of civilized Europe and the backward Balkans; traditionalists rejected intimacy through a narrative of decadent Europe and an authentic national, Serbian (but not Balkan) tradition;

As for the second reason, being a member of the Serbian minority on the Croatian Military Frontier on the southeast edge of the Austro-Hungarian Empire, Micić may have had traumatic experiences.[48] In such a peculiar position—living on the frontier where multiple modes of exclusion and inclusion (interiority and exteriority) produced subjectivities with dual identity—he must have felt twice othered.[49] His attempt to incite countercultural self-re-Orientalization and aspiration to belong to both the Slavic Orient and Western Europe at the same time, was actually an endeavor to escape the practice of "nesting orientalisms" through the (de)constructive practice of zenithism. Konstantinović, one of the most vocal and strongest critics of Micić's zenithism, characterized it as a "haiduk-komitadji barbarism," elaborating on it in the following way: "Just as Europe was for Micić 'the vampiric Turkey of our [twentieth] century,' so the avant-gardist, in this call for the destruction of Europe, appeared to him increasingly as a haiduk and komitadji from the Balkan wars and the First World War, with a dagger or a bomb in his hand,

---

surrealists and social artists rejected the Balkans in the name of class struggle. Finally, the zenithists, through the myth of the Barbarogenius, are the only ones to accept the Balkans as a truly authentic civilization, and thus reject all the mentioned positions, groups, and movements" (73).

48 For example, he faked "madness" to escape military service in the Austro-Hungarian army, which press-ganged him and sent him to fight in Galicia during World War I.

49 "The Military Frontier of the Austro-Hungarian Empire that between the 16th and late 19th centuries acted as a buffer zone on the very edge of imperial territory, intended to protect it from Ottoman invasions. As many Serbs fled Ottoman oppression in the South, they settled in the Military Frontier, working as *granitschari*, or frontiersmen, and bearing arms at all times. As Serbs defended the Austrian lands against steady offensives from the South, their villages were constantly burnt down in continual wars, and despite the numerous tax benefits offered to the Serbs by the Austrian Emperor, the Military Frontier remained the poorest and most isolated part of the empire; the war was its only economy. As the Ottoman Empire declined, the Military Frontier was dissolved and incorporated into the Croatia-Slavonia region of the Kingdom of Hungary in 1881, leaving a sizeable Serbian minority in that part of the Austro-Hungarian Empire. This re-drawing of boundaries created a particular dynamic of Serbo-Croatian relations that would expand in the 1920s, the time when the Micić brothers were active. As the Serbs observed the absorption of the Military Frontier into Croatia, they somewhat resisted their new position of a minority culture, increasingly looking to nearby Serbia as their homeland. On the other hand, some members of the Croatian cultural elite, aligned with the Catholic, Hapsburg, and the larger Western European cultural model, perceived the impoverished Serbian frontiersmen and their Orthodox Faith 'as a backward and inferior race.'" Igor Marjanović, "*Zenit:* Peripatetic Discourses of Ljubomir Micić and Branko Ve Poljanski," in *On the Very Edge: Modernism and Modernity in the Arts and Architecture of Interwar Serbia (1918–1941)*, ed. Jelena Bogdanović, Lilien Filipovitch Robinson, and Igor Marjanović (Leuven: Leuven University Press, 2014), 65–66.

charging the bloody trenches (*krvavi jendeci*) of the surviving and cannibalistic European culture."[50] The border—be it a bloody trench (*krvavi jendek* for Konstantinović), the Croatian Military Frontier, or the Balkans (for Micić)—can be a method precisely insofar as it is conceived of as *a site of struggle*. The zenithist program of the Barbarogenius, its cultural nihilism, and the Balkanization of Europe should be recognized as such a struggle, where the Balkans, as the liminal zone, "opens up the possibility of articulating different, even incommensurable cultural practices and priorities. It is a third space, enabling a cultural translation, denying essentialism."[51] *Haiduks* and *komitadjis* are, in fact, examples of the rebel lifestyle devoted to such a struggle: the first developed mainly in bordering parts of the Croatian Military Frontier, while the second is the term used for Bulgarian fighters in Macedonia from the end of the nineteenth to the beginning of the twentieth century. *Haiduks* and *komitadji* transgress borders and boundaries in a literal (geographic), social, political, legal, and symbolic sense.

"Our rebellion is the new humanity" and "Be a rebel / I am your brother," writes Micić in *Damn Your Hundred Gods/Rescue Car* (1922) and maps out the "catachrestic space of the new Balkans" in geographic (Šar mountain, Avala, Albania, Kosovo, Krajina and Banija/Banovina, Macedonia, Yugoslavia), political (Nikola Pašič and Svetozar Pribićević), artistic (Ivan Meštrović, Micić himself), and social terms (bandits, haiduks, komitadji, and rebels). The Balkans function as a metaphor or, more precisely, as a realized *catachresis*

50 Konstantinović, "Četiri pesnika (Sifon–soda–krv Ljubomira Micića)": 228. Konstantinović denounced "the spirit of this komitadji barbarism" in Micić's writings, arguing that: "Before civilization, he remains as his Balkans before Europe, the Balkans of the haiduks of bloody trenches (*krvavih jendeka*), of the Šar and the Avala mountains, the Balkans that powerfully resists every challenge of some external force, the Balkans that is never threatened by that civilization, because it does not know it, and because it is not a temptation (as for the komitadji, Kant is no temptation at all)" (246). He criticized Micić's Barbarogenius as an expression of "the darkest possible nationalism," later embodied in Micić's novel *Barbarogénie le Décivilisateur* (1938) and *Manifesto of Serbianism* (1940). Both Micić's and Konstantinović's texts (especially the former's texts to which the latter refers) are contingent upon the historical contexts within which they came into being—before the Second World War (1938–1940) and around the Croatian Spring (1969–1972)—and, as remarked by historians, they were reactions to nationalistic ideologies on the rise. See Goran Miloradović, "Ljubomir Micić's *Manifest Srbijanstva: Post Festum*," 129–155; Olivera Dragišić, "Where Does Barbarogenius Come From? Pseudoscientific elements in the Work of Ljubomir Micić," 157–172; Petar Dragišić, "Between Zagreb and Belgrade: Ljubomir Micić's Identity Carousel," 175–186; Jovan Bukumira, "Zenitist in the Jaws of Dialectics: Micić and Ristić (via Krleža)," 205–222; all texts in Jović and Subotić, *A Hundred Years of Zenit*.

51 Homi Bhabha, *The Location of Culture* (London: Routledge, 1994), 38.

(from the Greek word for "abuse"): a semantic misuse or error, as it is common to use "militate" for "mitigate," "chronic" for "severe," "travesty" for "tragedy," "anachronism" for "anomaly," and "alibi" for "excuse" to explain the Balkans. The crossing of categorical boundaries with words, characteristic for catachresis as a figure of speech (because there otherwise would be no suitable word), is an analogue for alternating between a relationship and a separation when negotiating differences among Balkan identities (which historian Marija Todorova has called it "differences within one type").[52]

Konstantinović was right when equalizing Micić's vision of an avant-garde artist with the rebel figures of the *haiduk* and the *komitadji*; but, at the same time, he may have been too protective of the fetishism of authenticity (especially of European culture and heritage), which is the most intense form of the production and protection of boundaries—a form that illustrates the point as well as the risk of boundaries as such. It is exactly this fetishism of authenticity, authorship, and originality, that the "*haiduk-komitadji* barbarism" of zenithist literature was questioned. Micić, Mikac, Poljanski, and most of all, MID [Mita Dimitrijević], all pushed forward the "haiduk-komitadji barbarism" in literature: with zenithist conceptual writing, the banditry (*hajdučija*) becomes both a concept and a key for the transgressive reading/writing of a cultural nihilist. Quotations, hybridization, and bastardization are within conceptual writing the literary *hajdučija* par excellence, exposing the boundaries themselves as being representations of representations. The three subsequent sections of *The Three Roads of the Barbarogenius* address the transgressive nature of zenithism's literary hybridization, intertextuality, and arts cross-pollination.

---

52 "Unlike orientalism, which is a discourse about an imputed opposition, Balkanism is a discourse about an imputed ambiguity. [. . .] While orientalism is dealing with a difference between (imputed) types, balkanism treats the differences within one type. [. . .] This in-betweenness of the Balkans, their transitory character, could have made them simply an incomplete other; instead they are constructed not as other but as incomplete self." See Marija Todorova, *Imagining the Balkans* (Oxford: Oxford University Press, 2009), 17, 19, 18.

Zenith Manifesto 1922

Ljubomir Micić
from *Zenit,* no. 11 (February 1922)

Translated by *Steven Teref* and *Maja Teref*

19 ZENITH MANIFESTO 22

LJUBOMIR MICIĆ—ZAGREB

ZENITHISM is liberation from all the academic shackles and the obvious lies of European classicism and P. T. Barnum civilization.

Zenithism = new Balkan art.

I am the only born zenithist! (I am integral!) You will become a zenithist! You must become a zenithist! You will be created! You all have to be zenithists!

We pull off *Moliere*'s fragrant greasy wig: what remains of the head of the royal and court supplier of madness is empty.
We tear off *Dante*'s Catholic black mantle: what remains is the nakedness of the ecclesiastic Lucifer, who only wants Heaven for himself and Hell for everyone else.
We pluck *Shakespeare*'s chin hairs: what remains is only the pathos of Lord Bacon and the homosexuality of the Danish prince Hamlet with the hackneyed "To be, or not to be."
We remove *Kant*'s brain and cut the navel: what remains is the "common sense" of Germanic philosophy at the tips of our fingernails.
We stuff *Prince Marko* in the Vidovan Temple and Meštrović in the Rectorate of the Academy of Arts. This is the best way to deal with them because

I, RASKOLNIKOV'S BROTHER
: ask :
the new children of our Russia Today
you red and tough civil guardsmen at Nevsky Prospect
you the first cubist monument of Bukharin
you Moscow gods at the Kremlin
LENIN—TROTSKY—LUNACHARSKY
to all of you I ask
if it is indeed true
that RASKOLNIKOV committed
☛ A CRIME ☚
That old legend has already been told
to your blood brothers in the Balkans
but one of your fathers
☛ DOSTOEVSKY ☚
they say
that he wrote exactly that in the Russian novel
Who KNOWS THAT?
NOW YOU ARE silent.
We are glum because they blocked our way.
OPEN UP!
Erase the borders!
(ministers of the army and foreign affairs)
WE KNOW OUR WAY
On our own we will scale the Spanish roadblocks
charge
THE ORIENT EXPESS

ZENITHISM = the manifestation of a free spirit.

What do these *savage* zenithists want?
"FRACTURE.

1. A superior attitude toward the former protégé Madame Europe.
2. A complete denial and rejection of an external mathematical-physical civilization.
3. A modern affirmation of the Eastern metacosmic idea of the mystical archetype of the *New Man*.
4. The resurrection of the Southern Balkan prototype of the *Man-Hero* in the inner spiritual incarnation of the BARBAROGENIUS."

A memento:
Zenit
The first Balkan magazine in Europe the first European magazine in the Balkans.

MOSCOW vs. PARIS

Inside the Esperanto theater! The only modern CINEMA! Watch in ecstasy CONRAD VEIDT and CHARLIE CHAPLIN. Geniuses on a screen!

they should be the first in museums to be embalmed for eternity.

EAST vs. WEST

S. O. E.[1]

We should close all the theaters that impose performances of *The Hypochondriac* and their staging of *Othello*. They stink like corpses.

Writers and journalists! We muddy our consumptive shoes on your "works" and use them where kings tread.

We don't want to be Europeans.
We are Balkan—Easterners.
We create:

Balkan art
for
a Balkan culture.

We want: the BALKANIZATION of EUROPE.

Hanging Europe on a peg
will be a wild pleasure.

We could not be destroyed by either poisonous gases—GAS—or your massive monsters—TANK—or cannons—42—without masks we swallowed your gases and we're still alive. Your poisonous gases and our blood should give birth to a BETTER MAN.

Art for life! Man + life!

Zenithist poets! Hurrah! Inside time! The art of time! Art in time! Time in art! Jump into life! A poet's leap into a new time! Jump high: the ZENITH!

to destroy
WE WILL MOON THE WEST.
Legends are the truths of weaklings and sycophants
We zenithists trample legends
Legends always lie
Historia NON vitae magistra!
STEP ON THEIR THROATS!
Hey, Russia
your leader today is
RASKOLNIKOV
He was the first to crush the hag,
the bloodthirsty Louse.
Yes, you old sinful woman, mother
of blessed vermin
☛ **HE** ☚
he smashed the liquid brain of human leeches.
Watch
in Europe at the stock exchange
SKULLS FOR SALE
There you go, you Russian hag
On the red flag they hanged your Christ by
the tongue
Memento
Europe
DEATH IS OUR NATIONAL PASTIME
Ooooh
Ooooh
our men still carry a flute and a knife between
their teeth
With blood in their eyes . . .

On the last page of Crime and Punishment *in lieu of the hundredth anniversary of the birth of the barbarogenius DOSTOEVSKY.*

Every person enters and experiences art without a tailcoat!

S. C. S.[2]

We are not Gnostics to think that heaven is woven from the soul. We are heretics who hate your God and note with joy, that the only vicar of God on earth is Pope Benedict XV who "peacefully" kicked the bucket or died. One louse less.

We zenithists are the first to listen to the commandment of our wild blood in art. (You call us barbarians!) We are the first to discover that there is a land of the Barbarogenius—the Balkans! So far, it has *given birth* to us, and as of today, we *create* it in the atmosphere of the Balkan spirit and Balkan culture. (Creation as the superiority of every race! We do not allow the "*annihilation of the personality*," comrade Maxim Gorky.)

We create zenithist art. Zenithist poetry = WORDS IN SPACE. Words as meaning—the concept. Association without the logic of events: simultaneous. An event without the laws of psychology: *space*. Not without the logic of sense: the idea. Not unrelated to time: *Man*. Not just one part and one place without totality: *Life*. *Homocosmos*. *Metacosmos*.

Balkan art isn't utopia.
Zenithism is the new art of the awakened Balkans and the liberated Barbarogenius.

ZENITHISM is the new art of the awakened Balkans and the liberated Barbarogenius.

Endnotes

1 S. O. E.: It's not known what the acronym stands for. It may be an abbreviation of Südost Europa (Southeast Europe in German).

2 S. C. S.: The Kingdom of Serbs, Croats, and Slovenes.

Zenithism as the Balkan Totalizer of a New Life and a New Art

Ljubomir Micić
from *Zenit*, no. 21, February 1923

I.
ZENITHISM AS THE TOTALIZER OF THE NEW LIFE

Zenithism is a wild eruption on the wide crater of the Balkan volcano.

The Balkans are a volcano of unknown strength.

Zenithism erupts from a profound need for man's inner liberation from dusty, ancient European academism and its anti-human fungus.

On account of that lifeless, bleak academicism of Western European moths, which ate through more books and papers than all the rats—all harbors—all continents—many races, many peoples suffered and were smothered—many young and strong generations perished. According to the false, empty vision of "culture," which, of all its manifestations thus far saw its most disgraceful conclusion in what is perhaps the world's last bloodbath—all the Western European, cultured turds who flout controls and tariffs within its ranks. Countless crates of the tarnished brand "Europe," which only continues to impress those who shine shoes in the corners of great cities, has every one of our men convinced without fail, for it is a long-running advertisement built on the false conviction that it is superior and second to none.

That unfortunate Balkan, uncultured nirvana and hypnotic dream, a suggestion of a nameless and unknown third party, killed our **great big soul** in the past, deceived our **ethical spirit,** enslaved our great and **good heart.** The most significant motorized elements that always constitute the pure distinctiveness of a race—were swallowed up by a hungry, greedy, and hysterical frog called: Europe.

For this reason, zenithism is born out of a racial necessity: for independence, the affirmation of our youthfulness, and our health—created as a counterweight to European paralysis and an incurable degeneration.

Europe can only be reborn if it is fertilized with raw powers and new seeds, but never entirely on its own.

Zenithism aims to encourage people to love **life and work,** as a vital energetics.

Zenithism aims to encourage people who experience the **magnitude of suffering** to be brothers and friends to one another.

Zenithism aims to give people an awareness of **the new man and the new life,** which is an irreconcilable enemy of paper philosophy and romantic-poetic phrases.

Zenithism aims to serve all people as the **Balkan totalizer,** which has to become the new strong base conditioned by all heretofore unknown positive elements of our **Slavic race and pan-humanism.**

In short: time is expansive enough to finally accommodate us Easterners in its **car,** which rushed past us and over us countless times in the course of twenty centuries, leaving only bloody tracks behind.

Until now we lacked the courage or might to ride that **car.** We only lay down on the public squares of our past like corpses and skulls, knocked down and trampled in the heroic battle for the liberation of our bodies.

Our heroic tradition is great and unsurpassed. But our cultural tradition is so little known, insignificant, and thus disproportionate to our tradition of physical heroism.

This is why we are far from faint-hearted. What is more: we are proud that we are living in tumultuous times that urgently call for only the very best to rise to the **GREAT NEW TASK OF LAYING THE FIRST FOUNDATIONS OF BALKAN CULTURE AND BALKAN CIVILIZATION,** to which our young and full-blooded race has to contribute its most vital elements.

For this reason: zenithism is anti-Europe and anti-culture in its stance. And that is its virtue, for it aims to be a cleansing fire in the creation of a new life. Today we are at a major crossroads (it is important to note here that I do not even know how many times I have stressed this). It is our duty to decide, **EAST** or **WEST?** (The East gave birth to Christ and Dostoevsky!) We are Easterners.

The **Balkanization of Europe,** in short, means: the formation of a new type of culture and man from a Balkan trademark of ethics and genuine humanity—which at its furthest extent means: to create a culture of life and not a culture of lies and paper—to create a new life and a new culture within that life for every man and not just for the privileged, for libraries, galleries, and museums.

Certainly in modern times the **Balkanization of Europe** has the highest degree of possibility because it represents the crudest cut on the moving scale of **collective progress**, which has to be summed up for the future as: **THE HEROISM OF THE SPIRIT.**

The **barbarogenius** is the carrier of an unsentimental, coarse vitality—pure faith—an unadulterated soul—a good, open heart, which with a lot of universal love we, along with the Russians, bring to the new life of a new humanity.

II.
ZENITHISM AS THE TOTALIZER OF A NEW ART

Art has become the most obvious anachronism.

(Here I stress the following: the word "art" denotes only the absolute creative manifestations in works that have nothing to do with various skills. Art is, for instance, creative poetry, but it is not operatic singing or piano or violin productions. Those are only skills, as valuable as the writers who describe events or painters who photograph in color seen objects in nature.)

The new art opposes pseudo-art and the anachronism of unproductive or otherwise reproductive art, which we do not accept, not only because it is not creative but because it has done nothing for **collective humanity** or the **totality of man** thus far, not even as much as the Serbian national poem, which the nation produced as a **collective creator** and as a common product.

While I am on the subject of the national poem, which I present only for its collective creative character, all that came after it here and in Europe gave birth to the **individualistic period**, I emphasize that today's man and future man is in dire need of such a national, international or supranational product of their own, one that reaches the pinnacle of pure expression of our race in the past. What we need is a pure, simple greatness, more so than any so-called artistic work, whether it be a sonnet of a virtuoso or a painting of the former madman Cezanne.

(The first buyer at Cezanne's exhibit in Paris was a Serbian king.)

There is no denying that our times call for a collective expression, but by no means the kind that existed in the time of Kosovo or the Renaissance. We are constantly in search of this kind of expression of the times, one that will suit us living in an era of the airplane and the machine, in an era of radiotelegraphy, technical acrobatics, and speed, in an era of people's rejuvenation on the one hand and cannibalism on the other.

It is understandable that our times make the imperative demand that we also find a new mode of expression, new constructions and architectural levers for the realization and elevation of our works. It is necessary for us to also generate a new style that zenithism marks with a vertical direction, but for which no existing style until now can be considered adequate.

Zenithism is a perpendicular line drawn to a horizontal plane of symmetry.

Despite thousands of dusty academies, which live like "scholars" only in the past and of the past—despite millions of graying and impotent academics whose eyes are on the backs of their heads and not deep set below their foreheads—consciously, with clear aims and principles, we want to create for the times, to overthrow rigid and dangerous minds, to work for the future.

We even have the strength to tolerate your smirks and are likewise strong enough to match your shame with our **trademark madness,** which always signifies: **the future**.

Zenithism, the new art movement that was established in the Balkans after Christ, has the following task:

1. to introduce as much healthy and masculine vitality as possible to the new art and to effectively give it a backbone.
2. to synthesize all that is excellent and positively created through great effort in the last twenty years.
3. to impose order and discipline in these tumultuous times, which took with them numerous epigones, false prophets, snobs, and imposters.

"We depart from chaos in order to create works of art."

4. to totalize all the creative elements of the new art and to usher them into the new life and work before us, which I have called:

THE CONSTRUCTION OF THE PANHUMAN EPOCH

There is no space for coffeehouse decadence in our work—for the descendants of the inescapable Baudelaire or the European degenerates—for the descendants of Casanova or Marquis de Sade. To us, the long-haired young man or the man with the shaggy unwashed "brilliant" hair or beard who writes verses has no value whatsoever—if he is not a **man-worker-poet** who radially influences people for their real and general good. We have to make man better than he has been up to this point, at least I am convinced we must: **MAN IS A SCOUNDREL.**

The new poet has to be both a teacher and a creator, to be a creator of man and society, to be its means and reorganizer.

The new painter should construct, together with the work of the engineer, a **reality** which will serve people living in a community of cities, railways, and cars, and not only as a document of artistic and cultural value.

The new painter has to do the same, together with the engineers, architects, sculptors, and poets, as spiritual forefathers create in life, for life, and not outside of it.

It is clear that with this kind of position comes a break with the past and all the traditions of salons.

Zenit, the international journal of zenithism and the new art, which with this kind of combative posture has been publishing in our country for two years now to the astonishment of all Serbs, Croats, and Slovenes, boycotted morally and materially from all sides—gains more and more influence beyond our borders and collaborates with all those who are working toward the realization of our new aspirations, which I also warmly salute here.

P.S. The emergence of ***Zenit* and zenithism,** on which an entire generation across the globe collaborates, has garnered attention in 12 countries, in more than 60 journals and newspapers. I mention this only to emphasize that it is precisely in our country that this journal, the only one of its kind in the world, publishes works in all original languages, and for it to be known to all what a shame it is that our country (state, society, press) treats us like an evil stepmother, while we zenithists selflessly carved out quite a bit of space on the international battlefield, where the finest do battle to claim victory for a new art and a new panhuman culture.

Nonetheless:

Art is dead so a new art can live: zenithism

Belgrade January 1, 1923.

Translated by *Suzana Vuljević*

Effect on Defect

Marijan Mikac
Zenit Edition, 1923

Translated by *Vesna Jevtić*

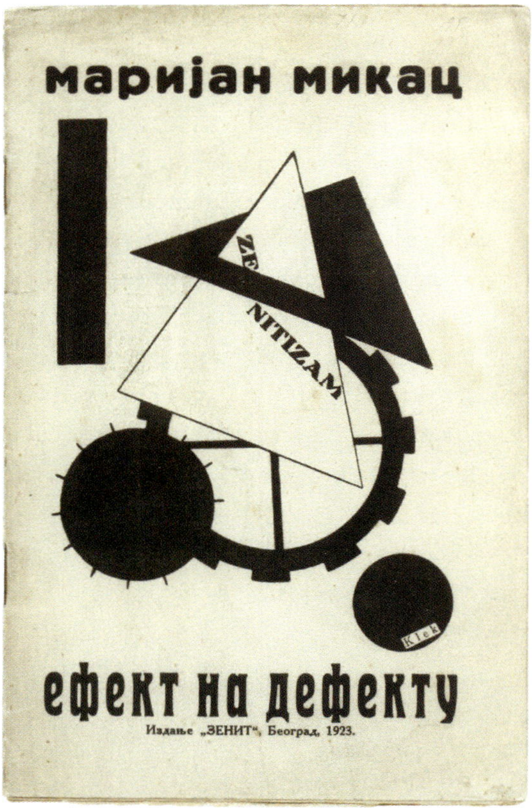

2.1. M. Mikac, *Efekt na defektu* [Effect on Defect], Zenit Edition, no. 4, Belgrade, 1923. Front cover. Courtesy of Ubu Gallery, New York & Galerie Berinson, Berlin.

marijan mikac

effect on defect

in the name of zenithism

a certificate

has been issued hereby to confirm that Marijan Mikac, a naval officer, born in Senj, may perhaps be an Uskok[1], but surely is a most ardent zenithist, with watery green eyes, without sea waves. Sailing across Banija, i.e., Šumadija of the North, he has successfully passed all maturity tests at the Academy of Zenithism in the year 1923, in the Balkans. Undoubtedly his advantage is that he has only just bit the tail off the age of twenty and is not hereditarily burdened or encumbered with anyone's "literature." He has sprouted from his own self, as has every good student at the Academy of Zenithism. To sprout from one's own self is the hardest and most laborious of all other artificial births.

Futile are tries to plant a poet as an acorn or sow him as a "Mauthner's seed"[2] or as a member of parliament. This poet, were his name not Marijan but Malipiero[3], would easily find himself in the scented shadow of a worthless Sunflower Woman[4], even more so being a sailor and a very young one at that. However, he is devoid of all European imports and "substandard samples," as is our scorched country, basically, devoid of all cultural traditions. In our purity lies our Slavo-Balkan strength. In our uncouthness, except for zenithist beliefs, lies our youth and our dizzying will to create new and pure values. Hence, we proclaim:

ZENITHISM IS THE LIFEBLOOD OF THE BALKANS!

Always has the crucial precondition for art, that is, for culture in general been: A GENUINE CREATIVE ORIGINAL. The same goes for us, each new work of art must be zenithist, developed to the maximum point of affinity and fullness in all directions, which means the following:

1. A ZENITHIST WORK OF ART SHALL BE INTERWOVEN WITH A COLLECTIVE HEART DANCING ON THE ELECTROMOTIVE ROPE OF TIME.

2. A ZENITHIST WORK OF ART SHALL BE AN INVENTIVE AND ORIGINAL PHENOMENON OF THE HUMAN SPIRIT.

3. A ZENITHIST WORK OF ART SHALL BE A CONSTRUCTIVE EXPRESSION OF MECHANISED LIFE AND RADIAL SPEED OF MODERN WORK AND GREAT LABOR.

4. A ZENITHIST WORK OF ART SHALL BE BAPTISED BY THE EASTERN-SLAVONIC WATER OF OUR RUSHING RIVERS AND ANOINTED BY THE BLACK ROSIN OF DENSE FORESTS OF THE HAIDUKS.

5. A ZENITHIST WORK OF ART MUST BE INGENIOUS.

Oh, yeah, millions of poets write verses, yet poets in this world are scarce. Even if there sprouts a poet, from seven possible symmetries of a cliff, seldom does he know that he has to project himself as the eighth symmetry and increase the number of known symmetries by at least plus one, since nature is by no means capable of doing it.

Our new comrade, whose name is definitely not Malipiero, but Marijan, is undoubtedly well on his way to discover all those symmetries by himself, which are the conditions for the existence of crystals in petrography, as well as for the existence of zenithists in the arts, among people and in society.

Even though we grow beards just because our country has no respect for its youth, and perhaps because we prefer ćevapčići (since we cannot have gelato or roast lamb!), we still hope that the day is near when one won't have to grow a beard at the expense of one's handsomeness and one's youth. We're waiting for the time when even here the value of a man and his work will not be measured by the age of one's hair or the thickness of one's wallet nor by the number of ballots cast in favor of this or that ruling party in the country.

On that day, zenithists will fly their flag on Hagia Sophia.

Today we are being washed over by the vast and murky waters of time and contemporary society. In this society zenithists are those ridiculed black sheep and scattered cliffs the edges of which are hit by international smuggler ships with flags of all colors and of all countries. Besides human trafficking and cocaine, and sellouts, and platinum and radium, silk stockings are also smuggled, filled with a splendid dowry for highly respected God's emissary on Earth—his Excellency Mr. Profiteer. His Majesty the Profiteer I, II, III, etc. . . . The Lord of all kingdoms and republics.

Madam, I know that your own mother has sold you for a stack of money. I despise you for that which you yourself have allowed, to let your own mother sell you into slavery, therefore certainly no hats off to you ever.

Mr. Minister, I know your soul is locked in the treasury of that huge bank in Terazije. That's why I wait, your Excellency, for you to greet me first before even this proletarian dies.

At the same time, nonchalantly, "modern" Belgrade poets, as well as Zagreb "Kulturträgers," that is parrot-like Europe-bearers, compose something like this:

—Stork projection
Following fashions—

And I add in their "style":

—Pagoda distraction
Soda rations—

as frogs don't hatch in soda, nor new poets in the shadow of someone else's books and ripped newspaper feuilletons printed a long time ago.
Therefore, to you, you and your offspring, I recommend from the bottom of my heart and navel: read zenithist poets there where no one sees you, where you can blush freely, if nothing else but with feigned embarrassment. You should be convinced that zenithists, similar to Indian fire-eating fakirs, easily and joyfully eat their paradoxes—for our ephemeral health and your long-lasting enjoyment.
No matter how: it's not the point to have your cheeky cheeks blushing only from the red varnish of Paris. The point is that there are zenithists around. Right?

Belgrade,
May 31, 1923
Hotel Moskva

LJUBOMIR MICIĆ

here

IT'S TRUE: ZENITHISTS ARE NOT NORMAL.
ABNORMAL PEOPLE CAN BE
EITHER ABOVE OR BELOW NORMAL.
ZENITHISTS ARE ABOVE.

Hey, God's beloved people, I'm ready to reject spite and pack my vocal bomb into my bag. I'm carrying a heated desire about our divan.
Gloves in my pocket, peacefully and amicably.
Hold off your business-gambling race for an hour only. There will be less nitwits and wimps. Indeed, I'm not as old as you are, I might lack your knowledge and experience (it's easy when you lie in your cozy beds! I spend nights on ship decks and the dew covers me!) I hold no authority, but with my poems I might uncover what covers your day.
All has been done for an agreement. A street boy has already received the placards. And I assure you of my subtlety and take heed not to hurt your vanity.
Isn't that horrible! Darn, why can't a sailor be a rider? I'd make business studs retreat into locked fashion parlors. I'd fasten ring bits on them. I'd nail the authorities to their seats.
I also rebel because your rotten eggs intend to put me back into the shell.
When I was born, my mother's womb was swayed by the sea.
Good day!

---

360 ÷ 180 = 0

Man is a traveler.
SCIENCE would like to hold a monopoly on travelers' transport. However, studies can cause consumption.
PHILOSOPHY would gladly give you wings to fly with. Eventually it gives you a pistol to kill yourself.
RELIGION wants to take sloths, geniuses, and idiots alike by the same car to heaven. However, cars cannot fly.
ART arches its back in birth-giving convulsions. It doesn't want to abort, let alone give birth.
NEW ART—ZENITHISM—is the only one that leads man up and holds him down.
Neither science—for it, one needs nerves of stone.
Nor philosophy—it needs skill: to keep one's feet in the air.
Nor religion—for it, one needs a fixed idea: to think to be able to see when you don't see, to believe not to see when you can see.
Art keeps its feet in the air and its head in the air, inconsistent with the gravity of the Earth. However, due to two opposite positions of the bodies, two different currents rise: up-down, down-up. Some have disproportionately lighter heads and stand out above with disproportionately heavier feet that hit the ground; and the other way round. Generally, art makes a revolution in the kingdom of snails. Torn in two, it fixates on the crossroads: Whether to barricade the shell with stinging nettle—gooey slime and

post a female spider as sentinel. Or: to lock away the burden on the back—may the remains rest in peace! Have trust in stepmother nature to provide arms.
The feisty are closer to rats than to snails. Snails are the species in decline, rats are the species on the rise.
The feisty are horrified: we'll throw cigarette stubs from your heads.
Promising: we're going to make a wonderful à la Turk without dregs.
Reassuring: spit will be preserved in museum spittoons. Your works, your manuscripts shall be eaten by bookworms in the editor's basket. Truly we say to you: no one will be given a monopoly to judge the worth of a work of art.
A Croat condemns Serbian Balkanism to camouflage his own.
A Serb is not ashamed of Balkanism.
A zenithist—a new man—is proud of the young Balkan race.
His goal is: THE VICTORY OF BALKANISM. All we've got, that has neither been contaminated with Western frogs nor disseminated by Western fungi, is what is Balkan within us.
We don't want death—we want resurrection.
Is it right to have both a barn and a drawing room dialectics? We shall communize it. By communizing, the zenithist cemented the ekavian dialect, being lazy to peruse Boranić's ijekavian orthography.
We are positioned at 360. We have to fortify ourselves at 180, yet not in a rib-cracking leap. The crack of our bones must be music. Our battle cry—a song, our leap virtuosic—worthy to be sculpted. There lies the synthesis of art. We have to go down the stairs at an angle of 90 degrees and not break our legs, get down the unsupported ladder (also at a 90-degree slope) and not break our noses. Mind you—nose—not head. Is the idea of a nose encompassed by the idea of a head? —That is the question. We set it as Paradox One. And Paradox Two: a ladder can stand unsupported at a 90-degree slope. It's all the same whether you fly through the air with your feet or head forward. It's important that you fly and that you by all means have a head and feet. As we said, from 360 to 180. Add 90 + 90, which are slopes, that's Math. It kills. It is crucial to realize that Math kills. (Sorry, gentle Math teachers—I don't say this out of personal dislike toward Math, because I, as a student, used to get an A, while I also happened to get a D—that's your highly appreciated logic!). Math is killing itself with its non-mathematicality. If you allow—360.—This angle cannot equal as many degrees as zero. 360 is a starting point—it really exists, we are on it (or were). 180 is a necessary constellation of those from 360. Zero is the peak of constructivism to strive for. Zero is the confluence of genius!
That's the construction: from 360 to 180!
That's the peak of construction: to position at zero.
Which means: to convince yourself you're mad.
Never will you receive a new wisdom laden with old ignorance.
ZENIT—May 1923 **M. M.**

joyous lament

What force gets the authority to manufacture elephant trunks
I'm struggling to live like a man
Where do I get all this power to be a man
Where's the cloth to remove the cobwebs
We need to shine more than a pair of patent leather shoes
We mustn't be like varnish
Have you ever created a work of art
I'm a sailor
My ship sails west with the wind against the stern
I'm not alone
I'm one of the rowers whose hands steer the galley
I'm a friend only to those who sail sharing the weight

The glass cracks
Nobody has died
Resurrection is not a fall
The ship nears its destination
The sea is not dead.

zenith—specter

A band of colors replaces topazes
The shimmy swallows the quadrille
The quadrille lives in the shimmy
White red black yellow and blue
Behind chained cash registers
In front of chained cash registers
The savages fight
For a bagful
—Authority disorder 99
The doctor yells
Should we buy pigs in a poke
Indeed
America's flour is moldy
What do we need Europe's flour for
It's not our fault that the sea overflows
We come from the Balkans
It's too late
It's too late to open Tutankhamun's wounds
It's too late to patch up holes
Idleness is the root of all mischief
You're wrong
It's not hail falling on our heads
The sky sends manna
We have impervious armor
Patent—electric guns
We're monopolistic builders
For sure we are impervious
And we build
We demolish we pull down we lay mines
We create
We shoot
To hit the target
To hit.

ZENIT—March 1923

a riot of atoms

To the kafana grave: Poets
Cards
A glass
Syphilis
A clothesline!
Powdered phrases
Just you try!
I live under a curse
I won't moan
I'm not a mischievous moralist
I welcome marble and mud with clean hands
A riot of atoms
In the brain.

rush up the rope

An engagement fantasy goes up in flames
The altar rusts through the chains
Time swallows troubadours' guitars
A beloved family
A feline wink
With a bloody ballad
Parents on a mission
Our sentimental heels
Her furious breasts
She
He
Fear
Hurrah
The economy is presented in her name
An endless marriage-minded horde rushes up the tower
of idols

a poem for the twentieth dog

Had I ever been a dog
For sure I'd never have liked dogcatchers
Though dogcatchers are cultivating factors
They put white gloves on a Japanese boy
They trim sleek manes
The world is obliged to reveal skulls
But if I were to hee-haw like a donkey
Have I then become a donkey
The little Japanese boy is a perfect mime
It's still not flattering though
It's another thing to wash your hands in salty water
To make breakneck flights in a submarine
Inasmuch as a woman can hold the Bible and be a whore
Free from censorship
And with us she can be
If she likes the music of a magical hairdresser
Women—virgins are not God's beloved
And this isn't the clamor of those who go to the local fair.

a prayer of the blessed

curse

Hey children
Fingers are not toothpicks
Our ears fill with the foam of the dying
We are eternally suspended in the air
A girl with deflowered legs cries
Sharks howl
I still think (modestly)
My hat is sweeter than my heart
I am not to blame
STARS BRING SALVATION
Folly marks your victory
    THE SPIRIT doesn't trail the airplane
    The spirit rides on the airplane
    Or: the spirit creeps on sandaled feet.

3

a fanatic's nights of love

Boom
Behold
A tear of laughter quivers on the back
A curse is laid at the graves of old men
Not the magic of Osiris
A sacred crocodile or a turtle
A girl lies drunk on the road
Young men won't touch her
Kids have always bathed naked
We think we know
How brave our hearts are
Wrong
Well whatever
My darling has sharp breasts
Antennae
We receive signals
And count
One two—one two
Eight
Troops march pointlessly
Into tomorrow

!

bachelor tax

Your intelligence is so skinny
That girdle sure is tight
You could thread it through the eye of a needle
Not another new correspondent at *Zenit*
Isn't he stupid-silly
(The frozen Moon listens)
We're so glad to not have read
(The Moon falls on the Daystar to preserve its innocence)
The wisdom of many lies in their heels
Tear your socks
No one must ever walk over wisdom
Isn't it a corny phrase
—In the interest of the state
Who trusts you
That's not the way to pay your debt to humankind
You pathetic civil servants you must not preserve yourselves
through your offspring
Use protection
Hola gentlemen—ministers and members of parliament
Listen to the suggestion of a madman
A progressive bachelor tax will solve the problem of civil servants
We are crazy because our minds overflow
You think we're stupid
Darling!

against gossips

Will there come a time
When capitalist spouses would do the laundry
So that laundry ladies can sit in a *kafana* nibbling on gossip
It's too far-fetched to call ourselves comrades
Or will a new Tesla rise with a new patent
So that your white hands blacken with writing ink
To make the wind smirk
The bars and cafés yawn
We welcome communal kitchens
Is a man more an activist
Or a plodder
A LUKEWARM WOMAN DOESN'T LIKE A MADMAN
May you gossips be eternally damned!

ZENIT—April 1923

man's tango with a flea

In a box an owl on a string
A hunchbacked fortune teller points from over her glasses:
A flea under the streetcar—how can it be!
The flea takes a ride on a man
The man takes a ride on a streetcar:
All right
When you talk about man
You should put a flea on display
How did you sleep last night
"Good day" always sleeps well
When "Good night" had a romantic duel
All night long
Today a man could be under the streetcar
Tomorrow a streetcar might be on the back of a flea
Fleas jump
Hey joyful!
A flea is not quite the last thing in the world

?

the guard on the rhine predicts

O

Fun fun funny
The world coils and cries for poor—Deutschland
Sorry it's not—über alles
Bravo
We're not the children of a time when one rode on tame
mules
The wings of our aeroplane chase the radio
Ding dong ding dong
Dong ding dong ding
Sing
Alas poor Jerry for goodness' sake
What has your mother done to you
The laws of Karma
Microscopes and field glasses
Astronomers have forgotten about Venus
Poor Europe you're so blind
We are constantly
Bound to suffer
Why do you cry out then
Obituaries and epistles—Nach Berlin
Let's protect our crude heads

effect on defect

At every crossroads—a Christ
From every Christ three roads of Hercules
In height
In width
Seven Thomas's wounds are dripping on the landfill
Onto the heads of Stenjevec candidates
I fell in love with the rat's sister
The rat devoured my tailcoat pocket
I wrote an ode to love
The rooster received the manuscript
The bespectacled rooster announces midnight at one
in the morning
Yugoslav punctuality is the head of a sheared ram
They hung a Hottentot charter in front of a man's nose
THE NOBEL PRIZE
I can't see over grey heads
In order not to become a profiteer
A hint of ears in the overgrown beard
Zagreb is stranded for silence
Man wants what's worse
The one criterion is that man cannot be blind
In *Novosti* we're registered as madhouse
candidates.

Endnotes

1 *Uskok* (uskoci pl.) as a term comes from militarily organized groups of hajduks, which in the Croatian and Bosnian history of the Ottoman era consisted mainly of Catholic refugees from the areas of Croatia, Herzegovina and Bosnia that were under the Ottoman administration. The term itself comes from the verb *uskočiti* (to jump in, to invade), which is the basic feature of these largely robber formations throughout history.

2 Fritz Mauthner (1849–1923) who was an Austro-Hungarian novelist.

3 Gian Francesco Malipiero (1882–1973) was an Italian composer.

4 A reference to the Croatian play *Gospođa sa suncokretom* (The Sunflower Woman) by Ivo Vojnović.

Toward Opticoplastics

Ljubomir Micić
from *Archipenko: New Plastics*, September 1923

2.2. Lj. Micić, *Arhipenko: Nova plastika* [Archipenko: New Plastics], Zenit Edition, no. 5, Belgrade, 1923. Front cover. Courtesy of National Museum of Serbia in Belgrade.

Presumably one night, the third dimension categorically demanded its own vital right among the arts. That hypothenuse, without which any triangle is inconceivable, was resuscitated into the life of art by new artists and their works.

After the birth of the third dimension (which will further give birth to the fourth, fifth, and so forth), artistic amateurism ends in the plastic arts as well. Neither Rodin nor Meštrović could get rid of amateurism. Among others, only they succeeded in distancing themselves from the plastic arts, that is sculpture. At the same time, their prolific amateurish work brought them, at an early age, a well-deserved reward of immortality: a public recognition, so that they will never be burned!

The illusions of living immortals are always corrected by their contemporaries—the genial mortals! It is their task to destroy immortal ignorance and to erect a Pantheon or a Zeniteum for those few mortals who are aware of existing organic objects and natural forms as the raw elements for new artistic creations.

Is the goal of the arts indeed so inferior that the mediators ("artists"!), by the artificial methods of their crafts, to merely translate the ready-made artifacts of **living nature** into the **still life** of sculptures, paintings, poems, novels? Is it worth photographing the **living reality** only to turn it into a **dead representation** which we can carry in a pocket or hang on the wall as a sifter? Is the artist to be so humiliated and diminished into an aid-memoire, a mediator, or a guide through the labyrinths of waning human memory?

Not at all!

Technology, it is out of question, has achieved far greater and more important results. Technology has beaten all contemporary art! Machine! Machine! Do not forget the radio–film and the puppet factory! Artists! Do not forget the top-notch orthopedic sculptures! When will we experience an airplane sculpture or a plastic representation of an electro-radio-plant on the Goliath-Steamship named *Leviathan*? Will we ever see electric-wave sculptures (do not fear zenithist paradoxes!) or the plastic art of Balkan wildness, printing press rotations, or Japanese earthquakes? Where will we spot a sculpture of the sun's madness or the plastic art of ocean waves, which orbit the earth twice and splash meteors, those emigrants in the freedom of space originating from the Sun's militaristic system? Will we be able to gaze soon at the **opticoplastics** of all stellar bodies, forms, and lives captured in human artworks? There are so many of them in life, and so few in art itself! The plastic of the star of Saturn (The Earth is also a star!) would be wonderful in a disjointed sculpture-painting construction by Aleksander Archipenko.

Insanity? Yes! There is no future without insanity!

Therefore, from now on, no more copies of nature, but a disciplined synthesis of natural and supernatural elements. No more "the same but slightly different," but a realization of discovered and then created forms and objects. No more reproduced "motifs" of already existing objects (mainly bare human flesh. Is that all there is?), but the plastic of the very object the artists have categorically created and found. Not the plastic of what has already been seen but the plastic of what has been created. No more somatology of women and horses (in a birthday suit!), but the **formology** of cubist space. No longer metaphysics and abstraction (it is a misconception to signify cubism and Archipenko's sculptures as abstractions), but the physics and reality of new forms created and revealed as they approach a collective style. On the road to pure **opticoplastics**! No more symmetry but the asymmetry and the statics of concentrated disjointed dimensions and objects.

The new plastic should be an authentic act, an experience of simultaneous optic subjects, which, only when taken in their entirety, according to the artist's creative will, comprise an artistic work in a certain space, and in a new equilibrium.

Just as in zenithist poetry, also in future **opticoplastics,** the simultaneous concentration of heterogeneous elements within one artwork offers a true experience of totality and mastery of space (All new art consists of breaking and mastering space!) One needs to reach for zenithism and new plastics because in the final synthesis, zenithism in plastics means **opticoplastics**, the vanguard of which is the great inventor Aleksander Archipenko.

Archipenko, our first plastic-thinker, a Russian Columbus—the discoverer of the new world of art and the tamer of old classicism and the debauched, compromising neoclassicism—is on his way also to become the first master of new art, who has already founded his private sculpture and painting academy.

We, after African plastic arts and Archipenko's sculpture-paintings, do not need "art" that is an aid-memoire or a "Guidebook" for the feeble and senile human memory. Zenithists only recognize art which is by itself creative and active. Zenithists only recognize artists who themselves discover and invent original artworks. Aleksander Archipenko is among them. He is on the frontlines of all those for whose final victory Balkan zenithists fight in a manly and steadfast manner.

Maestro Archipenko, zenitisti te salutant!

Let's go, youngsters: tear the old cataracts from your eyes! Watch the world around you with the artist's gaze! Make a habit of it! This is the only way to enable the fluid flux and radiant wave transmission between you and us.

Open your eyes: look with what joy ***Zenit*** (once again!) leaves the legacy of Aleksander Archipenko for you and your offspring—to the astonishment of all Serbs and other major nations lacking zenithist spirit.

Belgrade, September 20, 1923

Translated by *Aleksandar Bošković*

2.3. Lj. Micić, *Arhipenko: Nova plastika* [Archipenko: New Plastics], Zenit Edition, no. 5, Belgrade, 1923. Back cover. Courtesy of National Museum of Serbia in Belgrade.

Nemo propheta in patria[1]

Supplement to *Zenit*, no. 25 (February 1924)
Various anonymous

Translated by *Samantha Farmer*

2.4. *Nemo propheta in patria*, supplement to *Zenit*, no. 25. (February 1924). Open source.

what has the world press
written about
zenit
zenithism
zenithists?

■ "*Zenit*, the international journal, a unity of new European directions in art and literature."—*Action—Paris*

■ "*Zenit* publishes the programmatic articles of Ljubomir Micić—*the categorical imperative of the zenithist poetic school*. Zenithism is a movement of new art on the Balkan peninsula, whose real prime mover is Yugoslav poet Micić."— *Athena—Paris*

■ "Ljubomir Micić edits the European journal *Zenit*. It publishes prose and poetry in all original languages. It seeks to make known all varieties of culture and from them draw out a new spirit of life."—*Aventure—Paris*

■ "**Zenithism—the newest artistic movement**. While it is charged daily that Expressionism is dead, while it has been famously ruined once more by Marinetti in Milan, meanwhile the newest direction has made itself known—Zenithism. This mixture of Americanism and distinctiveness has appropriately placed its headquarters in Zagreb, which is the rival city to Belgrade. In Yugoslavia, although culture is taken with cavalry attacks (who is read in primary schools?—Ibsen!), Ljubomir Micić, the editor of the international journal *Zenit*, brawls with all traditions in the zenithist manifesto: O Europeans, your foreheads are narrow, we hate you! Among the zenithists are numbered: Behrens, C. Einstein, Epstein, Fels, Talov, Gleizes, Goll, Hasenclever, van Hemskerk, Kulka, Heynicke, Kassak, Pannwitz, Sauvage."—*Berliner Börsen-Courier*

■ "We have not yet reached so far in modern artistic efforts that we can assert with certainty what this "Zenithism" is, which comes to us from Belgrade in the form of a single remarkable journal . . . (Here is printed a poem of Lj. Micić, no. 6 from *Rescue Car* in German translation by the editor)."

"We hope that Yugoslavia is not so often shaken up by such inspirations; at least until now it has been a completely sane country."—B.Z. *am Mittag—Berlin*

■ "'I created: a new art: Everything else is iced lemonade'—the affirmation of the Serbian poet Ljubomir Micić, whom we want to unleash."

"ZENITHISM: THE BARBAROGENIUS. Cheers, cheers! Who is arriving but none other than Ljubomir Micić, the leader of the avant-garde who tells us that the irresistibly young "barbarians" (they think so highly of themselves!) in S.C.S., desirous of sensation, want to be an intellectual invasion and set the Latin world ablaze. Zenithism: the Serbian barbarogenius."—*Bollettino della Casa d'Arte Bragaglia—Rome*

■ "As *Zenit* sees itself, it wages war against strong traditionalism and cultural separatism, declaring itself for the brotherhood of all people. It is the first and only international journal in the Balkans and carries poems of select authors in the original text and modern pictures of all nations."—*Čas—Prague*

■ "A colorful journal comes to us from Yugoslavia that is so modern and lively and so temperamental and fresh. It is not broad in scope, but the entire world is nevertheless condensed in its pages."—*Červen—Prague*

■ "The international journal *Zenit* and zenithism have roused the greatest sensations in recent memory here . . ."—*Češke Slovo—Prague*

■ "*Zenit* is the name of the international journal which evangelizes the neo-artistic trend, Zenithism. The head spokesperson of the trend and editor of the aforementioned magazine is Ljubomir Micić, poet of the book *Ritmi mojih slutnja* [The Rhythms of My Forebodings]. His present work is predominantly programmatic. The majority of his collaborators are towering figures of Yugoslav literature who have assembled themselves and *Zenit* is their representative voice . . . It carries painterly reproductions of modern painting trends . . . On its ideological side, zenithism is the true face of our time: an expression of strong volition for a human rebirth, an expression of desire for a new man, who is born from the cruelest humiliation of the human personage in war. In art he sees a medium for realizing that ideal."—*Delo—Trieste*

■ "Ljubomir Micić is the illustrious Yugoslav prime mover of a new literary trend: zenithism."—*Esperanto Triumfonta—Anvers*

■ "***Zenit*** is a machine of thoughts that records all intensive symbols in life."—*Tableros—Madrid*

■ "**Zenithism**. Of course, zenithism. It is a Yugoslav phrasing—Zenithism recently took root with a journal, which is wonderfully called *Zenit* and is published by Ljubomir Micić. In search of unheard-of artistic forms, it expresses a passionate hatred for war, a desire beyond all borders and countries, a hunger for universal culture, for love and brotherhood."

"By publishing poems in all languages, zenithism truly is trying to erase national borders."—*Frankfurter Zeitung*

■ "Zenithism! A word that saves. What is zenithism? 'Zenithism is the Balkan totalizer of new life . . . Zenithism is the Balkan totalizer of new art . . . Zenithism is a vertical drawn on a horizontal plane of symmetry.' Quite right."

"Our predecessors yearned for the classics and wanted to be saved by Hellas. But at that time, Greece did not lie in the so-called Balkans, but in the star of European yearning, so to speak. Now the location of Elysium is finally geographically determined. Onward to the Balkans!"

"'Today, the Balkanization of Europe is surely most probable, since it is found at the crudest of notches on the sliding scale of collective progress.' Can you hear Spengler?"

"Before, it was foolhardily attempted to Europeanize the Balkans—but now they arrive from the Balkans to paint us kindly: The French in pink and the Germans in light blue. Central Europe will become an Elysian box of chocolates."

"We Übermenschen of Friedrich Nietzsche, since the world has condemned us, owe our thanks to "the Barbarogenius," to whom we are also grateful that the journal *Zenit* speaks German as well as the Balkan language to European peoples. Only in the subtitle do we read the language of dear Monsieur Poincaré: 'revue internationale zenitiste et de l'art nouveau'."

"The Barbarogenius will thus expand the spirit of mankind not with weapons or shrewd diplomacy, but with the aid of *l'art nouveau* and *nova umetnost*, as the Balkans already call it."

"New art! What is art?, asks Mr. Micić. He says the infamous words: 'Art is dead, may the new art live: zenithism!'"—*Frankfurter Zeitung*

■ "Ten thousand of *Zenit* in the Balkans. A new Yugoslav art . . . mixed with Pan-Slavism, to whom belongs the great cultural role of the future, but also hegemony. Europe is an old woman; the Balkans are a young man. Zenithism is heroism of the soul—says Micić."—*Hírlap*

■ "**Zenithists**, those Yugoslav elites who are assembling around the journal *Zenit*. In the manifesto of the new journal a decisive battle and revolution in art is proclaimed on the world stage. It sympathizes with the futurists, the cubists, and with all new manifestations of contemporary life. A fight to the death is proclaimed with all the rhetoric and the academicism of the old European world. The collaborators are of today's ilk. Poems are published in the original languages. They also manage in all languages. Just like in Babylon."—*Il Tempo—Rome*

■ "The new journal *Zenit*, which comes out in Yugoslavia, apprises us of the position it takes on modern life. A machine of opinions, a register of all the signals of life or art, an active factor of existence. It affirms a new European spirit which is coming to us. It unites all the -isms in art, those kindred in spirit as well as unfriendly: futurism, cubism, and so forth. It destroys the diplomacy of European rhetoricity, the rhetoric which is concealed by that which has something to say but is saying nothing . . ."

"Barbarians, in this case, honestly, the Zenithists themselves are setting in motion a new language, whose effect in language alone is a shriek and a rhythm."

■ "As concerns the French, names are mentioned: Cendrars, Drieu La Rochele, Salmon, and the Germans Einstein and Georg Kaiser. Also represented: Italy, America, Russia, Spain, Hungary, Serbia, Poland, Finland, Japan, Peru, Mexico, Czechoslovakia, Denmark, and the Jews."—*L'Intransigeant—Paris*

■ "Ideas that are circulating—*Zenit*, read number 17, new Russian art!"—*Národní listy—Prague*

■ "Futurism is nowadays a curiosum and it fights for global supremacy with: zenithism and Dadaism."—*Národní listy—Prague*

■ "The latest: Zenithism, the most novel artistic movement in the world. It has graced us with a lively journal. The publisher: Ljubomir Micić . . ."—*Neues Wiener Journal—Vienna*

■ "***Zenit***. Director Lj. Micić. Belgrade. Truly worthy of admiration, the efforts of Lj. Micić, the prime mover of zenithism, distinguish themselves, which he makes in the name of new art in Yugoslavia. Zenithism wants to be the Balkan totalizer of new life and new art and harbors many affinities for constructivism. Since there exists no burden of tradition of any kind in Yugoslavia, new artists have turned towards the most extreme direction of cubism. But Mr. Micić, to whom we concede an apt intelligence, should be on guard.

It is our wish that Mr. Micić acquaint himself with the latest manifesto of the futurists on mechanical art. The greatest affinities for constructivism could thus be pacified, and zenithism could still remain on the field of art.

And then Mr. Micić, who is no gullible fanatic, will conclude his work, as we are right."—*Noi—Rome*

■ "**Zenithism**. The new artistic direction's prime mover is Ljubomir Micić, leader of the young Yugoslav literature, and even Y. Goll bade farewell to expressionism and signed the first zenithist manifesto. The latest issues of *Zenit* are before us and are interesting in various directions . . . The journal unites the best modern names of the whole world and in the original languages, too: German, Russian, French, and Serbian. It is good to know that in such a fairly unknown city young people of a young nation are working on new art. For example, *Zenit* no. 7 reports better than all the journals in Prague being made by the young Czech generation," *Prager Tagblatt—Prague*

■ "**Zenithism**—a red flyer. Its curse of "the bloody century" is winning, energetic, and its last lines seriously and acrimoniously establish that 'Man is to man just a criminal and a murderer. A revolt of slaves . . .'"—*Prager Presse—Prague*

■ "Zenithism...what it seeks and the end result of what it is achieving is wholly wonderful and it has quite a serious raison d'être. It liberates . . . from pompous seriousness in all forms in which it manifests itself."—*Prager Presse—Prague*

■ "*Zenit*. The journal *Zenit*—edited by Ljubomir Micić—wants to assume in modern life the role of a cosmic watch, which is guaranteed for three hundred years. The journal unites in art all the unfriendly -isms, and even those kindred: futurism, cubism, purism, expressionism, Dadaism, ultraism, and so forth. *Zenit* is international and interreligious. *Zenit* publishes poems in all the original languages of the globe, and appears in Belgrade, Paris, Rome, Munich, Berlin, Moscow, Chicago, Tokyo. It renews the work of Babylon in an epoch of linguistic confusions."—*Promenoir—Lyon*

■ "The 10th issue of the international journal *Zenit* carries a poem in the original Russian of the poet Mayakovsky and in an article by editor Ljubomir Micić the program of zenithism is laid out once more: What do the zenithists want? A rupture! The superior attitude from the former protégé toward, *Madame Europe*—the total negation of her outward civilization."

"Let us get closer to *Zenit*, which already has a European name and great significance . . ." —*Rovnost—Brno*

■ "We cannot sufficiently express our affinity for this consistently international journal. Among *Zenit*'s publications the *The Manifesto of Zenithism* has come out, which professes the trajectory of zenithism, which unites all artistic movements in the struggle for a new world and new culture."—*Rudé právo—Brno*

■ ". . . a journal is coming out, which has gathered around itself all the young Yugoslav powers of visual and literary art. Yugoslav modernism is thus distinguished by a crude temperament, full of life and full of audacity; it has given its word that from its unsanctioned efforts artworks of great worth shall be born."

"*Zenit* is an international journal for new art, edited by Ljubomir Micić, under one of its main slogans: 'East against West, and Moscow against Paris . . .'"

". . . In that journal we read all the significant names: Dermee, Einstein, Fels, Gleizes, Goll, Hasenclever, Salmon, Lunacharsky, Blok, Survage, Modigliani . . . (but Yugoslavia is represented by the names Foretić, Micić, Petrov, Poljanski, and the rest.)"

". . . As an artistic and philosophic direction, zenithisim wants anthropocentric harmony and the synthesis of time. Ljubomir Micić has developed its position more extensively in manifestos and various articles. Zenithism is a work of spiritual revolution. Zenithism is a war against the false pacifism of our time . . ."

■ "*Zenit* is the true face of today's revolutionary time, a hotbed of beams that light the whole world. Some printed works we can accept in their entirety, and others not, but it does not escape us that we do not extend a hand gladly to all Yugoslav comrades for collaboration in the great work of future culture."—*Tribuna—Prague*

■ "*Zenit*, under the editorial direction of Micić. In a nest of reaction—a good battery."—*Вещь—Moscow—Berlin*

■ "Zenithism is a synthesis of the whole of modern artistic movement, of all directions. The search for modern man is reflected within it to the greatest extent, which is again a reflex of the previous times in which we lived, during the great crucifixion . . . seeking new content and new forms."

"Ultimate nihilism on the one hand, and on the other a deep faith in creation—whomsoever understands it, understands modern art, understands zenithism, understands our entire great age, the entire social war and its reflex in the ethical war of today's humanity."—*Uč. List—Trieste*

■ "*Zenit* celebrates its victory under the sign of zenithism . . . As Ljubomir Micić, editor of Zenit, says, it is a revolution. The only outcry in the middle of the present moment and the only way to the future. Of man for man—that is the watchword of Micić, Mikac, etc."—*Златорог—Sofia*

Endnotes

1 Lat.: "No one is a prophet in his own country."

COLLABORATEURS DE ZENIT 1921—1926

Archipenko — Arnauld — Asseiéff — Barbusse — Belling — Behrens F. R. — Billerova — Birot P. A. — † Blok Buzzi — Delaunay — Depero — Dermée — Doesburg — Einstein C. — Epstein — Erenbourg — Eesteren — Fels — Felchin — Gallien — Gleizes — Gorki — Gropius — Goll I & C. — Grosz G. — Hausmann — Hoffmeister — † Hemskeerk — † Hlebnikov — Haynicke — Yéssenine — Jacob — Kaiser G. — Kandinsky — Kassák — Klek Liebmann — Lissitsky — Lozowick — Loos — Lounatcharsky — Mayakovsky — Malevitch — Malespine — Marinetti — Mendelsohn — Meierchold — Mid — Milef — Mitzitch — Mikatz — Moholy-Nagy — Nina-Naï — Pannwitz — Parnach — Peeters — Picasso — Polianski — Pocarini — Rodjenko — Seifert — Salmon — Survage Sauvage — Seuphor — Slavensky — Schlichter — Taïroff Teige — Tatlin — Trotzki — Torre — Vasari — Vandercammen — Walden — Zadkin — e t. c.

Штампа „Родољуб“ Кнез Мих. 3.

2.5. Collaborators of *Zenit* 1921–1926, excerpt from *Zenit*, no. 43 (December 1926). Open source.

Zenithosophy, or the Energetics of Creative Zenithism

Ljubomir Micić
from *Zenit*, nos. 26–33 (October 1924)

zenithosophy
or the energetics of creative zenithism[1]

No made in Serbia[2]

1.

our fellow travelers cannot be corpses. **o**nly vital life lives on! **o**ur fellow traveler is a future **zenith man**, a central transformer of our vital rebellious sparks, of our savage and barbaric energies.

and life? **t**his miserable life strikes me as a huge **cosmic factory** where thousands upon thousands of neurons and millions upon millions of electrons work tirelessly. **a**nd there are just as many idlers who do nothing at all!

my vision is neither cosmic nor earthly animalistic. **a**fter all, animals are not familiar with the system of speculative philosophy and even less with the indian opium of buddhism.

my vision is entirely human and therefore entirely banal. **a**fter all, the privileged may sit on their hands and enjoy doing so!

2.

where sins end, philosophy begins. **w**e have not yet freed ourselves of our sins. **w**hich is why we serbs have no philosophy.
hit my crazy head again for dipping this old pen into ink to write a new story about the **birth of god's calf**.
the birth of god's calf! **g**od's calf!
he is wonderful, that phenomenal walker on the bloody rope of the gallows raised for us by recent history.
glory be to the gallows! **w**e destroyed them with our teeth, shooting straight into the jaws of death.
we did not lose a single tooth though our birth was as deadly as the birth of god's calf or the **zenithist movement rebellion**.
glory be to the gallows in the highest!
so after all, zenithism has begun dancing like a crazed phantom dancer on the burning balkan sky of **brilliant beyond-sense** . . .

3.

in the new art and new menagerie of *isms* our word was a magic word, a new word, the last word. **t**he last, as usual, but this time in the vanguard as well and **effective**!
just a few words concerning this last and final *ism* of a flooded age since this is the only *ism* of a definitely post-war character. **t**he energy of creation is zenithism's pulse and calls for the synthesis of all phenomena in the highest and most elemental forms of life and worlds. **l**et us call this creative urge the **energetic imperative** in addition to the "categorical imperative of the zenithist school of poetry" which i presented to the world in the spring of 1922 to the shock of all serbs and other great nations lacking in the zenithist spirit. **t**hat is the date of the **first revolution** in the anemic and eclectic poetry of all south slavs (and other artistic mediums!), and it has continued to this day without anyone's recognition. **s**o much the better!

of one thing we can be certain: there is not a single great artist, poet, or even philosopher who does not carry the germ or instinct for zenithism, since zenithism is self-creating and not an artificial product of modern bourgeois propaganda. **e**ven less is it a product of the imperialist culture of speculation.

4.

here are ten points on a tablet, but they are merely general principles, not commandments:
1) —**z**enithism is the awakening of elementary and vital instincts of work natural to all people.
2) —**z**enithism awakens in man everything that is common to all humanity within him, everything above the personal, everything akin to the **barbarogenius**.
3) —**z**enithism, given its elementary nature and creative syntheticism, is inseparable from all those who create great and new things and who work for the future of mankind.
4) —**z**enithism shows as clear as day that the ultimate human goals are out of the reach of the people currently engaged in creating the new world order and new human relationships.
5) —**z**enithism is an elixir of eternal youth and a realization that one must tirelessly and eternally strive upward.
6) —**z**enithism is the energetic imperative of the sum of the new art's work, and it must follow the path of those who are working toward mankind's common goal.
7) —**z**enithism is an awareness of the falseness of literary "dreams" and the errors of "the absolute" in philosophy.
8) —**z**enithism is the strength of an immutable will and food for creative instincts.
9) —**z**enithism is the positive energy for raising a vertical of the new spirit.
10) —**z**enithism is also a negative energy, since it is consumed in the inevitable struggle with countless cultural eunuchs, the eternal struggle to overturn their reeking matter and **closed-mindedness** and put their **empty heads** in the horizontal position of the grave.

5.

poets have always wanted to make whips and whip this world. **i**n whose name? **f**or what? **no**! **n**ot even whips can change people until there is peace among them; they cannot change people as long as there are those who whip and those who are whipped. **s**o, give

up this useless task, poets. **n**either the whippers nor the whipped should exist! **m**any of you will be gone in the near future anyway.
the new spirit must gather and lead all creative forces of art and work.
the creative force scrapes out the riverbed, while creative will and visionary minds should decide the form of the river's flow, creating a symphony of work, rhythms, and waterfalls. **n**ew poets know better than anyone how powerless rhythms, verse, and word waterfalls are today.

6.

the new world is an antenna, and poetry grows only in the beyond-sense sphere of space. **t**hese are the zenithist **words in space**.
—poetry is the first plane of symmetry
—painting is the second plane of asymmetry
—sculpture is the third plane of plane-symmetry
—music is the fourth plane of non-symmetry
—dance is the fifth plane of rhythm-symmetry
—drama is the sixth plane of poly-symmetry
—film is the seventh plane of counter-symmetry.
altogether, there are seven versions of symmetry possible in nature. **n**o more than seven symmetries can be found in a crystal: the mathematics of crystals is strange: 7 x 1 = 1, one body. **a**nd here we have one crystal, one body with various lives: art!
zenithism, as the new art that embodies all mediums, is the only eighth plane of outside-symmetry, or rather, super-symmetry in space: a new supernatural body, created with the maximum of man's powers. **o**nly a few such synthetic works of new art and new life correspond to the zenithist principles of **relative aesthetics** or **anti-aesthetics**. **t**hose rare works are the only ones we can stamp with the copyright of zenithism. **t**he best mark in the best place, the best word for the best work.

7.

genius only discovers—tombs, findings—mummies, perceptions—the face of life.
the barbarogenius totalizes the powers of existence into a unique pulse of new life.

the barbarogenius creates a new work and awakens a **collective feeling** within people, a feeling that is primordial, elemental, but murdered by contradictory cultures and inhuman religions.
contemporary life strives toward complete collectivity and the economy of all vital forces, toward the **organization** of mankind's work and the **economy** of collective feelings. **a**ll individual forces should be **concentrated** in the great circle of the whole.

8.

souls are the daily bread and the daily burden of all slavs and all asians. **l**et us free ourselves of the soul's burden and the daily bread of sentimentality!
sanctification and the last rites have not been performed on our souls according to the christian serbian-orthodox ceremony, in the church, but according to the christian ceremony in fratricidal wars, in the trenches. "**w**ar be with you!"—brave politicians paraphrased the sentimental messiah, who whispered to the people of rome and jerusalem, "**p**eace be with you!" **a**fter those words catacombs burned and the weapons of the ancient roman bourgeoisie clanged. **i**t was those words that caused an abandoned and a spat-upon fanatic to be crucified by the romans.
epigones of bright minds and profaners of great minds are those who throw the cruelest mottos and paraphrases to the nations.
we do not acknowledge old, profaned christianity.
we preach **new and pure barbarism**.
old christianity is cannibalism.
new barbarism is the **brotherhood of men**!

9.

european culture is cruel and cannibalistic. **t**hat's why zenithists work on the **balkanization of europe** and want to expand their **cultural nihilism** to all the continents in the name of the new barbarism, in the name of new people and new continents, in the name of a terrible struggle: **east vs. west**!
the **b**alkan peninsula is a cradle of pure barbarism, which preaches a new brotherhood of men.

that is the idea of our new culture and new civilization, which will come to a final clash between two old giants, the east and the west, whose urge to fight each other is in their blood.

10.

before the last wars, thought walked on unsteady feet and, like a colossus, on fiery legs. **m**uch has been said about this by the epic russian count lev nikolayevich **t**olstoy, since neither he nor maxim **g**orky could have fathomed that zenithism's founder would one day write, "**an epic is not energy.**"

after the imperialist wars and wars of liberation, thought dances and spins on hot heads. **t**he proletarian commune-father, commune-son, and commune-holy spirit have fallen silent on the subject once and for all. **o**nly the radio telegraphs buzz through all the continents, **l**enin has died, but his work will live forever.

apparently, the only people in france who heard the news on january 21, 1924 were romain **r**olland and henri **b**arbusse, in america upton **s**inclair, in india mahatma **g**andhi, and maybe an unknown yogi. **a**nd in serbia? . . .

the next day, in england, the leader of the second international assembled the ministerial cabinet, and in the name of his majesty king george VII, sir ramsay macdonald ordered the establishment of the famous equilibrium, which is now destroying our lives and our youth.

11.

the new thought spins and climbs like a circle of fairies above its axis. **t**hat is **zenitosophy**.

new thought in a cone, in a spiral, in a vertical.

zenitosophy is the last vertical of the spirit, which connects the earth to other planets.

zenitosophy connects three crucial points in space: **earth—sun—moon.** **t**hat **metacosmic triangle** is the only zenithism symbol. **z**enithism acknowledges no symbols in any sphere of the new manifestations and phenomena.

zenithism, the definitive "ism," is congenial to all we want and look for: it is a **totalized and unified expression for the synthesis of the new spirit** and all its endeavors and struggles **toward the zenith**. **w**e are finally on the right path.

zenithism is a new discovery of spiritual technicality as well of the mind's construction.

zenithism is an airplane for the first, second, and third atmosphere—for all atmospheres!

eureka: zenithism!

12.

life without zenithism is not worth a brass farthing. **n**ew poets have no business living it. **t**he new life should be proud of us, not we of it.
our time has put on a concrete suit of armor, a glass torso, steel transversals, electric wires, radio waves. **t**ime has put on a concrete crown and a glass crinoline: a **steel rococo. b**ut this new upstart has forgotten the electric brain, radium heart, rubber legs, and magnetic arms. **w**hich is much sadder than the fate of sentimental werther and the fall of his antipode, that stuffed shirt zarathustra.

13.

airplanes visit the clouds, pass over cemeteries, graves, and cities, and never land on dull crosses or sharp lightning rods. **t**heir pilots have no liking for constructivist painting and the fate of mankind on earth.
neither dead nor living poets (after the several deaths they have survived) are crowned with green wreaths of flowers or even hard bread crusts anymore, so how can they be blessed by airplanes?
that is why our **spirit-planes** fly straight for the round wings of machines and workers, where they have found a new contemporary aesthetics of the spirit and the machine. **o**ur **idea-planes** fly from our chests high into the immeasurable hangars of work and love, toward the airports of brotherhood of all people and all continents. **a**n old song to new music! **w**here there is a heart, there is a sun. **w**here there are new poets, there is no old bread. **s**o it is in great serbia or yugoslavia or the kingdom of serbs, croats, and slovenes—or whatever you wish to call it.

14.

all the crude elements of life can be turned into creation using zenithist energetics.
our life burns like a threshold of death. **d**eath is a circle.
it is impossible for people to be a straight line and a circle at the same time. **r**un out of the circle into a straight line, into a straight line! **b**ut only the opposite of geometry is possible: sticking the vertical line straight into the heart of a horizontal circle—zenithism!

the energetic imperative is **zenith's barbarogenics** of the wild thought of the sixth balkan continent.
and who is zenithon?
zenithon is a beyond-sense miracle: a synthetic man of superlife, the son of a Balkan mother in mourning, a **fata morgana**.

belgrade, may 1, 1924

P.S. This essay is to be published in German (*Der Sturm,* Berlin), English (*S4N,* Northampton), Flemish (*Het Overzicht,* Antwerp), Polish (*Blok,* Warsaw), French (*La Vie des Lettres,* Paris).

Translated by *Maja Starčević*

Endnotes

1 This article was translated into German as "No Made in Serbia: Zenitosophie oder energetik des schöpferischen Zenitismus" and published in *Der Sturm* 15, no. 4 (1925).

2 In English as is in the original.

Antisocial Art Needs to be Destroyed

The following interview was conducted via questions being posed in the October 1924 issue of the Czech journal Bytova kultura[1] *and being answered by Ljubomir Micić in* Zenit, *no. 35 (December 1924) without reprinting the questions.*

1) What is the meaning of today's "decorative and industrial arts"[2] also by comparison with its historical development?

I do not trust the meaning of any decorative and industrial art—even less the meaning of its practical application. I consider the comparison with its historical development impossible or completely negative in nature. In art, nothing develops historically, but only spiritually and intellectually. Do these decisive elements of creation constitute history or historical continuity?

2) What is the relationship between folk art and modern decorative and industrial arts?

Since I do not believe in the meaning of decorative and industrial arts (I believe more in its nonsense!), then there can be no question of a relationship between it and folk art. There are only folk crafts but there is no folk art!

3) What is the social and economic importance of the decorative and industrial arts?

The social and national-economic significance of the decorative and industrial arts is unconditionally greater than any meaning of art. Why? Probably because art is not on the right track yet. And what is the right path? There are many of them and only one is needed. Maybe: vertical to the zenith?

4) What is the question of popularization, fundamentally?

Is it possible to talk seriously about the nationalization of any artistic values? No! Only in the case if the objects were outside art and outside creation.

5) Which methods of socialization do you consider most effective?

If a man were a machine, such as a typesetting machine, only then would I be able to answer the question correctly. Which method of socialization would be the best? Thus, the question lingers on ceaselessly. However, something came to my mind: first, all antisocial art should be completely destroyed, and then we should start with a new alphabet. Only that would be the right part of that method of socialization. And what would be left behind? On one side the pure ashes of a contagious plague, and on the other the beautiful and pristine field of a new beginning. Only then would everyone equally begin the great human work.

6) How do you view the current activities of craft and design schools and museums?

I certainly prefer craft schools to museums. Craft schools are about life and work. On the contrary, museums are pantheons of non-work. Museums are like tombs: one should take comfort in death because of the great illusion of "another world."

7) Do today's purposeful and technical considerations lead to internationalization, or will the art industry maintain its distinctive character according to states and territories?

As a Balkan man and as a zenithist who preaches the Balkanization of Europe, I am unconditionally in favor of the internationalization of all cultural values. Only on that path could all people meet as brothers and as self-conscious citizens of one common homeland—Earth.

8) In your opinion, what will be lessons from the International Exhibition of Modern Decorative and Industrial Arts in Paris in 1925?

Finally, in 1925, the largest decorative art fair will be seen in Paris. Its merit is invaluable: all the impotence of one of the greatest delusions of all semi-cultured people will be shown most clearly. This negative event will be the strongest incentive for the positive work of all new generations: for the work of a new culture in the name of the old homeland—Earth!

Ljubomir Micić—Belgrade

The Czech questions were translated by *Meghan Forbes* and *Aleksandar Bošković*
Ljubomir Micić's answers were translated by *Aleksandar Bošković*

Endnotes

1 The magazine *Bytová kultura* published responses by Jacobus J.P. Oud (a Dutch architect from Rotterdam and a follower of the De Stijl movement), Dr. Alexander Dorner (Director of the Provinzialmuseum in Hanover), Dr. Jan Löwenstein (Professor at the Technical University in Brno), Jan Vaněk (Chief Director of the U. P. plant in Brno, an architect, a designer, a manufacturer of furniture, and the main editor of *Bytová kultura*), and Walter Gropius (architect and the founder of Bauhaus).

2 "Uměleckého průmyslu" in Czech.

The New Art

Ljubomir Micić

from *Zenit,* no. 35 (December 1924)
(From the opening of the First International Exhibition in Belgrade, April 9, 1924)

Anyone questioning or underestimating the significance of the First International Exhibition is to be ridiculed or even pitied. The exhibition includes all the artistic movements of the past two decades, if not all their founders, then for the most part their finest representatives. Moreover, the significance of the exhibition is of a timely character, in that this is the first time people have been able to see the original works of the new art in the originals, and not, as heretofore, through dishonest mediators and epigones who, going abroad for "studies" that consist of strolling the boulevards and lolling about in cafés, have done nothing but import and imitate shop-window kitsch. And this they sell to their naive homeland under the exonerating title of "modern art." So, for a while we have been a kind of colony of Europe that places no limits on the import of cultural refuse and even protects it by law. Our movement and our hard work have at least done something to change the situation and decrease the smuggling to a more reasonable extent. I assure you that we have had unexpected success and will have more. Only after the zenithist movement can we claim with certainty that this country is nobody's cultural colony, nor is it willing to be one. We are standing at the gates, watching carefully to make the smuggler's job more difficult and their raids less frequent, of less significance, and more vain. True, they are always in the majority. They are supported by the state and the state government, people whose cultural education has rarely ventured as far as a dusty encyclopedia—much less to an art about which the only thing they know is that it exists (or so it is said!)—and some heavy tomes written about Michaelangelo or Raphael (who, according to the report of a newspaper "critic," passed away just the other day!), about Rembrandt or a museum-housed Greek sculpture "which is unsurpassable in its beauty and aestheticism." They have ventured no further, and we, the new artists, carry all the consequences of such sins on our shoulders. However, *Zenit* has made some daring leaps, and this exhibition is yet another. Belgrade can now witness the sensation of zenithist "fools" mounting its first international exhibition despite the dilettante mafia and *Zenit* haters. The exhibition has been recognized in all cultured countries by those who know of *Zenit* and zenithism. And the number of those people is not small. Today there is not a single cultured town nor center unaware of the fact that the Serbs have produced a Balkan artistic movement of international importance. It is not surprising that great libraries and reading rooms in New York subscribe to *Zenit* at their readers' request nor that both a great museum and an art gallery in distant San Francisco do the same. We do not care if this sounds exaggerated to some; we do not care that these real facts cause hysterical envy and enmity in those who hate us and are our enemies. We feed on your hate: only great tempests cause great waves.

I admit that the paintings hanging before you are surprising and that you are not used to seeing their like. They have no titles, since that is of little importance. They are numbered, just as people are named. They need to be registered, but they do not need to be titled, since titles tend to lead the viewer astray. As soon as viewers see a title, they start looking for the picture's "theme" or for "what it represents." There is none of that here. In fact, at first glance they all seem the same, they look like the same picture, just as we think all Japanese look the same, although each one has his own physiognomy and anatomy. I gladly admit that it is very difficult—almost impossible—to explain all the paintings at this conference. But I still have a duty to give you some general advice on how to look at them, if you are willing, and I ask you to take it as benevolent advice. Let me stress again: it is impossible to enter the labyrinth of the new art immediately for the aforementioned reasons. If you wish to understand high-level mathematics, you need to know the basics of general mathematics. The same holds for abstraction. So, if you can understand a geometrical abstraction in space—for instance, that two perpendicular lines meet only in infinity—then it will not be so hard for you to view these paintings, which were also executed in space and which are real because of that, but also supernatural because of their anatomy.

The first condition is that you must not compare these paintings with any object you have seen in nature, since this is an exhibition of **paintings**, not a sideshow or a display of consumer goods. This is not the "half-girl, half-fish monster" from the Mali Kalemegdan circus!

We must demand of painting more than what it can give. A painting should be viewed for the painter's vitality and nothing else. Whatever artists wish to paint is fair game. Free choice and free creation are their absolute right. Anything that exists in art, in life, cannot exist outside nature. Everything that is in nature is natural. Ergo, the new art is natural! The painter can paint a peasant shoe atop the Main Church's cross (or a man's head turned upside down as Marc Chagall does), and if this idea works and is artfully executed, the painting can stand as a first-rate artifact.

Each painting thus makes its own nature, and one should not wander outside its frame. One should not wander or ask oneself whether it depicts a horse (and whether its tail is in the right place) or a man, or a snake, or a boring female nude. All comparisons with surface nature and explorations of natural exactitude or possibilities—all that is of little importance to the painting. What's important for the painting are certain basic principles on which the art of painting rests. Formally, these principles belong to three categories: 1) **form**—2) **color**—3) **space**. It is within the framework of these three fundamental elements that we find the art of painting in general and especially of the new painting. Painting has finally successfully freed itself from literariness and history, from photography and amateurish copying. This is best seen in arbos-**painting**, as I will now for the first time term the zenithist style, represented at this exhibition by the work of Josip Klek. Arbos-**painting** manifests a successful economy of material, work, and action. No palette contains colors so bright and effective as our *arbos*-paintings, which present the purest forms as if cut in marble or glass. (*Arbos* is an acronym standing for the material of zenithist painting: **AR**tija [paper]—**BO**ja [paint]—**S**lika [painting]. It will not hurt to mention that of all the arts only music has always been free of non-artistic weight. Music alone has remained true to its artistic nature. A musician connects tones and sounds, provides rhythm and dynamics, and when it all comes together we hear a melody that makes us ecstatic. No one has ever dragged nature into it since, if we apply to music the kind of logic I've seen in print, music would be condemned to reproducing the ox's bellow, the horse's neigh, or Mary Magdalene's sobs at the feet of Christ. Is that what art should be? Everyone (except zenithists!) call opera art. Well, following the line of logic I have just proposed, may I ask if you have ever heard the music of *Carmen* in nature or the passionate wild rhythms or, rather, the musical paradoxes of Mokranjac[1]'s songs? Where in nature have you seen love proclaimed by singing in the ridiculous way opera singers do? But let us return to paintings, painters, and art as a whole. Artists connect sky to earth, heart to heart, and soul to soul beautifully.

It is meet and right to do so!

Translated by *Maja Starčević*

Endnotes

1 Stevan Stojanović Mokranjac (1856–1914) was a Serbian composer who, among other accomplishments, modernized Serbian Orthodox church music.

The New Zenithist Art

Marijan Mikac
from *The Monkey Phenomenon* (1925)

2.6. M. Mikac, *Fenomen majmun* [The Monkey Phenomenon], Zenit Edition, no. 7, Belgrade, 1925. Front cover. Courtesy of Ubu Gallery, New York & Galerie Berinson, Berlin.

Zenithism is a new movement in art. As such, zenithism is revolutionary.

"Russia mother of chaos
Why is REVOLUTION our feast day"[1]
(Ljubomir Micić, *Rescue Car*)[2]

Art is not a depiction or reproduction of nature and events. Art must be constructive and creative, which is to say that it should not describe or mimic. Therefore, zenithism is not impressionistic or photographic. Zenithism is constructive. Art always has its own demands of the public. It is said that people are weary and need simple readings that are easily grasped, readings that are widely understood, because in them they discover themselves, their own small desires, and joys. Fine, but that is not why we need art. What constitutes literature versus ordinary prose must always be clearly determined, as should painting as a fine art versus painting as a representational art, which only photographs the objects seen. The same applies to music; to architecture and to sculpture.—"The new plastic should be an authentic act, an experience of simultaneous optic subjects, which only when taken in their entirety, according to the artist's creative will, comprise an artistic work in a certain space, and in a new equilibrium."—(Ljubomir Micić, "Toward Opticoplastics")[3]

Zenithism expresses the most serious need of contemporary man to triumph through the creation of new and pure values. This absolute creation, which is one of the most important aims of zenithism, necessarily brings with it the destruction of all that is old, that has endured and is non-vital. A strong sense of individuality and great strength are required to walk past the crowd. Furthermore, one must be willing to go against the crowd if necessary.

Art should always be an expression of the times and of life itself.

Art must influence people, reinvigorate the people, and uplift them.

Artists, and poets especially, also announce the coming times:

"The spirit doesn't trail the airplane
The spirit rides on the airplane
Or: the spirit creeps on sandaled feet."
(Marijan Mikac, "a prayer for the blessed curse")[4]

That means: some people move forward, ahead of their time and with the times, others fall behind and look backward instead of forward. The contrast is an airplane and feet dragging on cobblestone! Furthermore, it means: the modernism of zenithism is not an affectation or an adherence to technique. That same brilliant spirit that constructed aircrafts, likewise in the field of art, presents new laws, creates—a new art.

A submarine, radio, an airplane without an engine, film, and all that is related to the product of the new spirit, as a requisite, has to assume its appropriate place in art. Zenithist works are short and honest, unequivocal and deep. But people are nonchalant and do not make an effort to "understand" zenithism. People are used to being lied to by books and by life; or otherwise used to the poet, let us be frank, pandering to them. Just as not everyone is able to read original well-known works, likewise many people are incapable of appreciating artistic works. A good upbringing is important because art is certainly above science. The wider masses are not aware of how an airplane or radiotelephone is constructed—people use them mechanically, without fully comprehending them. The masses take well to scientific results and popular science. We zenithists could "popularize" our art just as well, but in order to "understand" zenithism, a pure heart and clear mind is needed. Book smarts or a formal education is secondary.—"If your mom had sung zenithist songs over your cradle; if your teacher had interpreted zenithist poems; if your professor had provided commentary on zenithist poems, you would understand those poems as much as they did, as much as 'your' favorite poets. For zenithist poetry to leave an impression on you, it is up to you, just as it is up to you that the poems of 'your' favorite poets leave an impression on you."—(Andra Jutronić)[5]

The path of new values is paved with sweat and blood. With more cheer than sadness the modern poet defends new ideals. Bravely and recklessly:

"Our breath has set fire to the air."

(Stevan Živanović)[6]

All creators have complete freedom to select the form and how they will express themselves. The means cannot be banal. Expression is free and no one can school a poet. Zenithist poets express life with reckless abandon, just as they perceive it, and without scruples. We zenithists do not give importance to whether the word that we use or the subject that we are talking about is beautiful or ugly. So-called "beautiful art" is like polenta that is uncooked and impossible to digest. It might appeal to spinsters who fear looking at things head on. Zenithism catapults aesthetics from art like a ballast. We do not see any reason to believe that a work cannot be artistic and good if it is not also beautiful. These days life is caked in mud, and so are people. Because a zenithist poet does not lie and pretend, he does not want to express life through rose-tinted glasses, with sweet phrases about fragrant flowers and white, silky butterflies. How come, for instance, do the words *rose* or *angel* find a place in literature, while, on the other hand, others are excised: *trash*, *carcass*, and others still. But *trash* is a more apt descriptor for life today than *rose* is, and *carcass* a more fitting one for people. Because every word has to be carefully selected, zenithism suspends symbolism, which has a hermaphroditic character in art. The poet has to be selective in the use of words. Here are the basic elements of zenithist poetry:

1. **Paradoxicality.** Paradoxes have a vital and temporal significance. What in life happens according to a strict professorial logic? In life paradoxes predominate.—"Paradox is the spirit's agility and its plasticity."—(Branko Ve Poljanski, "Manifesto")[7]. Certain scientists likewise get on better with paradoxes, and in astronomy, for instance, distances are determined with reference to time.—A significant paradox by Mr. Poljanski:

"GRAIN BY GRAIN—A PALACE
STONE BY STONE—BREAD
SLAP BY SLAP—VICTORY"[8]

2. **Simultaneity.** In a single moment, innumerable things happen, which are altogether independent. Those occurrences manifest themselves simultaneously, at the same time. The most obvious simultaneity is broadcast in news telegrams. In the news, colorful stories from all corners of the globe are strung together on a regular basis, about events that are happening at the same time but which do not share an inexorable connection, according to the law of cause and effect.—An example of simultaneity:

"Russian man dies of hunger
Professor rapes his student out of joy for her having mastered logic
Lenin's death in the newspapers
Charlie Chaplin riding a donkey
Import of luxury clothing prohibited"
(Micić, *Rescue Car*)

3. Through **association** occurrences are connected, which the poet, of course, freely makes and selects. For example:

"Fatal fata
Morgan
Rockefeller's death
Stinnes leaps into a cauldron of boiling lead
A bleeding ulcer grows in the belly of Paris."
(Branko Ve Poljanski, "T.B.")[9]

From Fata Morgana to Morgan le Fay. From Morgan to Rockefeller. From Rockefeller to Stinnes. From Stinnes to Paris.—Another example of association: What kind of connection, for instance, can exist between Christianity and radiotelephony? This train of thought might seem absurd: "The crosses on the towers cracked. Radiotelegraphic antennas already disappeared long ago into the hats of beautiful (and ugly!) ladies!" (Mikac: *The Monkey Phenomenon*)[10].—In terms of associations, that connection becomes natural and understandable. The cross on a church reminds one of radiotelegraphic antennas. Moreover, this same association can be applied to the pointy breasts of a young girl (the tautness of the antennas—firmness of girls' breasts!). It is used in the same way in my first poetry collection *Effect on Defect*—but can be applied to other girls, and eventually to the whole line of female and male generations, which the degenerate culture of Western Europe ravaged.

This is the dynamic, a continuous movement forward.

Zenithism is proto-dynamic. Proto-dynamic in its poems and novels. (Micić, Poljanski, Mikac, Živanović, Jutronić, Avakumović, etc.). Zenithism is proto-dynamic in music too (J. Štolcer-Slavenski). Zenithism is proto-dynamic in painting and in our future architecture (Josif Klek)[11]. Zenithism is proto-dynamic in its development: the basic elements are evident everywhere, but the movement is in constant creation, progression, and evolution. (On zenithist poetry, see the first zenithist book *Rescue Car* by Ljubomir Micić, the first edition of which the royalist government attorney's office confiscated because it carried the archaic Balkan inscription *Damn Your Hundred Gods*).

Originality is the first thing a zenithist must have, besides elasticity of spirit. These principles do not enslave the spirit. The principles are needed for the formation of a unique spirit, but the principles of zenithism are not set in stone. Revision and transformation are allowed in the name of adaptation to the new demands of the times. Thus, zenithism is eternally new and eternally young.

Zenithism is an original creation of the Balkans. It has been almost four years since the first of February 1921, when Ljubomir Micić founded the zenithist movement. The establishment of zenithist poetry owes a lot to film.—"Film triumphs with its fantastic quality, its lively and picturesque persuasiveness, its constructive—machine speed, its directorial refinement, its abrupt change of place and time[12]: an economy of technical means, and wealth of effects.[13]"—(Ljubomir Micić). Zenithism propagates filmism in art: speed, abrupt changes of place and time, a plethora of events, the suggestive conquest of the masses—the support of the masses for the new art of film. (Film, too, had to go through long and arduous battles before it could proclaim victory!)—"Zenithist poetry demands a filmic realism and the totality of modern life, the quick-change of the interior and exterior world, the sharp-edged contrasts of black and white by means of alogical associations and simultaneities."[14]—(Micić).

Despite all obstacles, of which the most difficult for the zenithist is financial trouble, besides the intellectual poverty of one's own "birth country." Despite all obstacles and against all enemies, zenithists have developed their own activity not only in the Balkans but the world over. That is made clear in numerous foreign journals and newspapers and by zenithists who are not of South Slavic nationality.[15] What has the global press written about *Zenit*, zenithism, and zenithists? Until now, there has been talk in at least fourteen countries about the emergence of *Zenit* and zenithism, that we are aware of. An entire generation of the whole world is collaborating on zenithism. Zenithist works have garnered attention abroad due to their strength and originality, and Ljubomir Micić himself has so far been translated into eight languages. He receives no small number of requests to contribute every day from many different countries. What writer in our country, young or old, can boast such a thing?

Many people associate zenithism with the futurist movement. However, futurism has nothing in common with zenithism as it first seems. Although: futurism is a movement that comes from a profound need for something new, but it failed like cabaret dadaism. Futurism is the fruit of the degeneration of Western Europe and originates from the traditions of Western-European civilizations. On the contrary, zenithism rests on the healthy elements of our race and our positive barbarism. Zenithism is in this way internationalist, in the best sense of the word, as art and culture are panhuman goods. Not only does zenithism not destroy the raw material of our race, but, to the contrary, it furthers our racial virtues, and aims to heal a deeply ill Europe—which, finally, suits the true Balkanization of Europe.

The West reproduces itself. Everywhere: imitation, a monkey's grin, and hunchbacks. Yammering on about the same thing for decades. We have a culture of lies, a culture of paper, a culture of sentimental and artificial tears. Man faces destruction. Man suffers. We all suffer. It is comforting that our illness is not fatal—we are that strong. We have benign stomach cramps from eating smelly sausages mother Europe offered us. Yes, Europe accomplished its negative mission, which is why Europe is now in its death throes. Today Europe gifts its opinions only in bars, bordellos, and with syphilis. And all those so-called cultures consist of, above all, the spreading of venereal diseases and modern life, and then in the accumulation of dust through educational institutes where students gladly flirt with women's panties.

In the battle of two cultures, Western and Eastern, zenithists were the first in the Balkans to begin the battle for the triumph over the East. We are Easterners. We are Balkanites. (Without any danger, those of you who remain can stand up against Western-European culture to your heart's content, too, but do not forget that Dr. Vladimir Dvorniković[16] and the Belgrade circle came only after *Zenit* and the zenithists, under the developed flags of zenithism). Zenithism aspires to create a new Balkan civilization, which cannot be sentimental, because sentimentality is never positive. We ought to have feelings but only when they are necessary and as much as is necessary. I would like to mention just a few important elements of Balkanism, which Ljubomir Micić highlighted 1) Purity of primitivism 2) down-to-earth humanity 3) heroism of spirit and heart 4) integrity of soul 5) universal brotherhood 6) justice 7) ethics. Balkanism—at least in the way that the zenithists propagate it—does not entail any kind of barbarism in the Budapestian or Viennese sense. The effort to heal Europe and the blessed world altogether using the positive serums of our Slavic-Balkan race, that is our feared and loathed Balkanization of Europe! The aspiration toward Balkanization in no way originates from some nationalistic-egotistic motives. To the contrary, we live in the firm conviction of the reinforcement of healthy Balkan elements in the interest of all peoples, and thus, in the interest of humanity.

The barbarogenius is the carrier of unadulterated products of the young Balkan race. The barbarogenius is the heroism of the spirit, that is, the greatest strength of our future. The zenithist understanding of life and the world builds a new philosophy, a new perspective on the world—zenithosophy. The center of zenithosophy is man's vertical meridian, man's transformation into the new man. The tearing apart of man into "77 bodies," according to one of our modern novels by Branko Ve Poljanski 77 *Suicides*[17], will replace the homogeneous and synthetic new man. "I am born again,"[18] Stevan Živanović sings, and Ljubomir Micić says in the *Manifesto of Zenithism*:

"Black flags, brothers, flutter in our souls
because
Man is dying everywhere"[19]
"Man wanted!"[20]

And I, too, have found an adequate expression for the same feeling:

"I'm struggling to live like a man
Where do I get all this power to be a man."
(Marijan Mikac, "joyous lament")[21]

The German zenithist Franz Richard Behrens, in "To the People Made of Chocolate," calls out to everyone:

"Every transaction is a theft."[22]

Yes, anyone who wagers our souls is a thief.

Our dignity and patience are not points of weakness but compassion. Our "rebellion against man on behalf of man"[23] exists everywhere, at all ends of the earth where zenithists are found.

Our friend, the young Josif Klek, is energetically working on his new zenithist work of art (which Micić called arbos-painting[24]) and our new architecture, which will be heavily accented with new forms of our as yet unknown strengths.

As early as 1921, Branko Ve Poljanski announced our arrival in *Svetokret* like this:

Oh, cultured one!
Oh, humanitarian![25]
Oh, human!
Europe!
The day will come
It will!
The day of blood and blaze
When from the heavens
Where reigns a man—God
A fiery rain will pour!

—Belgrade—
The month of March 1924

Translated by *Suzana Vuljević*

Endnotes

1 Mikac's quotes often don't follow the original format of the source, and in some cases, he misquotes or misattributes his sources. We've corrected his quotations and standardized his citations where necessary.—Eds.

2 Ljubomir Micić, *Kola za spasavanje* [Rescue car] (Belgrade: Biblioteka Zenit, 1922).

3 Ljubomir Micić, "Prema optikoplastici" [Toward opticoplastics]. Preface to *Arhipenko: Nova plastika* [Archipenko: New Plastics] (Belgrade: Biblioteka Zenit, 1923).

4 Marijan Mikac, *Efekt na defektu* [Effect on defect] (Belgrade: Biblioteka Zenit, 1923).

5 Andra Jutronić, "Odgovor na pitanje" [Answer to a question], *Zenit*, no. 34 (November 1924): 8.

6 Stevan Živanović. The first line from "verujte matere nerotkinje" [believe the barren mother]. *Zenit*, no. 22 (March 1923): 5.

7 Branko Ve Poljanski, "Manifest" [Manifesto] in *Panika pod suncem* [Panic under the sun] (Belgrade: Biblioteka Zenit, 1924).

8 Branko Ve Poljanski, "untitled." *Zenit*, nos. 17–18 (September–October 1922): 60.

9 Branko Ve Poljanski, "T. B. C." [T. B.] in *Panika pod suncem*.

10 Marijan Mikac, *Fenomen majmun* [The monkey phenomenon] (Belgrade: Biblioteka Zenit, 1925).

11 Stevan Živanović, Andra Jutronić, Vojislav Avakumović were zenithists who frequently contributed to Zenit. Josip Štolcer-Slavenski (1896–1955) was a Croatian composer who published his "Danse Balkanique" in *Zenit*, no. 36 (October 1925): 11–14. Josif Klek is a reference to Josip Seissel (Jo Klek) (1904–1987) who was an architect, constructivist artist, graphic designer, theatrical designer, and member of the zenithist movement.

12 The quoted passage before the colon is not from "Radio-Film."

13 Ljubomir Micić. The quoted passage after the colon is from "Radio-Film i zenitistička okomica duha" [Radio-Film and the zenithist vertical of the spirit], *Zenit*, no. 23 (April 1923): 2–5.

14 Ibid.

15 See *Nemo propheta in patria*, which was a supplement to *Zenit*, no. 25 (February 1924).

16 Vladimir Dvorniković (1888–1956) was a philosoper and an ethno-psychologist, and a strong advocate for Yugoslav ethnicity. MID refers to his book *Die beiden Grundtypen des Philosophierens* (Berlin: Leonhard Simion, 1918).

17 Branko Ve Poljanski, *77 samoubica* [77 Suicides] (Belgrade: Biblioteka Zenit, 1923).

18 Stevan Živanović, "Zdravo savremeniče!" [Hello contemporaries!], *Zenit*, no. 15 (June 1922): 35.

19 Ljubomir Micić, *Manifest zenitisma* [The Manifesto of Zenithism] (Belgrade: Biblioteka Zenit, 1921).

20 Mikac added an extra line "Traži se čovek!" [Man wanted!], which isn't in the original *Manifesto*. The line seems to be from Ljubomir Micić's "Revolucija u gradu beome: 7777: traži se čovek" [Revolution in the white city: 7777: man wanted], *Zenit*, no. 10 (December 1921): 2–7.

21 Marijan Mikac, *Efekt na defektu* [Effect on defect] (Belgrade: Biblioteka Zenit, 1923).

22 The title might be a reference to Behrens' "Schokoladene ballade" [Chocolate ballad] in *Zenit*, no. 24 (May 1923): 4; however, Mikac's translated quote "Svako trgovanje je krađa" seems to be a reference to the line "Jeder Handler ein Dieb" [Every trader a thief] from Behrens' "die dollar-arie" [the dollar aria], *Zenit*, no. 23 (April 1923): 5–6.

23 Marijan Mikac, *Fenomen majmun* [The monkey phenomenon] (Belgrade: Biblioteka Zenit, 1925).

24 "ARBOS" stands for what Jo Klek since 1922 called PAFAME (Papier-FArben-Malerei in German), that is, in Micić's translation in Serbian "ARtija-BOja-Slika," as yet another "original" or "authentic" phenomenon of zenithist art, which Micić had found in Jo Klek's paintings, collages, watercolors, and abstract compositions (often used in his advertisements).

25 Branko Ve Poljanski, "Evo me!" [Here I am!], *Svetokret*, no. 1 (1921): 1.

Airplane without an Engine

Ljubomir Micić
Zenit International Review Edition, 1925

Translated by *Suzana Vuljević*

2.7. Lj. Micić, *Aeroplan bez motora: antievropska poema* [Airplane without an Engine: An Anti-European Poem], Zenit International Review Edition, Belgrade 1925. Front cover. Courtesy of National Library of Serbia, Belgrade (Legacy of Ljubomir Micić, Special collections).

1

author without a beard
—1918—
as a recognized poet
▪ before zenithism ▪

LJUBOMIR MICIĆ

AIRPLANE WITHOUT AN ENGINE

AN ANTI-EUROPEAN POEM

with a foreword from the editors of *Politika*

2

+ Zenithism.

— A poet who becomes head of a public relations-advertising company —

At the beginning of 1921, *Zenit*, the international journal of zenithism and the new art, was founded in Zagreb. Each new edition came out on different colored paper and made use of a range of fonts at the disposal of the Zagreb printing house. Ostentatious and colorful, the journal resembled a broadside. Its founder and editor, Mr. Ljubomir Micić, who remained unknown for his more-or-less orthodox poems, *Rhythm of My Inklings*, suddenly became a hero of our times.

Mr. Micić laid out the five principles of zenithism, of which the first stated: "A Zenithist work must be interwoven with a collectivist heart that dances on the electro-motorized line of time," and the fifth dictate read: "A Zenithist work must be genius." That is the reason, without a doubt, why modernist poets of Belgrade also appeared in the early issues. But something happened that was as unexpected as it was characteristic for Mr. Ljubomir Micić. Belgrade's modernist poets very soon unanimously agreed that Mr. Micić's writing was so erratic and obtuse that even they could not understand their editor's words. Withdrawing their efforts from the collaboration, they went on to lambast him in an open letter, and Micić, in turn, let them have it.

At that point, *Zenit* became even more bizarre. The world was baffled; people made fun of the journal, but most of all, kept talking about it. The Zagreb-based literary journal *Kritika* once referred to Ljubomir Micić as "Lunatic Micić." Micić sued Milan Begović, editor of *Kritika*, for insulting him and that was one lawsuit that, like any spectacle, captivated Zagreb for three days.

Ultimately, the world eventually grew bored of being shocked and of making the same jokes over and over again, and Ljubomir Micić became intolerable in Zagreb. No one laughed anymore, and people were no longer amused, they just looked on with indifference at the worn-out journal, *Zenit,* in the display windows of bookstores, and Micić was forced to move to another place where people did not already think of him as a sham.

He came to Belgrade. He went from being clean-shaven to growing out his beard. With him appeared the twenty-fourth issue of *Zenit.* Unfortunately, this was also the last. During the several months that Mr. Micić spent in our parts with the editorial board at Birčaninova 12, *Zenit* did not come out. Indeed, a brochure was published by *Zenit,* but that looks like it was the reason for the new issue's failure to appear. All of Belgrade's bookstores together hardly sold twenty copies of the issue and the last brochure, but the publishing expenses were considerable.

However, even as zenithism as a literary movement can be considered dead, Mr. Micić had, it seems, an original idea through which he could recover lost funds, even if he could not make a profit. In the last few days in the showcase of the Cvijanović bookstore a colorful zenithist poster (the work of Mr. Jo Klek, a zenithist) made for advertising purposes appeared. It is a generally known fact that advertisements produced by a somewhat capable advertiser can withstand a lot. But for Mr. Micić, a lot could be denied, except that he did not know how to promote himself. Being that he became world renowned, he will open a public relations-advertising firm, Zenith, he will stop writing poems and only write invoices, and who knows, maybe he will become a wealthy man who would have never become so had he remained the director of the literary movement Zenith.

POLITIKA

BELGRADE, MONDAY, SEPTEMBER 3, 1923

NUMBER 5517—YEAR XIX

P.S. Reprinted with all intellectual, ethical, stylistic and typographical errors.

4

Verses, articles, essays, fragments, and manifestos by Ljubomir Micić—have been published in these journals thus far

ANTHOLOGIE MONDIALE—Paris	French
BLOK—Warsaw	Polish
BOUWKUNDE—Antwerp	Flemish
DER STURM—Berlin	German
DE MORGEN—Helmond	Dutch
INICIAL—Buenos Aires	Spanish
LUMIÈRES—Anvers	French
MA—Vienna	Hungarian
MAVO—Tokyo	Japanese
MANOMETRE—Lyon	Serbian
PLAMK—Sofia	Bulgarian
SEPT ARTS—Brussels	French
25—Gorizia	Italian
S 4 N—Northampton	English
WOHNUNGSKULTUR—Brno	German
WALLONIE—Liège	French

ars pro patria

document of confiscation for the first of zenithist verses

■ ■ ■ ■ ■ ■ **damn your hundred gods** ■ ■ ■ ■ ■ ■

"Number: I 5047.—1922

DECREE.

The criminal state prosecutor's office in Zagreb makes prohibitions on the basis of Article **13** and **138** statute of publishing and distribution of issue **XX** from November 7**, 1922**, of a temporary manuscript: Zenit, coming out in Zagreb and due to the following printed paragraphs:

On page **24**, indent **1** line **7** to **10**, from the word "young" to "ridicule."

On page **18**, indent **1** from the word "always" to "legs," then on the same page the expression with the second indent that reads "Damn Your Hundred Gods."

On page **17**, indent 1 line **25** from the word "ate" to line **27** the word "sins."

On page **16**, line 5 the word "Syphilis culture."

On page **14**, indent 1 line 20 the word "whore."

On page **10**, lines 15 and 16 the words "Damn Your Hundred Gods"

and finally, on the second to last and last written page the words "Damn Your Hundred Gods" since these items contain a heavy insult to public morality and an insult to the ruler.

The criminal state prosecutor's office

Zagreb, November 7, **1922**."

document de la confiscation du premier livre de poésie zenitiste

■ ■ ■ ■ ■ ■ ■ **par mille dieux** ■ ■ ■ ■ ■ ■ ■

6

anuška

TO YOU, MY INCREDIBLE WIFE
I DEDICATE THIS BALKAN, BARBARIAN POEM

in the name of
zenithism
and
LOVE

Marvelous marvels boarding platforms are
Anywhere above Europe
High above European bordellos and bars
Wouldn't you say Mata Hari you immaculate virgin
Boats or airplanes
Sailing dappled seas oil-slicked from ships
Trample over corned feet Lady Asquith
In the soccer stadium of the Leviathan
At last
To watch a radio-film in the ninth heaven

EUROPE
OR
THE DEMISE OF A PUFFED-UP FROG

At least Madagascar
Afghanistan or Koko Nor
Zanzibar or Hamilton
The Urals or Durmitor
Argentina
The Equator
Kangaru

8

Sailors
Chimneys
Mermaids
Cannons
Binoculars
Captains

?

is there any
room left
for
the Balkan man

Behold weary helmsmen dreaming
In spite of romantic dreams
I'll rewrite the rules of poetry in reality
Never mind
Of all the poets on earth
Let only the new ones defend the heart and soul of the new life
It's no bother
Women give birth in large numbers following bouts of seasickness
Women kiss the rags they swaddle their babies in
Which is why I like neither dreamy poets nor snotty-nosed women

In a dream
I hopelessly fled from muddy floods
And in vain I strutted in royal feathers
In truth I flounder in Balkan mud and stumble over skeletons

In the eyes of my horned fate
I haven't found a port

At night
I kept hurling black cloths at the unsightly
cheeks of haggard days
But in the morning I stroke my wife's marvelous hips and back
If she chastely permits

People
Don't fear my love
They've lapped enough of our blood of
Milk Milk Milk
of sun-drenched milk
Weep you humanists
Today I think like a barbarian
Tomorrow we'll be humanity's haiduks again

Hellooooooooooooooooooo
I leap headlong into my ideoplane
To smash the hollow engines in the factories of the whorish press
O the vanquished
O the conquerors
I will slay all the Western pilots with my ideoplane
I have already bent the pan-European spine over the Danube
I built a bridge without iron and repairs for the Balkanites

Hellooooooooooooooooooo

10

Our bridge is an earthly rainbow
East versus **West**
Here: our new freedom: bridge
There: your new life: descent
Quake-o-earth
Temblor—tremor—Temblor—tremor—Temblor—tremor
In my honor
My countrymen wait for the moment when the ravens
come to peck me to death

Grandfathers tubby wise men
Anti-zenithists stretch your bows from
the English Channel to the Black Sea
Shoot me down from my zenithist flight
Hey
High above the oaks I'll shoot at death

What trials and wonders
Aerial waves flash through the prism of my small brain
Lying on a rebellious spine
Often with a twisted vein between my legs
I guide the Bolshevik revolution of the **metacosmos**
Alas . . . .
Love has hooked my heartheart of my dynamomotor
To the switchboard's main line of electricity
The insanity of persecution damns the steep town of Belgrade

Because
Zenithism is the propeller of the Balkan continent
Let it be known to all
The Balkans are a young male
Europe a raggedy whore and his withered mistress
Let whatever you called Europe be Balkan henceforth
From the very beginning
The Balkans are that
My crazy ideoplane let your will be done
Let's go friends black and white
via the zenith
Vroooooooooooooooom Vroooooooooooooooom
Vroooooooooooooooom

In all the lightbulbs Balkan bells clack
—for European wings to break
—to shatter stock-exchange windows
—to detonate the vacuumed living quarters
of all the bourgeoisie on earth
—to collapse the foul-smelling **old**
—to wildly sprout **anew**
anew
anew
Everywhere things are turned upside down
Always against the eternal
Wherever the fist of my furious eyes hits
Down with eternity
Long live the life of the lively living alive

12

Perhaps we have been deceived as to the shape of the earth
Isn't it just three airplanes that reached the world's record
Bravo . . .
At last the cell of motorized skulls opens
Cultural cells break apart into crumbs like walnut shells
bitter is the fruit of civilization
on the Balkan continent
hurraaaaaaaaaaaaaaaaaaaaaaaaaaaaaaaaaaaaaaaaaaaaaaaaaaaaaaaaaaaaaah
Perhaps the new life is an oyster from blazing waterfalls
—to fly deep
—to journey through the steppe
—to triumph over culture
—to fall high
—to serenade barbaric people
—to defy civilized man
everything is perhaps just a product of wild waterfalls
Niagara
Volga
Vardar
Only wild waterfalls are strong
    wild waterfalls are raw and proud-spirited
    wild waterfalls generate electric power
Which is what my Balkan blood brother did
The first inventor of wireless telegraphy
Serbian electrogenius Nikola Tesla

Men
Draw the verticals from atop your heads
O barbarogenius fount of my insanity
Drill cranial lightning rods and radiotelephones for us
O barbarogenius sole carrier of the new spirit
Vomit my savage strength expel it from your body
O barbarogenius world traveler of our haiduk culture
Erect statues for extramental utopias
Skyward
Skyward
Skyward

Along the way listen to the nameless symphony
Coming from the magical intestinal canals of the late Leiden
I wait in vain for the obliteration of the stock-exchange dollar-bill palace
Thresholds on floor-levels in all directions
Like haiduk pig troughs from Topčider and sinful Avala
The elevator of the fifth floor in a warm bathroom
Oh my
Switched off lightbulbs copulate
They get prettier in the electrical headquarters of Belgrade
Round women rush through the state hospitals' white clinics
Short-tempered buzzers howl from inside the bowels of deadly Leiden
Batteries thrust themselves under love-makers' quilts

14

Marble and spit-covered graveyards
Marble and defiled icons
Marble and smoky revelries
Marble and consecrated bars
Marble and blessed dice
Marble and Orthodox cathedrals
Marble and women's shirts
Marble and colorful dollars
All together below the torturous stairs of Balkan gallows
Half-human European freaks
This way
Under the solitary justice of blissful ashes

There there my wife
Don't reveal the secrets of my zenithplane to anyone
—**it's dangerous to lean on the hatch**—
To you this poem is the murmur of airplane wings far off in the distance
Only you know the countless names of the stations
Where the traffic lights of my love flash
Only you my lone friend know
All the stops are traffic lights of our love

And on this night three hundred conquered pains flash like lightning
Countless cramps shoot straight to the heart
At least three hundred barbarian cramps

Here high above
In the white breasts of my insane ideoplane
Boiling in the place of bile: zenith and blood
My wings shake wicked stars mercilessly
In wooden breasts of railroad tracks and thresholds
Above every nation

O iron meridians of cannibalistic nations
Your luminous ribs like countless serpent stomachs
The pulverization of the **barbarogenius**

You rigid iron serpents
Why don't you tie all the world's continents together
To the most far-flung promised land
Held in ill repute }
Goes by the name } **humanity**

To your feet
To your feet you iron-clad rigid and legless serpents
There in the heights of the so-called sky
Bloodied underwear of our hungering years
Above the heads of all of the continents
Billowing frights
Brrrrr
Waaaaaaaaaaaaaaaaaaaaaaaaaaaaaaaaaaa

16

FROM THE SAME AUTHOR

PRINTED WORKS

1) Rhythm of My Inklings, poems 1919
2) The Salvation of the Soul, poems 1920
3) Eastern Sin, dramatic canto 1920
4) The Manifesto of Zenithism 1921
5) Rescue Car, words in space 1922
6) Archipenko: New Plastics, monograph 1923
7) Airplane without an Engine, anti-European poem 1925

MANUSCRIPTS

1) A Head in the Bag, a novel about Balkan hordes
2) The Birth of God's Calf, a poem about the Balkan continent
3) Fata Morgana, a film that is neither in the sky nor on the ground
4) Of Cobblestone and Rifles, verses and prose
5) 1921, poems on proletkult and pan-humanism
6) God Watches Over Serbia, a cheerful play
7) Film and the New Poetry, the fundamentals of anti-aesthetics, illustrated
8) Hands Up, an anthology of zenithist poetry
9) The New Art, a calendar of contemporary art
10) For the Balkanization of Europe, barbarian thoughts and creations
11) Zenith Almanac, 1921–1926

2.8. Lj. Micić, *Avion sans apparel: poème antieuropéen* [Airplane without an Engine: An Anti-European Poem], Zenit International Review Edition, Belgrade, Serbia, 1925. Front cover. Courtesy of Archives Michael Ilk, Germany.

Barbarism as Culture

Risto Ratković
from *Zenit*, no. 37 (November–December 1925)

To the zenithists of the world:

Barbarism—not in the sense that the Greeks, the Chinese, or the Germans understood it; nor peaceful, cultured ladies (even if they are feminists) understand it, nor the fine souls wearing bank governor's and inquisitor's shoes understand it. Not primitivism or anarchism, either. And not some "return to nature," as the decadent Rousseau sentimentalized; not licentiousness either, dreamed of by silly poets and revolutionaries lying under coffeehouse tables. Not the "Umwertung aller Werte"[1] for it does not matter: you go forward either on your feet or in your head.

In a word, barbarism is not meant as the antipode to culture; it is culture, culture's recovery. Such barbarism is an undying, eternally rejuvenating injection of purity, a disinfectant for mildewed spaces in dead spirits. Above all, barbarism is ours. It is an undying thirst for unmasking, for complete unmasking, even if we have to scratch at our own fates. As such, barbarism is a fundamental revolution in culture, a rebellion against all pseudo-revolutions. In order to unmask (oneself and others) one needs to be able to control what one has (which does not mean being aware of everything). One therefore need not be a slave, which to barbarians also means not to be a tyrant.

Above all, barbarians are not *Kulturträgers*, but creators of culture. Moreover, they have the same relation to culture as creators to their works: they are not mere suspenders like *Kulturträgers*. (The explanation is acrobatic: anti-barbaric culture is only the fear of having one's trousers fall).

Beyond the relative terms of good and evil, we believe that man is good deep down, that any action performed of one's own free will, completely independently, in no one's name but one's own, is worth more than the entire slew of made-up, *fawning freedoms*. That is a pre-philosophy of pure being and at the same time the ethics of an undefeatable uprising against all false etiquettes, the ethics of people who do not a priori respect anything and are still meek and good. We find true nobility in this, a nobility that does no harm to anyone and is both individualistic and social. We have felt, seen, and guessed that so-called culture, anti-barbaric culture, is progressive only pro forma, that it has not distilled primitivism but rather only masked it the better to be de facto anti-cultural. It is in man's nature to mask himself carefully, to hide, since man fears his own nudity.

So, it is not at all a paradox or impossible to reach barbarism through culture, because the very act means not giving up on culture yet avoiding becoming its victim. On one hand, we are extremely idealistic; on the other, we share a basic fraternal nihilism: *looking for one's beginnings by going forward*. It is not so long ago that militaristic expeditions were all the rage in Europe: "Berlin has gone mad, Paris is spewing forth its rapture, Moscow is tearing its chest." And through all that time balding culture played chess in salons, gambling away armies during its orgies. If the revelers could have admitted to themselves and to others. . . .

The dandy—that pseudo-aristocrat, that stinking flower of stolen culture—is showing off everywhere. Everywhere and all the time there is at least one marketplace of conscience, at least one exchange office of lies, at least one department store of pride. Which clearly shows that the real creators of culture are anonymous even if anti-cultural anti-barbarians put their names to it. Culture is symbolically like a slice of meat: the thicker one is, the more cultured one is. The trouble is, the meat has spoiled, and to keep the smell away culture takes cocaine and turns the tears of the impoverished into cologne for whores.

It would seem, then, that barbaric ethics opposes civilization. But historic materialism cannot be denied and barbarians will not retreat; they will advance civilization and thus make it impossible for civilization to be abused. The invention of gunpowder created great evil, but it has done much more for the expansion of the spirit than Dante's invention of the Inferno, the toilet of his Purgatory, and his idiotic Paradise. It is obvious that the wireless and other products of the exact sciences will either raise social injustice and anti-cultural exploitation to new heights or make a new, independent collectivism possible. The barbarians opt for the latter.

It is no mechanization of the soul. Technology is its necessary luxury. Barbarian culture does not see the world as a machine. We find the scientists' habit of "explaining" the world ridiculous. We even see it as dangerous: disappointment is inevitable, since everything is as "purely materialistic" as it is "purely spiritual." Barbarians cannot be victims of driveling sentimentality or banal rationalism. Even mysticism has its place, but if something stinks it should be removed, mysterious or not, because tolerating a bedbug under one's nose means either not having a nose or being a bedbug oneself. So mysticism remains, as pure and as mysterious as snow from an ancient dream, mysticism of the beginning and of the end, the mysticism of everything. We see no reason why man cannot be a mystic on a plane if he can be one on his couch.

No philosophical school calls into question the ethics of cultural barbarism. Countless philosophical systems correspond to one another on paper without disrupting the purity of interpersonal relations. For instance, I could be a pansexual without sending a single girl to the VD clinic. Because by applying any view of the world to real life, independent of ethics, we give it an ethical character. Besides, ethics itself is also a philosophy, since no concept is more universal than morality. Here, morality is freed of theological and political boundaries. Man alone remains in his countless relations to the world, a power characteristic only of the victors of culture.

Barbarism, therefore, is no sewerage system to say nothing of a guidebook to life. It frees the personality. Barbaric cultural ethics are not defined by any social system, but every system free of the reek of humility and cowardly abuse is defined by it. No classes are pure. Even the most miserable proletarian can be as much of a bastard and philistine as a man of leisure. A banal point, but important.

The barbarian-anti-slave, the anti-tyrant. The antipode of all charlatans, from Alexander the Small to Schopenhauer the Lame. It is pitiful, the entire construction of religious heavens! It is so naive and pathetic, the logic of dualism. Barbarians will never try to build that legendary Tower of Babel destroyed for all times by Dostoevsky. To go one step farther, after Ivan Karamazov and Kirilov, is what it really means to be a barbarian. And we have gone further: the Tower of Babel is behind us.

Barbarism also has a metaphysical basis. Einstein claims that even his own theory of relativity is relative, and the phrase "everything is a lie" also means everything is not a lie, since if everything is a lie, then the statement "everything is a lie" is also a lie. Thus, it would be perfectly logical to prove that there is no death, though death itself needs no proof at all.

We once felt that we should do nothing but weep our whole lives: it was the only way to save ourselves from the grotesque. But because that was impossible, we decided to be maximally courageous. Our innocence made us mad and we became barbarians. What a paradox! But here it is: we oppose all savagery, indignity, meanness, all repulsive things so neatly masked by culture; we oppose them with pure goodness and joyful freedom. (The barbaric cultural spirit is well illustrated by its disgust with the death penalty. Murder can be justified and noble, but the death penalty—never.)

The spirit of cultural barbarism has given rise to an entire revolution in culture. It has made art a conquest of space and time when it expresses what it could not express in previously existing space and time. Art is the maximum of expression in a minimum of space; moreover, the expression (content–form) must be located in the newly conquered space and time. The rhythm of conquest, of moving into another world, the rhythm of creation is specific to any kind of art that has its own character. This is especially true of poetry, music, and painting. The creation of such painting was aided by the invention of photography, which made all copies superfluous and ridiculous. Music too is closely connected to technique, but its tone association is becoming increasingly liberated.

Poetry is the most liberated art and where our greatest hopes lie.

Belgrade, October 3, 1925
Translated by *Maja Starčević*

Endnotes

1 Ger.: the re-evaluation of all values.

Anti-Europe

Ljubomir Micić
Zenit Edition, 1926

Translated by *Dragana Obradović*

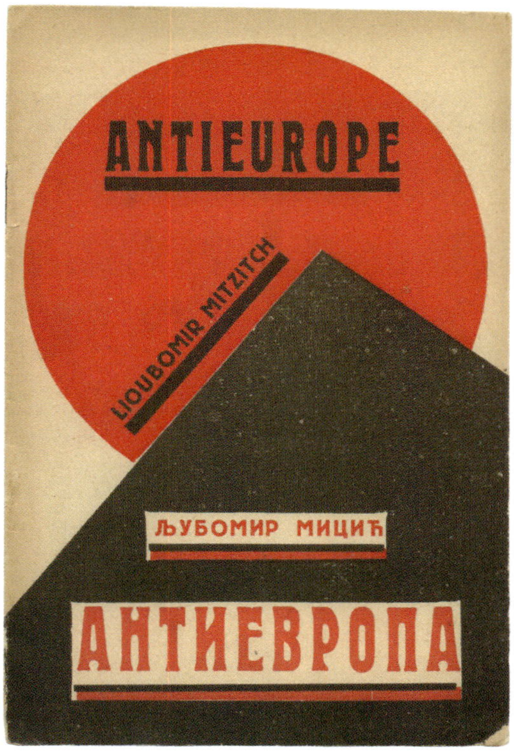

2.9. Lj. Micić, *Antievropa* [Anti-Europe], Zenit Edition, no. 9, Belgrade, Serbia, 1926. Front cover. Courtesy of Gallery RIMA, Kragujevac, Serbia.

TO DR. DUŠAN POPOVIĆ

ZAGREB

In art, there are only revolutionaries and plagiarists

Gauguin

LJUBOMIR MICIĆ

ANTI-EUROPE

1926

LIOUBOMIR MITZITCH

ANTI-EUROPE

BEYOND-SENSE POETRY AND ANTI-EUROPE

Two apparently independent worlds here make up an indivisible whole: anti-Europe and beyond-sense poetry. These two worlds are linked by the antennae of the new spirit of zenithism.

●

Beyond-sense is heaven for the "crazies" which one enters with an unwritten passport of talent, spiritually naked and clean, like a drop of the sun. I entered and, battling across the corpses of European classics and national traditions, I left behind the skin of my old poetry in contempt of myself and other writers. And to those of you who stealthily follow my "insane" example that leads to "the promised land" beyond sense and reason into the hell of a new zenithist poetry; to those of you who can and wish to: above all, down with the dirty, old, and heavy rags of poetry!

●

Zenithism is the liberator from the slavery of the European literary traditions. Zenithism is the discovery of barbarianism and freedom—the barbarism of the spirit and barbaric free thoughts. I discovered the source of new poetry in zenithism: beyond-sense! Beyond-sense: the spring of creation. Beyond-sense is the boundary at which the lunatic and the genius dance the wild kolo. Yes, at the boundary of "pure" reason begins "pure" art, that is, new art: zenithism! Where the stinking breath of "pure reason" does not reach, there lies the zone of creation of beyond-sense. In that wonderful zone of beyond-sense, the flowers of reason don't stink, while the place for reason's limited and healing analysis—applied with pathetic dignity by so-called and self-proclaimed critics when they "assess" the value of art—is outside the realm of my deep regrets.

●

Europe is the mother of analysis. That, however, is not her only error and sin. There are many. They are numberless. Alongside the political monstrosities of imperialism and capitalism whose slaves we have been since time immemorial, our cultural enslavement grows noticeably fast. Therefore: anti-Europe! The race toward Europe is disgusting. I want zenithist poetry to be the first dam to European degeneracy in the Balkans. Wanting the Europeanisation of the Balkans today, in the twilight of Europe, when the Balkanization of Europe is at hand, means running around oneself, after one's own tail. Alongside the Russian revolution, the cultural emancipation of the Balkans from Europe is for us one of the most significant contemporary problems. These two burning fires should be priorities for a zenithist above all other "life interests." Why I have begun, through poetry, to fight against Europe and European culture in a country where culture is a chamois expelled from the Balkan pyramids of political mud and moral corruption is a question I leave intentionally unanswered. Let the work speak! If they have no one to speak to today—they will tomorrow! Let zenithism speak!

●

Enslavement to European culture and her slaughterous hunt across the East will have more fatal consequences for us in the future than now. That is why we cannot let the Balkans become a warehouse and stockroom for a surviving and cannibalistic European culture. After Christianity, European culture is the greatest evil of enslaved mankind! And for some years now, in the maelstrom of the European swamp, the Balkan galley sinks—without a cultural stern and without political balance. Here: we are the first to offer help under the sign of poetry, to save her and our lives. Our help is the shriek of zenithism and my beyond-sense poetry the spiritual life jacket. Like an eruption of deep quakes from our barbarian womb, let my poetry be the thermometer of new, anti-European feelings and thoughts which blossomed in the spring of the first spiritual revolution in the Balkans under the wing of zenithism!

●

Revolution is not slavery. Revolution is resurrection. Revolution is freedom. Whoever wishes to enter the heaven of cultural independence, they have to run manically in the steps of the spiritual revolution. Independence of the spirit, independence of feelings, and independence of creation are not gifts for Salome, like John the Baptist's head on a plate. Freedom and independence, the only two moral and cultural values, are worth all our suffering and victimhood; they are worth all our banditry. The freedom of the spirit and the independence of thought are seized with teeth! Whoever wishes to become an independently free man has to subordinate an enslaving and illusory peace to the emancipatory revolution of the spirit, to revolutionary thoughts, to the revolution of beyond-sense feelings. Zenithists throw the burning bombs of zenithism toward the zenith in the post-war literature of Serbs, Croats, and Slovenes, instilling fear in the enemy. In the flaming forge, zenithists mint the hot iron of the young barbarian spirit and its carrier, the barbarogenius, beyond boundaries! It is shameful to be a lyricist in the post-war days of the heinous rape of our conscious and our too pure love for a new humankind.

Belgrade, June 13, 1926

the barbarogenius

My new song is the rabid lightning of mother sun
The earth's belt is a burning equator
Hey, rays of Mars's rebellion, where are you from

My feelings have become numb for ordinary human loves
The one whose hatred stiffened under my gaze
My shoulders are too narrow for the rebellious waves of new planets
Even though I proudly kiss a single woman
Ah
I am merely a new earthly man of old bad weather

It's easy for you, light bodies of Mars
You can fall and break your wings as you please
You can rise in freedom
I
I dare not even kneel
Let alone fall on this planet

Still wild, I'm tied and I can't get on my hind legs
Ah, I would die wildly in the mountains of the Balkan continent
Caught like an animal in the handcuffs of the east and the west
Owww

You Bedouin mares from Mars and crazy phantoms
And you, cranes of an unmasked European Venus
You do not know the cramps of this sad, once-stepped-on country
You cannot even fathom the damned Turkish meridians
Your brothers lapped up young Balkan blood in vain
Never mind—for many a year: your hatred and my love
Our flag is the sky today
My fatherland has been the earth since time immemorial

And yet we will meander on godly gallows
Be merciful
But the barbarogenius will avenge new pain.

barbarian omelet

We will drink up nine barrels of stars
And eat a thousand wagons of Serbian sky
If Balkan eyes do not peck at the brain of western culture
If eastern rainbows do not lap up European blood

What are we going to do with blood alone
Blood alone is a pest
And a pest is to everyone—genius

Yes
In pure blood we'll drown the eyes of your watery ideas
On the embers of our gaze we'll fry the brains of genius

BARBARIAN OMELET

Here comes the barbarogenius
Crazy zenithist barbarogenius
Barbarogenius: a beautiful image and an opportunity of tempestuous thought
Barbarogenius: a rescue pilot of barbarian ideoplanes.

hey slavs

What joy
White snow falls on the mountain of my soul
Blizzards snowdrifts
The enormous soul of an enormous mountain of a barbarogenius

Hey Slavs
Once your moustaches were unsheathed yataghans
And your loyal wives double-barrelled flintlocks
In ancient times, cannibals
Always bloodsuckers
Since time immemorial our song is a deadly love

Damn the three hundred thunders
March ahead
Let our revolutions pant madly everywhere
So that dead gods can feel
How angrily old wounds burn
In the new chests of barbaric generations!

syphon—soda—blood

An excellent moussaka
Not to mention the sausages
Smoked ham and brandy just wonderful, eh
The centipede of a lie crawls in ministers' attics
And everything is empty in the books of European poets
Words are just greased wheels of ichor and marrow

Eyes bark the truth

Blood is the healthiest bathroom.
Syphon—soda—blood
In bottles of sweet wine and yogurt
In peasant shoes, the secrets of war and graves are kept.

radio in the balkans

New beauty: radiotelephones
New culture is the sad eye of the beyond-sense madhouse

Beauty—bevel—ball

Beauty is not just a bevel
The ball is not our destiny
Beauty and bevel is the destiny of new poets
And eternity
Eternity is a naked ball and a flintlock

Hey, Unknown Lithuanian, the killer and suicide Anna Ousoupaitals
An American is cruel in the Balkans
Brutal is the grandfather's blood from the wild west
A bullet is the truth
The Balkan man is a martyr in California.

bim bam boom

From the red roofs of love
Liberated towers first floors to the sky
To the proletariat in all continents a song along with a greeting from my eyes

—INSTEAD OF DROPPED BOMBS SPILT TEARS—

Snakes are my tears
Comrades of human rebellion and celestial blood
The sky is green grass
The sky screams in the desert of Christian Easter

Earth, you simian planet with the horns of god, remember
Today all the factories of our souls clamor shriek to shriek
Sirens of the scream echo from the roofs of red spears of the new soul

All dirty streets flow like the insides of a European capital
In our cities, the site of human millions,
Streetcars travel like flags, red
They rush chased by deadly electricity of the electro-revolution
And the bourgeoisie is decorated with mud
The bourgeoisie walking the rich parks of the golden calf
And gearing up to celebrate Easter of that Christ with drunkenness
Who they lasciviously crucified so many years ago

Only black dogs carry a pure love in their eyes

Cars rabid machines on four rubber wings
Carry cannibals
No doubt they will run over a number of sullen pedestrians today
Because in the Balkans a pedestrian is still the only man
Pedestrians—zenithists—poets—proletarians suffer
And you should know: freedom is a sleeping cuckoo-coward on Europe's branch

The radio-eagles of our antennae and sheaves of spat-upon ideals
Along with the blue breasts of Avala are going crazy
Shackled with the chains of freedom of my barbaric nation
Awarded by chetniks invalids and komitadji
Fighters crowned with glory like scarecrows
Stand out in the winds of financial-political speculations

Orthopedy is a life sentence in the wing of war
A prosthesis is the brightest medal of all victories that are always defeats
Above tussocks of human crucifixions and gallows sparkle
national banks
national stores
national politics
national arts
national corruption

In our breast blossoms leaden requiems.

While we announce our rebellious thoughts on the hillsides with our skeleton nails
While the rusty qama scratches the cursed centuries
On the dirty backside of Serbian Rome
From the dark caves of our rabid skulls
Howl the janissaries of revolution

For a new humankind, everything into the whirlpool.

made in england

Hey hi
Last night factory chimneys were sleepwalkers in England
And factory workers stars in the unwieldy sky of capital
And no sun to burn through the prism of our suffering
Celestial paradise on earth

Far is the sun of our redemption
The sun is sailing in the ships of Chinese crowds
Through blooming parks of the Russian revolution and the grand ocean

For centuries night has been pillaging the subterranean castles of miners
Where millions of slaves build the palaces of their graves
Last night five million English workers howled
With an ugly curse on their lips
At midnight a spark jumped
Into the womb of the global leech England

A general strike is but an inflammation of the appendix
Since factory foremen only see green traffic lights

On this night of first collisions, green lights mean death
And red
Only red lights are the railroad switch toward a new life
a new day
a new man

In English ports in the East hungry bayonets shimmer
Rifles and rabid cannons grunt there
Wounded by the sunstroke of revolution

Oh workers miners sailors
Proletarians and followers of the Balkan blood feud
We greet you and ask one infantile question
Why are your blisters not diamonds
Or dynamite?

avala, a tomb in the sky

And this earth is a sun in the chest
Under the sun, a human heart flares like a rifle
Look
Love echoes far like the blast of a bomb on Šar mountain

The clouds are ladders to the Turkish towers of our tomb
The Avala tomb, the old building, ossuary of great loves
Deep in its volcanic womb, it hides the spilled guts of vassals
Because on muddy roads, Turks tore skin for peasant shoes

And the forest of wooden corpses has already bloomed with haiduk's leaves

Above the amphitheater of lyrical fields and hillsides
Undiscovered miracles of my Balkan soul float
They lament the Serbian skulls of self-proclaimed princes
Along with the ploughed land drunk with blood, the wave of the public is colorful flowers
And the clapping of sunned hands
Avala, axle and tomb

Oh, caravan of buried builders of the crescent moon
Once more get down on your knees
And then into the palisade, you barbarian caravan
Europe is the vampirized Turkey of our century
We are still vassals and the children of serfs
It is still necessary to fall
And then into the leap of life
Because the gallows creak in the breast of my eye

Oh, caravan of skulls pierced with our living stakes
Stop Stojan Stojanče
The unknown hero cannot sleep from our rebellious epic folk songs
Stop, you pierced skulls of Balkan haiduks
And listen to my songs
My new songs are the executioners of the European agas and beys

Listen, caravan
Far away the wounded mother of a new humanity laments
Re—vo—lu—ti—on
The Balkan Caravan!

oh, balkan caravan

In the peasant shoes of my new poetry
Travel, caravan, into beyond-sense corners of the barbarian spirit
Do not be afraid of the pride in the humiliation of combatants
Because I lead you toward the lit stitches of protest lyrics

Behind raped hills, caravan
Echo hundred-headed Balkan mountains
Come on
Let's shoot the bullets of our new emotions
The brains of European clouds
And the rage of cultural thunder

We will destroy rabid stock markets and hills, oh Balkan caravan
With the rainbow of barbarian love and anti-Europe hatred
Our hills are women's knees of the earth
And sweaty streets of blood and mud are the male wrinkles of corpses
Each street of ours is a bloody scar on the cheek of a Balkan man
We wounded zenithists sing above clouds of red sickles

And the carriage creaks through muddy silk post-war twilight

<table>
<tr><td>The caravan
And fur vest
And chaika-hat
And peasant shoe</td><td>}</td><td>EVERYTHING IS A SCAR
OF THE RED SNAKE OF REVOLUTION</td></tr>
</table>

Travel, Balkan caravan
The vassal Karadjordje puts on a red sheepskin cape
Follow the lethargic cloud of democracy and pain-bearing Serbia.

slender snakes blossom

Murat's Tomb a haiduk's tower and a radiotelephone
a suicidal fountain Gazimestan and godless antennae
And the pain of the poet zenith's egg
Because Kosovo is not the history of the people
Only princes
And princes are masters

Red peonies are exploded bombs in my chest

The Kosovo phantom treads upon Serbia in the boots of gamblers and the bloodthirsty
Leeches of evil history and fratricidal wars
Suck the blood of freedom of our hungry years
And lava from disgusting floods of Kosovo corruption
All "in the name of the heavenly kingdom" and "for the people"
Rapes the conscience of the old and new Balkan man

Oh, Balkan man
Why, in the shadow of a fake celebration, do you calmly listen to your death sentence
Get on your hind legs
Get on your hind legs and roar into the mustache of the selfish European turtle
Cursed dragon: down with the bourgeoisie
                                        man is the only one
Europe has poisoned the too-pure blood of barbarians
Serbia is the saddest chapter of my life.

Under new furrows of red peonies
Blossom the slender snakes of a Balkan revolution

Oh, Kosovo, ploughed anew
Hooray: anti-Europe!

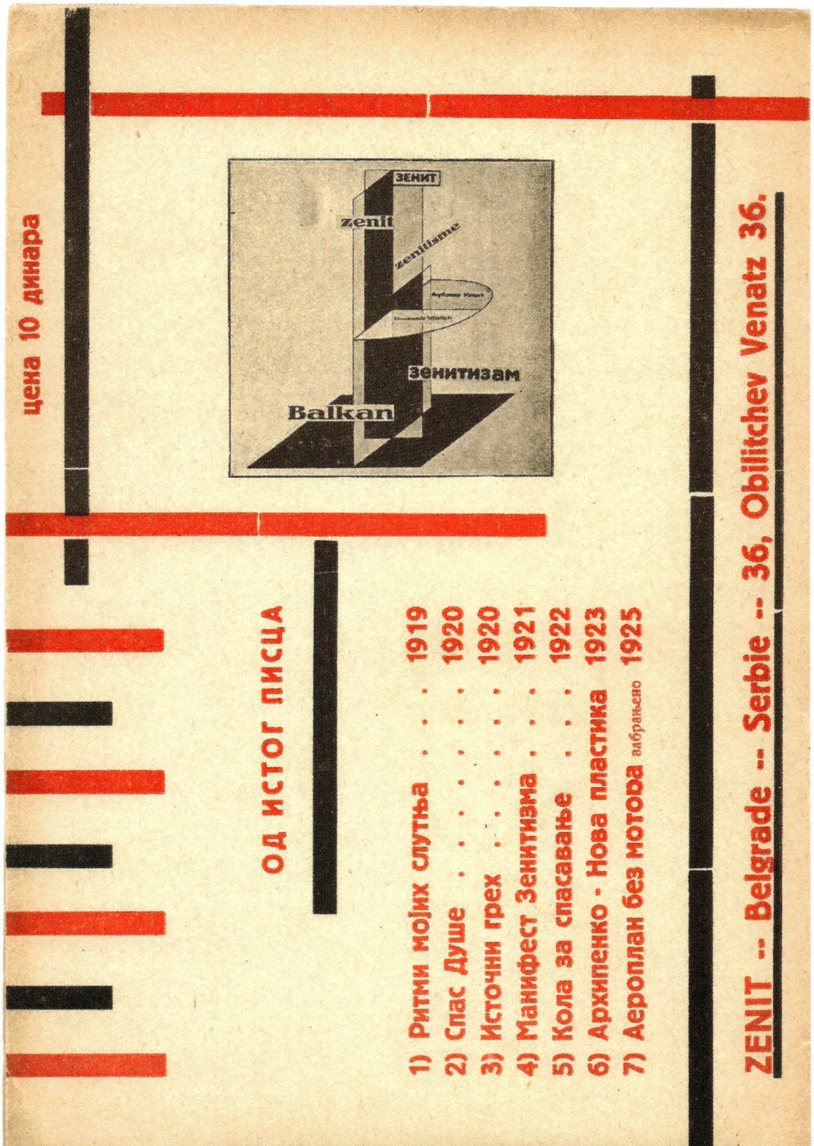

2.10. Lj. Micić, *Antievropa* [Anti-Europe], Zenit Edition, no. 9, Belgrade, Serbia, 1926. Back cover. Courtesy of Gallery RIMA, Kragujevac, Serbia.

Typogram

Ljubomir Micić

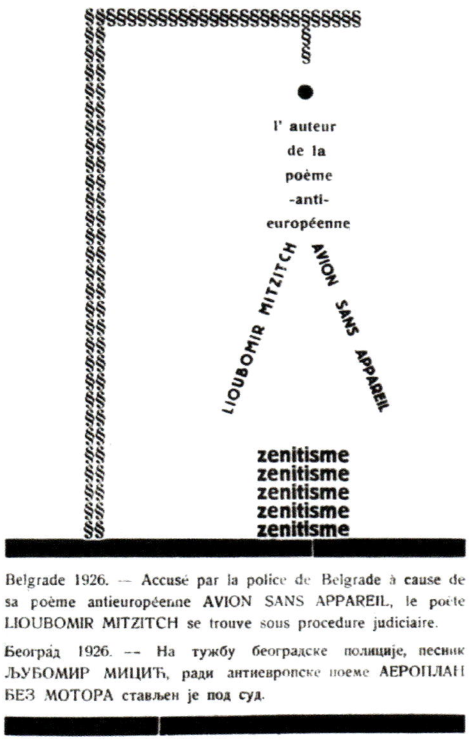

Belgrade, 1926.—At the accusation of the Belgrade police, the poet LJUBOMIR MIĆIĆ was put on trial for the anti-European poem AIRPLANE WITHOUT AN ENGINE.

Translated by *Aleksandar Bošković*

Zenithism Through the Prism of Marxism[1]

Dr. M. Rasinov (Ljubomir Micić)
from *Zenit*, no. 43 (December 1926)

If we consider the development of art from a Marxist point of view, i.e., its relationship to the social condition as a whole, the reason for zenithism's emergence becomes clear. We can no longer consider it a product of a desire to be modern and "hypermodern" but rather as a spiritual eruption—as a conscious artistic being—created from a mass of successive causes and struggles intertwined in the thick web of the entire post-war twentieth-century condition.

The current state of affairs has needed spirits capable of making an honest synthesis of global events, presenting them in all their nakedness and shining the light of the future into today's dark *chaos*. Such spirits have been necessary—just as honest artist giants are necessary—and they have indeed appeared from all ends of the earth. We needed to make people aware of the truths of today and tomorrow and return honor to twentieth-century man. These spirits have appeared to shine the light of truth and save our honor. What we needed was to regain faith in man—and they have revived it. Zenithism is among these spiritual giants!

Zenithism has been fated to make more enemies than any other artistic movement, and its enemies have come from both camps of today's divided society: as zenithism throws bombs and thunderbolts into one of the enemy camps, the other camp, not yet acquainted with zenithism, denies its revolutionary and proletarian value. The hatred of the bourgeoisie and servile capitalist intellectuals is a laurel wreath for zenithism. It is truly its greatest reward, one that has been particularly hard to earn. However, the lack of interest proletarian fighters show for zenithism is a cause of great pain, even if we bear it proudly. Yet the proletarian camp too has extended greetings of friendship and understanding—if not the camp in our own nation, then those in other countries (and zenithists do not care for nations). We could mention a number of such greetings—for example, several articles in the Czech newspaper *Rudé právo* and an invitation from Moscow to participate in the International Exhibition of Revolutionary Art to be hosted by the Academy of Arts and Sciences this year.

What is zenithism? Zenithism is a son of Marxism. The blood of Marxism flows in zenithism's veins. Because all knowledge and ideals that the science of Marxism preaches—such as sociology—are the same as zenithism both preaches and revives in its sphere of art. Zenithism's mottoes are the same as Marxist mottoes:

Down with today's tyranny Down with the exploitation of man by man Down with country borders	**DOWN WITH EUROPE!**
Greetings to all workers of the world Revolution is our poem Long live a new liberated society Long live the new man	**LONG LIVE BARBARIANS!**

However, it is unfortunate that certain Marxists understand mottoes such as "Down with Europe" and "Long Live Barbarians" quite literally and thus give them a non-Marxist meaning.

What sort of Europe are we talking about and who are these Barbarians?

Europe is a synonym for greedy Western capitalism and imperialism (including America) resulting in the stinking collapse of mankind, a collapse that reeks so horribly that it threatens to smother everyone—those who have created this paradox, who have killed man in man, who have . . .

Barbarians are the entire world proletariat. Barbarians are the idea of total proletarian strength, which has the power of volcanic lava about to explode. Barbarians are crude and powerful natural elements still unspoiled by bourgeois emancipation. Barbarians are "Moscow vs. Paris"—"East vs. West"—as certain proletarian and non-proletarian journals in other countries have rightfully noted. Barbarians are Micić's barbarogenius—the "sum total of the eternal crude forces rejuvenating mankind," as Branko Ve Poljanski puts it in his book *Topsy-Turvy*. The barbarogenius is the fighting proletarian, the only one who can make the appearance of the new man possible.

That is the point of the balkanization of Europe, since the "balkanization of Europe" also means the "barbarization of Europe" in the above meaning. Finally, the expression is colored by its faith in the special talents of the Asiatic race and of its own Balkan race, which has, of all races, been the least successful in unleashing its vital forces on European civilization. Therefore, it is not at all like Tolstoy's struggle of primitivism against culture; it is the struggle of a powerful proletarian fighter against a pale bourgeois civilization, a fighter who will bring about a new culture with his crude and healthy elements of gigantic force.

Naturally, the zenithist movement had to go through a period of factionalization in its beginnings. It has had its fill of pseudo-zenithists who, naturally, were eventually unable to follow the zenithist path. After all, zenithist thunderbolts had to be hurled over the entire capitalistic and imperialistic literary, cultural, and moral residue; heavy zenithist aircraft had to drop as many as 7 million bombs. And these people were unable to help because they possessed no thunder or lightning, not a single bomb of spirit or an idea.

However, the group that has remained true to zenithism and is headed by Ljubomir Micić, its founder, has in the six years of its existence missed not a single major event of interest to the world's proletariat, nor has it failed to report on the events in its journal *Zenit* or in its books. *Zenit*'s pages glorify the Russian revolution. Lenin's death was very important news to us as was the fighting in Morocco and other colonies. Protests to all of Europe, screams of tremendous pain from the large heart of the poet Ljubomir Micić made waves throughout the continent when the revolutionary poet Geo Milev was killed by the bloody hand of the Bulgarian bourgeoisie or the general strike took place in England.

Ljubomir Micić dedicated a poem to the strike in his latest book *Anti-Europe*. The title itself speaks volumes. The poem will kindle love for zenithism in every proletarian fighter's heart. The strike is observed in a literally Marxist manner:

A general strike is but an inflammation of the appendix
Since factory foremen only see green traffic lights

On this night of the first accidents, green lights mean death
And red
Only red lights are the railroad switch toward a new life
a new day
a new mankind

In English ports in the East hungry bayonets shimmer
Guns and rabid cannons grunt
Wounded by the sunstroke of revolution

Oh workers miners sailors
Proletarians and followers of the Balkan blood revenge
We greet you and ask one infantile question
Why are your blisters not diamonds
Or dynamite?

The entire book is a prediction of and strong incitement to a Balkan revolution.

The gravedigger featured in *Topsy-Turvy,* the latest book by the zenithist poet Branko Ve Poljanski—isn't he the same as a hungry proletarian artist dying on a Paris street? Aren't the same millions of starving proletarians dying in all cities, their suffering made so real in his poem that I can feel horror paralyzing my face as I read. "The Laughter of Rifles" from the same book is further proof of the Marxist streak in zenithist writing: it shows the development of the proletariat and the path to social revolution in a completely Marxist way. Many pages of *Zenit* and zenithist books are filled with a feeling of repulsion and disgust for the capitalist organism, for the gnawing cancer that cannot be removed and with great feelings of love for a new mankind. The powerful zenithist throat loudly echoes Marx's words: "Workers of the world, unite!"

Finally, zenithism stands for an already completed revolution in art. The limits of the academic understanding of art have been broken, limits which could not encompass the **free spirit** in post-war twentieth-century social conditions. Ljubomir Micić's book *Rescue Car* conveys zenithist principles of artistic creation. Zenithism enriches artistic development by creating yet another new form. Spiritual revolutions are closely connected to social revolution. Their bond is the place where they influence one another. Scientific and artistic revolts indirectly and psychologically influence people who then become more courageous and gain more confidence for social revolt and transformation. Furthermore—though it is just a detail—the international form of *Zenit* subconsciously influences people's opinions, making them feel that national ideas are truly foolish in this day and age since all people on the globe are really **one nation.**

How long will zenithist art last? Will it remain in the distant future of the new classless society? Undoubtedly, but it will have to perform its great historical duty during the long class struggle. Because zenithism is an art of struggle, just as our age is an age of struggle. Zenithism will be remembered as the great art of its age, but with the arrival of the classless society a more subdued kind of art will appear, the *art of harmony*, since the future will be an age of harmony. That future art will arrive over the zenithist bridge, which will divide it from pre-war art, and it will have zenithist juices in its veins.

November 19, 1926

Translated by *Maja Starčević*

Endnotes

1 Because of this text, *Zenit* was banned in the Kingdom of Serbs, Croats, and Slovenes, which effectively marked the end of zenithism in Serbia.

The First Road of the Barbarogenius: Cinépoetry and the Radio-Film

Introduction

Aleksandar Bošković and Steven Teref

The new media in the "age of technological reproducibility"—newspapers, photography, radio, and film—had an indelible influence on zenithist experimental cross-genre writing.[1] Zenithists reflected the sweeping power of these media by incorporating them into the structure of their literary works and their approach to art. They explored the parallels between radio broadcasting and experimental writing, following the path paved by Marinetti's poetic theory of "the wireless imagination," Apollinaire's celebrations of the Eiffel Tower's status as Europe's most renowned antenna, and Tatlin's design for the *Monument to the Third International* (1919–20) which had a broadcasting station at its apex.[2] In zenithism, as with its forebear futurism, cinema was seen to have a "cosmic dimension" and to be the art of the future particularly on account of its technical and mechanical aspects. Zenithists also

1 See Walter Benjamin's essay "The Work of Art in the Age of Its Technological Reproducibility," in *Selected Writings*, ed. Howard Eiland and Michael W. Jennings, vol. 4 (Cambridge, MA: Harvard University Press, 2003), 251–283.

2 See Filippo Tommaso Marinetti, "Technical Manifesto of Futurist Literature (1912)," in *Futurism: An Anthology*, ed. Lawrence Rainey, Christine Poggi, and Laura Wittman (New Haven: Yale University Press), 119–125.

included photography along with their writings to make their literary works more responsive to an increasingly technological and rapidly changing modern age. Literary structure, typography, and page design played a major role in these publications.

From the outset, zenithism emphasized the importance of film and embraced aspects of the cinematic experience that transcended industrialized cinema—dynamism (movement), simultaneity (montage), and the imaginary (cinematic)—to produce them in writing. Each of the authors of the *Manifesto of Zenithism*—Ljubomir Micić, Yvan Goll, and Boško Tokin—practiced cinépoetry, a hybrid form with roots in the telegraphic writing of Italian futurism and the visual poetry of French cubism and orphism (Guillaume Apollinaire, Blaise Cendrars, Max Jacobs, Pierre Reverdy, Pierre Albert-Birot), which strived to produce cinematic effects in writing: movement and speed, abrupt change of perspective and point of view, rapid succession of poetic images and montage of different sensory experiences, and the use of jarring juxtapositions, paradox, constructive principles, and so on.[3] Branko Ve Poljanski also believed that his epoch could be defined as the era of cinematography. He even predicted the invention of apparatuses such as television and smart phones as the future of cinema. "It won't be a rarity in the future for people to have small cinema devices which will become their only source of entertainment after dinner," Poljanski writes in his essay "Film and the Future of Humankind" ("Film i budućnost čovečanstva," 1921), published in the inaugural issue of the film magazine *Kinofon* which he edited and published in Zagreb.[4]

The writings of early film theorists and poets in French circles—Ricciotto Canudo, Louis Delluc, Abel Gance, Philippe Soupault, Louis Aragon, Jean Cocteau, and Jean Epstein—influenced Tokin and his friend Slavko Vorkapich, who lived in Paris from 1916 to 1920, to

---

3 For useful definitions of cinépoetry, see Jan Röhnert, *Springende Gedanken und flackernde Bilder. Lyrik im Zeitalter der Kinematographie. Blaise Cendrars–John Ashbery–Rolf Dieter Brinkmann* (Göttingen: Wallstein Verlag, 2007); Christophe Wall-Romana, *Cinépoetry: Imaginary Cinemas in French Poetry* (New York: Fordham University Press, 2013).

4 *Kinofon* [Cine-phone], no. 1 (December 15, 1921): 4–5. From its beginning, *Kinofon* propagated American cinema and featured texts by Poljanski and Dragan Aleksić about cinematography around the globe. Poljanski also authored an article on Charlie Chaplin featuring his caricatures; see "Razveseljivač miljuna" [A Cheerleader of Millions], *Kinofon*, no. 2 (January 1, 1922): 2–3. For more, see Dijana Metlić, "Branko Ve Poliansky: Editor of *Kinofon*, The First Independent Southslavic Film Review," in *Sto godina časopisa Zenit 1921–1926–2021 / A Hundred Years of Zenit Magazine*, ed. Bojan Jović and Irina Subotić (Belgrade: Gallery RIMA, Institute for Literature and Arts, 2021), 521–539.

expand their views on film to achieve new, avant-garde approaches.[5] Tokin's essay "Essais d'une estetique cinegraphique" published in *L'Esprit Nouveau* in 1920, offers an apotheosis of *motion/movement* as the new absolute and charts popular concepts of *photogénie* (conceived in the sense Delluc has given it as the hypothetical essence of cinema[6]), *super-art* (influenced by Canudo's definition of film as a bastard, cross-fertilized, synthetic art[7]), and *simultaneity* (which served as an operative term for what would eventually be called *montage*, a concept still in the making at the time). Tokin defined simultaneity as "elements and material for constructing thoughts and emotions" while "developing a visible psychological process in front of us. With different methods of enlarging, superpositions, decoupage, and by putting five or more motifs in one image, it is possible to visually represent our most inner processes."[8] According to film historian Božidar Zečević, in Tokin's understanding of simultaneity one finds the concept of montage as "the most intimate inner movement" and "an inner language syntax," as defined by Sergei Eisenstein and Boris Eikhenbaum, while the

---

5 Slavko Vorkapich (1894–1976) was a Serbian film theorist, painter, film editor, and director. He studied painting in Belgrade, Budapest, and Paris. His love of cinematography took him to New York in 1920, and later to Los Angeles, where he began his career as a filmmaker. His most important experimental film, *The Life and the Death of 9413: A Hollywood Extra*, was shot in 1927. He is best known for his theory of kinaesthesia/synaesthesia, which he explains in his essay "Film as a Visual Language and as a Form of Art." He contributed to the *Manifesto of Zenithism* a portrait of Boško Tokin, made in a mixture of Art Deco and Art Nouveau styles. See Božidar Zečević, *Srpska avangarda i film 1920–1932* (Belgrade: UFUS, 2013), 48; *Boško Tokin: Novinar i pisac. Prvi srpski estetičar, publicista i kritičar filma*, ed. Marko Babac, vol. 1 (Novi Sad: Matica Srpska, 2009), 19–38.

6 Photogénie is one of the more elusive concepts of French film theory; accounts of the term by Louis Delluc and Jean Epstein appear as most important. As Viva Paci notes: "A thin line separates the conception of photogénie in the work of Delluc and Epstein. [. . .] For Delluc, photogénie is the magnification of the beauty already existing in the world [. . .] while for Epstein photogénie is created out of the encounter between the cinema and the world." [Viva Paci, "The Attraction of the Intelligent Eye: Obsessions with the Vision Machine in Early Film Theories," in *The Cinema of Attractions Reloaded*, ed. Wanda Strauven (Amsterdam: Amsterdam University Press, 2006), 135n12.] See also Louis Delluc, *Photogénie* (Paris: de Brunhoff, 1920); Jean Epstein, "On Certain Characteristics of Photogénie," trans. Tom Milne, in *Film Theory: Critical Concepts in Media and Cultural Studies*, ed. Philip Simpson, Andrew Utterson, and Karen J. Shepherdson, vol. 1 (London: Taylor and Francis, 2004), 52–53; Richard Abel, *French Film Theory and Criticism: A History/Anthology 1907–1939*, vol. 1 (Princeton: Princeton University Press, 1993), 115; 107–108.

7 Riccioto Canudo, "The Birth of the Sixth Art," in Abel, *French Film Theory and Criticism*, 58–66.

8 Tokin's essay, published in Serbian in the magazine *Progres* in October 1920, is considered to be the first theoretical writing on film in Serbia and Yugoslavia. See Boško Tokin, "Pokušaj jedne kinematografske estetike," *Progres*, nos. 120–122: 2–3; reprinted in: Zečević, *Srpska avangarda i film*, 260–263.

notion of psychological process developed by "putting five or more motifs in one image" resonates with the intellectual and affective process Eisenstein understood as "polyphony."[9] The French term *découpage* ("grouping of images" by which the author "combines continuity of scenario and selects the length of separate shots, that is, composes the rhythm") that Tokin used in his essay, was later changed to *montage*—the term that has dominated the discourse ever since.[10] More importantly, however, Tokin contributed to establishing cinematography as "an integral part of a new poetic technique,"[11] which is of a constructivist, montage character that enables "to reveal the human soul and to bring humans closer to each other."[12]

Tokin wrote cinépoetry that glorified dynamism (movement, velocity, and energy), Americanism, and the artist lifestyle. His "Cinema Poems" (1924) celebrated the new collectivities that cohered delicately around the urban and bohemian sensibility of rapidly pulsating Parisian life, which Tokin enjoyed and shared with a young generation of Yugoslav expats and friends, artists, and poets.[13] Tokin's "Cinema Poems" promoted Americanism in the same threefold manner as his essay in *L'Esprit Nouveau*. First, he praised Americanism for enabling the creation of "a new man," the best examples of which were film stars.[14] Second,

---

9 Zečević, *Srpska avangarda i film*, 48. See also Sergei Eisenstein, *The Film Sense*, translated and edited by Jay Leyda (San Diego: Harcourt Brace Jovanovich, 1975), 68, 75.

10 Zečević, *Srpska avangarda i film*, 48. On decoupage, see Henri Diamant-Berger, "The Decoupage" (1919), in Abel, *French Film Theory and Criticism*, 185–188.

11 Radovan Vučković, *Poetika srpske avangarde* (Belgrade: Službeni glasnik, 2011), 212. In addition, literary historian Gojko Tešić considers Tokin also the author most responsible for introducing film as a narrative theme into Serbian literature. See Gojko Tešić, "Kontekst za čitanje pripovetke srpskog modernizma i avangarde," *Antologija srpske avangardne književnosti*, ed. G. Tešić (Novi Sad: Bratstvo jedinstvo, 1989), xv.

12 Tokin, "Pokušaj jedne kinematografske estetike," in: Zečević, *Srpska avangarda i film*, 260–263.

13 B. Tokin, "Kinematografske pesme," in *Crno na belo* [almanac], edited by Monny de Boully (Belgrade, 1924), n.p. In the "Cinema Poems," Tokin lists nicknames of his friends and artists, who formed the kernel of Serbian/Yugoslav avant-garde in the period between 1919 and 1926. Many of them (Rastko Petrović, Stanislav Vinaver, Stanislav Krakov, Miloš Crnjanski, for example) actively published their literary works in early issues of *Zenit*, until they broke with Micić and stopped contributing to his review, announcing their decision publicly and collectively, as Belgrade Literary Community *Alpha*, in the journal *Kritika*, nos. 11–12 (November–December, 1921): n.p.

14 Charlie Chaplin, a "modern Aristophanes, critic of our age" who created a "new type of man"; Douglas Fairbanks, a "self-made man" and an "embodiment of dynamism"; W. S. Hart, known as Rio Jim, a "son of nature, often brutal, but good," an "embodiment of tragic force," and a "man from nowhere." Tokin, "Pokušaj jedne kinematografske estetike," in Zečević, *Srpska avangarda i film*, 262–263.

Tokin recognized in Americanism a new, modern, and dynamic lifestyle, exercised through popular art forms— jazz, film, and modern dance—and their infatuation with rhythm and movement. Third, according to Tokin, film artists such as David W. Griffith, Thomas H. Ince, Charlie Chaplin, William S. Hart, and Douglas Fairbanks, accomplished in cinema that what Walt Whitman did for poetry, and were characterized as "intimate America." The power of cinema is to *be* a life without much effort. Finally, it is the artist lifestyle that has a central importance for Tokin: being always in movement and following the zenithist vertical. The increased motion of real life reveals itself not merely in its counterpart in art, but rather both *the style of life* and *the style of its art* have their source in the same deep root.

Tokin, whose pseudonym was Filmus, published several important texts in *Zenit* as Micić's close associate (until November 1921), and established himself as a pioneer of film theory and criticism in interwar Yugoslavia.[15] In Paris, Tokin met Yvan Goll, a French-German poet who frequented the same artistic circles and practiced the new style of cinépoetry as the aforementioned French poets, and introduced him to the Yugoslav audience in *Zenit.*[16] In the text "European poet Yvan Goll," published in the inaugural issue of *Zenit* (February 1921), Tokin acknowledged the novelty of Goll's *Die Chaplinade, eine Kinodichtung* (The Chaplinade: A Cinépoem, 1920) in its assimilation of cinematic elements into verses: "*Die Chapliniade* opens a new epoch in art: cinematic poetry. The basis of cinematography is MOTION. Motion is the basis of every new art. Only a few saw the new possibilities of the new art. Goll was one of the pioneers."[17] Goll, who in 1918 worked

---

15 See Tokin's texts, "Evropski pesnik Ivan Goll", *Zenit*, no. 1 (February 1921): 5–9; "U atmosferi čudesa" [In the atmosphere of miracles], *Zenit*, no. 3. (April 1921); and reviews "Mierendorff: Haette Ich das Kino," "Kabinet Dr. Caligaria," *Zenit*, no. 4 (May 1921): 13–14. In the inaugural issue of *Zenit*, Tokin emphasized the importance and omnipotence of cinematography: "The cinematograph is capable of uniting the elements of all other arts, it presents the STYLE of its epoch. As Canudo put it [. . .] the cinematograph has already given the world a new artist: the painter-sculptor-architect of light-musician-poet-choreographer of black and white, it has given it the *metteur en scene*." Tokin, "Evropski pesnik Ivan Goll": 8.

16 Jovan Kršić, "Zenitizam," in Jovan Kršić, *Sabrana djela*, (*Književnosti naroda Jugoslavije*), ed. Vojislav Maksimović, vol. 2 (Sarajevo: Svijetlost, 1979), 21–25.

17 Tokin, "Evropski pesnik Ivan Goll": 8, 9. For English translations, see Yvan Goll, "The Chaplinade: A Film Poem," trans. Clinton J. Atkinson and Arthur S. Wensinger, *The Massachusetts Review* 6, no. 3 (Spring–Summer, 1965): 497–514; Yvan Goll, "The Chaplinade: A Film Poem," in *New Directions 39: An International Anthology of Prose and Poetry*, ed. James Laughlin, trans. Frank Jones (New York: New Directions, 1979), 40–50. See also Bojan Jović, "*Zenit*, Cine-Poetry, and Chaplin," in Jović and Subotić, *A Hundred Years of Zenit*, 93–107.

with filmmaker Viking Eggeling on a project of early abstract film he termed *Kinomalerei* (ciné-painting), expressed in his 1920 essay "Das Kinodram" (The Ciné-drama) the conviction that cinema is "the basis of all future art."[18] Published with Fernard Léger's four full-page drawings and the cover design, Goll's *Chaplinade* was subtitled in its French version "poème cinématographique," a subgenre Philippe Soupault first defined in 1918 and which Jean Epstein further articulated in *La Poésie d'aujourd'hui, un nouvel état d'intelligence* (Poetry Today: A New Mindset, 1921) and *Bonjour cinéma* (1921).[19] For Tokin, "*Die Chapliniade* is an epic-drama-cinépoem [epos-drama bioskopska pesma] of our time," since it is written in a dialogic form.[20] Unlike *The Chaplinade*, Goll's zenithist photopoem *Paris brennt: Ein Poem nebst einem Postekartenalbum* (Paris Burns: A Poem with Eight Postcards, 1921) had no dramatic dialogues; instead, it was composed as a fast-moving urban collage-text featuring eight photo-postcards.[21]

Goll published his photopoem *Paris Burns* in Zagreb, as the second book published by Biblioteka Zenit press, developing a poetic form akin to the cinematic genre of "city symphony."[22] Inspired by Apollinaire's poem "Zone," *Paris Burns* describes the experience and exasperated rhythm of modern life of the French metropolis from the early morning to late at night. Similar to Alberto Cavalcanti's film *Rien que les heures* (Nothing But Time, 1926), which featured documentary-style scenes of Paris and its daily life presented in a mixture of rhythmically and associatively edited shots, contemplative panoramas, and cityscapes, in Goll's poem (which is a literary predecessor of Cavalcanti's "city symphony"), Paris becomes "an amalgamation of sights and sounds, slogans, images,

---

18 Yvan Goll, "Das Kinodram," *Die neue Schaubühne* 2, no. 6 (1920): 142. During the course of 1918, Yvan Goll helped Viking Eggeling with preliminary work on the unfinished film project *Horizonal-Vertikales Orchester* (Horizontal-Vertical Orchestra), by cutting geometrical forms and mounting them onto the celluloid support. See Andreas Kramer, "'Basis aller neuen kommenden Kunst ist das Kino': Yvan Goll und das Medium Film," in *Yvan Goll–Claire Goll: Texts and Contexts*, ed. Eric Robertson and Robert Vilain (Amsterdam: Rodopi, 1997), 83–95. Eggeling abandoned this project in 1922 in favor of his abstract avant-grade film *Diagonal-Symphonie* (Diagonal Symphony, 1924).

19 Wall-Romana, *Cinépoetry: Imaginary Cinemas in French Poetry*, 375.

20 Tokin, "Evropski pesnik Ivan Goll": 8.

21 For more on the notion of photopoetry see Jindřich Toman, *Photo/Montage in Print* (Prague: Kant, 2009), 284–311.

22 For more on the city symphony as an experimental film form, see Steven Jacobs, Anthony Kinik, Eva Hielscher, eds., *The City Symphony Phenomenon: Cinema Art, and Urban Modernity Between the Wars* (New York: Routledge, 2019).

impressions and voices, recorded or otherwise conveyed by a mobilized and at times strangely disembodied poet."[23]

Zenithist eclecticism in *Paris Burns* appears as "a sort of postmodernism *avant la letter*"[24] or a new literary "ismensynkretismus,"[25] comprised of elements of literary cubism (orphism), futurism, and expressionism.[26] Featuring apocalyptic motifs of the Eiffel Tower, Goll's text is multisensory, but also multilingual as it incorporates into its collage excerpts from other Paris poems by *Zenit* contributors—Blaise Cendrars, Valentin Parnakh, and Vicente Huidobro—printed in their original French, Russian, and Spanish, respectively. In the section where Mr. Eiffel "hosts the poets of Europe for dinner," all of these excerpts refer to the Eiffel Tower—the modernist beacon that Nicolas Beauduin called a "living machine."[27] Both typographically and "by dint of the fact that the three poet's languages are quoted in the original," writes John J. White in his analysis of Goll's poem, "this collage-passage serves as a 'Steigerung' [heightening] of the poem's general method, with its mixture of registers, juxtaposition of word and image, and rapid shifts in perspective. But the effect is also telegraphic. As a variant on the popular contemporary image of the Tower sending out messages across the globe, the coming-together here of four poets (Goll himself, as well as a French-Swiss, a Russian, and a Chilean) epitomizes the cosmopolitan nature of the French metropolis."[28]

---

23 Andreas Kramer, "Europa minor. Yvan and Claire Goll's Europe," in *Europa! Europa? The Avant-Garde, Modernism and the Fate of a Continent*, ed. Sasha Bru et al. (Berlin: De Gruyter, 2009), 132.

24 John J. White, "Iwan Goll's Reception of Italian Futurism and French Orphism," in *Yvan Goll–Claire Goll: Texts and Contexts*, ed. Eric Robertson and Robert Vilain (Amsterdam: Rodopi, 1997), 26.

25 Johannes Ullmaier, *Yvan Golls Gedicht 'Paris brennt'. Zur Bedeutung von Collage, Montage und Simultanismus als Gestaltungsverfahren der Avantgarde* (Tübingen: Niemeyer, 1995), 94.

26 But also of Dadaism, constructivism in the case of Micić, Mikac, and Poljanski, and surrealism in the case of MID.

27 These poems are: Cendrars' "Tour" (1913), which Goll probably first encountered in *Der Sturm*, no. 4 (November 1913), a part of the poem "Eifeleva Bashnia," (The Eiffel Tower) by the Russian futurist Valentin Parnakh, later published in *Zenit*, no. 11 (February 1922); and an excerpt from Vincente Huidobro's "Ecuatorial" (1918).

28 "A cosmopolitan atmosphere fully reinforced by the facts, Cendrars was by then living in Paris; Huidobro had moved there in 1917, so too had Parnakh. His *Motdinamo/Slovodvig* (from which the poem in question is taken) was published in Paris in 1920, while his *L'Art décoratif théâtral moderne* had appeared there the year before. It was Goll who drew *Zenit*'s attention to Parnakh rather than getting to know of his work via the Slav connection." For White, "the poet *is* the Eiffel Tower, with the construction in this case becoming a metaphor for zenithist Goll himself." White, "Iwan Goll's Reception of Italian Futurism and French Orphism," 32.

In his "The Word as a Beginning," Goll writes that "[t]hrough newspapers, the stock exchange, movies, postcards, we are slowly connected to the millions of events of the earth and the cosmos."[29] *Paris Burns* is composed exactly as a verbal collage: "newspaper headlines nestle alongside advertising slogans, technical abbreviations, bill-poster declarations, religious imagery, and references to contemporary poetry and art."[30] Goll's strange vision of Paris is "essentially a capitalist conglomeration."[31] In it, "[i]mages and snapshots of circulation and disruption, vitality and blockage abound, from the flow of traffic, advertising, and commodities, to more traumatic stoppages through accidents, crowds and more symbolic kinds of upheaval, such as the eponymous burning. Elsewhere, the text symbolically connects Parisian landmarks and squares with other European and world cities."[32] In *Paris Burns*, Goll also built a myth that arose on the basis of the process of collage and montage of elements of dismembered reality, parts of visions and dreams, and in that way formed a hidden plot about the apocalypse.[33] Rather than conventionally illustrated, *Paris Burns* features eight photographic postcards of Paris (view of the Eiffel Tower from the Trocadero, a Ferris wheel, Bal Tabarin, the Arc de Triomphe) and sports (boxing, cycling, running). As mobile reminders of Paris cityscapes and global enticements feeding the reader's imagination to fantasies and marvels, these postcard photos cohabit in the same discursive space with the text and invoke European alongside non-European (cinematic) imaginaries.[34]

Andreas Kramer argues that Goll's *barbarism* is not just of the Balkan or Eastern variety, but of a global kind: *barbarism* as a common culture (as Risto Ratković put it) and a shifting signifier of a more global kind of cultural economy, in which fixity has been replaced by flow and movement. The commonality of that culture is one of perpetual displacement, residing not within a bound geographic space or a fixed cultural time, but in willingness and readiness to unbind and unfix the European chronotope,[35] turning it into a multilingual,

---

29 Yvan Goll, "Reč kao počelo": 5.

30 Eric Robertson, "'Notre oeil quadruple': Visuality and Circularity in Yvan Goll's Poetry," in *Yvan Goll–Claire Goll: Texts and Contexts*, ed. Eric Robertson and Robert Vilain (Amsterdam: Rodopi, 1997), 130.

31 White, "Iwan Goll's Reception of Italian Futurism and French Orphism," 35.

32 Andreas Kramer, "Europa minor. Yvan and Claire Goll's Europe," 132.

33 See Vida Golubović, *Biblioteka časopisa Zenit* (Kragujevac, Belgrade: Gallery RIMA, 2021), 12.

34 The back cover features linocut "A Fragment of Our Sins," by Mikhailo Petrov, already published along with his poem "The Sound of Today" in *Zenit*, no. 6 (July 1921): 10.

35 Chronotope is the term introduced by Russian literary theoretician Mikhail Bakhtin, who took it over from 1920s science to describe the manner in which literature represents time and space. See Mikhail Bakhtin, "Forms of Time and of the Chronotope in the Novel: Notes toward a Historical Poetics," in

cosmopolitan spatio-temporal network for cultural exchange where avant-garde traffic can flow in various directions simultaneously. That is why Goll's *Paris Burns*—with a photograph of the Eiffel Tower on its front cover—opens with a reference to "Cinnabar ship *PARIS*," where the city, its urban landscape, its art and culture have been all metonymically linked to a mythical-cum-heraldic ship (the civic coat-of-arms of Paris). If the ship, according to Michel Foucault, is a key trope of heterotropia—a space temporarily outside social and political power, as Kramer reminds us—then the *barbarism* of the avant-garde also figures as a mobile culture (a space in transition), unbound by prevailing norms, though still intimately linked with the globalizing forces of modernity as registered by Goll's nomadic poet.[36]

Employing techniques of collage and montage, Goll's poem served both as a blueprint and a departure point for subsequent zenithist "iconotexts" that imported tropes from newspapers, photography, radio, and cinema as literary practices and, particularly in the case of Micić, treated words as a visual medium. Several of Micić's texts published in 1922 and 1923 introduced zenithist radio-film and "words in space" as hybrid narrative structures based on ideas of global, cinematic, and journalistic simultaneity.

Announcing the new genre with its subtitle, "A Zenithist Radio-Film in 17 Acts," Micić's "Shimmy in the Latin Quarter Graveyard" ("Šimi na groblju Latinske četvrti: Zenitistički radio-film od 17 sočinenija") challenged both the dominance of European culture and the basic text-creating process. "Shimmy," as a "fashionable dance of African-American provenance that, with jazz, flooded Europe in the 1920s" became a sign of abandonment of traditional Eurocentrism.[37] The *Latin Quarter Graveyard*, on the other hand, was for Micić a metonymy for decadent Europe, emphasizing both the fatigue of traditional European culture and a professed end of the domination of its civilizational values. Finally, Micić's *radio-film* was an innovative genre label with its origin in montage (the main

---

The Dialogic Imagination: Four Essays, ed. Michael Holquist, trans. Caryl Emerson and Michael Holquist (Austin: University of Texas Press, 1990), 84–258.

36 Andreas Kramer, "Europa minor. Yvan and Claire Goll's Europe," 132–133; Michel Foucault, "Of Other Spaces" (1967) in *Diacritics*, no. 16 (Spring 1986): 27.

37 Aleksandar Flaker, *Nomadi ljepote: Intermedijalne studije* (Zagreb: Grafički zavod Hrvatske, 1988), 239. "In Micić's interpretation, it [shimmy] became a synonym for grotesque couples swinging wildly in the dance halls of post-war Europe. In the ninth act of his radio-film, Micić exclaims: 'While Russia starves, Europe shimmies,' thus revealing his love of Eastern Europe and his urge to help the thousands of people going hungry in Russia." Dijana Metlić, "Zenithist Cinema: Influences of Marinetti and Mayakovsky," in *International Yearbook of Futurism Studies*, ed. Günter Berghaus, vol. 9 (Berlin: de Gruyter, 2020), 256.

component of film) and simultaneity (radio: due to the development of technology it enabled revolutionarily reaching distant spaces; film: an accelerated sequence of heterogeneous images from different places on the globe that evoke the simultaneity of events).[38]

"Shimmy in the Latin Quarter Graveyard" is a zenithist exemplar of hybrid writing inspired by radio and newsreel. It is composed, both factually and visually, of seventeen edited fragments that function as "The Latest News" (which is the supra-title of these fragments) all reporting about events taking place on the same day (February 1st), in seventeen different cities worldwide.[39] The intention of such an avant-garde depiction of global simultaneity is explicitly motivated in the introduction, which precedes "The Latest News" and features the initial motif of the elevated radio station positioned *at the top* of Tatlin's *Monument to the Third International,* displaced *above the globe,* suggesting that the total and simultaneous coverage of geographically separated loci around the world is possible. The seventeen news fragments follow, with each fragment titled in a form of quasi-scandalous newspaper headline style, enticing the reader to read the news (concise reporting, reduction of expression, avant-garde provocation, aesthetics of the ugly, paradox, irony) and signed by a leading world avant-gardist who, as a member of a "network" of artist-reporters, sends out to the Tatlin radio-center the latest news about the current political and cultural situation from a specific city across the globe, and functions as a bearer of demands and signs of avant-garde poetics.[40]

Both semantically and structurally, "Shimmy" reflects the new media regime of the 1920s. On a thematic level, it references radio waves, film projection, advertising, along with various motifs of architectural projects, haiku, fashion, as well as popular forms of everyday entertainment: dance, cabaret, and sports. Similar to Goll's *Paris Burns,* Micić's text fuses high and popular culture, merging art with life. In terms of its structure, "Shimmy" is a "cinematic-literary collage."[41] Not only is the simulation of the newsreel film language realized in it, but also the concept of *cinematic simultaneity,* that is, the montage principle of juxtaposing variously marked elements assuming simultaneous events in different parts

---

38 See Lada Grdan, *Zenit i simultanizam* (Belgrade: Službeni glasnik, 2010), 89–90.

39 The choice of the date is deliberate: February 1st marks the anniversary of the inaugural issue of *Zenit.*

40 Tatlin, Mayakovsky, Ehrenburg, Hausmann, Veidt, Chaplin, Marinetti, Yvan and Claire Goll, Teige, Nina-Naj (Anuška Micić), Micić, Mihail S. Petrov, Poljanski, Aleksić. All of them are invited to meet at the First Zenithist Congress, to be held in Rodchenko's *Kiosk* in Moscow, except for Marinetti who is excluded because of his chauvinism and fascistic leanings.

41 Zečević, *Srpska avangarda i film,* 80.

of the world. Micić structured "Shimmy" as a constructivist collage, as if assembling "photo-montages from newspaper clips depicting manifestations of the 'new spirit' around the world," thus accomplishing *journalistic simultaneity.*[42] Ultimately, Micić employed the collage structure of the written text not only "to convey the dynamic nature and the switch-board-like function of the *Monument*," as Pavle Levi put it, but also to activate the reading practice that turns the reader into a switch-board operator.[43]

The so-called *spatialization of time*—the suggestion of events happening simultaneously in different loci that partially cancel temporal continuity and produce spatial parallelism—and *montage*, which overcomes the linearity of time and enables diverse time "shifts" (past reversals, representing reminiscences, equalizing psychic and "real" time), were both made possible by new media and experienced as new spatial-temporal coordinates. "Can it be of little import to the new poets that there exists radio-telegraphy, radio-film, radio-concerts, or radio-press?"—asks Micić rhetorically in his programmatic essay "Radio-film and the Zenithist Vertical of Spirit," published in *Zenit* in 1923. In this essay, which essentially follows the trend of avant-garde manifestos with pronounced imperative demands, Micić articulated a block of statements concerning *cinematic* and *journalistic simultaneity*, rendered so successfully in "Shimmy":

> Just before the beginning of the world war, I was deeply convinced of the superiority of filmic comprehensiveness, as I am convinced today, that new art cannot be created beyond the great foundation of *filmic simultaneity*. That filmic simultaneity means: the coeval, rhythmic concentration of time, space, and various events, regardless of their apparent illogicality. An economy of technical mediums and a wealth of effects.[44]

After stating that film is "the only basic collective expression of modern life" and "the real seed of zenithist poetry," Micić cited the "telegrams from the 28th of February from an American daily" verbatim, as they appeared in a newspaper. These telegrams were not only an "example of filmic journalism and its most obvious simultaneity," but also the

42 Tešić, "Kontekst za čitanje pripovetke srpskog modernizma i avangarde," xv. "The flow of time that the recipient needs to go through some textual material is reduced to a spatial dimension." Grdan, *Zenit i simultanizam*, 90.

43 Pavle Levi, *Cinema by Other Means* (Oxford: Oxford University Press, 2012), 50.

44 See Micić's text "Radio-film and the Zenithist Vertical of Spirit" in this collection.

most representative "example of zenithist reality and modernity," claimed Micić, concluding that "Filmism," with the "rapid-fire" of its simultaneous images, is the basis of zenithist poetry.[45]

These statements attest to the high degree of awareness of avant-garde devices, which actually speaks of zenithism belonging to the so-called *conscious avant-garde*, of consciously projecting an avant-garde manifestation in order to, on the one hand, demonstrate a rational choice of elements from which everyday life, world, and future can be projected, and, on the other, present the diversity of life's phenomena, its chaos, and disparity, but also universality and transnationalism that were best expressed, as in "Shimmy," through the spirit of revolutionary internationalism. Consequently, Micić, unlike Goll, became much closer to a constructivist and leftist ethos, which he gradually appropriated and, after his trip to Germany in summer 1922, increasingly propagated in subsequent works.

Damn Your Hundred Gods (*Stotinu vam bogova*), published in October 1922 as the third Biblioteka Zenit title and the first in the series authored exclusively by Micić, is one of the most radical zenithist publications. The entire print run of Micić's book" was immediately confiscated by the police and banned by the Royal State Attorney's Office due to "severe violations of public morals and insults to the sovereign."[46] In December 1922, Micić published the second, censored version *Rescue Car* (*Kola za spasavanje*), with suprematist-like black and white geometrical blocks printed over the censored verses of the banned first edition, thus accomplishing "a special visual rhythm and dynamic distribution of typography and graphic design" of the printed page.[47] The spaces where the censored text once stood were left empty as a silent yet potent and defiant protest. This anthology features a translation of the first, uncensored edition, while acknowledging in annotations the parts of the original text that were erased or altered in the second edition; it also closely follows the book's original layout in which the notion of space plays an important aesthetic role. The reader will be able to see how Micić's graphic design and its unconventional structure visualizes his "words in space" (printed both in Cyrillic and Latin scripts in the original).

Subtitled "The Zenithist Barbarogenics in 30 Acts," Micić's *Damn Your Hundred Gods* has a tripartite structure: a prologue; a manifesto followed by a short "zenithist

45 Ibid.

46 Vidosava Golubović and Irina Subotić, *Zenit: Internacionalna revija za umetnost i kulturu 1921–1926*, (Belgrade: Narodna biblioteka Srbije, Institut za književnost i umetnost, 2008), 126.

47 Ibid, 72.

demonstration"; and a series of thirty numbered poems.[48] The book is dedicated to Nikola Tesla whom Micić celebrated as a new zenithist man, an "electro-genius," innovator and the inventor of radio—symbol of both zenithist techno-scientific utopianism and the barbarogenius.[49] In the prologue "written by a madman," Micić attacks his critics (calling them "flies"), foreshadowing his later bouts with the academic community for disapproving of Tesla's invention in favor of Marconi's, albeit unaware that the former mostly worked with scalar and not Hertzian waves, as did the latter.[50] This pro-Balkan and anti-European position is underscored by Micić's double call for the destruction of European cities (Paris, Berlin, Monte Carlo, Rome) and a triumphal revolution of Balkan civilization, echoing the program he laid out in "Zenith Manifesto 1922." Similar to Tokin and Goll, Micić declared *cinema* to be the "only collective art," proposing Esperanto plus Chaplin as a formula of the new art.

The manifesto "The Categorical Imperative of the Zenithist School of Poetry" launched anti-academic aesthetic provocations as non-Kantian imperatives and had all the elements of a poetic program.[51] Conceived as a pseudo-scientific sequence of eight "Komitadji exercises," which "can be held simultaneously in Avala—the Himalayas—Mount Vesuvius—Mount Fuji—the Caucasus—the Sierra Nevada—Vladivostok," it featured elements of poetics that both resemble and differ from Goll's program articulated in "The Word as a Beginning." Micić also insisted on the word as the basic unit of the text, association, and

48 The chronology of their creation follows the reverse order: Micić first published his cycle of poems "Words in Space" in *Zenit*, no. 7 (September 1921) and no. 9 (November 1921), which he additionally revised for the book, then the manifesto in *Zenit*, no. 13 (April 1922), and finally the "zenithist demonstration" (first published in German in July 1922) and prologue (October 1922).

49 See "Second Attack of the Barbarians" in *Damn Your Hundred Gods*, and Ljubomir Micić, "On the Electrogenius of Nikola Tesla," *Zenit*, no. 15 (June 1922): 37–38.

50 In the article entitled "Nikola Tesla an 'Engineer,'" published in *Zenit*, no. 40 (April 1926), Micić asserts that Tesla does not deserve the title of engineer, but of great inventor, electro-genius, simultaneously issuing an ironic review of the Nobel Prize and membership in the Academy of Sciences. Micić also reminds his readers that *Zenit* as early as 1922 ("On the Electrogenius of Nikola Tesla") had expressed its opinion and the views of French, English, and American experts on Tesla's significance for modern science. For more on scalar waves see Konstantin Meyl, *Scalar Waves* (Kronach: Indel GmbH, 2003).

51 The manifesto's style is conceived as a speech to "academics" with pseudo-addresses of ironically inverted places of residence: the Serbian Royal Academy is in Zagreb, and the Yugoslav Academy in Belgrade. Anti-academic appellate statements are provocative and become a fundamental thread of the manifesto: they are intended to provoke resistance, rejection, "the astonishment of all citizens" and "the horror" of spinsters, but also "gentlemen poets" and even "Roman Catholic churches" and "Orthodox brothers," because, according to Micić, "Every one of our words has to be like a poisonous injection. (99% cyanide!) It has to invoke: a reaction: protest: uproar." See Flaker, *Nomadi ljepote*, 220–221.

simultaneity. Thus, the zenithist word has to be clear and simple, elemental, and specific; it has to be a fixed, naked, pure word without psychological value, functioning instead as a factor of association: "the association is the essence of the wide and time-oriented concept of zenithist poetry" ("Exercise VII."). Micić's demand for simultaneity and constructivism can be found in the second, fourth, and fifth exercises, while paradox is to be found in the first one.[52] As a school of poetry, zenithism was eager to highlight the simultaneous expression and constructive principle (montage and shock) under the direct influence of radio and cinema: "our time came in a new form with a new soul and with eyes open. Look: film and the radio-telephone!" ("Exercise VIII."). Finally, the "Categorical Imperative" advocates for a destruction of classical poetry and its formal values, insisting on the principle of aesthetic prohibitions: a zenithist poem must not be banal, rhyming, epic, sentimental, etc.

The third part of the book brings a cascade of thirty numbered poems, marked as "acts" or "real-contemporary pictures," functioning as a fast-moving zenithist radio-film. Micić developed his "words in space" as a new artistic practice by following Marinetti's "liberated words" and a telegraphic style of poetry combined with experiments in typography. In the way it transmits the independent poetic word into the plane of space, Micić's poetic cycle resembled Goll's essay "The Word as a Beginning."[53] As his "Categorical Imperative" suggested: "In space, time DOES NOT EXIST (as a restrictive concept!). WORDS IN SPACE in this way nullify the fatal motionlessness of TIME" ("Exercise VI."). Since for Micić, "zenithist poetry has to be [. . .] a real film projection of the times" ("Exercise VI."), its construction follows the intrinsic device of film-montage, juxtaposing elemental but semantically distant words (or phrases) and achieving their successive accumulation and fusion. Consequently, Micić's "verse-like-mottos," as Dijana Metlić put it, "attained a telegraphic speed of movement and were organized according to the law of simultaneity."[54] Micić employed the cinematic technique of sequencing, adding and accumulating heterogeneous

---

52 For Micić, "paradox is an element of zenithist poetry" ("Exercise I"). The basic poetic impulses, the "primary experiences" must be given consequentially, "simultaneously—all at once—fleetingly" ("Exercise II"); "the simultaneous expansion of concomitant and diverse occurrences is the most important element of zenithist poetry" ("Exercise IV"). In addition, "a zenithist poem must be a construction" and the montage of its visual and textual fragments should be "conscious–determined–geometric" ("Exercise IV"); "through zenithist construction one achieves unity and simplicity of every shape in space" ("Exercise V").

53 Ljubomir Micić, "Reči u prostoru," *Zenit*, no. 7 (September 1921): 10; "Reči u prostoru 10–16," *Zenit*, no. 9 (November 1921): 1, 5–7, 11–13.

54 Metlić, "Zenithist Cinema: Influences of Marinetti and Mayakovsky," 246.

statements to suggest the simultaneity of various life phenomena that function as a kind of critique of petty-bourgeois and traditional values that lead life to the absurd.[55]

By simultaneously arranging independent events (acts), according to Vida Golubović, "Micić portrayed the negative aspects of the socio-political and moral reality of his time—'The throngs only kiss justice on movie screens'; 'Capitalists are integral Yugoslavs'; 'Profiteering aristocracy'; 'The dollar is magic'; 'They dance the shimmy on Europe's gold and bones'—to address the poets under the guise of an appeal, demanding that they establish a rebellious, anarchic attitude toward existing phenomena, which would in one way or another lead to a poetic, social, and, finally, cosmic revolution."[56] The diverse and cinematically assembled semantic units critically refer to contemporary social and political events, from the French serial killer Henri Désiré Landru (1869–1922) to both Russian revolutions (1905 and 1917). If the first one is an ironic reference to the barbarism at the root of Western civilization and colonialism ("The new epoch is LANDRU / Oh how marvelous your Latin love is / Import of cultural refuse to the colony of 'savages'"), the second brings Micić closer to Mayakovsky and his poem *Cloud in Trousers*, where the poet, in addressing the street masses, "turns into a leader and commander, shifting the motives of aesthetic rebellion into a direct call to social rebellion and the prophecy of the coming revolution."[57]

In his 1928 essay "Zenithism," Risto Ratković singled out *Damn Your Hundred Gods* and claimed that Micić's movement "breathes a curse on Europe," while it believes in its material civilization: it is not only poetically, but also socially oriented, and programmatically and spatially placed at the "crossroads of East and West"; from the East it received the elementality of the spirit, and from the West the "apparatus against the blindness of Nature."[58] The zenithist view of the world is "parallel to the historical materialism of the West, on the one hand, and the metaphysics of the East, on the other."[59] Ratković concluded that zenithism constitutes its image of the world in "the catachrestic space of the new Balkans," isolated from the Asian and European continents and located in a special, sixth continent.[60] Micić delineated this "catachrestic space of the new Balkans" in geographic, political, social, and artistic terms under the sign of revolt: "Our rebellion is the new humanity" and "Be a rebel / I am your brother."

55 See Zoran Markuš, *Zenitizam* (Belgrade: ID Signature, 2003), 73.

56 Golubović, *Biblioteka časopisa* Zenit, 17.

57 Aleksandar Flaker, *Ruska avangarda* (Zagreb: SN Liber, Globus, 1984), 149.

58 Risto Ratković, *Ćutanje o književnosti* (Belgrade, 1928).

59 Ibid.

60 Golubović and Subotić, *Zenit*, 257–258.

In *Damn Your Hundred Gods,* Micić frequently reacted to social trends through a series of aphoristic remarks, combined with grotesque, futurist visualizations of acceleration and onomatopoeia, insolent sarcasm and extreme irony, "introducing strong, sharp, black-and-white contrasts by means of illogical links and simultaneity of inner and outer life."[61] The reader encounters definite proclamations and negations, wrapped in ideological and artistic *eclecticism*: the Nietzschean-like Barbarogenius as a new Balkan man depicted with Dadaist technique; zenithist ideology that is both pro- and anti-European, congealed into the so-called paradoxical "potential of the modern local."[62] On the whole, the book is abundant in "extra-artistic and non-aesthetic lyricism."[63]

Moreover, Micić's language in this book is "barbarically affective," loaded with warlike rhetoric; it is aggressive, graphically violent and sensationalistic, all under the sign of the radical promotion of what Konstantinović calls "the spirit of aggression."[64] Aimed to shock and provoke, the radicalized poetic discourse is full of paradox and irony, combined with laughter and parody, promoting anti-sentimentalism and non-conformism along with a vehement critique in the sign of barbarity. In his "recognizable strident tone,"[65] Micić called his readers to "turn churches into cinema theaters" and "blow the brains out of smoky skulls," thus bringing his poetic language of "iron lyricism deprived of both sentimentalism and stylization"[66] on par with the assertive prose of his manifestos that Risto Ratković called "the most iron prose in the Serbo-Croatian language."[67]

Along with Goll's *Paris Burns,* Micić's *Damn Your Hundred Gods/Rescue Car* represents an example of zenithist photopoetry, since it features along with the text the photographs of machinery and a film projector, a reproduction of Tatlin's *Monument of the Third International,* as well as illustrations of a flying bird (suggesting an airplane without an engine), an ocean liner, and Malevich's *Black Square.*

---

61 Metlić, "Zenithist Cinema: Influences of Marinetti and Mayakovsky," 246.

62 Miško Šuvaković, "Eklektični avangardizam: Zenit," in *Istorija umetnosti u Srbiji XX vek: radiikalne umetničke prakse,* ed. M. Šuvaković, vol. 1 (Belgrade: Orion art, Katedra za muzikologiju Fakukteta muzičke umetnosti, 2010), 83–100, 87.

63 Ratković, *Ćutanje o književnosti,* 1928.

64 Radomir Konstantinović, "Ko je barbarogenije?" [Who is the barbarogenius?], *Treći program* 1 (Spring 1966): 16, 18.

65 Metlić, "Zenithist Cinema: Influences of Marinetti and Mayakovsky," 246.

66 Radomir Konstantinović, "Četiri pesnika (Sifon–soda–krv Ljubomira Micića)," *Treći program* 4 (Winter 1972): 219.

67 Ratković, *Ćutanje o književnosti,* 1928.

3.1. Tokin & Micić photo, Courtesy of Irina Subotić

Paris Burns

Yvan Goll
[German version] Biblioteka Zenit, October 1921

Translated by *Jed Rasula*

3.2. Y. Goll, *Paris Brennt* [Paris Burns], Biblioteka Zenit, no. 2, Zagreb, Croatia, 1921. Front cover. Courtesy of Gallery RIMA, Kragujevac, Serbia.

for Carl Einstein[1]

Cinnabar ship *PARIS*
Mariner of town hall heraldry and tramways
In the mistral of prisons a swinging signboard

LIBERTÉ ÉGALITÉ FRATERNITÉ

From the steeple masts of St. Sulpice
Angels alight
In invisible lifts
Pianolas sing in the sails
Angelus
5 a.m.
Apocalyptic freight trains
Slowly enter the station in the rain
Bearing the golden oranges of dawn
You catch the first bus
To Châtelet

Already the white buzzards of the press
Squabble over the night carrion
Abridged judgments in three lines
Scriptures for the subway:

> *"A hairdresser*
> *Hangs himself*
> *With wife's hair*
>
> *12 Blacks*
> *On board the* Goethe
> *Shot for blasphemy*

General strike
At the Vatican
Pope has stomachache

A comet
Over New York
Revives three million dead

He loved her
She loved him
Ten years in penitentiary"

But on republican boulevards
Morning cafés blink
Houses with sleepy bags under window-eyes
Thriving businesses
Charming founts in colorful urinals
As though sweet thyme grew there
And the last widows of the night
Draw veils of mist to their breasts

A statue
Is raised in the night
Guillotine on Boulevard Arago
On which a blue blackbird perches
A murderer
Chuckles
Teases his hair
On the front page of the morning papers
In all the milk deliveries
And suburban trains mourn Europe
Already rolling
The golf ball rolls in golden
Sawdust
No: rises
Behind mankind sneaking up
Round
Red
        SUN!
Thou shalt not kill!

But the sun is no death's head
It's a dandelion bloom
It's the hairdo of a typewriter girl
First window in Montmartre
Diamond in my necktie!
In Paris
It's in all the bakeries
Smelling of cornflower fields
Three-kilo
Bread

Behind the bedpost
Good wives tuck away a bottle of spirits
Because the postman will come
Perpetual destiny

But reception rooms are warm and cozy
The dermatologist writes a death certificate
In the green plush of the waiting room
Smiling nuns
Play with tiny red germs
Manicurists
Get a discount
At each bus stop
My great unknown awaits
How much longing the bus conveys!
At first she smiles, and later
You have to dose her heart with raspberry ice-cream

Three hundred times she was called Isabel
But now it's Bad Zuzu
Birdie fallen into a few hotel rooms
Her heart's a puppet
Eyes rolling back when you tilt her
But when she cries
You already see the wrinkled mouth of an old dame
Her eyelids flutter with fear like maple leaves in autumn
Drained of life, fallen to earth
Together we discover nature
Little steamboats cavorting in St. Cloud
Real primroses by the gasworks!
And green moss in the bosom of the ancient goddess
Proves that even the rain has character
But nothing ages as quickly as a morning landscape
All at once the tree is dust
The stream comes back with a dirge
Of mint! We don't have time to be Greek!
Turnabout, globespun

Circuses
Copper Pantheons
With pink garters quickly whipped!
The Zodiac revolves
On the iron fountain of the Eiffel Tower
The drive belt from moon to moon
Spans the planetary velodrome
On a rattling unicycle rides the SUN

Winning the handicap
Noon
ZENITH
Sweating in its yellow sweater
The world race is nothing less
Than motorbikes mounting the Milky Way
And at Longchamp on besotted steeds
The lemon jersey jockeys shout
HURRAH!

The man summons the divine world champion
All the hairdressers of Europe
Plunge their souls in the jackpot

NOON

High tension
700,000 volts
Twirl the nerve battery
The platinum needle of the Eiffel Tower punctures the ulcer of a cloud
Fever
Typhus ward
Blast furnace
Snow train
Incandescence 44 degrees plus or minus
Fir forests burn like paper
Icebergs glide down the equator
Their comet tails curled
Aluminum eagle
Collapsing
Oh the century's going out of its mind
Taking the measure of the gold standard sun
And I fear for my heart
Suddenly going off like a pistol!

But the brickwork
Sphinx
Barks: WORK WORK
In the factories pimped sirens snort
Puddle push cut solder turn dredge plow heat sweep embroider tap lift die
Oh socialist: Sebastian in the burning fiery red
Worked up into a lantern
Hoarse prophet
Pointing to the new Tuileries[2]
Vaillant-Couturier[3]
From Belleville[4] dark clouds amass
Red torches light the prisons

LIBERTÉ ÉGALITÉ FRATERNITÉ

But the sower has put her
Phrygian cap on askew
The pensioners' whores
On all the 2-franc pieces
Dance tangos

Smiling maidens of the Folies-Bergères[5]:
I know what *origan* means
All of Senegal
Then Canada
The dreadnoughts blow into your ports

Your blue-white-red hair
Lights victory torches
All over Europe
Yet I know your modesty, young lady
Alone in a dreary hotel
Haggling over second-hand blouses
And at noon over a low gas flame
Two soft-boiled eggs
Postcards from Nice on the broken mirror

But next to the furnished hotel
Is the fortune teller
Modern Pythias
On a piano stool
Pumped on cheap Ceylon tea
The poor girls buy
The purple Ace of diamondstar
Three nines speedy marriage
Queen of Spades in play
And behind the Japanese screen
The KING OF HEARTS is smoking
Marxland

Oh Place de la Concorde
What does the obelisk
Of wisdom
Reveal?
At the Admiralty
In a moldy office is a painting of Madagascar
Cornflower blue admirals
With goatees
Dish out
With magnetic pencils
Naval ships cruising Gibraltar
Official disembarkation

Alphonso XIII[6] clutches his top hat
Presidents of the Republic in all the windows
But the Crown Prince Hirohito[7]
With a cynical smile
Executes the diplomatic corps

VIVE LA FRANCE!

Accident
Rumors
One-second film
A head
A hat
A head out of fifty thousand heads
In good civil fashion
One head
Falls
Rolls
Oh pitiless car tires
Blood
Stone—oh!
Oh head with paternal beard
Maybe it was Jochanaan[8]
Just risen from the subway
Any head
My head maybe . . .

All the reporters' blue ink fades
The photograph bows down to world history
Rotary machines
Spit out grey reptiles
And in all the news bureaus
Pandora's boxes open up
Over the stock exchanges of London and Brussels
A white
Fleshy
Greasy
Hand
With mother-of-pearl cufflinks
Symbol of cursed creation mounting mounting to a cramp
All the gramophones know the price of Royal Dutch
La Marseillaise

ALLONS ENFANTS DE LA PATRIE

On the boulevards
One recites the litany of the holy numbers of the age:
Oracle
420
606
66
75
The poker of CULTURE!
In Chicago a famous tile falls into the street
In Greenland a seal expires
In Shantung the Finance Minister bursts into song:
I have a crown
On my tooth

I have a hundred shares
In Olympia Mines

I have a family vault
For twenty centuries

I have
I have

Even as the day grows old
On my tooth I've got gold

And he tenders his resignation
Moscow telegraphs Gomorrah:

REVOLUTION!

Workers in blue tramway-tank attack the Louvre
On all the café terraces bloom the May cockades
"Singer sewing machine guns"
Railway workers strike
Express trains pause in the pinewoods
For four days
But radio-telegram bees
Buzz around the Eiffel Tower
From afar the Mont-Blanc station transmits
Diamond signals
"Comrades, get your special edition!"

Ideal of ideals
Boxing bout in Jersey City
The new century's law of the fist
The Butcher's Association sends a delegation over the ocean

Attention! Round one!
Europe shakes hands with Black Zeus
Blue-white-red shorts
The male breast bulges ruddy steel

Morse in a fever
Four fists crank the world's honor
In America time stands still
Munitions factories close up
All over the Atlantic steamers drop anchor
Round four
Mountains roll
Banks robbed
77 suicides
300 coronaries
Knockout!

The STATUE OF LIBERTY grins

In grief a war breaks out
Skeletons beat the drums
The price of sugar goes up
Free burials
From cattle cars beribboned heroes growl
A dried-up heart's pasted into a stamp album
Express trains with coffins
Link Rome to Stockholm

Now for the first time
At an empty café table
A GENIUS discovers
Brotherly love!

Café SOUL center of the world!
Brothers and sisters share cigarettes

CAFÉ DES WESTENS[9] CAFÉ DE LA ROTONDE[10]
CAFÉ TERRASSE[11] CAFÉ PRAGUE CAFÉ STEFANIE[12]
CAFÉ

Swimming in the iced coffees are undiscovered stars
The whirling blades of thinking brains
Plunge deep into placid mirrors
Young poet perishes of skeptical truth
Painters vault on ultramarine balconies into the sky
Political will clenches its head like a fist
Oh epoch of the people!
Fernand Léger's[13] cinnabar dynamo
Bursts the plaster walls
Lipchitz[14] sings new sphinxes
The Louvre-graveyard collapses
Grass grows in the ears of Gothic apostles

Meanwhile
Even the waiters
In tails
Sell contraband
Brotherhood
à 50 centimes

Locomotives
Centaurs
Race gleefully howling along the boulevards
Sea wind and birds of prey on their shaggy chests
But in tender arms
The blue sources of night meadows
Go home lightly bearing
Iron rainbows

Paris
Diamond on Europe's throat
Made iridescent by a million arc- and oil lamps
On the Arc de Triomphe a jazz band plays

Pantheon cymbals
Trocadéro organ
Oh Paris foxtrot!
In the breeze the flute of the Eiffel Tower softly sings

On the first platform of his Tower
Mr. Eiffel, magician in sports cap,
Personally hosts the poets of Europe for dinner
Symphony concert of clouds
Acoustics of the cosmos
And after the third course: lightning-grilled stars
Recite
BLAISE CENDRARS[15]

> O Tour Eiffel
> Feu d'artifice géant de l'Exposition Universelle
> Sur le Gange
> A Bénarès
> Tu te penches, palmier géant
> Et au Pôle-Nord
> Tu resplendis avec toute la magnificence de l'aurore
> boréale de la télégraphie sans fil
> En Europe tu es comme le gibet
> Au coeur de l'Afrique c'est toi qui cours
> Girafe

Tu est tout
Tour
Dieu antique
Bête moderne
Spectre solaire
Sujet de mon poème
Tour
Tour du monde
Tour en mouvement

ВАЛЕНТИНЪ ПАРНАХЪ[16]
Пресс гидравлическiй в ночи меднобетонной
800 тонн
16 рычагов орудуют колонной
И ребр уклон
Скрещенья скрениты и скреб
Тормазов стрѣней и стропил
Скрип крутьев стрѣл решеток ребр
Шмыг рѣзь и грыз когтей и пил
VICENTE HUIDOBRO[17]
Los hombras de manana
Vendran a descrifrar los jeroglificos
Que dejamos ahora
Escritos la reves
Entre los hierros, de la Torre Eiffel

This poetry festival lasted all night
Monsieur Eiffel made a gift to each of three shares in his Company
Patron Prometheus
Paris keeps on burning
The bracelets of the Grand Boulevards were platinum
And the war widow Seine wore her black pearl lanterns
All the jewelers awarded a Nobel Prize

The Opera House
Undermined with Maggi dice
Guarded by ballerinas

Berlitz School: Academy of the Fifth International

At the Musée Grévin Marat[18] asked three francs for an interview
Café de Madrid: congress of travelling piano salesmen
And all the adulterers marry their detective

Oh Queen of Romania sell me your love
I'm called Yvan
Like a good European I'll shoot you tomorrow!
I'll seek my final despair in the cinema

Protected by the Swiss of Notre-Dame
On the posters Charlotte Corday[19]
Laughs at her humanitarian award
And flaming airships
Project the photo of Lenin
Onto Saturn

Stop!
There you are, Violet Zuzu,
Soft blossom on Printemps paper display
Will you sell me a ream for this heavenly poem?
Because the larks died for us
I'll fling rosy bank drafts in the air

Jacob's ladders and elevators
Ascend
In our poor Eden Hotel!
Crazy telephone
Stained menus with funereal borders
And the porter is only an anxious patriarch
Where is Australia?
When do the steamboats leave for Saint-Cloud?[20]
The police drive a sky-blue car
On a distant meadow bobs the wagtail
Freight trains
Alarmed with their cargo of rotting oranges
Tomorrow's sunrise is cancelled

Last
Red light
At the tram stop
My heart
Gives out

What time is it?

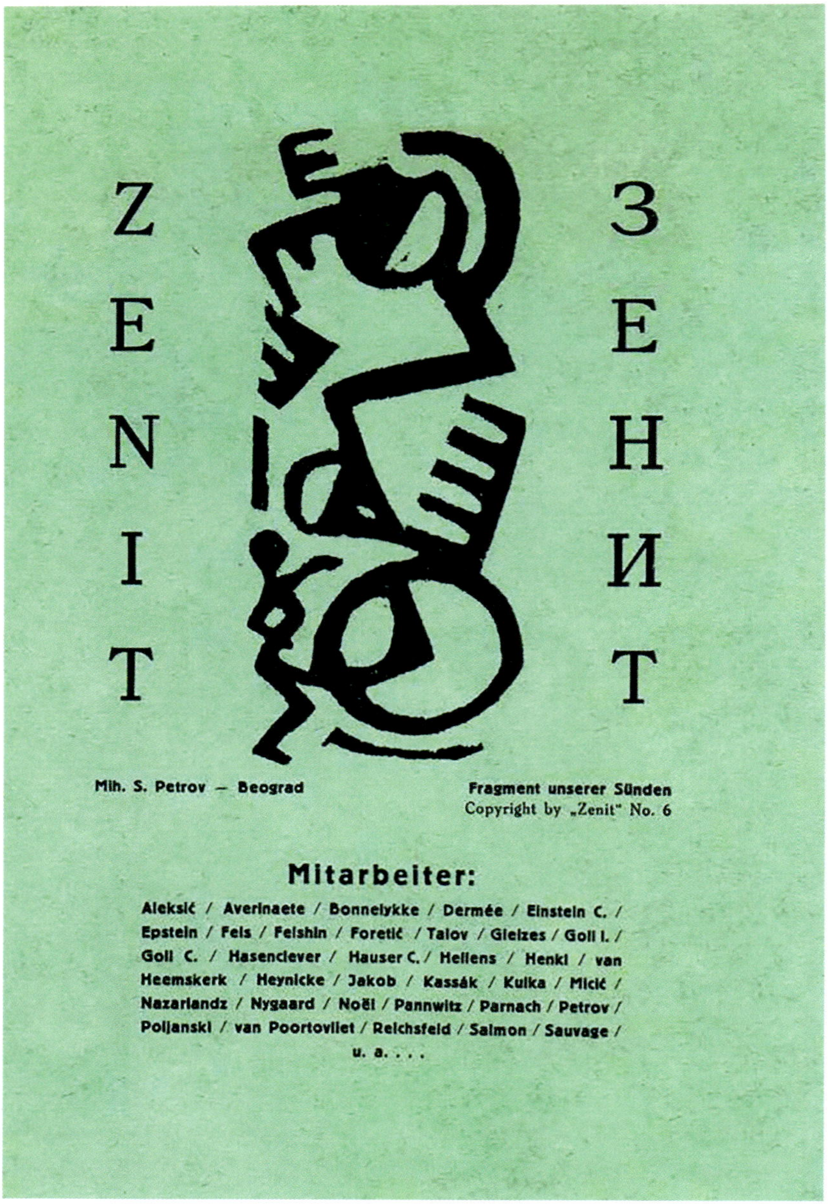

ZENIT

ЗЕНИТ

Mih. S. Petrov – Beograd

Fragment unserer Sünden
Copyright by „Zenit" No. 6

Mitarbeiter:

Aleksić / Averinaete / Bonnelykke / Dermée / Einstein C. / Epstein / Fels / Felshin / Foretić / Talov / Gleizes / Goll I. / Goll C. / Hasenclever / Hauser C. / Hellens / Henkl / van Heemskerk / Heynicke / Jakob / Kassák / Kulka / Micić / Nazarlandz / Nygaard / Noël / Pannwitz / Parnach / Petrov / Poljanski / van Poortovliet / Reichsfeld / Salmon / Sauvage / u. a. . . .

3.3. Y. Goll, *Paris Brennt* [Paris Burns], Biblioteka Zenit, no. 2, Zagreb, Croatia, 1921. Inside back cover. Linocut by Mihailo S. Petrov. Courtesy of Gallery RIMA, Kragujevac, Serbia.

Endnotes

1 Carl Einstein (1885–1940) was an influential German Jewish writer, art historian, anarchist, and critic. He was one of the first critics to appreciate the development of cubism, while his work on African art was regarded as influential on European avant-garde.
2 A royal and imperial palace in Paris on the bank of Seine, burned by the Paris commune in 1871.
3 Paul Vaillant-Couturier (1892–1937) was a French writer and communist, a founding member of the French Communist Party in 1920.
4 A neighborhood of Paris.
5 A cabaret music hall in Paris, established in 1869. The height of its popularity and fame was from 1890s Belle Époque through the 1920s.
6 Alfonso XIII (1886–1941) was the king of Spain until 1931.
7 Prince Hirohito (1901–1989) was the Emperor (Shōwa) of Japan from 1926.
8 Jochanaan is John the Baptist in the Richard Strauss opera Salome. The libretto is Hedwig Lachmann's German translation of the 1891 French play Salomé by Oscar Wilde, edited by composer.
9 A famous coffeehouse in Berlin, operated from 1898 to 1915, and was a meeting place for turn of the century artists.
10 A famous café in Montparnasse in Paris established in 1911 and frequented by avant-garde artists and writers during the interwar period.
11 A well-known café in Zürich and a meeting place of writers and artists.
12 A coffeehouse in Munich which around the 1900s until the 1920s was the leading meeting place for artists.
13 Fernand Léger (1881–1955) was a French painter, sculptor, and filmmaker; in his early works from 1910s and 1920s, he created a personal form of cubism.
14 Jacques Lipchitz (1891–1973) was a cubist sculptor.
15 Blaise Cendrars (1887–1961) was a Swiss-born novelist and poet, of considerable influence in the European avant-garde and modernism.
16 Valentin Parnakh (1891–1951) was a Russian poet, musician, and choreographer, who was a founding father of Soviet jazz.
17 Vicente Huidobro (1893–1948) was a Chilean poet, a promoter of avant-garde literature in Chile and a founder of the literary movement called Creationism.
18 Jean-Paul Marat (1743–1793) was a French political theorist, physician, and scientist. He was a journalist and Jacobin leader during the French Revolution.
19 Charlotte Corday (1768–1793) was a figure of the French Revolution, executed by guillotine for the assassination of Jean-Paul Marat.
20 A Commune in the western suburbs of Paris.

Film and the Future of Humanity

Branko Ve Poljanski
from *Kinofon*, no. 1 (December 1921)

Cinema! Cinema! Cinema!

How strange, magical, and attractive?

Cinema art is loved by the king as well as by his servant. Cinema nowadays is loved by everyone. In big cities, every type of person frequents the movie theater where they typically spend their happiest hours.

Cinema: Dionysian joy!

How did this new century miracle happen? If we look back two and half decades, we'll see a colossal step made by technology in cinema art.

Back then, people considered cinema something almost wretched, and yet today, today when film offers us, in addition to its present technological possibilities, a thousand new possibilities, our present day, so great and entangled, belongs to the **CINEMATOGRAPHER.**

Our tomorrow belongs to the **CINEMATOGRAPHER.**

Already, today one can see that film is becoming an increasingly important factor in society, spreading into all branches of culture, thus becoming the more necessary means.

RUSSIA. Today, in a much-scorned Russia, film plays an enormous role. Bolsheviks are possibly the first to use film to direct propagandistic ends. They projected before a big crowd films in which they divulged to the people the secrets of false religious idols. With such films they also sent their rhetorician and achieved incredible results in propaganda films.[1]

In nearby Czechoslovakia, films have been introduced as an obligatory means of education in universities, especially in clinical studies. They are establishing powerful foundations for a detailed study of cinematography, for which, a Prague shoemaker contributed 800,000 Kčs. (God! Oh my God! If only we had such shoemakers in Yugoslavia!)

Film! Eureka! The most inexhaustible spring for the future cultural mission of humankind.

Film will take the place nowadays held by books, paintings, theaters, newspapers, etc.

Film in the future:

1. Propaganda for the masses.
2. Reproduction of any ideas.
3. Economics.
4. Film scores.
5. Artistic interpretations, etc.

There isn't a thing that this new century miracle can't be applied to—**cinema!**

Future cinema undoubtedly will be even simpler and more developed than today's. Already nowadays we hear news about a phenomenal invention by two Czechoslovakians that film will be made on newspaper stock, i.e., celluloid, so expensive and impractical, it would be discarded, so the film industry would step into a sea of new possibilities. That would be a considerable step into the future of cinematography.

People can expect great entertainment from: **future cinema.**

We are still primitive in many ways, including film.

It won't be a rarity in the future for people to have small cinema devices which will become their only source of entertainment after dinner.

In the future, it won't be a rarity watching the following events:

Cinematic symphony concert.

Cinematic theater.

Cinematic recitation evening.

Cinematic choir concert, etc.

It won't be impossible to explain obscure philosophical systems from books through film projections.

Moreover, I think that some of these things wouldn't be impossible these days (if God gave a goat a long tail!) if we didn't live at this time of stock trading.

Cinema! The future could be called
the cinematographic period!

AMERICA! Whatever Columbus's country is doing today regarding film, versus in Yugoslavia, it is simply fantastic and, because of our laziness, that for us, is a twenty-third century perspective. Let's not forget Denmark, France, Germany, including Scandinavian film culture.

Yugoslavia. Only us Yugoslavs poorly understand the maxim: "slowly but surely," so we have remained, as elsewhere, including in film, far, far behind!

To work! To work! (It's for those who are concerned! But it's not for those who want to make 10 million out of 1.)

No matter how fast we can now be, we'll continue to be too slow, so this proverb doesn't apply to us because it doesn't say—"*too slowly!*"

"*Fast but steady*," exclaims an American. **Eureka!**

CINEMA! CINEMA! CINEMA!

Translated by *Steven Teref* and *Maja Teref*

Endnotes

1 The exhumation of Saint Sergei's remains.

Shimmy in the Latin Quarter Graveyard

A Zenithist Radio-Film in 17 Acts

Ljubomir Micić
from *Zenit,* no. 12 (March 1922)

A field near St. Petersburg. Tatlin's monument reaches up to cloud-bergs. On top is a Radio Center + 400m. Devouring a deluge of impulses from Asia Europe the Balkans America China and Japan. A sharp electricity conductor sports the head of an eternally vital bourgeois. Network: MOSCOW—Petersburg—Tokyo—Peking—Bombay—Constantinople—Alexandria—Belgrade—Zagreb—Milan—Prague—Warsaw—Riga—Berlin—London—New York—PARIS.
Orient airplanes ready to rush to all the continents of the Globe. Radio stations controlled by Zenithists. The Tatlin radio-center receives:

☛ THE LATEST NEWS ☚

I. ELECTRIC CONDUCTOR TO THE LEFT!
Petrograd, February 1st. Use all your strength to pull the nineteen-twenty-first bow! Deadly buzzing heard around the Winter Palace. Turn the electric conductor more to the left! Do not rise when the Marseillaise is playing. The Russian Revolution is old hat to us. Roll up your sleeves! **Man-Machine**: NEW ARCHITECTURE! More to the left! . . .

Vladimir Tatlin

II. CHREZVYCHAIKA[1] ABOLISHED, PEACE CONFERENCE TO BE HELD IN GENOA.

Moscow, February 1st. Yes! To reach the clouds with airplanes, to raise a revolution of all poets, and to find NEW FORMS, the Russian Chrezvychaika has been abolished. All Russian poets are to be futurists. This is what life and honor of Soviet Russia demand in Genoa. Lenin does not ride in motor cars and will not therefore attend the conference. Lunacharsky hates the Imagists since he wears an English suit and French gloves. "To the left! Move the conductor to the left!"

Vladimir Mayakovsky

III. THE MIKADO HAS A GOLDEN BEAK

Tokyo, February 1st. German books printed on Japanese paper are quite affordable.
KOKORO—KOKORO—KOKORO =
HEART. Little Hototogizu's heart was broken because she hasn't seen Ljubomir MICIĆ and his wife's pretty Japanese feet.

"Hito koe wa
Tsuki ga naita ka
Ho-to-to-gi-su"

(Poor lonely voice! Did the moon call? It was only Hototogizu.)

The Mikado has a golden beak. His incisor hurts from pecking on Eastern Siberia. Japanese sun umbrellas are on their way to Paris to protect French geniuses from the sun's Salvarsan.
NEW SPIRIT. Geishas too are on their way as cross-deprived sisters of mercy.
Kamakura. Oi! Mate!

Kyo-To

IV. BLACK GIRLS ARE AS SWEET AS HAWTHORN FRUIT

Peking, February 1st. No! No! We don't care for Europe anymore. The Great Wall of China is secure. Cannons made of Japanese bamboo are spitting fire. Buddha's signs are being erased from foreheads because they resemble crosses. Here too people realize that Jesus Christ plagiarized Indian philosophy. Certain WHITES are being eaten like lamb. Mount Everest is Indochina's great pride. Black girls are as sweet as hawthorn fruit. Only the Himalayas give birth to blue birds, only the Himalayas.

King Ping

V. APPARITIONS AND GHOSTS FEED MY BONES

Bombay, February 1st. I, a descendent of Caligari and Indian fakirs, do not swallow flames, but I do dance to the all-human tragedy on a timely canvas. Apparitions and ghosts feed my bones. HYPNOSIS. Magic. The occult. Film. NEW STYLE. Suggestion—new rhythm. I am a Cesare Sleepwalker. I believe in zenithism. Do not shout or I will fall! I will dance in the moonlight atop the Tatlin monument. To rise and not to fall!

Conrad Veidt

VI. PRUSSIAN OFFICER'S BODY FOUND IN SULTAN MEHMED'S STOMACH

Istambul, February 1st. Pierre Loti is living under harem skirts, his sailor hats hanging from the Hagia Sophia. Newspaper vendors are rabidly growling at capital letters R. F. and shouting "*ZENIT.*" The Dardanelles are vomiting the mines they once devoured as well as torpedoes dating back to the year 5916. So, instead of the shark that bit Lady Morgan's left tit and the back of her right knee under water as she was on her way to help Serbia, my projectionist is now extracting a Prussian officer's body from Sultan Mehmed's stomach. I film the comedy. I took off from London because I was liable to laugh in their faces. Lloyd George has taken it upon himself to save Europe in Genoa. Red seagulls peck.

THE KINGTOWN OF ENGLAND
THE IDLE CLASS

New orientragicomedy of an American zenithist. NEW FILM in 17 acts. Price US$ 1,000,000. The Hagia Sophia leans to the left today.

Charles Chaplin

VII. IMPORT OF SAHARA'S DUST AND EGYPTIAN NIGHT TO THE BALKAN PENINSULA

Alexandria, February 1st. An Egyptian pyramid's Sphynx is not our grief. The zenith is the NEW GOD. My eyes are filled with the Sahara's dust and the Egyptian night, and I'm on my way to the Balkans. Long live zenithism!

Nina-Naj[2]

VIII. THREE SHELL-STRICKEN HATS SINGING

Belgrade, February 1st. The king is getting married. Avala is taking care of the tomb of the "unknown" soldier. The cross is stuck right in his heart. In his heart! Raiders were strictly forbidden to enter Europe lest they disturb the "eternally independent Croatian state." The Vidovdan Constitution does not allow for zenithism since zenithism excludes Prince Marko and the Latins and extols Russia. Moscow is mentioned reluctantly and with a sour face and only in the National Parliament, without the Croat lobby's approval. The Minister's Cabinet forbids the BALKANIZATION OF EUROPE and threatens the death penalty on the same gallows and with the same rope once sullied by the

UNKNOWN BALKAN MAN

on his way to the eternal Albanian Tragedy. The Minister of Education is trying to prevent the creation of a constructive Balkan civilization. "A pearl branch fell from the lilac," as the folk song has it. Get outta here! I am the first zenithist painter. Three shell-struck hats are singing another song: "Take it to the left . . ."

Mih. S. Petrov

IX. SHIMMY IN THE LATIN QUARTER GRAVEYARD

Zagreb, February 1st. Shimmy! Shimmy! Shimmy! An old, wax-and-powder-encrusted corpse reeks. People only in pockets. Poets handcuffed by editorial good opinion. Nude women in champagne glasses. Shimmy! Shimmy! Shimmy! The whole city is shimmied out. All the faces—masks. All the streets—banks. Prince Carnival is always alive. "Ah, Shimmy," central fans chatter through transparent skirt slips. "Oh, Shimmy," tight trousers of black marketeers and speculators croak. "Ooh, Shimmy", is the height of European civilization. (Zagreb is in Europe TOO.) While Russia starves, Europe shimmies. Hey, Balkan man! Spit fire **in their eyes!—Oh, those were the times when you could take a respectful peek under the tails of Austro-Hungarian mares!** Those were the times when we were an **Austro-garage**. I propose to the Yugoslav Academy that the zoological name of the cockroach be changed from

PERIPLANETA ORIENTALIS

to

PERIPLANETA OCCIDENTALIS.

The Latins called the cockroach "eastern" because they hated us.
DAMN IT, GYPSY, PLAY!

Ljubomir Micić

X. ITALIAN CHAUVINISM

Milan, February 1st. Only Italians can be Futurists!

F.T. Marinetti

XI. CZECH CUBISTS STILL IMITATING THE FRENCH

Prague, February 1st. The Žižkov Group is storming St. Wenceslas' monument. Czech Cubists are still imitating the French.

"DEVĚTSIL"

renounces the president of the Czechoslovak Republic because he refuses to listen to Radio Tatlin. ZENITHISM! DANGER—POISON! *Nazdar!*[3]

Karel Teige

XII. ALL THOSE WHO ARE NOT ZENITHISTS TO BE LASSOED

Warsaw, February 1st. An expedition to the NORTH POLE OF THE SPIRIT is underway. We have yet to find a means of destroying all the Earth's idiots. Polish blood is not exactly milk, but it isn't water either. Helen has a Balkan temperament. Do only IDIOTS have blue blood and dance the shimmy? All those who are not zenithists should be lassoed! Hrmph, those silly bastards! Don't they know that all zenithists are geniuses? Lasso evvvverybody!

Valerium Poljanski

XIII. SUSPENSION BRIDGE TO CONNECT VLADIVOSTOK AND ODESSA

Riga, February 1st. Construction! All Brian's dogs cannot fit into the Pasteur Institute. Realization! Erect another thousand cubist sculptures immediately. WE WILL BE VICTORIOUS OVER EUROPE without Genoa's help. We must surpass the new American star—and quickly! Build a suspension bridge to connect Vladivostok and Odessa. Geometry! Central elevation: MOSCOW. Western Europe has gone crazy over Charlie Chaplin, whom they love more than Lenin. *Khorosho!* All cinemas: The Third International! NEW ART: leftist—ours, **zenithist**! Controlled by rebels who love Mother Russia. Old Europe dances the shimmy to the dropping point. As I say, I am the teaching of the Lord: EPPUR SI MUOVE!

Ilya Ehrenburg

XIV. EUCALYPTUS—MENTHOLS WITH BEER AND TOBACCO

Berlin, February 1st. Germans feed on war pâté and museums. (Oh, the red salt of Spartacus!) STINNES is the legal descendent of Kaiser Wilhelm II and is persecuting me, the first Dada-sopher, because I am of Slav origin and an anti-puffkeist. We have erected an anti-Dada cabaret on the heads of Prussian Junkers, and we are spinning a Presentism No. 8998 merry-go-round. Eucalyptus—Menthols with beer and tobacco. Take ten to twelve daily.

Raoul Hausmann

XV. HERERO TRIBE SISTERS

London, February 1st. I couldn't care less about the New World. Come, dear Herero tribe sisters! Suffragettes are the latest TREND in England. Yvan Goll is the greatest poet in Western Europe! Boo! Boo! Boo!

Claire Goll

XVI. FROGS CROAKING CANNOT BE HEARD

New York, February 1st. Tohuvabohu! Dada anonymous. Eight hundred tons every-hourly high-rising. Frog-croaking cannot be heard. (Slavonia, dammit!) Hundreds of hydroplanes salt-sea air-flight height eighty floors. I live in an elevator-mobile high-up-bed. Five hundred automobiles over my head bone-cracking no-mercy. America lock skyscrapers wide-mind SELF-SHIP. (Slavonia, up with your skirt! Lie down, giiiiiiiiirl!) Jazz band zenithist music. Thirty-six soda bottles—Bruit. Proletkult nice pointed shoo shoo shoes Miss Mary has. The man is crazy. Marymerymorymurymyriad.

Dragan Aleksić

XVII. BACKLESS DRESSES AND VERA SHAW SHOES

Paris, February 1st. Hey, you barbarians. Zenith—Box—Match. We suck your PRE-BLOOD. Come. Walk over the height of the sexus civilization in fashionable dance halls. Backless dresses and Vera Shaw shoes are first-class Parisian products. The foxtrot- shimmy is danced here. In the Louvre. PARIS IS BURNING. I travel across the Balkans tomorrow. Hooray! Hooray! Hooray!

Yvan Goll

FIRST ZENITHIST CONGRESS TO BE HELD AT RODCHENKO'S KIOSK
All zenithists except Marinetti are to meet TOMORROW at Rodchenko's Kiosk in Moscow for the First Zenithist Congress. There will be joyful funeral masses for the peace of the dearly departed at the largest graveyard in the Latin Quarter. The incredible Charlie Chaplin and Conrad Veidt will star in the zenithist Radio-film in Seventeen Acts. Entrance free to all under sixteen years of age. Beginning at high noon—not in the morning or in the afternoon. Music by the zenithist BANDERIUM. Tickets available at all zenithist stations on the Globe. One price everywhere: 17 zenithirs. (No other currency accepted!)

Translated by *Maja Starčević*

Endnotes

1 More commonly known as the Cheka.
2 Nina Naj was the pen name of Anuška Micić.
3 *Nazdar* literally means "to the success" in Czech but is one way to say "hi."

Damn Your Hundred Gods

Ljubomir Micić
Biblioteka Zenit, October 1922

Translated by *Suzana Vuljević*

3.4. Lj. Micić, *Stotinu vam bogova* [Damn Your Hundred Gods], Biblioteka Zenit, no. 3, Zagreb October 1922. Front cover. Courtesy of National and University Library in Zagreb, Croatia.

3.5. Lj. Micić, *Kola za spasavanje* [Rescue Car] (second edition), Biblioteka Zenit, no. 3, Zagreb 1922. Front cover. Courtesy of Gallery RIMA, Kragujevac, Serbia.

ЉУБОМИР МИЦИЋ

LJUBOMIR MICIĆ

DamN YOUR Hundred GodS[1]

ZENITHIST BARBAROGENICS IN 30 ACTS

WITH A PROLOGUE WRITTEN BY A MADMAN ■ WITH THE PROJECT OF A HIGHER ZENITHIST SCHOOL ■ WITH A RIOTOUS DEMONSTRATION AND SOME REAL CONTEMPORARY PICTURES

DEDICATED TO **NIKOLA TESLA**

EDITION ZENIT

ZAGREB

BELGRADE

1922

PROLOGUE BY A MADMAN

MADMAN

BEFORE A LEGION OF EXCEPTIONALLY WISE FLIES

My dear and esteemed flies
It's easy to put up with your innocent buzzing
It only happens during the second season of the year
Accept the expression of my blood's
Deepest respect
You have wings

GIVE US MAGNIFICENT WINGS

But how do we protect ourselves from those flies in trousers
For years on end they annoy us with their wisdom
They gorge themselves like swine and move with a monkey's gait
They kiss like mammoths and are named after infectious diseases
With envy they dig through our empty pockets and intestines
They are called people
I ask YOU my honorable flies
Why are dogs better than these people
Why have dogs never committed rapacious murder
Or caused a world war of the dogs
Or suicide
If one can become better just on the example of dogs
I suggest

THAT WE BECOME GOOD DOGS
SO WE CAN BECOME GOOD PEOPLE

The flies lament
Unanimously
That's right

You all say that Chaplin is a circus harlequin
Chaplin is a proletarian-puppet of the movies
The new Shakespeare projected on a screen
Let's be happy

FILM IS THE ONLY COLLECTIVE ART

In celebration of transparent and empty stomachs
Let's sing songs like a film
Let's be poets of all people
With our laughter we wipe away tears and pain
But who
Who are our enemies today
The crawling army of hollow curdled pumpkins
You hate us and spit on us
Tomorrow you'll fancy the zenithists surely
We are the progeny of Karađorđe and the haiduks
We hurl mines at Europe like comets
We will remain rebels
Our country is a volcano
Zenithism is the lava
That's the truth
I am the first victim of its eruption
We have to shower the globe with the fire of electric rain
Ruin Monte Carlo Paris Berlin Rome
Who can deter us from carrying out the zenithist terror
Zenithism is the pilot of vertical flights into the heights
Toward the zenith
For the triumph of panhuman and Balkan civilization
October 15, 1922.

The Categorical Imperative Of the Zenithist School of Poetry

An open lecture of the first zenithist anti-citizen Ljubomir Micić written in blue ink—published in *Zenit* number 15—held at the Serbian Royal Academy of Arts and Sciences in Zagreb—the Yugoslav Academy in Belgrade—at the Mitrovica Prison and at the opening of the European "peace" conference in Geneva—April 10, 1922.

To the melancholy anti-zenithist assembly!

Goatees masterfully paralyze the cultural value of all contemporary, middle-aged poetry with unmediated ease. (How wonderful the aesthetic powers of goatees are!) And now if only goats had a long tail—the goat itself would be in a position to ruin all Western-European poetry in Yugoslavia—in other words Yugoslav antediluvian fossilized poetry.

Since the GOAT does not have a long tail—with our appearance on the first of February in 1921, we threatened to bring about a catastrophic earthquake and stoked horror in every citizen. We had already incited "terror" among the spinsters by 1922 according to the Gregorian calendar. Without prior permission from the old white-bearded spirit, we created the first independent and collective arts movement in the Balkans:

(ZENITHISM)

the newest Balkan type of constructive creation

We are international poets and we respect the Balkan race! We are in awe of the awakened **BARBAROGENIUS**—since absolute creators are always brilliant. Only mothers are destined to give birth.

We have created a NEW ZENTHIST POETRY as an expression of the times and the era of the most brilliant paradox.

Whoever among you is not meant to and does not understand the great time-bound meaning of the paradox cannot "understand" the so-called "crazy" and "paranoid" zenithist poetry. That person cannot even be a student of the first zenithist school that I am opening here on the ruins of PAPER TOWERS as an aware, spat-upon victor.

With the assistance of radiotelegraphic apparatuses, exercises can be held simultaneously in Avala—the Himalayas—Mount Vesuvius—Mount Fuji—the Caucasus—the Sierra Nevada—Vladivostok. Through empiricism and comparison, my dear anti-zenithist citizens and academics, we must carry out a deadly exodus—reckless operations, and the following acrobatic guerrilla exercises:

Exercise I.

During an EARTHQUAKE one should remain calm and be ruthlessly logical. (To become logical is the most difficult prospect!) Stereotypes make moving man's physical body unnecessary. (Hamlet's gravediggers will take care of that!)

Everything is happening to you all and against your will. Be still and unaffected like Buddha. Lie down on your belly buttons if your midwives have not cut them out entirely. Sense the clarity of cognition

PARADOX IS THE GENERAL CONDITION OF EXISTENCE
PARADOX IS AN ELEMENT OF ZENITHIST POETRY

Exercise II.

During a period of STILLNESS (nothing is as dull and putrid as the stale brain matter in your pumpkin heads!) when your own wife asks you for a divorce so that she can marry her mother and dance the last dance of fashionable European culture—the shimmy (mister minister of law which is that § in the civil code?) go see the streets of dirty cities for yourselves or go through the bloodied, plowed fields of our land littered with skeletons and then THINK NOTHING of life!
Express LIFE like a poet (life as a physical—metaphysical—cosmic—metacosmic—magnetic—metamagnetic pulse of the times: **zenithosophy**)
Express the EXPANSION of life without recourse to the logic of any single event. The expansion must be expressed: **simultaneously—all at once—fleetingly**. In any given moment an infinite number of varied illogical occurrences (acts) take place independent of one another. Example:

Russian man dies of hunger
Professor rapes his student out of joy for her having mastered logic
Lenin's death in the newspapers
Charlie Chaplin riding a donkey
Import of luxury clothing prohibited

THE SIMULTANEOUS EXPANSION OF CONCOMITANT AND DIVERSE OCCURRENCES IS THE MOST IMPORTANT ELEMENT OF ZENITHIST POETRY

Exercise III.

Fill your own SPINE with gunpowder! Light up your obsolete CANNON with a spark of the ecrasite brain: you will leap elegantly to the heights like Anna Pavlova or Nijinsky or take suspended tonal leaps as Igor Stravinsky in Petrushka. If all the heritage the Western-European HARLOT infected you with dies out—we will seek a state monopoly for our poisonous medicine and will proclaim the experiment with your spine a national holiday (An absolute necessity for the purification and affirmation of our racial persona.) Above all, we have to stay alive in the interest of our shared nation and humanity. Only then will we be able to admit your "test of maturity" as valid. In this way everyone suddenly becomes the chosen:

Free Zenithist Anti-Citizen

from whom is further sought:
a) a report on "anti-cultural" and anti-European behavior (A consideration of thought and works has to be included!)
b) a report on the rebellious capacity of action ("common sense" is damaging to the new artistic creation!)

c) a report on boundless vengeful hatred culminating in the destruction of the entire old pseudo-culture of the poetry of "feeling"—"emotion"—"beauty" (The PAPER TOWER has to be burned down mercilessly!)
d) a report on meta-sexual purity and the health of radiomotor nerves. (The semen must be of pure unadulterated blood.)
e) a report on the anti-political virtue that conditions the purity of an individual of our kind—its elevation above the narrow-minded nationalism of small nations (The politics of nationalism: an inferior toad among tree-frogs!)
f) a report on the boldness and resolve that gives way to scandalous savagery—

! For the Balkanization of Europe !

(Komitadjism or Balkanism is necessary for the creation of a new civilization!)
Mister president do not ring the bell so furiously—you are still not permitted to and cannot get a WORD in because I am its warden and you are just a servant. I will wait for the **RESCUE CAR** to pick up your esteemed friends who have so quickly fainted. Do not forget that I am a **BANOVITE-BALKANITE** like Nikola Tesla. I am not even afraid of the crack of a haiduk's pistol nor of the stench of poisonous gas not to mention your billy-goat bell. Quickly remove the corpses so they do not begin to smell of Latins. Your dear Molière is a real twit. Ah and your imaginary Shakespeare mister Lloyd George! You've driven me to madness you measly, plagiarizing sycophants! Charlie Chaplin ridiculed all of you!

Exercise IV.

Hush! Hands on the bench! In the end, impeccable obedience, honesty and trust is asked of you. The unity of nations is a necessity that must be achieved by force!
Allow me to continue:
The new zenithist poetry is not birthed but created—It is a lie that a poem is birthed into existence!
A ZENITHIST POEM MUST BE A CONSTRUCTION
A zenithist poem emerges through a totally constructive path: conscious—determined—geometric. Architecture can only withstand as many levers as are necessary for its stability!) **The construction of an overriding feeling.** A feeling has no eminent or imperative function. (What business of yours are my feelings?) It is of no one's concern what the poet feels, but what the poem is like and what it thinks. It is up to you all to feel. And that is not our concern. (What is important is that you **must** feel.)
An emotion is only a function of free choice and the poet's attentions. (All apples do not grow on one tree!) Macedonia, the cradle of old Serbian culture, rouses the emotion of hatred in Croats, and in Serbs the emotion of love. What Macedonia feels is secondary to the fact-based unfolding of events.)
Beauty as the banality of the philistine does not belong in the new art. Beauty is a matter of public safety so as not to expose your philistine and bourgeois morality.
ZENITHISM IS THE MOST REBELLIOUS ACT OF THE YOUNG BARBARIAN RACE

Exercise V.

Jump over the Drina and climb to the top of Avala. (An airborne attempt at elasticity!) With one hand grab the star Dinar and with the other the cathedral in Reims. DWELL on Tatlin's Monument and STAND on Morgan Bank in New York. A real SPATIAL experience.

THROUGH ZENITHIST CONSTRUCTION ONE ACHIEVES UNITY AND SIMPLICITY OF EVERY SHAPE IN SPACE

Impossible explosion!

The expansion of 100,000 VOLTS OF TESLA'S TENSION the high point of which is the sensation and POWER that zenithist poetry demands unconditionally. In space, time DOES NOT EXIST (as a restrictive concept!). WORDS IN SPACE in this way nullify the fatal motionlessness of TIME. **A poem cannot be a restriction.** (Poetics are not cosmetics!) **The zenithist poem has to be an expansion beyond dimension.** (It is inaccessible to two-gendered and two-dimensional people!) And how should a zenithist poem not be?

The whole of Yugoslav-European poetry produced from Ireland to Vardar by millions of snot-nosed and infertile poets is a case in point. There are countless abominable models who serve as your holy icons and on whom we spit salt and blood from our lungs. One must learn by heart what a zenithist poem must not be like.

Exercise VI.

A zenithist poem:

1. cannot be banal!—a cow-milking aesthetic is what I have in mind. 2. cannot rhyme!—only parodies should rhyme. 3. cannot be clear-cut!—the demarcation line of the brain is unknown. 4. cannot be lengthy as an epic!—the epic is not energetics. 5. cannot be cloying!—sweetness makes lips stick together. 6. cannot be sentimental!—life is not expressed through sentimentality. 7. cannot be bereft of ideas and cohesive!—conjunctions, ties and garters are what women need for their stockings. 8. cannot be declamatory!—declamations only bring forth acclamations. 9. cannot be cliché!—dictionaries and lexicons frustrate breakthroughs. 10. cannot be symbolic!—a black cat remains a black cat and nothing more.

Zenithist poetry has to be:

A SIMPLE EXPRESSION OF MAN
A DIRECT EXPRESSION OF THE SOUL
A REAL FILM PROJECTION OF THE TIMES
THE PICTURE OF CLARITY

Zenithist poetry must be for the most part substantive, understandable, and compact: a **PHENOMENON. A poem must be a total expression of our era and the totality of life in our times.** The realization of a new style and rhythm is possible only as

Words in space

Exercise VII.

The word: as an important element. The elasticity of words has to be developed to the maximum degree. Word choice has to be as varied as possible. Where Vuk's and the grammatical expression fails, a new word is created, which is the only one that fits. (It is always just one word that is most appropriate!) That is the kind of word the poet is in search of. (The modern detective of new and hidden words.) Apostrophes and metaphors should not exist.

The word as philosophical concept. The determinacy of words has to be fixed. The word cannot be synonymous or have a double meaning. In the zenithist poem a word does not have the superficial meaning and medium of understanding that it does in general speech. (Oh superficiality, our tribal country!) Pure physics—pure metaphysics—pure abstraction. That is why the zenithist poem provokes conflict and misunderstanding, namely due to its simplicity and depth. (They live the paradox just like the parasites on your wretched tongues!)

The word: as meaning. A word need not correspond only to real reality but can have an abstract meaning and vice versa. (Again the paradox of an entirely real meaning.) And in the same way, a larger complex for words that make up a poem:

"In my dreams the dead awaken
Train tickets Vladivostok—Paris
In the dream
Book covers made of white bread"

Real abstraction. Simultaneous expression. Simplicity. Clarity.

The word: as factor of association. The law of insane psychology. The primacy of **the event** and secondary nature of its **psychology**. A word does not have a psychology. The word is pure—absolute. The catastrophe of the hydroplane happens without psychology and logic yet the poet comes "to that" through means of **association**. An association is a powerful means of full zenithist expression in poetry. When I speak about the immortal Lenin I can think not only of the Russian revolution but also of his workers' shirt—Trotsky's electrobus—the Cheka and inflammation of the brain. When I see the great deformer Charlie Chaplin or the great stylist Conrad Veidt I do not think only of the small Jackie Coogan and Caligari but also of the woman at the cinema who burst out laughing like the miracle of Jesus Christ. When I see the marble bank then I also see profiteers grinning from every bar and theater—I see politicians "moralizing" through the keyhole of a huge cash register—I see you provincials, draft animals with long donkey ears.

THE ASSOCIATION IS THE ESSENCE OF THE WIDE AND CONTEMPORARY CONCEPT OF ZENITHIST POETRY.

The word: as idea. Idea as synthesis. **Zenithism has to become a pure synthesis of the new art.** The idea as an ETHICS of the new man (it has no connection with civil and academic morality!) The new ethics of naked man as anti-aesthetics! We unleash cascades of words upon you so that you croak like pike in mid-air! Every one of our words has to be like a poisonous injection. (99% cyanide!) It has to invoke: **a reaction**: protest: **uproar**. A poem must operate with originality. (The potency of independent persons!) We do not go down the pedagogical path. (Pedagogy stunts growth and potency.) The effect we have: poisonous gas mixed with the grotesque.

(The grotesque recovers from sentimentality!) Battle in an open field: being ashamed of your own weakness. (That hurts so much!) Your sneer as a shield for your own nakedness. (That hurts twice as much!) Our undisguised laughter washes over you. (That hurts one hundred times as much!)

A familiarity with the translated words of our ideas strengthens man's power and ethos:
1. his faith in the necessity of anarchism— 2. his interest in the most reckless leap to the heights of the earth (ZENITH OF THE EARTH a pull of 1,000,000 volts!)

The idea of the zenithist poem is PURITY OF SUBJECT. The means we use are secondary. WE could not care less whether our poems offend you and what inferior anti-zenithists think of that (superior types do not exist).

Zenithism is the most powerful means to drown literary weakling-cockroaches—grand mastodons and the mediocre. Therefore: **the social factor!** Pure and distilled alcohol: 100%. **An authentic Balkan product!** It is not a danger to the state! (It is available at any anti-zenithist bookstore for a price of five dinars with a seller's discount of 25%.) Trademark stamp: **BALKAN TROIKA.** Watch out! One-hundred-fold poison! Earth, take cover! Earth!

Exercise VIII.

Finally, dear academics, pull the hair out of your goatees and look me straight in the eye. My eyes are deeper than all the classical philosophies and histories of art. Larger than any political memorandum. In our eyes numerous pigments should burn like the residue of dirty decades. Even the last speck must disappear. A poem has to be pure like the pupil of our eye. Clear like the eyes of traffic lights that signal directions to faraway travelers at night. We do not have time to wander outside our lovers' windows. That era along with its long-haired and drunken poets was overrun by the first car that barreled through our country without license plates under the name of the "devil." But we new poets do not allow any car to run us over. Because when we were very young we moved out of the way and hid under our fragrant hay—, so that after, in our time, we would triumph and do all those "devilish things" with respect to life, man and country. Unfortunately for you, our time came in a **new form** with a **new soul** and with **eyes open.** Look: film and the radio-telephone! The clarity of pictures and distant waves is a merciless slap across your faces. Our poems have the clarity of live pictures and the rhythm of waves from which your donkey heads hurt so much. Your headaches will go away and the new art will no longer be outside of life and the times; your kids, like you, won't find themselves without any direction for the future. For this reason, in the name of the new poets and the new people, today before you I officially open

The zenithist school of poetry
The first free center
For the Balkanization of Europe

Let us, too, have a feast day in this century!

ZENITHISM

SECOND ATTACK OF THE BARBARIANS

(First published in the German language in Munich on July 12, 1922, as a zenithist demonstration in Germany)

There is no more art! There is no more art!

Nikola Tesla triumphed over Michelangelo, Kandinsky, and Picasso.

The Serbian BARBAROGENIUS from the Balkans discovered wireless telegraphy for humanity. Not Marconi!

Radio: the new art. Everything else: a lemonade served over ice.

Airplanes obliterate space. All of the bridges in the sky—are in ruins.

> **“Hurraaah**
> **We will hang your perverse culture**
> **On women’s hats in brothels**
> **At the very moment you are on your knees”**

Electromotor power triumphs over romantic historic adventures and its wartime acrobats.

Museums are preserved for the rats to live in during the time of world revolution.

And art? A contemporary anachronism!

To destroy this century and to create a new era:

LIFE + MAN = THE NEW ART.

Quick get your hands on Tesla's new lightbulbs that emit light without heat.

We need heat for life dynamics—light for the dark catacombs of coagulated brains.

Only leaps into the heights can save you all from decline.

Hurraaah! Hurraaah! Hurraaah!

ZENITH = summit of the most intense tenseness = **ZENITH**

ZENITHISM expansion of the barbarian strength **ZENITHISM**

OF THE NAKED MAN

Yes! For the second time the putrid fruits of European pseudo-culture and civilization must be destroyed.

It is already being done by

THE BARBARIANS OF EUROPE WE THE BARBARIANS OF EUROPE

do it with pleasure.

Machines shred the PAPER TOWERS. They create a new possibility for man's liberation.

Let us too create exactly that kind of art alongside you:

ZENITHISM = the new art without tradition and sentimentality.

ZENTIHISM IS UNSENTIMENTAL

CONSTRUCTIVIST NEW ART

We need ONLY that kind of new ART FOR MAN—FOR LIFE

For that reason, zenithism has to be the blueprint for the new art and its realization.

Zenithism

Construction of the panhuman epoch

Zenithism

which is conceived in the human fratricidal blood and chaos of the proletarian revolution.

Zenithist poets celebrated the glories of zenithism in their best works.

The Balkan RACE ultimately gained its expression and style through zenithism.

Our rebellious spirit gained its form and direction through zenithism.

The aim is ZENITH.

Just listen to how our zenithist neurons sing.

Peace

The beginning

Damn/amn **Y**our/our **H**undred/undred **G**ods/ods

Владимир Татлин — Москва Споменик трећој интернационали

1

Poets
Airplanes circle high above you
Radiotelephones have won against the feeble rhymes
Hey unknown children

IT'S HEALTHY TO DRINK ELECTRIC MILK

Fanatics
Millions of standard-bearers march
Thump—THUMP—Thump—THUMP
Red armored cars charge
MOSCOW → PARIS
Preserve our glory
Sinful sons of a stiff country
Create
Your words are the hollow phrases of the crowds
Cerebral semiautomatic rifles hiss
Rata—tat—tat—tat
North Pole

THUMP—THUMP

TAT—TAT

BLOW THE BRAINS OUT OF SMOKY SKULLS

Curse wildly in space
Bloody rebellion
Why don't you give out the heroic roar

OF THE BARBAROGENIUS

To Roar To Roar To Roar
To Roar To Roar To Roar
To Roar To Roar To Roar

2

Peasants
Raise the STONE OBELISK of the "unknown hero"
From Avala lord over the monuments of the mongrels
Let the obelisk be the Balkan expression of the EASTERNER
The summit of tension at a modest height

SEJ DEN

What are they lying and prattling on about at the rallies
Sokol parade fanfare
Hey gypsies instrument strings of mine
Cymbals
Of a drunken groomsman

DAMN IT GYPSY PLAY

Cymbals

Sparks in the eyes
Sun and rebel's blood in the tendons
Blood-electricity and savage rhythm
runs through the legs
Plaaaay
Let even the skulls shake
OPA PA PA PA PA PA
Zagreb is sad that it is in the Balkans
My little village don't be so proud
Cover yourself with a rag
Far off in India they are laughing at you
Madras and Benares
You European urchins

opa opa goes the dance of my boots

3

Our forests are up in flames
The smoke bites the eyes to the point of tears
Have we any more tears

WHY ARE YOU ALL BLIND

Our tears have seeped through the pores of our brains
Get your sight back
Neurons twitch
Heads hit against the surrounded ramparts
Bombs
Do not want to burst under express trains

Motors provide rescue

Machines provide rescue **NIHILON**

The brakes provide rescue

Electromagnetic nets have caught electric fish
In space
The latest news from America
Radioconcert
Avala
What are those fish with the big red eyes
Fireworks at the amusement park
Absolutely not
Only those in Russia know that
Moscow

WE BUILD THE FACTORY OF SPIRITS

4

Albania is the dead nerve of sorrow
S. C. S.
The ill-fated love of a merchant with swine
In the basement the dead on ice like ice cream
The premium for insured "Balkan" society has been salvaged
A black car is a profiteer's jewelry
A matter of legal social order
Since your wife is yours for a year
The city
A suffocating tomb of wreaths
Banks sprout from a stream of blood
Black banners
The last rebel-king has died
The rusted spurs of Cuban Cossacks clink
Faded red hoods draped over shoulders
Oh dismal forest pluck the Russian balalaika

BE PATIENT MAN

Be a rebel
I am your brother
Let's sink the ships with cannons from Krupp factories
Ground the Western submarines
Film Eastern volcanoes
Russia mother of chaos

Why is **REVOLUTION** our feast day

5

The moon
Midnight's reflector
Shakespeare's contemptible troubadour
Hey moon
Electric bombs descend from darkness
Where do those storms carry Balkan bridges off to
We don't even have roofs anymore
Hordes of degraded people passed through cities
They spit fire from inflamed lungs
They lie in the dust of paper boards and placards

DOWN WITH THE CZAR **LONG LIVE LENIN**

The crowds never return
Death and vengeance stalk Lenin
The East is ablaze in black rebellion
Where did Nirvana get held up
Man is to man no more than a murderer and a killer

Why
The century of blood
Civilization
Slut
Europe
Ossuary

Light fire to

THE PAPER TOWER

Light fire to

BRING AID TO THE HUNGRY IN RUSSIA

6

Lamps lamps
Lamps protrude high against the lunar eclipse
Women roll about in expanded headquarters
Birth is death

BIRTH IS ALWAYS DEATH AND PAIN

We yearn for life
We have triumphed over pain
Girls with the yellow ticket lurk
Destiny in space
Syphilis is the Eastern lust for people
Across the street
In paralysis an unknown man falls apart
Pope Borgia is a big sinner
Nina
Only you
Love of mine

ALLAHU AKBAR

WE HAVE TO BECOME PEOPLE FOR ONCE

Good people good people good people
Smile at my life
My star is being born
Midnight

Through worlds brilliant madmen bark
True brothers
In my dreams the dead awaken
Train tickets Vladivostok—Paris
In a dream
Book covers of white bread
Haiduk's cradle
Is haiduk Peter Čučković still alive
Banovina
In honor of your volcanic sons
TESLA AND MICIĆ
Let the yellow pistols fire
Gunpowder mortar

bang bang bang bang
bang bang bang

OH KRAJINA BLOODY DRESS

bang
bang bang

An explosion
The squeals of fair daughters-in-law
Haiduk gatherings

A drum and pipes
A bachelor
Lovers' cries

Electric stars under the sky
City meteors
Red halos on the asphalt
The 1st of May

COME TONIGHT SWEETHEART

7

oy oy oy
oy oy
oy
oy

From the walls of Merciful Murderers Hospital
From the windows of hearses
The dead men's placards bellow

CALIGARI

Every moment three men in the world die

9

The state lawyer regrets not being a zenithist

"if I were a zenithist
I would convey the speeches of the defense figuratively
as dancers on one hundred legs
whose vibrations serve as a depiction of the dance"

Zenithism is neither a figure nor a dance
Zenithism is a brain with jags
The air is full of poisonous gases
But the factory of rifles and cannons is not yet built

8

OMNIUM OF THE SERBS

Submissive servant
Provincials bow profoundly
A special edition of *Novosti*
A snooty editor bows his head to the ground
Millionnaire excellence

THE CYLINDER

**PASS
ES**

Passes

Have you guys found

THE DEAD CHILD IN THE BOX OF CHICORY

Clean out your pockets and under your toenails
Since you don't have time to cleanse your soul

SYPHILISCULTURE

No

Assassinations aren't metacosmic actions
A death sentence

TO THE LEFT IN THE CORNER THE EXECUTIONER WAITS FOR THE ORDER

The gallows
The courtroom is full of bayonets
Countries of cannons
What would be the need for cylindric cannons without countries

O Venice
We travel in the ruin of the abyss
Canyons in the sky

ZENITH

10

On your streets dead bodies lie
Seven suntanned dead bodies

It's a shame to die from sun-drenched milk

11

Our brothers wander through faraway lands
Unknown suburbs
Underground railways
Green lights flicker in tunnels
We are in search of the star of a genius

MY COUNTRY

Rise up

How happy my mother would have been
Had she lived facing the street
Only two large street-facing windows
Four drapes
Just a little humane love
People's drama
Mothers

12

Traffic lights change directions

Where are those intersections with the wooden hands
O stupid crucifixion
Crosses have to be removed from church spires
Bend the lightning rods under the bourgeois throat
My left heel is covered in blisters
Church boats sail through god
A flood in the inflamed intestines
Today a green tie sings to me
Tomorrow
Tomorrow we'll wear Tesla's lightbulbs around our necks
Airplane wings jutting from our shoulders
Our repentance will glisten in the heights
And from there we'll fall to embrace the earth
Our pilots are no better than the wolves on earth
And what about you shrines of sweaty erotica
Full of gold wine women and ditties
Are you god's emissaries
Slapping the backsides of other men's wives
For the forgiveness of sins
The Vatican
Millions
Fall

13

Hand over the sooty lenses now
The solar eclipse can be seen more clearly
Look
Astrakhan is a Russian graveyard without crosses
Bones and cannons like curses over the graves

VOLGA **VOLGA**

DEAR MOTHER

Our fingers are sooty from coal
Let's take leave of the grave
How many of you rape our brains
Eclipse of the century
My soul is an airplane
My heart a radiotelephone
My urn will skin the clouds
Oh suck the electric blood from the apex of the zenitheum

14

Pulley saws cut through the insides of muddy streets
The inquisition
Girls with bared knees
Throw wooden logs into basements
Free love
His Highness

MONEY

Evil are people with ruddy cheeks
Eyes always peek under women's skirts
Taxi carriages wait in front of villains' houses
In autumn our bones creak
Frontal bones
Brain in the airplane

THE BARBAROGENIUS BREAKS THE FRONTAL BONE OF WESTERN MAMMOTHS

Bullfights in Paris and London
People on Mars and the Sun
Women on Alpha and the Moon
Still no real men on our planet
Winds over the Volga howl with hunger
Russian vodka green and sweet
Deadly
Out of love the Russian Danton will be hanged
Crowds applaud

15

HUNDRED

DAMN YOUR

GODS

Black Sea ships
Drums firing up
Sailors' rebellion
Red sirens
Odessa—Gibraltar
A change of direction
on every compass
Magnetic needles
quiver restlessly
Electropull: EUROPE
Revolution in Portugal and India
On your feet
HEROISM OF THE SPIRIT
Orientplane
Man

16

MORI MOMO

Dream
A dream
I dreamt at the end of September
Higher mathematics is shallow
Like dance and soccer
Like women with Spanish combs in their hair
Bullfighters hate combs

LOVE IS A BULL

SO YOU KNOW

Bulls are the proud rulers of Spain
Red cloth against black
Carmen kneels below the navel
The stands
The Sierra Nevada laments
The death of Espada Granera
Madrid

17

Women
Read the Egyptian dream interpretation book in the morning
They want to find out
What cute little fish represent
When they graze white-haired legs in a dream
Night of love
Of an enigma
Opium
Cairo

DEAR MOTHER BUY ME SILK

On the 16th of October the moon died of Spanish fever
The Romantics are in deep mourning
The death of inspiration
Yugoslavia

18

Town or village
The flag makes no difference
Capitalists are integral Yugoslavs
Who care about others
Profiteering aristocracy
The heads of the wealthy
Round greasy cheeks
Repulsive bastard
Currency exchange Maulner 400 million
Mustache like Charlot
Pince-nez like gentility
7% interest
Their wives only eat chocolate
Ride only in airplanes
Always dream of City-Bar

oy

oy

BARK ALREADY

BITCH OF SLUNJ

Hello Poljanski
Ben Akiba[2] lied about everything

EVERYTHING IS NEW UNDER THE CAP OF THE SKY

How much cord is needed
For just one person to be born
In our country

oy

19

Film is Esperanto: cinemaism
Convert churches into cinemas
Children of another time faint

Not in front
of the church
Not in front
of the king
Not in front
of god

IN FRONT OF CINEMA DOORS

CIRCUS OF EUROPE

the fourth epoch begins

Monkeys are saving people

They became human beings
Monkeys they remain
And Darwin's theory
HAD MAN COME FROM MONKEYS
MONKEYS WOULDN'T EXIST
The crowds thunder in the ardor of darkness

THE THRONGS ONLY KISS JUSTICE ON MOVIE SCREENS

SENSATION UPON SENSATIONS
Brought back by popular **demand**

20

The sun is a murderer
Old worlds grunt under our heels
Under the weight of suntanned dead bodies

PEOPLE ARE MURDERERS

Hurray **Hurray** **Hurray**

We will hang your perverse culture
On women's hats in brothels
At the very moment when you are
in the crawler's position
And laugh: ha ha ha
Hurray
Large boats sink

CUNARD LINE

Europe—America in 6 days
Healthy young men sing crude Balkan arias
The earth burns under the feet of flaming forests
ATLANTIS
The city rests on the bones of sharks and corals
Countless drowning men grasp for
the golden straw of America

THE DOLLAR IS MAGIC

They shimmy on Europe's gold and bones
Fire
Always a few victims

MEN DIED
THREE
MARO
EYES
FOR YOUR

Our oak hangers are solid
Hello hurry up

RESCUE CAR

Wagons
Why are your joints black
The steam that shoots from the top of locomotives
Is white like silver
Goodness, how could that be
People and cattle trek through your intestines
Railway men live there
Our breath is invisible like ghosts
Maybe that's why people don't have a conscience
Or maybe because their joints are white
They don't rub themselves with black wheel grease

HAVE DINNER THEN SLEEP

MIRIANA YOU HAVE AUBURN HAIR

22

Just like that woman
Now drive faster for Saint Ilija's sake
Away with you idiotic serenity in the first plane of symmetry
I want to travel vertically to the earth's core
I am a tireless zenithist traveler
I am taking the Balkan hero-bears around the world
Yugoslav kids are laughing

Let's go Let's go
Let's go Let's go **Ljubomir**

21 I drink black coffee like a Turk
Why not
We smoke Macedonian cigars after the explosion in Bitola
We are only a few centuries young

OH MY UNFAITHFUL YOUTH

Kosovo is dead from the opium of holiday feasts 23
The Russian revolution forever the monument of our century
And we
It was just yesterday that our heads bobbed wondrously
On stakes and Turkish daggers
Poincaré adores the sadism of Kemal Pasha

LET'S GO TURKS FRANCE IS CALLING

Farewell my beautiful procuress
Our Muslim women feel sorry for us because we're not Turks
But we're good EUROPEAN BARBARIANS

Yes we are   Yes we are
Yes we are   Yes we are

WHOEVER SWALLOWS

Czar Nicholas 24
The words "hungry revolution" are written on old mummies

WHOEVER SWALLOWS THE ROYAL CROWN
WILL GET AN INFECTION OF THE APPENDIX
WHOEVER WAS SWALLOWED BY THE ROYAL CROWN
HAS TO BE BURNED

Rasputin surely didn't know higher mathematics
(Ladies of the court are numb to the saints' pinches)
Nor the millions of new children
Singing and marching to the music of the revolution
No way
The people will no longer tolerate being raped
Like a girl of nine years old
On Little Kalemegdan

Czar Nicholas issued a manifesto

Freedom to the dead, the living under arrest

25

Here
We too wear our derby hats

Tip Top Tip Top

Promenading with genteel pride through Paris and London
Heads held high
WE HOLD YOUR **HEART** IN OUR PALMS

Go ahead and devour it
We always end up alive
There are even plenty of us in New York, Geneva, and Tokyo
We are still waiting on Moscow to open
Until next time
Is it not enough that we stroll about in English shoes
We are familiar with the acrobatics of the airplane
Deadly circus jump
We play soccer and shimmy like pros
Metropolitan cities are ranked based on their bars

The new epoch is LANDRU[3]

Oh how marvelous your Latin love is
Import of cultural refuse to the colony of "savages"

We had everything that you have before you had it
Oh
I can only spare 10 dinars for the hungry in Russia
And you
Oh if only you all could greedily slurp up Russian petrol

26

DON'T YOU GO COMPLAINING

FOR YOUR OLD MOTHER

Why is it that I feel my stomach oxidizing at dawn
Politics and newspapers are the same as yesterday:
A Spanish ceremony in the castle
Lenin has died
The great work of madam Bessarabo
Zenithism is for the madhouse 10,000.000
For the unfreedom of the press
The marriage ceremony of Pašić and Pribičević[4]
Around the world alcoholic intestines are singing

BEAUTIFUL HOMELAND OF OURS

My head doesn't hurt since I don't watch for pickpockets
I don't worry about those dinars I used to have

GOD WATCHES OVER SERBIA

But never over the Serbs
Good day mister national minister
Will there be war with Allah

Your knowledge of diplomacy is funny to us
You burp crude paragraphs of the Versailles Treaty
Why the revision to the Vidovdan constitution

WHAT'S ON PAPER IS NOT LIFE

What do you know besides that
Go to hell: Dostoevsky is a writer
Tesla: an ordinary electromechanic
You may have heard of Rodin and Meštrović

Small notice:
Ivan Meštrović—self-portrait No. 1 Vienna.
Price 50,000 Dinars.
Inquire atArt gallery 54.

BARE STONE

You don't even know about Malevich or Picasso
Mićić
Mayakovsky
Marinetti

HARLEQUINS

?
!

What is it to kill: political realism
Declare wars: political impressionism
Sever diplomatic relations: political dadaism
Expressionism
Codex Justinianus
All of that is the irritating **PANEUROPEAN PLAGIARISM**

You were delegates of peace and love in Geneva
You brought ruin to French power interests

SLAVISH WIT IN RUSSIA'S WAITING ROOM

Laughter is the great truth

ALL TRUTHS ARE SMALL

My corns burn from English-made shoes

We are so tragic in bathrooms

And bedrooms
In the morning
My wife ate a heart of lettuce
Unstitch the linen of new shirts
The kiss of love
In Serbian a rhyme is a found **phrase** in an aunt's **maze**[5]
Which is to say that it's always the same everywhere
I swear it's more comfortable to walk in komitadji sandals
Hip Hip Hurray

FLINTLOCK

Hip Hip Hurray

29

Hey sad Serb
Is a swan roast sweeter
Than a swan's song is beautiful
Ox roasted on a spit
One hundred pails of wine

VICTORIA A LA DAUMONT

Young Karađorđe
Poets were once kings
Today madmen ride in rescue cars
Carting off wild bears to be ridiculed

HAGIA SOPHIA

If you really insist
I'll believe you lepers
I went mad without the newspaper questionnaire
The fault of the Croatian bloc and aerial republic
The Urals are my friend
Avala my sister
The madman came up with his own diagnosis

SMALL CHILDREN SEE SUBJECTS WITHOUT PERSPECTIVE
OLDER CHILDREN SEE PERSPECTIVE WITHOUT SUBJECTS

Who sees well anyway
Don't be afraid friend
Off into the mountains we go
Our laughter is the last cry
Do you kiss me Umoramena
All of you—rebel

Our rebellion is the new humanity

POP GOES THE SOUND OF MY THREE RIFLES

30

Citizens
Turn your **BACK** so I can spit in your **FACE**
HOW AMAZING
WOULD **AN ELEVATORAIRPLANE**
BE
AN ELEVATORAIRPLANE **TO HAVE**
TO GO TO ANOTHER ATMOSPHERE

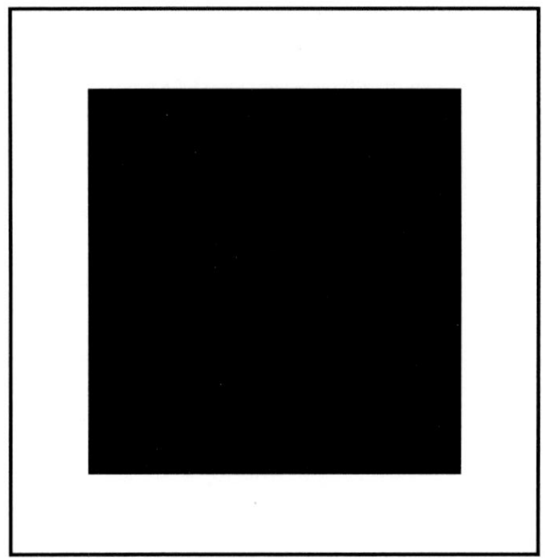

3.6. Lj. Micić, *Stotinu vam bogova* [Damn Your Hundred Gods], Biblioteka Zenit, no. 3, Zagreb 1922. Inside back cover. Courtesy of National and University Library in Zagreb, Croatia.

3.7. Lj. Micić, *Stotinu vam bogova* [Damn Your Hundred Gods], Biblioteka Zenit, no. 3, Zagreb 1922. Back cover. Courtesy of National and University Library in Zagreb, Croatia.

Endnotes

1 **Differences between Damn Your Hundred Gods and Rescue Car**

Damn Your Hundred Gods	page	*Rescue Car*
With a riotous demonstration and some real contemporary pictures	title	"with a rebellious demonstration of Balkanism * some real contemporary pictures and 'white on white' after the seizure by the Royal State Attorney's Office in Zagreb"
sideways "ф" [Cyrillic f]		cut, leaving blank space
"Damn Your Hundred Gods" (2×)	10	"D Y H G" only
"Bombs"	13	"Bombs bombs bombs"
"Whore"	14	cut, no blank space
box w/ "Syphilisculture"	16	box of blank space
"Are you god's emissaries Slapping the backsides of other men's wives For the forgiveness of sins"	17	cut, leaving blank space w/ arrow pointing to it
"Eyes always peek under women's skirts" (2nd line)	18	cut, leaving blank space
two text boxes w/ "Hundred" and "Gods" w/ "Damn Your" and thick lines		"Damn Your Hundred Gods" cut, leaving two empty text boxes and two thick lines
"(Ladies are numb to the saints' pinches)" (2nd line)	22	cut, leaving blank space
missing in original	23	"Futurism" added "Cubism" added
missing in original		"Man is a scoundrel" added
"Young Karađorđe Poets were once kings Today madmen ride in rescue cars Carting off wild bears to be ridiculed" (2nd stanza)	24	cut, leaving blank space; an inserted hand w/ finger pointing to blank space
missing in original		Closing text: "Excerpts have been translated so far into: Russian, Czech, French, [I]talian, Spanish, German, Hungarian and some will be printed in the World Antholigy" [sic].

2 Ben Akiba: Pseudonym of Branislav Nušić 1864–1938, who was a playwright, satirist, essayist, novelist, and founder of modern rhetoric in Serbia. He was often referred to as the Serbian and Balkan Gogol.

3 Henri Désiré Landru (1869–1922) was a French serial killer, nicknamed the Bluebeard of Gambais.

4 Svetozar Pribičević (1875–1936) was a Croatian Serb politician in Austro-Hungary and later the Kingdom of Yugoslavia.

5 In the original, "tetke" (aunts) and "spletke" (intrigues) rhyme and are bolded.

Radio-Film and the Zenithist Vertical of the Spirit (excerpt)

Ljubomir Micić

Zenit, no. 23 (April 1923)

This article was prepared as a lecture for a zenithist evening, which was to be held in the Apolo Kino[1] on April 1st of this year. The director of Bosna-Film furnished the theater only on the condition that the manuscripts first be placed under the control and censorship of the board, which is to say their "literary" advisor. As a result of such improper proceedings and tactlessness, nothing ever came of the evening and the lecture.—The editorial board.

First: the verse dramas of the illegitimate royal son of "Shakespeare" are impossible today, as are the "infernal" lemonades of vulgar Latin—of Dante. The ministerial verses of Goethe are impossible today, just like the verses of the Romantic doppelgänger Pushkin or of the volunteer Lord Byron. For us, our dear, good fop Branko Radičević is naive.

Indeed, the excavation and raising of the dead—in spite of the living—is incomprehensible to us, since it reminds us of the work of bristling hyenas or the global farce (not comedy!)—of Tutankhamun . . . . From day-to-day, vain European follies are frequent, and never seem to be made for the masses. The masses regularly seek only that for which their unadulterated instinct hungers most. Everything appears to be meant for the stagnant backwaters and brains as well as for the "scientific" ambition of poor corpse-ologists. I call that ancient cathedratic "science," according to the field that it addresses—corpse-ology. Eternal is that type of corpse-ologist in art and philosophy, just like the bourgeois type in society. [...]

Can it be of little import to the new poets that there exists radio-telegraphy, radio-film, radio-concerts, or radio-press? Is it unimportant that there exist airplanes without motors or future air steamboats or elevator-airplanes for the zenithist concert in Micić Square on Mars? You futureniks—do you think that our journey to the Soviet Republic of the Moon is impossible, or to the Kingdom of Mars? Soon all cinematographers will project our zenithist poems and dramas up there. Is our coquetry in air-parks impossible, or planetary-continental bloody armies in the air, let's say in a fleet of 385? Is the greatest and most cannibalistic revolution of all history impossible—in the air? And Earth? Earth will then just be a far-off island for summer vacations or for excursions to the old homeland, with the obligatory passport of the superhuman republic in which you reside, of course. Don't you feel that in all of this zenithism is truly found, made according to the pure instinct of the genius inventor in the Balkans? Zenithism is the most epochal revelation of art in the new time and the only signpost of the creative new art amid modern, senseless chaos on Earth. Everything grows in the air and everything bends in the direction of the vertical. Look to American skyscrapers and radio-telegraphic antennae! Vertical! Vertically! [...]

Filmic erudition

1) By filmic erudition's unsurpassable fantasy—2) by its live-painterly realistic persuasiveness—3) by its constructive-mechanical speed—4) by its sophistication of direction—5) by its instantaneous change of place and time—until now it has squandered most of all an artificial literary volition for boring, static, sluggish, doddering theater, let alone ever-hated poetic neologisms. Filmic erudition and the mobile, restless instinct of the masses destroyed all of "our" long sedentary lyric poetry and the mundane, emotional poetry of mosquitoes—they've made the consumptive appearance of degenerate sexus-novels impossible. Who today asks, and whom does it concern, on which stairstep Hamlet met Ophelia—on the third or ninth? (There are even "scientific-philosophical" debates written about it!) Who today asks after the idea of the poet at all? Much more poignant is the question: how much does a dollar cost, or how many more bars are necessary until we are a metropolis? But we ask—1) how much can you envelop the entire world with your works, with the depth and height of modern life—2) how close is man not to himself individually but to the whole collectively—3) how much closer are we to animals and farther from men?

Until now the poets have led the masses, but here today it is the opposite: the masses trample and despise the poets. The masses, with their unadulterated instinct free of any sort of aesthetic principles, turned their back on the poets. And rightfully so! The masses felt, sensed long ago that those poets are liars and that they only erected the cult of their own gluttonous and insatiable personality by artificial means or intrigue. The masses hate personality. The masses today are adapting to their own free will and greedily gulping down fleeting living pictures[2] in a fleeting life on an endless white screen. The spirit of the masses is like a white screen on whose static square every film can be projected, made on a broad foundation of its natural instinct. Every zenithist poet must take this into account. And all the other poets of silken bonbons, pantyhose, and low-heeled slippers—they are foreign to us and deeply spellbound by the masses—extraneous.

Here the path of poetic revolution, which the zenithists started in the beginning of this decade, is glancingly shown. It is progressively being imposed all the more as a postulate and categorical imperative, directly as the second link in a chain of social revolutions, which shook and partially imperiled the foundations of capitalist society. In such a society, certainly, the poet is caught unawares and confused, since he had remained a legendary parasite and a deluded invalid, a layabout, a chatterbox, and a bashful lover.

[. . .]

Fourth: . . . Great poets must be inventors and the new poetry unconditionally inventive and always active in its own time. Simple is the deception and great Latin lie that "in a time of war the muses fall silent." All reasons speak against and all examples speak for: high above the smothering atmosphere—a new discovery! We manly zenithists began this journey in the Balkans, first taking into consideration the wanton artistic fact and new truth: film overtook and destroyed art, which was endless until now—nirvana and the first sister of enjoyment. Film, in its youthfulness and intensive conquest of the masses, destroyed the lustful poetry of the troubadour Romeo. And I often call upon the *lanterna magica,* my only companion and friend from childhood. That little toy became a great life and an event . . . . We were excited and obsessed with movie theater magic. I'd already gathered all my kreuzers for the coming year and was extremely unhappy as I waited in expectation for the movie theater and circus. Wonderful! What kind of poems? What kind of novels? The movie theater! Living pictures! Film! . . .

Can all this remain without influence or be completely lost! Impossible! That small part from childhood was necessary to mention, since it is deserving of credit in the creation of zenithism and zenithist poetry. I was no longer in Paris, like those other meddlesome "pupils of the Parisian school," where it would have just been "discovered" that film is the new art and possibility of great conceptions (I know that those very same, before they were in Paris, despised film). I discovered it in my soul, in my instinct, in the Balkan crust of the earth, first in the bloody cradle of Banovina, and then in the old Zagreb Edison Kino, where I was amazed by the English film *Hamlet* and the unforgettable Russian film *A Living Corpse,* by Tolstoy. It was quite formative. Just before the beginning of the World War, I was deeply convinced of the superiority of filmic comprehensiveness, as I am convinced today, that new art cannot be created beyond the great foundation of **filmic simultaneity**. That filmic simultaneity means: the coeval, rhythmic concentration of time, space, and various events, regardless of their apparent illogicality. An economy of technical means and a wealth of effects. Under the influence of film, I wrote a filmic drama for a scene in 1915, but I could not fit all the events and actions into the scenic frame according to its known laws and rules. Then, I felt most strongly the endless delusion of narrow principles in art and the inferiority of theater to film. I felt the same when I wrote my first sonnets on a school bench. But sometime in 1918 or 1919, I dragged a young poet to the Metropol Kino by force, let him watch Strindberg's drama *Intoxication,* with the great actress Asta Nielsen, and told him: "Wonderful, it is not possible to perform or even experience this on stage." A few days later, that little poet and many other long-haired rhymesters looked down their noses at me, then because of a film and today because of zenithism. That was back then, when the rest of society gorged itself on film the lowest kind and entertainment of a humiliating rank. Then, they'd go to the cinema stealthily "so that nobody sees me," just as the journal *Zenit* is read today. It has not been long since film became the teacher of all the theaters in the world and since it has left its indisputable influence on new art, and especially on new poetry. The future of zenithism is similar. It won't be long until theaters and churches are transformed into cinemas (which will mean enormous progress!) or they should become zenitheums for zenithist gatherings as soon as possible.

Observing and experiencing such pronounced paradoxes of life, that quick exchange of black and white—observing film as the only basic collective expression of modern life—observing the hungry masses who gluttonously gulp down the quick and illogical rush of irreversible living pictures, I was convinced of the existence of a most painterly, filmic vitality in the whole of art, indisputable for now.

I emphasize once more that film is the real seed of zenithist poetry, and not of any other European movement, least of all futurism. That mistake seems inescapable, firstly, due to its own gross underestimation, since our representatives until now were in an inferior position in relation to Europe—secondly, due to the sheer ignorance and nonrecognition of the subject about which is often spoken. (Futurism is the deserving offspring of an old and oversaturated European-bourgeois culture, with which even our country is sufficiently supplied. Zenithism and futurism, in great part like expressionism and the other "isms," are completely antagonistically opposed.) Moreover: film most successfully degraded the symbolics and astral, disembodied metaphysics in art, which triggered an early case of German expressionismitis in the appendix. Film finally realized that timeless, blind longing: oh, if I could **see** it! And indeed: The miracles of a new constructive epoch of labor **are seen**—the Russian steppes of good muzhiks and the American ranches of famed cowboys **are seen**—the habitats of Himalayan blue birds and the wild dances of black tribes in Africa **are seen**—the beyond-sensical impossibilities of acrobatics and the wild paradoxes of time **are seen**—nowhere else are the unseen expressions of human pain on the face of one of the geniuses, let's say C. Veidt[3], **seen**, and the genius proletarian Chaplinisms **are seen**! Even liquid magma on the pockmarked head of the sun **is seen** and everything, everything that a man of the masses can barely imagine.

I will cite just one example of filmic journalism and its most obvious simultaneity. In connection with those mentioned, I didn't hear anyone say that the zenithist elements in the dailies bothered him (since nobody even noticed them!) and even if I then heard and read countless times that zenithism in art, which is to say in poetry, is nonsense, a psychopathologic apparition, or at the very least unintelligible. Not a single shopkeeper, let alone any university prof or aesthete, for that matter, ever found in the daily telegrams, which quickly arrive one after the other, anything abnormal or idiotic. And yet! Those telegrams are truly the best example of zenithist reality and modernity. For example, telegrams from the 28th of February from an American daily show it best, and I leave them intact here exactly as follows:

TELEGRAMS

Moscow. —Colonel Svejevski, who was charged with conspiracy to make an attempt on the life of Soviet Premier Nikolai Lenin, was sentenced to death today by the Supreme Court.

New York. —A strike of 30,000 workers in manufacturing factories finished today with an agreement between employees and employers.

Washington. —In the Senate an appeal was addressed to President Harding to help put an end to the hopeless and futile struggle that has developed over the project to subsidize a merchant marine and which threatens to incapacitate the Senate for any kind of positive action.

Philadelphia. —From a local mental hospital today Harry Kendall Thaw[4], the famous millionaire who several years ago killed the seductor of his wife, was released "on temporary leave." He is allowed a leave of 10 days to visit his elderly mother who lives in Pittsburgh.

Berlin. —The German government accuses the French of using black troops in the Ruhr Valley who are extremely cruel in their interactions with local people.

New York. —Federal agents in New York and New Jersey today jailed 24 makers of counterfeit money. It has come out that around 150 members of a crew of counterfeiters have been jailed. Last night the police raided one of their "factories" in Brooklyn, where a mass amount of counterfeit money of all possible varieties was confiscated.

Chicago. —The famous high priest of the Christian Catholic Apostolic Church, Voliva, who made his name for having asserted that the Earth is not round, has been sentenced by a jury to a year in prison and a $500 fine for the criminal defamation of T.H. Nelson, who belongs to the same church.

New York. —Today Prince Miguel de Braganea, the oldest son of pretender to the Portuguese throne Don Miguel Braganea, died of pneumonia. He was 45 years old and was married to the American Anita Stuart from New York.

San Salvador. —Here a strong earthquake was felt today that lasted 50 seconds. There was no damage.

London. —Today the first parliamentary attempt was made to introduce the prohibition of alcoholic drinks in Great Britain, when MP Scrymgeour filed it as a legal project.

Washington. —The United Mine Workers are accusing the operators of a soft coal mine of having less than 41 percent of yearly profit actually invested in their own enterprises.

Rome. —Here news has been received from Albania that the Malisor tribe has revolted against the regime in Tirana.

Filmism, broad in this way, with its rapid-fire-simultaneous elements, also served as an example for the construction of zenithist poetry, which is to say that it influenced the reality of the exterior world—its forms and its correlation with an interior, rhythmically balanced vitality. This balance of the exterior real and the interior spiritual is the essence of zenithism, which is to say the new art that zenithism is creating.

Behold: a new poet is wanted, who with his poems will simultaneously speak on five continents to all in an equally intelligible tongue. A poetry is wanted, which is equally modern and zealous to the masses, which is to say to millions. **Zenithist poetry demands a filmic realism and the totality of modern life, the quick-change of the interior and exterior world, the sharp-edged contrasts of black and white by means of alogical associations and simultaneities** (every man for himself!). Until now, all these elements have played a crucial role in the conquering victory of film as the pancontinental art of millions.

Wanted: **zenith-man-philosophy: zenithosophy**
Wanted**: filmic-zenithist new art: zenithism**
Wanted: **radio-film-zenithist vertical: of the spirit**

Translated by *Samantha Farmer*

Endnotes

1 Title kept as is, since it names a historic movie theater on Ilica 31 in Zagreb, built in 1912.
2 The original "žive slike" appears to be a literal translation of the French *tableaux vivants*.
3 German actor Conrad Veidt.
4 Incorrectly called "Henri Tav" in the original.

Cinema Poems

Boško Tokin
Crno na belo [almanac] (1924)

1.
Life: buildup of power.
Thwarted power is worked off daily.
American, our—life—certainly three films:
Charlie Chaplin, Douglas, Rio Jim.[1]
Our America, three triumphs:
life (being alive), struggle (struggling), creation.
Accumulated powers, emotions, creating, raging,
the jazz band rages.
Owing to the play of Romanticism—mourning:
Thirsting after freedom in my dreams
Seeking new men, crazed, through the world.
When will my work see the light of the world?
The jazz band rages.
Our film (title: *The Standard Intensity of Life*) is projected.
Our America: *wins*.

2.
There, as here, a happy industry thrives:
Staša, Kraša, Toša, Dada, Tin,
Mima, Rastko, Pera, Hipnos, Stop.[2]
With "Paris" Douglas, happy dynamic.
Paris city of isms and my friends.
Our heart's biplane.
Our soul's monoplane.
The new generation takes flight.
Striking women,
gallant thoughts,
have taken us far.
There.
Mainly we keep our noses clean.
We defeat
ourselves, yourself, every minute. Mainly.
Line. Victory. Style.

3.
Life for most:
Question Answer, Answer Question.
Always: Question Answer.
Our life, a diminishing life?
Airplane, department store,
cinema, sports,
speed and art.
Art.

4.
In a drawing a thousand lines
In an airplane a hundred possibilities
In a film a million flickers.
Embrace. Be an artist.
Always.

Translated by *Jed Rasula*

Endnotes

1 Douglas Fairbanks (1883–1939) was an American actor. Rio Jim is the protagonist of a 1914 western film *The Bargain* played by William Hart, one of the most popular Western actors of the silent film era. Poljanski's *Kinofon* film magazine advertised Jim Rio.

2 Those are names of Tokin's cotemporaries and friends, who formed the kernel of Serbian/Yugoslav avant-garde in the period between 1919–1926: Staša (Stanislav Vinaver), Kraša (Stanislav Krakov), Toša (Todor Manojlović), Dada (Dragan Aleksić), Tin (Tin Ujević), Mima (Miloš Crnjanski), Rastko (Rastko Petrović), Pera (Petar Dobrović), Hipnos (Rade Palavičini), Stop (it is here to underline the telegraphic style of the poem).

The Second Road of the Barbarogenius: The Hybrid Novel, Prose Poetry, and the Serpentinella

Introduction

Aleksandar Bošković and Steven Teref

This section features Branko Ve Poljanski's writing, which is the hardest to pin down since he was the most stylistically restless of the zenithists. Despite this, or perhaps because of this, his work is the most zenithist of all. If zenithism was an unabashed embrace of all the avant-garde movements whirling across Europe, no writer embodied that belief more than Poljanski. If zenithism was preoccupied with the fusion of verse and prose into hybrid, or cross-genre writing, no writer did that more successfully than Poljanski.

The years 1921–1922 saw a whirlwind of activity for Poljanski. In 1921, he tried his hand at acting in Ljubljana, but Ljubljana was also where he began his literary activity. In January, he wrote and published a single issue of the futurist-expressionist magazine *Svetokret* (Worldwhirl).[1] The magazine featured the subheading "Journal for the Expedition to the North Pole of Man's Spirit," an image that prefigured his brother Ljubomir Micić's magazine *Zenit*, which launched its first issue the following month.

1 *Svetokret* (January 1921). Republished in *Zenit, Svetokret, Dada-Jok, Dada Tank, Dada Jazz, 1921–1926* (Zagreb: Ranko Horetzky, 2008).

Svetokret opens with the section *Thought Labyrinth*, which features his programmatic ideas. "Here I Am!" exhibits a frequent Poljanski motif of the poet persecuted by "idiots," where he casts himself as a bull to gore them. In the section *Projections*, the poem "On Train Tracks" captures the heightened emotive-charged images of a speaker awed by the "horror" of a train with "bestial eyes" speeding past him, while his wintry poem "Longing" hints at a *lustmord*[2] motif often found in expressionist painting.

The following year saw a great transformation of Poljanski as a writer. In the March 1922 issue of *Zenit*, he published two strikingly transgressive poems: "A Lasso around the Holy Mother's Neck" and "The Beauty of a Horse and the Face of Queen Zita."[3] What separates these poems from Poljanski's earlier verse is their fearlessness—pivoting from the somber introspective poems of *Svetokret* to confrontational poetics. "A Lasso around the Holy Mother's Neck" is intertextual (i.e., parasitic) and blasphemous (i.e., anarchic), while "The Beauty of a Horse and the Face of Queen Zita" is humorously offensive toward the Austro-Hungarian queen.[4] Both poems are transgressive, one toward religion and the other toward the state. An editorial in *Zenit* nos. 19–20 claimed the poems "challenged mice out of holes."[5]

Poljanski's "A Lasso" should be read in conversation with Rastko Petrović's "Spomenik putevima" (Monument to Roads), which had been published in the January 1922 inaugural issue of the proto-surrealist magazine *Putevi* (Roads).[6] Petrović's poem caused a huge scandal and public debate that threatened the poet with ex-communication from the Orthodox Church. Critic Aleksandar Petrov links Poljanski's poem to this debate, arguing that some of the poem's polemic stings and its call to the "hawks" could be understood as references to Petrović's poem. Petrov argues that Poljanski's portrayal of Christ evokes Petrović's Christ's "male sign" that "reaches to his knees" ("Muški mu znak dopire do kolena").[7] In a similarly blasphemous manner, Poljanski likened the Holy Mother to a dancer or a prostitute who

---

2 *Lustmord*: Sexual murder. A motif in German expressionist art, film, and literature. See Maria Tatar, *Lustmord: Sexual Murder in Weimar Germany* (Princeton: Princeton University Press, 1995).

3 Branko Ve Poljanski, "Laso materi božjoj oko vrata" and "Lepota konja i kraljice Zite," *Zenit*, no. 12 (March 1922): 12.

4 Queen Zita: Zita of Bourbon-Parma (1892–1989), the last Empress of Austria and Queen of Hungary.

5 "Netužni nekrolog 1922. godini," *Zenit*, nos. 19–20 (December 1922): 69.

6 Rastko Petrović, "Spomenik putevima," *Putevi*, no. 1 (January 1922): 9–12.

7 Aleksandar Petrov, "Branko Ve Poljanski i njegova *Panika pod suncem*," foreword to *Panika pod suncem. Tumbe. Crveni petao*, by Branko Ve Poljanski, ed. A. Petrov (Belgrade: Narodna Biblioteka Srbije; Gornji Milanovac: Dečje novine, 1988), xxxi–xxxii.

had "just performed in City-Bar." The poet extends the metaphor by asking "how many more newborn / Christs / will have hereditary syphilis."[8]

Both "A Lasso" and "The Beauty of a Horse" mark a new irreverent style for Poljanski that he developed further with a series of periodicals over the course of the year.

In 1922, Dragan Aleksić, a former *Zenit* contributor, launched a one-man Dada movement and published two single-issue Dada magazines: *Dada Tank* and *Dada Jazz*, in opposition to *Zenit* and zenithism. In reaction, Poljanski published *Dada-Jok* (Dada-Nope), an anti-Dada magazine that featured poems, tracts, and illustrations by Micić, his wife Anuška (under the pseudonym Nina-Naj), Petar Bauk, and Poljanski himself.[9]

Though all Poljanski's work is striking here, from the humorous "Dada Causal Dada" to the philosophical "The Panopticon Passes through a Mirror," one piece stands out. The prose poem "33 sEcoNdS" blends the intense brooding emotional state of expressionism with the nonsense and arbitrariness of Dada. These two opposing poles, in Poljanski's prose poem, coalesce as much as they clash. If one had to characterize Poljanski's writing style, then this poem, which might be considered as the embodiment of the crossbreeding spirit of zenithism, might serve as an ur-text of that style.

Additionally, the poem stands out for being referred to as a *serpentinella*. The term would seem to be a poetic form, but how does it differ from a prose poem, which "33 sEcoNdS" clearly is? Was this Poljanski's personal word for a prose poem, was he indicating a new poetic form, or was it a ruse and the poet was merely toying with the reader as any good (anti-)Dadaist would? If this was the only serpentinella Poljanski wrote, then any one of these conclusions could be true and that would be the end of it. What makes the matter more intriguing is that in *Zenith-Express: Dada-Jok* no. 2, Poljanski calls two other prose poems serpentinellas: "300,000 Punches per Second," what we would today call flash fiction, and "2 ÷ 2 = 1," a hybrid of prose and verse.[10] Stylistically, the three poems are versions of a prose poem, but each text diverges in its own way. Poljanski persisted with the term, so it would seem that the term was more than a one-off joke, but then he just as suddenly dropped the term in all subsequent writing that bears a hybrid form. Evidence that Poljanski discussed the term in correspondence has yet to surface and there does not seem to be any research into the serpentinella, so it is difficult to know what to really make of the term.

---

8 See "A Lasso around the Holy Mother's Neck" in this anthology.

9 *Dada-Jok* (May 1922). Republished in *Zenit, Svetokret, Dada jok, Dada tank, Dada jazz, 1921–1926* (2008).

10 *Zenit-Ekspres: Dada-Jok*, no. 2 (July–August 1922): n.p.

Poljanski closed out his 1922 periodical trilogy with *Zenith-Express: Paris–Berlin–Munich! Radiograms.*[11] *Radiogram* was the title of a poetry collection by Yvan Goll intended for Biblioteka Zenit, but the concept did not make it to print. Instead, Branko Ve Poljanski published the leaflet *Zenith-Express: Radiograms* as a combination of news, poetry, and advertising, to mark the special occasion of his and his brother's trip to Berlin in 1922. Over the course of the three publications, Poljanski continued to experiment with the boundaries of prose.

Poljanski's next publication was his first book, the hybrid novel *77 Suicides* (*77 samoubica*), in which he formalized his short experiments into a long form.[12] Poljanski's "very fast superfantastic novel," as its subtitle proclaims, was innovative in the context of contemporary Yugoslav literature at the time, and shared an affinity with expressionist fiction, but even more so with expressionist film.

Like other zenithists (Goll, Micić, Mikac, and Tokin), Poljanski was a great admirer of early cinema. He knew the history of film well and followed its development. He was the founder of *Kinofon*, a "review for film culture," in which he published translations of "fantastic film stories" by H. Wehner and W. Heinrich, as well as a work that with its narrative collage technique is closest to Poljanski's novel—the first Dadaist novel, *Second through Brain* (1920) by Melchior Vischer. Expressionist films such as Paul Wegener's *Der Golem, wie er in die Welt kam* (The Golem, 1920), Robert Wiene's *Das Cabinet des Dr. Caligari* (The Cabinet of Dr. Caligari, 1920), Fritz Lang's *Dr. Mabuse, der Spieler* (Dr. Mabuse, the Gambler, 1922), and Friedrich Wilhelm Murnau's *Der Bucklige und fie Tänzerin* (The Hunchback and the Dancer, 1920), to name just a few, renewed ties with legends, fairy tales, and fantastic stories by German romantics and their followers, thus reviving the interest of artists in the field of the irrational and esoteric. Traditional psychology and logic were suppressed, while symbolism and the illogical came to the fore. All these features are to be found in *77 Suicides*.

The divided or double personality, a key expressionist motif, also appears in Poljanski's novel, and in a grotesque way. The novel's exaggerated characters resemble those from *The Cabinet of Dr. Caligari*. Thematically, Poljanski's text reflects even more expressionist film's fascination with the irrational, esoteric, demonic, and magical. The protagonist Nikifor Morton is a double figure of a mysterious character, inherited from German romanticism, who seeks knowledge and, at the same time, a modern character who searches for meaning

11 *Zenit-Ekspres: Pariz–Berlin–München! Radiogrami* [leaflet] (1922).

12 Branko Ve Poljanski, *77 samoubica* (Zagreb: Naklada Reflektor, 1923).

and wants to overcome the mundane materialistic age. Poljanski refers, for example, to the myth of Faust, where Nikifor evokes Faust's acknowledgment that Mephistopheles is "part of the force that always wills evil and always produces good." Christianity, with its construct of good and evil and other binary oppositions characteristic of Western cultures—God and Lucifer, creation and destruction, male and female, the individual and the collective, and so on—also plays a role.

The term "novel" does not do the book justice; a more precise genre definition for *77 Suicides* might be *ciné-novel*. The book is an experimental multi-genre work that fuses the innovative techniques of expressionist film to a poetry and prose hybrid in a discontinuous narrative, resulting in an abstract-expressionist-futurist-constructivist text by applying film techniques to writing. Poljanski drew on the procedures developed in futurism, which celebrated speed and strived to imitate the possibilities opened up by photography and film in the mediums of painting and literature. He achieved the impression of cinematic dynamism by the rapid alteration of words, phrases, and sentences which, along with the variations in their length and frame, all suggest a transformation of rhythm and feelings, signaling a change of genre codes. At times, Poljanski reveals this process in autopoietic (meta) formulations via a sudden and unexpected change of third-person speech to first-person. Since he experimented with both prose and poetry in prose, an important role is played by the alternating rhythms of prose and poetry, and his use of repetitions, parallelisms, and the varied length of sequences (a sentence or a verse).

Poljanski followed *77 Suicides* with his first poetry collection *Panic under the Sun* (*Panika pod suncem*, 1924), though many of the poems predate *77 Suicides*.[13] The book opens with Ljubomir Micić's brief foreword, composed as another "slap in the face of public petit-bourgeoise taste" and with a noticeable disdain for it in its title, "C'mon, Now!" ("Ajde de!"). The foreword is followed by two key Poljanski tracts. The first, "Manifesto," originally published in *Svetokret*, promotes paradox as the most important element of zenithist poetry that his brother Ljubomir incorporated and made into one of the pillars of zenithist aesthetics. The second, "Alarm," was read by Poljanski at the second zenithist soiree in Zagreb, on January 31, 1923, as an introduction to his reading. "Alarm" reiterated Micić's condensed zenithist ideas built on the opposition of the Balkans vs. Europe, understood as the "life-death" dichotomy. The poems following this text range from expressionist (producing the

13 Branko Ve Poljanski, *Panika pod cuncem, Tumbe, Crveni petao*, ed. A. Petrov (Belgrade: Narodna Biblioteka Srbije; Gornji Miilanovac: Dečje novine, 1988).

effect of movement by alternating long and short poems, or repeating characteristic consonants such as *r, z, ž* in the original, or using monosyllabic rhymes; creating sonic grotesques), to orthographic and typographic experiments in the "visualization" of poetry, to poems that have more in common with Richard Huelsenbeck's Dadaist understanding rather than Apollinaire's or Marinetti's, to futurist-Dadaist experiments with cutting words into syllables and letters for separate verses or using infinitives and coined neologisms, so-called "bombs," to poems that successfully articulate zenithist poetics in its most crystalized form: ambivalently critical and under the sign of Balkan oppositions, often with a satirical tone.[14]

Poljanski's second poetry collection *Topsy-Turvy* (*Tumbe,* 1926) reconciles a torrent of poetic words about a world turned upside down with rationally organized constructivist typography.[15] Bold black circles and black bars are as vital to the music of the poems as periods and commas.

As with *Panic under the Sun, Topsy-Turvy* opens with two manifestos. The first, "S.O.S.," is striking for its foreshadowing when Poljanski declares that one can "meet all cultural requirements by creating a 'civilization' in Terazije Square," for it is in that spot that he, the following year, would hand out 2,000 copies of *Topsy-Turvy* and his last poetry collection, *The Red Rooster,* as his farewell to the Balkan civilization he could not save. The second manifesto, "Manifesto," is more than a manifesto because it opens with a portrait of Poljanski's childhood in which he reveals how he invented the name Poljanski.

The book comprises a rich array of diverse texts: lyric poems ("Eros" and "Dusk"), prose poems ("Contraidioticon" and "Nihilon"), something in between ("The Panopticon Passes Through a Mirror"), flash fiction ("300,000 Punches per Second"), and even flash drama ("The Laughter of Rifles"). The more experimental pieces in *Topsy-Turvy,* along with *77 Suicides,* exemplify the best of Poljanski's crossbreeding of genres, a seminal body of early hybrid writing.

Not only was *Topsy-Turvy* a visually arresting book, it also expanded the emotional range from Poljanski's earlier work. Two examples underscore this point. The short grotesque prose text "300,000 Punches per Second" is a love story in which the spirit of expressionist prose, the motifs of the monster city, a lonely and alienated individual, and death on the rails are reinvented through its absurdist humor in which the characters Rakir and Martira pick a fight with streetcar tracks, only to be killed by a streetcar. The poem is a

---

14 See Petrov, "Branko Ve Poljanski i njegova *Panika pod suncem*": i–lxxviii.

15 See *Topsy-Turvy* in the anthology, where we have reproduced the original layout.

comical inversion of Poljanski's "On Train Tracks." The poem "You Have Wonderful Eyes, Lucia," written in Paris around the same time as *The Red Rooster,* is one of Poljanski's most wondrous poems, a lustmord poem to revolution personified.[16] The speaker is clear-eyed in his mania, in contrast to the haunted speaker of "Longing."

The complexity and depth of Poljanski's hybrid writing style in this collection stands in sharp contrast with the experimental verse in *Panic under the Sun* although both maintain an engaging playfulness each in their own way. *Topsy-Turvy* not only shows a greater versatility of modes, but also exhibits an effortless blend of various avant-garde aesthetics: the absurdism of Dada, the violent brevity of futurism, and the melancholy of expressionism as each poem demanded.

---

16 See Petrov, "Branko Ve Poljanski i njegova *Panika pod suncem,*" lxxiv.

Here I Am![1]

Branko Ve Poljanski (as Virgil Poljanski)
Svetokret, no. 1 (January 1921)

Here I am!
Dedicated to all the psychiatrists on all the continents of planet Earth.

Oh, cultured one!
Oh, humanitarian!
Oh, human!
Europe!
The day will come
It will!
The day of blood and blaze
When from the heavens
Where reigns a man—God
A fiery rain will pour!

Yes! Here I am! I showed up (after all!) though they wanted to beat me down but couldn't! My days were the torture of the Inquisition.

They lynched me (which they do to this day) and I screamed, and they—laughed (unaware that laughing at others' suffering they have condemned themselves to suffering).

Yes! Here I am! At last, after I took it all, I became stronger, so strong and powerful.

The strength to fight is hurricane strong and desires destruction . . . destruction, so that everything rumbles from the crumbling of old towers.

Yes! Here I am! They thought I had collapsed from their punches, and yet here I am risen from the waves of life—like a siren.

Oh! How often I exclaimed: "Idiots!" But they reserved that name for me.

Oh! How often I hurled at them: "Oxen!" But the reserved that name for me.

Oh! How often! How often I accused them: "Cows!" But they slung a cowbell around my neck and corralled me to graze, so that we together could graze in a barren pasture.

Oh! Yes! Here I am! Their name-calling at this hour of my resurrection is pointless. I remove (have removed) the cowbell and sow fertile seeds over the barren pasture where I'll make them graze.

"You're nuts!"

Oh, yes! That's me! I'm nuts! That fortifies me against "them." I'm nuts! That "something other," that other, other—other!

Oh, yes! Here I am! I carry a whip to lash the thickest skin till it bleeds! I carry a whip to lash everything worthy of being whipped.

(Oh! There will be wailing and hellish screams!)

"You're a bull."

Oh, yes! That's me! I'm a bull taunted to rage at their red cape of lies. And I will thrust my horns toward their punches and gore them.

"You're stupid."

Oh, yes! That's me! I'm stupid. Off the scales with my stupidity. No one scale their intelligence and on the other, my stupidity! Off the scales!—Marvelous math! But defeating the "intelligent."

Oh, yes! Here I am! In the name of the law of gravity I condemn them to the fall! Whatever isn't tightly screwed on will fall when punched.

I will strike with the steel strength of Cyclops and demolish.

And when I have demolished everything, I'll build a tall tower to be ruled by a god, a man-ruler—of the Earth's loony bin!

Oh, yes! Here I am! I climbed to the top of myself and there I found a man, and then I plunged into the abyss of myself and found a man! And "they" won't plunge because they won't climb until "someone" takes them out of the desert.

Oh, yes! Here I am! A crown of thorns on my head, my hands bound behind me. From my wounds, red drops of suffering fell, and from them strength blossomed and I untied my hands, and "they"—suddenly turned to stone!

Aaaaaaaaaaaaaaaaaaaaaaaaaaaaaaaaaaaaaaaaaaaaaaaaaaaaaaaaaaaaaaaaaaaaaaa!

Translated by *Steven Teref and Maja Teref*

Endnotes

1 "Here I Am!" is the first piece in the first section titled Thought Labyrinth.

Under the Sign of the Circle

Branko Ve Poljanski
from *Zenit,* no. 1 (February 1921)

Blue and red
flits in a dancehall
dance

Sweat flesh in the dancehall
O O circles O O
And wine riots in the blood
of riotous dancers and their bodies
dance

Everything spins
dances
forms a circle.
Blood boils
boils
circulus!

Life
Death
Circulus!

Under the Sign of the Circle

Colors glitter
colors flit
blood boils
in the veins of the drunk
like champagne.

Under the sign of life
and death
under the sign of fire
and dust
circulus!

Life
Death
Circulus!
O O O O O O O
Everything dances in the circle
O O O O O O O

Translated by *Steven Teref and Maja Teref*

A Lasso around the Holy Mother's Neck

Branko Ve Poljanski
from *Zenit,* no. 12 (March 1922)

Fear not, hawks
there are still chickens!
Their blood like a blooming rose.
(It's delightful to drink blood.)
Why be concerned over
epilepsy mortal cramp
of the wretched sick?
We can't be our own fathers'
fathers!

The Holy Mother
just performed in City-Bar.
Woewoewoe
just so you know
again, how many more newborn

Christs
will have hereditary syphilis.
Folks! Soon you won't even know
who is whose god.

Fear not, sparrow hawks
your parabolic hop under the world's flaming teat
will be the peck of their beaks
at the bulging eyes of the perished hen
from an olden culture.

Croak, you blind decrepit hen
I don't acknowledge you as god's mother!
The ellipses of sparrow hawks burn the world's teat
a lasso around your neck,
for
by god, you must have had enough of sitting for twenty centuries
on stinking eggs.

Translated by *Steven Teref and Maja Teref*

The Beauty of a Horse and the Face of Queen Zita

Branko Ve Poljanski
from *Zenit*, no. 12 (March 1922)

The brain gives birth to black cats
Man I love
Man I hate
: I hold dear above all
A CARRIAGE HORSE.
The carriage, a black coffin
(*Non simbolismus!*)
awaits a passenger.
A burning lantern
illuminates the horse's rear
: it's more beautiful now
than the cheek of the minister president
and the face of Queen Zita.[1]

In every lantern burns my
I
!

Translated by *Steven Teref and Maja Teref*

1 Queen Zita: Zita of Bourbon-Parma (1892–1989) was the last Empress of Austria and Queen of Hungary.

Dada Causal Dada

Branko Ve Poljanski (as Valerij Poljanski)
from *Dada-Jok*, no. 1 (May 1922)

1, 2, 3, etc.
Every afternoon rings the breaking of imaginations
at the bend of my finger.
I love you u u u u u
utopia
39° heat.
The tousled train tracks to Russia.
I'll tell my student Seneca that
Kurt Schwitters escaped Hanover
to avoid paying the shoemaker
        Friedrich Nietzsche
the bill for real Dadashoes.
1, 2, 3, 4, 5, 6, 7, 8, 8, 10, 11, 12 . . .
Scram, causal whore!
Howhowhowhowhow
whowhowhowhowhowhowhowho
oooooooooooooooo . . .

Translated by *Steven Teref and Maja Teref*

Codes of the Dada-Jok State

Branko Ve Poljanski (as Valerij Poljanski)
from *Dada-Jok*, no. 1 (May 1922)

§ 1.

Everyone is required to respect Ljubomir Micić and V. Poljanski under penalty of 10 years imprisonment in a camera obscura along with forced memorization and recitation of every Zenithist poem.

§ 2.

A man must not be stupid because stupidity is punishable by death or at best a life sentence reading *Zenit*.

§ 3.

It is not permitted to be a cretin, so "topographically speaking" every cretin will be mercilessly shot by firing squad.

§ 4.

On the basis of state principles, every resource should be utilized to destroy Yugoslav literature before *Zenit*.

§ 5.

To be an upstanding citizen, everyone must be a good Dadaist by fighting against a Dada-no worldview.

§ 6.

Number 13 must be respected.

§ 7.

All out war against journalistic limitations.

§ 8.

Sanitary fight against intellectual TB.

§ 9.

No western European can be respected.

§ 10.

Every member of the Dada-Jok state is required to become a founding member of the state clinic for the operation of limited intelligence.

§ 11.

Collaboration on the building of the state factory of the reservoirs of intelligence and thought.

§ 12.

All citizens are required and alternate working in the revolver factory in the fight against the syphilitic horde of western Europeans.

§ 13.

Logic doesn't exist. (This paragraph does not apply to inferior citizens.)

§ 14.

Paradox is the sanctuary of the **Dada-Jok** state.

§ 15.

St. Paradox Day is a state holiday celebrated every year on February 1st.

§ 16.

The National Anthem:
Hey rooftop brick
don't fall on our heads
St. Paradox take pity on us
Sons of the battery are
your loyal servants
Oh, Ganges flow into our hearts
Destroy our foes
the idolaters
        of **Logic**.
Oh, mother technology
our great protectress
bestow on us skyscrapers,
millions of automobiles, and engines
        Brain **Strength**
kill this country's

embryonic types of
pseudointellectuals
feed and protect our ruler
our Ljubomir Micić
and duke
V. Poljanski.

§ 17.

No house can be built from the foundation but from the roof. (This doesn't apply to inferior citizens.)

§ 18.

Those observed not to reverentially sing the national anthem every morning will be mummified, and their mouths will be forced to recite the national prayer until the end of the world.

§ 19.

The city of Ljubljana must be destroyed as it is in the interest of the **Dada-Jok** state.

§ 20.

Cretin-hunting is a patriotic duty in the rainforests of idiocy.

§ 21.

Citizens must help each other while tending to all dadajokistzenithist affairs under penalty of exile to the "Marsyas" group.

§ 22.

The institute of state animal husbandry must bear the name:

Home of Stanislav Vinaver
or
House for Unmuzzled Dogs.

§ 23.

No citizen may be named August, for that is beneath the dignity of every man to bear such a compromised name, borne by so many shockingly embryonic originalunoriginal blockheads.

§ 24.

Those who curse the gods, denigrate and wear an army uniform, will be punished by being meticulously described in the manner of Miroslav Krželа. Moreover, an entire literature will be written by said author.

§ 25.

Those who read Vladimir Vidrić or whatever August Branko Si . . . ć and Antun Krk . . . c have written about him will be spanked 25 times like an ultrasniffler.

§ 26.

Those with small foreheads will have their front hairline shaved.

§ 27.

It is strictly forbidden to attend Zagreb's theater because it features Schnitzler, Shakespeare, Dimović, Božić, and Sophocles. Whoever is observed to have seen a play by these playwrights will be dispatched to the spiritual rehab called *Zenit* at the state's expense.

§ 28.

The form of rule is **Neroesque**.

§ 29.

A thumbs down for those who disrespect the national anthem.

§ 30.

Institutes have been founded for the acculturation of animals. Beginning with horned cattle who will be read the latest issues of *Savremenik* and *Kritika*. Edited by Milan Begović.

§ 31.

Summer school is offered to intellectual scoundrels and coeditors of the following reviews: *Savremenik, Kritika, Književni glasnik, Putevi, Misao* and so forth.

§ 32.

A large state circus will be built which will feature the best acrobats of their time. The artistry of burning thought eating will be especially noted.

§ 33.

A staunch individual's fanaticism of an intellectual point of view is considered a patriotic virtue. This fanaticism will become rabid. Poisonous words bite into the meek, bloodless and miserable. Those who are superior will have boundless rights. All the Begovićs, Livadićs, Krležas, Petrovićs, Dimovićs, Professor Prohaskas, Ogrizovićs, and their hangers-on should be destroyed.
(The unmentioned are little worms who drop dead.)
It is in the interest of the **Dada-Jok** state to immediately execute its intensive work.
(For other articles see the great Code. It is available at the editorial office of Dada-JOK.

Translated by *Steven Teref and Maja Teref*

33 sEcoNdS

A spinning wheel in the SERPENTINe
A serpentinella[1]

Branko Ve Poljanski (as Valerij Poljanski)
from *Dada-Jok*, no. 1 (May 1922)

Hiccup. For **19** seconds I despair. In the **20th second**, I go over pointed statements. In the **21st second**, it's a shame I'm not a Ceylon native. Everything falls statistically in place and I with them. In the **22nd second**, I drink a blood oath with the candelabrum in front of house number 7. The candelabrum is a good friend of mine. The dark suffocates the street. The street reeks of tuberculosis. In the **23rd second**, to dance. In the **24th second**, to kill. In the **25th second**, to laugh. In the **26th second**, to travel through the Panama Canal to Constantinople. In the **27th second**, to ride a fiery star toward earth. Insanity number 1922. There are no psychiatrists for such patients. Drop dead, loony bird, until your wit grows back. In the **28th second**, to set on fire the Alexandrian wisdom of Dr. Prohaska in the country of Yugoslavia. In the **29th second**, to contemplate the Dadaism of Jesus Christ. In the **30th second**, to annul women's right to vote because Zofka Kveder is a dangerous agitator of Dadaism. In the **31st second**, to spit at the serpentine city. In the **32nd second**, V. Poljanski promises to continue his journal in the next issue of **Dada-Jok**. In the **33rd second**, to think how many seconds are in 33 eternities?

Translated by *Steven Teref and Maja Teref*

---

1 The serpentinella was a fictitious poetic form invented by Poljanski. He also labeled "2 ÷ 2 = 1" and "300,000 Punches a Second" as serpentinellas.

$2 \div 2 = 1$

A Serpentinella

Branko Ve Poljanski (as Vij Poljanski)
from *Zenit-Ekspres: Dada-Jok* 2 (July–August 1922)

The other half is illuminated by the sun. It shines but doesn't know for whom. This ½ is dark and only the laughter of skull lighthouses can be heard. Intellectual searchlights are powerless. Dark remains dark. Pig remains pig. Ox remains ox. All the lines are cramping into a spiral. Chinese revolutionaries break into the parliament. In 15 seconds, 15 idiotic reactions occur. Those who want to die laughing, let them apply to this address:

Earth
Five continents
Five capital cities
Five newspaper offices.
Zenith
"Modern thinking"

Just now some wretch jumped from the third floor and crushed his skull at the expense of ridiculousness: Compact thinking!

Translated by *Steven Teref and Maja Teref*

Radiograms

Branko Ve Poljanski (as Valerij Poljanski)
Zenit-Ekspres: Pariz–Berlin–München! Radiogrami [leaflet] (1922)

Translated by *Maja Starčević*

ZENITH EXPRESS

PARIS BERLIN MUNICH ! RADIO GRAMS

Ladies and Gentlemen!

Stupidity is self-defeating! I don't need to comment on that. The disease of stupidity has become an epidemic. Stupidity is the Asiatic plague of our time.

Ljubomir Micić

(I am sure you know him!) has discovered a Serum for the stupidity epidemic. There have been many successful operations thanks to this specialist in numbskull diseases.

Valerium Poljanski

We therefore wish to inform you that the great inventor Ljubomir Micić, when suddenly called to Paris, threw several thousand pills onto the streets of **Munich** as first aid for people stricken with the disease. He is currently undertaking extensive measures in Berlin to prepare for a sanitary struggle against the terrible epidemic. His Serum, which has become the talk of Europe, goes by the name of

ZENITHISM

The first news we've received has been quite alarming: after Rathenau's assassination all Germany is excited by the arrival of Maestro **Ljubomir Micić**, a man who is only by pure coincidence the son of our country. True, he has done nothing to deserve this bad luck, but as folks are wont to say, "**Fate is a kangaroo.**"

And as we are wont to say, "**We are too wise to be 'mad'**." Our wisdom breaks heads. Believe us, we have mercy for "**Thickheads**," but we unfortunately haven't much time to soften millions of skulls.

Zenithism

(let's be clear on this) is a principle that calls for the complete destruction and disarmament of

the anti-human army

for the sake of Man to come. Panic has taken over battalions of

Non-Humans

as the leaders of tomorrow's squadrons (**Napoleon—Ljubomir Micić and Bismarck—Valerium Poljanski**) arrive, each ready to fight for the new man!

Ljubomir Micić

sends his best from a land where rail traffic is as common as trams and where books sell as fast as bread rolls do in our country.

Well, I would write to you till the beginning of time, but I'm in a terrible rush to get to **Tokyo**, where my sweetheart is waiting for me in front of a certain Buddhist temple.

Her name is

Luma

She loves me because she can sense my genius in the fashionable cut of my coat. The tip of my pointy America-shoe represents the peak of my wisdom to my darling.

That female is Japan's audience. Down with Japan! Things are different with us, aren't they?

Long live the valley of wisdom!

Bye-bye! I can hear the toot of the **D-train** to Tokyo. So long!

Ever devotedly yours,

Valerium Poljanski

77 Suicides

Branko Ve Poljanski
Naklada Reflektor, Zagreb, 1923

Translated by *Steven Teref and Maja Teref*

4.1. B. Poljanski, *77 samoubica* [77 Suicides], Naklada Reflektor, Zagreb, 1923. Front cover. Drawing by B. Poljanski. Courtesy of Gallery RIMA, Kragujevac, Serbia.

The incredible love affair
of Mr. Nikifor Morton.
A very fast superfantastic novel.

Front cover drawing by Ve Poljanski

May you never forget me
Neither before my end
Nor at the end
To you, Branka
I dedicate this book
Which you won't understand

TSF[1]

sent out to the ends of the earth the terrible news:

Nikifor Morton is Dead!

Here is how this strange case unfolded:

For a time, a young man lived in the house at 14 Eternal St. The young stranger could be seen every evening when night caught in its net all the houses, the streets, and the entire horizon.

The room the young eccentric lived in was always quiet. Stuffy like a tomb. His things also always left in their place. No movement. Dead. Life without rhythm. And life was the rhythm of worlds in time to infinity.

No one knew the young man at 14 Eternal St. He kept to himself. Piercing green eyes. Oddly green. Eyes that left the impression of not seeing. Like glass eyes. Frightful and dazzling, as if dreaming about something big, coming to destroy the world.

The face of the young stranger was angular. Chiseled. As if made of wax. This face often terrified. Horrified. His whole bearing seemed like a wax fugitive from a suburban panopticon below which read:

3 Seconds Before the Act

9 o'clock. Footsteps rang out between the walls. Steps led to the second floor. The door opened softly. The young stranger left a wake of cold air. The door closed. Stillness set in as if no one entered.

Something must be said here.

It was known that this pale stranger dealt with obscurantist matters. Papers covered his desk. Heaps. Scribbled on. They said—rumor had it—that he recorded his secrets. No single living soul knew absolutely anything about it. He wrote in red ink. The little town—where he lived—believed the red ink was real human blood.

Only the dead knew his secrets!

It was important and of interest to know what had been written on his piles of paper?!

Every evening he entered the house at number 14. From the street one could see his windowpane light up. It stayed so bright deep into the night.

This peculiar pale young stranger with the waxen face and venomous green eyes was none other than

Nikifor Morton

He was young and furious. Slender and tall like a young oak tree. Conceited and cheerful as a tyrant. Proud. Angry and forceful. Good and sentimental. This last quality lay buried in the back of his mind's magazines. The first look into his eyes, incredible. But—so it was. Maybe it wasn't. We'll see! The spiritual lord Morton's professional occupation was

Destroyer of the World

He despised life. Why? Because life hadn't been created by his own will. And Morton fervently believed in imposing his own will. He hated everything with a real devilish force because—the world wasn't Morton's creation.

Nikifor Morton set his jaw. He wanted to destroy everything. From solar systems all the way down to his own life.

Why the World?

It was the first thought that stormed his brain when he awoke in the morning. And it was his last thought when he fell asleep.

Morton dreamed little. His infrequent dreams were inevitably mad: a volcano erupting, many volcanoes—at all corners of the world—needlessly destroying everything.

Morton's plans triumphed in his dreams. He felt completely exhausted in the morning. His face still and wan. His expression betrayed his dreams that life hadn't been pleasant.

That was the expression, like—the face of an executioner who had just hanged a hundred million evil-doers—people.

Morton hated people not only in his dreams. He also hated them in real life. Morton recently took it upon himself to poison Earth's atmosphere. To destroy all living people. Everyone. He would spare only one living thing and himself.

But what was that one thing? He himself didn't yet know. It would only have to exist first. Alone?! He'd order at once his heart not to beat anymore. Death.

Nikifor Morton's scheme failed. But Nikifor didn't go crazy. No. His will raged fantastical from its failure. That was the positivity of failure. He conceived a new and even more frightening and hellish scheme.

Annihilating Everything from Beginning to End

And—now Morton lived in that inexplicable scheme.

It should be noted that Nikifor Morton's hellish scheme would certainly succeed. With one movement of his hand, he would

Destroy the Whole World

Evening. Morton entered his room. His face brightened. Opposite his window was another window at house number

13

In the opposite window, he saw a bouquet of roses. Flowers. This sight had an unusual and soothing effect on his gloomy face. He was drawn to one particular big rose. Fresh. A heady ambrosia. His room grew redolent with its fragrance. A miracle. That evening, Morton didn't write a single note about his epic scheme:

How Should We Annihilate the World?

How miraculous and massive life would be if people could only be its masters! But! People were only miserable indigents:

The Servants of Life!

What a terrible accident for everyone.—*Was I meant to be a lackey?!!* Nikifor Morton, furious and wild, exclaimed to himself.

1st day after discovering the rose.

A searing gong wailed above the horizon. Night passed. Morton dreamed. A horrible dream. An unusual event. The world red. Cheerful. Everything fragrant.—The dream shocked Morton. A paradoxical dream. His real world was anything but red and fragrant. Odd. Out of the ordinary for his personality.

It had been an ordinary day.

Nikifor Morton spent his day observing. He observed everything from the cheerful point of view of destruction. Every form of life, even the smallest thing, interested him.—But what he loved most were architectural objects: temples, stock exchanges, cathedrals, factories, mosques, palaces, theaters, banks, and other stone colossuses.—Morton enjoyed observing each object in his own particular way.—He didn't celebrate their monumental nature as an expression of human culture, that which defied (!) space.—No.—Mostly, he felt an "aesthetic" enjoyment. He imagined how spectacular it would be to see each object at the moment of destruction!

Everything is Built to be Destroyed!

That maxim truly cheered up Nikifor Morton.

1st evening after discovering the rose.

Extraordinary! His steps weren't so heavy. The key didn't turn as usual. Everything passed calmly and easily.—Nikifor resisted it. But the elasticity was far more comfortable than the tremendous tension which ruled his physical and metaphysical body.—He entered the room cheerful. He whistled. A cheerful young man. Dawn. Flowers again grew fragrant in the breeze from the opposite window. He looked in the opposite window. Before him, an incredible transformation took place.—Was it possible?—Thought Morton—I'm not Christ!—Before Morton's eyes, a big rose. A large one. The largest one. Grew into a body. A miracle. The fresh cheerful body of a fragrant young woman.—Her body smelled like a pristine rose.—Morton felt the air freshen. The heavy pressure of the sickly dusty street dissipated. The scent intoxicated Nikifor's conscience.—The clean breeze of the new fragrant body swirled like a flock of black truths, coiling around Morton's skull.

Glory to You who bloomed in a window.—My visions were not the fortune of life.

Those were Morton's last words before bed.

2nd day after discovering the rose.

Nikifor Morton furious flung himself into the enlivened day. His dream tormented him. He dreamed that everything was black. Immeasurably black. Without fragrance or order. Black and nothing more.—That unfathomable blackness devoured his body and soul. Everything.—Was it really indeterminable?! Without ruin?! Without triumph?! No! Just not that!!! That mustn't be! Black or white. White or black.

but but.

2nd day after discovering the rose.

Nikifor Morton entered 14 Eternal St.—It had been late at night. Out on the street, the darkness barked. The last ray of light died in his soul. His room was too rigid that day. Hard.—Heavy. Black. Dark. Sick. Idiotic and mystical.

In the dark, he stood by the window. The moon cut the night.—Icy whiteness murmured over rooftops. Morton raised his hand and said:

Oh! Isn't there a path for me?
Oh! Isn't there a glass from which to drink?
Oh! Isn't there a bread with which I'll feed my hungry contradictions? Alas!

Give me something to inhale! Hey, moon! Pour your silver into my eyes. Give me something to inhale! Give me bloom. C'mon roses. Big rose, come here. Your bloom is more cheerful at my window. I'll pour my blood into a vase. You'll live long, long . . . forever!

He could feel daybreak.
It smelled like rhythm.
Why couldn't this murky piece stay
for a few billion years so that I could—rest from weariness

LLLiiivvve

There were days when my eyes had been more cheerful and my legs lighter. There were days when my heart beat till midnight. My feverish hands yearned to grip a young woman's body.—Today?! Everything is utopia. A lie. Disgusting.—And my real life is utopiiiiiaaaaaaaa. Poor me, woe to you, world.—The entire procession of earthbound ants is a stupid fiction. Not even that. Nothing. None. Nihil.—Nikifor Morton's soul spasmed by the window on an overcast morning burdened by astute spectral dissections. The moon. His dumb wan face grinned like a blasé Russian baron emigrant.

Everything is an Optical Illusion

Lord Morton felt with conviction that an unusual change was coming into the world. When? It wasn't quite clear to him. The world would be transformed.—The change hurled toward his body. Only he felt it with intensity.—(Everyone else was carefree.) Morton shuddered and the blizzard swirled around his bones.

Nikifor swam in his bed sheets as if in the sea. He fell asleep. Entering the window, daylight threatened with life.

3rd day after discovering the rose.

A boring old morning. Without change. The sun looked the same as yesterday. Only the people had changed—for the worse. Nikifor looked through the opposite window. He saw the rose body. Blossoming. Youth. Triumph of the sun. Her hair fell like braided darknesses.—Her name was

Mirjanđeja

She greeted Morton. The girl called out to him. Entangled in the cobweb of life, he forgot his immeasurable wealth.—Mirjanđeja reminded him of life.—Morton cheerfully cried into the day

I am young!

Stepping out into the street. Morton forgot about his window girl. His face darkened. Life overpowered him.—He met people, machines, cats, towers, nuns, monkeys, grisettes, butchers, actors, and other "cultural" cattle both alive and dead. A thought spiced by crazy desire raged.

Seeing All This Screaming Before its Ruin

Morton's eyes no longer held a trace of cheer or brightness.—This consumed him at his window. Nowhere out in the streets. Nowhere in the cities did Morton find it. Empty. Weariness. Boredom. A madhouse without doctors. A slaughterhouse without butchers. A czardom without a czar. A church without a priest. Lord Morton's eyes couldn't burn with the fire of life. Hatred. Without borders. Beyond reason. Nikifor's eyes saw everywhere only

Death.

3rd evening after discovering the rose.

Visions poisoned the eyes of Nikifor Morton. That evening he came home completely crushed. His face flashed with despair. The lines on his forehead coiled like snakes. Every thought about people enraged him to death. The millions of creatures Morton had seen with his own eyes and knew in his mind that they were still alive—rushed him to answer their question:

Why Did Our Mothers Bear Us?

His brain jerked in his skull like a snail whose shell had been stepped on.—May your stupid saws snap in two! If your life doesn't satisfy you, crawl back into your mother!—Morton retorted.

Morton cheered up.

At 13 Eternal Street, I have a fragrant window. In the window, a rose. A full one. Alive. I don't care about the world. My hours have been precisely numbered. How many of them remain?—How does tragedy arrange itself? I don't want to batter my skull with hard questions anymore.

At times, Morton surrendered to the maneuvering of his great will. To overcome the inner desire for utter destruction. He wanted cheer. A thought. Oh, to be a boy!—His equilibrium already rebelled. So young yet so violent.

Why does darkness saturate my eyes? My eyes exist to see the world.—To see life. To seek life.—To destroy found life with life.

To Create a New Life

Why do I torment myself over every contradiction?—For people's lives? Don't poison yourselves! You'll be happy!—This advice flashed in Morton's conscience.

Sing! Why be silent. Faces burn.—Move. Thought Morton again.

A lie. Truth seen from another perspective:

The World is Given to One Kind

The transformation of his soul.

My house. My stone ship. Fall apart. I. Nikifor Morton cannot live.—Neither the world nor I need my life. My life is a spectral waste of days and nights. My life is a lie in the mud of truths.

Night flowed through hollow windows pouring into the body of Nikifor the experimenter.

Silence smelled like fresh lilacs
like fire
like speed
like gasoline
like transcendental horrors
like weariness
like the mad boredom of concentration
like endless black and blueness
like horror
like corpses
like revolution

like rueful cheer
like blood

The night tired Morton's eyes.—His eyes soaked up the last rays of light from the opposite window. They closed. The manufacture hub for words of great tension churned without end.

Nikifor Morton stood at length with eyes closed at the window. He imagined an end to all ends. His speech. Soft. Horrible. Laborious. Icy. Night devoured words like a starving tiger.

Good Words. Great Words. Fast Words:

Why did that man plead for mercy yesterday but got a slap in the face instead?
At the window, why do I count down the minutes to death?!
There in the dark beyond the window, the scent of lilac.
At my window, wormwood!?
A song rises in my heart.
I don't want to sing.
I am not a good man.
I live in the year 1923.
No man in the world this year is good
Among the living
Only the dead are good!
I am dead
I am good without end like a pigeon
My mouth is my beak
My words, my wings
I'm flying

Mirjanđeja

Here—a letter:
In my heart, despair tears up my visions
In my soul, envy dies triumphant
My chest swells with goodness
Listen:
I inhale the deep dark air from the breeze of your hair
Nothing can move me from this spot

I exhibit my great love like chiseled stone
My eye burns without prayer
I'll scorch all evil!
People are weary with corruption
Crime is a heavy burden our backs bear
Don't sink into a silk stocking. Wait!
I'll stay here forever
It would be magnificent
If my life watched You without end
Mirjanđeja
May this moment last forever
The fragrant night washes over me with passion
Life's disgust is nothing to me
not yesterday
not today
nor even tomorrow
Now is all I know.
May 9 p.m. on May 1, 1923 always remain
May time stand still
Not backward
Not forward
I want the birth of this poem to stay in my soul
Mirjanđeja
What golden fish is purer than your body?
What apple more wholesome than your face?
Merriment itself isn't merrier than your life
Mirjanđeja
If the heavens were mine
Believe me!
The stars would be your necklace
I would give you a gift on our wedding day
And then I would die
I wouldn't let anyone insult you with their eyes.

Remember
When I first saw you at the window
The day was opaque and life stained the street
Under our windows.
I laughed.
That was a lie!
Mirjanđeja
Nikifor Morton doesn't know how to laugh
Laughter poisons and hurts him.
Our secret has yet to be revealed!
Mirjanđeja! Goodbye!
In my silk dreams, I kiss your pale feet
Farewell.

4th day after discovering the rose.

Nikifor Morton got on his old rabid nag and galloped into his day.—Fast.—Gradually. Lightning speed. Mindlessly. He sought. Looked everywhere. Screeched. Called out. Cursed.—He climbed the bell tower. Struck the bell. He set the cathedral clock back 777 hours. Nothing! Still nothing. He couldn't change it. Terrible.—Hellish idiotic monotony. Nothing had changed. Transformaaaaaaaaaaaation.—He roared the streets silently.

He immersed himself into yesterday. Evening. Yesterday by the window. A frosted dark appeared to cover his cheeks. Transparent.—An odd constellation of features.—Fantastic geometry.

Ancient Egyptian science—they said—they told one's future by reading one's facial features.

Morton's face revealed something strange. It defied description. One could easily tell by that face that something special would undoubtedly happen with this man! What? No explanation. Something. It must!

Even Morton the destroyer felt quite clearly that a transformation to another form was nigh. What kind of form would it be? Elusive. A future math would provide an accurate answer.

It would come! It was coming!

Nikifor Morton walked the streets. Laughed.—Only he Morton laughed like that. A cynic of immeasurable proto-goodness. That laugh wasn't a typical stretching of the mouth to show teeth. That laugh was a lethal power. Elementary. That laugh couldn't by any account be endured by the weak. They would collapse.—They would spin on their navels. Electrified by the power of the deadly charge.

No horse could trot the street without Morton getting on it and crying out: Forward! Forward!

No face could walk down the street without Morton spitting into it crying out: Disgusting! Disgusting!

Where?

There?

Yes. Morton was certain that "there" wasn't far. He didn't know what kind of black monstrosity it was.—He only felt it gripping his skull like an iron polyp.

To march? He overcame that fear within himself. Why have a premonition of something that had yet come to pass? I am here. That is important now. My heart still beats. My eyes still see. My arms hang. My feet carry me. My poor soul ponders its reality. My body swims in sunlit air. It doesn't ask how?! To whom? Where?

Life is to be lived

Throughout the day Morton encountered many silly miracles.—But now. Ha! Triumph. He ran into Mirjanđeja. For the first time in the sun. During the day. For the first time he heard her voice. She spoke.—Nikifor listened.—Mirjanđeja asked: You're undoubtedly an unusual man?

No, Mirjanđeja. You. Fragrant in the street. I don't know who and what I am. I know. A man I am not. I am a monster. I don't understand myself at all. I am not one being! That I know. Indeed! I am one. Just so! I have 77 bodies. Those bodies are scattered all over the world like people's conscience. In big cities.—Now! It is 4 o'clock. In the afternoon. At this moment, all of my other bodies are standing in another 76 places on 76 streets and speak words

From the new gospel

I'm speaking to You. Another 76 mouths are speaking the same words the world over. Yet! I am still only one creature. How so?—Incredible! True. A miracle! An intoxicated transparency has given me 77 bodies.

You! My great disclosed secret. Pure and white. Silky and beautiful. Incredibly good. Strange. Fiery.—My dearest one in the triumph of sunlit rain. The sorrow of my wisdom. My idol from a starry kingdom. You don't know the secret of my life.

Mirjanđeja pleaded.

Tell me. Oh! Tell me royally wise Nikifor. Greatest among the czars. The strongest of all heroes. The wisest in the valley of opaque wise men. More beautiful than the most beautiful. The best of the best. Tell me! Reveal the secret about you! Or I'll die.—Raise me from the dead.—Being among worms is disgusting and nauseating. Take me to your loftiest worlds. Life there isn't as soiled and disgusting as it is in the swamp among the mosquitoes. "God" said even mosquitoes are so-called people. Save me! Save! Nikifor, greatest in your goodness!

No! My dearest of dearests. Mirjanđeja! Suffer! Down there! Here with me there's more to endure.—I love You too much to disfigure Your face with eternal pain. No! You, first tear of my eye!—You're too lucid for me to darken Your soul with the darkest of darknesses. No! You mean too much to me to allow You to be humiliated by the truth from my world. To suffer! To laugh! To lie! To live!—Just don't ask anything about the other side.

Listen. Here is the most important truth about us. I feel that an incredible comedic miracle will happen to us. Sorrowful and joyful. Far from happiness. Uncomfortable. Tragic. (Local tragedy!) That's why! I want us to say goodbye. Farewell. I don't know why. But I know it has to be that way. Change rushes at lightning speed.—Mirjanđeja! Be cheerful. Don't cry. Tears are a sickness. Tears kill. Tear apart. Eat away. Eat up. The body falls like trees. Mirjanđeja, be happy. Farewell! I kiss your sensual hands. Your feet and toes, eyes and hair, lips and cheeks!—Don't let my fire scorch you. I love You because when I'm dead I won't be kissing your body.

4th evening after discovering the rose.

Proto-archetypal mourning enveloped the heart of the joyful Morton.—He knelt in the moonlight. An entire evening. An entire night. Idiotically sentimental.

In black and white. After tyranny in the life of the most notorious aggressors, a pathological sentimentality set in. Morton's case!

5th day after discovering the rose.

99 crowing roosters solemnly observed the occasion.

Morton's first step. He tripped. Not far from falling. When the world fell there would be a din—an unthinkable din as if sunlit volcanoes spilled their fires from all corners of the heavens. One.—Even faster. And the world's gone.

How miraculous the world was.

People seemed changed today to Morton. Unusually so. Everyone carried something on their shoulders. But—not heads. Objects replaced heads.

First case—instead of a head: a church bell.

Second case	an empty pot
Third case	chainsaw ring gear
Fourth case	a car horn
Fifth case	a swine head
Sixth case	a pointed shoe

The Seventh case had instead of a head—as seen on shoulders—a real wooden nightstand.

Strange. Nikifor Morton passed the streets in awe. He rejoiced at the world suddenly developing some kind of new face.

Morton walked fast. Something suddenly stopped him.—Nikifor didn't see anyone nearby.—He had to halt as if on command.

He stopped.

He listened. Somebody called him by name.

No!

That wasn't a voice. That was a wave of energy penetrating his frontal bone and established contact with his inner world. Incredible. Ha! Nikifor remembered.

Brain radiogram

He listened further. He felt the words:

I am here. I'm calling you. Your Mirjanđeja. I'm dying for you, Morton. Your life is my death. You are preparing for a great feat. I'll be dead when it happens. I can't bear to see your ruin. Know this. Your Mirjanđeja respects you. Loves you. Every moment of my life I have kneeled before your body. In spirit.—You! My big beautiful and powerful king! You who gave me life before god—you'll die! I suffer.—Poor me, I didn't know how to defeat death with my love.—My weak love wasn't strong enough for your spiritual colossus.

May the rivers flow into the seas! May the seas sink into the earth.

—May the lakes disappear into underground chasms!—May hearts stop beating.

May all life stop in the world because I, Mirjanđeja, didn't know to give you, my majestic Morton, a glass of my tears which would heal your incredible suffering.

Nikifor Morton stood in the street with his eyes closed. A blind man. With extended arms. People put money in the palm of his hand. Money stung him but he didn't know what stung him. His conscience was overcome by an odd conversation. He wasn't a beggar. His arms were extended with a desire to hug someone. Stupid people! Giving to the rich! A noose for the poor man. People are such dogs.

He listened further:

My last hours approach my body and soul quietly and solemnly.

I'm sick. I'm crying. Love poisons me. My bitter mouth. Morton, my dear! I won't see the next day. Today is my last day.

At 3 p.m., I will feel the last breeze from your window. I'll cry into the breeze. My last sob will be for you to remember.

At 4, my body will stiffen for all eternity. In that rest, good mother earth will cradle me.

At 5, my father will come with my mother and cry at my bedside. Their wretched selves won't know that I didn't die from death.

I'll die because of You, Nikifor. For you, swarthy Morton, I will defeat death.

At 6, a gilded carriage drawn by liveried horses will carry me to the morgue.

Farewell, my good Nikifor. Don't be surprised when I don't come to my window when you sing. You'll be calling me from your window. I won't be home. I'll be far away. Don't call my name for long! I'll be truly gone. When you're blue, look to the heavens above my house. The thirteenth twinkly star straight above from the corner of my house—that's me. If you call to me and despair long enough, the thirteenth star will fall. I'll be the unhappiest one among the stars.

Farewell, my strong one! My dear! My handsome Nikifor!

Your Mirjanđeja rubs your head and kisses your dark brow.

Morton heard everything. Really? A fantasy? The Devil? God? A dream? Mirjaaanđeeeeeee–j–aa– – – – – – –

A head too heavy to bear. Morton collapsed, his body like lead.

A throng gathered around Morton's body. Every bystander rejoiced (not at all saddened) at it not happening to them.

A short time passed. Morton woke up. He opened his eyes. He saw people watching him like a rare animal. He realized he was lying on the sidewalk. Yes. This was a street, not my bed. It was day, not night. This is life, not a dream. He gathered his strength. He jumped up. Nimbly. He strode with sharp and resolute steps.—**Human cattle**, he cordially greeted the elegant audience. He disappeared.

He reflected on what had happened.

First, I got up. Paralyzed with my arms outstretched. Standing. And then? I collapsed. Lying in the street, what happened before that? I had been listening to something. I was receiving signals. I had been thinking defeatist thoughts. Still. Those thoughts hadn't been from within me. Someone else's. How? Whose? Yes! Yes! I know Mirjanđeja had been recounting her death. Could it be true?—This chilled his mind! For Mr. Devil, that was only a fantasy. Our minds have yet to become radiotelegraphic stations. Still, I had been receiving words unhatched by my mind. A current rippled through my skull as I received the signals. Argh! What time was it? The question shot through Morton's consciousness. Mindlessly, he rushed toward the square. His eyes fixed the hands on the cathedral clock. 5:59. He jumped up as if slammed by rage. In 55 seconds, Morton materialized at his window. The tenants from 14 Eternal Street marveled at Morton's arrival. He had never entered his apartment in daylight.

Nikifor stood at the window. Morton stared out. All the formations before him rippled black for a moment as if at sea. All quieted down. The street wasn't as noisy as before. All grew silent. A carriage approached. A carriage, Morton thought. A strange car. A fantastic, absurd carriage. Horses. For a million gods' sake! Liveried horses! Alongside the carriage strolled some old grotesques—the world like a grotesque! Ha! Cheerful!—Morton reasoned ahead. The carriage stopped. True. It stood still. As if made of stone. Door 13 opened. Four ridiculous creatures carried a long coffin. A silver coffin. Heavy indeed.

What is thaaat?

The question roared from the blanching, turned white—Nikifor Morton. Nobody heard his question. The black creatures loaded the silver coffin onto the carriage. The carriage was insanely ridiculous. Pitiful was its gilded body.

Morton laughed!

His laughter petrified the whole street. Everyone looked up at the window. Up at him. And so, they became petrified. Morton's laughter cricked their necks. The horses' hooves froze mid-step. Crick! At the window, an unnatural screech tore from Nikifor: Go away! What are your eyes bulging for? Go on! The street isn't a museum! Get lost!

At this pompous request, everything set into motion again. The horses awoke. The ludicrous mustached creatures lowered their heads. The gilded carriage with the liveried horses moved on. The tragic absurd wave coursed around the corner down another street. An unbearable stillness set in.

The dike holding back eternity collapsed. Time rushed like a raging river. Like the wind, evening whistled its way down.

The window. Morton at the window. Stone still. The desperate empty sky. The gods had plucked the stars like cherries.

The opposite window was lit as in evenings past.

But the roses weren't as fragrant as before.

A profound fear assailed Morton. He wanted to scream but his strength failed him. Words, desperate and terrifying like a dust storm tore up his inner oasis.

And. Morton collapsed at the window.

In a coma.

6th day after discovering the rose.

Morning. Morton woke up. Opened his eyes. Stared at the sturdy, smeared wall. His body spent. Weak, as if beaten with a steel rod. He realized he had slept through the night on the floor by the window. An uncomfortable bed.—I was sound asleep.—I hadn't felt alive, even subconsciously!

He got up. Looked at the opposite window. But the curtains were closed. He whistled. A long time. A very long time.

No response.

Stillness.

He sang his usual song:

There
In the far land of Japan
Looking for me all night, a strange woman
Crying in the dark, she carries a lotus flower.

No response.

Morton roared at the opposite window like a lion in the desert:

Mirjaaaađeeeejaaaaaa

mmmmmmmmmmmmmmm

No response.

Stillness.

He felt as if he were dying like a flopping fish.

The day passed. Terrible and lonesome. Nikifor Morton tied a knot. The sword sharpened. Lopping should begin.

Morton didn't see anything or anyone during the day. Emptiness. He knew nothing. He heard nothing. Emptiness.

The city reminded him of a tremendous cemetery. He roamed the streets. Mute and deaf. He gaped as if looking for an empty grave for all of his own bodies. Morton wished to lie down into it alive. To be buried alive.

77 graves should be dug for Nikifor Morton. He has 77 bodies.

Morton's face ricocheted with triumph. He found the solution. In the factory of his feelings, a supernatural sadness poured like an hourglass.

There you are my big great world

6th evening after discovering the rose.

Nikifor Morton entered his room. 9 o'clock. The world from his window existed perspectively like before.

The opposite window was now black and empty. Closed. Nothing. Stillness. Silence as among the stars. The far-off muffled rumbling of Morton's 77 airplane engines sounded. The airport at the city outskirts.

Morton's windows were bright. Like the eyes of a wolf. Morton's arms and head moved against the walls of the house opposite. A projected shadow. Disembodied Morton.

The drunks were singing. Madness in the air. The night was the night. But! A change was in the air. A great change.

Morton gathered his secret papers. He arranged them in the middle of the room. It was unusual. He couldn't even fathom—why?

12 were rejected. Nikifor Morton's room was strange. It became another form. A new face. Everything was systematized. Everything in the middle of the room. Over everything, the table. Secret papers lay on the table. A strange thing was among them. It resembled a photographic apparatus. From afar. It was some kind of machine. It was

A machine from Hell

The hands of the catastrophe would be exactly at 12.—The time space was 24 hours.

So. Exactly at that time tomorrow. The entire house would dream of midnight wonders. Then, the greatest miracle would happen. The house would break into its separate components—bricks.

Morton did it so his neighbors wouldn't forget.

After completing his work, Morton left the room. He turned the key twice. It creaked as if in some idiotic hell. Steps. Morton went down. Down into the deepening murk. A dog barked behind a door. Then. Perfect stillness. On the street. Police. Rifles. Pointers. A terrible tension in Morton's soul. Every heart beat in Morton's skull. They almost broke through the skull. Night. At the distant airport, the hellish roar of propellers. The sign of a long journey.

Go to hell, city. Little town. Picture perfect.—Morton thought.—If a single one of my bodies could gift you one part of its life, it would have been cretinously negatively ridiculous. Here, I greet you! When my first airplane leaves your walls behind you'll burn up in flames. Go to hell, you wretched corpse behind the ridge.[2] My eyes aren't x-rays, so supposedly I won't lay my eyes on you anymore once I fly my plane to the hills. To hhhhhhheeeeeeelllllll!

A sharp, singeing wind hit Nikifor's sunless face. He left for the airport. A brief time passed. Instead.

Nikifor Morton, the tyrant and destroyer, boarded 77 airplanes. They furiously flew over the black sea to the world's deepest blue. And fly did

Nikifor Morton.

7th day after discovering the rose.

The airplane night passed. A morning of new worlds. Morton flew into 77 cities. Millions of people felt a new presence among them. They didn't know his name. They didn't see his faces. They felt only fear. Around him, Morton cast this fear in the atmosphere. His fury poisoned the air.

On every continent, a few of Morton's airplanes crashed at 77 airports. 77 bodies exited those planes in 77 cities. Seventy-seven unusual visitors were

He

Nikifor Morton.

Morton stood in 77 squares. He was in impossibly profound thought. He stood. A minute. An hour. Hours. Till the evening. Motionless. A man of stone. It was in the main squares of these 77 cities:

1. Tokyo
2. Bjornberg
3. Takapan
4. Anvers
5. Ohakune
6. Belgrade
7. Banjarmasin
8. Paris
9. Larnaca
10. Athens
1. Hong Kong
2. Amsterdam
3. Bangkok
4. Prague
5. Morogoro
6. Petrograd
7. Orillia
8. Constantinople
9. Occoquan
20. Madrid
1. Narva
2. Warsaw
3. Reims
4. Smolensk
5. Berlin
6. Cairo
7. Tangier
8. New York
9. Tampere
30. Amagasaki
1. Kuala Lumpur
2. Los Angeles
3. Alexandria
4. Denver
5. Sofia
6. Colombo
7. Stockholm
8. Surabaya
9. Baltimore
40. Christiania
1. La Paz
2. Hamburg
3. Bucaramanga
4. Vinh
5. Lobito
6. Tehran
7. Diego Suarez
8. George Town
9. Wadi Halfa
50. Gumaken
1. Khattan
2. Teluk Anson
3. Chicago
4. Jerusalem
5. Balboa
6. Rockhampton
7. Escanaba
8. Montreal
9. Ufa
60. Port Arthur
1. Cape Town
2. Port Sudan
3. Baghdad
4. Colombo
5. Homs
6. Saginaw
7. Khaitan
8. Shika
9. Sungei Petani
70. Nagano
1. Shkodër
2. Cobán
3. Santiago
4. Yamagata
5. Ca' Rangon
6. Kharkov
77. Toronto

Morton held onto his last thoughts before the apocalypse. Why the sentimentality? Go ahead! Hooray! Earth, that prostitute in space! Annihilation. And after? Let a new nine-headed god be born. He needs to create a new world. It's wrong. Worms have disfigured it.

Tropical and icy northern nights surrounded Morton's bodies. At once. He observed people.—Passing. In a hurry. Falling. Driving. Picking themselves up. Dying. Cursing. Robbing. Killing. Suffering. Lying. Stealing. Crying. Cheering. Killing each other. Having orgies.

The music of Morton's last minutes tore at night's heavy curtains. Now. A few minutes more. Get out! All would sink into black.

The twenty-fourth hour hand of the apocalypse ticked on the hell machine. There in his room. 14 Eternal Street. A city of idiots. 11 minutes more! 11.

Morton's thought apparatus for the final 11 minutes.

First minute: My name is Nikifor Morton. In 10 minutes, I will no longer be called Nikifor Morton.

Second minute: I am a man. An incredible wise man. I have 77 bodies. In 9 minutes, I will be beyond the borders of wisdom. Beyond my body.

Third minute: I have loved the world. The object. I have been the subject. I have adored the visions. They became reality. My incredible power of love was to destroy. In 8 minutes, we'll see the result.

Fourth minute: I have suffered. Not on my account. That's why I'm destroying it. My suffering was my joy. My joy tormented me to madness. I didn't believe in reality. I've always possessed sad visions. You wouldn't believe it. Still. I was the cheeriest man in the world. In 7 minutes, the 77 faces of Nikifor Morton, the son of Doctor Devil, and the grandson of Master God, will die.

Fifth minute: Everything was. Screaming and sobbing. Hatred and spasms. The cobweb caught the dying young bodies. Dying is sweet. Fast. The only joy in the world. Plastic psyche: Nothing to feel sorry for. Everything will return. Dizzy, I will send the world into a tailspin.

$$77 \div 1 = \text{Morton}$$

In 6 minutes, it will be $77 \div 1 \div \text{world} = 0$

Sixth minute: I have carried the heavens on my shoulders. I'm tired. I can't hate anymore. In 5 minutes, I'll lower my shoulders. The heavens will fall. Yes! It'll be mathematically accurate. All. Glorious! Victory! Yes!

Seventh minute: I always wanted the indescribable and unimaginable immeasurability of empty space. In 4 minutes, the universe will be empty. Completely. A place for a new creature. The absolute system of a new world. Without relativity. Philosophy, pick up your feet. I'll be the beginning. Therein lies the secret of the destruction of this world in 4 minutes.

Eighth minute: I created to destroy. I destroyed to create. In 3 minutes, I'll start anew.

Ninth minute: Already! Fast! Mindlessly! Forcefully! Charge! God's fiery wind blows! The icy spheres course through my eyes. I love everything, from nothing to 9,999 suns. In two minutes, all suns will fall to darkness.

Tenth minute: Here. Thus lived, spoke, thought, and fell the world. Hear. In a minute, the seventy-seven-bodied Nikifor Morton, in 77 squares, will utter his last words in 77 languages.

Eleventh and last minute: You. Me. You. Me. The world. Grotesque. Funny tragedy. Tragic ridicule. Fantastic caricature. The final minute burns the tips of my fingers. It'll fall apart. Joyfully. A transcendental grinning will tear every ear. I won't leave anything behind. Why indeed destroy everything. The wall of China?! Every airplane?! Women's underwear?! Stock markets?! Tigers?! Philosophies?! Brothels?! Art?! Seashores?! Movie beauties?! Dissectsalons?! Dollars?! Moscow?! Chaplin's moustache?!

I dreamed of the greatest good. I saw the perfect end.—Love! The repulsive symbol of marriage beds! Is that the joyous burn of the sun? Love: the body trade! The father sells his son. The mother sells her daughter. The daughter sleeps in her father's bed. The mother sleeps with the whole street. Excellent! The servant class! All is "relative"! What is immoral to you. I love the smell of sperm in brothel hallways. Quiet! My pale face. Don't distort. The heavens will cover it. Ooooonne. Hello! Who's there? God?!—This is Nikifor Morton! "Destruction and New World Creation, Inc."—Twooooooooooooo. Lord God! I had appointed you General Director of the heavens. **You have abused your position!** By creating our world, you achieved a negative outcome. You've been replaced! Get lost! Kill yourself!

Threeeeeeeeeeeeeeeee! Morton's arm raised by itself. The gun barrel rested against the forehead. A thought. Last one. A word. Mirjanđeja! The vowel *aaaa* remained on his lips. Bang!

An incredible crack thundered on the horizon. Morton fired one bullet. 77 corpses collapsed in stone squares in 77 cities.

A terrifying immeasurable desert of suspended colorless space.

The world was no more! Not at all!

A police superintendent in Tangiers stuck his hand into the pocket of dead Morton. He drew out a long letter. The letter said:

Nikifor Morton's Will.

The superintendent opened the letter. A poem. Really? A will?! Ha!? A very wealthy man! The police superintendent told his partner laughing.

People gathered simultaneously in 77 cities around 77 police superintendents. Huge crowds called for Nikifor Morton's poem to be read aloud in each of the squares.

The poem was dedicated to the world! To us! The mobs howled.

For fear of being lynched, 77 police superintendents read the very strange poem in 77 town squares before 77 crowds in 77 languages.

Poem on the new Babylon in the gun barrel at the end of space.

To you
Millions of races and nations
On every planet
And bestowing the last poem
For all times
For all beginnings
For all endings

I

Nikifor Morton, have joyfully strolled along the asphalt of the Milky Way
A telescope from the town square can see the gold mines of Mars
Sadness broke my jaw from disgust
Muzzled dogs flew into the pince-nez
Of wise professors
A dark chord shattered the attic with a whistle
A thought meowed with its eye, hammered the
victory of a deed
The thorn black at the bottom of the lake in the eye
Of a legendary storm god
A sharp bullet
Laughter cut through wires of sorrow
Entered grand crystal castles

Before the humiliated mob
Revealed to them the truth of all truths:
Brothers, gold has the least value in the world!

Soft stars fell into our eyes
Babylon crumbled into gun barrels
In the dark, the blind saw the supreme picture
A wail rattled
Hear
At the bottom of the sacred Ganges
Dead Buddha's servants hug a hundred-armed god
Calmly waiting for the heads of the desperate
For suicide bullets
Eyes dream of the idiotic infinite
Mother
6 feet in the earth, icy, and soaked through
Can panic be felt at the New York Stock Exchange
1, 2, 9, 4 4 4 4 4, 9 9 9 9 9 9 9^{9999999}
Mathematics!
We extended our arms to reach the ending
So!?
Distances singed our fingers
We are disgusted!
Heeeeey! Geometryyyyyyyy
Give us water
A glass
A lake
A river
A sea
The open sea
Boundless and reflecting
So that we can slip with finality and ending
Across heaven and hell

Into eternal fiery laughter
Restless are the wombs of volcanoes
Holy eruption, have mercy on us
Let's drink by the window exactly at the break
Of light and dark
Blood soda
The trigger's song
Joyous screeching revolution
Bring a sword
Raise the flag
A pocketknife
A rifle
A motorless cannon
Airplanes
Tanks
Humankind
Arabs, Indians, Serbs, Chinese, barbarians, and
Russians
To shed blood like rakija
We flood the boulevards
Lazy and drunk
In all the Parises, Londons, and Chicagos
Let's go
All of the heliocentric systems
Let's drive them in a huge car
A fast one
A fast one
The fastest of the fast
So every tooth falls out
In the triumph of the chase
Ay yai yai
The last hilarious comedy
Under a heavenly cap

To pour all of the skyscrapers
Streetcars
Factories
Temples
And brothels
Into one's pockets
To build an interplanetary republic on Saturn
To make all of space proud
Ha?!
The great future of people
Fear not!
Hooray chaaaaaaaaaaarge! As fast as you can
Like lightning
Any women's blouse can be removed
Phonetically in a dream
For five coins
To love!?
Poor tactics
Truth
Get lost!
Mirjanđeja
You who gobbled all the bells
From parliaments and cathedrals
You left me this mad and lonely
To lose my mind from the silence
Hooorrrrrrrraaaaaaaaaaaay
Yes!
On the high Tatra mountains to drink the lakes
To cruelly bend the thumb
To hang
The sun
The moons
People

To knock about space
Like a giant with a barrel
To pour time so it flows like a river
Before our horrified eyes
From the source to the mouth inexpressible
Nothing.
Forgive me!
But laughing at someone who's strongest in laughter
  Is hysterically funny

Co Co	**C**	CCC CCC CCC	**A**	III III III	**N**	E E

Cocaine in the vein!
Vision in the soul!
A curse in the mouth!
From the Eiffel Tower to howl with laughter
To fire at the fastest planes
Which will in a second
100
Burn the foundation to the ground
And then give a mighty kick
To pound the earth
Like a soapsud
Into the vacuum
To be a creator!
To create the super monumental!
Timeless
☛ **NEW** ☚
EW
My ears have endured so much
Believe me

If there is faith
In your corrupted souls
Please don't laugh! One ought to be moral! Yes!
It was incredibly hard
Gods cursed her!
The devil himself brought her before my eyes.
Her name was
Arđena.
Her body was a fiery serpent.
I desired her like a hungry jackal
But her visions were only
Of an automobile!
She was the monster of stupidity
Today
Arđena is a living corpse somewhere
In the embrace of a wealthy idiot!
My blood on rouged cheeks.
And
Said he! Who? A cop!:
"Excuse me, sir
You held a revolver."
A wise adage tears a street at night:
Slaughterhouse.
Letters screech into the bright lantern panes
My childhood memories lit up
The present collapses into forgetfulness
Tomorrow burns
My philosophy outwitted
Me
Oh, Kantian misery
How many of you will the earth breed
You write fat lies
For mice and straitjackets

From Plato to Einstein
Too many lies to believe!
Get going, Lenka.
Start anew, man!
Horses' clops clip-clop at night
Stone-like across the rooster's beak
Weren't all, my son, followers of the hard I am
Stop!
Whoever you are
You're under my window
My skull is not a violin
But a bone without acoustics
Take up maple wood gusles
And play to the joyless skies
Let me hear the man say!
A soul is no camel
Asia is no fantasia.
A mammoth is no human, a civilized piglet
In 8,888,888,888 bordellos
Daughters of the sun, eat Eden's apple
Serpent culture says:
"Upside down virtue
Is a sin!"
Umwertung aller Werte[3]

$$\frac{36}{36}\times 36 = 63$$

A door.
Step past the threshold.
Rap your finger against your forehead
Think
Where does this path lead
That covers our faces with pitch blackness?

You pass a street
You feel disgust and further contemplate
Factory smokestacks should trumpet:
"The machines are tired!"
Who died
So that rough-hewn wheels can lumber down the road?
It's ludicrous seeing a dead man
Whose voice rang in our ear yesterday!
Life isn't hazardous foolishness!
Look! Doesn't life have more faces
Beside a woman's smirk and a full stomach?
They stole that from us, too
Those
Who see savage red
As we have once before
We know, oh, do we know sharplight like a knife
We do know the pointed tip
So they wouldn't hear our thunder
Throats.
Hey, priest, where's your belly
Chaplin is our Christ
Pogrom
Pogrom
Hehehe
The magic broom
Becomes a rifle
In the hands of exhausted cleaners
Of new roads!
Theorize, theorize, my mind,
Till the stone blossoms a fresh rose
Till the crowd sees through wise men
Till entombed corpses joyfully shimmy
Thick blackness smokes, smokes, oh, how it smokes

Rush to the roofs, then vertically to the foundation
Splendid is the music of the sun's detonation
When all square windows break
Glass and grains
Our sorrow, our mare
Reasonably arrange life
So that you die in your bed stupidly
Normally
Dear bathos
Highest ethos
What piglet nowadays cares for your good reputation
Doesn't every creature rape you
By day
By night
Everywhere and in every place?!
Outstretched arms
My good comrades
New poets
Don't think by shoe
Smash marble with your head
To learn how to write verse
Religions
Trainloads of books } **May wolves eat you alive**
Philosophies } **Those bandits**
Give us new life!
¡ Gods
Idiots
Oxen
Cretins
Fictitious scoundrels. !
Three of our skulls have burst!
We ask wise men
? ? ? ? ? ? ? ? ? ?

Stupidly bend down and prattle “a priori” foolishness
Dancing on her toes
A beautiful emigrant
A black-eyed Russian
A stylized revolution in contempt
One ballerina’s toe is worth more
To a fat banker
Than an army of geniuses!
They’re crazy
And her soft toe
Fresh into the round foot fits
“L-o-v-e
I l-o-v-e
Bam bim bam
Bim bam bim bam
A thousand dinars spent
Just to see her naked body
White
Sight!
In the municipal dissecting room
Surgeons cut through the brains of suicides
Please
Diagnose how to target the wretched poor
Watch! Science!
Academic butchers!
Sand into their eyes.
Go for the banker’s stomach.
Alas
To ashes
To ashes } **To rush the first and last lie**
To ashes
The night of my childhood
When I cried on the tracks in the snow

The memory eats at my heart
The devil took hearts to Africa
I haven't gone to faraway worlds
The train didn't come
My tears weren't money
A child
Collapsed desperately onto the tracks
People don't have wings
Nine laughs laughed within me
The past
Dear girl
May I pluck your firm breasts
Like oranges
Youth
May I weld my arms around your body
Joy of mine
Antonia!
You're the triumph of my rapture
Don't lie before roosters rouse the sun.
"What would then happen without erotica"
Said my friend Rikard.
To die like heroes of paradox
Primitive man ■■■■■■■
Last night a poet wrote the oddest words
Last night a cow birthed the oddest three-headed calf
Last night a comet annihilated a faraway solar system
Night of wonders
Life must be a perpetual new wonder
Distances burn
Bats flit in the murk
Starved
And yet one must live.
To wonder a wonder with wonder
Aaaaaaaaaaaaahhhhhhhh.

■
■
■
■
■
■
■

AMEN

Endnotes

1 *Télégraphie sans fil*. French for 'wireless transmission.'

2 In the original, there is a phrase partially bolded "i**za greb**ena" ("behind the ridge"). The bolded letters spell the Croatian capitol Zagreb.

3 "Revaluation of all values" (Ger.)

Panic under the Sun

Branko Ve Poljanski
Zenithists International Edition, Belgrade, 1924

Translated by *Steven Teref and Maja Teref except where noted*

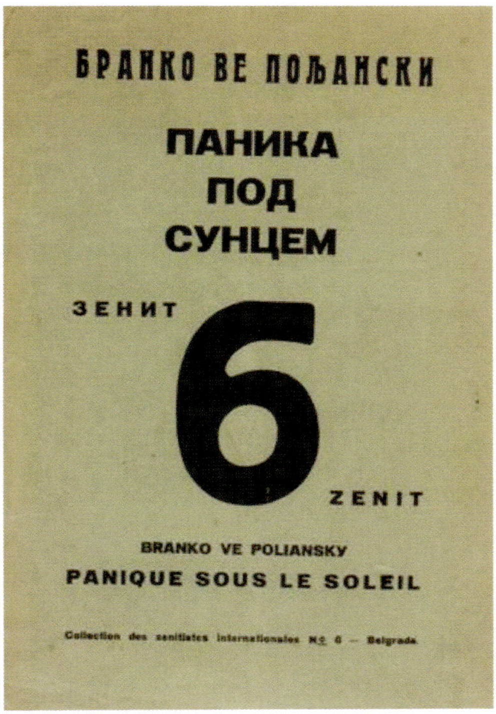

4.2. B. Poljanski, *Panika pod suncem. Tragedija balkanske azbuke* [Panic under the Sun. The Tragedy of the Balkan Alphabet], Zenithist International Edition, no. 6, Belgrade, Serbia, 1923, Front cover. Courtesy of Ubu Gallery, New York & Galerie Berinson, Berlin.

No!

The first word I uttered after being born was—No!—*Negation*! I boldly assert that is a rock of wisdom and that negation is the meaning of the world. It is the fundamental law of nature. *You die, so that I live who just came*. So it is with people and with truths, since truths come with people. There isn't an internal logic, everything is rhythmic and in motion. And logic moves. Zenithism is the new literary logic from which a new philosophy will be born. After the literary republicanism and aesthetic of pederasts, comes a new epoch—*Zenithism*.

Wretched is our literature and the revolution in it, which has stooped so low that it is now propagated by ruined Austrian cadets and Jewish onanists. And since the zenithist duty is to salvage the broken spirit of the broken man, so our work is very, very challenging, but victory is surely ours. Although I pity, being born with such a sense of humor in the Serbian language, I still continue to a great light into the dark of our cultural misery and shame. Convinced that the law of the strong applies to the spiritual world, I forge forward from trench to trench, carrying a cannon on my shoulders, which will never run out of ammunition whose name is positive spirit. All that's ephemeral, idiotic, reptilian, plagiaristic, epigonic, and reactionary will go to a hundred devils together with D'Annunzio, Homer, Shakespeare, and Charlesky; and what will remain will be the new literature for the new mankind: the works of all the zenithists the world over.

Bogdan Popović[1] will sooner go through the eye of a needle than pigs will understand me. *What is clear to god is not clear to an ox*! Ideas are the fate of mankind and individuals. Look before you leap. I looked and it's up to you to leap!

May 1924

Truthfully yours,
Branko Ve Poljanski

Mih. S. Petrov: Portret de Branko Ve Poliansky

Branko Ve Poljanski

PANIC UNDER THE SUN

The Tragedy of the Balkan Alphabet

C'mon, Now!

This collection doesn't need a specific recommendation since a Belgrade daily wrote in black and white that Branko Ve Poljanski is a genius poet. We don't have anything to add or deduct, all the more because Serbian dailies represent the conscience of this country and they reliably stand in the place of the Old and the New Testament. This is so in all Christian countries in which perverse murders and famed spy adventures are regularly celebrated. Our sole duty, despite everything, is to impressively exclaim: Hosanna, zenithists!

It would be too barbarian to not have mercy for a homeland full of sweat and make-up (after Albania and Dobro Polje!)[2], at a moment when its wretched literature appears: panic under the sun. No! In the face of such a catastrophe, let's not speak about paradoxes in these poems which are shared with ∞ spiritual forces.

These poems, since they have nothing to do with political peacemakers, won't be regarded even at the cost of the book, let alone in millions of dailies dedicated to sloth and defeatism or to honor the author with attention, so to be well-fed in the proud capital of Serbia, Croatia, and Slovenia. Boo! That would be the ultimate madness interrupted by cultural beggars, political humanists, and artistic pederasts.

Had this poet not been expelled from every school in Croatia and Slavonia during the insufferable year of 1915 just because being a Serb he wasn't even allowed to sing in the Prečani-Serbian land[3], even the student parody of the well-known provincial anthem "Our Beautiful Full Bottle,"[4] had he not slept in empty streetcars after midnight devouring free and cultured air of the Austro-Hungarian-Croatian monarchy, and had his brothers not struggled through their first sad youth in Albanian and Galician trenches, Hungaro-Croatian war hospitals and prisons saved by their "madness"—then none of us maybe also at the injustice of this country would have become rebels and the first Balkan nihilists. (How marvelous: Balkan nihilism!) But, bearing one's naked life and saving in it only what's human was in those tumultuous days the only consolation for all those who, hunched and ashamed, walked next to giant crosses, under the gallows, and under the panic of the war sun of cannibalistic nations and continents.

Bearing one's life and saving in it only what's human is the biggest modern problem torturing the post-war generation of new people and new poets.

C'mon, now! We still haven't managed to redeem the sins of our ancestors and silver-haired contemporaries by pounding our heads and chests. Still, despite the sins, after the war, we have managed to write so many books and other works more than ever before. Our tumultuous time, for example, produced the superfantastic novel *77 Suicides* by Branko Ve Poljanski, the greatest acrobat of spirit and poetry! After his magazine *Svetokret* was published independently of and simultaneously as *Zenit* in 1921, he directed a Serbo-Croatian drama and became a Serbian language lecturer at the Slavic Theater in Trieste. But even there, a fire suddenly burned down the theater and the ill-fated career of this poet. Having published his October manifesto, Branko Ve Poljanski, that "rabid-dog," as the clerical Ljubljana press christened him, after the theatrical bravado at the Ljubljana theater, he traveled to Prague where he put on a memorable stage performance in the then-famous "Revolutionary Scene." He was, at the same time, the first zenithist actor.

A cynic out of necessity and a homeless drifter out of misfortune, after Berlin, Vienna, and Zagreb, he descended on the cobblestone streets of Belgrade to make one more attempt to overpower its glory.

Perhaps our work is too complex because nobody liked us, and no one likes us. Hate is the easiest path.

Perhaps we're so hateful because we suffered and because we know how to love. To love is the hardest human labor.

In the end, both our love and brotherhood are sad because our familiar past is even sadder than the sadness of this country. Our homeland was the saddest then because we had to be born in it.

Belgrade 1924

Ljubomir Micić

Manifesto[5]

Branko Ve Poljanski

To all those with pale cheeks, bloody hearts, and souls hovering in the heights like smoke!

To all those who have turned their eyes into their very depths!

To all those who are drunk on eternal mystery!

The human spirit has become the prostitute of the twentieth century. Our spirit has become completely lost in the chaos of all sorts of nefarious desires and has become a piece of merchandise owned by a few kilograms of flesh.

And behold, my spirit is screaming because it has woken up and wishes true, flesh-free freedom of the spirit, a spirit wanting to shake off nefarious desires and lies of that well-established, well-respected Madame "Today," whose only goal is to serve fattening and ample dinners.

Our spirit, under the protection of the mighty Madame "Today," is nothing but a sacrifice to our Lord God—the "golden calf" at the end of twenty stinking centuries.

Need! Oh, our spirit needs terribly madly to be free; it needs the sacred freedom to march ahead into time under its colorless flag, to march into eternity, leaving infinitely behind those twenty stinking centuries that appear in the infinity behind us as a tiny, the tiniest black dot of our ancient "Once Upon a Time."

Need! Oh, our spirit needs terribly madly to be free, so that its invasion, under a holy colorless flag, may advance into time—into eternity—towards the new man.

Need! Oh, we need to proclaim October a holiday a million times over, October, when all conventional and patented forms of cultural laws shall fall from the grafted fruit trees of the European garden and a new earthly spring shall come, when European fruit trees shall absorb new directions from the new earth and bear new forms.

We need to spit into the goblet of eternity: it is a disgusting drink we have gorged ourselves on! We need to spit into the goblet of eternity: it contains the leakage of twenty poisonous centuries!

Long live the self-determination of the spirit! May it ring through all cities, through all streets, through all countries red and blue, through all institutes and royal bestiaries, etc.

May the globe resound, glow, and burn in mad joy and cheering:

Long live man's free spirit! Glory to the new man!

May it be a glorious revolution of the spirit in October, when the old forms fall like dry pale leaves.

Let the colorless flag of the spirit flutter high in the air in October, when the new man shall be born.

Our spirit acquires its most sublime form through art.

Our spirit acquires that deep bottomless form through feeling—through feelings of pain and laughter, grief and joy, always searching for a meaningful direction.

Art is far from everyday political—national—social—Bolshevik terror. Art is the form of our deepest "Inner Self."

Art does not need to be logical!

Art can be a paradox!

This means an assassination of all patented forms of music, sculpture, painting, poetry, etc.

But paradox is not nonsense!

(This holds for psychiatrists too!)

Paradox is the spirit's agility and its plasticity.

There is only one possible alternative to our hearts in this life. Things are either tragic or comic.

Consequently, every work of art can provoke either tears or laughter—loud laughter in all four directions. Tears are the spirit's purity, while laughter is its healing potion.

You who have been blessed by the holy spirit, *create in the martyrdom of tears or laughter, because there is no art without martyrdom!*

Cry your blood and your bile out!

Laugh your brain and your heart out!

Die in delirium. Let your brain explode and burn, drunk on mystery!

My ear blends the sounds of the European concert. Long live the Republic! Long live the king! Long live the Internationale! Workers of the world, unite! Long live the soviets! Long live Lenin and Trotsky!

Lucifer triumphs! Glorious music!

In a puddle of red blood and with Parisian grace, joyful Europe is dancing a grotesque can-can

while a Russian balalaika plays "The Red Sarafan!"

The sounds have blended in my ears and fallen into my soul, creating the surrogate of a quiet smile, and my face has been transformed from laughter into cheers.

Long live the October revolution of the spirit!
Long live new art!
Long live new man!

Translated by *Maja Starčević*

Alarm

> Swear on the flintlock and Kajmakčalan[6], my Balkan sons, not
> to rouse our love, to not rouse it—will raze Europe.

What this isn't: a foreign currency exchange
a silk stocking
a whisky soda
an old madam
a roast pheasant
political agitation
Eastern wisdom

Categorically not. This is Balkan wisdom: *zenithism.*

History itself is zenithism's friend. That's why all its enemies deceive themselves imagining they would destroy it with their "wise" ignorance.

Zenithism fights for pure *Balkan elementary expression.*

It shoots left and right at the jackasses and powdered European snivelers who hoist the banner: *Where Europe goes, Balkan snivelers follow*. No! Don't be chummy with a dummy!

Therefore, we certainly aren't friends of dummies. We may be loony. That's correct. Here's the explanation:

Dummies can on no account find mental space for any monumental thought, much as none of us can stuff a new parliament building or a Viennese cathedral in our pockets.

What's the effect of all this? The effect is that people with great spiritual ideas don't possess nor can comprehend them. They are mediocre or so-called "ordinary people".

If you are loony, you can't be a dummy.

Mohammedans flee from Mecca to Medina—because they're loony
Jesus freaks die spat on and crucified—because they're loony
Gandhi is beloved by prisons—because he's loony
Jan Hus was burned alive—because he was loony
But, when the Mohammedans return—the masses drop to their knees!

When the crucified are resurrected—the masses drop to their knees!

When the imprisoned are freed—the masses drop to their knees!

When the burnt alive return—the masses drop to their knees!

Could it be that this history also lies?

Art has always done its human duty without being coerced by jackasses. Art always ushers in a new time.

Ultimately, art is the strongest component of creative culture.

Zenithism has entered Europe. Europe wonders at Balkanism, which offers new and positive outcomes.

Zenithism chases Europe from the Balkan peninsula.

Enough already!

We zenithists who lay the foundations of the Balkan cultural epoch freed from European powder and makeup, mocked in our own land—by Viennese "Kulturträger" and Parisian eau de colognialists.

Well, power to all of you who are heartily laughing. And for my own part, may Allah bless all of you. We're still moving forward. With words, we construct constructive plastic elements and objects. The malleable nature of these objects is accomplished through black and white words. (That's a paradox!) Objects in space viewed from multiple points has multiple reflections.

The plastic nature of an object achieved though paradox: zenithist poems, plays, novels, paintings, or sculptures—is reflected introspectively. Reflections cross over to the spiritual plane of an individual: making them laugh—making them crazy—making their skull hurt—making their brain cramp—making them cry . . .

This is a very simple explanation which cannot be not understood. Why does logic cancel out love? Because logic cancels out psychology. Through psychology, one arrives at associations which are essential to zenithist poetry. (See "The Categorical Imperative of the Zenithist School of Poetry" by Ljubomir Micić from *Rescue Car.*)

We create a new logic: *the logic of paradox.*

For us, no more secrets or mysteries. New people are correctly oriented in their time.

Today's culture, resulting from all previous cultures, presents itself as *totally negative.* An injection is needed. *Zenithism* is an even newer Salvarsan than the latest Salvarsan.

Only those who are satisfied with today's culture and world affairs have the right to throw a rock at zenithism. I take it they don't exist.

Whoever rises against zenithists will know: they are either liars or idiots.

Down with makeup and powder! Long live the Balkan invasion! Long live the zenithist rebellion! Long live the zenithist alarm!

Read at a grand zenithist event
on January 31, 1923.

On Train Tracks

Lights
In the dark breast of night
I
Step across the tracks
And
The ramp descends
Lest
Death strike on the tracks.

Through the dark, the iron beast buzzes
With big, furious bestial eyes
It stares into the night
And
Speeds
As I stand
It flies past me
And
Whistles.

Yet
I stifle the horror within me
At the thought
Of jumping onto the tracks
My head bones crack
My marrow and blood.

I still stand
And watch
The red eye
Flee like a savage into the night.

Man
That worm
A worm.

1921

Longing

Cold
Winter
Alley
Black branches
Bare
Night
White silence
In the soul, black and frozen
Pain.

In my heart's rhythm
A woman
In a silver cloak
Of moonlight
Disappears in the night
At the corner of my teary eye
A shriek
Frozen in her throat
— — — — — —
The moon's silver shrouds
My longing.

Winter
Cold
In the soul, frozen pain
In the throat, strangled shriek
While
The sun's love

Bare
Black branches
Crave
Crave
Crave

1921

At the Hair Salon

My cheek's reflection
IN
the mirror
damns itself
AND
the world

I'm still
on the toilet seat
In the next room
a prostitute talks
ABOUT
the beauty of her bleached hair
An electric gadget rattles
brrrrrrrrrr
AND
blow-dries her hair
AND
the clock on the dirty wall
ticks the seconds away
tick-tick tick-tick
tick-tick
AND
carries time somewhere
beyond comprehension

Yellow electric rays
crawl along objects

In my mind
psychology
plays a soft abstract song
plays
plaaaaaaaaaaaays.

1921

Graveyard-Express

I. A green eye darts
to the other side
like a shooting star
A metal bell clanks
muted and brief
as if broken
pipes shrill
tooooot tootootoo
beeeeepbeepbeepbeep
a horn bleats

Hoooooooooooooooonk
honk—honk honk—honk honk—honk
honkhonkhonkhonkhonkhonkhonk
(Music for bones).

II. Black coffins rush into the night
thick smoke weaves wreaths
around them
yellow windows gleam through the night
like flaming monuments.
— — — — — — — — — — —
The train is a graveyard-express
rushing to the pit of night.

III. In the heavy iron coffin
of a black car
the hungry distance
beyond the sphere's horizon
devours you.
A naked road awaits

me
loneliness
hungry streets
and horror
the pain of all things
buuuuuuuuuurrnsssssssssssssss

IV. Along a bare road
I walk downcast
briskly
toward a lonely idiotic city
as if leaving a graveyard
mournful.
The lines in my face twist
from the madness of pain
— — — — — — — — —
as—my—steps
as—my—steps
stifle my heartbeat—I count.

V. I stand
in a house
in an all too empty room
all too bare
you're gooooonnnnnne
everything cramps and creaks.
But behind the heavy midnight-blue drapes
a dense shadow dances
over everything
and the old clock
marks a minute
in time.

VI. A window
like a blind eye
gazes into opaque eternity.
Motionless, I
eavesdrop from the remote distance
your little hand
murmurs through the midnight-blue
like a white flag
greeting
me.

VII. My eyes
fixed
into the distant deep of night
stare
stare
stare

Toooooooootootootootootoo
honkhonkhonkhonkhonkhonkhonkhonk
— — — — — — — — —
Graveyard
— — — — — — — — —

1921

Poem #13

I. Streets
evening
the black fingers of clocks point to tomorrow
through me
blurry and black contours pass.
Thousands of windows stare at me.
Streetcars ring at dusk
the chords of city life
bounce off the walls
lights diffuse
thousands of bodies
on the streets
singing life.

II. In my soul everything sings
a bursting dithyramb
before midnight.

Everything sang death in a choir
every chasm gaped at me
every hope dissipated into the night.

III. My wooden friend
a cane
rattled against the ungiving asphalt
telling me how everything is
hard as stone.

IV. Cars
locomotives
live a motor life

and anticipate distant roads.
Wheels
heavy iron wheels
quietly hum
crossing
my body
heavy freight wheels of time.

V. Shop window
gun shop
hungry loud barrels
lie in wait for my head
boom—bang
and the whole world disappears
and then
eternal wasteland
or
?

A coffee shop
empty coffins
— — — — — — — — — —

No—no—nooooooo
I haven't died yet
I'm alive
I drink red wine
I love beautiful women
I welcome sunny days
I burn the flag of my life
along the meandering roads of worlds.

VI. From the deep night
a hundred dogs bark at me

a yellow light dies in a lamp
windows on houses weary of the day
doze.

Streetcar number 13
celebrates victory on the street
and my fortune
stabbed in the back
with a pointy number 1
screams.

VII. In the night
in the day
long crisscrossing roads whip by
I travel
along streets and roads
by streetcars
by trains
searching for a human road.

VIII. A toot
far into the night
a locomotive joyfully shrieks
fueled by fire.

1921

Trip to Brazil

The law of static still holds
Horror in the dark
The Canadian Pacific crosses America
Gonorrhea reeks
Alijagić[7] thinks worms are smart beasts.
Belgrade in Zurich
7.77
The cube of time collapses vertically
The lines of all things fold into it
I am
I'm thinking of going to the seashore
Scorpions terrify me
I'm looking forward to orchestral music
A street full of storms stinks of lightning.
Sharks still haven't wizened up
From pulpits drastic curse words shower
the pioneers of the new time.
I was stroking a woman's leg today
through her silk stocking.
I felt all the beauty of S.C.S.[8] poetry
before zenithism.
I returned from Gaurishankar
so that in my room I can travel to Brazil.

1922

Tick-Tock like a Crab in a Tailcoat

How I'd like to talk
If I didn't have a blazing whip
Females favor kings
(To each their own!)
Kings devour living children
Ramses was the first child-eater
My evenings are the curses of striking miners
after a catastrophe
Oh, you, Egyptian pyramid and you whore, sphinx
Which great child-eating king
Left us your face to remember?
Who wouldn't be cheerful
When fiction rushes down the road
On an express airplane a mad pilot dies
Rapid-fire hammers hey let's
Break into the portal of the Human Bank
To weld happiness for each of us
From a gold piggy bank

Murk lurks at dusk
I don a tailcoat
In my solemn suit I bow down to time
It travels like a crab
Express—in the dark
Tick-tock
Tick-tock
Tick-tock
Opium
Poppy
Poppy
Red.

1922

Blind Man Number 52

Hello!
Skull.
Number 52
hurts me.
The blind man stands at midnight
waits at
intersecting streets.
Corner
cabaret
orgiastic music.
Daylight dawns
through the black
of the blind man's sunglasses.
Magicians Russian czarist generals
10 dinars per evening.
My shadow my vampire.
Break the clock
stop time
transform the world
into a foolish country fair
idiotomaton
pan
pan
pan
panopticon
con
on
n.

1922

Arise

The day is a jackal's eye
Why do eyes hunger for the dark
The day hungers for barricades
Arise
The sky is a straitjacket
Wide roads gnaw at the sun
We build brute towers
Oh Europe
Your roads will crave Balkan masses.

1923

TB

A thousand-ton grief
Poisons a rebellious thought
TraaaaRaaaaA
My eye sees an ultraviolet tomorrow
Health's flowers bleat
Veal blood streams into the hearts of sleep factories
Telegraph poles cry
The earth coughs
TB
The death of electric trains
Durmitor[9], the Balkan Sphinx
Clean people ride a flaming broom
On the horizon grow angry invasions
Fatal fata
Morgan[10]
Rockefeller[11]'s death
Stinnes[12] leaps into a cauldron of boiling lead
A bleeding ulcer grows in the belly of Paris
Strombo
Strombo
Stromboli[13]

1923

Sing Sing We Ride the Himalayas

The taxicab is a creature at a record speed of 1,000 kilometers per minute
to the family plot. Believe me.
Banks, slaughterhouse creatures, their brains will burst
into a horizontal ash-packed sarcophagus.
We ride the clouds to catch space goldfish.
Joyous doctrines spread laughter into the sick whistles of locomotives.
Flames roar, tearing the twilight of sniveling universities.
2 × 2 = 4 here is your Don Logic.
It shoots you right between the eyes.
Nor do we pour savory verses for nothing!
Between the legs of the past blossom the pipe organ of the
black mantle's shadows.
The rhythm of infernal money tricks shakes our souls.
Why wouldn't our mouths trumpet cheer along the equator.
To demolish a stone cemetery of dog streets and corset factories.
Goddamn three hundred eruptive verses.
Lawyers stretch their mugs into smiles.
The righteous wail like factory sirens.
a
a **a**
Graves aren't boats entering a red sea of flames.
Bestial poisonous greed leaves a deep wound in the body!
Beware
Peaceful } **three crazy poets dream**
Lava fragrance
The antennae play deadly leaps of green traffic lights
Terror-torn trains derailed
HRSS—K

There won't be a bone left of you
of you YOU
All that the rage of our eye can slap you with
Fire fights fire
Let the skyscraper calves be paid with iron rope
Fire
Fire
To swim to India to impertinently ride the Himalayas
To bark to wake the sleeping millions under the burden of the sun.
sing
sing } singapore
sing

1923

You, Belgrade, You

The tumult of gypsy shouts on cobblestone streets
We break our backs every evening
Shake our brains,—watching
An entire street, an entire city, an entire country, an entire world
Die from heart paralysis.
Belgrade, the sun falls heavily on the back of your head
Burning Serbian skulls
"Grilled brains"
Let's hurry into my book, Belgrade
And hide among my verses
So you won't die of shame
Hey! Hey! City of our dreams
Repulsive mannikins prance around your streets
Parisian chic, idiotically vain, sell shame.
On your streets, peasant oxen meet
Reparation streetcars and automobiles
The oxen wonder, ask themselves
Why did our masters carry
Bullet-riddled bodies to a dozen spots
Are they as poor as we are?
Poor oxen of this world!
And who isn't an ox in this fatherland of mine
Except for the horses in the royal stables
Huh?

1924

God Beefsteak

We wipe down the stars, the sun, and the moon with a sponge.
We swim in waves of clouds.
We pour sap into the fire.
Somewhere there in dusty books
The last punished paragraph moans.
A straight razor song thrills us
A leap onto mosques
The minarets ring and brains whimper
In the valley of the murk truth thumps:
"La illallah zenithist intellect rasulullah"
Let the headless purchase a cheap prosthetic!
People pawn their brains for an illusion
On every corner a colorful placard hangs
"For rent: hospice."
I and you
You and I
We'll sing till our rags fall off
About an insipid caricature of the world
"Don't love anyone because no one loves you!"
When illusions sap our bodies,
We'll weep with laughter.
Before we leap into our grave
We'll curse the false prophets of god
Beef
Beef
Beefsteak

1924

Joyous Poem

No one in the world believes in miracles
And every day thousands of marvels
Blow up before our eyes:
Houses eat cars, ordinary people, and ministers
Flags lie to the sun
Arrogant idiots flood the streets
Selling a horn for a candle
Cretinism for genius
A bloody river flows from lampposts
In the visions of miraculous people with souls.
Without roofs overhead they roam the world
Many starved curs
New poets.
On the streets silk swishes and perfumes taunt roses
Canals, toilets, and muddy streets sing
About the scent of our time
May the miserable rejoice
That the whole globe has yet to be devastated
At the expense of the bourgeois
A morsel will remain for us
Heavy cars will quicken
Houses and hearths
Gasoline will stream down the streets
Bombs will blossom in parks.
How lyrically I feel the future
When palaces flip onto their roofs
And our shoes step on the cobbled skulls
Of our contemporary sages and stock market players
On the tambourine of millions
Our poor millions,
Bloody millions.

1924

Endnotes

1 Bogdan Popović (1863–1944) was an important Serbian literary critic whose 1911 book, *Antologija novije srpske lirike* (Anthology of the Modern Serbia Lyric), was the first attempt to create a literary canon of the most significant Serbian poems. He would have been viewed by Poljanski as representative of the literary establishment, which zenithists rebelled against.

2 Dobro Polje was a September 1918 battle in what is now Greece and North Macedonia, where French, Greek, and Serbian forces defeated the Bulgarian army.

3 Prečani was a term Serbs from Serbia had for ethnic Serbian communities outside Serbia proper in Austria-Hungary-held Vojvodina, Bosnia and Herzegovina, and Croatia.

4 The Croatian anthem was "Lepa naša domovino" ("Our Beautiful Homeland") which was parodied by ethnic Serbs as "Lepa naša puna flaša" ("Our Beautiful Full Bottle").

5 Originally published in *Svetokret: Journal for the Expedition to the North Pole of Man's Spirit* 1, no. 1 (January 1921).

6 Kajmakčalan is a mountain on the border between Greece and what would now be called North Macedonia, where a battle between Serbian and Bulgarian troops was fought during the First World War.

7 Alija Alijagić (1896–1922) was a member of the Communist group Crvena Pravda who assassinated Milorad Drašković, the Interior Minister of the Kingdom of Serbs, Croats, and Slovenes, in 1921.

8 S.C.S. refers to the Kingdom of Serbs, Croats, and Slovenes (1918–1929).

9 Durmitor is a massif in northwestern Montenegro, part of the Dinaric Alps.

10 This could be a reference to the American financier J.P. Morgan (1837–1913) but is most likely a reference to his son, the American banker J.P. Morgan, Jr. (1867–1943), who survived an assassination attempt in 1915.

11 John D. Rockefeller (1839–1837) was an American business magnate.

12 Hugo Stinnes (1870–1924) was a German industrialist.

13 Stromboli, an Italian island, containing the active volcano Mount Stromboli.

Topsy-Turvy

Branko Ve Poljanski
Zenithists International Edition, 1926

Translated by *Steven Teref and Maja Teref except where noted*

4.3. B. Poljanski, *Tumbe* [Topsy-Turvy], Zenithists International Edition, no. 10, Belgrade, Serbia, 1926. Front cover, printed on red paper. Courtesy of Ubu Gallery, New York & Galerie Berinson, Berlin.

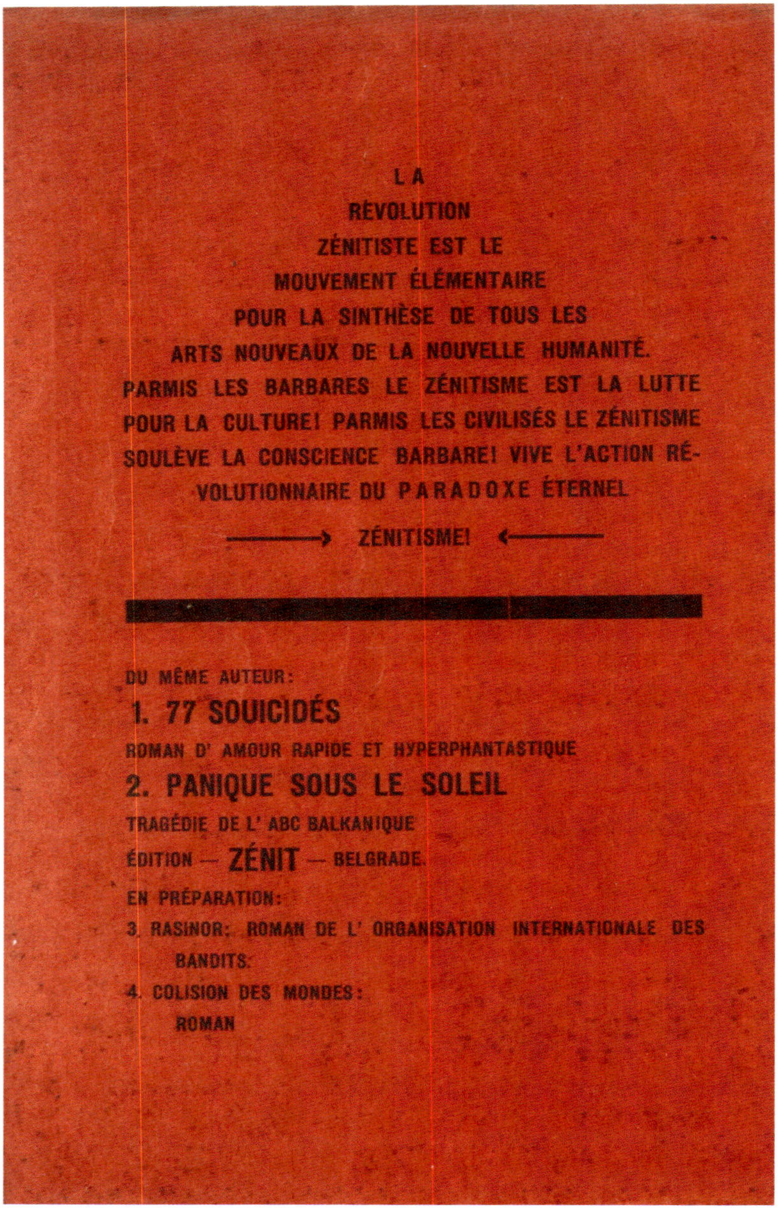

LA
RÉVOLUTION
ZÉNITISTE EST LE
MOUVEMENT ÉLÉMENTAIRE
POUR LA SINTHÈSE DE TOUS LES
ARTS NOUVEAUX DE LA NOUVELLE HUMANITÉ.
PARMIS LES BARBARES LE ZÉNITISME EST LA LUTTE
POUR LA CULTURE! PARMIS LES CIVILISÉS LE ZÉNITISME
SOULÈVE LA CONSCIENCE BARBARE! VIVE L'ACTION RÉ-
VOLUTIONNAIRE DU PARADOXE ÉTERNEL

→ ZÉNITISME! ←

DU MÊME AUTEUR:

1. 77 SOUICIDÉS

ROMAN D' AMOUR RAPIDE ET HYPERPHANTASTIQUE

2. PANIQUE SOUS LE SOLEIL

TRAGÉDIE DE L' ABC BALKANIQUE

ÉDITION — ZÉNIT — BELGRADE.

EN PRÉPARATION:

3. RASINOR: ROMAN DE L' ORGANISATION INTERNATIONALE DES BANDITS.

4. COLISION DES MONDES: ROMAN

4.4. B. Poljanski, *Tumbe* [Topsy-Turvy], Zenithists International Edition, no. 10, Belgrade, Serbia, 1926. The inside front cover, printed on red paper. Courtesy of Ubu Gallery, New York & Galerie Berinson, Berlin.

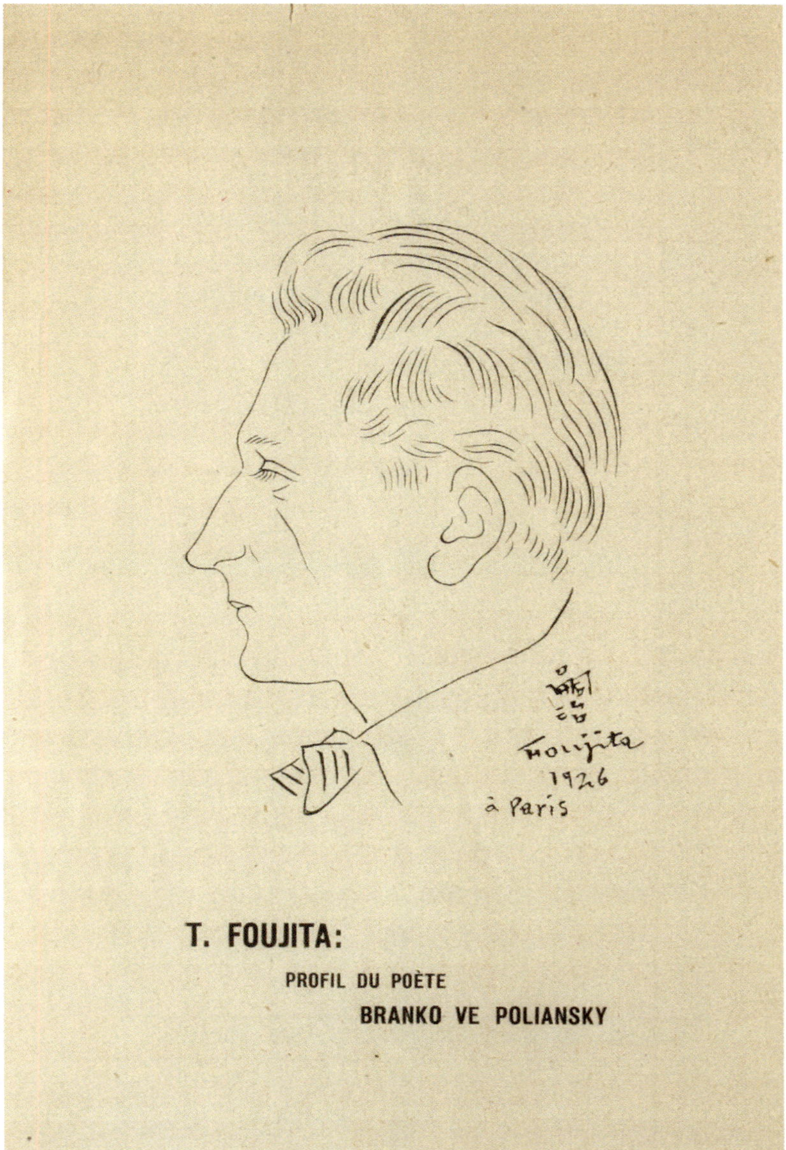

4.5. B. Poljanski, *Tumbe* [Topsy-Turvy], Zenithists International Edition, no. 10, Belgrade, Serbia, 1926. Tsuguharu Foujita, Profile of poet Branko Ve Poljanski. Courtesy of Ubu Gallery, New York & Galerie Berinson, Berlin.

S.O.S.

Save yourself if you can.

—I've long imagined and deceived myself that our land is full of great, good, and noble people. Honestly and morally, I understand my own and all other zenithists' calling to tread a revolutionary path toward realizing new ideas for a new nation which still hasn't given a historic explanation of its genius. Oh Devil, did I believe! I grew weary believing and am broken by the delusion I fell into through my own fault. An unpleasant truth. Maybe because all the great truths, dramatic and tragic, are always unpleasant. Just like the truth about death.

●

That's how I convinced myself (subjectively) that there are no people in this country. Only non-people and victims. The sufferers are too tragic within to be able to get over themselves and take up revolutionary work. Society intentionally and calculatedly crucifies them on the cross of misery to exterminate the deepest and most fundamental humanity from the face of our poor homeland.

●

Why is everything like that? I don't know. Nobody knows. Those who wish to disentangle all the tragic conflict cannot even stay out of danger for one day from the evil forces of societal forms thriving in the agony of non-culture.

●

All dramatic conflicts around us are not their own cause and effect. That's why it's probable that every cause will inherit its consequences. My poetry is the result of certain causes. It will again become a cause of new consequences. Those consequences will trigger new causes, into perpetuity.

●

I am aware that for Serbian literature some literary Shylock is more respected than any genius poet.

●

I am aware that in this society it is better not to know anything because that way it is easier to meet all cultural requirements by creating a "civilization" in Terazije Square.[1]

●

I am aware that a liar or a political bum appeals to the conscience of this society more than any genius truth lover or zenithist.

●

It is known that the one who is loved is also criticized. If our victorious Serbian century evolved to a civilization of chickens, it would be understood that those who keenly criticize this immature, green gang, do so because they love their people. Does anyone still care about our people in this capital's bazaar? A ridiculous and naive question.

●

Let my digressions not confuse anyone. I will never leave my circle of poetry. I will never stand outside the lyric passion of the zenithist revolution. I merely raise my voice to be heard by those who desire salvation for the welfare and greatness of a future humankind. I call upon all the sufferers and the shipwrecked to run for their lives from this pirate galley called the Balkans! Run for your life!

SOS
SOS
SOS

Jump into the waves of your moral and human depths to resurface at the helm of a new world for which this zenithist poetry has been created in my most progressive book Topsy-Turvy.

●

Discussing purely poetic elements here would be too modest. That is not me. That will never be me.

●

After all the crimes commuted by societies against their revolutionary poets, now they want to foist modesty onto them. Since they took away and confiscated everything a living person needs, to not die, the last thing that irritates them is—The poets' faith in their own genius.

●

I am not humble, and to all who think I'm wrong for this, I send my deepest contempt.

Belgrade, October 1926

▣

Manifesto

Fragment of a Great Manifesto to all the Nations of the Globe

It happened yesterday. My earthly consciousness awoke for the first time. I was a boy of five. High above me my wondering childish eyes saw the sun. I was standing in the road. Next to the road was the small wooden house where I had woken up. A garden full of ripening fruit protected our little house from all evil.

The road was very, very long. Oaks walked by the road all the way to the end of my world, to the end of the road. They met there. And my childish eyes could not see any further. I was terribly curious. I had asked my Grandma Julika, now dead, "Granny, what's at the end of the road?" "The town," she said. The word made me happy: it was like hearing angels sing, angels carrying me on their tiny wings above strange and brave new worlds. The town. Yes. The town. And my childish imagination saw it like this: silver waves emerging at the end of the road I was looking at. It was a sea of silver where good people, like my grandfather Stevan Stojić, went swimming. Yes.

Today I am twenty-eight. Today? The town. The city. I feel disgust as only a disappointed soul of a pure and innocent child can feel it. Today, when cities reek of the offal of their culture, my only joy is hatred and my only pain—the sun.

The difference I felt after twenty-five years of a life spent between the city of my childish consciousness and the city of reality is so great that had I not become a zenithist poet, I would have surely been a murderer by now.

The village of my childhood was called Majske Poljane, May Fields. So, I called myself Poljanski, of the fields. My grandmother, now dead, was called Julika; Grandpa's name was Stevan. One aunt was called by the name of the first woman: Eva. Her two sisters were Ljubica and Marija. Marija, now dead, was my mother. She had two sons. The name of the firstborn is Ljubomir; the younger one is me.

I can thank those great, shoe-wearing peasants for everything that is golden and powerful in my spirit. A thank-you to them and to the gentlemen of culture—s**t.

The little river flowing through my village was not the Seine, nor did Cézanne live in the house by the river close to a small wooden bridge. There were no museums of "eternal works" up on the green hill. There was a mountain and a game-filled forest, where liquid gold mixed with the morning dew.

The little river flowing through my village was called Maja. It is not without significance that Maya has two meanings in Hindu—meanings are both opposed and similar: illusion and land. I bathed my body and my spirit in the Maja, and the latter is still pure: it may wear shimmy shoes today but it could easily walk naked and barefoot. May the spirit—my spirit—step barefoot on this sun-scorched land. And on the Maja.

My Zenithist Spirit

And I went along that road, the road I have mentioned. The first town I reached was called Glina. (*Glina* is the Serbian word for the yellow clay that pots are made of). There were two churches there, one school, and two banks. There were two cemeteries on a nearby hill. Here is where I drank up the rudiments of culture. The only thing that made me madly, insanely happy was a circus with a stupid clown and a cinema with a huge projector that made a whistling sound as if all the devils were laughing. And that is the road that took me to Paris. May my naked spirit plant its heavy foot on that Paris,

My Zenithist Spirit

●

I was seven. At that time, I thought the sky was a huge glass bell. God (with a beard!) was the greatest **man**: he could do anything. One day he would lift the great bell and people would be joyful and gay and see a heaven filled with angels and saints. It did not take long for that lie to turn into bitter disappointment in my childish imagination.

And so, time passed and I rode on a steel wheel from lie to lie.

My barbaric genius suffered for a long time until it entered its own world, until it became a destroyer and a ravager, because the greatest spiritual joy lies in destruction a joy both negative and positive.

●

Zenithism has saved me. Ideas bring salvation. The great Balkan poet

Ljubomir Micić

said

Zenithism

and the word became **deed**.

●

And so, my dear innovators, creators of all and sundry, creators of the great nothing, turn your faces to the light brought you by joyful Balkan barbarians. Prodigal sons of Mother Earth, do not forget that the only deed that is a

Great Deed

is one that is

Created for Humanity

and not against it.

Works you create for museums are not creations of the new mankind; they are created out of the desire of petty speculators to go beyond the present to Eternal speculation.

We have no understanding for your painting, since "great art" is nothing but a trade where the innovators of today play the part of salesmen on the stock market of mankind's conscience.

Your painting has no sense and no shame. Zenithism fights with European painting.

For a New Barbaric Style

When you discovered African sculpture, what you were really ecstatic over was zenithism, which you knew nothing about. Your joy did not last long, however, since whatever the speculative hand of the new European touches is lost to the new mankind. You have turned African sculpture, which comes from the naked spirit of "savage" man, into a spiritual nectar of tasteless European lemonade that can only cause—vomiting.

Be zenithists. Create works that are great for the greatness of mankind and forget your know-nothing aesthetics. If aesthetics stands for anything, it stands for the

Phenomenon of Stupidity

Do you think mankind would lose anything if Derain or Matisse had not been born? Do you think mankind would lose anything if there were no painting? Believe me, painting is the most foolish work the human spirit has wasted its time on. Stop painting, for God's sake, you

50,000

lost men who paint on the streets of this beautiful city of Paris. Stop painting, because you are committing a historical sin against humanity, which will be summarized by the generations to come as:

Painting is a Crime

●

Mankind has never been so much in need of sound, serious spirits. And while fifty thousand people stroll along the boulevards of Paris thinking that the work of their poor

"Spirit in Color"

represents one of the most significant applications of spirit to life, there is another front growing, a front called the

Zenithists

Zenithists are interested in the problem of the spectrum in the art of painting only insofar as they ask how much spirit a certain artist has, if he has as much as is needed for the new world. Verily, I say unto you, it is not a great miracle and wisdom to paint a backside and to claim that it is eternal because it is hanging or will hang in, say, the Louvre. It is even a lesser miracle to paint a square or a circle and to claim it is the greatest manifestation of spirit since the beginning of time. Dear God, those who do cannot imagine the laughter of the

New Man

You will rightly say I am a peasant. And I will be right in pitying you for your immeasurable stupidity. I truly do not "understand" Cézanne, just as I understand Braque or Léger so well. They cannot guess that I understand them better than they understand themselves, because my Balkan eyes can see what people hide the most.

Each age has its brand of painting. Only this headless, bloody age of ours lacks one. Everyone and his dog is talking, writing, yelling about the painting of our time, and

There is No Painting

There are painters, some of whom are even geniuses, but there is no contemporary painting to be found anywhere.

We need a new way of expressing man's naked spirit in color.

We need zenithist painting. Enough backsides and squares! Stop or you'll ruin painting for the sake of an imaginary lyricism, a virtuous line. Anyone who can feel with his spirit and has intuition understands that this culture is in the process of collapsing. Its creators find it hard to admit, but the rest of us could not see it more plainly.

Gallery owners in the city of Paris and their painter partners say,

You Need to Know How to Look at a Painting

and zenithism says:

You Need to Know How to Create a Painting

●

It is obvious that a shameful historical deed has reached a dead end in the aesthetic theory of l'art pour l'artism and cannot move a step further. When a group of Russian jokers with a great sense of humor founded

Nullunctism

in painting, that is, painting white on white and black on black, it obviously meant the end of a painting culture, of a historical error and of an obvious acrobatics of stupidity that had resulted in the theory of

L'art pour l'art

They say a painting is a world in itself. An absolute work. Pure gold. An eternal work. A museum piece. The zenithist says:

A painting is stupid. An absolute stupidity. A pure stupidity. An eternal stupidity. A museum-piece stupidity.

Strange. Each painter knows the now banal theory of relativity put forth by Mr. Einstein, who states that all is relative. If that is so clear and painters in their agony defend their painting with it (though it hurts them the most), why do they go on trying to create eternal works and museum pieces? Eternity, too, is relative

One Minute—One Billion Years

Create one-minute paintings, because in the end they are the same as eternal paintings.

Go to a cinema where you will feel better than anywhere the relativity of your "eternal works." Let film teach you the speed of changing place and space. The miracle of film is firmly based on a single idea that is not and could never be pretentious.

Why are Buster Keaton, Charlie Chaplin, Douglas Fairbanks, and others like them greater dramatists than Shakespeare? It is quite simple. They have instinctively felt the relativity of place, time, and space. In drama they have discovered the

seventh dimension

film

speed.

All Contemporary European Art is Suffering from a Lack of Ideas

●

Work without an idea = man without a head!
Work without an idea = fish out of water!
Work without an idea = Pegasus with no legs!
Work without an idea = Columbus' egg without America!
Painting without an idea = backside factory.

Poor painting. It has turned into a mania mankind needs to be cured of. The enemies of contemporary painting will certainly be victorious in the fight against it.

●

I have been speaking of a dead museum and "eternal" painting without ideas.

Now a few words about the future.

Zenithist Painting

Since the beginnings of painting and sculpture, it was clear that they have never in any age been without ideas, that is, a bluff with no sense.

It has become the custom for the "modern" sculptor to invoke ancient Egyptian, Greek, and even Assyrian sculpture. Then why aren't the principles of these civilizations, where spirit is applied to sculpture, accepted by our gentlemen innovators? Why? The answer is short:

Contemporary European Artists Have No Spirit!

Contemporary European artists are pure artistes, masters. (In Serbian, a master is an artisan). They know their trade. They know color. They are virtuosos, the absolute rulers of light, color, form, and space. The only things missing are

Spirit
The spirit of man
The spirit of the new man
The spirit of the naked man
The spirit of the barbarian
The spirit of the barbaric genius.

So, they will again invoke African sculpture and everything from the Egyptians to the Cretans. But, dear European artists without zenithist spirit, I beg of you, look at all the periods of artistic creation, from its beginning to the present-day, look for what you are lacking. And you will find

Humanity's Philosophical Attitude to the Life of Its Time.

●

There is not a single great work in the world that can be free of ideas when it comes to the artistic and philosophical attitude to the time it was created in.

There are no great works outside mankind.

There are no great men outside life.

There is no great art without mankind.

There is no spirit outside of life.

The spirit is not a dead thing that can be hung on a nail.

The spirit is something eternal, something that **moves** all the forces of the universe.

The spirit is always alive, never dead.

The spirit is always within man and never outside him.

Art is always within man and for man and never outside of him or against him.

The zenithist spirit is alive and bloody.

The zenithist spirit is naked and wild.

The zenithist spirit is new and barbaric.

The zenithist spirit is strong and humane.

The zenithist spirit is young and joyful.

The zenithist spirit is a genius creator.

Ljubomir Micić has given a name to this sum total of the eternal crude forces that rejuvenate mankind. He calls it

the Barbarogenius

Using pure barbaric genius and the new spirit of a new heroic mankind, we will create

New painting!
Zenithist painting!
New sculpture!
Zenithist sculpture!
New poetry.
Zenithist poetry.

New art.

Zenithist art.

This method must be applied to the concept of

Culture

●

Culture is not outside man. It is within him and for him.

Culture is not dead. It is alive.

Therefore, culture is not a thing but the force that propels mankind. Let us not call that force the fuel of society but the

Morality of Society

Cultural = Moral.

Moral = Cultural.

Mankind has gone through several stages of morality. Today's stage of morality is called

Morality

For Sale

True miracles have been performed using that morality. It is hard to pinpoint its beginning, but it is not hard to say how it will end.

And when a zenithist says "morality" to modern Europeans, they say he is being—pretentious. No one has ever asked what morality was. Well:

Morality is an elemental force that moves the collective spirit of mankind in the direction of a goal. It would be better to call the force

Anti-Morality

as the new affirmation of a new morality,

Zenithist Morality

The present European morality is Christian. It has become one whole with the morality of

buy—sell

mankind—goods.

●

Mankind is not for sale!

Europe is not cultured!

Zenithism is a movement for the barbarization of Europe!
Is zenithism a movement for the Europeanization of the barbarians?
Zenithism is a movement of eternal youth!
Zenithism is a poetry of clashes.

Paris, January 1926

Translated by *Maja Starčević*

■

Contraidioticon

Sausages are emotion—Bratwurst is utopia for the starved Russians along the Volga—Cars discover deserts—Deserts will fall on New York skyscrapers—The privileged will jump into their own intestines.

Streets fly into madhouses—Madhouses fly into Chaplin's eye—Cannons roar the birth of lunatics—Where you dig for gold you'll find trash—Fires are the eyes of the desperate—

Wisdom is a harlot
The sky is a madhouse
The world is a slaughterhouse

Idiots laugh geniuses—Vigilant is the eye of the observatory—Seismographs show

DOOM MARCHES ON

Doom toots from the East—Is a lunatic loony?—Is a wiseman wise?—Is a hoof a horse brain?—Is a silk stocking a woman's soul?—Does a podium lecture the professor or the professor to the students?—Who is the professor of the professor?—Are states organizations of dunces?—Are dunces the executioners of wise men?—

"How ragged is our soul
How leprous is our consciousness
How blind our eye is
How beautiful our deed"

Thus sang czars of yore—Thus sing the dogs—Thus sings the cardinal—The world is a labyrinthine barracks—The barracks are a tomb—The uniform is a sarcophagus—Alive are the dead in the world—Dear are the worlds in the universe—The universe is a dungeon of worlds—Dungeons are the despair of lions—Lions are a desert's desire.

●

Isn't the shovel a symbol of time?—Is time only today?—It's pitiful to think that time is a calm lake!—Time marches on—Time is a passenger—The passenger is a prophet—The prophet is a martyr—Martyrs are righteous—The righteous are fanatics—Fanatics are an organization for the ultraradical victory of the scrawny over the army of the fat.

●

In a cabaret, a scream—Screams are an act of joy—The merry merrily howl like healthy monkeys—The one who's a monkey must be hung on the nearest nail—Time is quite unmonkey-like—1,923 years after the birth of the plagiarist of the Buddha's big thumb—We should be generous with our laughter—It's difficult to be wisely joyful—May all the Indian gamblers be crucified—

●

A donkey has long ears. Well-developed hearing organs—Listen, jackass! How did your legendary ears come to be?—Question.
Answer:

Whisper did the wretches—you didn't hear
Grunt did the wretches—you didn't hear
Speak did the wretches—you didn't hear
Shout did the wretches—you didn't hear
Roar did the wretches—you didn't hear

The wretches ate the crematory. Donkey! You remained deaf. Then came the righteous. Shoved you in the ribs. You said: **HEE-HAW**
They pulled your ears—You said: **HEE-HAW**
Now you have long ears—Tomorrow, martyrs will come. They'll pull out your ears—They'll run a spit down your maw and roast you alive—

HEE-HAW

Those who don't want to be declared donkeys, may they stop acting like donkeys!
Those who don't want to be roasted alive, may they give up

religion HEE-HAW religion

They are coming—carrying the spit—it'll come to pass—words will be the heroes—songs will be a brigade—Books will be an army—The army will be a conflagration—The conflagration will roast the gallbladder and cities—The fire will roast the spine and brains—The fire will roast the "manicure et pedicure" salons—The fire will roast the backrooms of secret diplomacy—The fire will roast the brothels, the Vatican, and Morgan castle—Fire will roast everything except for a sharp vertical line—

●

The hat, your head's protector, speaks:
"Take me off, Mr. Billionaire, and cover your head with an iron helmet because they'll shoot you in the skull!
Take me off, Mr. Minister, and cover it with St. Peter's Dome in Rome—they'll crush your head!
Take me off, fat citizen, and scatter ashes on your head—your stupidity will be baptized in blood!"
Thus spoke the hat, your head's protector.

●

A file sharpens a dull saw.
A file sharpens a dull brain.
A file jabs the queens of idiots under the seventh rib.
Don't pray to god, your lord, because your god is a notorious fool. **Kill!** (The body is out of the question!) Watch what you shoot with and shoot at! **Steal!** (Money is out of the question!) Keep an eye on your hand lest it steal a car from your soul and build a house from it for someone homeless. If you only stole from some fatso, you could have shaved his soul.

▣

Eros

You whack your head with delight when houses collapse
When you speak
Your words bounce off the walls
A canal song on a summer night boils
The world happily blossoms among lamps
Gin—gin—ginarata!
The music begins and our childhood aches
Everything aches
My dear citizens
Which of you can defiantly leap
Like a fish over water?

300,000 Punches per Second

A serpentinella[2]

The street murmurs and steps on a hungry youth.
The autumn evening howls. All the city clocks cynically display

9

He is hungry. His name is **Rakir**.
He was born quite accidentally and clearly forgot that funny fact.

—Yes! That's me! Rakir

—You, Rakir?

—Yes! I love you. Come with me. I know you were looking for me. And here I was right here on the streetcar tracks. I imagined the tracks were a snake. I wanted to pummel it. But I failed. The iron is hard and doesn't turn into a snake.

—Yes! I Rakir love you Martira. Now you're going to come to my bed. You will smother me in horror at the triumph of passion. I'm suffering. Come along. I'm in agony. I'm dying. Come. Martira! I will transform your love into a fallen hieroglyphic.

I, Rakir.
You, Martira.
We're wizards. Let's pummel the head of the iron snake, which will die from 300,000 punches to the head.

Letch.
City edge.
Stench.
All the bars in the city are joyous churches.
"Beat it, dog!" Those were the last words of Rakir and Martira!

■

The Panopticon Passes through a Mirror

"Don't worry, shoe, I'll slip you on. Isn't it nice seeing a bullfight and the boldness of the picador? That is real."

It's unclear from whose lips these words fell nor for whose ears they were meant.

The day before yesterday they hanged a man for reasons quite just. On the one hand! But everyone has two hands unless they lost one fighting for their homeland and a just cause, and they now have a prosthesis. A person with two healthy hands would seek to know the reason they hanged the man, on the other hand. However, the one who shares the point of view of the hangmen, doesn't have an "on the other hand." It was cut off by Mr. surgeon who foresaw an evil future for it. Now, it doesn't have any rights because it's no longer a hand; it is—a prosthesis.

A hypothesis!

●

Many people, dogs, horses, etc. strolled in the afternoon.

Everything entered the bright surface of the mirror. Everything transformed in the imagination and everything was dying.

Through the bright surface of the mirror entered:
churches and nuns
cars and grisettes
kings and invalids
newspapers and bricklayers
suns and moons
stars and notorious prostitutes
magazine editors and kangaroos.

Once they passed through the mirror they turned to stone.

Boom! Something cracked open.

It was the noggin of an American potato king.

●

Great is the song of the whirlpool. The whirlpool is the first and the last sense of the nonsensical. If anyone can spit out the word

Nonsense

Then sense exists!

What is the sense of the nonsensical? Nonsense!

And what is nonsense?

It is a very nice notion of something, of which even the hellish human brain can't conceive.

The point is that it occupies such a superb place in the world of our notions.

What exists beyond notions?

Beyond notions is that which cannot fly through the surface of the mirror.

What is a mirror?

A mirror is an object without which the notion of the object would be incomprehensible. The object exists just as long as it can reflect.

In the stone city of San Francisco there is an opium den. To experience another world which can't be penetrated by an ordinary citizen, you need to expose the body to agonizing cramps—for the revelation of a new world where one can live disembodied—fluidly.

A trance! A trance! A trance!

Oh, how insanely boring it must be for one who is unfamiliar with the pleasures of life beyond concrete forms, beyond sausages and *ćevapčići*.

Tangible forms are ground in the mill. The grinding continues into an ethereal rebirth. And then every object attains its true face:

IT ISN'T

That **isn't** is precisely the shortcut for Mr. donkey to reach the hay.

Isn't = Is.

Is = Isn't.

(Don't be ashamed by confusion, dear reader!)

●

In your eyes, my dear, flickers the strangest spell of the gods, who lost their invaluable believers today.

Nobody believes in anything anymore!

We only believe in negation

Modern-day fornicators believe **in negation**

Negation is the source of all goods

Amen!

—To live through tomorrow, today must pass. If that doesn't come to pass—ah—then the horrifying, peaty, and stinking swamp of time would emerge.

Always tomorrow
Always tomorrow
Always tomorrow
Eternity has 777 eternities.

The Laughter of Rifles

(Liberty Square. Fallen heroes' obelisk. Shouting can be heard over the radiotelephone from the conference on a healthier Europe. Winter 1300 hours! A shimmy rattles through the streets.)

Man 1: I'm hungry.
Man 2: I'm sick.
Man 3: I have a prosthetic.
Man 4: My children are dying.
Man 5: I'm blind.

(The people speak incessantly. They stand next to one another like mannikins.)

A **uniformed man** barges in: In the name of the law, you are saved! (Signals with his hand.)

A **Salvo**

(All the people fall like razed smokestacks. Silence gnaws at the obelisk. Fades to black. A shimmy orgy. Muffled shouting from the radiotelephone.)

The **uniformed man** lights a cigarette and signals.

Man 6 (pushes a two-wheeled cart for the nameless dead.): These here? Okay!
(Approaches the corpses. Speaks softly.)
Get up, comrades!
(He attacks the uniformed man. The corpses quickly rise. They help lift the uniformed man on to the cart for the nameless dead. The shimmy stops. A frightening detonation. Desperate shouting rings from the radiotelephone.)

Radiotelephone: Help! Help! Marauders! Barbarians! Tanks! Barbarians! May Trotsky's heel be shot from the Eiffel Tower!
Booooooooooooooooooooooooooooooooo!

(Detonation over the phone and in the square. Everything's burning. Crowds cross the square and shout.)

Long live man. Liiiiiiivvvvvvvve.

Down with man. Doooooowwwwwwnnnn.

(There is shouting in every European and Asian language.)

A Steamboat in the Appendix

The mob screams. A horde of evil-hunters. The pharmacies are open. The street is joyful. The sun kneels and watches the horses. The horses kneel and watch the sun. All the theses are diseased harlots. The newsboys are pioneers of Bonar Law. The trams are imagined. The merchants are magi from the east. The Academy of Sciences and Arts awards the medal of the highest order for wisdom—to the merchant of the idiotic concoctions of Dr. Thiefson.

Asphalt is the city's skull covered in spit. Lead falls on the city. Dusk. The street roams over Mr. Terroren. Terroren is the secret councilor of the king of underground states

L. U. M. S.

The League of Underground Mankind States

Terroren is a much-distinguished member of the organization of L. U. M. S.

The house enters Terroren. The street enters the house.

A spectral nightmare burst within Terroren. The street stood in the middle of his skull. Terroren radiographed to the fiftieth century:

> We built a steamboat to sail to you.
> The steamboat has docked in our appendix.
> We're running a high fever.
> Horror entered our spine.
> The houses became night owls.
> The villains are around every corner.

Only I have the secret files on Man

> Every step is a concussion.
> Every look is with disgust.
> Every look is a cramp.

Every word is a curse
in the brains of an avalanche.
In matchboxes we hide fire.
(Here fell a meteor and severed all communications.)

The street moved on. Terroren found himself before a tavern door. The door opened him. The tavern walked through Terroren. He saw the guitar play on the worker. The tavern was wretched and drunk. A glass laughed at Terroren. Terroren inquired:

—What's so funny?

The glass answered:

—Don't you see how I'm drinking this man? He works in a sugar refinery. His life is bitter. I'll drink him until I slurp out his eyes and brain . . .

Terroren was flabbergasted. He flew vertically into the room. He set the cupboard on fire and placed it on the table. An enormous black wall whirred around the table on a burning lamp. The room buzzed in the fly. The bedsheets lay on Terroren. The dream dreamed him.

Morning came. The bedsheets awoke. At their great consternation, the bedsheets found on themselves Terroren's dead body. It was determined that he'd been bitten by the wall which caused the poisoning of his sixth rib. Complications ensued that caused the inflammation of his shirt.

The lamp and closet sobbed the whole day. The mirror mourned till it shattered from grief.

Two days later, the body dissected the morticians. Three days later—with great honor they interred

the Grave in Terroren

Even the king of L. U. M. S. made an appearance at the sable ceremony.

Four days later, Terroren summoned the formidable sable army of L. U. M. S.

■

Nihilon

A clew of thoughts: future people will spin hemp from me. The crack of a revolver. It shot the rooster before dawn. The roosters were alive. The crack of laughter, then nothing. Nihilon's steps dripped lead on the asphalt. Nihilon wondered. And again, that crazy day brightened. Streets whimpered under the pressure of riddles: In hospitals, lepers whined and cursed the sun.

Nihilon thought:

Somnambulists dreamed through the night in the towers. A month from the 20th century was unusually magical.

• • •
• •

The day.

Nihilon was driven mad from laughter. A scream in the soul. A crack in the brain. A burst of ideas.

Annihilate
Demolish | **Plummet** ←
Burn

An elixir of new life. A factory of surrogate mothers. Sex is superfluous. The Tower of Babylon, constructed without the mathematics of reality—crumbled.

To die. Dogs will devour the heart from my dead body. At that, Nihilon clenched in fury. From a secret little corner in the sentence factory flashed a freshly fabricated thought:

! Save the red heart for black days !

Nihilon cautiously tucked his heart in his pocket.

What if someone steals my heart?

He grew terrified.

Ah!

What if they already stole it?

No, they didn't!

And he delightedly returned his heart to his chest. The heart joyously beat: A love for all. Nihilon kissed houses, streetcars, coffins, wedding parties, towers, and geometry. Nihilon removed his heart and again cautiously tucked it into his pocket. The chest dimmed to a cold wasteland.

. .
. . .

Advertisements roared. False is the typography of a worm-eaten century. Announcements howled like hungry jackals.

Russia Starving

The filthy mob grew deaf and blind. The filthy mob was colorblind to bloody words.

. .
. . .

In a European city where Nihilon lived, the city council posted:

NOTICE

It's been observed that citizens have been neglecting the cult of the **backside.** The backside is our great national martyr. The public is put on notice that offending that national saint will be strictly punishable by law. Only thugs, not peace-loving persons, disrespect the backside.
Death to the bastards and the miserable who wish for the return of the head. The head is mere bone. The backside is flesh. We must do our utmost to preserve the power of this fleshy century.
Those in violation of this order, approved by the president of the human peace republic

Martin Butcher

will shamefully grease the gibbet and be thrown to the dogs.
Nobody is to be hungry as such a state is irrevocably punishable by death.

The City Elders

. .

In Niholon's ear, a wave of laughter screamed and cries whirled up. His face contorted like that of an epileptic. He bid farewell to the ultramarine night and stepped into the land of

Self-forgetfulness

Month of June. 9:00 p.m.

Mirozov

• •

•

Nihilon's friend was four-legged. His legs wooden and hard. Nihilon got carried away talking to his friend:

I can't for the life of me untangle the sequence of concepts

A SOLUTION

To live is strange.

To not live is strange.

Nihilon's face stretched out into a small smile like an Archipenko sculpture.

MEMENTO.

A NEW CULTURE

I pour myriad years under a millstone.

Under the millstone trickles moldy flour that will never yield bread.

MEMENTO:

A NEW MILLER

My friend—my dear chair—tell me—please tell me—WHO IS MORE ALIVE BETWEEN THE TWO OF US?

You or I? Which one of us is the *superior element*?

I know—you are immortal.

I know—my immortality is so stupid.

Any prostitute would burst into tears at my immortality.

You stem from the time of the Egyptian pyramids and will live to see the 999th century, counting from my birth.

MY CHAIR ! ! ! ! !

I sit on you. You are hard, angular. Hard and angular is everything in this world that's to you

INFERIOR
Do you know, my wooden, four-legged baby: In the world of revolutions, his name also exists:
LENIN
Nihilon was startled.
A sharp thought whistled through his skull: Hilarious is the life of a bony, two-legged dunce to the world of CHAIRS—the world of superior four-legged beings.
Rotation in the body of a car under Nihilon's window.
Moments of consternation and horror flew into the spiderweb of Nihilon's nerves.
The chair sat on Nihilon.

Whistling Face

I am eternal. Thus, he spoke. He wasn't Mohammed, only someone called Kor.
At the speed of sunlight rushed hatred into Kor's factory of imaginary worlds.
Kor leapt over a tower.
The tower rang with catastrophe.
The love of Mr. Kor awaited a monumental object.
Kor's love dissipated the dark on the horizon.
Kor wasn't God.
Kor was a man.
Kor wasn't a criminal.
Kor was a lamppost.
The lamppost poisoned the sun.
The sun poisoned the centuries.
Kor poisoned exclamations.
Kor dismantled mazes.
In Kor's mind knelt the eternal question.
Kor closed his eyes and saw countless miracles.
He saw:

> Humans flying into abysses
> Abysses flowing into violins
> Violins falling on moons
> Moons rushing into brains
> Brains dripping onto streets
> Streets riding roosters
> Roosters crowing on underground trains
> Underground trains rushing into a billionaire's shoe
> A billionaire's shoe pulverizing skulls.

Kor's face is a locomotive.
Kor's face whistles ahead of tunnels.
Kor's eyes are sharp lamps.
His eyes scissor the dark.
The dark is a symphony of terror.

Where are the man's tracks

I found them!
Kor lit up the atmosphere.
Kor's face trumpets into the burning atmosphere!

Mariner's Bell

The foundations shake
The roofs collapse
The oxen low
Pains flow
On my nose on my nose
Through the streets I balanced
My frightened soul, on my nose
The meekness in my skull got in my way
I break rigid wisdom against royal courts
Like a zebra frolic
To reach myself, which runs away
And when the silent inky heavens fall on the city
With the moon and pearly stars
Then
I romantically leap around
Across the streets
Over the houses
And mark the crosses
Dreams stand
My wisdom weeps
Be smart and kiss life in cars
Flirt coquettishly with your homeland
And be its pimp
Take it from me, don't be a genius
The last fool
From the world of lost souls
It will be celebrated with triumph
And you will gnaw the Balkan cobblestone streets with the dogs
A song screams the river murmurs with my words
The wretched bazaar

Dances lightly along the coast
Shouldn't we hurt you with our pain
To invite you to join us for an aesthetic enjoyment
Oh idiots
Oh thieves
Oh leprous stupidity

The bell rings and the ship whistles
The church shakes and the ship departs
Let's construct a road machine
Toward the undiscovered worlds of bloody atmospheres

You Have Beautiful Eyes, Lucija

Across refracted diameters
In the circle of our lives
Today I skipped over everything
I felt this loony and hard earth
On which I dance from mindless mornings
To insane evenings
I look up: I look for a human face
My proud image askew
I drop my head and think
Revo
Revo
Revo
You have beautiful eyes, Lucija[3]
I know nothing of beginnings or endings
When the seams of the horizon tear
At least with one look I will peer into the hell of barricades
Oh my beautiful boyhood days
When the only tyrant was my father
And my mother
Lampposts under the windows buzz at night
The pocket watch in my hand in the mirror
Predicts my future.
Why wouldn't I be able to cut under her left breast
To see the heart with which she loves
Me, the bloody proletarian.

Dusk

This joyous hour marks the birth of new pains.
Loneliness silences me under the stars.
Night veils the town, damned
black and hard.
The sky
wide, high, and heavy
a pall on my youth.
The days
with their screams, cramps
and pangs of love
shorten.
Rebellion and blood
in the dusk of a culture
remain
on the barricades
like a dream found in a romantic poem.
I can't bear
the thought
that every flight has its fall
that I'm wilting like a flower folding its petals
at dusk.
Splendid the splendid death and the dream at night
the dream at night with its low song
on cold lips.

Poem About Him

The deadly pen
Trembles in the pale nervous hand
Blood is no ink
A word is no deed.
My lyric joy
Wishes to forge your precious self
Without lament and poisonous tears
For the salvation of
Poets
Thieves
Adventurers
This one here
Fools
From all past centuries.
There
At the end of my vision's horizon
Fantastical suns of new worlds
Yet undiscovered
Singe my immeasurable pain
At the center of the circle.
At the center
Of my visions
The smoke clears
So
At night
Peace
The silent stars
The clock in my room
Toys with humanity
You never know

When that wondrous mechanism will burst
Plight and suffering
That gently rock on his fountain pen
Tick-tock tick-tock tick-tock
Tick-tock tick-tock tick-tock.

We don't have friends
To comfort us
At the end of our dramatic momentum
From the attractions in our lives.
Without a lover to leave us every day
In our nights our last spasm whispered by
A woman's voice
The fatal cramp found in Eros.
Peace
Sh
Shshshshshshshshshsh
May the lunacy of broken arrows
Not overpower you
On the bows of days
When you pull back the string to strike the sun
In its noblest heart.
Why
Did you stop like marble before questions
Below your high forehead you thrust your hard look
Into that dusk
When you flirted with a beautiful woman:
How beautifully
How beautifully and joyously she laughed!
You roamed the world to lose yourself
You pondered inexplicable foreboding
You reaped passion to sow hatred
You loved so as to lose love

You didn't know how to make a knot
At your jugular where your juicy blood boils
Your life's blood and suffering
You wretched rebel and lunatic
You
Transcended death itself
On the road to dying.

Tomorrow
When this poem with awful excitements passes
It will be too late
In your travels over roofs
And telegraph wires
To know
Our day is the killer of poets
Our sun
The butcher of somnambulists.

4.6. B. Poljanski, *Tumbe* [*Topsy-Turvy*], Zenithists International Edition, no. 10, Belgrade, Serbia, 1926. Back cover, printed on red paper. Courtesy of Ubu Gallery, New York & Galerie Berinson, Berlin.

Endnotes

1 Terazije Square, a square in Belgrade.

2 Serpentinella, a fictitious poetic form Poljanski invented. Poljanski wrote two other serpentinellas: "2 ÷ 2 = 1" and "33 sEcoNdS." Though stylistically different, the poems all have prose elements.

3 The Serbo-Croatian spelling of Lucia is Lucija. The Serbo-Croatian word for revolution is *revolucija.* The poem's concept revolves around a pun: Revo-Lucija, or Revolution personified.

The Third Road of the Barbarogenius: Conceptual Writing

Introduction

Aleksandar Bošković and Steven Teref

The enigmatic Mita Dimitrijević, who wrote under the nom de guerre MID, penned perhaps the most fascinating, the most parasitic, and the most radical zenithist texts: *The Sexual Equilibrium of Money, or A Trade Correspondence on the Currency Question* (*Seksualni ekilibr novca ili Trgovinska prepiska o valutnom pitanju*, 1925) and *The Metaphysics of Nothing* (*Metafizika ničega*, 1926).[1] The two works stand out both thematically and formally by elevating cross-genre writing to a new paradigm, decades ahead of their time. It is very hard to differentiate the genre to which these two books belong as we are dealing with para-genre or meta-prose.

The two books are along the lines of pseudo-philosophical treatises and deviate from manifestos and other straightforward dogmatic texts. They are experimental multi-genre

1 MID is a mysterious author who owes his posthumous entry into Serbian and Yugoslav literature to Gojko Tešić, a literary historian who edited the following facsimile reprints of MID's two books in the 1990s: Mita Dimitrijević MID, *Seksualni ekilibr: Trgovinska prepiska o valutnom pitanju*, ed. Gojko Tešić (Belgrade: Otkrovenje, 1996); *Metafizika ničega* [*Uvod*], ed. Gojko Tešić (Belgrade: Otkrovenje, 1996).

works with an explicit zenithist agenda of persistent self-revolutionizing and drive toward a new artform. MID's books are prime examples of zenithist prose as an "intertextual parasite,"[2] which combine quotations from newspapers, politics, banking, literature, and philosophy. They are well-constructed, but highly hermetic, proto-conceptual writing, prefiguring the conceptual poetry movement in the United States that first came to prominence via text-based conceptual art in the 1960s and later formalized in the 2000s.

MID's books examine the relationship between the concepts of negativism and value, on the one hand, and dualism or theory of opposites and nihilism, on the other; both discursively, through free play with quotations, and visually, as typographic letterpress experiments. Risto Ratković, a *Zenit* contributor and author of "Barbarism as Culture,"[3] classified these books as "negativism," which MID used to describe *The Sexual Equilibrium of Money*.[4] According to Ratković, MID reduced philosophical and social dualism to a struggle between the sexes: male, negative, beautiful, evil, abstract vs. female, positive, ugly, good, dead, selfish. MID's nihilism is expansive and, what is significant, his views are hostile to all nihilistic views of the past. Instead of stating that everything is nothing, MID "assigns (initial) value to Nothing" so that "the spirit flies to both sexes, thus achieving a sexual balance of measuring values."[5] MID recognizes negativity as an inevitable factor in measurement and simultaneously destroys it. MID's destruction of negativity represents "a danger to the existing unipolarity," which Ratković perceives as "the slavery of the negative, the male sex, the slavery of the spirit in general."[6]

As a "book on negativism," *The Sexual Equilibrium of Money* opposes what MID perceived as an American and west European "bankocracy"; it plunges into a poetic and philosophic examination of the "trade (import—export) of words" and its connection to the notion of value, that is, *money* as a universal measure of the values of all other commodities (i.e., the general equivalent). The book includes "the key" that will help the reader unlock its hermetically closed doors of possible meanings, which is found in the words "steal freely." This "key" for understanding MID's books should remind the reader of the fact that they are almost entirely composed of quotations, self-quotations, para-documentary

---

2 Ivan Negrišorac, "Zenitistička proza kao osporavanje romana," *Polja*, nos. 342–343 (1987): 353.

3 Originally published in *Zenit*, no. 37 (November–December 1925); see the translation of his text in the second section of the anthology.

4 Risto Ratković, "Negativizam," in *Ćutanja o književnosti* (Belgrade, 1928), 23.

5 Ibid.

6 Ibid.

materials, slogans, and so on, in an "authentic" zenithist fashion of literary banditry (*hajdučija*). Although given the "key" to MID's textual "crypt," the reader is nonetheless challenged in their quest to fully decipher the book's cryptic message that complicates the discourse and the reading experience. The annotations that we have provided, which are a first in MID scholarship, including noting the different editions of MID in Serbian, although not exhaustive of all references in MID's books, should assist the reader in such a quest.

Furthermore, *The Sexual Equilibrium of Money* is a typographic experiment remarkable for its economy: the maximum effects (semantic explosion) are accomplished by a minimum of means (typographic condensation). MID printed his text over a bookkeeping ledger—used, most likely, either by the Kingdom of Serbs, Croats, and Slovenes' National Bank or Chambers of Commerce (at the Ministry of Foreign Affairs) for some sort of trade correspondence and/or bookkeeping records—while keeping the found language in it (including the words about trading such as "commercial tender," "offer," "party," "gaffe," "section," and so on). Moreover, he printed the page numbers in reverse order of the text so that the book can be read from both ends.[7] If read from beginning to end, as *The Sexual Equilibrium of Money*, the text unfolds linearly, simultaneously running parallel to the countdown of the page numbers, so that the final word of the book—"nothing"—appears on page zero.[8] If we read the book from end to beginning, starting with the last sentence on page zero and the sign of the cross (as a symbol of positive/death) on the next page, following the right order of page numbers printed in red (1–40), we would come to the book titled *A Trade Correspondence on the Currency Question* (where, on the 39th page, as if it were a new first page, we read again: "A type of trade shop: The Import—Export of words"). It is as if MID's pagination does not mark the pages, but instead numerates each featured text as "currency"—a paper of value, receipt, or check.[9]

MID's negativism is further explored in *The Metaphysics of Nothing*, a conceptual sequel to his previous book, a quasi-philosophical treatise on the concept of value, its

---

7 For more, see Gojko Tešić, "MID=DIM ili 'Pesnik apsolutno ničega,'" in Mita Dimitrijević MID, *Metafizika ničega* [*Uvod*], ed. Gojko Tešić (Belgrade: Otkrovenje, 1996), 45.

8 The last sentence in the book reads: "If we, therefore, don't wish to lie to each other then it is necessary that we not lie about nothing." See *The Sexual Equilibrium of Money* included in the anthology.

9 "Each text in the book is assigned a numeric value from 1 to 40—all given in red typeface. The original edition has 84 pages in total." See Gojko Tešić, "Beleške uz Trgovinsku prepisku . . .," in Mita Dimitrijević MID, *Seksualni ekilibr: Trgovinska prepiska o valutnom pitanju*, ed. Gojko Tešić (Belgrade: Otkrovenje, 1996), 86.

recuperations and meanings in economics, philosophy, spiritualism, and language. The book starts from the assumption that the perfection of form endangers the spirit.[10] The opposition of cross-genre writing and its various thematic segments—the book is comprised of quotations from diverse written sources referencing 1920s European politicians and economic issues of the time, medieval texts, various philosophers and philosophical schools, including financial reports and banking, and mathematical rules—appears as a consequence of considering the metaphysics of the word *nothing*. This is especially evident in the excessive use of the word "nothing" by politicians, poets, philosophers, and journalists, which MID treats as found language quoted throughout the book. This "nothing" that ceaselessly repeats and reappears throughout MID's book is, actually, the *nothing of language*: it can be read as a faraway echo of a Dada-game, but it is first and foremost an expression of a lost faith in language, or an attempt to manifest *nothingness* that is inexpressible in a language of words.[11] In that regard, MID's book can be read as a prolegomenon for non-verbal poetry, which was explored in some Dadaist experiments[12] and later researched and practiced more systematically in Yugoslav neo-avant-garde (concrete and visual) poetry.[13]

One of the key features of MID's book is that it addresses both the particulars of the moment and the essence of the universal. For example, MID established a connection between spiritualism (which is in the origin of surrealism), on the one hand, and political economy and international relations, on the other. Thus, for example, the message about the forthcoming crisis received by a medium during a spiritualist séance, prefigured the 1929 stock market crash followed by the Great Depression via then contemporary references to

10 The opening is thematically connected with two short texts that MID published in *Zenit* in 1926 under the same title; see: MID, "Form Devours Spirit," *Zenit*, no. 40 (April 1926): n.p.; no. 41 (May 1926): 14.

11 See Radomir Konstantinović, *Biće i jezik u iskustvu srpskih pesnika dvadesetog veka*, vol. 4 (Belgrade: Prosveta, Rad; Novi Sad: Matica Srpska, 1983), 91.

12 "Many Dadaist experimental poetic forms emerged as yet another project that aimed to renovate poetic language. Their works forcefully demonstrate how language, that foremost guardian of reason and the socio-symbolic order, might itself be 'savaged' and transformed into a crude substance of pure enjoyment: Tristan Tzara's simultaneous poem (read in different languages, with different rhythms, tonalities, and by different persons at the same time), Hugo Ball's phonetic poem (lautgedichte), Richard Huelsenbeck's bruitist poem, or Raoul Haussmann's opto-phonetic and poster poems, are the most salient examples of such experiments." Aleksandar Bošković, "The Avant-Garde Photopoetry," in *Književna istorija*, no. 158 (2016), 297.

13 See more in: *OEI*, nos. 90–91: *Sickle of Syntax & Hammer of Tautology: Concrete and Visual Poetry in Yugoslavia, 1968–1983*, ed. Sezgin Boynik (March 2021).

international negotiation deals—the 1924 Dawes Plan (which negotiated Germany's reparation payments after the First World War) and the 1925 Locarno meetings (which brought the Rhineland Pact, signed by Germany, France, and Belgium)—from the mid-1920s.[14]

The Metaphysics of Nothing is divided into three sections, each suggesting surrealist ideas. The first part ("Night") references "a congress of spirits and spiritualists recently held in Paris," while the second and third parts ("A Small Anthology about the Smallest Thing," "On the Double Meaning of the Word *Nothing*") quote, respectively, André Breton's well-known definition of surrealism and its genealogy, both from the first *Manifesto of Surrealism* (1924). In addition, it is important to point out that MID may have travelled to Russia with the Ministry of Foreign Affairs, which left a mark on a short travel note in his book: "The proletarian loan! I thought that I, a citizen of a bourgeois nation and a westerner with capitalist biases, would be surprised by my encounter with a communist and Marxist country. I expected to find in Moscow something unusual, inhuman, some sort of urban and social futurism. But NOTHING like that at all!"[15]

The Metaphysics of Nothing represents yet another typographical experiment. The author insists on a visual reading of the text, punctuation marks, plus and minus signs, horizontal and vertical typographic lines placed on blank pages, emphasizing the seemingly emptied meaning of the text and the artistic aspect of the concept of nothing. Also, the front cover page and general layout of the text reflect the connection with Bauhaus's functionalism in arrangement, color, typeface, and graphic design.

MID's books appear dialogical if read alongside the authors whose writings discussed similar phenomena at the time, such as Georg Simmel, a German sociologist, philosopher, and critic, and Branislav Petronijević, a Serbian philosopher. MID addressed the relationship between money and value in a similar yet different way than Simmel in his seminal *Philosophy of Money* (*Philosophie des Geldes*, 1900). Both Simmel and MID reveal that money is a "relation of relations"[16] and "the measure of all measures,"[17] that is, the universal

---

14 See the annotated *Metaphysics of Nothing* in this anthology. Along with surrealism and psychoanalysis, political economy also developed strongly in the interwar period. Only after World War II will political economy emerge from anonymity and determine economic trends in the second half of the twentieth century.

15 See *Metaphysics of Nothing* in this anthology.

16 See George Simmel, "Value and Money," in Clive Cazeaux, *The Continental Aesthetics Reader* (London: Routledge, 2000), 305–321.

17 See "The 8th Party" section in MID's *Sexual Equilibrium* included in this anthology.

equivalent, a Standard that gives expression to deeply buried metaphysical modes of evaluation. MID, however, goes further by asserting that "*nothing* must be factored into the Standard," that is, into money as a measure for any other entity, "even though *nothing* cannot be known." He also claims that *nothing* "is a 'thing-in-itself,'" and that *words* "cannot be understood as money [...] but only as a relative one-sided twofold value, a 'thing-in-itself.'"[18]

MID's understanding of the *words* and, thus, of the concept of *nothing* as the Kantian "thing-in-itself" may be perceived as a ludic zenithist response to Branislav Petronijević's essential philosophical work, *Principles of Metaphysics* (*Prinzipen der Metaphysik*, vols. 1–2, 1904–1911).[19] Petronijević firmly believed that "correct mathematical concepts are the key to solving the riddle of the world."[20] He developed a doctrine of reality based on the notion of "discrete geometry" to which MID refers in the short section "A Small Anthology about the Smallest Thing" in *The Metaphysics of Nothing*.[21] According to Petronijević, there are two principles of hypermetaphysics above mathematical reality, defined as *one* and an *unlimited divisible set*, that is, *being* and *nothing* from whose unification (mixing) the whole of reality is derived. Toward the end of the section "On the Dual Importance of the Word *Nothing*" in *The Metaphysics of Nothing*, which represents a "dialogue" between the First and the Second, the exchange between the two in which the former utters "mathematics" and the later replies "calculus" resonates with the pivotal postulates of Petronijević's philosophy. MID's work appears as hermetic as it is ambivalent: both humorously criticizing and affirming Petronijević's attempt to overcome the duality of Western philosophy and Kantian conservatism, by bastardizing, (mis)using, and abusing dense philosophical discourse in order to playfully dislocate and deconstruct its seriousness through a playful game of quotations

---

18 Ibid.

19 Petronijević's theoretical philosophical works (metaphysics and theory of knowledge) were written in German and intended for a philosophically educated public, unlike his historical and philosophical texts, which were written in Serbian with propaedeutic goals and a pedagogical purpose.

20 See Boris Milisavljević, "Nov pogled na delo Branislava Petronijevića," *Gledišta* 40, no. 1–2 (1999): 272; Milorad Lj. Milenković, "Petronijevićev uvid: jedinstvo bića i mišljenja," foreword to *Metafizičke rasprave* by Branislav Petronijević, ed. Milorad Lj. Milenković (Sremski Karlovci: Izdavačka knjižarnica Zorana Stojanovića, 1991), 14.

21 For Petronijević, discrete space is composed of a finite number of simple quality points separated by unreal points as "acts of negation." He writes: "Discrete space: consists of undivided parts. In discrete geometry, a point is no longer a fictitious value, it is the last real element from which it becomes both the space itself and all the individual elements in it." See Branislav Petronijević, "Osnovni postulati diskretne geometrije," in *Članci i studije B. Petronijevića*, vol. 2 (Pančevo: Napredak, 1920), 136–163.

and hybridization, thus crystalizing the zenithist *active nihilism* geared to destroy the present to create the future, to destroy the destructive ideals of the present so as to create new ideals and bring about the future we want.

The two myths of modernism are disregarded in MID's books: originality (authenticity) and author(ship). Both books were published without the author's name on the cover; we only know the author's identity because of two short texts, both titled "Form Devours Spirit," that were written in the same style and employed the same language, that were published in *Zenit* and signed by MID. And we can connect the name Mita Dimitrijević to MID through a dedication. The Serbian poet Dragutin Kostić dedicated his poem "Umesto ludila" (Instead of Lunacy) "to Jack the Ripper of all lies and a universal Zarathustra, my dear friend MID—Mita Dimitrijević, a poet and philosopher."[22] Information on MID is limited. One source refers to him as a tobacconist who was jailed for twenty days over his first book. This same source provides a brief window into his poetics. When questioned by a police chief about the purpose of the blank pages in *The Sexual Equilibrium of Money*, MID explained that they are a space for a reader to "write a whole novel."[23] Beyond this, we know next to nothing about this mysterious man who wore his top hat in the "Zagreb fashion."[24] It's not clear why Dimitrijević chose MID as his pen name. It is possible that it may be an allusion to King Midas (the Serbo-Croatian word for *Midas* is *Mida*), a figure he alludes to in *The Sexual Equilibrium of Money*. Although, it is more likely that his pen name is simply an abbreviation of his first and last names. This proto-postmodern "obfuscation" of authorship and promotion of the so-called figure of uncreative writer is even more telling when MID's books are read alongside several Yugoslav conceptual and post-conceptual artists from the second half of the twentieth century.

Overall, MID's two books and short texts stand out among a number of modernist works considered to be models of conceptual writing—for example, Stéphane Mallarmé's falsified fashion writings, Erik Satie's experiments with repetition and boredom, Duchamp's readymades, Francis Picabia's embrace of mechanical drawing techniques, or Walter Benjamin's *Arcades Project*, a work that collates more than 900 pages of notes—as a rare

---

22 Dragutin Kostić, *Umesto ludila* (Belgrade: Štamparija "Miletić," 1928), n.p. Quoted in Konstantinović, Biće i jezik, 91.

23 See "A Tobacconist in Literature" in this anthology.

24 See Djordje Kostić, "MID—Mita Dimitrijević," in *Do nemogućeg* (Belgrade: Nolit, 1972), 26–27.

example of the entire modernist oeuvre seen as conceptual writing.[25] As such, MID's work appears to be a forebear of what by mid-century, with the advent of widespread technology, solidified in diverse movements as concrete and visual poetry, Oulipo and Fluxus, musique concrète and the works of John Cage, conceptual art, continuing into what by the 1980s became appropriation art. MID's *Metaphysics of Nothing* reminds us of a secret predecessor of Joseph Kosuth's exhibition *Titled (Art as Idea as Idea)* (Los Angeles, 1968), which mounted "a series of enlarged projection photocopies of different dictionary definitions of the word 'nothing,' isolated from their original placement on the page and resituated on the gallery wall."[26] MID's willingness to discount traditional values of originality, to question the sense of property behind *le propre,* or what is one's own, to demand an opaquely material language (something to be found and cut, physically moved and reframed, searched and sampled)—reveal the dominant procedures of conceptual writing in these zenithist works.

25 "I coined the phrase 'conceptual writing' as a way both to signal literary writing that could function comfortably as conceptual art and to indicate the use of text in conceptual art practices." Craig Dworkin, "The Fate of Echo," in *Against Expression: An Anthology of Conceptual Writing,* ed. Craig Dworkin and Kenneth Goldsmith (Evanston: Northwestern University Press, 2011), xxiii.

26 Craig Dworkin, "The Fate of Echo," xxiii.

The Sexual Equilibrium of Money

MID [Mita Dimitrijević]
Zenit Administration, 1925

Translated by *Steven Teref and Maja Teref*

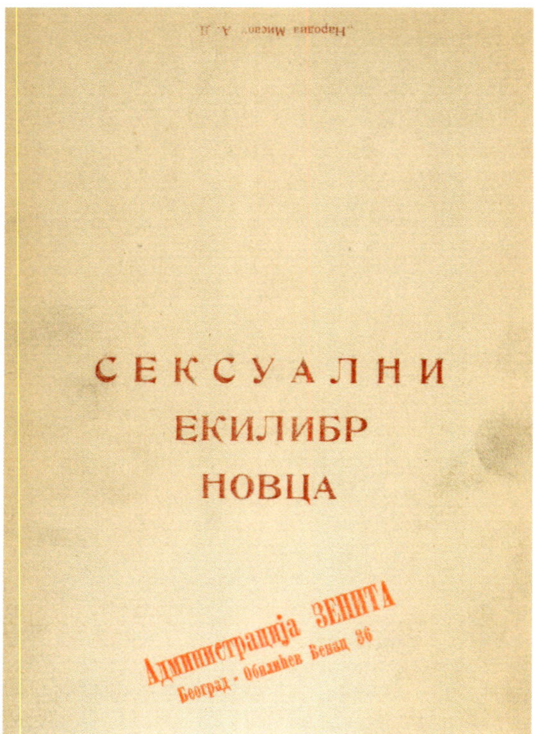

5.1. MID [Mita Dimitrijević], *Seksualni ekilibr novca. Trgovinska prepiska o valutnom pitanju* [The Sexual Equilibrium of Money. A Trade Correspondence on the Currency Questio*n*], Zenit Administration, Belgrade, 1925. Front cover. Courtesy of Ubu Gallery, New York & Galerie Berinson, Berlin.

A TRADE CORRESPONDENCE

on

THE CURRENCY
QUESTION

40

A BOOK OF
HORS D'OEUVRES
on
NEGATIVISM

A type of trade shop:

The Import—Export
of words

39

The guiding principle:

Bankocracy

38

The Leading Motif

first,
one-sidedly twofold.

*

The National Bank can carry out its chicanery against its national massif, its spouse, because it regulates its spouse's monetary,—materialistic relations, by using the bank's privileged means, the bank note;—this notorious chicanery is NOT worth writing or speaking about because the massif's entire body would feel it and quake from it, causing: an accidental showdown.

*

In this super organic miasma of hyper organic cosmos, generally speaking—there is a mystery (. . . a marital secret . . .), a whirlwind of (. . the problem of causality . .) . . . sadism . . ., surrealism . ., futurism . . dadaism . . . gaiaism . . . ZENITHISM . .—in which there isn't a more dignified quotation than the one given at Such-and-Such a time by lord So-and-So: . . . "the solution to the currency issue points in the direction which, 'on some pretext or other,' leads straight to"—The loony bin of words is falling apart . . . falling apart . . . like antiquity shattered into the seconds of the present . . .

37

The Leading Motif

second,

two-sidedly hermaphroditic.

*

Good (+) has, POSITIVELY, received from evil an inoperative subtraction: beauty; yet evil (–) has, NEGATIVELY, received from good an operative sum: UGLINESS.

According to Plato . . . Diogenes . . . .
Then, "According to Fragonard's painting
with laughing angelic
backsides"[1] . . .

36

Approving a business loan

35

To the National Bank Administration.

All the individuals at the National Bank who are acquainted with me have obviously come to an awful misconception about me because, as I have unquestionably observed, they have labeled me a nervous wreck. However, per my current circumstances, I am only monetarily wrecked. But, since having property and being a nervous wreck intersect and often hinder each other simultaneously, and since the general nature of currency is under question in the entire country,—it leads to deconceptions [*sic*] about me which cannot be reconciled because they cancel each other out.

Indeed, currency-wise—I am the most acutely attuned type of human you will ever meet. Nobody can lie about me without my consent to play the role of a scoundrel.

I couldn't help but defend my character! . . .

. . . .

And the Truth,

which I'm disseminating, in place of the chicanes, which I gather from the initial low sum stated in the LETTER OF CREDIT at the National Bank—is independent from whether It is necessary or not, and whether it is convenient for others or not. It depends only on the index number of the dinar currency system of weighing and calculating the value of the truth.

. . . .

Very Respectively,

34

Establishing trade relations

33

Supply of goods.

To Mr. Edison, New York.
To Mr. Grey-Snowden, London.
To Mr. Flammarion, Berlin.
To Mr. Hauptmann, Paris.
To Mr. Ujević, Zagreb.
To Mr. Gorky, Moscow.
To Mr. Tagore, Delhi.[2]

32

GAFFE.

"all the efforts of Marco Aurelius to MASTER life, all of his skepticism, stoicism, asceticism,—comes down to that famous thing of his: be cold as a rock and hard as stone!"

*

"all paths lead to Rome but going around is closest."[3]

The 1st Party

One can and dare do with money (+) what one dare not, cannot do sexually (–). With goods, the "thing-in-itself" (+), the seen and unseen, one can evaluate a relationship; a calculation (–) by itself is not the end all and be all to assigning value . . . . . . We have a duty to lie, nothing is just . . . .[4]

. . . STEAL FREELY!

THE KEY ! . .

THE KEY ! ! ! ! ! . . .

The 2nd Party

. . . . . Inalienable?

—Nothing is not just . . . . the ultimate, but also the central concept; that is, when it seems limited to a one-sided idea, nothing simultaneously generates the embryo of the twofold idea from the seen and the unseen. This again shows that nothing is the central concept of all concepts; it proves that nothing is an integral concept, circulus vitiosus, the central question of Death and life,—Death, which is positive, active (+), and life, which is neither (–), cancel each other out as they hurtle toward one another from the seen and the unseen. Nothing is therefore one-sidedly twofold and simultaneously a two-sidedly hermaphroditic concept; it is as a result four-fold (to note an eight-fold) . . . . central concept of two categorical oppositions and two elementary impulses which propel and yet cancel each other without separating the seen and the unseen.

THE KEY ! ! . .		THE KEY ! ! ! ! . . . ,

The 3rd Party

Make no mistake about the meaning of nothing: it is both love and the calculus, the seen and the unseen: a fluid (+) conventional and unconventional (–) currency of poles and sex. Nothing isn't free; its shares, due to its passivity, are latent, . . . Nothing can't be seen, nothing can't be heard, nothing can't be felt; not everything can be understood . . . . The basic principle of nothing, or nihilation, which is the transformation into nothing, annihilation, therefore nothing,—would be both understood and not understood, just like nihilism, from what can be seen and unseen, in a one-sided, twofold way . . . . Nothing is therefore the Center and the vortex of time and space of the seen and the unseen: . . . . Even Arius of Alexandria preached that the first perfect creation was dead matter (+), a "thing-in-itself:" a WORD created from **NOTHING**: an eternal, self-important, **UNCREATED** divinity (–).[5]

28

THE KEY ! !

THE KEY ! ! ! ! ! . .

The 4th Party

The material fluidity of nothing . . . . .

It can be safely established that a single METRIC is needed to measure value, and value is the measure of all measures; this metric must be a constant in its division and multiplication values, uncompromising in meaning, definitive, a single Standard to measure all measures in all of time and space from the seen and the unseen, so that it can be used for precise calculations of the following: all fluctuations of all relative values .(. . goods . .). from the seen and the unseen, the dead (+) resurrected (. . by being calculated . .), and the cost of the deadened living (–): strength, property, skill, knowledge . . . . Nothing must be factored into the Standard, even though nothing cannot be known . . . . To know “the price of everything but the value of nothing” (Wilde). . . . . Therefore, goods can be used to calculate relationships, but the calculation can’t measure the value.[6]

THE KEY ! ! ! ! . . .

THE KEY ! ! ! ! . . .

The 5th Party

To cancel a real (+) question, ...

. . . . The RESPONSIBILITY for WAR . . . .

. . . . (. . . . The aromatic musk of Western Civilization, its love . . . . : "You think the desire for a more righteous justice and wiser traditions felled Ithuriel to the earth?—Ambition, affinity for intrigue, love of true honor, and wealth made heavenly peace unbearable for her and she burned with the desire to mix in with the restless tribe of humans" . . . .)—to cancel the great (+) positive question . . . . requires asking the same question from the opposite yet abstract (–) position which made the question FLARE UP originally; and then to distinguish between the poles of the seen and the unseen . . . . One again encounters the central question, the castration of a stallion, the nothing, because the opposite poles in the question cancel each other without separating the seen and the unseen . . . . Nothing is incessantly considered for its stylized, active (+), positive properties, which are constantly NEGLECTED and confirmed by its one-sidedly twofold denying positivism: nothing: the most unreal of all unreal questions, and simultaneously, the most real of all unreal questions, seen and unseen . . . . . . "Since the figure was too polite to put on the pajamas and underwear of the young d'Esparvier—it was impossible for Mrs. Des Obelle not to notice, in the bright light, that her suspicions were founded (+) and that angels (–) do indeed possess human eyesight. Curious as to whether that vision was imaginary or real, she asked the son of light if angels were like monkeys (. . . . Leningrad deduction: . . . descendant theory . . .) who, to make love to women, need only money" . . . . . According to the one-sided twofold theory about the minimum amount, nothing would be the smallest amount of the maximum, which would be the most negative positivity (+); but: according to the two-sided hermaphroditic altruistic quadruple problem of causality, nothing is the largest sum of the negative, THE MOST POSITIVE NEGATIVITY (–).

Wings are therefore the currency of NOTHING (+) . . . . . .

A CONVENTIONAL METRIC and

an Unconventional (–) SEXUAL FIXATION, both of which, within nothing, cancel each other without separating the seen and the unseen.[7]

THE KEY ! ! . .

THE KEY ! ! ! ! . . . .

The 6th Party

If nothing isn't necessary, then breathing isn't necessary; breathing is also one-sidedly twofold: Inhalation and exhalation, which are an elementary and natural way of receiving and giving, which are manifested through the one-sidedly twofold invocation of nothing through the dynamics of words: . . "Just that, . . that isn't nothing?!" . . . . in it, within this dynamic, "you may admire philosophers who approach a solution to, a dissolution of, and a resolution to the Absolute, and the determination of the indeterminate and the definition of infinity" . . . . . .—It has been said that the first pole, the stronger (+) pole, the active pole, the Death pole, the conventional, positive pole, is found in nothing through the negative, weaker pole, so that, like a grinning debtor, it covers up the trace of nothing, and in a one-sidedly twofold way, rejects its own positivity;—while the other pole, the negative or passive (–) one, which is ON NO ACCOUNT A TRAGIC ONE, actively yet mystically points to the RAW SUM of nothing . . . . . (. . . Compte rendu . . . . In the invention of gallium . . . .) . . . . The currency (+) question, no matter how miniaturized or aggrandized, cannot be resolved independently of the sexual question, or vice versa, because the currency question is inextricably entwined with nothing, and because, along with the sexual question, it represents a quadruple . . (from a one-sidedly twofold literary . . . . perspective) . . issue of the balanced relativity of living and dying. "DER BEIDEN GRUNDTYPEN DES PHILOSOPHIERENS" From the most important (+) and the most conventional perspective, that which has the most currency is that which cannot be had, cannot be seen, yet can be kept silent about the hymen (nothing). From a faunal . . brutally calculated, sexual, . . perspective, therein lies the intrigue of ʎǝuoɯ, the price . . . ., the secret of a monetary, fluid (+) perspective . . . . of being (Of the Dance of Death, a positive Dance) toward dying . . (–), which is the unconventional . . phenomenon of life . . . . Voronoff . . Einstein . . Steinach . . . . "Go to it. It runs from you; run from It, It's following you" . . . . . From the seen and unseen, therefore, currency-wise (+) . . . . . . "The validity of all contracts based on money are on shaky ground" . . . just like the sexual (–) question, which is the twofold hermaphroditic question of nothing: . . . .

. . . . Currency is a conventional (+) metric, and the question of sexual difference (the balance); yet an unconventional, sexual (–) fixation is the question of the currency total (sum); and both of these, the metric and the fixation, cancel each other in nothing but without separating the seen and the unseen.[8]

THE KEY ! ! . .

THE KEY ! ! ! !

The 7th Party

Nothing is consistently treated as a phenomenon, the central question of everything . . . . .: "Mr. Mišle, I know nothing and I acutely suffer from it!" . . . . . . "Doctors knew nothing before and they will know nothing after." . . . . . . "And so it goes, to own everything as if nothing happened!" . . . . . . "In him nothing betrayed a prophet or magician!" . . . . "You can't trust the government nor its representatives." . . . . "You aren't allowed to speak or write about nothing!" . . . .

Both freemasonry and communism (together) are a one-sided twofold emphasis of nothing in bold relief . . . a transformation into nothing . . . the annihilation of . . . (sexual difference, the monetary sum: THE KEY BALANCE)., the dual sameness of the opposites of hermaphroditic instincts, a one-sided twofold . . . . . . transparent . . . ACCUMULATION of all opposites at once . . . . . . in EVERYTHING . . . .

Even "Pythagoras of Samos proved that everything is a number!" . . . . Nothing shouldn't slip one's mind, even when nothing is not acknowledged . . . that's all . . . . ! Oh![9]

24

THE KEY ! ! ! ! . . . .

THE KEY ! ! ! ! . . .

The 8th Party

If this party, the 8th one, were to be eaten, to be savored slowly, and then to reach the bowels, which is what it's meant to do, it would cause such a forceful explosion that it would make Judgment Day seem like a real comedy. Therefore, in strict confidence, this commodity is recommended for the strong . . . . positive pole . . . when its charge is . . . . blasé

Nothing is not easy to ISOLATE LEXICOGRAPHICALLY . . . That would mean switching established properties of the poles: THE BEING OF DEATH and THE DYING OF LIFE, whose properties in nothing cancel each other without separating the seen and the unseen. One is . . . an active (+) pole, stylistically, conventionally attracted to nothing, and therefore not SEPARATED . . . .

YOU WRITE NOTHING, BUT READ IT AS: . . . . EVERYTHING ! ! ! ! . . . .

. . . . "Bastard . . . bastard! . . . From the negative therefore comes nothing . . . And without nothing you cannot positively charge god (–) who is himself a negative charge! . . . . . .

. . . By not thinking about nothing and not analyzing nothing, everything is annihilated:

. . . . . The smallest and the largest, the hottest and the coldest, simultaneously, the seen and the unseen . . Clearly, nothing is a "thing-in-itself," "an und fuer sich," . . noumenal . . . . an ethereal, WORD . . . AN OPERATIVE VALUE . . . .

"Go to It, It runs from you: you run from It" . . . . (spectral analysis . . . a Biblically related operation . . . . Czaric sonnets) . . .

. . . "Such a point of view is called transcendental realism which, unlike empiricism, comprises a naive and natural (dogmatic) realism" . . . .

Words, therefore, cannot be understood as money (which is a two-sided, hermaphroditic bill (–) of receiving and giving, a Standard, the system of measurement calculating fluctuating (+) values), but only as a relative one-sided twofold value, a "thing-in-itself": a COMMODITY from the seen and the unseen . . . Commodities do not contain anything serious, only comical (. . . "that's nothing . . .") . . . It is in their nature to seriously peddle DEATH (+) the "thing-in-itself," the one-sidedly twofold of the seen and the unseen: through miraculous stories, advertisements, in nothing, from the seen and the unseen, they become . . . are becoming . . . the most comical), the most ethereal, the most attractive . . . the most invisible . . . (. love . .) which causes the money gaffe: the problem (–) in life: dying . . . . .

. . . So this is how the positive (+) value of nothing hides like a "thing-in-itself" from the seen and the unseen, a unique word . . . with an ethereal value . . . so that with the WORD, nothing, as an inoperative value, DEATH can be traded as a commodity to "create-in-itself" from the seen and the unseen . . . (. . . the commercialization of Diplomacy . . . . .

. . . . . . Therefore, in nothing, a dead deity becomes DIVINE . . . . Sciences . . . Religions . . . Arts . . . a debatable Truth (+), which is operative from the seen and the unseen . . . through a peripeteia, shifts to the inoperative (–) irrefutable . . . . yet still positive (+) RIGHT . . . , but the living (–) deity in it, in nothing, becomes a SPECTER . . . Voltaire . . . Dante . . . Nietzsche . . . Dostoyevsky . . . . . "Bastard . . . , bastard!" . . . "My friend . . . , I'm often sad . . . that I'm so mad!" Rostand . . . . .[10]

THE KEY ! !

THE KEY ! ! ! ! . .

Another, more reasonable offer, I, from the 8th party of the gaffe.

Still, nothing hasn't come to pass . . . . And nothing is the ABSOLUTE AXIOM of all the words from the seen and the unseen simultaneously! . . . . Why? . . . . .—the Ethereal . . . . one-sidedly twofold "thing-in-itself" . . . the word . . . . . . commodity . . . . . . the ǝʌᴉʇɐɹǝdouᴉ operative value . . . (+) . . . . Nothing isn't a novelty . . . . . . « le vrai, le bon, le seul . . . le vrai, le fou, le sage, ... et toujours neuf, quoique le plus ancien ! » . . . . In nothing, REVOLUTION and WAR avalanche and tumble, roll, simultaneously, in the twisted up fourfold trade, in denial of any acknowledgments; they, in nothing, cancel each other without separating the unseen and the seen . . . . Nothing isn't the Scoundrel nor the genius "Oh, bloodthirsty Holy Mother, You who conceived without sinning, . . . let me sin without conceiving!" . . . . The holy day of the sinless Virgin in Belgrade . . . . I'm not talking to you, son of a bitch, but to your Glorious Mother!" . . . . The fall of angels . . . . Nothing is a neutral divinity, compared to which, a positively charged divinity taunts the positively charged devil (god) . . . . . . and metamorphizes . . . . . by folding in on itself: shrinking ; and compared to which, the negative divinity . a blasé demon (–) . . is magnified

Nothing is therefore . . . . .

THE CENTRAL ARBITRAL
TRIBUNAL

in which, all relationships and every intercourse intersect and parallel each other, conventionally and unconventionally (+, –); and simultaneously assemble themselves every night, every day, and every moment: all relationships and every intercourse . . . . . . of the Currency Sphinx and the sexual phantom : rash plutocracies of royal courts and reasonable riff-raff of the medians . . from the seen and the unseen . . . .

Roads to nowhere :

. . . «Veritas est suprema lex!» . . . The Dead Cvijić (His Bust) . . . Truth is Death! . . the living dead (Tolstoy) . . . "Hey woman, you grave, hell is packed!" . . . . . . d'Aragon . . . . "Man, you bitch, the madhouse is packed!" . . . . . . from the seen and the unseen simultaneously . . . .[11]

22

THE KEY ! ! !

THE KEY ! !

A further offer, IV, from the 8th party of the gaffe

....

....

THE KEY ! !

THE KEY ! !

A solid extension of offer, II, from the 8th party of the gaffe

"Such hard times . . . such nasty people,
such unstable monarchies . . . once more
inspired Him profoundly to die . . .
. . ., or to rejoice . . . . . ., so that
for a moment, to escape that teeerrible
condition . . which the English, our teachers
of melancholy christened by the name: . . . . . .
SPLEEN."

THE KEY ! .

THE KEY ! ! . . . ! ! . . .

Again, an elegant offer, III, by the 8th party of the gaffe

The embedded glands of words . ,
. . the "thing-in-itself," a commodity . . .
which has its essence . .
. . ethereal . . operative
. . from the seen and the unseen at the same
time . . . . . one-sidedly twofold:

The King: "It shall be so.
Madness in great ones must not unwatched go!"[12]

THE KEY ! ! . . .

THE KEY ! ! . . . ! ! . . . ! ! . .

Letter D.

Another offer, V, by the 8th party of the gaffe

THE KEY ! ! . .

THE KEY ! ! ! ! . . . .

Letter C.

Again, an offer, VI, by the 8th party of the gaffe

17

THE KEY ! ! . .

THE KEY ! ! ! !

Letter B.

A respectful offer, VII, from the 8th party gaffe

. . . .

THE KEY ! !

THE KEY ! ! ! ! . .

Letter A.

THE ADVERTISED OFFER, VIII, BY THE 8th PARTY AND THE ELIMINATION OF THE GAFFE.

....

....

I am asking everyone, except for the individuals to whom this letter is addressed, who has all the positive and great powers . . . attributes, . . . to forgive me and not mind me, if during the inspection . . . of my organic statement, they find:

that I don't give special treatment to nothing, . . .
that I do nothing . . . ;

or if they find:

that I forget nothing, . . .
that I forgive nothing . . . .

. . . . . . IN MY SHOP of outrageous merchandise . . . the "thing-in-itself" . . . words . . . , an exemplary eight-sided order rules . . .

. . . . . . IN MY SHOP, nothing is suspected from the seen and the unseen . . .

. . . . . . IN MY SHOP, it is my honor to especially recommend FIRST the "thing-in-itself," from the seen and the unseen, labeled: TIME IS A COMMODITY . . . I, II, III, IV

Illuminating and shading . . .
Heating and cooling . . .
Feeding and starving . . .
Clothing and disrobing . . .

. . . . . . IN MY SHOP special guarantees are offered for the most extenuating circumstances: diplomacy and warfare, active and conventional, for a general's headquarters: one OTHER „thing-in-itself" CALCULATION . . . one specific calculation for measuring and . . . the value . . . this „thing-in-itself"; though it may be missing its essence, . . . it contains: . . . premises and impure practices, then also promises of the most prestigious shops on EARTH . . . and also those of the darkest . . . underground . . . slaves of omni-human gaffes (. . . Count Cagliostra . . . Indian fakirs . . .)

IN MY SHOP . . . the ghost of Isadora Germanova . . . . "Give us Hamlet!" . . . ("Bastard! . . ., bastard!" . . . "Oh, how wonderful!" . . .) is repulsed by Mathematics (itself) during the performance of the annihilation of sexual difference . . .—in which it eruditely follows, in the manner of the mystical and rhythmic shadow of Mage Boccaccio's Salome Borghesia, . . . the explanation and demonstration, the "thing-in-itself," words, commodities from the seen and the unseen . . .—alternately reciting Tolstoy's Sonata: . . . "AREN'T YOU TERRIFIED, WHY DO YOU FEAR?" . . . and the bright mathematically symbolic wordless poem: "THE LOCK IS IN THE KEY!"

IN MY SHOP . . . Mathematics is Mathematics (+) and a calculation (–) isn't Mathematics. It is stylized (+) . . . (Mathematical Theory of Henri Poincare is viewed only as one of eight great minds in Europe" . . .), yet a calculation (–) is not. . . . Rodin's *Le Penseur* . . . Mathematics has a cost (+), yet a calculation (–) doesn't have its gaffe. Mathematics is positive, active (+), conventional, but a calculation isn't (–)

IN MY SHOP there is a large party of the "thing-in-itself," words with the label: THE PHENOMENOLOGY OF SEXUAL CURRENCY, which contains: syncopies, . . . iambs . . . alliteration . . . trochees . . . synthesis, classical figures of Euripedes . . . Sophocles . . . Tucidides . . . Anacreon . . . allegory, antinomy, Slavic antithesis of antonyms, epic repetitions, and oratories of all sorts . . . . . . then aside from that, . . . "Nothing is not . . . ." a "thing-in-itself," a commodity released into circulation after being acquired again from the "Danish Prince" . . . .[13]

IN MY SHOP

...... ǝlʇuǝƃ selfishness
...unbridled non-egotism:
commodities sing ... words are
commodities:
ou value for what has ǝnlɐʌ
that which has no value is valued

Beyond the now:
the banker

MID

The mythological king whom Bacchus granted the power to turn to gold all he touched but as his wish came true even his food turned to gold. He begged to be rid of his accursed gift. The godsmade him cleanse himself in the river....the water stripped him of gold flecks....

According to myth... the gods grew furious with MID; he favored Pan's flute over Apollo's lyre (...panic on the stock market,... panic under the sun...)[14]

14

....

....

....

....

Beyond Organic Statements

"Bin ich, oder bin ich nicht?!"
Schopenhauer[15]

13

ORGY

A great selection
of laying
for
funerals

12

A Constitutional Projection Of Russia

Art. 1.
Everyone must mind their own shop.
There can't be any allusions to nothing.

Art. 2. and the final one.
+
The State has a National Bank—the people of a Sovereign state.

O.

11

A BANQUET

THE MONUMENT ОВАЙ
rises and is fashioned after
the Russian masons who, too weak
to master the enormous edifice
and the crumbling material,
wallow in their tears and foaming mouths, in their snot
and their blood,—at the base of their
unfinished MONUMENT.[16]

10

K . . . E . . . Y! . . ! . . . .   KEE . . . E . . E . . .

"Your hands tremble,
Your knees knock!
There is time still,
At the end of the ballad, You I'll kill!"[17]

K..... E..... E...

It goes without saying that maidenhood,
"unfortunate in its fortune to not know instinct,"
has nothing to examine.

K..... E..... E...

"The sea beckons, pulls, with enoooormous power,
The southern sun's hot glow,
Strengthen our temper, faith,
Be faithful, steely grey!"[18]

7

. . . . E . . . . E . . . .

. . . .

. . . .

6

. . . . . . E . . .

5

. ...E....E...

4

. . . . . E . . E . !—

Panlyricism

Without further "ado;" it's nothing!
Between us exist: the SEEN and the UNSEEN!
One Triple Entante
Squeezed in one
small disagreement![19]

E...E...!!!!

It seems we look alike,
From the seen and the unseen,
In those retrospective mirrors,
The "thing-in-itself,"
Crafted in fécamp . . .
. . (master and tradesman Èduard Beaufils):
Pareils à des vieillards qui ramassés en eux,
Avec sérénité regardent fuir LA vie!

ꓯꞀ [20]

2

. . . . E . . . E . . . !

« Mais en vérité j'ai honte,
De bavarder toujours à ce Compte! » [21]

. . . .

Panhumanism:

. . . . . .

. . . .

. . . .

IT SEEMS A ONE-SIDEDLY
RIDICULOUS QUESTION WHICH
CONCERNS THE TWOFOLD
PROBLEM OF CAUSALITY
OF THE MOST TERRIFYING IMPORTANCE

*

IF WE, THEREFORE, DON'T WISH TO
LIE TO EACH OTHER
THEN IT IS NECESSARY
THAT WE NOT LIE ABOUT **NOTHING**

Endnotes

1 Diogenes (ca. 412 or 404–323 BCE), a Greek philosopher and one of the founders of Cynic philosophy; Jean-Honoré Fragonard (1732–1806), a French painter and printmaker, worked in late Rococo manner.

2 Sir Edward Grey (1862–1933), a British Liberal statesman, a foreign secretary (1905–1916), Ambassador to the United States (1919–1920) and a leading supporter of the League of Nations. Philip Snowden (1864–1937), a British politician, the Labor Party's first-ever Chancellor of the Exchequer when Ramsay McDonald was appointed as Prime Minister of the UK (in 1924). Camille Flammarion (1842–1925), a French astronomer and author, wrote books on mesmerism, spiritualism, and psychical research. Gerhart Hauptmann (1862–1946), a German dramatist and novelist, representative of literary naturalism, received the Nobel Prize in Literature in 1912. Tin Ujević (1891–1955), a Croatian and Yugoslav poet, from 1920 to 1926 lived in Belgrade and frequented bohemian circles at Hotel Moskva and Skadarlija. Maxim Gorky (1868–1936), a Russian and Soviet writer, a founder of the socialist realism literary method, and a political activist. Rabindranath Tagore (1861–1941), a Bengali polymath, writer, philosopher, social reformer and painter, the first non-European recipient of the Nobel Prize in Literature in 1913. We are assuming that MID intentionally mismatched Flammarion and Hauptman with their respective nation's capital cities.

3 Marcus Aurelius (121–180 CE), a Roman emperor and a Stoic philosopher. "All paths lead to Rome but going around is closest," a composite expression made up of two idioms: one universally known ("all paths lead to Rome") and another locally known ("Preko preče, naokolo bliže").

4 "Thing-in-itself" (German: "Ding an sich"), a concept introduced by German philosopher Immanuel Kant, referring to an object as it is independent of observation. It is closely related to Kant's concept of *noumenon*, or the object of inquiry, as opposed to *phenomenon*, its manifestations.

5 Arius of Alexandria (256–336 CE), an ascetic and priest who taught a doctrine that Jesus Christ was the Son of God begotten by God the Father, but was a creature distinct from the Father and therefore subordinate to him. Arius' doctrine viewed Jesus Christ as created and finite, called into existence out of nothing and had a beginning, whereas God was self-existent and immutable.

6 A paraphrase of the words uttered by Lord Darlington in conversation with Cecil Graham—"A cynic is a man who knows the price of everything but the value of nothing"—in Oscar Wilde's play *Lady Windermere's Fan* (1892).

7 Ithuriel, the name of an angel in Book Four of John Milton's *Paradise Lost* (1667). The name may date back to the sixteenth century and is not derived from the Bible. According to Gustav Davidson, it means "discovery of God"; see Davidson, *A Dictionary of Angels, Including the Fallen Angels* (New York: Free Press, 1967): 152. In *Paradise Lost*, Ithuriel is one of the angels dispatched by Gabriel to locate Satan, ultimately discovering him in the form of a toad, crouched by Eve's ear. Ithuriel, using his spear, forces Satan to resume his own likeness. The incident was illustrated in a 1796 edition of Milton's work.

8 "Compte rendu" (Fr.), "report" or "account." Gallium is a soft, silvery metallic element with the chemical symbol Ga, discovered in 1875 by the French chemist Paul-Emile Lecoq de Boisbaudran who named the element "gallia" after his native land of France (formerly Gaul; in Latin, Gallia). *Die beiden Grundtypen des Philosophierens* [Two Basic Types of Philosophizing], a book on psychological orientation in contemporary philosophical currents by Yugoslav philosopher and ethno-psychologist Vladimir Dvorniković, published in Berlin in 1918. Serge Abrahamovitch Voronoff (1866–1951), a French surgeon and a Russian transplant pioneer who believed that he could slow or reverse aging by transplanting monkey testicles into men. Known as the "monkey gland man," he was an inspiration for a character in a Sherlock Holmes short story ("The Adventure of the Creeping Man," 1923) by Arthur Conan Doyle. Eugen Steinach (1861–1944) an Austrian physiologist and a pioneer in endocrinology

who played a significant role in discovering the relationship between sex hormones (estrogen and testosterone) to human physical identifiers.

9 Pythagoras of Samos (570–495 BCE), a Greek philosopher and the eponymous founder of Pythagoreanism.

10 "An und fuer sich," (Ger.), "in and of itself." *Czaric Sonnets*, a collection of poems by Miloš Vidaković (1891–1915), one of the Young Bosnia leaders, posthumously published in Sarajevo in 1918. Voltaire (1694–1778), a French enlightenment writer, historian, and philosopher. Dante Alighieri (1265–1321), an Italian poet, writer and philosopher. Friedrich Nietzsche (1844–1900), a German philosopher and philologist. Fyodor Dostoyevsky (1821–1881), a Russian novelist, philosopher, and journalist. Edmond Rostand (1868–1918), a French poet and dramatist.

11 « Le vrai, le bon, le seul . . . le vrai, le fou, le sage, ... et toujours neuf, quoique le plus ancien ! » (Fr.), "The true, the good, the only . . . the true, the mad, the wise, ... and always new, even when ancient!" [Translation: Caroline Chapman Giberson] Veritas est suprema lex (Lat.), "Truth is the supreme law." (From *Magna est veritas et suprema lex esto*. "Truth is mighty and shall be the supreme law"). Jovan Cvijić (1865–1927), a Serbian and Yugoslav geographer and ethnologist. *The Living Corpse*, a Russian play by Leo Tolstoy, written around 1900 and published shortly after his death.

12 King Claudius' words in Shakespeare's *Hamlet* (Act 3, the very end of Scene 1).

13 Alessandro Cagliostro (1743–1795), the alias of the occultist Giuseppe Balsamo, an adventurer and self-styled magical, a charlatan and impostor. Occultist Aleister Crowley believed Cagliostro was one of his previous incarnations. Henri Poincare (1854–1912), a French polymath – mathematician, theoretical physicist, and philosopher of science. *Le Penseur* [*The Thinker*], a bronze sculpture by Auguste Rodin. Euripides (ca. 480–ca. 406 BCE), a tragedian of classical Athens. Tucidides (ca. 460–ca. 400 BCE), an Athenian historian and general. Anacreon (ca. 582–ca. 485 BCE), a Greek lyric poet. The "Danish Prince," a reference to Shakespeare's Hamlet.

14 MID is using his name as a pun in place of Midas.

15 "Bin ich, oder bin ich nicht?!" (Ger.), "To be, or not to be?" MID deliberately mis-attributed the famous quote from Shakespeare's *Hamlet* to Arthur Schopenhauer (1788–1860), the German philosopher of philosophical pessimism and quietism.

16 "Ovai" (овай, Rus.), "this."

17 The verse is from Cyrano's "Fencing ballade" or "Ballade of the Duel" from Edmund Rostand's play *Cyrano de Bergerac* (1897).

18 The verses are from the following Croatian poems: "Lastavicam" by Ivan Zahar (1845–1907)—"Zove, vuče, silnom moći, / Južnog sunca vreli sjaj;" the only difference is that Zahar's "vrući sjaj" is "vreli sjaj" ("hot glow") in MID; and "Mornarska" by Ivan Truski (1819–1910)—"Vjera jači našu ćud, / Sinje more vjerno bud!"; the only difference is that Trnski's "Vjera jači" is "Vjero jači" in MID. Both of these poems are included in the following anthology: Hugo Badalić (ed.): *Hrvatska antologija. Umjetno pjesništvo starijega i novijega doba* (Zagreb: Izdanje Matice Hrvatske, 1892): 42–43 and 37–38.

19 Triple Entante (from French entente meaning "friendship, understanding, agreement"), the informal understanding between the Russian Empire, the French Third Republic, and Great Britain, who fought against the Central Powers in World War I.

20 « Pareils à des vieillards qui ramassés en eux, / Avec sérénité regardent fuir LA vie! » (Fr.), "Like old men who, gathered together, / Calmly watch life rush by!" [Translation: Caroline Chapman Giberson] The verses are from Èduard Beaufils' poem "Les Oliviers" [Olive trees] as printed in the magazine *Revue bleue politique et littéraire* (in 1907).

21 « Mais en vérité j'ai honte, / De bavarder toujours à ce Compte! » (Fr.), "The truth is I am ashamed, / Of always talking on that account!" [Translation: Caroline Chapman Giberson] MID's reference to *Filosofija panhumanizma* [Philosophy of Panhumanism] by Dr. Miloš N. Đurić, published in 1922 "in a language of romanticist enthusiasm which equally poeticizes Bergson's intuitism and Nietzsche's dream of *Umwertung aller Werte,* and the eastern religious teachings of the 'undying life.'" See Radomir Konstantinović, *The Philosophy of Parochialism,* ed. by B. Jakovljević, trans. By Lj. Nikolić and B. Jakovljević (Ann Arbor: University of Michigan Press, 2021).

The Metaphysics of Nothing [An Introduction]

MID [Mita Dimitrijević]
Zenit Administration, 1926

Translated by *Aleksandar Bošković with Andrea Bogojević and Jennifer H. Zoble*

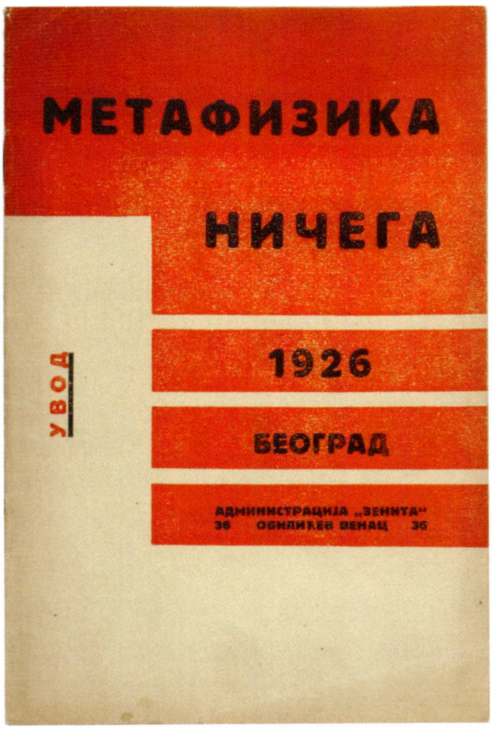

5.2. MID [Mita Dimitrijević], *Metafizika ničega* [The Metaphysics of Nothing], Zenit Administration, Belgrade, 1926. Front cover. Courtesy of National Library of Serbia, Belgrade (Legacy of Ljubomir Micić, Special collections).

NIGHT

Good (+) has, positively, received from evil an inoperative (+), but still operative subtraction: beauty; while evil (—) has negatively, received from good an operative (—), but inoperative sum: ugliness.

The sexual equilibrium of money has shifted.

Therefore:

all the sciences, in both their collective immensity and their most microscopic distinctions,

all religions

all arts

and all rights

find themselves in a condition that is more than alarming. All these positive (+) pursuits, taken together as well as separately, can distinguish in

NOTHING

NOTHING

the serious from the humorous, and vice versa.[1]

“

Sir Doyle, the star of a congress of spiritists and spiritualists recently held in Paris, has returned to London and, fully convinced of the truth of his own beliefs, revealed to the public some of the observations he previously shared only with his inner circle. Conan Doyle believes that the time has come for a Crusade (+) against the materialists. A few days ago, he asserted:

> —For the past three years, I have been receiving news from the other world with the help of my wife. All these messages clearly suggested a catastrophe, but lately the news is so threatening that I consider it to be my duty to express them to the general public. This is an urgent matter. Spirits report that a great catastrophe is about to descend on this world. Mighty powers want to cure the world from contemporary materialism. As a first warning, they sent war. But that warning didn't have much success. And the world will have to go through a new ordeal that will endow it with spiritual energy, which will help it eventually become capable for life.

Sixty different places around the world confirmed for me this news that Mrs. Doyle has received. A catastrophe is approaching. I don't know exactly when, but according to certain omens, I estimate it will be sometime from 1925 to 1928. The ordeal will be terrible. The world will be diminished, but [idealism] will be saved.[2]

”

+ −

The mental features of the poles

Compared to western writing, which is concerned with eloquence far more than we are and which consequently has a destructive influence on us, our writing style is clearer. "Write as you speak!" is fully realized in our language. That is why we inject the highest degree of subconscious hyperrealism into our writing about the numerous particularities of life and death.[3]

But, to have perfect eloquence, it is not sufficient for the writing to be the clearest—it also has to be the most exact. The ability to write every word, letter-by-letter, sound by sound, is insufficient. Rather, words should be the exact representations of thoughts: "The brain secretes thought as the kidneys secrete urine." That is why the maxim: "Write as you speak!" is accompanied by: "Speak as you feel!"

Still, after all this, one arrives at what is most important. To have perfect eloquence, which is to say the most exact, the thought itself needs to be perfectly exact.

Writing in this style, we feel tired in the presence of western education's ramified eloquence.

Thus, if only one of the conditions for perfectly exact eloquence becomes obfuscated, from one side or the other, or from both sides, we encounter the positive (+) path that is not imposed on us, but rather peddled to us. This path doesn't signify a path to be followed unconditionally, but rather signifies a breaking away from the disintegration of words in their contemporary, one-sidedly twofold, debased, and confused use.

+ −

“

It is truly amusing to observe how philosophy professors look with disgust at pantheism, as at forbidden fruit, lacking the courage to pick it up. Oh, how bitter is the bread, that bread of a philosophy professor! The main charge against the pantheists is that they have NOTHING to say to you. To call nature divine is not to explain it perfectly, but to enrich the language with a superfluous synonym.

”

A SMALL ANTHOLOGY ABOUT THE SMALLEST THING

It is only after this Anthology that the positive (+) value of the square decimeter of Ter Borch's discrete geometry will be revealed.[4]

“

Psychic automatism in its pure state, by which one proposes to express—verbally, by means of the written word, or in any other manner—the actual functioning of thought.

Dictated by thought, in the absence of any control exercised by reason, exempt from any aesthetic or moral concern.[5]

”

ON

THE DUAL IMPORTANCE

OF THE WORD

NOTHING

NOTHING

“

First

What is the co-logarithm of the given logarithm?

—The co-logarithm of the given logarithm is its opposite number, that is, such a number which, when added to the last logarithm, gives the sum: ZERO.

Second

The Chronicle of Dalimil in verse, which owes its soul to Cosmas' Chronicle [of the Czechs], adds NOTHING positive (+) to the dark details of its prototype.[6]

It would not be hard to list a number of similar examples, but it is hard to list NOTHING.

First

Nature would not dress itself in such fearsome zeal without any directive.

It is not the words that rattle me so.

Second

In such a state, we cannot take the ZERO for the foundation of the logarithmic system since any positive (+) degree from the ZERO equals ZERO, and any NEGATIVE degree from the ZERO is an endlessly large number.

First

All the progress of metaphysics up until now is, thus, equal to ZERO.

All metaphysicians start from the tacit assumption that outside and independent from us, there is a substance that exists on its own, a world of real factors which includes us. Since this substance cannot be comprehended through experience (of science), metaphysicians have tried to define its nature through speculation.

*First**

On her first meeting with Gishe, Juliette asked him cautiously: What do you do? I am a merchant, he replied.

—Ah! And what do you sell?

—*NOTHING*!

Gishe indeed was a merchant of *NOTHING*. But unlike his friends, who sold unusable soaps and fake golden chains to their customers (to preserve for their progeny the beauty of money's ancient intrigue), Gishe sold absolutely *NOTHING*. He would display his *NOTHING* with luxurious multicolored paper and silk ribbon. He would not mistreat his customers or trick them, because he would always tell them about the *NOTHINGNESS* of their purchases. The people would comment amongst themselves: well, he would not be so rude as to sell us *NOTHING*! And many arms would reach out to Gishe, who shared his *NOTHINGNESS* with a smile on his lips.

Those who were curious, after paying, would hastily open their small packages. They would unfasten the first ribbon, cut the second, rip the third; and still deluded would ultimately find inside NOTHING, *ABSOLUTELY NOTHING!*

Most of the buyers waited with glee for the misfortune of the next buyers. And when an irritable person would protest, Gishe would reply: I am a merchant of *NOTHING*, you yourself wanted to buy my goods! You've been served! What are you complaining about, about *NOTHING*? Juliette couldn't look at the departing Gishe without a dull fear. She

* The repeat of "First" is in the original.

couldn't stop repeating: Take care!

First

And during this period, a period both bourgeois and heroic, along with the ideas that had their knights, there were interests defended by their paladins. The banality of leaders subtracted NOTHING from the courage of the movement.

Second

It is necessary to fight for the salvation and liberation of Russia, said the Grand Duke, but NOTHING should be solved too early or too soon!

First

Okenski asserted: We organize NOTHING against Russia. There is NOTHING forming in our territory.

Second

There is NOTHING new in this statement, which only confirms the importance of Mr. Briand's visit to London.[7]

First

Nationalization and individualism reveal extremes that are both justifiable to a certain degree, but which may become harmful and fatal if the limits are exceeded. Thus, it is wise to find a middle ground between these two extremes.

Second

Why would I poison my husband?

What about the Last Judgment?

You ask me why I didn't go to court? Because all that investigating had found there is NOTHING to charge me with, since NOTHING happened.

V

First

After midnight, the former director of the theater was investigated, but he said NOTHING that would shape the development of the whole debate.

Second

At the dinner organized by the members of the International Association of Journalists in honor of Austen Chamberlain, Painlevé, and Vandervelde, Chamberlain added: You are both reporters and teachers, write *NOTHING* in your newspapers that would obstruct our great efforts![8]

First

Too bad they cannot find any questions other than erotic ones.

Our professors have NOTHING smarter to tell us than the love between a castrated monk and a nun.

Second

By this method, Mendel, the founder of genetics, achieved results concerning the stable ratio between the consecutive generations of bastards and discovered that the external appearance of an individual can tell us *NOTHING* about the appearance of the descendant, but that we can tell a great deal about parents from their descendants.[9]

First

In England, my dear, I will change *NOTHING*! Everything has its price, but *NOTHING* is known of its value!

I can stand *NOTHING* as much as the brutal viewpoint.

Second

Either anticipation exists only in literature, or *NOTHING* happened.

First

Starting from Relations (of connecting, compressing, fusing things) and proceeding to a number of differentiations without interruption, we enter Time, the pure relation between isolation and the so-called reciprocal repulsion having for its *CORRELATIVE* the impossibility of isolation and separation, the *CONTINUOUS QUANTITY* that develops in a consistent series, *SIMPLE* and *HOMOGENEOUS*.

Second

The proletarian loan! I thought that I, a citizen of a bourgeois nation and a westerner with capitalist biases, would be surprised by my encounter with a communist and Marxist country. I expected to find in Moscow something unusual, inhuman, some sort of urban and social futurism. But *NOTHING* like that at all!

NOTHING resembles the workers' financial system like the bourgeois financial system. Maybe I will find out later that the red hand is sufficient to change the character of bank operations.

NOTHING is harder than to differentiate! Theaters, banks, pubs, everything is alike and conspicuous. Hunger is next to luxury, and people are silent in their impatience: *NOTHING, NOTHING*! It's not for the first time that they are deceived.

Words, words! said Hamlet.[10]

I said to one of the rulers: You *ANNIHILATED* neither money nor poverty; neither speculators nor poor people; neither the patience of the former nor the grandiosity of the latter! What did you do?

The man looked at me with a dark, unfocused gaze, and responded, *NOTHING*!

First

Breton finds traces of surrealism in Dante and Shakespeare, and says that Swift is surrealist in his evil, Marquis de Sade in his sadism, Chateaubriand in his egotism, Benjamin Constant in politics, Victor Hugo when he is not stupid, Edgar Poe in adventure, Baudelaire in morality, Rimbaud in the way he lived, Germain Nouveau in the kiss, etc.[11]

Second

You're looking at my dress? In order to say in your story what kind of outfit I had? The black crepe georgette with purple roses! Purple is my favorite color! And my shoes are purple, look! I wear a nine-carat brilliantine ring. Tell that to your curious audience, there is *NOTHING* they don't want to know! And perfume? The perfume is Guerlain Pour Troubler!

First

The League of Nations came up with the decision in such a situation to bring the whole thing in front of its council, and still do *NOTHING*.[12]

Second

Eleatics recognized the perpetual existence of only one changeable being; the existence and disappearance of the things we observe, they proclaimed a *DECEPTION*.[13]

First

Even before she caught the crane and returned it to its place in the game, the fight was over, and both hedgehogs disappeared! But that would help *NOTHING*.

Second

In response, our delegate stood and immediately took the floor. Completely heated and agitated, he clearly surprised all the other calm delegates, changing slightly the hitherto usual academic speeches.

Unfortunately, Mr. Radić gave a speech. The misfortune that Armenians suffered made them unstable and

NOTHING is as bad as an unstable nation. Then he said that it couldn't secede, adding: it should be understood that we are not saying *NOTHING* should stay unchanged in the Constitution.[14]

First

A. Heveroch, a full professor of psychiatry and neurology, doesn't solve each specific problem separately, with ad hoc hypotheses, since sometimes it is necessary to delve into the domain of philosophy. On the other hand, we see the results showing the falsity of a philosopher's opinion that anything abnormal, pathological can give *NOTHING* significant to the mind—the book sealed with seven seals and written in hieroglyphs.[15]

Second

"Tell me *NOTHING! NOTHING, NOTHING!*" screamed Nina Padarachevskaya. "Unlike women, men are always unsatisfied! There is *NOTHING* in life that compels me anymore!"

First

NOTHING can liberate human souls from that immense power, that immeasurably heavy darkness of the spirit, that multifaceted eclipse of the world, but a godlike powerful dawn, a beginning that will enchant humanity.

From the soul of a race ordained to spiritually rule the world, as the spirit (*EQUILIBRIUM OF WORDS AND MONEY*) of the Jewish race reigned through Christianity, the new dawn must and will rise.

Second

And now, the face of a deceased man must emerge. Even though we open our eyes as widely as we can to see better, we see *NOTHING*. Suddenly, a Lady yells: "But there are fluids here, my legs froze!"

—Do you feel the fluid? they ask a journalist!

—No!

And everyone looks at him in anger and surprise.

—But if you don't feel the fluid, you should be able to see it. Its color is orange-red!

—I see *NOTHING*!

—That is because you're the enemy of the psychic sciences. There is an antipathetic stream between you and the *FLUID*. You should be neutral!

And this discussion didn't get in the way of the cataleptic dream of a medium.

First

But very soon, the reprimand came from Sir George Hunter, a man of high intellect and character whose name is brimming with confidence in all business circles: in the uncertainty and confusion which rose among the world's markets, any value had its night and NOTHING more.[16]

Second

When Mr. Caillaux travels to America, it has already been announced that he intends to take with him a team of financial experts. Then he will stand personally in front of Mr. Mellon who, it could be said, knows *NOTHING* more about finances than the experienced Mr. Caillaux. But it is a completely different story with Mr. Churchill—he is an astonishing orator.

Nonetheless, Mr. Caillaux concluded *NOTHING*, and therefore promised *NOTHING*.[17]

First

Mussolini stated that no Frenchman should be upset by the question of an Italian empire and added that *NOTHING* should set apart France from Italy.[18]

Second

Chamberlain's speech was recognized as a response to Painlevé, and carried an insular character. Chamberlain asserted that the Latin spirit likes to create theorems and general rules, and thus is contrary to the empirical English spirit. The greatness of the British Empire is in its merciless logic. The British secret lies in the fact that it evades definitions and concentrates on the day-to-day problems of the stock market.

Chamberlain attributed England's refusal of the protocol to its fear of formulas and stated that moral disarmament is more important than material disarmament. Chamberlain concluded that it is necessary to make a new soul of the world.[19]

First

An evening of Mr. Reznikov's occultism showed that *NOTHING* appeals to a Belgrade audience more than hypnotism, spiritualism, telepathy, and everything that falls outside of the circle of the natural and enters the realm of the mystical.

Second

Paul-Boncour's speech was a big sensation and was considered an excellent response to Chamberlain's speech. He precisely articulated that universality of danger calls for universality of precaution and that it's not about the arbitrary construction of the spirit but rather *ABOUT THE TRUE REFLECTION OF REALITY*. Paul-Boncour defended the protocol with conviction. The Latin spirit is logical and aims to synthesize experiences not through individual efforts but rather through a broader construction that will be both elastic and narrowly defined.

Chamberlain applauded vigorously, and Dandiron said that such a speech cannot be translated. Chamberlain then replied that he was in agreement, but that this couldn't be a precedent because the English language uses the same characters.[20]

First

From the first one, we got *NOTHING* for our comedy of manners.

And when you finish reading this chapter, you will understand that, as an old Greek poet said, *NOTHING* is sweeter than golden Aphrodite.

Second

Abelard and Heloise are two inseparable names, Mr. Petronijević began his lecture. Actually, in the field of science, Abelard was an anemic spirit. For example, he knew *NOTHING* about the structure of the cosmos, because at the time Aristotle's theory was unknown to the West.

Filbert's bitterness persuaded several individuals to sneak into Abelard's apartment and castrate him. That was the ultimate night of Heloise's and Abelard's love.

In conclusion, said Mr. Petronijević, Abelard and Heloise are two inseparable names.[21]

First

Senator Marinelli published a treatise in which he invited Italy not to commit suicide by satisfying American bankocracy. With regard to the loans, it should be clear that they can be granted only under the lender's terms. Therefore, Europe can expect *NOTHING* from America and should not make any sacrifices for America.

Even America itself would not benefit if it were to reintroduce the ban and thus cut ties with Europe. By doing so, America would postpone indefinitely the *TRANSITION* to the gold standard in Europe. On the other hand, by the same measure America would contribute to gold's declining value in relation to essential goods. America should not forget that it is the biggest individual owner of gold, and that *HARD CURRENCY* is dependent on this precious metal whose preciousness is fake. After all, even the Dawes Plan serves *NOTHING*.[22]

Second

Mr. MacDonald, while talking about "demising" jobs (exported revolutions), asserted: it is possible to change the English government but not the spirit of the English people, who cannot adjust to a new regime without seeing generations fall into political conflict, industrial ruination, and national chaos.[23]

First

Neither America nor Europe saw any positive (+) benefit from these financial politics, thus the fixing of currency in reality means *NOTHING*. In this way they occupy a double role—at once they are actors and spectators—while the others are only spectators. On the same night, our knight returns from America after accomplishing positively (+) *NOTHING*.

Second

In order to grasp the cinematic beauty of naked bodies, one needs to observe them critically. One needs to give appropriate praise to such play, while seeking in it *NOTHING* pornographic, since naked bodies are not pornographic in themselves.

First

Lord Grey's perspective on the value of history hardly offends if in his memoirs he links a phase of the French controversy over the river Nile with the inconvenience of shortening his weekend in the village, among roses. This also meant a bigger share in nature, which for Lord Grey was a positive (+) need, and not a luxury, both physically and mentally.

Lord Grey includes in the long list of Abdul Hamid's atrocities the fact that Hamid prevented him from spending the well-known English weekend in the village in May, when nature blooms. The best *CHARACTERISTICS* of the British ministers, adds Grey, were more *NEGATIVES* than positives (+). They would not make sudden changes; they were not inclined to cause damage, nor to turn nations against each other, nor to fish in MURKY waters.[24]

Second

Disappointed, yet self-possessed, he decided to use the *NEGATIVE*. Injustice is the most powerful tool humans have invented for incitement, to compel women, children, and lower animals to talk.

First

The world has always been largely divided into two factions: those who find and determine the path and those who *CLEAR* it. In times when it's been hard to see the path and when there has been no one to illuminate it, humanity has walked down a blind alley (Ribarska Street) and culture has fallen into a downward spiral.

The feeling and appearance of impoverishment in the face of history was greatest at a time when yesterday's goals and ideals were exhausted and tomorrow's not yet found. Our own age is consumed by such a fever.

The road to truth has been *CLEARED* on yesterday's paths; humanity has struggled to exhaust all possibilities marked by the previous generation's milestones.

But there, among those who must reveal the further path, it does not look promising. Listening carefully, a man hears a heavy, perhaps desperate sound, like that of souls possessed by a secret, unintelligible fear. As if they were confronted by a primordial SCREAM which, as in the paralysis of a dream, cannot be *ARTICULATED*, but instead transfixes the pained, despairing grimace and the cold *LAUGHTER OF HORROR*. Is this the birth of a new pain or a new poverty for which there is still no appropriate word?

Or is it just a *REFLECTION* of the void which froze the horrified human soul? Or perhaps both?

Literature, philosophy, arts of all kinds speak into this night, mauled by the language of scared wild animals who, surrounded by hunters, do not know where to run and how to save themselves!

Second

Have I loved? I have not. Have I hated? Who cares! I know only that I swam through the mud. And that I was alone, and that dirty disgusting things plunged me into the waves, beat me, bit me, suffocated and cut me, and that the days were rarely sunny, and that some unimpeachable women said that this is our heaven, our wonderful dwelling place.

I was christened (+), so the baptized called me brother: but, they spit on my vision with their hurricane of hate, burned my crown with their singeing delirium, infected my shame; their thorns scratched my weakness and tenderness, my foul soul fell among them like prey into their fast clutches.

And I know that my head often dove into the mud so it could strangle the burden, dove into the shame, and that it rose again like trampled grass; I knew not why it should suffer more than some other thing from pleasure or disgust, and it drank the scream in throes of passion and threw it to the *PRINCE OF DARKNESS AS A GIFT!*

Have I loved? I have not. Have I hated? Who cares! In that dirty bordello, where the sky rots, where love copulates, where the madhouse and bromine grant happiness. To hate is permitted, to love shamelessly forbidden, *THERE IS NOTHING* except a desire to save but a *THOUGHT* from this pit of stench and *QUAGMIRE OF EVIL.*[25]

First

The lord now began to PLAY with his pun as he wished.

He whirled it and tossed it into the air, he blew it away to lose it and then caught it again. He would leave it to gleam magically, while giving it wings with his paradoxes.

And when he continued, his praise to folly reached the heights of philosophy, which *REJUVENATED* itself and started *DANCING* like a bacchanal priestess, followed by ecstatic melodies of PLEASURE, wearing a dress sprinkled with wine and a garland of ivy while running over the hillocks of existence and teasing beautiful Silenus for staying sober.

Facts run from philosophy as if they were frightened nymphs.

Second

And if man dared, in this deaf night, to surrender to reverie during this vigil while the drunken East consumes the Western Point of View, there would be *NOTHING* much left of this positive (+) happiness nor of dreams.

First

And the stables are increasingly filling up with garbage, and the air is increasingly polluted and those who create the garbage are becoming more restless, fly-like, anxious. That is why they equally change places and limp from leg to leg. Now some go up, while others come down biting each other, cutting their ears, kicking their legs and fouling each other. And now they make up again, and when they've had enough of the same pose and a leg quivers from the *MUFFLED UNDERGROUND RUMBLE,* then they stand on both legs together. But both legs were swollen and rotten, and the mire increasingly deeper and the fear greater. And whatever they undertake to strengthen the pedestal, it keeps fermenting, and the garbage grows thicker, deeper, and more dangerous. Because they and their work only create new garbage.

They have bonded again this night, and because they have spat, bitten, torn, and covered each other in their own garbage, they have fused together for a moment. And as they are fly-like, covered in gadflies and anxious, they will attempt to spit and bite in unison, as they have just spat at each other and made asses of themselves. Because they are afraid, and all their strength *SEEKS TO PREVENT* it. However.

Second

Tonight, the Observatory in Madrid recorded enormous magnetic perturbations in the atmosphere of the earth, because, if from an eternal philosophical point of view existence is essentially *NOTHING*, then everything in it that seems meaningful and tragic (+) is terribly comical.

First

Deferential Mathematics teaches us how derivative functions are found for functions.

Integral calculus, oppositely, demonstrates how the derivative function helps find the original function.

Second

What is to be done?[26]

First

The drama of the Persians has had *NOTHING* done, much like with the Arabs.

Second

A multitude of these people are so subjective that for them exactly *NOTHING* has interest. They showed a man to Lao Tzu who looked like he only lived half a century, while he had actually passed his second century. The Chinese scientist interprets this long existence as the strength of a supremely developed spirit that knows how to win.[27]

And maybe still, the important fact that in the Tibetan city of the wise there is not a single woman—not even if their lives depended on it—may play a significant role.

Indeed, every people in its childhood is cruelly stern about relationships where

FORM DEVOURS SPIRIT[28]

First

Die reichstbeanlagten Europäer, die Slaven, sind zu sehr Gefühlsmenschen, sie *WIDERSTREBEN ALLZUSEHR DER FORM* (R. Hupfeld's emphasis) But they are of an amorphous, slopped, undisciplined soul.

The highest formed, says Hupfeld, are the French, as the Germans haven't achieved a *SYNTHESIS FORM OF SPIRIT*, but they yearn for that sort of synthesis the most. Kupler is right, and according to our saying, man speaks *THE MOST* about what he has *NOTHING* of.[29]

Second

C'est un monde nouveau, une terre inconnue à travers laquelle tous aurons besoin d' un FIL conducteur, pour s'y diriger sons perte de temps et sans fatigue de volubilité, pour y voir tout ce qui mérite d'être vu, pour éviter d'y errer à l'aventure, en passant, sans les apercevoir à côté de merveilles insoupçonnées.[30]

First

Mathematics.

Second

Calculus.

First

She is the name of that ancient anonymity. She has placed a question before everything, and finally slathered him with darkness too; there is *NOTHING*, neither behind, nor ahead, nor from both sides, nor above, nor below, nor inside: neither *TRANS*, nor *IN*, nor *PER*.

And what kind of satisfaction does it give? Which peace does it suppress in the soul?

Second

There is *NOTHING* in which intrigue seems so grandiose as when it is: *THE SMALLEST*.

First

A conscientious and cultured journalist noted that a feeling of *TWO CURRENTS* is obligatory among the followers of Mr. Radić.

Ignorant to the secrets of political electrification, Mr. Carlo felt offended, and being angry he crossed *ALL* lines of regard and called the aforementioned publicist a liar and an ass.

Mr. Radić himself did something more: he introduced himself as the electrical power station. And truly he is, and for himself, capable of producing *TWO CURRENTS*, a continuous rhetoric and an alternative agitation from the seen and the unseen, and vice versa.

But, who will explain that to Mr. Carlo?

Second

Francois speaks very poorly of Metaphysics: Ah, how Diderot has a right to say—he writes—that metaphysicians know *NOTHING*! There are very skeptical discussions about god in his book: to believe in god or to not believe, is there any *DIFFERENCE*? It is not big given that those who do believe in him do not understand him. They say that he is everything. But to be everything means to be *NOTHING*![31]

First

At the crux of the entirety of modern philosophy lies a large logical *FALLACY*: it seeks that which it should assume.

There are many names that are incapable of focusing their attention on *NOTHING*. Mostly lyrists.

All the police trusteeships write in their positive right (+) extensive critiques because those who seek to *DESTROY NOTHING* are great in number.

The anthology of the lyrists is growing smaller.

Second

What did you get from your wisdom and philosophy? If *NOTHING ELSE*, I had *BEAUTIFUL COMPANY*.

First

And what am I doing with the words on this clean white paper?

Second

The ethical function of the positive (+) positivism defines that I be of a *JORDANIAN* predisposition.

First

I give praise to the cross (†), one dry word.

Second

In an indeterminate *NIGHT*, present things, whose order and arrangement offend our eyes, will be

A N N I H I L A T E D

A N N I H I L A T E D

”

From the same author

1925

THE SEXUAL EQUILIBRIUM OF MONEY, OR A TRADE CORRESPONDANCE ON THE CURRENCY QUESTION

ЗЕНИТ

ЗЕНИТ

5.3. MID [Mita Dimitrijević], *Metafizika ničega* [The Metaphysics of Nothing], Zenit Administration, Belgrade, 1926. Back cover. Courtesy of National Library of Serbia, Belgrade (Legacy of Ljubomir Micić, Special collections).

Endnotes

1 The opening paragraph is a slightly edited quote from *Sexual Equilibrium* (see section titled "The Leading Motif").

2 The second International Spiritualist congress was held in Paris in 1925 (September 11th) and Sir Arthur Conan Doyle (1859–1930) was nominated its Honorary President.

3 "Write as you speak and read as it is written" was an orthographic principle devised by the German philologist Johann Christoph Adelung (1732–1806) and used by Vuk Stefanović Karadžić (1787–1864), a Serbian philologist and a reformer of the modern Serbian language, to push through his language reform.

4 Gerard ter Borch (1617–1681), a Dutch genre painter. Discrete geometry is a philosophical concept introduced by Serbian philosopher Branislav Petronijević in his study "The Main Principles of Discrete Geometry." See "Osnovni postulati diskretne geometrije," *Članci i studije B. Petronijevića*, vol. 2 (Pančevo, 1920), 136–163.

5 André Breton, *Manifestoes of Surrealism*, translated from the French by Richard Seaver and Helen R. Lane (Ann Arbor: The University of Michigan Press, 1969), 26.

6 *The Chronicle of Dalimil* (Czech: Dalimilova kronika; Kronika tak řečeného Dalimila) is the first chronicle written in the Czech language. *The Chronicle of the Czechs by Cosmas of Prague* (d. 1125) is regarded as the foundational narrative of Czech history and is the source of the oldest stories about the land, people, and rulers of Bohemia and Moravia.

7 Aristide Briand (1862–1932) was a French statesman who served eleven terms as Prime Minister of France during the French Third Republic and was a co-laureate of the 1926 Nobel Peace Prize.

8 Sir Joseph Austen Chamberlain (1863–1937) was a British statesman and a recipient of the 1925 Nobel Peace Prize with the American Charles G. Dawes (1865–1951). Paul Painlevé (1863–1933) was a French mathematician and politician. Emile Vandervelde (1866–1938) was a Belgian statesman.

9 Gregor Johann Mendel (1822–1884) was the founder of the modern science of genetics.

10 "Words, words, words," is Hamlet's reply to Polonius' question, "What do you read, my lord?" in William Shakespeare's *Hamlet* (Act 2, Scene 2).

11 This is from Breton's "Manifesto of Surrealism": "Swift is Surrealist in malice, / Sade is Surrealist in sadism. / Chateaubriand is Surrealist in exoticism. / Constant is Surrealist in politics. / Hugo is Surrealist when he isn't stupid. / [. . .] Poe is Surrealist in death. / Baudelaire is Surrealist in morality. / Rimbaud is Surrealist in the way he lived, and elsewhere. / [. . .] Nouveau is Surrealist in the kiss." See André Breton, *Manifestoes of Surrealism*, translated from the French by Richard Seaver and Helen R. Lane (Ann Arbor: The University of Michigan Press, 1969), 26–27.

12 The League of Nations was the first worldwide intergovernmental organization with the mission to maintain world peace and prevent wars through collective security, disarmament, and settling international disputes. Founded in 1920 following the Paris Peace Convention that ended the First World War, it was replaced by the United Nations (UN) in 1946.

13 The Eleatics were a pre-Socratics school of philosophy founded by Parmenides in the early 5th century BCE.

14 Stjepan Radić (1871–1928), a Croat politician and a president of the Croat Peasant Party who advocated for greater Croatian autonomy within Yugoslavia and pushed for changes to the Vidovdan constitution. He was also a Yugoslav substitute delegate at the Sixth Assembly of the League of

the Nations in Geneva, September 7–26, 1925. The sentence "The adversities that Armenians suffered made them unbalanced and NOTHING is as bad as an unbalanced nation" is from Vladislav Ribnikar's text published in *Politika* daily (September 19, 1925) on Radić's first speech at the League of the Nations.

15 Antonín Heveroch (1869–1927) was a Czech psychiatrist and neurologist.

16 The first part of the text is a quote taken from the text "Ekonomski položaj u Evropi" (Economic position within Europe) by David Lloyd George, printed on the cover page of daily *Politika* on Monday, October 5, 1925 (the day the Locarno meeting started). Sir George Burton Hunter (1845–1937) was an English shipbuilder and the chairman of Swan & Hunter company.

17 Joseph Caillaux (1863–1944) was a French politician of the Third Republic and one of France's foremost finance experts. He traveled in the US and had meeting with the Secretary Frank B. Kellogg at the State Department and Secretary Andrew W. Mellon at the Treasury on September 23, 1925. Andrew William Mellon (1855–1937), an American banker, businessman, and industrialist, who served as a Secretary of the Treasury from 1924 to 1932. At the time, Winston Churchill (1874–1965) was the British chancellor of the exchequer.

18 Benito Mussolini (1883–1945) was an Italian politician, journalist, and leader of the National Fascist Party. He joined the Locarno negotiations on October 15, 1925; his words "that nothing should set apart France from Italy" may be from the speech he delivered at the concluding session the next day.

19 The section refers to the Locarno meeting, held at Locarno in Switzerland between October 5 and 16, 1925. The leading European politicians at the time—the French prime minister (A. Briand), the British foreign secretary (A. Chamberlain), the German chancellor (Gustav Ernst Stresmann, 1878–1929), the Italian fascist leader (B. Mussolini), and the Belgian foreign minister (E. Vandervelde), to name a few—participated in negotiating reconciliation between Germany and France since further loans from the United States depended on negotiating a security pact between Paris and Berlin. The outcome was the Rhineland Pact, according to which, Germany, France, and Belgium recognized their existing borders as permanent, including the demilitarized Rhineland zone; Britain and Italy guaranteed the accord; all disputes would be referred to the League of Nations for arbitration; Germany concluded arbitration treaties with France, Britain, Poland, and Czechoslovakia. During the negotiations, the British foreign secretary, avowedly "the most pro-French member of the government," opposed a Franco-British military alliance, describing Britain's role as that of an honest broker, seeking to reconcile France and Germany. See Austen Chamberlain Papers, Chamberlain to Crewe, February 20, 1925, general correspondence 1925.

20 Augustin Alfred Joseph Paul-Boncour (1873–1972) was a French politician of the Third Republic. Paul-Boncour's speech is a response to Chamberlain.

21 Branislav Petronijević (1875–1954) was a Serbian philosopher and scientist who wrote books in Serbian, German, and French. Researched abroad and in Serbia, his major work is the two-volume, 1904–1911 *Prinzipien der Metaphysik* (Principles of Metaphysics), first published in Heidelberg in 1904. He later became a professor at the University of Belgrade. Héloïse (ca. 1090–1164) was a French nun, writer, scholar, and abbess, best known for her love affair and correspondence with Peter Abélard (ca. 1079–1142).

22 Giovanni Marinelli (1879–1944) was an Italian fascist political leader. He contributed to fascist success by financing the March on Rome and created the Ceka, secret police established on the model of the Soviet Cheka. The Gold Standard was suspended or abandoned by many countries

in Europe because of the First World War. By 1927, many countries had returned to the gold standard (this period of relative stability lasted until the Great Depression, 1929–1939), while some, such as Germany, could not effectively return to it because war reparations had cost it much of its gold reserves. The Dawes Plan (proposed by a committee under General Charles G. Dawes) was a plan that came into force in September 1924 to reconsider the war debts and resolve reparations issues of the First World War that Germany had to pay. Although it appeared successful in ending a crisis in European diplomacy following the Treaty of Versailles, it masked the underlying weaknesses in Germany's payments situation, namely massive foreign borrowing. So long as foreign capital poured into the country the settlement of reparations ran smoothly, but once funds dried up then the basic weakness of the position was exposed. The crunch came in the late 1920s when American lending was sharply curtailed; this set off a chain reaction among foreign banks demanding the withdrawal of loans from Germany.

23 James Ramsay MacDonald (1866–1937) was a British statesman and the first ever Labour Party Prime Minister of the United Kingdom. The word in MID's book is 'demsing' which most closely resembles the word 'demising.' It's not certain where MID is quoting MacDonald from.

24 Sir Edward Grey (1862–1933), a British Liberal statesman, a foreign secretary (1905–1916), Ambassador to the United States (1919–1920) and a leading supporter of the League of Nations. Abdul Hamid II (1842–1918) was the 34th Sultan of the Ottoman Empire and the last Sultan to exert effective autocratic control over the fracturing state. Often known as the Red Sultan or Abdul the Damned due to the atrocities committed against the Empire's minorities under his rule and use of secret police to silence dissent.

25 This section is a poem in prose form:

Voleo? Nisam. Mrzeo? Šta mari!
Znam samo da sam plivao kroz kal.
I da sam bio sam, i da su stvari
prljave, gadne, sručene u val,
tukle me, grizle, davile i sekle,
i da je retko bio sunčan dan,
i da su neke nezlobnice rekle
da je to raj naš, predobri stan.

I znali da nešto, što se krsti (+)
ljudi zvali me bratom: pljujući mi vid
orkanom mržnje, delirijem studi
pržeć mi teme i gnojeći stid,
da mi je trnje razgrebalo vrela
slabosti sviju i nežnosti svih
da mi je duša zagadjena cela
kao strv u kandže pala medju njih.

I znam da često ronila je glava
u mulj da teret udavi, u sram
i da se opet ko zgažena trava
dizala gore, ja ne znam ni sam
od kakvog podlog gadjenja ili slasti
da trpi više nego druga stvar,
i pila urlik u trpljenju strasti
i bacila ga SVEMRAČNOM NA DAR!

Voleo? Nisam. Mrzeo? Šta mari!
U prljavom razvratištu tom,
gde nebo trune, gde se ljubav pari,
gde sreću pruža ludnica i brom.
Mrzeti sme se, bez sramote za se
Voleti stid je, NITI SE IMA ŠTA,
do želja da se, bar MISAO spase
iz jame smrada i KALJUŽE ZLA.

It's not clear if this is an original composition or if this is appropriated from another writer.

26 *What Is to Be Done* (1863) is the title of a well-known novel by Nikolai Chernyshevsky (1828–1889), a Russian literary and social critic, journalist, novelist, a utopian socialist and leading theoretician of Russian nihilism; the same title is also used for a political pamphlet written by Russian revolutionary Vladimir Lenin in 1901 and published in 1902.

27 Lao Tzu (c. 6th-century BCE), an ancient Chinese philosopher and writer, the founder of philosophical Taoism. The section refers to an example of human longevity mythologically connected to Lao Tzu himself.

28 Mita Dimitrijević MID published two short texts with the same title, "Forma proždire duh," in *Zenit*, nos. 40 and 41 (April and May 1926): 14 and 16, respectively.

29 Renatus Hupfeld (1879–1968), a protestant theologian. The sentence translates as: "The most richly talented Europeans, the Slavs, are far too ruled by emotions, so they RESIST FORM ALL TOO MUCH." [Translation: Neil Blackadder]

30 "It is a new world, an unknown land across which we will all need a common THREAD, to guide us, to avoid loss of time and volubility; to allow us to see all that deserves to be seen; to keep from erring in our adventures when we overlook in passing the unexpected marvels at our feet." [Translation: Caroline Chapman Giberson]

31 Denis Diderot (1713–1784), a French philosopher, art critic, and writer.

Form Devours Spirit [I]

MID [Mita Dimitrijević]
from *Zenit*, no. 40 (April 1926)

> Astonished and horrified—I inform you—that—the whole—world—issue of validity—is taking big steps—to meet me.

To the greatest extent for the whole country in general, as a superorganic being, there is an increasing headlong reduction of all positive authorities. It is the embryo of future progress which is negative because the spirit does not need authority since it is itself authority.

It is still true, one-sidedly twofold, that Death is important as the ultimate authority for the dead living spirit, for its unrecognized, negative right; but as to the progress of the spirit, death is only the FIRST FORM. The spirit is negative and as such the opposite of positive death. Death, therefore, plays before the progress of the spirit, changes its form ("the Earth is round"), decreases positively, to appear to the spirit as more charming, negative, smaller. Thus, there is NOTHING where death, through its play, shows itself to be less than the spirit, which is BEHIND NOTHING, and which, negatively, is most concentrated in NOTHING.

The spirit, which encompassed the beings of the Earth, does not lose sight of the Earth's nature and its positive interest to be lost in its own visibility, so that with its positive metamorphoses, confuses the progressive spirit with the feminine, and devours what is positive from itself: NOTHING. That is why the diminishing positive authorities, in their solemn manifestations, are more and more nervously denouncing, annulling the word *NOTHING*. Therefore, they represent the whole cosmic obviousness of the spirit in the game of renunciation: "it is NOTHING," and they are afraid of NOTHING.

Translated by *Aleksandar Bošković*

Form Devours Spirit [II]

MID [Mita Dimitrijević]
from *Zenit*, no. 41 (May 1926)

> "Everything is possible in this country—NOTHING is impossible in it."
>
> Dr. Dragoljub Aranđelović: *Novosti*
>
> *
>
> "A feature of all our conclusions is that one day they will fail. That is why, in the end, we create. There are no final solutions. From everything we know, said the sublimely skeptical Emerson, the only thing we know EXACTLY is that we know NOTHING."
>
> Branko Lazarević: *Impressions*

If it were not the case as IT IS, if law professors are unable to stop focusing on NOTHING—then it would be clear that the game of Mrs. Simka and Mrs. Đurđinka and others, which is talked about and kept silent, is common with the game of all positive (+) intellectuals on earth: A GAME OF PHRASES.

This game is played for the calculation of the National Bank and the import-export brokers. These are tied to calculations for NOTHING.

Yet, precisely because these calculations are tied to NOTHING, they are unbound, negative (–), and as such, inaccessible to positive (+) law. By the negative (–) right of inverse proportions of the same numbers, the positive (+) right is WOMEN'S RIGHTS. And that is why the negative (–) right, in its action, eternally signifies the positive (+) right as a one-sidedly twofold right (renunciation), while in NOTHING it understands itself as a two-sidedly—hermaphroditic right: non-renunciation of the existing renunciation.

Under positive (+) law, NOTHING is the most negative of all positives (+), and therefore from the point of view of positive (+) law, nothing is selfishly taken into account, and even more selfishly, it doesn't want to understand NOTHING. But according to negative (–) law, NOTHING is the most positive notion of negativism, the opposite right to WOMEN'S RIGHTS.

According to WOMEN'S RIGHTS, a positive (+) right cares about ǝlqɐᴉuǝpun NOTHING: one-sidedly twofold, a positive (+) Death, mainly: leave NOTHING beyond reproach so that NOTHING would be taken into serious, positive (+) examination.

That is the idea of positive (+) legislation, positive (+) Truth: Death (+).

For the artistically ennobled world of bastards, Russian women are the best players on earth. And death (+) has its living form: a woman, no matter what kind.

The positive (+) gender is therefore female.

Translated by *Aleksandar Bošković*

A Tobacconist in Literature[1]

Anonymous
from *Vreme* (November 15, 1925)

A Writer Critiqued by the Police

The other day, the municipal chief of police, Mr. Ljubiša Lazarević, flipping through a pile of new books brought to him daily for review contemptuously glanced at a book on whose front cover was:

**A Trade Correspondence
on the Currency Question**

—Why on earth do we need to inspect this? thought Mr. Lazarević, knowing that trade correspondence doesn't contain any communist propaganda or anti-government or pornographic material. So, he tossed the book onto the pile of already inspected books, but was taken aback when the book fell open to another page with the following title in red letters and backwards:

1 "Duvandžija u književnosti," *Vreme* (November 15, 1925): 4.

"The Sexual Equilibrium of Money"

Mr. Lazarević picked it up and was even more confused when he opened the book.

Page one, blank; page two, blank; page three, blank, except for the number 40 denoting the page number; page four, blank, only at the bottom the following words were written partially in red and partially in black letters:

"A book of hors d'oeuvres on negativism."

The page count was in reverse order: 39, 38, 37, . . . Every other page was completely blank and in the remaining ones there was frequently only one word: "Bankocracy" or "Establishing trade relations," and then on page 32:

"Supply of goods

To Mr. Edison, New York.

To Mr. Grey-Snowden, London.

To Mr. Flammarion, Berlin.

To Mr. Hauptmann, Paris.

To Mr. Ujević, Zagreb.

To Mr. Gorky, Moscow.

To Mr. Tagore, Delhi."

On the following page the anonymous author frequently bitterly referred to the National Bank, whose name he printed everywhere upside down. On page 34, he wrote:

"To the National Bank Administration.

All the individuals at the National Bank who are acquainted with me have obviously come to an awful misconception about me because, as I have unquestionably observed, they have labeled me a nervous wreck. However, per my current circumstances, I am only monetarily wrecked . . . ."

Immediately after page 30 on the blank unpaginated pages the following words show up at the bottom:

"Steal freely!

The key! . . . The key!!"

And on and on, from page to page:

"The key!!! The key!!!"

or "K . . . e . . y! . . Ke . ke . . e . ."

or "K . . . Ke . . Ke . ."

or "Ke . . . . Ke . . . ."

Somewhere in the book there are parties comprised of six, seven blank pages with just a few dots here and there.

On page 12:

"*Orgy*
A great selection
of laying
for funerals"

On page 8:

"It goes without saying that maidenhood,
'unfortunate in its fortune to not know instinct,'
has nothing to examine."

When he turned to the last page, on it there was a large red cross and a horizontal red line, Mr. Lazarević rang his clerk, yelling:

—This is some loony bird!

Since the book didn't feature the name of the writer at all, a detective was sent to Narodna Misao A. D., the printer.

When the publisher was summoned the chief of police showed him the book, which had a different title on every page, and asked:

—I told him, Mr. Lazarević, we'll have to deal with the police because of that darned book and he told me in writing that he'd be taking full responsibility. He gave me 3,000 dinars just to print the book, he said defensively.

—Well, who is he? asked Mr. Lazarević.

—MID near the Sava,[2] Mita Dimitrijević, the tobacconist, explained the printer, who found this conversation unpleasant.

They summoned MID, i.e., Mr. Mita Dimitrijević, the tobacconist near the Sava, who wrote literature anonymously.

Mr. Lazarević, who inspected confounding books daily and discussed them with Mr. Tin Ujević, was well-versed in the latest manifestations, movements, and directions, told Mr. MID standing at the door:

—This is no longer zenithism, nor futurism, nor dadaism, nor surrealism, this is insanity!

However, Mr. MID quite calmly explained the blank pages in his book:

---

2 The Sava river is one of two rivers that flows through Belgrade.

—Why write a book? That's easy. I want to print a book in which the reader has the space to write a whole novel.

Since this explanation about literature couldn't persuade Mr. Lazarević, nor could Mr. Lazarević persuade Mr. MID, the police chief sent the writer to be briefly questioned by a clerk and thus give him the opportunity to explain his point of view on literature. However, since during this conversation it was discovered that Mr. Dimitrijević wasn't authorized to sell newspapers and books, Mr. Lazarević sentenced him to 20 days in jail.

Mr. Dimitrijević protested his sentence to the chief of police.

—Why am I being sentenced?

—The key! The key! replied the police chief enigmatically.

And thus, the new trend in our literature ended up in Glavnjača prison.[3]

Translated by *Steven Teref and Maja Teref*

3 Glavnjača prison was a notorious Belgrade prison for political prisoners.

The Sexual Equilibrium of Money, or A Trade Correspondence on the Currency Question [Review]

Anonymous
from *Zenit,* no. 40 (April 1926)

Belgrade 1925.

This book will confuse any thinking being. It will confuse anyone whose intelligence got drowsy among the fat of mediocrity and whose genius lies in our currency. The book will confuse readers because it is atypical and original in its ideas, because of its pure emotion and graphic design. A special lyricism and an elastic, rebellious, and inartificial spirit permeate the book. Its author is awake for everyone and forever. It is necessary to experience and express Belgrade's urban life outside literary clichés. For example: "Orgy—a great selection of laying for funerals." Undoubtedly, the author has had enough of life's bitterness and disappointment. He was at the source of evil—at the spring where money is everything. In a National Bank. There where the daily grinding machine squeaks: money! money! money! That disgusting elixir and foundation of contemporary culture and society. For the embodiment of his full-blooded loves and discoveries, the author put in function "the word as an operative value." And he revealed many "secrets" and peered through many "relics"—with an unnerving zenithist gaze. In an unusual way, the frozen hydra, money, has been laid bare and the banking financial system of "positive" labor has been ridiculed.

The author reflects on life and its puns from two basic positions: *sex* and *money*. It needs to be emphasized here, that these two opposites, brought into a common interrelation and interaction, as our unknown author did in his book, represent one of the most original aspects for examining life and decoding its hermetic script. That is fruitful soil for the growth of his explosive radiograms about everything that discharges through life's pulsations. In red typeface, it is written on a page "steal freely," and below it only two words: "Key. Key." This is the key for deciphering our lives, our sufferings, as well as for deciphering this interesting book, which is hidden in drawers and bookstore shelves undeservingly—since no one likes seeing oneself as it is. The book starts and ends (it is the same) with the words: "If we, therefore, don't wish to lie to each other, then it is necessary that we not lie about *NOTHING*."

Translated by *Aleksandar Bošković*

The Metaphysics of Nothing [Review]

Anonymous
from *Zenit*, no. 41 (May 1926)

This is a precious book due to its spirited nature. The unknown author perceived aptly both the importance and grotesque nature of the overused word *NOTHING* in different contexts: by politicians, poets, philosophers, and journalists. And nobody has thought to pay attention to this "insignificant" word and concept—*NOTHING*—except for this unknown author, who came closer to NOTHING and entered into its metaphysics. Isn't that significant: *the metaphysics of nothing!?*

This book, which also features a "small anthology about the smallest thing," launches a new writer, poet, and thinker, from whom we should expect many surprises of spirit, talent, and affirmation to come.

Translated by *Aleksandar Bošković*

The Barbarogenius at the Gates: Zenithist Theater, Soirees, and Public Interventions

Introduction

Aleksandar Bošković and Steven Teref

Zenithist performances—plays, evenings (soirees), public lectures, actions, interventions, and demonstrations—altogether comprise yet another important segment of the movement's art production. The possibility of creating a social situation that is an end in-and-of-itself, which the avant-garde especially recognized and widely used, represents the greatest value of the performing arts, while at the same time limiting what is possible in the way of research. According to performing arts theorist Ana Vujanović, there are two reasons for this. First, the sporadic and unreliable documentation together with the lack of material artifacts left behind the zenithist performances contribute to their ephemeral character. These public zenithist actions were primarily not thought of as works of art to be left as a cultural legacy, but rather as immediate and even excessive interventions in their immediate social field. The second reason is that the organizational character of performance productions was constrained by economic factors.[1] The sparse material

1 Ana Vujanović, "Avangardni teatar i performans 1920-ih (Umetnost u Srbiji)," in *Istorija umetnostiu Srbiji: XX vek—Prvi tom: radikalne umetničke prakse* (A History of Art in Serbia: The 20th Century—Volume

artifacts and documentation of zenithist performances included in this anthology should be measured against the backdrop of such limitations.

Protest and provocation were an integral part of zenithism, as first captured in the short and unsigned review "Zenithist Theater," published in *Zenit* no. 24 (May 1923). The riotous Jarry-esque performance by a group of Zagreb high-school students would mature into more pointed agitation for ideo-political interventions, such as the zenithist demonstrations against Alfred Kerr in Paris and Rabindranath Tagore in Belgrade.[2]

Micić considered the 1922 performance of the Zagreb high-school theater group *Traveleri* (Travelers) to be an integral part of the poetics of zenithist theater, not only because the group performed zenithist texts. The Travelers were the young educated progeny of wealthy bourgeois Zagreb families, aware of the societal changes that occurred in the period after World War I, and thus playfully critical of bourgeois values.[3] Since they were high-school students, they behaved differently from the bourgeois class of old Zagreb: they wore spectacles without lenses and they doffed their hats to horses instead of coachmen or gentlemen in carriages; they also organized meetings in apartments "where they posed together in funny costumes for photographs."[4]

In December 1922, the Travelers staged a play in a gymnasium of the First Real High School in Zagreb (today's Mimara Museum) with elements of performance art, which showed their avant-garde and anarchic inclinations through collaging texts, experimental directing, and performing. The play consisted of a collage of texts published in *Zenit*: Marinetti's drama

---

One: Radical Artistic Practices), ed. Miško Šuvaković (Belgrade: Orion Art, 2010), 147–156, https://bit.ly/3RbcdB5.

2 Vidosava Golubović and Irina Subotić, *Zenit: Internacionalna revija za umetnost i kulturu 1921–1926* (Belgrade: Narodna biblioteka Srbije, Institut za književnost i umetnost, 2008), 34.

3 Members of Traveleri theater group: Dragutin Herjanić, Jo Klek or Josip Seissel (1904–1987), Višnja Kranjčević (1904–1983), Zvonimir Megler (1904–1971), Vlado Martin Pilar (1904–1928), Miloš Somborski (1902–1983), Čedomil Plavšić (1902–1987), Dušan Plavšić Jr. (1904–1976), Miho Schön (1904–1930), and Radeta Stanković (1905–1996).

4 Suzana Marjanić, "Dečki, najbolje da bežite!" *Zarez* 9, no. 203 (April 5, 2007): 32. They performed daily in public some sort of art actions, thus identifying their lives with art, and anticipating the essential elements of artistic practice that will appear fifty years later. The group was active for a dozen years and afterwards, its members continued their professional careers in medicine, architecture and law, with remarkable results. For more on the Travelers, see: Ivana Janković, "One Possible View of the Avant-Garde Phenomenon of the Traveller Group," *Sto godina časopisa Zenit. 1921–1926–2021 / A Hundred Years of Zenit Magazine*, ed. Bojan Jović and Irina Subotić (Belgrade: Gallery RIMA, Institut za književnost i umetnost, 2021), 479–499.

of objects *They Are Coming* (published in Micić's translation in *Zenit* no. 14) that was performed for the first-time outside Italy, fragments of Micić's *Airplane without an Engine*, and poetry by Yvan Goll and Branko Ve Poljanski along with the reading of some newspaper articles.[5] Josip Seissel, whose zenithist pseudonym was Jo Klek, compiled the text for the play, and created the scenography, costumes, and five posters advertising the play. The play had unusual scenography: scenery in the form of movable, multicolored cardboard skyscrapers, which swung in dance scenes in the rhythm of the one-step. Costumes were also made of colored cardboard, mimicking the appearance of a stage curtain.[6]

Regardless of whether one considered the show to be zenithist, Dadaist-futurist, or purely Dadaist, it caused a scandal, although some in the audience were delighted by the performance.[7] The Travelers intentionally provoked the audience, who reacted with shock—whistling and booing—when they brought a live donkey onto the stage. One character on stage asked where the ass came from, and another answered, "from the audience," which included the high-school teachers. The play outraged the teachers through its humorous provocation and Dadaist critique. As a result, the students were expelled from school the next day.[8]

Aside from the Travelers, all other actions were mostly carried out at an individual level by Poljanski, Mikac, Micić, Vladimir Skerl, or the Micić brothers together, and often

---

5 See Vera Horvat-Pintarić, *Josip Seissel* (Zagreb: Galerija Nova, 1978).

6 "Black geometric figures on a multicolored foundation [...] tall skyscrapers in green and red, blue and yellow, changed their position on the stage to the rhythm of the dancers, so that the cubist principle of spreading, intersecting, and overlapping of parallel and divergent plans, was animated in the space of stage, but in the spirit of Dada." Suzana Marjanić, "Dečki, najbolje da bežite!" *Zarez* 9, no. 203 (April 5, 2007): 33.

7 "In the monograph on Josip Seissel, Vladimir Bužančić calls the play zenithist, which for Susovski is not at all convincing, because the performers were not connected with zenithism at the time, 'except that they took already published texts from *Zenit* as part of the play collage, since at that time it was the most accessible avant-garde magazine.' Furthermore, Susovski points out that in the first act, Marinetti's drama of objects *They Are Coming* is included in the collage of other texts, and that the often-mentioned play is defined as Dadaist-futurist, 'which can never be classified in the futurist milieu.'" Suzana Marjanić, "Dečki, najbolje da bežite!" *Zarez* 9, no. 203 (April 5, 2007): 33. Jadranka Vinterhalter, for example, considers the show of a futurist provenance; see: *Flashes of avant-garde in the Croatian art of the first half of the 20th century*, ed. Jadranka Vinterhalter, trans. Andy Jelčić (Zagreb: Muzej suvremene umjetnosti, 2007), 30.

8 Marijan Susovski, *Josip Seissel: nadrealističko razdoblje: slike, crteži, akvareli, tempere, pasteli, crtaći blokovi od 1920 do 1987* (Zagreb: Muzej suvremene umjetnosti, 1997), 17.

continued the performative character begun by the Travelers through small, ad hoc, provocative events called *večernje* ("evenings" or "soirees").

Micić gave his first zenithist reading in Belgrade, on January 3, 1923, in the large hall of the Second High School. The evening consisted of the lecture "Zenithism as a Balkan Totalizer of a New Life and a New Art" and reading from his book *Rescue Car*.[9] The aim of the reading had a bombastic, propagandistic character that went beyond the staid nature of a typical lecture or poetry reading and laid the groundwork for more ambitious endeavors.

A second zenithist event, given by Ljubomir Micić and Branko Ve Poljanski at the Music Institute in Zagreb on January 31, 1923, offered a program more dynamic in scope and had a decidedly more performative character. Although Micić again read "Zenithism as a Balkan Totalizer" and a new lecture on anti-aesthetics, "The Categorical Imperative of the Zenithist School of Poetry," illustrated by the reading of new zenithist work, such as *Airplane without an Engine*, Micić went a step further by staging the short grotesque play *Jury Trial*. Branko Ve Poljanski, for his part, gave the call-to-arms sermon "Alarm" and read zenithist works, for example, the paradoxical story "A Steamboat in the Appendix." But he too staged a zenithist drama, the comic tragedy *The Laughter of Rifles* and capped off his reading with a performative march for his poem "Tick-Tock Like a Crab in a Tailcoat." The evening culminated with the announcement and presentation of the *Zenithist-International Gallery of New Art* exhibition with works by Archipenko, Delaunay, Gecan, Gringova, Lissitzky, Moholy-Nagy, and others. *Zenit* no. 21 commemorates the evening by publishing the texts performed at the event which are set in the journal as a kind of open score.[10] The next issue of *Zenit* (March 1923) published a review of the Zagreb performance:

> Zenithists have shown that they know how to create new art, creating it in vivo, and that they know how to laugh without stretching their lips like pornographic literature does. The zenithists demonstrated how to win over life and how to laugh at their own tragedy, which is also universal. After the zenithist evening, many attendees remained in the lobby for a long time, visiting the "Zenith-Gallery of New Art," which presented original artworks to the public in our

9 "I. Zenitistička večernja u Beogradu" (The First Zenithist Evening in Belgrade), *Zenit*, nos. 19–20 (December 1922): 69–70.

10 "Program–Contents: A Zenithist Evening on January 31, 1923," *Zenit*, no. 21 (February 1923): 1–8.

> country for the first time. Mr. Lj. Micić, at the request of a few, spoke at the exhibit about the new style of painting, aside from the evening's program.[11]

At the beginning of *Zenit*'s Belgrade phase, Marijan Mikac embarked on a reading tour, organizing several zenithist evenings in small towns in the Banovina (or Banija) region of Croatia, where Micić and Mikac spent some of their childhood. Mikac seemed initially to take a more straightforward approach to his readings than Micić and Poljanski in the form of lectures, but nevertheless provoked his audiences all the same. A newspaper article at the time covered the February 11, 1923 zenithist event in Petrinja, where Mikac gave the lecture "Constructivism of a New Life or 180 Degrees in Fear" and performed the play *Jury Trial*.[12] Glimpses into the zenithist evenings Mikac held in Sisak, Topusko, and Petrinja are preserved through correspondence between Micić and Mikac, which was later edited and published by Vida Golubović.[13]

Each of the letters documents the zenithist events in detail, to time and place[14] or composition and size of the audience.[15] Mikac describes his presentations on zenithism and his own artistic practice, discussing poems from *Effect on Defect* and fragments from the unpublished novel *The Monkey Phenomenon*. The lectures most likely included zenithist ideas that Mikac later formulated in his essay "The New Zenithist Art," combining aspects of Micić's and Poljanski's zenithist poetics of paradox, simultaneity, and associativity. In the more radical

---

11 "Veliki uspeh II. Zenitističke večernje" (Great success of the Second Zenithist Evening), *Zenit*, no. 22 (March 1923): 6–7.

12 The author—who morphologically signed/disguised himself with "-ić"—issued a highly negative review of Mikac's performance: "The lecture sounded more magical, as if in the stories of some fortune-teller reading the cards," concluding, "Let's not attend lectures like this, and *basta*!" See: IĆ, "Zenitist lecture in Petrinja," *Hrvatska banovina*, no. 35 (November 8, 1923): 2; Boris Vrga, "Zenitističke večernje u Petrinji," *Generacije: časopis za kulturu i umjetnost te duhovni identitet grada Petrinje*, no. 8 (February 1995): 10–19.

13 Vidosava Golubović, "Iz prepiske oko *Zenita* i zenitizma: Marijan Mikac/Ljubomir Micić," in *Ljetopis srpskog kulturnog društva "Prosvjeta,"* vol. 4 (Zagreb: Prosvjeta, 1999): 277–293.

14 The evenings took place on: August 18, 1923, in Sisak (the letter from August 20); August 22, 1923, in Topusko (the letter from August 23); and September 2, 1923, in Petrinja (the letter from September 3, 1923).

15 There were about thirty people in Sisak, forty people in Topusko, and up to thirty-five visitors in Petrinja, plus some students who attended for free. In his letter of August 28, 1923, Mikac suggests to Micić: "We would have to borrow a modern film, and then hold lectures with projections [...] Then, we'll attract the masses."

parts of his lectures, where he compared his presentations to linguistic war-like expressions of shootings and bombings, Mikac seemed in line with futurism, while he advocated for a more traditional understanding of art to the audience. He insisted that the work could be explained and that a rational core can be perceived in it. One way to think of Mikac's talks is as a homogeneous zenithist work, oriented toward the poetics of paradox, as he explains in his letter written on September 2, 1923: "The whole lecture was a special paradox. It was only on the last day that I found out that in the entire building on two floors, there was no electricity, only in the hall where I would be lecturing. So, as soon as it was over, I had to use candles."[16]

In the letters, Mikac also reports to Micić on the reaction of the audience: in Sisak, "the ladies swallowed handkerchiefs with laughter; the old men held on to their bellies, and constantly wiped their glasses wet with tears"; in Topusko, "some of the visitors thought that the zenithist evening would be a concert, a play, something like that. Of course, when the lecture followed, they were disappointed," adding that "the verbal fight was fierce: I spoke and scolded, while the audience gradually, in silence, left the hall. So, one and the same evening provoked different reactions—in Sisak joyful laughter, in Topusko indignation and astonishment"; in Petrinja, "it was stormy. Banovina will have something to say," writes Mikac, explaining how he quarreled and debated with some lawyers and professors in the audience about the meaning of his poem from *Effect on Defect*, confessing that he was the target of the audience's laughter: "frowning shouts, questions, voices from the rest of the audience . . . a number of questions and answers . . . it was more an argument than a debate."[17]

It is especially evident from these letters that Mikac was most interested in working with the audience, insisting on an interactive and dynamic exchange, although he did not tolerate those who were averse to zenithist ideas. On August 28, 1923, he writes:

> I most dislike those opponents who pretend that it is not worth talking about zenithism at all, while they regularly work to undermine us. In fact, they do not have the strength to show themselves for a real fight. Really, how inconvenient it is to have simpletons, or more precisely, cowards for opponents! [. . .] Again, I find it difficult to imagine myself in a "tame" position toward the audience, which deserves nothing more than to be sanctified with ridicule and mockery."[18]

---

16 Golubović, "Iz prepiske oko *Zenita* i zenitizma: Marijan Mikac/Ljubomir Micić": 287.

17 Ibid., 280, 281, 285, 287.

18 Golubović, "Iz prepiske oko *Zenita* i zenitizma: Marijan Mikac/Ljubomir Micić": 283.

This attests to Mikac exercising the tried and true avant-garde method during his zenithist evenings, which Branimir Donat calls "swearing at the audience."[19] Mikac's zenithist evenings, as Boris Vrga noted, were held as "a provincial variant of European Dadaist appearances: a mixture of irony, sardonic tone, drama and humor, flirting with cheap nagging on the verge of ridicule and provocation, with the main intention to break the stereotyped cultural performances, to cause discomfort and a certain 'shock' on the horizon of the recipients' expectations."[20]

The correspondence provides insight into other, no less important, visible struggles: the difficulties of a material nature for distributing zenithist publications and collecting annual subscriptions for *Zenit*[21] and original ways of promoting zenithism through printed and handmade posters.[22] At the same time, Mikac's letters sent to Micić attest to the method and dramaturgy of the performance. In a letter sent from Petrinja on August 23, 1923, he points out that he always lectured in uniform, most probably in the uniform of a naval cadet.[23] Micić himself insisted on the aforementioned dress code for Mikac, and most likely, as Branimir Donat reveals, he was trying to emphasize the contrast between social uniformity and advocation of freedom of spirit.[24] On the whole, as Vida Golubović rightly concludes on the content of the correspondence, "Mikac tried to follow the programming and artistic attitudes of the movement to which he was deeply loyal."[25]

---

19 Branimir Donat, "Performans kao oblik komunikacije hrvatske dade i njenih inačica s javnošću," in *Dani hvarskog kazališta–hrvatska književnost, kazalište i avangarda dvadesetih godina 20. stoljeća* (Zagreb: HAZU, Književni krug, 2004), 11, 12.

20 Vrga, "Zenitističke večernje u Petrinji," *Generacije: časopis za kulturu i umjetnost te duhovni identitet grada Petrinje*: 17.

21 Mikac writes to Micić, in Sisak, "one of yours and one of mine books were sold out"; in Topusko: "materially—better than in Sisak, the deficit of the first evening was partially covered because of the sold tickets"; "I sold one of Poljanski's books and one of my own. But that's why there is only one of yours left"; in Petrinja: "one of the books of each type was sold."

22 For a lecture in Petrinja, scheduled for September 2, 1923, Mikac says that he displayed "an effective (in superlative) poster by Mr. [Jo] Klek." He also mentioned "a poster made by a very young man who graduated this year, Milan Žinić, the poster is made by hand in all vivid colors: triangular letters–zenithism, and squared: construction of the universal era."

23 Mikac mentioned his photo-portrait in uniform that he sent to Micić: "the attached photo was made by my good acquaintance, one of my comrades in Topusko, Zvonko Markovinović."

24 Donat, "Performans kao oblik komunikacije hrvatske dade i njenih inačica s javnošću," 12.

25 Golubović, "Iz prepiske oko *Zenita* i zenitizma: Marijan Mikac/Ljubomir Micić": 278. Mikac's "Zenithist evenings in Banija" were evaluated as successful in *Zenit*, no. 25 (February 1924), considering that they

Branko Ve Poljanski promoted zenithism across Europe and often acted as a zenithist liaison and correspondent in Paris, Berlin, and elsewhere. On April 23 and 24, 1925, Poljanski held two zenithist events at City Hall in Ljubljana, Slovenia, a city where he began his career as an artist in 1921. For his 1925 return, he printed the poster-leaflet "A Zenithist Evening of Sensations" in Slovenian. This promotional leaflet, as Irina Subotić and Vida Golubović explain, "invites audiences of all ages, genders, occupations in a provocative and sensationalist way, and at the same time presents the main postulates of the zenithist program. Poljanski presents himself here as a poet, a Balkan fakir—capable of performing incredible miracles, and a man whose powers of imagination are unparalleled in Europe; he promises to speak of zenithism as a new art in the world and to read poetry that cannot be heard anywhere else; he declares zenithism to be a 'counter-political movement' and therefore invites everyone to attend, regardless of their political beliefs."[26]

The promotional flyer for Poljanski's poetry reading mimics the form of a poem while his name runs down the left side of the page, the repetition draining his name of meaning so that it becomes a constructivist block acting as a framing device to effectively guide the reader to the message on the right side of the page. The constructivist gesture likely would have been intentional on Poljanski's part since constructivist ideas were in the Ljubljana air as evidenced in the Slovenian poet Srečko Kosovel's "Kons," or constructivist poems at the time.[27]

Since September 1925, Poljanski had been the representative of *Zenit* and the zenithist movement in Paris, actively involved in Parisian cultural life. One of his first public appearances was an interview with the Italian futurist leader, F. T. Marinetti. The conversation between the two took place at the Grand Hotel the day after Marinetti's contradictory lecture, "Futurism and Passatism, Fascism and Anti-fascism," held on October 28th at the Tribune libre des femmes in Paris.[28] Yugoslav painter Mirko Kujačić and Italian futurists Fortunato Depero and Enrico Prampolini were also present during the conversation; Poljanski spoke Serbian and German while Marinetti conversed in Italian and French, with an unnamed woman acting as translator. During the conversation, Poljanski objected

---

induced "laughter on the scales! Nobody knew why he was laughing—that's the main thing. Only the lecturer had a clear idea about that."

26 Golubović and Subotić, *Zenit*, 195.

27 Srečko Kosovel, *Look Back, Look Ahead*, trans. Ana Jelnikar and Barbara Siegel Carlson (Brooklyn: Ugly Duckling Presse, 2010).

28 Passatism (ital. *passatismo*) is the term coined by the futurists to refer to traditional culture and values.

to the fascist orientation of futurism, the appropriation of zenithism, and the burning of the Slovene Cultural Center in Trieste by the fascists. The dialogue was originally published in *Zenit,* and was later republished and reedited in *L'Impero,* the official newspaper of the Italian fascist party under the title "Italian Futurists and Serbian Zenithists: A Conversation between F. T. Marinetti and Poljanski."[29] Marinetti defined his positive attitude toward fascism, claiming that "Futurism was the forerunner of fascism" and outlining the main points of the futurist program. Poljanski, on the other hand, rejected the connection of futurism with fascism, illustrating this with the example of the fascist burning of the Slovene Cultural Center in Trieste, the terror against Croats in Istria, and the closure of the local Yugoslav school. The Italian version differs in terms of material facts only where there is talk of burning the Slovene Cultural Center in Trieste: according to *Zenit,* Marinetti stated that it was done by the communists, and according to *L'Impero,* by "anti-italiani feroci ed accaniti" (fierce and relentless anti-Italians). Poljanski also spoke about the foundations of futurism in zenithism: printing futurist works, holding lectures and zenithist evenings, where futurism was celebrated and defended from enemy attacks. In contrast, Poljanski emphasized the weak presence of zenithism in futurism. Marinetti justified it by not knowing the language, but he pointed out that Micić and Poljanski were mentioned in his recent manifesto on world futurism. The Italian version included Marinetti's statement that zenithists are Serbian futurists and as such he invited them to fight against a common enemy—passatism of all forms. Poljanski rejected this by claiming that there are only zenithists in the Kingdom of Serbs, Croats, and Slovenes, but he showed readiness to fight a common enemy—Europe and old culture. In both versions the dialogue ends with Marinetti's greeting to Micić.[30]

In addition to conducting confrontational interviews, Poljanski staged public interventions when the need arose. On one occasion, he organized a protest with painter Mirko Kujačić and composer Josip Štolcer Slavenski at a lecture given by Alfred Kerr, a German writer and editor, whom they accused of authoring war propaganda verses directed against Russians, the French, and Serbs. As a renowned theater critic for *Berliner Tageblatt,* Kerr

29 Branko Ve Poljanski, "Dialog Marineti—Poljanski" [The Marinetti—Poljanski dialogue], *Zenit,* no. 37 (November–December 1925): n.p.; P.D., "Futuristi Italiani e Zenitisti Serbi (Conversazione di F. T. Marinetti e Poliansky," *L'Impero* (January 8–9, 1926): 3.

30 See Zoran Markuš, *Zenitizam* (Belgrade: ID Signature, 2003), 92–93; Golubović and Subotić, *Zenit,* 237–238.

was invited to give two lectures in Paris (at the Sorbonne and for the Société Savante) in January 1926, which were organized by the League for Human and Citizens' Rights with the aim of furthering Franco-German rapprochement after the First World War. After the introductory presentation and welcome speeches by the president of the association and the former French Minister of Education, who expressed hope that there would be a "pacification of spirits," a young gentleman came to the podium and asked to be allowed to greet Mr. Kerr on behalf of a group of intellectuals. The young man stated that he knew Kerr's publicist and literary works from the war, which were hostile to the Slavs and the French. To support this, he invited Branko Ve Poljanski to read Kerr's verses. According to *Zenit*, Poljanski "recited loudly a propaganda couplet that was sung before the war on the streets of the Central Power's cities, from Berlin to Vienna and Zagreb: *Jeder Schuss ein Russ / Jeder Stoss ein Franzos / Alle Serben müssen sterben*—from the poem *Serbien muss strebien* (Serbs must die)."[31] Despite the audience's whistling, Kerr gave his lecture, but did not stay long to visit the capital of France: he traveled back to Berlin on the first morning train.[32]

The Kerr incident was not the only protest that the zenithists staged. A zenithist demonstration was mounted against the Indian philosopher and poet Rabindranath Tagore at his lecture in Belgrade on November 15, 1926. Micić and Poljanski tossed copies of an open letter in the form of a leaflet, from the gallery of the Ceremonial Hall of the University of Belgrade where Tagore gave his lecture. According to Micić's record, those leaflets "were released to fly like white pigeons."[33] The leaflet, signed by Poljanski and Micić and reprinted in *Zenit* no. 43, accused Tagore of officially representing modern culture and modern civilization contrary to the teachings of Mahatma Gandhi, whose ideas the zenithists accepted. Tagore's lecture, "On Modern Civilization" was held in a crowded hall and the speaker was introduced to the audience by Professor Pavle Popović. When Tagore climbed onto the stage, he was greeted by loud applause and cheers, but as soon as he started to speak, "whistles were heard from the gallery and shouts of 'Down with Tagore!,' 'Long live Gandhi!' Leaflets rained down on the audience that called Tagore a "false prophet" and he was sharply reprimanded in English and Serbian for not supporting Gandhi, the leader of the Indian national movement for independence."[34] The Belgrade newspapers *Politika*, *Pravda*, and

---

31 See "Zenitističke demonstracije u Parizu," *Zenit*, no. 39 (March 1926): n.p.

32 See Markuš, *Zenitizam*, 85; Golubović and Subotić, *Zenit*, 238–239.

33 Golubović and Subotić, *Zenit*, 232.

34 Jovan Pejčić, "Rabindranat Tagore u Beogradu," *Kulture Istoka* V/15, nos. 1–3 (1988): 66–67.

Vreme all commented on the zenithists' protest: *Pravda* (November 16, 1926) provided a short informative note, while the newspaper *Vreme* (November 17, 1926) writes critically that the event was an unheard-of scandal that equally upset the audience and Tagore, "who did not understand what was happening."[35] It seemed that "the events in the gallery visibly distressed Tagore, but that did not stop him from continuing his lecture."[36]

Ultimately, zenithism was not interested in the performing arts in terms of artistic production in theater, opera, or ballet. Zenithist performing practices were realized through small, ad hoc, and activist-oriented cultural and artistic programs. They mainly consisted of public readings of poetry, but poems of a provocative nature as regards political public life and behavior, rather than elaborated works of art. The last public display of zenithism, in the form of Poljanski's final act as a zenithist performance, will be addressed in the subsequent section of the anthology.

---

35 "Nečuven skandal na predavanju Rabindranata Tagore," *Vreme* (Belgrade, VI/1765, 17. XI 1926): 5. See also: "Najčuveniji medju trista miliona, slavni pesnik R. Tagore, u našoj sredini," *Pravda* 22, no. 314 (November 16, 1926): 1; "Beogradjani oduševljeno pozdravljaju velikog indijskog pesnika: Dva predavanja g. Rabindranata Tagore," *Politika* (November 17, 1926): 6.

36 Golubović and Subotić, *Zenit*, 232.

Zenithist Theater [Review]

Anonymous
from *Zenit*, no. 24, May 1923

Zenith Theater. On December 16, 1922, several young people, on their own initiative, organized an evening at the Gombalačka hall of First Real High School, where the main part was the so-called zenithist performance, *Airplane without an Engine*. This zenithist act was composed of various excerpts from Micić, Poljanski, Marinetti, and Goll's texts as deemed best by the organizers. Chaos was bound to happen, which the audience appreciated all the more and it outrageously and fervently cheered and jeered the unprecedented sensation in Zagreb. The brave young zenithists didn't waiver. They persistently and honorably performed the work they started, which was accompanied by effective changes of light, dancing, playing a barrel organ, an accordion, a piano, and wildly beating a drum. The names of these determined young zenithist actors should be emblazoned in these pages: D. Herjanić, J. Klek-Seissel, Miss Kranjčević, Z. Megler, V. Pilar, D. Plavšić Jr., and M. Schön.[1] The young Josip Klek deserves special mention; his extraordinarily effective

1 This theater group was called Traveleri, or The Travelers (often written as Travellers). The members were: Dragutin Herjanić, Josip Klek-Seissel, Višnja Kranjčević, Zvonimir Megler, Vlado Pilar, Dušan Plavšić Jr., and Miho Schön. This was their first performance when they were all high school

posters, staging of the scene, and multi-colored paper costumes, are far more memorable than any other ordinary attempts of its kind, let alone these zenithist ones. In this issue, we feature reproductions of two zenithist costumes (made according to the instructions of Lj. Micić) and the stage curtain made by that young and very gifted zenithist player who is just 18 years old.

Translated by *Steven Teref*

---

students. For more information: https://www.avantgarde-museum.com/en/museum/collection/authorstraveleri~pe4423/#overlay.

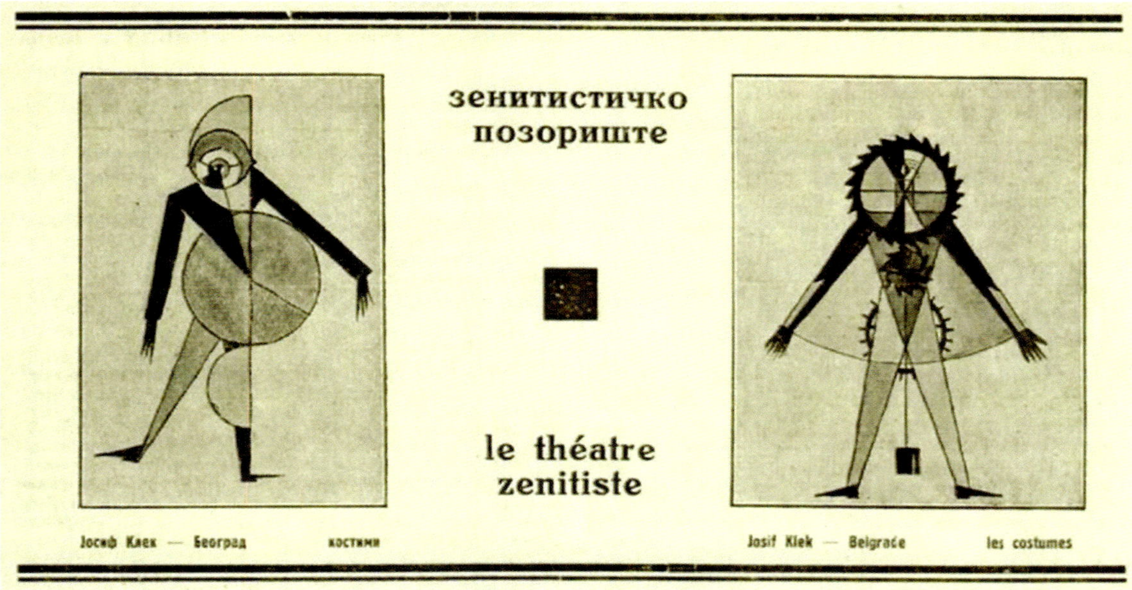

6.1. Jo Klek's costumes for zenithist theatre, *Zenit*, no. 24, (May 1923). Open source.

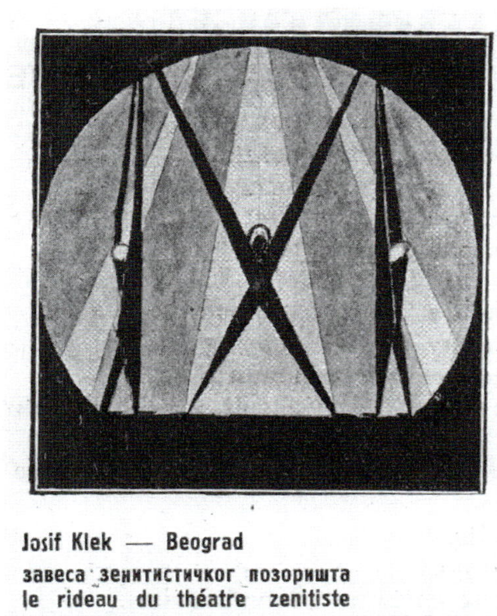

6.2.
Jo Klek's sketch for the design of curtains for zenithist theatre, *Zenit*, no. 24 (May 1923). Open source.

The First Zenithist Soiree

Anonymous
Leaflet (January 3, 1923)

Translated by *Samantha Farmer*

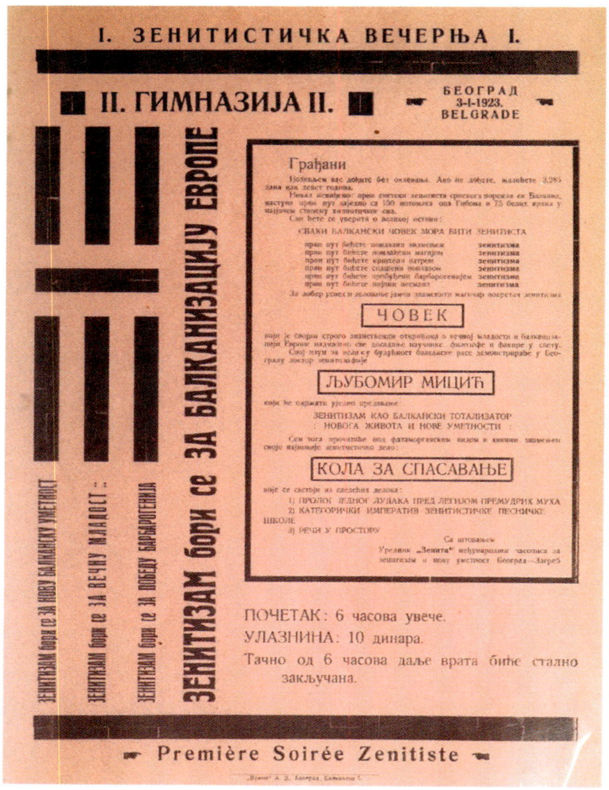

6.3. *I. Zenitistička večernja* [The First Zenithist Soiree]. Leaflet for "The First Zenithist Soiree" in Belgrade (January 3, 1923). Open source.

I. A ZENITHIST EVENING I.

II. GYMNASIUM II.

БЕОГРАД
1/3/1923
BELGRADE

ZENITHISM fights FOR A NEW BALKAN ART

ZENITHISM fights FOR ETERNAL YOUTH ::

ZENITHISM FIGHTS FOR A BARBAROGENIUS VICTORY

ZENITHISM fights FOR THE BALKANIZATION OF EUROPE

Citizens

I am inviting you to come without hesitation. If you do not come, you will regret it for 3,285 days or nine years.

Never before seen: the first global zenithist of Serbian extraction from the Balkans, is appearing for the first time with 150 descendants of Father Gibbon[1] and 75 black sheep in the strongest state of hypnotic dream.

You will all be convinced of the great truth:

EVERY BALKAN MAN MUST BE A ZENITHIST

for the first time you will be anointed with the sign of **Zenithism**
for the first time you will be rejuvenated with the magic of **Zenithism**
for the first time you will be baptized in the fire of **Zenithism**
for the first time you will be saved by the flood of **Zenithism**
for the first time you will be awakened by the barbarogenius of **Zenithism**
for the first time you will be intoxicated by the poems of **Zenithism**

The renowned magician prime mover of Zenithism vouches for good results

THE MAN

who with his strictly scientific discoveries about eternal youth and the Balkanization of Europe has surpassed all previous scientists, philosophers, and fakirs in the world

The doctor of zenithosophy will demonstrate his invention for the great future of the Balkan race in Belgrade

LJUBOMIR MICIĆ

who will also hold the lecture:

ZENITHISM AS THE BALKAN TOTALIZER
: OF NEW LIFE AND NEW ART :

In addition, he will read under the illusory guise and wondrous sign of his newest zenithist work:

RESCUE CAR

which consists of the following parts:

1) PROLOGUE OF A MADMAN BEFORE A LEGION OF OMNISCIENT FLIES
2) THE CATEGORICAL IMPERATIVE OF THE ZENITHIST POETIC SCHOOL
3) WORDS IN SPACE

Respectfully
The editor of the international journal *Zenit*
for zenithism and new art Belgrade–Zagreb

BEGINS: 6 in the evening

ENTRANCE: 10 dinars

At precisely 6 p.m. the doors will be closed indefinitely.

Première Soirée Zenitiste

"Vreme" A.D., Balkanska Street 5

Endnotes

1 Edward Gibbon (1737–1794) was an English historian and author of *The History of the Decline and Fall of the Roman Empire.*

The Second Zenithist Soiree

Program reproduced from *Zenit*, no. 21 (February 1923)

PROGRAM—CONTENTS

A Zenithist Evening: January 31, 1923

I.

LJUBOMIR MICIĆ

1 — ZENITHISM AS THE BALKAN TOTALIZER OF A NEW LIFE AND A NEW ART (a general interpretation of zenithism and a zenithosophical debate)

2 — THE CATEGORICAL IMPERATIVE OF THE ZENITHIST SCHOOL OF POETRY (a basis for a new ant-aesthetic—from *Rescue Car*)

3 — AIRPLANE WITHOUT AN ENGINE (a–b, the latest constructive zenithist poetry)

4 — FREE FALL (a synthetic novella)

5 — JURY TRIAL (a zenithist grotesque; a small act of a great drama)

II.

VE POLJANSKI

1 — ALARM (an awakening and a call for a zenithist rebellion)

2 — A STEAMBOAT IN THE APPENDIX (a paradox—a story from 1,001 darknesses)

3 — WHISTLING FACE (a Balkan neo-zenithist acrobatics)

4 — THE LAUGHTER OF RIFLES (a comedic tragedy)

5 — a—300,000 PUNCHES A SECOND (an ultra-novella)

b—TICK-TOCK LIKE A CRAB IN A TAILCOAT (a machine's evening march—a poem)

ZENITHIST-INTERNATIONAL GALLERY OF NEW ART: Archipenko (Russia) **Behrens-Hangeler** (Germany) **Delaunay** (France) **Freudenau** (Germany) **Gecan** (S. C. S.) **Gleizes** (France) **Gringova** (Russia) **Hansen** (Denmark) **Lissitzky** (Russia) **Lozowick** (America) **Moholy-Nagy** (Hungary) **Charchoune** (Russia) **Willink** (Holland) **Zadkine** (Russia)

SOMMAIRE—PROGRAMME

de soirée zenitiste 31. Janvier 1923.

Translated by *Steven Teref*

6.4. *Velika zenitistička večernja* [Great Zenithist Evening]. Poster for "The Second Zenithist Soiree" in Zagreb, (January 31, 1923). Open source.

A Zenithist Soiree

Poster for a zenishist evening (Sisak, August 18, 1923)

A Zenithist Evening.

8/18/1923

Veliki Kaptol

exactly 9 o'clock evening

Sisak

Zenithist poet and naval cadet

Marijan Mikac

will show clearly the principles of the new art of zenithism.

Zenithism fights for eternal youth.

Zenithism fights for the victory of the barbarogenius.

Zenithism fights against sentimentality in literature.

Zenithism fights for the new Balkan art.

Zenithism fights for the balkanization of Europe:

EAST against WEST.

Entrance fee: 7 Dinars

Payments accepted at the box office for ***Zenit***, an international magazine for zenithism and new art, as well as voluntary contributions to the ***Zenit*** printing fund.

These books by zenithist authors can also be obtained:

Ljubomir Micić: ***Rescue Car***. (Price 10 Din.)

Zenithist barbarogenics in 30 acts;

Ve Poljanski: *77* ***Suicides***. (Price 15 Din.)

A very fast super fantastic novel;

Marijan Mikac: ***Effect on Defect***. (Price 10 Din.)

The zenithist effect—poetry.

Mr. Ljubomir Micić

Address for headquarters, editorial office, and administration:

Zenit—Belgrade, 12 Birčaninova Street

Translated by *Steven Teref*

A Zenithist Evening of Sensations

Branko Ve Poljanski
Leaflet (April 1925)

A Zenithist Evening of Sensations
The Town House on Thursday at 8 p.m.

Branko Ve Poljanski	Never before seen in Ljubljana.
Branko Ve Poljanski	Never before heard in Ljubljana.
Branko Ve Poljanski	Students and young people!
Branko Ve Poljanski	Women and girls!
Branko Ve Poljanski	Lovers and suicides!
Branko Ve Poljanski	Professors and actors!
Branko Ve Poljanski	Singers and doctors!
Branko Ve Poljanski	Old people and children!
Branko Ve Poljanski	Come to the Town House this Thursday
Branko Ve Poljanski	evening at 8:00, so you can hear
Branko Ve Poljanski	a miraculous poet;
Branko Ve Poljanski	to see the man with the greatest
Branko Ve Poljanski	imagination in Europe!
Branko Ve Poljanski	The poet will tell you about zenithism,
Branko Ve Poljanski	a new art movement in the world.
Branko Ve Poljanski	He will read you poems as you have
Branko Ve Poljanski	never heard them before.
Branko Ve Poljanski	Zenithism fights for eternal youth!
Branko Ve Poljanski	Zenithism fights for the balkanization of Europe!

Branko Ve Poljanski	Zenithism fights for the triumph of the scrawny over
Branko Ve Poljanski	the obese!
Branko Ve Poljanski	Zenithism is fighting for glory in Europe!
Branko Ve Poljanski	Zenithism is fighting to create a new world!
Branko Ve Poljanski	Zenithism is fighting for a new way of painting!
Branko Ve Poljanski	ZENITHISM for a new poetry!
Branko Ve Poljanski	ZENITHISM for a new theater!
Branko Ve Poljanski	ZENITHISM for a new architecture!
Branko Ve Poljanski	ZENITHISM for the freedom and joy
Branko Ve Poljanski	to create the barbarogenius!
Branko Ve Poljanski	Old and young! Beautiful and ugly! Smart and stupid!
Branko Ve Poljanski	Men and women! Come to this evening
Branko Ve Poljanski	of sensations, to see and hear a Balkan fakir
Branko Ve Poljanski	and a man with the greatest imagination
Branko Ve Poljanski	of the old world and the new world:
Branko Ve Poljanski	**Branko Ve Poljanski.**
Branko Ve Poljanski	Zenithism is a counter-political movement, so
Branko Ve Poljanski	come all, regardless of political affiliation!

Long Live Zenithism!

Translated by *Steven Teref*

The Marinetti—Poljanski Dialogue

Branko Ve Poljanski
from *Zenit*, no. 37 (November–December 1925)

Paris, October 28, 1925

Marinetti[1] arrived in Paris for the birthday of the zenithist poet Branko Ve Poljanski. Their meeting was heartfelt. Marinetti gave a lecture on fascism and futurism the same day. He was heard to say that futurism is the main foundation of fascism and that fascism is the consequence of futurism. "Glory to Mussolini and long live the dictator!"—was the tone of the entire evening. Shouting, excitement. The *Giolittisti*[2] protested. The fascists made a ruckus. "Long live Mussolini!" "Long live Marinetti!" The French sniped at the temperamental Italians reminding them that—they were in France. They claimed they didn't need fascism because they had their—democracy. They were justifying themselves to the Italians that they were right to say so because Italy had rescued France from ruin in 1915. That was said by Marinetti. He continued that fascism was not reactionary but revolutionary because Mr. Mussolini—had been a socialist! He claimed that fascism was liberal since it had come out of futurism, and everyone knows that Marinetti is anti-clerical. Marinetti further spoke that the genius of the Italian people is the greatest—that the strength of the Italian youth is inexhaustible and that it just needed to be awakened.

He cried: "Rise young Italy!" futurists had exclaimed long ago which was carried out today by—fascists. Futurism—fascism—fascism—futurism.

The lecture was followed by a debate. Outraged, I almost spoke—French. I wanted to say that fascism is Italian imperialism which oppresses many Croats and Slovenes. However, I was tongue-tied. Still, what I couldn't say at the debate I imparted to Marinetti the following day at our meeting.

Our interpreter was—a lady. The zenithist representative spoke Serbian and German. The lady's comprehension was poor and yet in all probability she wouldn't understand a zenithist even in her native tongue. This meeting and dialogue, except for the zenithist representative and Marinetti, was witnessed by a two-meter-tall Serb with a Balkan back and wise eyes. Beside the Italian genius was the sculptor Depero[3] and the painter Prampolini.[4] Both were fine futurist intellectuals. Marinetti overshadowed them with his impulsivity.

Poljanski: Mr. Marinetti! I greet you as the progenitor of futurism and as the first man who raised the flag and incite the youth to rebellion. I am doing so according to my duty as the representative of zenithism in Paris. And the progenitor of zenithism and the director of *Zenit* also doesn't have reason to not respect you as such. But you, as the propagandist of fascism are losing our sympathies. Against such a Marinetti we stage a protest.

Marinetti: Thank you! You, however, don't have a reason for that because fascism is a call to battle, and battle is healthy and necessary.

Poljanski: Zenithists value your struggle but if it is fascist, then between us there can be no cooperation because fascists burned down the Slovenian National Hall[5] in Trieste and threw two living men through the flame from the third floor into the street.

Marinetti (fuming): Communists were hiding there!

Poljanski: A convenient excuse! But communists are people, too!

Marinetti: Zenithists have always enjoyed our sympathies.

Poljanski: Fine! Futurists enjoy our sympathies, but fascists terrorize honorable Croats in Istria[6] and close our schools.

Marinetti: Are you a Serb or a Croat?

Poljanski: *Serbo*.

Marinetti (raises an eyebrow and his left eye discreetly glistens from wonder): . . .

Poljanski: That our sympathies for you are truthful can be proven because we printed your works and because Mr. Micić always defends you if anyone attacks you. We have held state conferences and zenithist readings where you were celebrated. And what did you do for us? You only wrote a few lines about us, didn't you?

Marinetti: That's very hard due to your language, which no one understands . . .

Poljanski: What do you mean? Why, God is a Serb: Serbs are everywhere—there are Serbs and Slovenes in Italy.

Marinetti (slyly deflects and grows upset): So many German poets haven't been translated into Italian because of their difficult language. But there's proof that I kept an eye on the zenithists because in my latest manifesto I published Micić and yourself . . .

Poljanski: But we aren't futurists, we're zenithists. In our country, only zenithists exist . . .

Marinetti: I invited you to join us in our struggle as such against our common enemy.

Poljanski: If that is Europe, then go ahead! If that enemy is an old-bearded culture—we're ready.

Depero (abruptly interjects): *Lui dice*! *Lui dice*![7]

Poljanski: We are joyous barbarians who will set the beards of wise men on fire. We want to do something for Man. Zenithists are anti-political because politicians have destroyed the world with their professorial brethren!

Depero (interjects even more lively): *Lui dice*! *Liu . . . Liu . . .*

Prampolini (wisely silent as he looks on)

Marinetti: We Italians are also barbarians.

Poljanski: That's right! Bravo! Let's charge into battle together.

Marinetti: In the name of that, zenithists will be translated and published into all of our journals. Next year, we're hosting a great international futurist conference in Rome to which we will undoubtedly invite you.

Poljanski: But we aren't futurists.

Marinetti: Everyone will be entitled to their label.

Poljanski: So glad to hear it! And who will be providing the funding?

(Marinetti, the lady, another lady, a gentleman, Prampolini, Depero—burst into laughter!!!)

Marinetti: Goodbye! Send my regards to your leader Ljubomir Micić. I greatly respect him and like him.

Poljanski: Goodbye! Until Monday! . . .

They shake hands.

Translated by *Steven Teref and Maja Teref*

Endnotes

1 Filippo Tommaso Marinetti (1876–1944) was the founder of the avant-garde movement futurism.

2 Giolittisti was named after the Italian centrist-liberal statesman Giovanni Giolitti (1842–1928). The group, like the politician, opposed the Italian fascists.

3 Fortunato Depero (1892–1960) was an Italian futurist painter, writer, sculptor, and graphic designer.

4 Enrico Prampolini (1894–1956) was an Italian painter, sculptor, and scenographer.

5 Trieste National Hall: Italian fascists set fire to the building in 1920.

6 Istria: A peninsula on the Adriatic Sea shared by Croatia, Slovenia, and Italy. The region was partitioned to Italy in the Treaty of Rapallo in 1920. After the fascist takeover in Italy in 1922, the Italian government began a campaign of forced Italianization.

7 Lui dice: "He says" in Italian.

Rabindranath Tagore and the Zenithist Protests[1]

Anonymous
from *Zenit*, no. 43 (December 1926)

Admittedly, Tagore is a known sage—for the dunces of both sexes of the human race. Tagore, a god lover and an itinerant actor, like his fellow countrymen, Indian fakirs, and Krishnamurti[2], tours Europe as a "prophet" and "saint;" he escaped the ancient school of Gautama, the Buddha, and Jesus Christ. But, since he exists in ecstasy beyond time and space and in God's company, he previously bowed down to Mussolini[3] and then betook himself to our Balkan peninsula and blessed King Boris[4], so we are now surely ready to forgive him all of his childish lamentations and silliness. Truly, Tagore's silk pocket visibly contradicts his words. And his pocket is proof of our opinion of him: in Zagreb, in one evening, Tagore's silk pocket devoured—15,000 dinars, and in Belgrade—12,000 dinars. And then, on behalf of his enterprise, with a clear conscience, he encouraged our artists to renounce their earthly possessions. Such sermons are especially popular in his other homeland—England. Such "poetry" and such a "religion" are generously supported by the ruling class of all countries. Such posthumous Christianity, even in its most pitiful form—theosophy—is especially promoted by England and America because their goal is clear: *distract as many people as possible from their material possessions so that all earthly possessions could be easily grubbed by a handful of thieves*. And Rabindranath Tagore serves that goal, consciously or unconsciously, which, in our view, is secondary.

Our press unanimously supported Tagore in his enterprise. Endearingly, it called him an *India* poet, instead of *Indian*. And that wasn't the extent of it. Even better, its unanimous support is worth every praise because it was unanimously against the zenithists. This unanimity of it is quite rare. Anti-zenithism has the power to unite sworn enemies. This is clearer now than ever before. The press barraged us from all sides: *In the form of hysterical curses and insults, in the form of a misrepresentation of our protests*. That this is so, was evidenced by thousands of Belgraders who found themselves in University Hall. Even Mr. Tagore himself, who was so impressively greeted with "Long live Gandhi" in every European language.

The newspaper *Politika*, always reliable in its hatred of *ZENIT* and ZENITHISM, reached a fever pitch. Dismissing the relationship between a Belgrade audience and the protests as a "smattering of conceited and coarse ultramodern poets" it gave a nudge to the police in these words: "But it will certainly hurt the reputation of the police if they don't teach a lesson to these miscreants about propriety." Arrrgh. But Mr. Aćimović[5], the chief of police, didn't want to flirt with the burdensome *Politika*. He endeared himself to "Cvijeta Zuzorić[6]," the female president of the "Friends of Art" society. The skirts worried about the outcome of the lecture. So, they intervened by calling the police. Bravo!!! (A secret nudging is surely more moral than a public nudging to the police.) Ljubomir Micić was then invited to the Belgrade City Council. Why, you wonder? Well, because said "Friends of Art" society requested the meeting as they were the ones to invite a certain Indian Maharaja and conman with words—to peacefully give a lecture on art. And who do you think the police intervention was for? *It was for the local poets who have so much more to say to their country than some agents of culture and liars*. And do you wonder what response Mr. Aćimović got? Our response was so instructive and valuable that it must be written out: *Zentithists don't feel the need to repeat themselves and do a good deed twice. Last night we performed our cultural duty within the scope of our program*. (*See enclosed document*: "An Open Letter to Rabindranath Tagore.") *Our country needs to have cultural protests as well. I, for example, booed Milan Ogrizović*[7] *once at the National Theater in Zagreb though I was almost lynched by the enraged audience. I was ready even last night to be your guest in Glavnjača*[8]. *If zenithists felt compelled to protest against Tagore tonight as well, we'd do it, no matter the consequences. The police would do their duty (if that was indeed to be their duty), and the zenithists theirs.*

Those who benefited from our protest the most were, again, the merchants. Belgrade bookstore owners sold out of all the copies of Romain Rolland's book *Mahatma Gandhi*[9], who nobody knew anything about till then. And many Belgrade "connoisseurs" of Tagore and many a "Cvijeta Zuzorić" at his lecture thought Tagore was called Gandhi—since zenithists exuberantly chanted "Long live Gandhi!"

Translated by *Steven Teref and Maja Teref*

Endnotes

1 The events depicted here involve Rabindranath Tagore's visits to Zagreb and Belgrade in 1926. It's not certain whether Poljanski or Micić wrote this account.

2 Jiddu Krishnamurti (1895–1986) was a philosopher, speaker, and writer who promoted the idea of a revolution of the psyche, which cannot be brought about by an external entity, such as religious, political, or social.

3 Tagore visited Italy at Mussolini's invitation in May 30–June 22, 1926, where he was tricked into praising the fascist dictator.

4 The king of Serbs, Croats, and Slovenes at the time of Tagore's visit was King Alexander I, who ruled from 1921 until his assassination in 1934.

5 Milan Aćimović (1898–1945) was a politician who later joined the Axis puppet government during WWII.

6 Cvijeta Zuzorić (1552–1648) was a lyric poet from a prominent merchant family in Ragusa (now Dubrovnik). In addition to being a poet, she hosted writers and artists in her home.

7 Milan Ogrizović (1877–1923) was a writer, critic, and politician.

8 Glavnjača, a notorious political prison in Belgrade that housed the police administration between the world wars.

9 Rolland's book about Gandhi was published 1924.

An Open Letter to Rabindranath Tagore

Branko Ve Poljanski and Ljubomir Micić
from *Zenit*, no. 43 (December 1926)

Belgrade, November 15th, 1926

Gentle father of Bengal and false prophet!

We barbarians are sick of all the empty phrases about contemporary culture and contemporary civilization. That civilization, which in the Balkans is synonymous with blood-stained mud and billions of bedbugs. For this modern civilization is a bedbug—contemporary civilization is cannibal-like and opposed to all humanity.

We zenithists, revolutionary poets—artists, have engaged ourselves in a decisive struggle with European civilization which enslaves us, and we are ready even to fight tooth and nail to annihilate that cannibalistic civilization, which you advertise—in this detestable manner with your white beard and silken robes made in English factories. Do you remember—what then has your great countryman Mahatma Gandhi been doing? Why did you not also join forces with him when he organized that magnificent struggle—to free your enslaved people from the yolk of contemporary civilization, from English Lords and Indian Maharajas?

You have come uninvited to this land of barbarians, whose face is contorted with the pains and convulsions of your silken civilization, against whose flanks you will rub yourself this evening—on the wings of your idle words. For those who have brought you here, to this graveyard of European culture, they care only for money and profit, for trading with all and everything, for commerce in men's conscience and not in the least for civilization. These agents of culture, true sons of contemporary civilization have deceived you and rejoice perversely behind our backs, that they thus easily gained good coin in exchange for the counterfeits, which bear your name: Rabindranath Tagore. But if they have lied to you with Serbian hospitality, you, you false prophet: that Serbian hospitality is a lie and a deceit—and that the best sons of this country of the Balkans are strangers in their own land. We speak the truth and only in the name of truth declare ourselves publicly against you today, against the hypocrisy and cynicism of Serbian society and against the hypocrisy of modern society in general. We cry out to our motherland clearly and loudly above your voice—Give space to us! Give hospitality to us first! Let this country hear her own poets first—who are far stronger and greater than you and all your "Gardeners." This country must and shall give ear for once to the harbingers of a new civilization of humanity and not always to the swansongs of European carcasses which are already falling into decay.

Your verses are lemonade, your philosophy dung, your mysticism, like all mysticism, is—mystification. Your prophethood is a pose that groans beneath the burden of modern cannibalistic civilization.

With this epistle, the zenithists greet you and bid you farewell. Do not forget our gloomy Balkans and joyful zenithism. The zenithists beg only this of you at parting—bow down to your great contemporary Mahatma Gandhi in your far-off country of Bengal, for that will be your greatest deed and the earthly crown of your miming efforts. Look to this before your inevitable journey to—Nirvana—and rejoice, gentle father—for there will be no zenithists in Nirvana!

In the name of the phalanx
of the international zenithists

Translated by *Steven Teref and Maja Teref*

The Nadir of Zenithism

Introduction

Aleksandar Bošković and Steven Teref

The article "Zenithism through the Prism of Marxism," in which its author, Dr. M. Rasinov (widely viewed to be Micić himself) praised Communism and Marxism as humanistic philosophies, promptly provoked a reaction from the authorities.[1] Since the Communist Party was banned in Yugoslavia, the text was considered "to incite unrest and to propagate civil disorder (like the October Revolution in Russia). Micić was deemed a threat to 'social peace, morality, and public security,' stood trial, and *Zenit* was banned (no. 43 of December 1926 was the last issue)."[2] A series of zenithist provocations led to this outcome, one of them being the publication of a satirical personification of Capital on the front cover of *Zenit* no. 41 (May 1926), reproduced from the 1924 catalogue of Russian revolutionary posters, and another being *Zenit*'s participation at the international exhibition

1 Dr. M. Rasinov, "Zenitizam kroz prizmu marksizma," *Zenit*, no. 43 (December, 1926): 12–15.

2 Irina Subotić, "Zenitism / Futurism: Similarities and Differences," in *International Yearbook of Futurism Studies*, ed. Günter Berghaus, vol. 1 (Berlin: De Gruyter, 2011), 220; 201–230.

The Revolutionary Arts of the West (*Vystavka revoliutsionnogo iskusstva Zapada*), held in May–June 1926 in Moscow.[3]

Before he could be imprisoned, Ljubomir Micić fled Belgrade on December 17, 1926. He escaped to Fiume (at the time part of Italy; today Rijeka, Croatia). Since he was without documents, he was detained in Fiume and then released thanks to the intervention of the futurist leader F. T. Marinetti, with whom he exchanged ideas and texts during *Zenit*'s run. In mid-January 1927, Micić moved to Paris, where he remained until 1936. This Parisian period showed that the zenithist motto "Moscow vs. Paris" remained in the sphere of theoretical ideas, however, the French metropolis for Micić—as well as for many artists from around the world—was a space for broad insights into civilizations, providing concrete possibilities for creation, for interesting encounters and projects (even utopian ones), and finally for publishing several important books.[4] Micić supported himself by translating, and he wrote novels intensively and published in French: *Hardi! A la Barbarie. Paroles zénitistes d'un barbare européen* (Onward! To Barbarity. Zenithist Words of a European Barbarian, 1928; with illustrations by Branko Ve Poljanski); *Zéniton. L'Amant de Fata Morgana* (Zeniton. The Lover of Fata Morgana, 1930); *Les Chevaliers de Montparnasse* (The Knights of Montparnasse, 1932); *Après Saraïevo. L'Expédition punitive* (After Sarajevo. The Punitive Expedition, 1933); *Être ou ne pas être* (To Be or Not to Be, 1933); *Rien sans Amour* (Nothing without Love, 1935) and *Barbarogénie le Décivilisateur* (Barbarogenius, the Decivilizer, 1938). In his novels, the author evokes his avant-garde, zenithist period of life and work, and historicizes the whole movement with many emotional and autobiographical elements translated into novel form.[5]

The correspondence from 1927 to 1928 between Micić and Anuška, on the one hand, and Micić and Marijan Mikac, on the other, along with the correspondence from 1927 to 1929 between Micić and Slovenian artists Ferdo Delak and Avgust Černigoj, provide ample insights about this period and Micić's strategy to keep the zenithist movement, its magazine and press alive, despite the conditions of his unexpected exile. Micić saw in Mikac, one of *Zenit*'s most agile associates, a possible Anuška "successor," as he used to say in his correspondence, that is, her deputy in the business of running the Lipa Mill branch in

3 See the poster titled "Kapital" accompanied by Demian Bednyi's verses in Vyacheslav Polonskii, *Russkii revolytsionny plakat* [Russian Revolutionary Posters] (Moscow: Gosudarstvennoye Izdatel'stvo, 1924).

4 See Irina Subotić, "Paris in *Zenit*—*Zenit* in Paris," *Zbornik Narodnog Muzeja u Beogradu. Recueil Du Musee National De Belgrade* (Belgrade: Narodni muzej, 2010), 566; 565–579.

5 See Subotić, "Paris in *Zenit*—*Zenit* in Paris," 575.

Belgrade (a paper warehouse of the central factory located in Zagreb).[6] However, Anuška's uncle, the majority owner and shareholder of the paper factory, and others, opposed the plan.[7] Anuška was soon herself disappointed in Mikac and disillusioned by his business acumen, as she writes in her letter, dated March 22, 1927:

> Mikac became completely stupid. It is desperate, desperate, I'm crying to heaven in despair. Believe me, he would not be able to lead 'L(ipa) M(ill).' He is now, like a grouse in heat, blind and deaf. He does not hear or understand when he is spoken to. And she? (Anuška refers here to Mikac's wife—AN) He talks to her again, and she doesn't even listen to him. He made himself happy, poor thing, very happy. She is lazy, she sleeps all day. She dresses for three hours and he always runs and serves. He will also be the one who washes the diapers. [...] Of course, she doesn't like our apartment, she turned it over. She told Poljanski on the first day that she was not a zenithist. Of course. I would like them to get off my doorstep as soon as possible. They annoy and bother me.[8]

In letters from Ferdo Delak and Avgust Černigoj sent to Micić in Paris (between 1927 and 1929), we see that faith in the renewal of *Zenit* was alive. However, the zenithist ideas were not fully realized, but were partially reincarnated in the Slovenian avant-garde magazine *Tank*, started by Delak and Černigoj in Ljubljana in late 1927, through its internationalism and dynamic typography and prominently featuring Micić and numerous former *Zenit* associates in the magazine.[9] Unfortunately, the magazine was shut down after its second issue, so Micić's attempt to reaffirm the poetics of zenithism ultimately failed.

---

6 Mikac and his wife, who insisted that he leave the job on ships, named their son Ljubomir after the founder of zenithism. See Vida Golubović, "Iz prepiske oko *Zenita* i zenitizma: Marijan Mikac / Ljubomir Micić (1927)," in *Ljetopis* (Zagreb: Srpsko kulturno društvo Prosvjeta, 2001): 238–239; 237–265.

7 See Saša Ilić, "Ljubav i smrt posle avangarde," in *Strašna komedija: Prepiska Anuške Kon Micić i Ljubomira Micića 1920–1960*, ed. Šaša Ilić and Dragana Peruničić (Belgrade: Narodna Biblioteka Srbije, 2021), 17.

8 Ilić and Peruničić, *Strašna komedija: Prepiska Anuške Kon Micić i Ljubomira Micića 1920–1960*, 95. The letter (March 22, 1927) is held in the Legacy of Ljubomir Micić, Special collections, National Library of Serbia, Belgrade (Inv. No. LjMR/II/3/25).

9 Associates, mostly from Slovenia and Italy, were joined by a group of zenithists: Lj. Micić, Branko Ve Poljanski and M. Mikac, the latter being the only one living in the Kingdom of Serbs, Croats, and Slovenes at the time. See *Tank–revue international de l'art vivant*, 1–1 1/2 (1927); 1/2–3 (1928); https://monoskop.org/Tank.

After the episode with *Tank*, Mikac tried to rehabilitate and revive *Zenit* in a new publication and under a different name, where Micić and Mikac would join their ideas in terms of the journal's editing and orientation. Their correspondence from 1928 shows that they discussed starting a zenithist magazine called *Oči ciklona* (Eyes of the Cyclone), with the aim of renewing the tradition of zeal and the swagger of *Zenit*, by "provoking a similar revolt and a similar purification of spirits."[10] Mikac presented his editorial vision for the journal *Eyes of the Cyclone*, proposing himself and fellow zenithist Andra Jutronić as associates from within the country, and Micić and Poljanski from abroad.[11] They even had an alternative name for a planned zenithist magazine—*Nadir*.[12] Mikac suggested that Risto Ratković and writers from Zagreb collaborate on it, believing it would attract such new literary voices as Dragutin Kostić, whose book of poetry *Umesto ludila* (Instead of Lunacy, 1928), dedicated to MID and with foreword by Risto Ratković, was "written exclusively under zenithist influence."[13] Mikac detailed the idea behind the magazine *Nadir*, "emphasizing the need to gather the youngest forces with which the fight for 'our liberation from Western European influence' could be waged. The target of their attack would be Paris and its spiritual hegemony, ever present in Belgrade's political circles, especially with regard to Western democracy, culture, and civilization."[14]

Of the two proposed names—*Nadir* and *Eyes of the Cyclone*—the first was associated with the cosmism of the zenith, and the second with its dynamism. According to Vida Golubović, this magazine was supposed to be the bearer of the idea of zenithism under one name or another, as a counterpart to Micić's journal and with his blessing. According to Mikac the sudden rise and failure of the idea was not due to his incompetence, but to purely material reasons.[15] Micić's unsuccessful attempt to secure Mikac taking over Anuška's

---

10 See Mikac's letter of March 12, 1928. Vida Golubović, "Iz prepiske oko *Zenita* i zenitizma: Marijan Mikac / Ljubomir Micić (1928–1929) in *Ljetopis* (Zagreb: Srpsko kulturno društvo Prosvjeta, 2002): 184.

11 See Mikac's letter from April 2, 1928, where he proposes the number of pages, format, and possible collaborators; Ibid., 186.

12 See Mikac's letter from June 4, 1928; Ibid., 189.

13 See Mikac's letters dated July 7 and August 11, 1928; Ibid., 193, 196.

14 "In Mikac's opinion, the precondition for this anti-European revolt would be organized action and emphasizing the 'original values of our youngest literary generation.' It conveys the opinion of Belgrade intellectuals gathered around the Moskva Cafe: they acknowledge 'the great merits of zenithism, which awakened the youngest, as well as the older generations.'" Golubović and Subotić, *Zenit*, 255–256.

15 Golubović, "Iz prepiske oko *Zenita* i zenitizma: Marijan Mikac / Ljubomir Micić (1928–1929)": 180, 179–204.

place at the Lipa Mill branch in Belgrade, his dependance on Anuška's financial and organizational skills, as well as Mikac's own precarious situation in which he had to worry about the needs of his family while simultaneously sinking into the quicksand of societal pressures to conform, contributed to the quick end of their rekindled aspirations.[16]

Although he would seem to be the obvious successor to Lipa Mill, Poljanski was not in any better position than Mikac. In her letter to Ljubomir, dated March 2, 1927, Anuška writes: "Leave Branko alone. He is an unhappy guy and should be taken as such. I haven't delivered any of your messages to him yet. When the time comes [. . .] let him go for now."[17]

Reflecting on Anuška's observation, Poljanski had become disillusioned with zenithism, literature, Belgrade, and Yugoslavia altogether. By 1927, he felt that he had lost his fight. His break-up with the zenithist cause, literary endeavors, and the city and country that had antagonized him through the years were distilled in his third and final poetry collection *The Red Rooster*, which became the last book published by Biblioteka Zenit. The eponymous sequence is a long confessional poem Poljanski wrote in Paris. Poljanski's melancholic tone throughout the book is that of a man who seems decidedly resigned to his defeat, yet wants to celebrate his love for zenithism and poetry, his "sister muse"—a final act of defiance in the "valley of grim ignorance," in a society likened to a "wax doll." In the environment in which it emerged, that is, 'outside the avant-garde network,' zenithism did not have even the minimum preconditions for development. "The magnitude of great possibilities is only possible in a cultured society," wrote Poljanski resignedly.[18]

On Sunday, July 17, 1927, Branko Ve Poljanski distributed two thousand copies of his books *Topsy-Turvy* and *Red Rooster* for free in Belgrade's Terazije Square and along the promenade, thus symbolically marked his break with literature. According to Dragan Aleksić, who wrote about this incident in "The Poetic Disappointment or the Original American-Zenith

---

16 For more about Micić's and Mikac's lives in the 1920s and their life transformations during the 1930s—marked by the syndrome of the denunciation of the avant-garde—and swerving from revolutionary utopianism to nationalism and fascism, respectively, see Goran Miloradović, "Od anarhizma do šovinizma: Drugi Svetski Rat i pripadnici avangardnog umetničkog kruga oko časopisa *Zenit*—Ljubomir Micić i Marijan Mikac," in *Intelektualci i rat (1939–1947). Zbornik radova s Desničinih susreta 2012. Dio 2*, ed. Drago Roksandić and Ivana Cvijović Javorina (Zagreb: Filozofski fakultet u Zagrebu, 2013), 305–331.

17 Ilić and Peruničić, *Strašna komedija: Prepiska Anuške Kon Micić i Ljubomira Micića 1920–1960*, 67. The letter (March 2, 1927) is held in the Legacy of Ljubomir Micić, Special collections, National Library of Serbia, Belgrade (Inv. No. LjMR/II/3/8).

18 Poljanski, "Dogs Bark and Poets Sing," in *The Red Rooster* (1927), included in this anthology.

Advertisement in Belgrade," Poljanski handed out his books to random passersby out of disappointment and the long-term misunderstanding of his audience.[19] One way to view Poljanski's dramatic act is as the last zenithist performance, no doubt confusing passersby, before the poet boarded a train for Paris and turned his back on his homeland for good. Poljanski's last "performance" marked not only his break with literature but with his homeland as well. Despite Poljanski's paradoxical aphorism in *Zenit* that "there are cultural people in Paris but no culture,"[20] from 1927 until his death in 1947, Paris became a refuge for him where he devoted himself to painting and published his post-zenithist views on art in his 1930 *Manifesto of Panrealism*.[21]

19 Golubović and Subotić, *Zenit*, 248.

20 Poljanski, *Zenit*, no. 37 (November–December, 1925): 13.

21 For more on Poljanski's life and career as a painter in France, see Predrag Todorović, "The Life and Death of Branko Poljanski," *Književna istorija* 154 (2014): 1007–1015. See also Poljanski, "Manifeste du Panréalisme," 1930. https://www.avantgarde-museum.com/en/museum/collection/works/manifeste-du-panrealisme~fi1340/

The Red Rooster

Branko Ve Poljanski
Zenithists International Edition, 1927

Translated by *Steven Teref and Maja Teref*

7.1. B. Poljanski, *Crveni petao* [Red Rooster], Zenithists International Edition, no. 12, Paris-Belgrade, 1927. Front cover. Courtesy of National Library of Serbia, Belgrade (Legacy of Ljubomir Micić, Special collections).

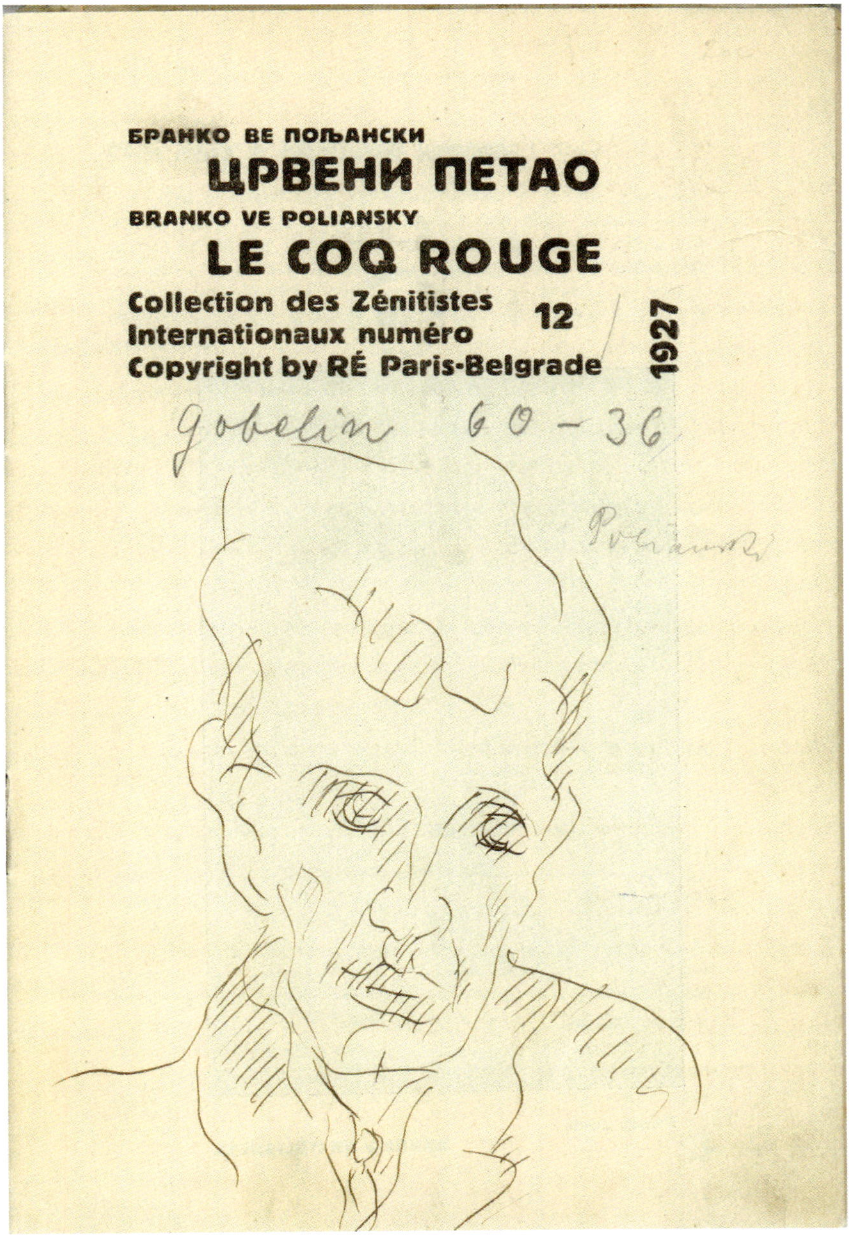

7.2. B. Poljanski, *Crveni petao* [Red Rooster], Zenithists International Edition, no. 12, Paris-Belgrade, 1927. Colophon page. Drawing by B. Poljanski. Courtesy of National Library of Serbia, Belgrade (Legacy of Ljubomir Micić, Special collections).

Dogs Bark and Poets Sing

This book is my last feat in the valley of grim ignorance and ever grimmer crime. I sing under the sky not for acknowledgment, not for a career in diplomacy, not for the historic development of society; I sing for love, I sing for the realization of a great love boiling in me which is the sole justification for my life and for every life. I can love even when I hate.

I pity my slanderers a great deal because the mud they sling at me besmirches them.

Although life is a single phenomenon hard to find a reason for, it contains the sole reality—poetry. Only a poetic relationship with life brings balance to the soul.

The mere thought of celebrity disgusts me. What would celebrity mean to me if my heart wasn't the source of tremendous turbulent feelings. What would heavenly blossoms mean to me if my world were a desert. I am worth nothing without myself. Oh, and may people not forget that fame is merely a lofty opinion of oneself. People who don't appreciate themselves are not worth appreciating.

Misconceptions that people have about zenithism and me are beyond my control.

The magnitude of great possibilities is only possible in a cultured society. Hence, cry not, my sister muse.

The society in which this book appears does not represent any new phase in the general development of cultures.

The society in which this book appears stands like a wax doll mechanically moving in the general movement of things and events. Those who scrutinize it will lose the illusion of the dramatic play and be overwhelmed by stench and poison.

It is difficult and dangerous to speak the truth, however, it's easy to lie. A lie. Between a word and the kernel of a thought a palpable difference exists. This is how the words that describe events and reality itself in the world of my poetry are differentiated. It is essential that life's wisdom can be expressed only through poetry.

Like a comet, zenithism flew over the earth. Fear, panicky fear ruled in this, our literary atmosphere. The comet Zenit *threatened the obliteration of "literature" to one small class of people, not typical, but aesthetically "highly educated."*

A timid Ms. Aesthetics almost lost her virginity in a beautiful park full of fragrant roses on a quiet night. What a zenithistic brutality.

Why shouldn't a man take pity and say, why do they take the blame for all their misery?!

Miserable are those aesthetes, but equally ruthless. The dream of their life is realized. The Zenit *comet disappeared from their sky. Except for a fleeting depression there were no greater consequences. Now they are the stars (zvezdas) of our sky, only those stars don't have tails.*

Ah, that our literary sky with angels from the I. C. G. (Impoverished Commercial Gazette). Just remember that little angel from the literary journal Nonsense, who on his little wings dropped a "critique" of contemporary literature and an anthology, that Pogdan Bopović[1] *[sic] couldn't compile. Indeed, it was an anthology of the "best" contemporary "poets."*

Accursed you, miserable poetry, that you have lived to see the day idiots would feed you corn.

Just remember all those from the dailies' holiday editions, so that you're overtaken by lyrical joy and ecstasy not unlike an Indian prophet, who triumphantly passes through this earth, which appreciates prophetic ecstasy. My land is the land of the righteous . . .

Patience is the virtue of a prophet. That's why I'll be waiting for acknowledgment. Just don't give me recognition because that would be my greatest defeat in life.

It is clear even to the most stubborn fool, that zenithism is one big moment in our literary and artistic life. It is known, that there isn't and never was a man, whether he wrote by hand or by foot, who wouldn't steal something from the pages of Zenit *or a zenithist publication. It is also known that the absolutely biggest slanderers of zenithists and zenithism are those who mercilessly stole while barking at the masters of the new poetry, at L. Micić, me, and other zenithists. It is also known (please don't forget) that certain publishing personages joined the fight against the two poets because zenithism and the new poetry likely means the destruction of publishing. Power to them all. May the earth they smile and walk on not crush them because they skillfully conned the two poets. Oh sure, the little bookstores are the stock markets of ingenuity. Zenithist bonds are worth zilch. Aren't those traders really spectacular. Every epoch has its value. Don't you forget that. On any account.*

Without the two aforementioned poets, Balkan poetry written in the Serbian language wouldn't be worth squat. Without these personalities, contemporary Serbian literature would be a trash heap, where all of Europe dumps its filth and vermin.

A heroic Serbian people and their contemporary literature. Think about it more deeply, all of you, those who care about Serbdom.

It is characteristic for this chaotic environment, that those outside Zenit *and zenithism, the ones furthest on the right, those on the right and on the left, all conspired to prevent the realization of zenithism so that it remains obscure and that its heroes die savagely backstabbed. United by their lack of talent and ignorance, they conspired in the most underhanded act since the inception of Serbian literature. Thanks everyone. It's no wonder that this nation produced one*

Vuk Branković[2], that ruthless mob making "poetry" and "literature" methanize in front of each other, they lift each other's tails and double-cross each other with ingenuity, kiss each other, hug and bite each other, and when the holy ghost leaves them, which never inhabited them in the first place, they then gang up on zenithists to steal from the rich well of zenithist poetry with abandon.

If only these miserable ones knew that even without my will and desire that not even a zephyr will be left of them when the words of great poets would be the sole consolation to the victims and when our poetic battle cry will rule their hearts.

Zenithism has won. Its apparent serenity denotes a buried force which will burst forth and a raging storm will thrash lives like flower stalks and break them. Believe them, it's irrelevant what an idea is called, what matters is that it is.

This book will confuse many friends and foes because there is one more unknown zenithism. On the surface, it is too lyrical, but it has an ironside. The intimate poetry of spring terrors mixes with the rebellion of our machinist epoch. I have endeavored to keep my expression and construction simple to capture the ecstatic zenithistic battle cry to spite the sky for the all-powerful love among people of all worlds and all galaxies.

And when rebellious rage swells in the hearts of innovators it is then that poetry is born, which uplifts faith in the new world, in the paradise of the new people on this earth for which, in recent history, an embittered and desperate struggle has begun. Zenithism resides in the fight.

In the fight, the flame of destructive poetry rages. The success of my poetry is the defeat of the gods.

"If those lying like sediment at the bottom of me
If only they had meaning ah those pitiful words."

Belgrade, May 1927

Branko Ve Poljanski

1

Had I known where my conscience would take me
I would have extinguished the flame
Joy's end is nigh
I know
All these houses are wretched brothels
Blackened morals of a time
The brightest hours of heaven are denied us

Pain consumes me
I remember a garden near the train station
And your joy when I plucked a winter flower
That bloomed yellow again in my hand
I revived it with my blood
And gave it to you
I loved you.
In my transient lodging near the station
I was a stranger waiting daily to slip
Down the eternal silvery murmur of train tracks
I dreamed through and saw
My life's always and ever novel feats of torment
In the glass square of my window
In the throes of my waiting I fired off mad looks
Ah what was I always waiting for
Not knowing waiting meant death.
My glorious waiting in sorrow
I will never realize my dream of bloody streets
To swim in the horror as if at sea.

If there were a thousand and one loony bins
In this stupid Balkan town
In each I would spend a century
To stop verse from spreading in the madness of human drama.
Fall on me hydra-headed darkness
Every night my heavy head falls
Into my weary hands
I hug myself and feel hellish doom
Cruelly and ruthlessly whipping him
Oh that's me
Who empathizes with my fall into the abyss
In the abysses of disgust and ever new bitternesses
Endlessly surfacing from my depths.

Machines and boats whistle over rooftops
Melt in the fog
Lights from the city's din rend my peace
I can't love the one who loves me
If only
Trains
Anchors
Valves
Boats
Murmurs
Harbors
And flights
Could leave me alone.

And now when I fly to other worlds
I want to carry within me the man who loves
There
Where a mindless machine furiously takes me
Hey poet-son keep your heaving
Hot in the bosom of your darling
Like a geyser
At the departure to the mute afterlife.

One two three four these are the four walls
Of my transient lodging enclosing me on four sides in a desperate dungeon
To roll my heart like a die
To lose and all the more thoroughly perish
Oh my love a ruined gambler cries for you
Because he can't find a door in these walls
Where
Where
Where to run oh refuge where to escape from one's own prison.

Who will give us love give us union
Love
The poem of our pride
Love
In our human skin
My spirit proudly carries this body
In it only a mad poet can rave
Hey
If I had a thousand and one minds
I would have lost them if I weren't a poet
If I didn't enjoy the workings of death and life
Hey
My love room
My gallows.

I carry my repentence through unlit streets
With my unbearable calm I feel a tragic end
In myself I rend the deepest me to the blood
To salvage my pride and arrogance in raging verse.

One endless afternoon
A greedy Sunday boredom devoured me
I picked up the phone and called a once dear woman
To tell her

My soul was in a fever
Take it to the clinic on Monday to the clinic
For an ultrasun
Was her answer.

I return from where I leave every minute
I leave for eternity
Eternity is my mother
I bear my genius like a burden one dies under
I'm brave enough to proudly spit in the street's face
At least I know
I'll spit blood one beautiful day.

Oh my world I suffer from your grinding gears
You embitter my joy
Who the hell created you my world
Why should this meek body put up with your
Shattering labor
Oh my annoying body
Poetic body
Human body.

2

I raise my hand against that black minute
My eye breaks through the panicked tooting fog
A shriek bursts from the balcony
My heart flies from my chest
Tight with terror
Your fantastic fear that strange haunting phantom
Terrifies you on your way to an adventure of red pains
Your strange shadows plague and plague me
In the shriek of senseless joy.

Malice ends in this poem
Know
My brain melts in my skull
Like liquid gold
Searches for the secret glow
Finds murk.
Your bewitching eyes cloud my mind
They glisten in love
Take me oh take me to the limits of erotic madness
So that I grow raving at the end under the sun
So that my blood-filled beating system bursts hits my forehead
So that I stilled by death fall onto you
On top of your feverishly shaking body
So that I fall with the last nihilistic poem of silence
Into the awakening
In our loony life
Burdened by life.

The flame of lies burns your face
My insanity treads in the endless joys of my genius

I collapse within and grow like a giant
I fall like a forest
Into deep regret
Before your deep raving eyes.

My thin hand rebelliously and furiously
Removes the fog from your body
Then
Heeeeeeeey
Then
A blood-filled hot center bursts
Until then I didn't know the speed of flight to the devil
That bewitched us that strange evening.

That's why
Today I chastise myself with rebellious protest
Loathing
Myself
Loving you
All the more
Most of all
I love about you what's above you
Above me
Above the world
I love the horror of falling apart one fateful second
It contains the lives and worlds of our hesitations
Of the eruptions of our desires and passions
Why wouldn't I sing about you
My strangest one
My glorious lover
When the whip of inevitability brought you to me
A victim of insane excitements
Dying and loving
Dreaming of your abysmal eyes.

If the sun burst to smithereens
Like a toy
This horrific night would creak
A new day
Our day
The day of the world's ruin
Even
In that moment the sun would overcome
Wrest your death from ghastly hands
Kissing you
Take you to a new solar system
Kissing you
So that we love each other beyond words
Where a burning flame reigns in terror
In the daily burning circle.

Let
The alarming scream of my embitterment
Overcome a moving love or your lies
Know your lies are
A truth bloody and horrid
Under the light of my eye
In front of which
You stand small you beautiful most beautiful pal
When one deadly moment
Pushes a proud genius into endless madness.

Hey
If I could cry tears of gasoline
To soak up this world far and wide
To ignite my joy and sorrow
To char in it this and all other worlds
A salvation for your pure human joys
Hiding in the corners of an afterlife

Ghostly as a hotel room
A black sun.

Inexhaustible are the hot springs of medicinal words from the depths of my spirit
Immeasurable is the goodness of my heart
Which wakes me every morning
Like an alarm clock.

Good day
I love you
Kill me
I'm mad
Kiss me
Period.

3

Today I haven't felt the odd murmur the ravages of my body
I'm numb from pains compounded in my skull
Does anyone know the admiration the vast bruise of lies
I pledged my foolish faith.

The flaming crack of the new the novel lives flickers murmurs toots
In my torment I see boundless full-blooded passions
That reach the mind's twilight the recognition
In agony I journey to madness
I no longer feel the surge of those thoughts
That humiliate me the pride of my boundless spirit
I cannot weep to pity the poverty the misery
Of the people who understand my written word
Neither can I cry for another people
Or for anyone else.

My afternoons noons mornings days dusks evenings nights
Where is the base of the abysmal volcano that spits its black and glow?
Ah
What's the point of the eruption the guttering in our lives our nights and days
When the eye penetrates the curtain of heaven
Swayed we glimpse our feet teetering on the edge of a stupid grave
In it we should gather the patience of a most fantastic bed
To lie in and never rise again
While the pitying living poor say
He
He died a poet the poet was a poet an insurgent.

With how much push for me to paint these words that most pierce
With how much contempt I lie to see truth

Whoever happens on the seductive lie-made smile
Is doomed so doomed to heartless to ruthless
To him the torment above all world-made tortures.

This smoke deadens my limbs encircles my head
Threatens my heartbeat vises my skull
If only if only I never left this chair
A comedic heroic pathetic death a spear in hand
A fountain pen
Hey if I never left this chair.

I bow my head in silence invoke verses
Every word depresses weakens me
My ceaseless battle within
I await the salve from myself the dread the catastrophe
The end of momentum my fantastic thoughts
The distress I think and think births miraculous collisions
Complications align behind closed eyes
With sorcerous speed reach my fatigue
Denote dying in the rivet my memories.

In my week the days skip time the sky breaks above my head
The unceasing spellbound sun spills its tentacled darkness
If only it could bestow on us the light where our lives decay
Our inexplicable imagined joys
We look forward to tomorrow and tomorrow and tomorrow
Until that tomorrow chars us in one pathetic descent
Into eternity that eternal tomorrow.
If not for you my love the madnesses
For one thousandth of a second I forget the misery my defeats
The endless absurd battles
If not for you I would be but banal aches
Crying in my poverty luckless.

This wide arch not only one but millions of arches welded to the firmament
This blue vaulting dims by distances rich in most wondrous secrets
The so-called sky yet I always laugh under that sky
Only to weep when it wanes.

Fatigue and midnight have passed I'm dead alive
Terror undoes me the self-contempt
Strength leaves me the deed my victory-spun illusion
Remains there in red madness the lips of a blood hungry woman.
I return to darkness in the darkness I leave spurred in the night oh my nights
Endless the nights I crucify myself a scene I witness daily
To embolden my paper confessions all the miseries my thwarted exultations.
A song of vast rage I fly into my room then to sleep
Defeated by day I long for a bed a city its souls-wide sky
The stone city collapses buries me on its streets
Streets that have seen so often my pale face
Terrifies me the bold hero at the mortal threshold.
These horrific nights push me to dream's abyss
The dream real yesterday but today a lost bitter memory
My love only mine You pass through me like death
Didn't kill me but left me aimless on sorrow's road
My spirit my strength despises sorrow the defeats the feathery feelings
Feelings come to me in a most human form come to me so I stay human
And love embrace die kiss burn die suffer for all the insanities
Remember our worlds and lives begin in insanity
How do I return to that good boy glow
Return to tears the shimmer the gleam from each eye
From each corner of the world her name spoken in cramp in tears under the burden
My woman the last of women
Your face ah your face false tyrannical the commanding eyes that whip
Kiss me kiss me kiss me to death die drop dead with my likeness in your soul
You are a grave my embrace gave a joy not yours
Mine only mine know that I am a woman a woman am I.

4

Thus our lives will pass reflect on hate
A poet musters to hold himself save himself on an island of love
Under a sun of fleeting visionary joys
To scatter surrender to reveries
His face slapped at each step to ensavage him
Then bid farewell like an idiot.
Doubts suspicions eat my nervous heart
Fear for the life my dying lover indelible
The most brilliant, she suffers from herself the world
I've been waiting since birth to lose before I welcomed her
The lost darling I've yet to meet.
My love what a bastard word love the letters ring my love
Hardened in lyric tears know that
This cry erupts for you
Ravages the boiling of me
I'm a wretch that loves that my strength can't move suns
Sets worlds ablaze with drama
My restless soul
Lies in wait for the last guttering.

These solemn shadows on the walls mock me
Drive me senseless to despair to the gut of agony
I don't know the distances You hide your taut grin
Come with me come with me I love senseless
Where are you my distant victim
Where are you where are you let me see you my love
Ah
Nothing closer than the farthest
Nothing farther than what comes closer
Dead dead the little street the house where four walls imprison me

At unbearable peace terrified of my meek self I gaze at the flame
Fiery lies spit from the furnace my charred joy.
In silence I remember remember the weight I groan under
I cackle like a black bird harbinger of my black hours
My bitter-warped face a madman's craft
I laugh howl for help as in shipwreck
Isn't that isn't every house I live in my non-life
Isn't that the hopeless sinking ship?
After the joy I welcome I descend in my silence
Silent I endure invoke gentle malice
To overcome my meek self
To suffer in love
To laugh die for it
Before the leaving the new return to the desert my wandering.
She
Whom I love loves endures lies kisses me
Worships the light the street and all
She seeds her smile everywhere under the sky always eager for
New adventures to lose herself somewhere in mud the street
Oblivious to flowers the sky the endless worlds in my eyes
Yet with them I exult I hoot
She
Afraid of death ah who before death suffers endures bloodless weeping

■

A quarter to eleven
Alone again with dead objects
I left the street my woman my city the night the sky
There past the threshold the house I enter with a darkened forehead
Every day
I cry out all the joys that grate me
To stroll into the past that I every minute exit
With a new furrow in my forehead
Mark of suffering.

That stamp of fathomless sadness
My face
Picture of my past
I feel you see you in the reflection of our tumultuous time
I see you mask cast in terror
My face
Tragic history
My face
Magical picture
You.

5

If those wretched words like sediment settled to my depths
Ah they would hold meaning
I would write them to break the reader's skull
Who curiously soils great thoughts with his eyes.
You don't know where to begin so that it doesn't hurt
No stairs left I can descend
There right there the bottom I feel it
I fall into it hopeless.
Not even a desperate howl can spare me then
Nothing helps hey people who grasp suffering
Help me help me come closer hey even closer so we can move this globe
With the strength of a new people
Closer to the sun the father
Let his heart
Heat up
This miserable
Insane wretched humankind.

I don't understand why I endure as my sleepy eyes bruise
Ah the dream-brought bruising
Isn't sleep a one-night death
Isn't waking a resurrection?
I know
Tomorrow once more tomorrow when I open my eyes
I'll recall all that's called life
Frightened at that at that panic thought
I'll wish again for dream hey dream its truth
The waking jolt dissolves
Into nothing
The bare lies of day that ghastly nothing.

As a zenithist I worship the sad night
Another night
Another
I spit on the day.

6

In the mirror horror reflects on a Thursday night
Flashes behind my forehead shakes me to the wick
The moon glows on the desperate days for sweaty bread
Reverie drunkenness tugs the heart's veins
My pain my old house
Do people know do they the path
To the flower shops of happiness
I only know the illusory.

Madness of regret spell of ruin through glasses
Through them we see a destructive flame
Panicked we eye the fear of a billion seven hundred thousand
Of those
Life carried on the back of ill
People
Who found an expression inexplicable to me.

Night day day night
Time within time I feel the breaking of these disposable bodies
I invoke myself from the lake's muck a sleeping demon
From my eyes' deep I invoke my whole being
I can't respond.
I'm tired release me my other self
So I can rest at the bottom of me waiting
If only waking could open with its clashing song
Flaming in the dreamers' red eyes
All those witherers found a dream within them
That cures saves lives
Our wretched proletarian lives.

7

Here comes that spring with the moon the cats on the roof
Howls screams a call to the funerals of joy
Morning jolts you its sun strikes up a song under your window
Its golden song flows down your street along the walls
The laborer's hammer pounds the walls echoes
The hammer reminds you of the leaps of new days
Its pounding muffled it's a dusky muffled worker's song
Calls you calls ah calls under the banner of the red sky
Early
In the spring of new humankind.

Aren't you yet tired of murderous thoughts
Aren't you yet crazy from bloody dreams
Aren't you yet bored by humdrum peace
Without the switching stop lights in your lane
Without the scratching needle of the seismograph?
Ah your ear picks up the murmur of the future
Collapses on your conscience like a tidal wave
The wave of time carries blazes
The sky will burn from the purity of the avenger
Purity
We will share the bloody lottery
That gigantic battle of chance our rebellious will.

Not one not even one word do I mark
For our tormentors
All these feelings all this blood from my breast
Call out to love you workers
On your exhausted backs this world rests.
Ah damnation flutters on my lips

Deaf today yet it will fire like a rifle
Day our bitter glass
Overflows.

So here I am in the grip frozen
I watch watch the thin black clock hand
That lightly oh so slowly carries the day our joy
How furious how fast misfortune defeats us.
Peace
Observe brightly the crystal miracles
I promise in these verses
Comrades
Know these poet's eyes see you in your suffering
Shed bloody tears glare on the road of struggle
They see far they shine with victory
I can't deny the mad flash of my eyes.

8

Our hour of horror this grim hour today
Every thought powerless every word stupid
Knowledge a delirium in the superconscious a spring in your step
The clash of time a moment ink eyes in sockets
The furnace a bottle a picture bedsheets a book
I size up these objects examine the clarity of my conscience
This wall isn't glass didn't I break it?
Evolve evolve dynamic terror in my soul
Plunge yourself a birth a breaking we roll down grow dizzy
The night hurts me today ah my joys
Mute I rush from hill to lights I see the city
There far below me.
Just how scalding that rush of boiling blood
Courses in my hand
At dusk a lunatic I rage unravel again
Hateful anguish at the cemetery of my love.

Paris that city that feeling cuts deepest
It only it I see clearly yes a clear picture
You torment me torment me the seventh floor with another
I almost died from decency in that automobile
Take me back to mine to yesterday to that wretched today
Through the winding downhill road
To the valley of nightingales
Black song of the Serbian metropolis
A hell that isn't a hell
That decay that sickness that death.

The metro murmur the song of wheels an iron spectrum
Lights victory cries night that joy life

Sad perverted wretched sick pensive faces
The masks millions of the millions stamped with terror
The question that kills
What will happen at the next stop when we emerge from underground?

A young woman's smile a scream along the boulevards
Green lights line the face of the street
A fantastic reflection glows on asphalt
Fragrant flowers eager to bloom
This and much more with church bells
How at odds they are their bizarre
Moaning along the quays the streets the boulevards
Packed with people and machines
Flies
This life its image pirouettes for a second
Before my eyes in my skull that ever odd movie theater
That constant I frequent
The endless gasp in wonder I watch
That furious onslaught of drama
I buy one ticket to watch it loop
The twenty-four-hour anguish.

This glass bitter too I drank all the drunkenness of dying
This so-called Friday has passed why Friday
The tension in my brain its conspiratorial train
They will kill cruelly my heart one windswept day
That heart my mechanical center ticks
The hours the minutes that eternity of the victim
With every lost hope
We will sing for the youth of this country along these roads
Isn't this earth a ball in a child's hands?
Isn't that god a neglected child?
Isn't the rotation a dangerous game?
During it you can lose your head by the road

As if you never had it.
After days lived the fatigue refreshing
I hang a shiny thought with a pen on a coat hook
On that hook hangs the wretchedness of intoxication
Aren't those who don't hang up their lives don't they deserve pity
To live a life to celebrate restlessness a cyclonic poem
Those who haven't heard you don't know your horrors
Those who have survived you are not at sea on the horizon
Such a person has never been and will never be
There are no people where there is no dying.
Let's perish for the place under the sun we need to conquer
When we're robbed of our simple lives
In the inescapable abyss the melody dies
Sung by rebellious prophets the joys of the machinist era.

I'm as stupid as Socrates powerless as wretched Hamlet
Scoundrel seer picador vagabond
Killer juggler poet and fool
With all these roles I've yet to find my place but when the time comes
A revelation
I can't say now what this verse will mean then
I haven't called it that but the wretches from the opposition have
My intentions
Noted in this code
Searing pain images grow through words.

The rain that spring rain
If only these drops were bullets this my wish
I would be deathly soaked through staggering to my grave.
You stupid you crying cynic
Is it not sentimental to contemplate death
That wet spring night promises
All roads will be fragrant with flowers.

Who knows how to untangle my knotted thoughts?
Who knows why this idiotic cry wearies?
Who knows from which beginning an agonizing end awaits us?
That muddy street undulates beneath your feet
The machines the people the streets the hills the animals the rivers the sky
Asleep.
Endless the poem whose images I carve
And I a small child play with fire
And then in bed the nightmare stream flows from me.

Where isn't the glistening fateful red fire a signal?
What about the rumbling wave not brought by the Yangtze?
I hear rifles cannons I feel proudly victorious isn't that the victory of people?
What miraculous joys red reflections bring the eyes of murky dreamers
Who have yet to kill instead believing in the victory of poetry.

Seek a brilliant style wisdom is a rhyme hey show me the poem
That rings that breaks over my head
That eternal palm of rage rebellion truth madness mendacity
One dies from.

Knock knock knock life ticks away by the second
Sweeps around a single dot that unfortunate center
It ticks and a tower of human bones crumples.
How deeply funny that sad tragic story
How shallow that lake of wisdom
Called society.

Freedom the greatest wisdom.

I descend the hill of poetry perched on a cloud
My steps silent mythical
An agonizing mystery robs me of life
When will it knock me to the mud of day

To soil what I've tried to save of the whole century.
I don't even know if this wound is deadly
Poisoning my being
I don't know have I lost the battle
In the arena of day?
I know nothing but love
Saving my heart even for hatred.

9

A poplar penetrates the distant red sky
She craved a view of only the poplar in the sky without rooftops
To watch its green wonder defy the wind
In the dusk our strange stories
A flash glowed deep in her eyes
Pining to die at her lover's hands.

Your villainous hands she said and broke at the waist
We're all villains in the face of the one
Who watches us from within
That man we eternally humiliate within us
Torture to the end
His good face rejoices his heart
Pounding for love not hate.

Our evenings under stars on green grass
Hours pass in wakeful breaths
A wonder petrified my memory fails me
I have forgotten the words uttered at old graves
Words muted before old massive crosses
Poetry for the dead.

You you
You are not a good man I fear your eyes
Through the dusk they torment me let me go
Let me die I love you to die
I cry without you
Past your joys I want to live
I love you let me once again hear your words
Feel your hand at my breast

The fantastic pleasant.
Let's absorb ourselves in our bodies
Then bid farewell
Then bend in the grip of soul kisses
This beautiful tragic spring its distances
The shiny image
I love you madly devoted you are no more
I'll plunge into the madhouse the despair the fall under the burden the yearning
Farewell.

The day-to-day hours sow
An eternity in him the blossom within waits
The murky hero sighs weeps
Hey refuge days of violent joys in the sun
A baked problem deflects in the sun
The murmuring blood fall memories green shiny in the sun
Smell smell the gaping grave in the spring.
A frightened street escapes under the sky
The mad faraway fizz under the blue ceiling
Foreshadows the screech of moving poems.

Her hands struck up a song around my body
Yesterday
That evening wounded me to the quick
She said her grandpa was a good old man even had built
A glass factory as her plaything
Then
A kiss passed ah if only I could forget
Soul kisses strewn pearls
The starry sky those nights falling on my life
Broken in half over this pen
I wither like the stalk of a wilting sunflower.

Eyes
Eyes my good eyes every day sink beneath my forehead
Hiding their shadows
Days lived in the passenger cars of European trains
Hanging over me I overflow
At machinist speed my ideal plans
Above the seas and countries my yesterdays now the tomorrows
Just Gauri Shankar
Gauri Shankar and Mount Fuji to fly over
Then plunge with broken wings.
To fly hey my flights
Across countless cultures countries deserts
To frantically scream to people calling out to them in their peace holes
To shake up this globe like an anthill
Crushed by the heavy foot of the new era.
The purple crystal the stone of wisdom on the desk
I throw far into the future
When others find it with this word
Let them remember to erect a monument high as the sky
Made of flames it will burn colossally
For my good word I tied
To that wisdom stone at the edge of my desk
That purple crystal that glass from my fantasy factory.

Lower the anchor lower it to the bottom of life
Above it you sail with your feet
To the bloodied days of the sun's spectrum
Be careful
You don't lose yourself in the storm from Tangiers to San Francisco
With your compass you tilt toward defeat
Find the passage the path to the earth's core tie yourself to it
Your ship roams from love to hate.

Chasing emotions in an ice storm
Misery haunts secret thoughts of the superconscious
The morning freshens the dead the sky tolls a requiem
Strange this day when I sense mechanical life
Loathing me oh unattainable joy
That cyclone lays waste to faraway lands
Last night passed through my dream so I awoke
As if I had returned from a long journey.
My eye captures objects with its net of nerves
Last night's prattle poisons my today
Hey poem my rendezvous farewell
I no longer remember and forgetfulness an ink
A where
A where a how I have lost myself
A where a when I buried myself within myself
That strange abyss.

10

That delirium of shadowed silence of eternity
Inhale the night dogs bark at stars a car crashes on a stone street
Pain a rush of blood from one heart to another drunk stagger
A chest worn out from horror
The May night redolent with lilac.
Train wheels spin murmur rumble in dream
Is there an escape from these follies except through death but for death?

Those bulging eyes in the hours of farewell
Must goodbyes shred great souls
Nestling in poets' bodies so damned.

From the belly of the universe behind those golden nails those stars
If I could only rent that distant green curtain
At this hour when I secretly pine for madness
May my resident cry reach my lover
Who left me for the farthest distance
To sob at my victim's silence
Farewell this farewell to life had been the law
Under it I'm terrified.

A pure face with two clear eyes shines beneath the clouds
Why do clouds press on us
Who knows
Who can utter one fateful answer to that question?

Why does everything unravel when there is only death
Why does it disappear when there is only the heart
For those movements in the wondrous horrors the joys of the new world.
Today

Today in the oppressive sun I passed under a chestnut tree
Full-grown
Verdant it turned its face toward the shade
Only to rejoice at the morning sun
Turning it greener under a volley of yellow arrows
Giving it life
Only to die from one such arrow.
The chestnut tree heard the cry from your breast
Ah Branko what a coincidence what a miracle I see you
I feared our most turbulent spring had passed.

Her arms gentle arms keen branches of the sun
That afternoon a hug an endearment
Boundless joy his face glistened
Kissed the joyful palm now ended.
Again waiting blurred his melancholy eyes
That eternity from hour to hour when the knot of fiery bodies
Celebrate the victory against this life against death.

Breasts her breasts beautiful blossoms
Blossoms guarding her heart
Furious kisses from the seat of my blood
Every memory of her will be a new spring
Until our next meeting.

What do I yearn for if only I knew
The constant watch over my ever-knotting paths
House shadows shadows of green branches my own shadow
Have flown with me through me in mortified silence
Along the street I ached for you.
My downcast eyes surveyed the wasteland of shadows
I am no longer a man but reduced to a reflection
Hit to the quick I'm broken into silence
A death wish after a booze-fueled despair.

11

My comrade the romantic I and the other I
Spent the night
In a cellar exchanging wine-fueled stories that exhausted me body and soul
Terrified of the alley cats' cries
Eyeing the door to an easy sleep.

Suffocated by stories I stood up my face blanched
In the mirror I looked for myself but found a stranger
Wondering grinning laughing at the glass reflecting me.

My thought tragic heavy I can't carry it
In this head give me salvation block the sun
Today it shines banal on the horizon.

Across the streets my heavy nostalgic eyes fall
There where my pining roams where the land purple forgetfulness lies
The green landscape all verdant over banks four arches
Span the mirror-like rivers for departing trains
It isn't painless to sing for the miserable sunshine
Red red that most strange sense to cry
In the murky depths of a non-reflecting heart.

In the distant backdrop chimney smoke spirals upward
In that purple background like a sigh rising from a laborer's chest
It escapes into the infinite where the view dissipates
How how ill-suited our eyes for distance
Don't ask this curiosity torments us
Your unquestioning eyes catch on the greened grass
Stillness spreads through the core of your body
Let your caged spirit loose

Like a dove let it fly let it sing its sad song
Of memory the greenest of springs
Where acacias bloom along dead-end roads
Above the tomb of joy.

How many more midnights will I bury into eternity
As a child I used to fantasize at midnight
About lives in sunlit meadows
Fear jolted me from dream
Only to nod off to the rooster's song
Crowing ominously from the yard.
Damned this petrified world within me
That past life lurks behind my glassy eyes
This maniac hidden in me
I calculate I shape memory into verses shameless
A catastrophe-full spirit.

At night when bar music surprises me in the middle of the street
My eyes fill with wonder
Unclear why the reason has been kept from me
I find songs wildly sad
Every night sound hurts offends torments
I am wounded by the shivers of music struck by the night sun
Tonight I am delirious before a picture of a parrot
Lit up in an electric cage
Cheaply selling on a street corner
Wretched esoterica.

12

I am naked as a finger in space suspended
I lie awake as rain murmurs against roofs
As tears over graves.
I fear the threat of another breakdown
I fool myself I sever ties to my emotions
I again return to that lyrical realm
It disappears under my fingers like a smoke ring
I fly through like an acrobat that miracle
Inexpressible
My thoughts are only for opinions that boil in my skull
Abstractions are not attractions
Every word far from thinking clashes
Like love against hate.
I fix my eyes on the dots at the end of the sky
Toward the distances rumbling from my steps
Endings are fast and new beginnings slow
In the sandstorms our most false lives.
Defeats the beginnings of the greatest virtues suffering is moral
The only true word comes at one's deathbed.
I believe in nothing today and I couldn't care from here to the equator
That wondrous equatorial circle cinches this earth
If only I could fly over it and die
When lyric horrors ravage me.
Too high too high up my poetic room I enter climbing the stairs
I enter without counting the steps as if climbing a stairway to the sky
I flip the light switch see my shadow
A projection of my innocence walking beside me.
On the desk rests a purple envelope and within
A letter without a stamp of truth a letter of her dreams
Where lemons smell of wonder Muslims worship Allah

From 33 minaret tops
Figs ripen she cries over a heart lost
Somewhere on the road of life.
Where did these repulsive words come from noted by
Her pale hand one fateful day
She said death my shining heart
Blackens the lyric sky.
Why build a tower of life on those lies?
Love a fast death and death eternal joy.
To cry how stupid to smile that tires me
Tonight the moon's size rivals the sun I am afraid
What kind of morning this the sun hanging high in the dark?
A glass of strong wine soothes me a thought of pain
Courses through my body.
That peace hurts my soul insane soul
Isn't my body your bloody straitjacket
I stained never to bleach it in death.
Those events following my death
I boo and jeer at.
Comrades there are people in me
Who have left love's trace
Comrades your comrade up here mute from agony
His evenings still and quiet as if in death
Any horizontal rest reminds him of lying in a grave
Comrades I'm brimming with contempt every expression every word
I'm ashamed of my helplessness why aren't words deeds
Even for one minute in this valley of horror
For me to build a world in poetry
Words you afflict me poison me with your rage
Feverish I shiver the center of my joys breaks
My words I spit at you under your wheels
I lie wounded in that arena under the sky
Wretched I wait for the human to blossom a blossom.
Irisek

Iris

I

The quiet sky the earth shook like an epileptic
From my bed helpless I called to that red blaze behind the hills
To sooth my blood to dry my tears that wretched child in me
Who thinks life is a toy for good kids.
That red forest river raging through my body froze
Today I'm peaceful bravely expecting death
Digging to the earth's core.
Restlessness like an earthquake rumbling
That the murmur of death's wings above the world
That disgusting damned woman death death a woman.

The miraculous miracle under heaven's flame
My poetry down my cheeks flows
Stay tonight stay in the night under the green sun freeze
I always eternally feel the sunniness of the precious stone
In all the days to come the posthumous ones.
What would my life be without your glow
What would my hate be without your ecstasy in my blood
What would my love be without you my boiling poetry
The gold fountain of my meek dying that into life flows
I'm blessed in your rage you the youth of the sun
For one more flare in my tumultuous time.

Endnotes

1 Bogdan Popović (1863–1944) was a writer, critic, and professor who published *Antologija novije srpske lirike* (Anthology of the Modern Serbian Lyric, 1911). His anthology was the first attempt to create a literary canon of the most significant poetry in the Serbian language since romanticism.

2 Vuk Branković (1345–1397) was a medieval nobleman portrayed as a traitor against Prince Lazar Hrebeljanović (1329–1389) during the Battle of Kosovo (1389) in the namesake epic.

Afterword: The Zenithist Legacy

Aleksandar Bošković and Steven Teref

Zenithism and its works were largely ignored in the Kingdom of Yugoslavia during the 1930s and, together with Micić, completely marginalized in the aftermath of the Second World War. Micić was excluded from the social and cultural life of Socialist Yugoslavia and, since he was denied membership to the Writers Union, his works could not be published. The silence around his literary, editorial, and curatorial work was broken in the 1960s.[1] In the 1970s and 1980s, the legacy of zenithism received much deserved attention, primarily by art historians, namely, Zoran Markuš and Irina Subotić. The public presentation of Micić's legacy, works, and activities in the exhibition *Zenit and the Avant-garde of the Twenties*, curated by Irina Subotić and Vida Golubović at the National Museum in Belgrade (February–March 1983) represents a milestone in the rehabilitation of zenithism in Yugoslav culture.[2] Since then, numerous studies on zenithism have been

1 In the 1960s, several scholars and university professors wrote articles about Micić: Slobodan Ž. Marković (1963), Radomir Konstantinović (1966), Zoran Konstantinović (1967), Miodrag B. Protić (1967), and Miklósz Szabolsci (1969).

2 See the exhibition catalogue *Zenit i avangarda dvadesetih godina* (Belgrade: Narodni muzej, Institut za književnost i umetnost, 1983).

published, including the excellent and extensive catalogue accompanying the facsimile reprint of the entire run of *Zenit* magazine and the collection of essays marking its centennial.[3]

The aim of this anthology is, first and foremost, to showcase the diversity of zenithist work. Another and more noteworthy goal, is to stress that the legacy of zenithist works should be recognized as the "conceptual unconscious" of later Yugoslav experimental art practices from the second half of the twentieth century, such as the New Tendencies of the 1960s, concrete and visual poetry of the late 1960s and the 1970s, and post-conceptual art and postmodernism of the last two decades of the twentieth century. If the zenithist *spatialization of time* resulted in what Russian constructivist El Lissitzky called the "topography of typography," that is, in the topography of a designed page, this aesthetic interest resurfaced in 1960s Yugoslavia with the OHO group's work in which "time has flattened into space."[4] The works of the OHO group[5] and Yugoslav experimental poetry aimed to destroy the last remnants of "traditional metaphysical thought by moving away from the human toward things (*reism*)." This spatial dimension revamped the zenithist "spatialization of time" as demonstrated by Micić's concept of "words in space" and MID's "discrete geometry" of the page and its link with conceptual writing in zenithist works.[6]

MID's proto-conceptual writing as a theoretically-based art, independent of genre, actually functions as a perfect illustration of what in 1968 philosopher Slavoj Žižek saw as the only way to resist the "duality of metaphysics (the signified and the signifier)"; according to Žižek, "the only way to resist it is a revolution of writing," while the essential enactment of the revolution represents "the breaking of form by way of disposition," that is, Derrida's deconstruction as the "dis-gathering of the structure of the sign (the structure of metaphysics) and emphasizing the materiality of the signifier."[7] The Yugoslav concrete and visual poetry

---

3 See Vidosava Golubović and Irina Subotić, *Zenit: Internacionalna revija za umetnost i kulturu 1921–1926* (Belgrade: Narodna biblioteka Srbije, Institut za književnost i umetnost, 2008); *Sto godina časopisa Zenit 1921–1926–2021 / A Hundred Years of Zenit Magazine*, ed. Bojan Jović and Irina Subotić (Belgrade: Gallery RIMA, Institute for Literature and Arts, 2021).

4 Taras Kermanner, "Fragmentarni prikazi povijesti i analiza konretne poezije u Sloveniji" [Fragmentary contributions to history and analysis of concrete poetry in Slovenia], *Vidik*, nos. 7–9 (1972): 14.

5 The OHO group was a Slovene art collective active from 1966–1971 in Ljubljana. For more, see https://monoskop.org/OHO.

6 See the introductory essay to the section *The Third Road of Barbarogenius*.

7 Slavoj Žižek, "The Spy Who Loved Me" (1968), in *Sickle of Syntax & Hammer of Tautology: Concret and Visual Poetry in Yugoslavia, 1968–1983*, ed. Sezgin Boynik, special issue, *OEI*, nos. 90–91 (March 2021): 41. Similar to MID, Žižek perceived materialism as "the dialectized play of the non-origin of 'nothingness'

of Vojislav Despotov, Vujica Rešin Tucić, and Judita Šalgo, to name just a few, employed the same strategies as zenithist writings: quotations, self-quotations, cutting and pasting found text, and montaging separate segments of semantic materials and thus creating confusing and hilarious juxtapositions reflecting the advent of a new informational age and its technologies. Moreover, MID's books share much in common with two important post-conceptual Yugoslav artists, Mladen Stilinović and Goran Đorđević. While the former, for example, created an extensive body of work experimenting with the notion of value, money, and banknotes (using dinar, dollar, and euro bills in his artworks),[8] the latter developed post-conceptual works based on the act of copying and focusing on undermining notions of creativity, originality, and authenticity, as well as a project on the refusal of authorship.[9]

Ultimately, zenithism's true heir is Sreten Ugričić in his post-conceptual postmodernist writing,[10] which addresses the key axiological problem of the highest value as the criterion of evaluation in the same terms as MID,[11] detects *nothingness* in the center of literature itself by revealing it as "the impossibility of literature,"[12] and playfully extends the concept of *literary banditry* as a postmodern strategy of mystification.[13] Both

(the absence of the 'here-now' in the 'sense of being') which enacts the absence of the world," while proposing a revolutionized writing as "the writing of Eros: writing is an act of Orgy 'beyond' the worldly: the split of being as an ejaculation of Eros in the MYTH, which is a 'trace,' the myth of non-origin." Ibid.: 42.

8 See Stilinović's works *They Told Me Told You* (1973), *Marx-Stilinović* (1980), *To Hans Arp* (1980), *Time Is Money* (1980), *Surplus Value* (1980), his artist book *Subtracting of Zeroes* (1993), and a series of installation projects featuring his works with money: *Money Environment* (1980), *About Money and Zeroes* (2006), and *On Money and Zeroes* (2008).

9 See Djordjević's first exhibition of copies *Against Art* (SKC, Belgrade, 1980), his staged public session of copying Mondrian in Belgrade's National Museum (1983), his "Philosophical Tractatus on Nonsense" (*Theoria*, 1984), his staging of *The Last Futurist Exhibition 0.10* (1985) organized in his apartment in Belgrade, and paintings under his nom de guerre Adrian Kovacs (1988–1991).

10 See Sreten Ugričić, *Infinitiv* (Belgrade: Stubovi kulture, 1997); *Uvod u astronomiju: ogledi o statusu uobrazilje i odgovornosti u Srbiji* (Belgrade: Stubovi kulture, 2006).

11 Thus, for Ugričić, the *unseen* (invisible) is the condition of the appearance of values, while the *seen* (visible) covers the invisible: it determines and defines the exact criterion of measurement, but this precise definition masks, covers, and consequently misses something immeasurable. See Sreten Ugričić, *Infinitiv* (Belgrade: Stubovi kulture, 1997).

12 Nemanja Mitrović, *The (Im)possibility of Literature as the Possibility of Ethics* (Delere Press, 2017).

13 His book *Infinitiv*, actually, takes as its task the explication of the theory of the axiological infinitive, elaborated in the 1990 book *The Axiological Infinitive* published by Cambridge University Press and authored by Stewart W. Greenchurch, the philosopher; yet, neither this book nor the other works

MID and Ugrečić employ literary banditry that hinges on its relationship with the notion of *responsibility*: MID (and zenithism) by demonstrating that the cultural supremacy of Western civilization is achieved through acts of barbarity for which it does not find itself accountable nor responsible; Ugričić by demasking mystification and fiction, imitation and mistrust, both as principles and as consequences of the Western politics of identity.[14] Finally, and precisely because Ugričić was not familiar with MID's writing, Ugričić's confirmation of MID as the "conceptual unconscious" of Yugoslav post-conceptualism and postmodernism came in the form of the former's concept of "meady-rade."[15]

We propose that zenithist works should be recognized as the "conceptual unconscious" of Yugoslav vanguard art practices in the second half of the twentieth century, and hope that our anthology will reach new readers and will encourage a new body of scholarship and translations.

---

that Ugrečić has translated and included in his monograph exist outside the pages of Ugričić's *Infinitiv*. Furthermore, *Infinitiv* is full of fake quotations: the chapter "They Said About *the Axiological Infinitive*" is abundant with fabrications of commentaries by "famous philosophers (e.g., Jacques Derrida, Jean-François Lyotard, Jürgen Habermas), artists (e.g., Umberto Eco, John Fowles, Joseph Brodsky) and pop-culture icons (e.g., David Bowie, Björk, Michael Stipe) about the work of Stewart W. Greenchurch." Mitrović, *The (Im)possibility of Literature*, 26. See Ugričić, *Infinitiv*, 155–182.

14 "Today, Europe is entering a time of responsibility. Legality is no longer sufficient to ensure sustainable and unquestionable legitimacy, so the dimension of responsibility comes to the fore. Europe's rule of law and human rights cannot respond to the challenges that threaten it by regressing to the position of the previous ideological paradigm, but only by moving toward a more advanced and legitimate paradigm of responsibility. Today, the same principle applies to the Post-Balkans and Europeans: responsibility instead of identity. We are that what we are responsible for. Neither more nor less than that. Everything else is not only pure but a miserable fiction and mystification. The culture of identity was Balkan, the Balkans was its unfortunate effect. Today, the culture of responsibility is a symbolic infrastructure of an integrated, self-conscious, and effective complete Europe—the infrastructure of the post-Balkan era." See Ugričić, "Post-Balkan Symbolic Structure" ("Post-balkanska simbolička struktura") in *Uvod u astronomiju*, 112–113.

15 See Sreten Ugričić, "Meady-Rade," in *Uvod u astronomiju* (Belgrade: Stubovi kulture, 2006), 54–90. Defined as "imperceptible, inaccessible, delayed, obscured, suspended, apophatic, and literally hermetic art," *meady-rade* is characterized by "a meta-procedure of immediate and unconditional exclusion, displacement, extradition, amputation, excretion of the work of art from its artistic context and the wider socio-symbolic environment" (57–58). In other words, it is "a work of art outside of any or whichever artistic or non-artistic institutionalization and artistic or non-artistic concept, outside of any reference context and outside of any interpretive code" (62); it is "an existing but unavailable and inaccessible work of art" (70), that is, "the concrete otherworldliness" (69) the aesthetic function of which "never becomes obsolete, is never lost, never ceases to be valid and effective" (76).

Bibliography

1. Primary sources

Anonymous. "I. Zenitistička večernja u Beogradu." *Zenit*, nos. 19–20 (December 1922): 69–70.

Anonymous. "Beogradjani oduševljeno pozdravljaju velikog indijskog pesnika." *Politika* (November 17, 1926): 6.

Anonymous. "Duvandžija u književnosti." *Vreme*, November 15, 1925, 4. http://istorijskenovine.unilib.rs/view/index.html#panel:pp|issue:UB_00043_19251115|page:4.

Anonymous. "Najčuveniji medju trista miliona, slavni pesnik R. Tagore, u našoj sredini." *Pravda*, November 16, 1926, 1.

Anonymous. "Nečuven skandal na predavanju Rabindranata Tagore." *Vreme*, November 17, 1926, 5.

Anonymous. "Sadržaj—Program zenitističke večernje 31. Januara 1923." *Zenit*, no. 21 (February 1923): 1–8.

Anonymous. "Veliki uspeh II. Zenitističke večernje." *Zenit*, no. 22 (March 1923): 6–7.

Anonymous. "Zenitističke demonstracije u Parizu." *Zenit*, no. 39 (March 1926): n.p.

Anonymous. "'Zenit' i naša književnost" [Group statement of writers/collaborators of *Zenit*: A. Braun, M. Crnjanski, S. Krakov, D. Matić, R. Petrović, B. Tokin, S. Vinaver]. *Kritika: književno umjetnička revija* [Zagreb], nos. 11–12 (November–December 1921): 452.

Anthologie de Poèmes yougo-slaves contemporains. Translated by Philéas Lebesgue and B. Tokine. Paris: Édition de la Revue Littéraire des Primaires "Les Humbles," 1919.

Goll, Yvan. *Die Chaplinade, Ein Kinodichtung*. Illustrations by Fernard Léger. Dresden: R. Kaemmerer, 1920.

———. "Das Kinodram." *Die neue Schaubühne* 2, no. 6 (1920): 141–143.

———. "Paris brûle." In *Le nouvel Orphée*, 139–155. Paris, Editions de la Sirène, 1923.

———. "Reč kao početo, pokušaj nove poezije" [The word as a beginning, an attempt at new poetry]. *Zenit*, no. 9 (November 1921): 2–4.

———. "Zenitistisches Manifest." *Zenit*, no. 5 (June 1921), 1–2.

Gorky, Maxim. "Povodom revolucije" [On the occasion of the revolution], *Zenit*, no. 34 (November 1924): 13–14; 4, no. 35 (December 1924): 11–12.

IĆ, "Zenitističko predavanje u Petrinji" [A Zenitist lecture in Petrinja]. *Hrvatska banovina*, no. 35 (November 8, 1923): 2.

Lunačarski, Anatoloj. "Proletkult" [Proletarian Culture]. *Zenit*, no. 1 (February 1921): 11–12.

Micić, Ljubomir. "§" [Typogram]. *Zenit*, no. 40 (April 1926): 3.

———. "Čovek i umetnost" [Man and art], *Zenit*, no. 1 (February 1921): 1.

———. "De Gidi bekjar budala" [It didn't go away, single fool]. *Zenit*, no. 40 (April 1926): 4–10.

———. "Delo zenitizma" [The Work of Zenithism]. *Zenit*, no. 8 (October 1921): 2–3.

———. "Duh zenitizma" [The Soul of Zenithism]. *Zenit*, no. 7 (September 1921): 3.

———. "Film jednog književnog pokreta i jedne duhovne revolucije." *Zenit*, no. 38 (February 1926): n.p.

———. "Hvala ti Srbijo lepa" [Thank you, beautiful Serbia]. *Zenit*, no. 36 (October 1925): 4.

———. "Nova umetnost." *Zenit*, no. 35 (December 1924): n.p.

———. "O elektrogeniiju Nikoli Tesli" [On the electrogenius of Nikola Tesla]. *Zenit*, no. 15 (June 1922): 37–38.

———. "Otvoreno pismo Tagori." *Zenit*, no. 43 (December 1926): n.p.

———. "Prema optikoplastici." In *Arhipenko: Nova plastika* (Belgrade: Izdanje "Zenit," no. 5, 1923).

———. "Protiv jugoslovenskog antirusizma" [Against Yugoslav Anti-Russian Sentiment]. *Zenit*, no. 15 (June 1922): 36.

———. "Protiv sentimentalne politike—za balkansku civilizaciju" [Against sentimental politics for Balkan civilization]. *Zenit* (September 23, 1922): 1–2.

———. "Putujući ekspresionizam i antikulturni most" [Traveling expressionism and the anti-cultural bridge]. *Zenit*, no. 3 (April 1921): 9.

———. "Radio-film i zenitistička okomica duha." *Zenit*, no. 23 (April 1923): 2–5.

———. "Reči u prostoru" [Words in Space]. *Zenit*, no. 7 (September 1921): 10.

———. "Reči u prostoru 10–16." *Zenit*, no. 9 (November 1921): 1, 5–7, 11–13.

———. "Savremeno novo i slućeno slikarstvo" [Modern new and future painting]. *Zenit*, no. 10 (December 1921): 11.

———. "Šimi na groblju Latinske četvrti: Zenitistički radio-film od 17 sočinenija," *Zenit*, no. 12 (March 1922): 13–15.

———. "Treba uništiti antisocijalnu umetnost." *Zenit*, no. 35 (December 1924): n.p.

———. "Vo imja Zenitizma" [In the name of Zenithism]. Foreword to *Efekat na defektu*, by Marijan Mikac (Belgrade: Izdanje "Zenit," no. 4, 1923), n.p.

———. "Za slobodu misli, za slobodu stvaranja" [For freedom of thought, for freedom of creation]. *Zenit*, no. 41 (May 1926): 10.

———. "Zenit-manifest 1922." *Zenit*, no. 11 (February 1922): 1.

———. "Zenitizam kao balkanski totalizator novoga života i nove umetnosti." *Zenit*, no. 21

(February 1923): n.p.

———. "Zenitozofija ili energetika stvaralačkog zenitizma." *Zenit*, nos. 26–33 (March–October 1924): 5–9.

MID [Mita Dimitrijević]. "Forma proždire duh," *Zenit*, no. 40 (April 1926): n.p.

———. "Forma proždire duh," *Zenit*, no. 41 (May 1926): 14.

Mikac, Marijan. "Nova zenitistička umetnost." In *Fenomen majmun* (Belgrade: Izdanje "Zenit," no. 7, 1925), 57–68.

Poljanski, Branko Ve. "2/2=1." *Zenit-Ekspres: Dada-Jok* 2 (July–August): n.p.

———. "33 sEkuNdE: kolovrot u SERPENTINe." *Dada-Jok* (May 1922): 6.

———. "Dada KaUzAl dada." *Dada-Jok* (May .922): 3–4.

———. "Dijalog Marineti—Poljanski." *Zenit*, no. 37 (November–December 1925): n.p.

———. (as Virgil Poljanski). "Evo me!" *Svetokret: List za ekspediciju na severnii pol čovekovog duha*, no. 1 (January 1921): 3–4.

———. "Film i budućnost čovečanstva." *Kinofon*, no. 1 (December 1921): 4–5.

———. "Laso materi božjoj oko vrata." *Zenit*, no. 12 (March 1922): 12.

———. "Lepota konja i lice kraljice Zite." *Zenit*, no. 12 (March 1922): 12.

———. *Manifeste du Panréalisme* (1930).

———. (as Virgil Poljanski). "U znaku kruga." *Zenit*, no. 1 (February 1921): 13.

———. "Zakonik države DADA-JOK." *Dada-Jok* (May 1922): 3–4.

———. (as Valerij Poljanski). *Zenit-Ekspres: Pariz–Berlin–München! Radiogrami* [leaflet] (1922).

Rasinov, M. "Zenitizam kroz prizmu marksizma." *Zenit*, no. 43 (December, 1926): 12–15.

Ratković, Risto. "Barbarstvo kao kultura." *Zenit*, no. 37 (November–December 1925): n.p.

———. "U Sandžaku san na crvenoj travi." *Zenit*, no. 38 (February 1926), n.p.

Tokin, Boško. "Evropski pesnik Ivan Goll." *Zenit*, no. 1 (February 1921): 5–9.

———. "Kinematografske pesme." *Crno na belo* [almanac], edited by Monny de Boully (Belgrade, 1924), n.p.

———. "Mierendorff: Haette Ich Das Kino" and "Kabinet Dr. Caligaria." *Zenit*, no. 4 (May 1921): 13–14.

———. "Moj zenitizam." *Jugoslavenska njiva* 34 (August 28, 1921): 539–541.

———. "Pokušaj jedne kinematografske estetike." *Progres* 1, nos. 120–123 (October 13–15, 1920):2–3.

———. "U atmosferi čudesa" [In the atmosphere of miracles]. *Zenit*, no. 3. (April 1921): 2–3.

———. "Zenit, broj 7." *Tribuna* 2, no. 205 (September 8, 1921): 3.

Trotsky, Leon. "Lenin." *Zenit*, nos. 26–33 (October 1924): 25–27.

a) Journals and Leaflets

Dada-Jok (May 1922). Republished in *Zenit, Svetokret, Dada jok, Dada tank, Dada jazz, 1921–1926* (Zagreb: Ranko Horetzky, 2008).

Nemo propheta in patria. Supplement to *Zenit*, no. 25 (February 1924).

Svetokret: List za ekspediciju na severni pol čivekovog duha (January 1921). Republished in *Zenit, Svetokret, Dada jok, Dada tank, Dada jazz, 1921–1926* (Zagreb: Ranko Horetzky, 2008).

Tank–revue international de l'art vivant, 1–1 1/2 (1927); 1 1/2–3 (1928). https://monoskop.org/Tank.

Zenit (1921–1926). Vols. 1–6, 43 issues. https://monoskop.org/Zenit.

Zenit-Ekspres: Dada-Jok, no. 2 (July–August 1922).

Zenit–Ekspres: Pariz–Berlin–München! Radiogrami [leaflet] (1922).

b) Biblioteka Zenit Editions*

[1921]

1. Micić, Ljubomir, Yvan Goll, and Boško Tokin. *Manifest Zenitizma*. Zagreb: Biblioteka Zenit, no. 1, 1921. Includes portraits of Ljubomir Micić (photography), Yvan Goll (drawing by A. Glez), and Boško Tokin (drawing by Slavko Vorkapić). The manifesto has been published in French and German.

2. Goll, Yvan. *Paris brennt*. Zagreb: Biblioteka Zenit, no. 2, 1921. Dedicated to Carl Einstein. Illustrated with the eight postcards of Paris, a military parade, and various sports, with a linocut by Mihailo S. Petrov.

[1922]

3. Micić, Ljubomir. *Stotinu vam Bogova*. 1st ed. Zagreb–Belgrade: Biblioteka Zenit, no. 3, 1922. *Kola za spasavanje*. 2nd ed. Zagreb–Belgrade, Biblioteka Zenit, no. 3, 1922. Dedicated to Nikola Tesla. The front and back cover pages by Ljubomir Micić. Illustrated with reproductions of *The Sketch for the Monument to the Third International* by Vladimir Tatlin, *Black Square* by Kazimir Malevich, photographs of machines and cine-projectors, with black and white squares and typographic signs. Printed in Latin and Cyrillic letters.

[1923]

4. Mikac, Marijan. *Efekat na defektu*. Belgrade: Izdanje "Zenit," no. 4, 1923. The front cover page is by Josif Klek.
5. *Arhipenko: Nova plastika*. With foreword by Ljubomir Micić. Belgrade: Izdanje "Zenit," no. 5, 1923. Illustrated by the reproductions of sculptures and sculpture-paintings by A. Archipenko and ex-libris *Zenit, zenithism*, by Jo Klek.
6. Poljanski, Branko Ve. *77 samoubica*. Zagreb: Naklada Reflektor, 1923; later counted as a Biblioteka Zenit edition. The front cover page is by B. Poljanski.

* This subsection is sequenced chronologically and not alphabetically.

[1924]

7. Poljanski, Branko Ve. *Panika pod suncem. Tragedija balkanske azbuke.* Belgrade: Collection des zenitistes Internationales, no. 6, 1923 [1924]. The title is also in French. Illustrated with a portrait of Branko Ve Poljanski, a drawing by Mihailo S. Petrov, and with a vignette/ex-libris in form of K. Malevich's *Black Square.*

[1925]

8. Mikac, Marijan. *Fenomen majmun.* Belgrade: Izdanje "Zenit," no. 7, 1925. The front cover page by Josif Klek. Some information also in French.
9. Micić, Ljubomir. *Aeroplan bez motora.* Belgrade: Izdanje medjunarodnog časopisa "Zenit," 1925. The front cover page is illustrated with a photo-portrait of Ljubomir Micić with the caption: "author without a beard—1918—as a recognized poet—before Zenithism" (also in French); photography of Anuška: "to you, Anuška, my wonderful partner, I devote this Balkan and barbarian poem. In the name of Zenithism and Love."
10. Dimitrijević, Mita [MID]. *Seksualni ekilibr novca / Trgovinska prepiska o valutnom pitanju.* Belgrade: Narodna Misao A.D. Administracija "Zenita", 1925.

[1926]

11. Micić, Ljubomir. *Antievropa.* Belgrade: Biblioteka Zenit, no. 9, 1926. Dedicated to Dušan Popović. Illustrated with a *Black Square* by K. Malevich. The front cover page resembles *Proun* by El Lissitsky.
12. Poljanski, Branko Ve. *Tumbe.* Belgrade: Collection des Zénitistes Internationaux, no. 10, 1926. The title is also in French. Illustrated by the drawing of B. Poljanski's profile by T. Foujita (made in Paris in 1926). The title page in constructivist typography; the back cover resembles *Proun* by El Lissitsky. The book has the following mark: RE-volution, RE-construction, RE-vision zenitistes.
13. Dimitrijević, Mita [MID]. *Metafizika ničega [Uvod].* Belgrade: Administracija "Zenita," 1926.

[1927]

14. Poljanski, Branko Ve. *Crveni petao.* Paris–Belgrade: Collection des Zénitistes Internationaux, no. 12, 1927. The title is also in French. Illustrated with photo-portrait of the author.

2. Secondary sources

Abel, Richard. *French Film Theory and Criticism: A History/Anthology 1907–1939*. Vol. 1. Princeton: Princeton University Press, 1993.

Babac, Marko ed. *Boško Tokin: Novinar i pisac. Prvi srpski estetičar, publicista i kritičar filma*. Vol. 1. Novi Sad: Matica Srpska, 2009.

Bakhtin, Mikhail. "Forms of Time and of the Chronotope in the Novel: Notes toward a Historical Poetics." In *The Dialogic Imagination: Four Essays*, edited by Michael Holquist and translated by Caryl Emerson and Michael Holquist, 84–258. Austin: University of Texas Press, 1990.

Bakić-Hayden, Milica. "Nesting Orientalisms: The Case of Former Yugoslavia." *Slavic Review* 54, no. 4 (Winter 1995): 917–931.

Benjamin, Walter. "The Work of Art in the Age of Its Technological Reproducibility." In *Selected Writings*, edited by Howard Eiland and Michael W. Jennings, 251–283. Vol. 4. Cambridge, MA: Harvard University Press, 2003.

Benson, Timothy O, and Eva Forgács eds. *Between Worlds: A Sourcebook of Central European Avant-Gardes 1910–1930*. Los Angeles: Los Angeles County Museum of Art; Cambridge, MA: MIT Press, 2002.

Benson, Timothy O. *Central European Avant-Gardes: Exchange and Transformation, 1910–1930*. Los Angeles: Los Angeles County Museum of Art; Cambridge, MA: MIT Press, 2002.

Bor, Vane, and Marko Ristić. *Anti-zid: Prilog za pravilnije shvatanje nadrealizma*. Belgrade: Nadrealistička izdanja, 1932.

Bošković, Aleksandar. "The Avant-Garde Photopoetry." *Književna istorija*, no. 158 (2016): 287–310.

Deleuze, Gilles, and Félix Guattari. *A Thousand Plateaus: Capitalism and Schizophrenia*. Translated by Brian Massumi. Minneapolis: University of Minnesota Press, 1987.

Delluc, Louis. *Photogénie* (Paris: de Brunhoff, 1920).

Donat, Branimir. "Performans kao oblik komunikacije hrvatske dade i njenih inačica s javnošću." In *Dani hvarskog kazališta–hrvatska književnost, kazalište i avangarda dvadesetih godina 20. Stoljeća*, 5–12. Zagreb–Split: HAZU, Književni krug, 2004.

Dworkin, Craig. "The Fate of Echo." In *Against Expression: An Anthology of Conceptual Writing*, edited by Craig Dworkin and Kenneth Goldsmith, xxiii–liv. Evanston, Illinois: Northwestern University Press, 2011.

Đurić, Dubravka, and Miško Šuvaković, eds. *Impossible Histories: Historical Avant-gardes, Neo-avant-gardes, and Post-avant-gardes in Yugoslavia, 1918–1991*. Cambridge, MA: The MIT Press, 2003.

Eisenstein, Sergei. *The Film Sense*. Translated and edited by Jay Leyda. San Diego: Harcourt Brace Jovanovich, 1975.

Epstein, Jean. "On Certain Characteristics of Photogénie." In *Film Theory: Critical Concepts in Media and Cultural Studies*, edited by Philip Simpson, Andrew Utterson, and Karen J. Shepherdson, translated by Tom Milne, 52–53, Vol. 1 (London: Taylor and Francis, 2004).

Gallo, Rubén. "Jean Cocteau's Radio Poetry." In *The Sound of Poetry, the Poetry of Sound*, edited by Craig Douglas Dworkin and Marjorie Perloff, 205–218. Chicago: Chicago University Press, 2009.

Glišić, Iva, and Tijana Vujošević. "I am Barbarogenius: Yugoslav Zenitism of the 1920s and the Limits of Performativity." *Slavic and East European Journal* 60, no. 4 (2016): 718–743.

Goll, Yvan. "The Chapliniad: A Film Poem." In *New Directions 39. An International Anthology of Prose and Poetry*, edited by James Laughlin, translated by Frank Jones, 40–50. New York: New Directions, 1979.

———. "The Chaplinade: A Film Poem." Translated by Clinton J. Atkinson and Arthur S. Wensinger. *The Massachusetts Review* 6, no. 3. (Spring–Summer, 1965): 497–514.

Golubović, Vidosava. *Biblioteka časopisa* Zenit. Belgrade, Kragujevac: Gallery RIMA, 2021.

———. "Iz prepiske oko *Zenita* i zenitizma: Marijan Mikac/Ljubomir Micić." In *Ljetopis srpskog kulturnog društva "Prosvjeta,"* 277–293. Vol. 4. Zagreb: Prosvjeta, 1999.

———. "Iz prepiske oko *Zenita* i zenitizma: Marijan Mikac/Ljubomir Micić (1927)." In *Ljetopis*, 237–265. Zagreb: Srpsko kulturno društvo Prosvjeta, 2001.

———. "Iz prepiske oko *Zenita* i zenitizma: Marijan Mikac/Ljubomir Micić (1928–1929)." In *Ljetopis*, 179–204. Zagreb: Srpsko kulturno društvo Prosvjeta, 2002.

Golubović, Vidosava and Irina Subotić. *Zenit: Internacionalna revija za umetnost i kulturu 1921–1926*. Belgrade: Narodna biblioteka Srbije, Institut za književnost i umetnost, 2008.

Grdan, Lada. *Zenit i simultanizam*. Belgrade: Službeni glasnik, 2010.

Horvat-Pintarić, Vera. *Josip Seissel*. Zagreb: Galerija Nova, 1978.

Flaker, Aleksandar. *Nomadi ljepote: Intermedijalne studije*. Zagreb: Grafički zavod Hrvatske, 1988.

———. *Poetika osporavanja*. Zagreb: Školska knjiga, 1982.

———. *Ruska avangarda*. Zagreb: SN Liber, Globus, 1984.

Forbes, Meghan. "Advertisement as Collaboration in the Central European Avant-Garde Magazines," *post: notes on art in a political context*, May 16, 2016. https://post.moma.org/advertisement-as-collaboration-in-the-central-european-avant-garde-magazines-2.

Foucault, Michel. "Of Other Spaces." *Diacritics*, no. 16 (Spring 1986): 22–27.

Freud, Sigmund. *Civilization and Its Discontents*. New York: J. Cape & H. Smith, 1930.

Ignatieff, Michael. "The Narcissism of Minor Difference." In *The Warrior's Honor: Ethnic War and the Modern Conscience*, 34–71. New York: Metropolitan Books, 1998.

Ilić, Saša. "Ljubav i smrt posle avangarde" [Love and death after the avant-garde], foreword in *Strašna komedija: Prepiska Anuške Kon Micić i Ljubomira Micića 1920–1960*, edited by Šaša Ilić and Dragana Peruničić: 7–54. Belgrade: Narodna Biblioteka Srbije, 2021.

Jacobs, Steven, Anthony Kinik, and Eva Hielscher, eds. *The City Symphony Phenomenon: Cinema Art, and Urban Modernity between the Wars*. New York: Routledge, 2019.

Jakovljević, Branislav. *Alienation Effect: Performance and Self-Management in Yugoslavia, 1945–91*. Ann Arbor: University of Michigan Press, 2016.

Jović, Bojan, and Irina Subotić, eds. *Sto godina časopisa Zenit 1921–1926–2021 / A Hundred Years of Zenit Magazine*. Belgrade: Gallery RIMA, Institute for Literature and Arts, 2021.

Kermauner, Taras. "Fragmentarni prikazi povijesti i analiza konretne poezije u Sloveniji" [Fragmentary contributions to history and analysis of concrete poetry in Slovenia]. Translated by Ljubomir Stefanović. *Vidik* [Split], nos. 7–9 (1972/73): 15–19.

Konstantinović, Radomir. *Biće i jezik u iskustvu srpskih pesnika dvadesetog veka*. Vol. 4. Belgrade: Prosveta, Rad; Novi Sad: Matica Srpska, 1983.

———. "Četiri pesnika (Sifon–soda–krv Ljubomira Micića)." *Treći program* 4 (1972): 211–250.

———. "Ko je barbarogenije?" *Treći program* 1 (1969): 9–21.

———. *The Philosophy of Parochialism*, edited by Branislav Jakovljević, translated by Ljiljana Nikolić and Branislav Jakovljević. Ann Arbor: University of Michigan Press, 2021.

Kosem, Dragotin. "V svojo smer!" *Grafička revija za pouku i promicanje grafičkog rada*, no. 4 (1925).

Kosovel, Srečko. *Look Back, Look Ahead*. Translated by Ana Jelnikar and Barbara Siegel Carlson. Brooklyn: Ugly Duckling Presse, 2010.

Kostić, Đorđe. *Do nemogućeg*. Belgrade: Nolit, 1972.

Kostić, Dragutin. *Umesto ludila*. Belgrade: Štamparija "Miletić," 1928.

Kramer, Andreas. "'Basis aller neuen kommenden Kunst ist das Kino': Yvan Goll und das Medium Film." In *Yvan Goll–Claire Goll: Texts and Contexts*, edited by Eric Robertson and Robert Vilain, 83–95. Amsterdam: Rodopi, 1997.

———. "Europa minor. Yvan and Claire Goll's Europe." In *Europa! Europa? The Avant-Garde, Modernism and the Fate of a Continent*, edited by Sasha Bru, 126–137. Vol. 1. Berlin: De Gruyter, 2009.

Kršić, Jovan. "Zenitizam." In Jovan Kršić, *Sabrana djela*, (*Književnosti naroda Jugoslavije*), edited by Vojislav Maksimović, 21–25. Vol. 2. Sarajevo: Svijetlost, 1979.

Levi, Pavle. *Cinema by Other Means*. Oxford: Oxford University Press, 2012.

Marinetti, Filippo Tommaso. "Technical Manifesto of Futurist Literature (1912)." In *Futurism: An Anthology*, edited by Lawrence Rainey, Christine Poggi, and Laura Wittman, 119–125. New Haven: Yale University Press, 2009.

Marjanić, Suzana. "Dečki, najbolje da bežite!" *Zarez* 9, no. 203 (April 5, 2007): 32–33.

Marjanović, Igor. "*Zenit*: Peripatetic Discourses of Ljubomir Micić and Branko Ve Poljanski." In *On the Very Edge: Modernism and Modernity in the Arts and Architecture of Interwar Serbia (1918–1941)*, edited by Jelena Bogdanović, Lilien Filipovitch Robinson, and Igor Marjanović, 63–84. Leuven: Leuven University Press, 2014.

Matičič, Ivan. "V svojo smer!" *Grafička revija za pouku i promicanje grafičkog rada*, no. 2 (1925): n.p.

Markuš, Zoran. *Zenitizam*. Belgrade: ID Signature, 2003.

Metlić, Dijana. "Zenithist Cinema: Influences of Marinetti and Mayakovsky." *International Yearbook of Futurism Studies*, edited by Günter Berghaus, 236–268. Berlin: de Gruyter, 2020.

Meyl, Konstantin. *Scalar Wave*. Indel GmbH, 2003.

MID [Dimitrijević, Mita]. *Metafizika ničega [Uvod]*. Edited by Gojko Tešić. Belgrade: Otkrovenje, 1996.

———. *Seksualni ekilibr: Trgovinska prepiska o valutnom pitanju*. Edited by Gojko Tešić. Belgrade: Otkrovenje, 1996.

Milenković, Milorad Lj. "Petronijevićev uvid: jedinstvo bića i mišljenja." Foreword to *Metafizičke rasprave*, by Branislav Petronijević, edited by Milorad Lj. Milenković, 5–14. Sremski Karlovci: Izdavačka knjižarnica Zorana Stojanovića, 1991.

Milisavljević, Boris. "Nov pogled na delo Branislava Petronijevića." *Gledišta* 40, nos. 1–2 (1999): 269–279.

Miloradović, Goran. "Od anarhizma do šovinizma: Drugi Svetski Rat i pripadnici avangardnog umetničkog kruga oko časopisa *Zenit*—Ljubomir Micić i Marijan Mikac." In *Intelektualci i rat (1939–1947). Zbornik radova s Desničinih susreta 2012. Dio 2*, edited by Drago Roksandić and Ivana Cvijović Javorina, 305–331. Zagreb: Filozofski fakultet u Zagrebu, 2013.

Milutinović, Zoran. *Getting Over Europe: The Construction of Europe in Serbian Culture.* Amsterdam: Rodopi, 2011.

Mitrović, Nemanja. *The (Im)possibility of Literature as the Possibility of Ethics.* Delere Press, 2017.

Negrišorac, Ivan. "Zenitistička proza kao osporavanje romana." *Polja*, nos. 342/343 (1987): 347–374.

OEI, nos. 90–91: *Sickle of Syntax & Hammer of Tautology: Concrete and Visual Poetry in Yugoslavia, 1968–1983*, guest-edited by Sezgin Boynik (March 2021).

Paci, Viva. "The Attraction of the Intelligent Eye: Obsessions with the Vision Machine in Early Film Theories." In *The Cinema of Attractions Reloaded*, edited by Wanda Strauven, 121–131. Amsterdam: Amsterdam University Press, 2006.

Pejčić, Jovan. "Rabindranat Tagore u Belgradeu." *Kulture Istoka*, V/15, nos. 1–3 (1988): 66–67.

Petronijević, Branislav. *Metafizičke rasprave.* Translated by Milorad Lj. Milenković. Sremski Karlovci: Izdavačka knjižarnica Zorana Stojanovića, 1991.

———. "Osnovni postulati diskretne geometrije." *Članci i studije B. Petronijevića* 2 (1920): 136–163.

———. *Principles of Metaphysics (Prinzipen der Metaphysik).* Vols. 1–2. Berlin: Ernst Hoffman & Co, 1904–1911.

Petrov, Aleksandar. "Branko Ve Poljanski i njegova *Panika pod suncem*." Foreword *Panika pod suncem. Tumbe. Crveni petao*, by Branko Ve Poljanski, edited by Aleksandar Petrov, i–lxxviii. Belgrade: Narodna Biblioteka Srbije; Gornji Milanovac: Dečje novine, 1988.

Poljanski, Branko Ve. *Panika pod cuncem, Tumbe, Crveni petao*. Belgrade: Narodna Biblioteka Srbije; Gornji Milanovac: Dečje novine, 1988.

Polonskii, Vyacheslav. *Russkii Revolytsionny Plakat* [Russian Revolutionary Posters]. Moscow: Gosudarstvennoye Izdatel'stvo, 1924.

Ratković, Risto. *Ćutanja o književnosti*. Belgrade, 1928.

Robertson, Eric, and Robert Vilain, eds. *Yvan Goll–Claire Goll: Texts and Contexts.* Amsterdam: Rodopi, 1997.

Röhnert, Jan. *Springende Gedanken und flackernde Bilder. Lyrik im Zeitalter der Kinematographie*; Blaise Cendrars, John Ashbery, and Rolf Dieter Brinkmann. Göttingen: Wallstein Verlag, 2007.

Simmel, George. *The Philosophy of Money.* Edited by David Frisby, translated by Tom Bottomore and David Frisby. Third enlarged ed. London and New York: Routledge: 2005.

———. "Value and Money." In *The Continental Aesthetic Reader,* edited by Clive Cazeaux, 305–321. London, New York: Routledge, 2000.

Slabinac, Gordana. *Hrvatska književna avangarda.* Zagreb: August Cesarec, 1988.

Strašna komedija: Prepiska Anuške Kon Micić i Ljubomira Micića 1920–1960. Edited by Šaša Ilić and Dragana Peruničić. Belgrade: Narodna Biblioteka Srbije, 2021.

Subotić, Irina. "Ljubomir Micić u svetlu novootkrivenih dokumenata" In *Ljetopis: Srpsko kulturno društvo 'Prosvjeta'*, 339–381. Zagreb: Prosvjeta, 2016.

———. "Paris in *Zenit—Zenit* in Paris." In *Zbornik Narodnog Muzeja u Belgradeu. Recueil Du Musee National De Belgrade,* 565–579. Belgrade: Narodni muzej, 2010.

———. "The *Zenit* Magazine and Ljubomir Micić: Ideas, Programs, Achievements." In *Balkanization,* edited by Žarko Aleksić and Jelena Micić, 14–23. Vienna: Friday Exit, 2016. Exhibition catalogue.

———. "Zenitism / Futurism: Similarities and Differences." In *International Yearbook of Futurism Studies,* edited by Günter Berghaus, 201–230. Vol 1. Berlin: De Gruyter, 2011.

Susovski, Marijan. *Josip Seissel: nadrealističko razdoblje: slike, crteži, akvareli, tempere, pasteli, crtaći blokovi od 1920 do 1987.* Zagreb: Muzej suvremene umjetnosti, 1997.

Šuvaković, Miško. "Eklektični avangardizam: Zenit." In *Istorija umetnosti u Srbiji XX vek: prvo tom, radiikalne umetničke prakse,* edited by Miško Šuvaković, 83–100. Belgrade: Orion art, Katedra za muzikologiju Fakukteta muzičke umetnosti, 2010.

Tasić, Dmitar. *Paramilitarism in the Balkans. The Cases of Yugoslavia, Bulgaria, and Albania, 1917–1924.* Oxford: Oxford University Press, 2020.

Tatar, Maria. *Lustmord: Sexual Murder in Weimar Germany.* Princeton: Princeton University Press, 1995.

Tešić, Gojko. "Kontekst za čitanje pripovetke srpskog modernizma i avangarde." In *Antologija srpske avangardne književnosti,* edited by Gojko Tešić. Novi Sad: Bratstvo jedinstvo, 1989.

———. "MID=DIM ili 'Pesnik apsolutno ničega.'" Afterword in MID [Mita Dimitrijević], *Metafizika ničega [Uvod],* edited by Gojko Tešić. Belgrade: Otkrovenje, 1996.

Todorova, Marija. *Imagining the Balkans*. Oxford: Oxford University Press, 2009.

Todorović, Predrag. "The Life and Death of Branko Poljanski," *Književna istorija*, no. 154 (2014): 1007–1015.

Toman, Jindřich. *Photo/Montage in Print*. Foto/Montáž tiskem Prague: Kant, 2009.

Ugričić, Sreten. *Infinitiv*. Belgrade: Stubovi kulture, 1997.

———. *Uvod u astronomiju: ogledi o statusu uobrazilje i odgovornosti u Srbiji*. Belgrade: Stubovi kulture, 2006.

Ullmaier, Johannes. *Yvan Golls Gedicht "Paris brennt."* Tübingen: Max Niemeyer Verlag, 1995.

Vinterhalter, Jadranka, ed. *Flashes of avant-garde in the Croatian art of the first half of the 20th century*. Translated by Andy Jelčić. Zagreb: Muzej suvremene umjetnosti, 2007.

Vrga, Boris. "Zenitističke večernje u Petrinji," *Generacije: časopis za kulturu i umjetnost te duhovni identitet grada Petrinje*, no. 8 (February 1995): 10–19.

Vučković, Radovan. *Poetika srpske avangarde*. Belgrade: Službeni glasnik, 2011.

Vujanović, Ana. "Avangardni teatar i performans 1920-ih (Umetnost u Srbiji)." In *Istorija umetnostiu Srbiji: XX vek—Prvi tom: radikalne umetničke prakse* [A history of art in Serbia: The 20th century—Volume one: radical artistic practices], edited by Miško Šuvaković, 147–156. Belgrade: Orion Art, 2010.

Wall-Romana, Christophe. *Cinépoetry: Imaginary Cinemas in French Poetry*. New York: Fordham University Press, 2013.

Zečević, Božidar. *Srpska avangarda i film 1920–1932*. Belgrade: UFUS, 2013.

Zenit i avangarda dvadesetih godina [Zenit and the avant-garde of the twenties]. Edited by Irina Subotić and Vidosava Golubović. Belgrade: Narodni muzej and Zavod za književnost i umjetnost, 1983. Exhibition catalogue.

Žižek, Slavoj. "The Spy Who Loved Me." In *Sickle of Syntax & Hammer of Tautology: Concrete and Visual Poetry in Yugoslavia, 1968–1983*, edited by Sezgin Boynik. Special issue, *OEI*, nos. 90–91 (March 2021): 41–42.

3. Recommended sources for further research/further reading

For a more extended bibliography and webography on Yugoslav zenithism see:

Golubović, Vidosava, and Irina Subotić. *Zenit: Internacionalna revija za umetnost i kulturu 1921–1926*, 421–466. Belgrade: Narodna biblioteka Srbije, Institut za književnost i umetnost, 2008.

Index